Margaret McPhee lo requirement for a train that her imagination romances she loves t she decided to put the ide her scientific life behind, retaining only the romance—her husband, whom she met in a laboratory. In summer, Margaret enjoys cycling along the coastline overlooking the Firth of Clyde in Scotland, where she lives. In winter, tea, cakes and a good book suffice.

**Don't miss these other Regency delights from
Mills & Boon® Historical romance's
bestselling authors!**

REGENCY
Debutantes

Margaret McPhee

MILLS & BOON

All the characters in this book have no existence outside the imagination
of the author, and have no relation whatsoever to anyone bearing the same
name or names. They are not even distantly inspired by any individual
known or unknown to the author, and all the incidents are pure invention.

Mills & Boon, an imprint of Harlequin (UK) Limited,
Eton House, 18-24 Paradise Road, Richmond, Surrey TW9 1SR

REGENCY DEBUTANTES © Harlequin Books S.A. 2011

The publisher acknowledges the copyright holder of the individual works
as follows:

The Captain's Lady © Margaret McPhee 2005
Mistaken Mistress © Margaret McPhee 2006

ISBN: 978 0 263 88735 8

052-0611

Harlequin (UK) policy is to use papers that are natural, renewable
and recyclable products and made from wood grown in sustainable
forests. The logging and manufacturing processes conform to the legal
environmental regulations of the country of origin.

Printed in the UK
by CPI Mackays, Chatham, ME5 8TD

The Captain's
Lady

Chapter One

November 1804

'Mr Praxton, you're mistaken in your assumption!' Georgiana Raithwaite staggered back from the hard thin lips pressed to hers. Her hand scrubbed at her bruised mouth as she attempted to escape.

'Come now, Miss Raithwaite, don't play coy with me. We both know the truth of your feelings on the matter.' Walter Praxton grasped Georgiana's wrist, the bones of his fingers biting into her. Relentlessly he dragged her closer until she was pressed fully against his frame.

'No! Let me go! I haven't encouraged your interest.' The dark green wool of his finely tailored coat scraped against her cheek, releasing a rush of cologne. 'We've been gone for an age and our party will be here at any moment.' She struggled harder. 'Leave me be!'

He sniggered, a harsh and petty sound against the rush of the nearby river, and his ruthless mouth touched the locks of her unbound hair. Her bonnet lay crushed amidst the hawthorn bushes where he had thrown it just moments before. 'Indeed, they will, my dear. Let them come upon our lovers' tryst.' His handsome face cracked with a smile that did not touch the coldness in his ice-blue eyes.

'How dare you! My papa won't believe your lies!' Georgiana wrenched her face away from his. 'Release me or I swear I'll scream.'

Even as she sucked the breath in to fulfil her threat, his left hand snaked around the slim column of her throat, crushing with a slow even pressure that ensured her silence.

He stared into her eyes, eyes that were wide and round with fear and loathing, and whispered softly against her ear, 'I won't brook such disobedience when we're married.'

The sound of voices murmured in the distance. 'Not long now, my dear. To be caught in such a compromising situation… You're fortunate indeed that I'm a gentleman and can be relied upon to do the honourable thing.' His mouth contorted into a sweet smile.

It was then that Georgiana understood the exact nature of the trap closing around her. Walter Praxton meant to have her for his wife, despite all of her refusals. It did not matter that he had callously engineered the situation for his own ends. Once Mama, Papa, the Battersby-Browns and Mrs Hoskin had witnessed her in this dishevelled state, with Mr Praxton's mouth upon hers and his odious hand kneading at her breast, nothing would save her. Her papa had worked hard to achieve a standing in society and nothing, but nothing, would be allowed to sully that, even her claims of assault. And Mr Praxton was so very suitable, the wealthy young owner of several paper mills in the area, respectable, influential. No wonder her family were irritated and incredulous that she saw fit to decline the gentleman's addresses. But to be forced to wed against her will, and to such a man… Georgiana felt the sensation starting in her toes. It crept slowly up her legs. Once it reached her head she knew that she would pass into the black realms of oblivion…leaving Mr Praxton's plan to successful fruition.

'Don't fight me, Georgiana.' Mr Praxton's voice scratched against her ear.

She knew she had but one chance, one hope of escaping this vile man and a life at his mercy. And she must take it now, if at all.

Her knee raised in a violent jerk, landing precisely in Mr Praxton's closely situated groin.

'Damnation!' Walter Praxton's body convulsed and he bent double, releasing his hold on Georgiana to clutch at the front of his breeches. 'Hell and damnation, you'll pay for that, you little bitch!' His cheeks paled and a scowl twisted his features.

Georgiana did not delay. Immediately his grip had released, she pivoted and ran.

His voice rasped thick, tinged with malice and pain. 'There's nowhere to run to. Unless you can walk on water, that is.' He leaned heavily upon his thighs and managed to straighten a little.

Georgiana looked beyond to the fast-flowing river, swollen from the heavy November rains. He was right. Dear Lord help her, but he was right. The small clearing was surrounded on three sides by dense shrubs. The gap through which Mr Praxton had coerced her was now firmly blocked by his enraged form. Her heart beat fast and furious as her skirts wrapped themselves around her fleeing legs.

'I fear that you've made a very grave error, my dear, and one for which I'll exact full payment, unless you make yourself amenable to me, Miss Raithwaite.'

In that moment Georgiana made her choice. There could

be no other. Before her courage—or foolery, as her papa would term it—deserted her, she leapt from the grass banking straight into the river.

Walter Praxton's mouth gaped with incredulity. Even the strongest swimmer would be hard pushed to survive such conditions. 'Stupid girl, you're going to drown yourself!' The realisation of just what he stood to lose loomed large in his greedy mind, not to mention Edward Raithwaite's reaction when he discovered that his stepdaughter had drowned whilst in Mr Praxton's care. 'Bloody hell!' he swore through clenched teeth, and scrambled about to find a branch to hook Miss Raithwaite back to safety.

The plan was not proceeding quite as Mr Praxton had envisaged.

A scream shrilled behind him. Mrs Raithwaite collapsed into a crumpled heap and Mrs Battersby-Brown appeared to be in the throes of hysteria, not helped by Mrs Hoskin's high-pitched screaming.

'Good God, man! What the…? Georgiana?' Mr Raithwaite looked at Mr Praxton, confusion clear upon his face.

Walter Praxton turned to the older man. 'Against my advice Miss Raithwaite insisted on examining the river at close quarters. Such a wilful girl! Sir, quickly pass me that large stick, and I'll fish her out.' Mr Praxton's fingers raked his perfect golden locks with ill-concealed agitation.

Georgiana's body submerged beneath the river, its freezing waters rushing to infiltrate the snug warmth of her clothing. Already it clung like a dead weight. Ice-cold water swirled all around, dragging at her skirts, conspiring to pull her beneath its bubbling surface to the dark unknown depths below. Her lungs constricted and would not function save but to gasp for air when there was nothing but water. She tried to scream, but could find no voice. Cold terror prickled at her scalp and her head ached where the freezing water beat her down. Her arms flailed, wildly seeking something, anything, on which to anchor, even as she sank lower. And, just as the darkness closed in upon her so that she could but look up to the lightness of the sky so very far above her head, her hand found purchase. Her fingers closed upon it, clinging for dear life to that saviour. With her heart pumping fit to burst, she pulled herself up and broke the surface, coughing while gasping in air that had never tasted so sweet. She embraced the clump of reeds, unmindful of its sharp-edged leaves lacerating the palms of her hands. Still the river fought to keep her, tugging mercilessly at her grip on that one small patch of vegetation.

'Catch hold of the end, Miss Raithwaite, and I'll pull you to safety.'

Fortunately, or as it now transpired, unfortunately, she was some way beyond the reach of Mr Praxton or, indeed, her stepfather. Through the soaking hair plastered across her eyes she saw Walter Praxton extend the branch towards her. Heard his cruel voice turned velvet with concern. Time stopped still. The river roared in silence, battering her body into numbness. Mama lay motionless upon the ground, and Mrs Battersby-Brown's and Mrs Hoskin's mouths moved in the shape of screams. But for that single instant Georgiana knew nothing, felt nothing, except the terrible certainty that by her own rash actions she had just played right into her unwanted suitor's hands. How well he feigned the hero. And how well her papa would reward him for saving her life. Walter Praxton knew it too. She could see it in his narrow calculating focus.

'Miss Raithwaite, Georgiana!' His honeyed voice pulled her back to consciousness. 'The stick…'

For all that she despised the man and his cruelties, she had not the courage, nor the folly, to sacrifice herself to the river. Death was more fearsome than Walter Praxton. Even as she reached to grasp the stick she saw the glimmer of a smile flicker across his lips, and all the while those cold pale eyes held hers, filled with the promise of what was to come.

Slowly, painfully, he dragged her closer, inching her towards the safety of the bank and the danger of what stood with such concern upon it. 'Nearly there. Just a little more. Hold tight, my dear.' Never once did she shift her gaze, fixed so markedly upon her rescuer.

'Do as Mr Praxton bids. You're almost within reach.' Papa's voice was relief edged with irritation. But then again, did he not always say she was a vexation to his soul, an inconsiderate stepdaughter with a selfish unruly streak?

'Georgiana!' The tips of Mr Praxton's long fingers reached to hers.

She was his. Caught. Landed with all the skill of an expert angler delivering a fine fat trout.

'Mr Praxton.' Her hand stretched towards him. Reaching for her captor. Her eyes closed in anticipation of the feel of his clammy skin. She heard a scream, felt the force of the rushing water pull her with a raging ferocity, saw Walter Praxton recede with the distant bank.

The woman was still yelling. 'Do something, Edward! Dear God, somebody help us!' Her mother's white face twisted with terror.

'Mama!' The word croaked from Georgiana's water-filled mouth as the river swept her downstream with an urgent insistence, ripping her away from the safety of her family and the threat of Mr Praxton. Mercifully Georgiana Raithwaite knew nothing more as the turbulent water claimed her as its own, within the scenic setting of Hurstborne Park.

* * *

'I dare say that you're right, Freddie, I should spend more time at Collingborne. Especially now, with all that's happened.' Nathaniel Hawke's grey gelding trotted contentedly next to the smaller bay.

Lord Frederick eyed his brother speculatively. 'Then you'll stay?' The question was pointless. He already knew the answer.

'I cannot, even if I wanted to. The *Pallas* sails in two weeks' time under orders from the Admiralty. There's nothing I can do to change that.' The reins tightened beneath his fingers, but his face did not betray any hint of the emotion that struggled within. 'Both you and Henry will be there to attend our father, and my presence is sure only to…aggravate the situation.'

'Perhaps you're right.' Lord Frederick sighed. 'But you'll have to confront him over this blasted nonsense at some point—he's threatening to disinherit you from all that he can.'

Nathaniel smiled grimly at the words. 'Have no fear for me, Freddie. I'm more than capable of making a success of my life without the Earl of Porchester's help. And now we should talk of more important matters.'

'More important matters?'

'Indeed. Just how do you mean to explain your *friendship* with Lady Sarah to Mirabelle! That lady will eat you for breakfast, little brother.' Nathaniel raised an eyebrow in wry amusement, and revealed his teeth in a broad grin, ready to hear the tale.

Freddie laughed, then suddenly stopped. 'Nathaniel, what's wrong?'

All traces of humour left his brother's face as he stared in the direction of the river.

'Nathaniel?'

Dark eyes opened wide in shock. 'There's someone in the river!'

The younger man's brow furrowed. 'But the water's too high and too cold for swimming.'

'I doubt that swimming is quite what he had in mind. Quickly, Freddie, there's no time to lose, the fellow will soon be drowned, if he isn't already dead.' Nathaniel spurred the gelding to a gallop and shouted, 'Head towards Holeham's Hook, wait for me on the bridge.'

'But where are you going?' Freddie's words flitted weakly into the wind. Worry growled in his gut. He hoped that Nathaniel wasn't about to do something foolhardy. But wasn't his brother's life a string of foolhardy ventures, with scant regard for the danger in which he seemed permanently embroiled?

Nathaniel's jaw set firm as he directed the gelding to the swollen river. Now that he had drawn closer, he could see that the boy had lost consciousness and was being dragged within the grip of the sweeping current. The slight body tossed and tumbled down the central line of the river beyond all hope of reach. Even as he weighed the situation, Nathaniel knew what he must do. Not once did he flinch from his purpose. He bellowed the words at Freddie's blurred image, 'I'll meet you at the bridge. Be ready to haul us out!' Urging the horse on, he raced alongside the river for some distance.

Just short of the muddied bank he leapt from his horse, snaring the reins over a bush as he ran. First his boots were discarded. Then his superfine coat. Just as the boy swept past Nathaniel plunged into the fast-flowing water. Icy shock bit deep and he schooled himself not to gasp. 'Hell's teeth!' The curse escaped him, but there was no one to hear him over the river's roar. With immense strength of will he forced his legs to kick and swam like he had never swum before in the direction of the poor battered body. The writhing water, pounding in his ears, stinging his eyes, transported him to his quarry.

He felt the slim arm before his saw it, and his fingers closed firm. *Not far to Holeham's Hook. Hold on. Kick hard. Steer towards the right-hand side.* The thoughts came with deliberate logic even as fatigue and pain assailed his body. *The lad's heavy, so heavy. Arms growing numb.* Determination focused as he fought. *Hold fast. Keep his head up. Nearly there.* Through the blinding water he saw the bridge coming up fast and braced himself. He turned his body to absorb the worst of the impact and grunted as it hit hard. His right hand shot up and grasped the sodden wood, striving for anchorage, pulling for safety. But the river would not relinquish her prize so readily, raging against his legs and the limp body he gripped so keenly. Slowly his fingers moved against the post, a minuscule motion, barely noted, but a portent of what was to come. 'No!' he cried out as his palm slid against the wood. And just as it seemed that the river had won, something warm and strong grabbed his wrist. Freddie.

After he had dragged them both out, she lay on the muddied grass beneath Nathaniel. Not a lad at all, but a young woman, her face deathly pale, her sodden clothes revealing a slim but shapely form, long dark hair splayed in the mud around her head. Working with a speed that belied his growing exhaustion, Nathaniel pressed his fingers to the side of the girl's throat and touched his cheek to her mouth. 'Her heart's weak, but she's alive.' He looked up to meet Freddie's concerned gaze. 'She isn't breathing. Help me lift her up.' Once she was cradled in his arms, Nathaniel let her head and chest drop back low towards the ground. 'Slap her hard on the back,' he instructed his brother.

Freddie looked dubious.

'Just do it, man!'

Freddie shrugged and did as he was told.

Water spilled from the girl's mouth as she coughed and spluttered.

'Thank God!' Nathaniel hoisted the slim body back up into his arms and looked down into the girl's face.

A pair of grey-blue eyes stared up into his, and in them he saw the mirror of his own surprise, before the fear closed in.

'Don't be afraid, miss. You're quite safe.' Water dripped in rivulets down his face, splashing on to her cheeks.

She tried to speak, her words but a hoarse croak.

Nathaniel's arms tightened around her. 'Your throat will be sore for a few days yet, but there should be no lasting damage. Don't speak until you're able.'

Her blue-tinged lips tightened and she nodded.

He stared down at her for a moment longer, then sprang into action. 'Freddie, take the girl up on your horse and transport her to Mirabelle. Whoever she is, we cannot leave her here, and the sooner she's dried and warmed, the better. Wrap your coat around her for the journey.'

His brother nodded, clambered on to his horse and reached down for the woman.

'I'll be right behind you.' And so saying, a shivering Nathaniel Hawke set off across the grass in his wet-stockinged feet to retrieve his boots, his coat and his trusty steed.

It was just as his toes squelched down inside the highly polished leather that he heard the shout.

'Excuse me, sir. You over there!'

Nathaniel looked up to see a robust grey-haired gentleman waving from the opposite bank. Two well-dressed men hovered at his side.

'Young man!' Mr Raithwaite shouted louder still.

'How may I help you, sir?' Nathaniel stood tall and, oblivious to his sodden state, executed a small bow in the man's direction.

Edward Raithwaite peered through the spectacles perched on the end of his nose. 'Your appearance suggests that you have just suffered an encounter with the river.'

Nathaniel resisted the reply poised so readily upon his tongue. Rather, he pushed his weary shoulders back and affected to be polite. 'That is indeed the case, sir. Have you an interest in the matter?'

'Yes, sir,' the corpulent man replied. 'I've lost my daughter. Silly chit walked too close to the river.' He glanced towards the young man behind him with blatant irritation. 'Mr Praxton here tried to help, but unfortunately the water took her before he could pull her out.'

Nathaniel's gaze sharpened with interest.

The young man pushed forward. 'Mr Raithwaite's daughter fell into the river about a mile upstream. Considering your appearance, we wondered if you might have tried to assist the young lady.' He gripped the older man's arm. 'Her father is most distressed.' Belatedly adding, 'This is Mr Edward Raithwaite of Andover.'

'I'm pleased to make your acquaintance, sir, and can put your mind at ease. I pulled a girl from the river not fifteen minutes ago.' Nathaniel shrugged into his coat. 'Suffering from cold and shock, but no worse hurts that I could see.'

Mr Raithwaite's elderly head sagged and he pressed his hand to his brow. 'Thank the Lord!'

The handsome man spoke again. 'We must be sure that it is Miss Raithwaite. Was she dark-haired and slender, wearing a yellow walking dress?'

Something in the tone grated against Nathaniel's ear. 'I believe the lady matched your description.' He eyed the man with disdain and turned to address his further comments to Mr Raithwaite. 'My brother has taken Miss Raithwaite to Farleigh Hall. It's situated nearby and she'll be well tended.' He climbed upon his horse and looked directly over at the small group of gentlemen. 'You're welcome to attend your daughter there, sir.'

Mr Raithwaite nodded and mumbled a reply. 'Got to see to the ladies first, then I'll come over.'

'You sent her to Viscount Farleigh's residence?' The voice was curt and heavy with suspicion.

Even Mr Raithwaite turned to look at the man by his side.

'Indeed.' Nathaniel raised an enquiring eyebrow. 'Why?'

Mr Raithwaite cleared his throat and touched a restraining hand to the golden-haired man's arm. 'Mr Praxton, don't worry so. This gentleman means to help us and I believe his actions to be nothing but honourable.' Turning to Nathaniel, he said by way of explanation, 'Mr Praxton has a great fondness for my daughter and is concerned for her.' Then, as if catching himself, 'Please forgive my manners. These are my friends, Mr Walter Praxton and Mr Julian Battersby-Brown.'

Nathaniel acknowledged the introduction with a quick nod of his head. 'Nathaniel Hawke, sir.' He looked directly at Mr Praxton. 'Viscount Farleigh is my brother.'

'*Lord* Hawke!' Mr Battersby-Brown uttered with reverence.

'Please excuse me, gentlemen. I've an inclination to change my clothing.' And with that he made off into the distance with some considerable speed.

Georgiana awoke to find herself tucked firmly into a vast four-poster bed. A fire leapt in the hearth and the room was quiet save for the crackles and spits that emitted from its warm golden flames. She remembered her arrival at the house with the fine young gentleman, but thereafter nothing. She wrinkled her brow in concentrated effort, but there was nothing except a haziness to recall. Sitting up, she became aware of the luxurious nightgown draped against her skin and that her hair was now dry, but tumbled around her shoulders. Just as her toes contacted the floor the door positioned in the far corner of the room swung open. In waltzed a petite lady wearing a fashionable dress of blue muslin.

'Miss Raithwaite, you're awake. Are you feeling better?' Without waiting for an answer, the woman wafted towards her in a cloud of fragrant lavender. Her lively cornflower-blue eyes dropped to where the tips of Georgiana's toes touched upon the carpet. 'My dearest girl, what can you be thinking of? You must not attempt to get up just now. Doctor Boyd has said that you're to rest, and rest you shall. You've suffered a shock and it's likely to take you some time to recover.' The lady chattered on.

Georgiana looked on in mild confusion.

'Now, pop your feet back beneath those bedcovers and rest against the pillows. I'll instruct Mrs Tomelty to bring you a little broth.' She pressed a hand to her mouth in sudden consternation. 'Oh, but whatever am I thinking of? You've not the faintest idea of who I am.'

'I—' Georgiana opened her mouth to speak.

'No, my dear. It's quite inexcusable of me. I'm Mirabelle Farleigh, wife to the brother of Nathaniel and Frederick, the two gentlemen who rescued you from your most unfortunate incident.' She smiled sweetly at Georgiana and helped to rearrange the covers upon the great bed. 'My husband is Henry, Viscount Farleigh.'

'I must thank you, ma'am, for your kindness and for taking me into your home.' Georgiana's voice was husky.

Lady Farleigh's golden ringlets bounced as she shook her head. 'Think nothing of it, dear Miss Raithwaite. You're very welcome.' Her small pink mouth crinkled into a smile again.

'You already know my name, ma'am?' Georgiana's brow lifted in surprise.

'But of course, Nathaniel has told us all. And let's dispense with all this "ma'am-ing", please call me Mirabelle.'

Georgiana smiled at the small woman before her. 'Thank you…Mirabelle, and, of course, you must call me Georgiana. But how did you come to know my name? Has my papa—?'

'Forgive me, my dear.' Lady Farleigh interrupted. 'I'm ahead of myself as usual. Let me retell the story in full just as Nathaniel did.'

'That would be very kind. Thank you, Mirabelle.' Georgiana's eyebrow twitched slightly, but she made no further comment as she leaned back against the pillows and prepared to listen.

Mirabelle settled herself into a chair close by the bed. 'I had just visited baby Richard in the nursery when—'

A brisk knock rapped and not one, but two, gentlemen entered the bedroom.

Georgiana pulled the bedcovers higher to meet her chin and eyed them with suspicion.

Lady Farleigh gave a squeak of delight. 'Nathaniel, Freddie! You've come to check upon poor Miss Raithwaite! What impeccable timing you have. I was just about to explain all about Nathaniel's meeting with Mr Raithwaite, but now that you're here I'll leave all that to you. Miss Raithwaite is positively agog to know how we came to discover her name.'

An uncharitable thought popped into Georgiana's mind.

Would Lord Nathaniel, whichever of the two men he happened to be, be able to squeeze a word in edgeways in the presence of the effusive Mirabelle? And then she had the grace to blush at her quite appalling lapse.

Nathaniel Hawke looked at the subtle play of emotions flitting so clearly across Miss Raithwaite's surprisingly fine features. Curiosity followed suspicion, guilt trailed humour. Mirabelle's chatter allowed him to study the girl with her pale skin and expressive eyes. Her long ebony-coloured hair splashed its dark luxury against the stark white of the nightgown, sweeping down to hang as two heavy curtains. Nathaniel experienced an urge to tangle his fingers in it. She was young, and a lady to boot. Two very good reasons why he should resist the compelling physical attraction he felt towards her.

Mirabelle had paused in her introductions and was pushing him forward with pride. 'Nathaniel really is quite the hero despite his protestations.'

The grey-blue eyes glanced up to meet his...and stopped.

'Miss Raithwaite, I'm glad to see that you're somewhat recovered from your ordeal.' He held her gaze, and smiled.

Georgiana's mouth suddenly felt dry, and the room hot. Indeed, her cheeks burned uncommonly warm. 'Sir,' she managed to croak at the man standing before her. She owed him her life, of that she was certain. It was his strong arms that had pulled her from the river, his courage that had saved her from a watery grave. Those same dark eyes that had held such concern on the riverbank were now regarding her with amusement. The hair that had hung in sodden strands now sprang in mahogany-coloured curls around his rugged face. She should have proclaimed her gratitude from the very rooftops. But Miss Raithwaite, who had been raised to behave with the utmost decorum, suddenly found that it had deserted her, along with every other rational thought. For Lord Nathaniel Hawke was having a most peculiar effect upon her sensibilities. And she was certain that she did not care at all for such a situation.

The wicked smile crooked upon his face deepened as if he sensed the riot of emotion that roared within her. Dear Lord, surely he could do no such thing? The mere thought heightened the intensity of the two rosy patches glowing upon her otherwise pale cheeks. She cleared her raw throat and struggled to regain some measure of composure. 'I'm very grateful to you.' She glanced towards Lord Frederick standing further back. 'I wouldn't be here if it were not for you.'

Freddie smiled and stepped closer. 'It was Nathaniel who went into the water to save you. My part was relatively minor in the whole affair.' He looked towards his brother.

'And where would both Miss Raithwaite and I be without your presence on the bridge?' Nathaniel demanded. 'I won't take the credit for your part in the rescue.' Turning once more to the girl, he offered an explanation. 'Freddie pulled us from the water. Indeed, we both owe him our lives.'

Freddie's face coloured in pleasure and he mumbled, 'Nonsense.'

It seemed that Nathaniel was determined to share the glory. 'Thank you both.' Miss Raithwaite smiled shyly.

Freddie's cheeks grew redder.

So his brother had noticed Miss Raithwaite's attributes. The girl was undeniably fetching, but as the daughter of the owner of several coaching inns, she was strictly off limits to both of them. Neither marriageable material nor otherwise. He had best have a word with Freddie.

'Miss Raithwaite,' he continued, 'before leaving Hurst-borne Park I had the good fortune to meet your father and his companions. Naturally they were concerned about you, and I reassured them of your safety. Your family know that you're here and will call as soon as possible.'

'Oh,' Georgiana Raithwaite said in a small voice. The memory of Mr Praxton's outrageous actions appeared with clarity. Having survived the river, she now felt that her biggest ordeal was yet to come. Just for a moment a look of horror and desperation flitted across her face before she masked it once more with polite indifference. 'Thank you, my lord, you're most kind.' She settled her wounded hands together in a demure gesture. Only Nathaniel noticed just how white her knuckles shone.

Nathaniel Hawke swirled the brandy around the finely engraved balloon glass. 'Our Miss Raithwaite didn't seem to regard being reunited with her family as entirely favourable. Did you see the expression upon her face when I mentioned her father?'

'Mmm.' Freddie regarded him quizzically as he lounged back in the winged chair. 'You think there's more to the matter than meets the eye?'

'Perhaps. We shall discover soon enough.'

Gravel crunched from the drive and a carriage emptying its passengers sounded through the library window.

'Mr Raithwaite,' Freddie said distractedly. 'Georgiana's a fine-looking girl, don't you think?'

Nathaniel's face became somewhat grim. 'Don't get drawn down that line, little brother. There's no dalliance to be had there. Miss Raithwaite is a coaching-inn owner's daughter, albeit a wealthy one. Our father would most heartily disapprove, and you don't want to risk becoming as black a sheep as me.' He twitched an eyebrow, and offered an imitation of the Earl of Porchester's voice, 'Think of the scandal, dear boy, the scandal.'

Laughing, the brothers departed the library and went to meet Mr Edward Raithwaite.

Georgiana's back scarcely felt the soft plumpness of the pillows supporting it. Nor did she notice the cosy warmth of the finely-stitched quilt covering the length of her body. Mirabelle had lent her a dressing gown and sent her own maid to dress her hair so that she might feel more comfortable with receiving visitors. But none of the small woman's kindness could obliterate the uneasy feeling in the pit of Georgiana's stomach. She stretched a smile upon her mouth and turned to face her stepfather.

'Georgiana, thank goodness you're safe and well. Your poor mother is distraught with worry. She's taken the headache and been forced to bed,' Mr Raithwaite chided his stepdaughter, but his relief was plain for all to see.

'Poor Mama, I didn't mean to worry her.'

'Quite so, quite so.' He nodded. 'I dread to think what would have happened without the quick actions of the two gentlemen. We would have lost you for sure.'

'I'm sorry to have caused such distress, Papa, but—'

'And how did you come to fall into the river? Do you know no better than a child?'

Georgiana lowered her eyes. 'I…' She paused. 'There…'

Mr Praxton stepped forward, looking immaculate in his green coat. 'I'm sure Georgiana has had ample time to consider her folly in strolling so close to the river's edge. She's given herself a nasty fright as well as the rest of us, and is not likely to repeat the same mistake again.' He touched a hand to Edward Raithwaite's sleeve. 'Mr Raithwaite, I beg of you, don't be too hard on the girl.'

'You're too damned soft with her, Praxton,' the old man growled, then spoke to his daughter once more. 'Do you hear how Mr Praxton pleads your excuses? And what have you to say in your defence?'

Walter Praxton threw a long-suffering smile at Lady Farleigh. The indulgent suitor to perfection.

It did not escape Georgiana's notice. Neither did Lady Farleigh's subtle knowing nod.

Her body tensed in anger. Walter Praxton was a conniving knave. And it seemed he had hoodwinked them all. Well, if he thought her fool enough to stay silent over the precise cause of her winter plunge, he had another think coming. 'Papa, I have no excuses, only reasons. As they are of a delicate nature, I would prefer to discuss them with you in private.'

Mr Raithwaite looked at her knowingly. 'Mr Praxton has already spoken to me of the matter, and, much as I cannot pretend that I'm happy with your behaviour—' he stroked his chin '—I understand that young women are somewhat excitable in response to such declarations.'

'Exactly what has Mr Praxton revealed?' Georgiana's greyblue eyes glittered dangerously, her temper soaring by the minute.

'Georgiana!' He glanced apologetically at Lady Farleigh. 'Have a care with your manners. Now is clearly not the time to discuss the matter.' His countenance was turning ruddier by the minute.

'Oh, please do excuse me, Mr Raithwaite, Mr Praxton, Georgiana,' Lady Farleigh said. 'I've just recalled a pressing matter downstairs.' Mirabelle fluttered out of the bedroom and straight to the library to apprise her relatives of the news that the delectable Miss Raithwaite had indulged in scandalous behaviour with Mr Praxton. And who could blame her with such a thoroughly handsome beau?

Georgiana looked from her father to Mr Praxton and back again. 'Lady Farleigh has left us. Surely we can speak of *the matter* now.' Her teeth gripped firmly together.

'You're trying my patience, girl. When will you learn to leave things be? Is it not enough that you've…that you behaved in such a way? Your mother would be shocked to hear of it. Mr Praxton and I have decided that Mrs Raithwaite should not learn of your actions prior to this afternoon's incident. We informed her only of the betrothal.' Mr Raithwaite nodded sagely.

She could feel the steady pulse beating at her neck, pumping the anger throughout her body. 'I don't know what untruths Mr Praxton has told you but be assured, Papa, that I've done nothing dishonourable. I'm neither compromised nor ruined, and marriage to Mr Praxton is not necessary. You may tell the truth to Mama.'

'Enough!' Mr Raithwaite said. 'I'll hear no more. Mr Praxton has confessed the truth of those stolen kisses. As a gentleman, he felt it his implicit duty to do so.' His cheeks bulged a puce discoloration. 'He will make you a good husband, Georgiana.'

Walter Praxton was fairly glowing with angelic piety. 'I'm afraid Miss Raithwaite has stolen my heart, sir.' He sighed and glanced down at the rug.

Mr Raithwaite looked at him strangely. 'Then you had best take more care of her. She is not yet your wife, Mr Praxton.'

Their eyes locked for a few silent moments before the younger man inclined his head in subtle compliance.

The elderly hand moved to stroke the grizzled beard. 'That said, I believe the wedding should be convened with some haste.'

The blood beat strongly in Georgiana's ears. How could her stepfather take the word of an acquaintance over hers? Did he truly judge her character so lightly? 'Papa,' she tried again.

Edward Raithwaite turned a steely eye upon his stepdaughter. 'Say no more, Georgiana. It's clear that your experience this afternoon has adversely affected your mind. I trust that a good night's rest will return you to your senses. I'll have the carriage sent round to collect you tomorrow.'

'Adieu, Miss Raithwaite, until tomorrow.' Mr Praxton bowed. Together the two gentlemen turned and left the room.

An irate Georgiana stared at the door that closed so firmly behind them. Her jaw clenched with determination and her fingers stole to worry at the lobe of her ear. If Papa thought the affair settled, he was to be grossly disappointed.

It was some time later that Georgiana heard the discreet knock at the door and found Nathaniel Hawke entering the bedroom for the second time that day. *The Italian* fell limply from her fingers, pages fanning open to lose the sentence she had been forcing herself to concentrate upon just moments before. She glanced up to find him walking purposefully towards her with a large tray in his hands. The elderly and rather rotund Mrs Tomelty hobbled in his wake. Setting the tray down upon the table positioned beside the bed, he gestured towards the cook. 'Mrs Tomelty has made you some of her famous broth. If you would care to try a little, I can personally vouch for its healing properties.'

Georgiana's gaze flicked from the strong tanned fingers that curled around the handles of the tray to the dark warmth of his eyes. Lord Nathaniel had brought her the broth, in person! Unwittingly a crinkle of suspicion crept across the bridge of her nose. She wetted her suddenly dry lips and looked at the cook.

'That he can, miss,' beamed Mrs Tomelty. 'Could never get enough of my broth, could Lord Nathaniel. Always had to have a bowl full to the brim every time he fell out of a tree or come off his horse. Never known a little 'un like him for getting himself into mischief. Why, I remember the time him and Lord Henry were swimming, bare as the day they were born, in the—'

'Thank you, Mrs Tomelty,' said Nathaniel rather forcefully.

A smile tugged at the corners of Georgiana's mouth. Suddenly the tall, athletic gentleman standing only a few feet from where she lay in bed didn't seem quite so intimidating.

Mrs Tomelty moved forward to pat Georgiana's hand. 'Now, duck, you eat that up, and it'll do you the world of good. I'll be just over there in that chair by the fireplace so that there won't be no problems 'bout Lord Nathaniel bein' in a young lady's bedroom.' The elderly servant remained blissfully unaware of the ghost of a grimace that flitted across Nathaniel's face. She hobbled the distance to the fireplace, eased herself into the rose brocade chair, and made herself comfortable.

'Please forgive my intrusion, Miss Raithwaite. I know that I should not be here, but I wished to speak to you…alone…to reassure myself that you are well.' There was a slight uneasiness about him, as if he wanted to say something, but didn't know quite how to go about saying it.

Georgiana's suspicion should have escalated, but it didn't. Instead, it fizzled away to be replaced with an intrinsic trust. *Has your experience with Mr Praxton taught you nothing of gentlemen?* the little voice inside her head insisted. But something outside of logic and common sense assured her that the man standing before her now was nothing like Walter Praxton. Mr Praxton revolted her, but Lord Nathaniel… A shiver tingled up her spine and she deliberately turned her mind from that vein of thought. 'I am very well, thank you, my lord,' she managed with a politeness of which Mama would have been proud.

He was looking at her as if he knew the words that tripped from her tongue for the lie that they were.

The pause stretched.

Georgiana felt the first hint of a flush touch her cheeks. Lord, but he couldn't possibly know the truth. She must stop acting like a ninny-hammer and pull herself together.

'I wanted to ask you about your accident. Were you alone with Mr Praxton when it happened?'

The gentle hint of colour in Georgiana's face ignited with all the subtlety of a beacon. Her heart set up a thudding reverberation in her chest. She swallowed once, and then again. 'Yes.' Her fingers moved to gather hold of Mrs Radcliffe's book lying atop the bedcovers. She gripped the ornately gilded leather and took a deep breath. 'Yes.' This time more strongly. 'Mr Praxton wished to show me an interesting botanical species that grows close to the river.' *Or so he said.* 'My parents and their friends were following in a walk of their own.'

One dark eyebrow raised in a minuscule motion.

Georgiana saw it and found herself swamped in a feeling of wretched shame and anger. She knew very well the path his mind was taking. 'We were not alone for long.' *Long enough for Walter Praxton to make clear the exact nature of his intent!* She knew she was only exposing her own guilt. Drat the man, why was he looking at her like that? She had a sudden urge to confess all, tell him exactly what Mr Praxton had done and why. But when all was said and done, Nathaniel Hawke was a stranger and a man…a very attractive man. And she couldn't reveal such sordid details, especially not to him.

'And what was it that you were doing to come to land in the river, Miss Raithwaite?' He stepped closer to the bed and lowered his voice.

'I…I was…' She glanced up to meet the strength of his gaze.

'Examining the botanical specimen?' he suggested.

'No.'

'Then what?'

She could give him no answer that would not compromise herself and she did not think that she could bear to see the condemnation in his eyes that was sure to follow. So she said nothing, just shook her head.

'And what was Mr Praxton doing to allow you to fall?'

I didn't fall, I jumped! And Mr Praxton was doing precisely as you suspect! she wanted to shout, but couldn't. 'We had a disagreement, and…that is when I went into the river.' Subconsciously her fingers slid to tug at her ear lobe.

Nathaniel took another step closer. He made as if to reach his hand out to her, then checked the action. 'Miss Raithwaite,' he said quietly, 'I have the notion that you're fearful of returning home. Who are you afraid of?' He waited, before prompting, 'If Mr Praxton has done aught that he should not have…'

The beautiful grey-blue eyes widened in shock and for the briefest moment he thought she was about to tell him something of the greatest significance. Then she faltered, and the moment was gone.

'No.' The temptation was great. She wanted to tell him. The words had crept to the tip of her tongue before she'd had the sense to restrain them.

'Then, your father?'

The intensity of his gaze made her shiver. It was as if he could see past her defences to the truth. She willed herself to stay calm. 'Why should I be afraid of my papa?'

'Perhaps he does not approve of your friendship with Mr Praxton.'

If only that were the case! Had she imagined his subtle emphasis on the word 'friendship'? She bristled at the implication. 'I have no *friendship* with Mr Praxton. My papa is more approving of our betrothal than you could possibly realise.'

Hell's teeth, but the girl was infuriating. He'd come here to assail the nagging doubt that there was more to Georgiana's story than she was telling—something that wasn't quite right. Fear, desperation, anger, indignation, he was sure he'd seen them all marked clearly on her face. Damn it, he hadn't even known her this time yesterday. Now here he was, behaving like the village idiot, in the chit's bedroom of all places, with the foolish chivalric notion that she needed his help. So Mirabelle had been right. Miss Raithwaite had been indulging in some compromising behaviour with the man and she was to marry him. The thought irked him more than it should have. 'You are betrothed to Mr Praxton?' He struggled to keep the scowl from his face.

'Mr Praxton is very determined to marry me.' She spoke so quietly that he struggled to hear her answer, strange as it was.

He thought he saw her lower lip tremble, but before he could be certain it was caught in a nip by her teeth. Praxton was clearly capable of eliciting strong emotion in her. Again that surge of disquiet made itself known.

Nathaniel looked at the girl with her flushed cheeks and glittering eyes for a moment longer. 'Then, you have my felicitations, Miss Raithwaite. I will leave you to your rest.' He bowed and strode from the room as if it was a matter of the smallest consideration. Georgiana Raithwaite's future was none of his concern. But he could not rid himself of the unsettled feeling for the rest of the day.

Chapter Two

Nathaniel Hawke dropped a chaste kiss on to his brother's wife's cheek, only to find himself embraced in a bear hug. Mirabelle's arms barely stretched around him and she stepped on the tips of her toes to reach up to him. 'Dearest Nathaniel, promise me that you'll take care on both your journey to Portsmouth and your voyage, wherever it may take you.'

His mouth opened to reply.

'And make sure that you send Henry back from Collingborne. He's been away for an age and I'm sure that your father will manage perfectly well with Freddie instead.'

Nathaniel's eyes crinkled with amusement. 'I'm quite sure that—'

'Shall we see you again soon?' Mirabelle disengaged her hold and launched herself in Freddie's direction.

'I'm afraid I haven't received my sailing orders yet so I cannot answer your question.'

Freddie suffered a similar mauling at Mirabelle's hands and grimaced when she pinched his cheek. 'You grow more like Henry every day!'

He groaned. 'Mirabelle!'

'Well, fortunately for you it's true. Now, off with you both. It's time for my visit to the nursery and I can hear Charlie and Richard bawling from here. Such lungs!'

Having taken their farewells of Mirabelle, their nephews and a rather wan Miss Raithwaite, the brothers headed out at a steady pace south along the Gosport Road.

Freddie screwed up his face. 'The prospect of an increasing similarity between Henry and myself is most depressing!'

Nathaniel laughed. 'Why? Surely a marked resemblance to our distinguished sibling can be nothing but good? I mean, Henry has wisdom, good judgement and a deal of sense. What more could a fellow want?'

'A sense of humour springs to mind, along with a number of other criteria. Henry's a fine chap and all that, but he's a trifle dull. All work and no play, *et cetera*, *et cetera*!'

'Beneath that stuffy exterior is a good man.'

'I know, I know. But can you imagine Henry jumping into the River Borne to rescue Miss Raithwaite? Poor girl would have drowned, and I wouldn't have had the pleasure of carrying her back to Farleigh Hall.' A wicked expression crossed Freddie's face. 'Delicious! Quite a figure beneath all those clothes!'

Nathaniel affected shock, but laughed just the same. 'Frederick Hawke, that's no way to speak of a lady.'

Freddie's grin deepened, and his eyes twinkled. 'But if Mirabelle is to be believed, our Miss Raithwaite is hardly a lady. Lucky Mr Praxton.'

'Ah, Mr Praxton. I'd lay the blame for Miss Raithwaite's misdemeanours firmly at his door. Taking advantage of the girl he is betrothed to.' Nathaniel looked directly at his brother. 'There's something rather unsavoury about the man, wouldn't you agree?'

'He seemed perfectly fine to me. Rather a fashionable good-looking chap. I wouldn't have thought he'd have too much trouble with the ladies, if you know what I mean.' Freddie winked.

'Perhaps you're right. But my instinct sets me against him, however unfair that may seem. Still, what's it to us? We shall likely never set eyes on Mr Praxton or Miss Raithwaite again.' He twitched the reins beneath his fingers. 'I wonder if she knows what she's getting herself into, tangling with such a man?'

Freddie snorted. 'You're growing suspicious in your old age. I think it must be time that we stopped for some refreshments to soothe your poor addled brain. The George Inn isn't far ahead. I'll race you to it!'

It seemed to Mirabelle Farleigh that Georgiana's health had suffered not so much from her plunge into the River Borne, but from the visit of her father and the man to whom she was betrothed. Subsequent to their leaving the girl appeared pale and listless. Scarcely a morsel of food had passed her lips since and she declined to be drawn by the brightest of conversation that her ladyship had to offer. Not that any sign of fever or pain could be seen to account for her behaviour. But something was wrong, very wrong. Georgiana wore the air of a woman condemned, not of one about to marry her lover. Lady Farleigh, who had an innate interest in such things, had every intention of getting to the bottom of the mysterious affair.

'My dear Georgiana, I've spoken to your stepfather's man and explained that you're not sufficiently recovered to travel home today. Why, such a journey would be sure to leave you with a chill, and is quite out of the question. The carriage has departed with a letter to your stepfather explaining my decision.' Mirabelle did not miss the brief flicker in Georgiana's bleak eyes.

'My father did not come in person?'

Mirabelle shook her head. 'No, my dear. I'm sure he must have important matters to deal with that prevent his presence. Don't concern yourself over it. It's well and good that he didn't come here himself, as he's clearly busy, and gentlemen do so dislike a wasted journey.' She adjusted her skirts and sat herself down on the bed. Taking hold of Georgiana's hand, she studied the girl's face with undue attention. 'I understand that you would be much happier to be going home today.'

A careful guard slotted in place over the white features.

'But can you reconcile yourself as a guest at Farleigh Hall for a few more days?'

The grey-blue eyes widened in surprise.

Mirabelle saw the blatant relief, felt the lapse of tension in the hand positioned beneath her own.

'Of course. Thank you, Lady Farleigh…Mirabelle. I have been feeling a little unwell,' Georgiana lied. The river experience had caused exhaustion, bruising, a sore throat and some cuts to her hands, nothing more. But the knowledge that Walter Praxton had tricked them all to force her into marriage affected her far more deeply. And the loathing that it engendered made her wonder just how she could endure such a thing. He stood for everything that she despised and now she had no choice but to marry him. 'No choice at all.' The mumbled words had escaped her before she realised what she was about. Her eyes slid to Lady Farleigh's in a panic and she pressed her fingers to her lips as if to stopper any further traitorous disclosures.

Her ladyship's bright blue eyes looked back, and Georgiana could have sworn that they held in them an understanding that belied the lady's blithe manner. She held her breath and waited.

'If something is wrong, Georgiana, you need only tell me and I will try to help.' Her small face was unusually still.

Georgiana pressed her palms to her forehead. Dare she trust Mirabelle Farleigh? 'I'm afraid that it's a matter of some delicacy, ma'am.'

Lady Farleigh gently touched Georgiana's arm. 'I thought it might be, my dear. Rest assured I won't discuss your story with anyone else.'

She so desperately needed to speak to someone, to tell another of Walter Praxton's lies. She remembered Nathaniel Hawke's concern and how he'd offered her the opportunity to confide in him. But he was a man, and a very attractive one at that. And she didn't doubt that he had mistaken her situation with Walter Praxton entirely. Why else had she been forced to reveal the wretched betrothal? Lady Farleigh was different altogether. She undoubtedly liked to chatter. That wasn't what worried Georgiana. The nature of her concern lay more in whether the lady's preferences stretched to gossip. She twisted her fingers nervously together and contemplated further. If that was the case, then the damage was already done, for Georgiana was certain that the conversation witnessed by Lady Farleigh could do nothing but lead her to conclude that Georgiana had indulged in grossly inappropriate behaviour with Mr Praxton. And that man's—she could no longer say *gentle*man's—manner had done everything to foster the impression that he was her suitor. Heaven forbid that Lady Farleigh thought Georgiana and Walter Praxton lovers as Lord Nathaniel had done! The greatest harm had happened. Telling the truth couldn't make it worse, and might even go some way to helping her situation. The prospect seemed appealing.

All the while Mirabelle Farleigh had sat, quietly watching the play of conflicting emotions on Georgiana's face. 'If you choose not to speak of what's bothering you, then I'll say nothing further on the matter other than there's always a choice, no matter what you might think, and you must always remember that.'

The words confirmed Georgiana's decision and with a sigh she uttered, 'There's so much to tell, I scarcely know where to begin.'

Mirabelle's curls swayed as she lowered her head. 'You must start at the beginning, it is usually the best place.' And, so saying, she made herself comfortable upon the bedcovers and prepared to hear Georgiana's tale.

It was some considerable time later that Lady Farleigh had heard it all. Her ladyship was fairly bursting with indignation. 'I cannot conceive that a gentleman could be so profoundly dishonest and despicable. Indeed, his actions are most definitely not those of a gentleman and I refuse to call him that.' She paced up and down the bedroom, her hands pulling at her skirts, her cheeks a blaze of furious colour. 'Of course you won't marry him.' She honed her gimlet eye upon Georgiana, who was already feeling much better for having unburdened herself.

'No. I had no intention of accepting his addresses when he indicated that his affections lay in my direction. I made sure that he fully understood that I wouldn't look favourably upon him—that's why he resorted to this scheme.' She had swung her legs from beneath the covers and was sitting on the edge of the bed.

Lady Farleigh struggled to understand the motivation behind such a dastardly deed. 'He must be mad for love of you; when he realised that you'd no intention of accepting his suit, it forced him to take desperate measures. What other explanation can there be?'

'I don't know.' Georgiana shook her head. 'But I cannot believe that he loves me, for all his declarations.' She moved her bare toes across the rug. 'Indeed, I cannot believe that he loves anyone other than himself. My friends, Sarah and Fanny, can barely contain themselves in his presence. They swear that he's quite the most handsome man they've seen. Their response seems ludicrous to me, for I cannot find him handsome in the slightest. He's a cruel and unfeeling man with no regard for the welfare of others.'

The small woman was regarding her quizzically. 'Have you seen evidence of his nature to reach such a conclusion?'

Georgiana stood up and found herself a full head taller than her hostess. 'Mirabelle,' she implored, casting her hands out before her, 'I've seen it with my own eyes. He owns the paper mill in Whitchurch and, because of his friendship with my family, invited us to visit. I attended with my mama and papa and explored all through the mill. Oh, Mirabelle, you wouldn't believe how that man treats his employees. It's truly awful. I saw one poor boy, who couldn't have been more than five years old, running around gathering any rags that had fallen on the floor. He was as thin as a stick and couldn't stop coughing. The child had the misfortune to drop a piece of material close to Mr Praxton—not that it touched him in any way at all. And do you know what that man did?' Georgiana's face contorted with anger. She swept on heedless of Mirabelle's reply, fuelled by wrathful indignation. 'He struck the boy hard across the head with his cane. Can you believe it?' Her breast heaved dramatically, leaving Lady Farleigh in no doubt as to the extent of Miss Raithwaite's feelings. 'Blood ran from the child's crown and the boy didn't dare to utter a sound. Not one sound. That is the essence of Mr Praxton's nature. Nothing excuses such callous behaviour.' Georgiana's eyes flashed with all the fervour of the stormiest sea, grey and green lights shimmering in their depths. 'These people have nothing, Mirabelle. They steal bread to feed their families, such is their plight. And for that crime, Walter Praxton would have them flogged as thieves. He was the one who reported Tom Jenkins, and you know what fate that poor soul met.'

Lady Farleigh nodded. 'Flogged through the streets before transportation for seven years.' She pursed her lips. 'Theft is indeed a crime, but the punishment seems a trifle harsh.'

'Harsh?' The word erupted from Georgiana with all the force of Mr Trevithick's new *Wylam* locomotive. 'That must be the greatest understatement I've heard.'

'Georgiana, I understand that you feel sorry for these people, but you're becoming distracted from the point. Mr Praxton is reprehensible to you. He's behaved abominably and it's quite clear that you cannot allow your stepfather to believe his lies.'

The fire surging through Georgiana's blood mellowed and she let out a sigh. 'I've tried. He won't listen.'

'Perhaps if you spoke to your mama, she would intercede for you.'

Georgiana wrung her hands miserably. 'Mama loves me dearly, of that I'm sure, but she would never stand against my stepfather, not for anything in the world. She says that a good wife must do her husband's bidding, for he always knows best.'

Exactly what Mirabelle Farleigh thought of that statement was written all over her face, but she made no mention of it.

'Please, Mirabelle, do not blame her. My own dear papa died when I was fourteen years old, leaving Mama and me quite alone. After his death she was so lonely and afraid…and then she met Mr Raithwaite, and everything changed.'

Mirabelle laid a hand across Georgiana's white knuckles

and said gently, 'Try to speak to your stepfather again. I'm sure that, once the truth is revealed to Mr Raithwaite, he'll send Walter Praxton packing with a flea in his ear. You must speak to him, Georgiana, even if he doesn't want to listen.'

Later that night, as Georgiana lay snug beneath the blankets within the four-poster bed she mulled over Mirabelle's advice. It was the most sensible approach of course. No more moping. No more lying in bed. Mirabelle was right. Papa would be horrified to learn that Walter Praxton had used them both miserably and all talk of marriage would be dismissed. But first she just had to make Papa listen; knowing what she knew of her stepfather, that was not likely to prove an easy prospect. It was very late before Georgiana finally found sleep.

Two days later, and Georgiana had left the sanctuary of Farleigh Hall. The clock ticked its frantic pace upon the mantelpiece as she faced her stepfather across his study. She stood tall with her head high, her hands held tightly behind her back, trying hard to convey an air of confidence that she did not feel. From the moment of her entry to the room, it was clear that Mr Raithwaite's annoyance with his stepdaughter had not mellowed since their last meeting in Farleigh Hall. He continued to write, refusing even to acknowledge her presence, never mind actually look at her. Georgiana waited in silence. The only sound in the room was the frenzied ticking. And still Edward Raithwaite concentrated on the papers lying neatly on the desk before him. Some fifteen minutes passed.

'Papa.' She uttered the word softly, as if to diffuse any notion of confrontation or insult it might contain.

Mr Raithwaite's flowing script did not falter, his hand continuing its steady pace across the page.

She thought he had not heard or was intent on refusing any means of communication with her when he placed his pen upon the desk with the utmost care. Finally he raised his eyes to meet hers and they were filled with such unrelenting severity as to almost unnerve Georgiana before she even started.

'Have you come to apologise for your appalling behaviour and the lack of respect with which you treated me the other day?' His thick wrinkled hands lay calm and still upon the polished wood veneer, a stark contrast to Georgiana's fingers, which were gripping onto each other behind her back.

'I meant no disrespect to you, sir, and I'm sorry if my words sounded as such.'

Mr Raithwaite's austere demeanour relaxed a little. 'No doubt the shock of falling into the river was responsible for your harsh words. And now that you've had time to reflect upon the whole affair, you see the error of your ways.' The elderly brow cleared a little more. 'Mmm.'

A woman was expected to be obedient and unquestioning, first to her father, and then to her husband. Her stepfather was an old-fashioned man, fully supportive of the view that his wife and children were merely chattels. Nothing would be gained by antagonising him, or so Georgiana reasoned. The best strategy was to agree with most of what he said, even though it rankled with her to do so, and then, when he was at his most amenable, to reveal Mr Praxton's lies. Not for the first time, Georgiana wished that she'd been born a man. The feeble weapons of women were not those she would have preferred to use. But they were the only ones available to her. She forced her face into a smile. 'Indeed, Papa. I didn't mean to be ill mannered with you. I know that you only have my best interests at heart.'

The old man nodded and looked at her with a strange speculative gleam in his eye. 'Never a truer word has been spoken, Georgiana. Your welfare lies at the heart of all of my actions of late. It's well that you realise that.' And then he looked away, and the peculiar intensity of the moment had vanished.

It was precisely the opening Georgiana was looking for. 'I never should have doubted it, and it's with such an understanding in mind that I must speak with you. I ask only that you listen to me, for what I have to say is the truth. I would never lie to you, Papa, you must know that.'

He cleared his throat, rose, and meandered over to stand before the window. 'Then say what you must, child, and be quick about it.'

The time had come. Now she would reveal Mr Praxton for the man he truly was. She pressed her cold clammy palms tighter and began to speak in what she hoped was a calm and controlled voice. Any hint of emotion could condemn her as a hysterical female, not worthy of Mr Raithwaite's attention. 'I'm aware that Mr Praxton has spoken to you regarding what happened prior to my accident. And I also know that you hold that same gentleman in high regard.' She swallowed hard. 'But I must tell you, sir, that Mr Praxton has not spoken the truth. I would never entertain an improper dalliance with any gentleman, let alone Mr Praxton. You know that I've never encouraged his attentions. Why should I then behave in the absurd manner he's claimed? I swear that I'm innocent of his charges. He's trying to make fools of us both.' Her heart was pounding and her lips cracked dry. She waited to hear his understanding, his proud belief in her virtue, his condemnation of Walter Praxton.

Silence, save for the clock's incessant ticking.

Georgiana longed to still its maniacal movement, but she waited with restrained patience.

Eventually her stepfather turned from the window to face her. 'No man, or *woman* for that matter, makes a fool of me.' His voice was slow and measured.

The breath escaped her in a small sigh of relief. The deed was done, the truth told. Mr Praxton would be banished from her life.

'How could you even think it?' He surveyed her with a closed look. 'Whether you did, or did not, indulge in unlady-like behaviour no longer matters. Your marriage to Mr Praxton has been arranged and in time you'll come to see that it's a good thing for both our families. Mr Praxton thinks very highly of you and I trust you will endeavour to become a good wife.'

A strangled laugh escaped Georgiana's lips as she stared at her stepfather with growing disbelief. 'He lied to you, tried to destroy my reputation. Does that mean nothing? You would still have me wed him?'

Edward Raithwaite's manner was carefully impassive. 'There was never any threat to your reputation until you started your foolish twittering in front of Lady Farleigh. Any damage to your reputation was effected by your own hand, my dear. But your forthcoming marriage will rectify any harm that has been done.'

'You cannot seriously expect me to marry him!' Georgiana's voice increased in volume and she placed her hands against the desk's cool wooden surface, leaning forward towards her stepfather.

'Sit down, Georgiana,' he snapped, 'and do not raise your voice to me.'

Georgiana took a tentative step backwards, but remained standing.

Mr Raithwaite's face darkened. 'I said, sit down,' and his enunciation was meticulous.

Her legs retreated further and she stumbled into the closely positioned chair.

Gone was the bumbling genteel man. Mr Raithwaite's eyes focused with a shrewd clarity. 'A woman must marry as her father directs, to consolidate power and wealth, to open up new opportunities for the family. It's the way of the world. If you're labouring under some childish notion of love or romance, then I'm here to tell you that it's nonsense. I didn't send you to that expensive ladies' academy to learn such foolishness. No, Georgiana. Walter Praxton is as best a match as can be expected. You will marry him and behave as behoves a decent young lady. And that, my dear, will be an end to the matter. Forget all else.'

Georgiana stared at Edward Raithwaite as if seeing him for the first time. A tightening nausea was growing within her stomach and she could feel the sweat bead upon her upper lip. The terrible sinking sensation arose not so much from what her stepfather had just said, but rather from that which he had not. Her scalp prickled with unease as she struggled to comprehend the enormity of what she had just learned. All his talk of childish notions and nonsense was a distraction, an attempt to divert her from the real issue. But Georgiana would not be distracted so easily. Her mind had grasped the problem in full. 'You knew,' she said in a quiet voice, and never once did her eyes leave Edward Raithwaite's face. 'You knew all along.'

Mr Raithwaite sent her a look that held nothing of affection. 'The water has sent a fever to your brain.'

The harsh chill of the truth seeped through to scrape at her bones. Now that she had started she could not stop. 'It was an agreement between the two of you. That's why you were so content to allow me to walk alone with him in Hurstborne

Park, even when you knew that I didn't want to go. The seduction was planned.' She stared at him, the full extent of the horror uncoiling. 'And Mama…surely she could not have known too?'

'Your ranting renders you fit for nowhere but Bedlam, an amusing spectacle for the aristocracy, nothing more. Be careful what you say, Georgiana. I would not have your mother any further upset than she already is. I must warn her to watch for any signs of a brain fever in you.' He sighed and, removing his spectacles, pinched at the bridge of his nose. 'Both Mr Praxton and I only want what is best for you.'

Her mouth cracked to form a cynical smile that did not touch her eyes, eyes that faded to a bleak grey-blue. 'How my leap into the River Borne must have dismayed you both.'

'You jumped?' Raithwaite's brow lowered.

Georgiana's smile intensified. 'Oh, yes, dear Papa, I'd rather face death in a swollen river than submit to Walter Praxton's cruel lips.'

'You're mistaken about him. It's a measure of your youthful ignorance, and I won't let you throw away the chance of a good marriage because of it. You're one and twenty, and in danger of being left on the shelf. This is the best opportunity you'll get.'

She shook her head sadly. 'He is not a kind man, Papa. How can you justify what you've done?'

Edward Raithwaite slowly sat himself down in the comfortable chair behind his desk. 'I said that my actions are for the best, and so they are. The end justifies the means, my dear. You'll thank me in the years to come. Now, our discussion is at a close. It would be well if you did not mention that of which we have spoken to your mother. I will not have you run bleating to her. Do not seek to flout my judgement, Georgiana, for, if you refuse to marry Walter Praxton, then I'll have you deemed of unsound mind, and I don't need to explain what the consequences of that would be.' His mouth shut in a tight grim line.

Indeed, he did not need to offer any explanation at all. It was with a very heavy heart that Georgiana made her way out of the study.

Nathaniel propped himself against the sturdy wooden gate and was content to enjoy the view before him. Collingborne was set amidst the soft rolling splendour of the Hampshire countryside, close to Harting Down. The green velvet of fields stretched ahead, dotted periodically with prehistoric mounds. Above yawned a rich russet canopy, its seasonal castings rustling gently around his feet. The air was damp and still, the sky grey with cloud. Within the hour the light would fade to darkness and the gentle patter of winter rain begin…and he would be back within the great house to suffer the hatred of his father. A robin flitted between the branches overhead, singing its distinctive call, alone in a field of crows and starlings and magpies. It was a feeling that Nathaniel knew well, and not one on which he wished to dwell. This was his respite, his time of peace, and from it he gathered the strength to face the sombre house once more. He would be gone tomorrow, and he could endure all that his father would throw at him until then. The leaves crunched beneath the soles of his riding boots as he strolled with purposeful resignation towards the place he could not call home.

'Mirabelle?' Nathaniel halted in surprise upon the gravel drive.

'Nathaniel!' His sister by marriage clambered down from

the travelling coach. 'You'll think that I'm following you! But I couldn't wait four more weeks for that dratted brother of yours to return. He sent me a letter saying that he couldn't leave until then. So I decided right then and there to come. And here I am. Won't Henry be surprised?'

Nathaniel thought that perhaps surprise might not be Henry's primary sentiment when he viewed the arrival of his wife and children. Not that his brother did not care for them, it was just that Mirabelle's presence was not entirely conducive to performing matters of business. Quite how the relationship between his straight-faced sibling and Henry's vivacious wife worked was something that Nathaniel was often given to speculate upon. Mirabelle certainly brought happiness to his brother. Perhaps there was more to the lady than her chatterbox ways would suggest.

Behind Lady Farleigh a stout woman had just emerged from the carriage carrying one small child wrapped within a blanket, and holding another by the hand. 'Unc Nath!' The child loosed Nurse's hand and threw himself towards Nathaniel. On reaching the now mud-splattered high boots, the small boy stopped, looked solemnly up with his big pansy-brown eyes, and raised his chubby arms towards Nathaniel. 'Up, please, sir,' he said in a polite voice, and waited patiently for Nathaniel to respond.

Nurse tutted and stepped forward to reclaim her errant charge.

But without a further thought Nathaniel lifted the child against him, unmindful of the buckled shoes scraping against his smart country coat, and the small sticky fingers pressing against his cheeks. 'Have you missed your uncle Nathaniel?'

The curly head nodded seriously.

'And have you been a good boy, Charlie?'

Again the head nodded and the arms tightened around his neck, rendering his carefully arranged neckcloth a mass of crushed linen.

'Then I think we'll have to play a game of horses.'

A broad grin spread across Charlie's face and he uttered with reverence, 'Horses, yes, play horses.'

To which Nathaniel set the boy upon the ground, turned around and crouched down as low as he could. Charlie clambered upon Nathaniel's back, gaining a firm hold around his uncle's neck. He was secured in place by Nathaniel's arms and then the pair were off and running, galloping up the broad stone stairs in front of Collingborne House, accompanied by Mirabelle's laughter and Nurse's snorts of disapproval.

Charlie's giggles reverberated around the ornate hallway, up the splendid sweep of the staircase and along the full length of the picture gallery, through the green drawing room and back down the servants' stairwell. The boy squealed with delight as his uncle attempted some neighing noises and stamped his boots against the marble floor to simulate the clatter of hooves. Just as they rounded the corner to head back to the blue drawing room and Mirabelle, Nathaniel stopped dead in his tracks. For there, not two feet in front of them, in imminent danger of being mown down by Nathaniel and his small passenger, stood the Earl of Porchester and Viscount Farleigh. Both heads swivelled round to view the intruders, the old man's face haughty with censure, the younger's gaping with shock.

'Charles?' Henry managed to utter, as he regained a grip on himself. His countenance resumed its normal staid facade and he raised his eyebrows in enquiry to his brother.

The earl said nothing, only looked briefly at Nathaniel with sharp brown eyes. His cool, unwelcoming expression altered as his gaze shifted to his grandson, and although it could hardly be described as a smile, there was a definite thawing in its glacial manner.

'Papa!' Charlie's sticky hands reached out towards his father.

Nathaniel shifted the child round and handed the small squat body to his brother. 'Mirabelle and the children have just arrived. She wanted it to be something of a surprise for you. I left her in the blue drawing room.'

'Quite.' There was no disputing the disapproving tone in the earl's voice. He did not look at Nathaniel.

'We had better take you to find your mother, young man.' Henry tried unsuccessfully to disengage his son's arms from around his neck. 'Be careful of Papa's neckcloth, Charles.'

Charlie completely ignored the caution and pressed a slobbery kiss to his father's cheek.

Henry sighed, but Nathaniel could see the pride and affection in his brother's eyes as he turned and headed off to meet his wife.

The two men stood facing one another, an uneasy silence between them. Up until this point they had managed to avoid any close meeting.

'You'll be leaving tomorrow?' the earl said sourly.

Nathaniel inclined his head. 'Yes, sir. My ship sails in one week and there's much to be prepared.' He looked into the old man's face, so very like his own, knowing as he did before every voyage that this might be the last time he looked upon it. 'I'd like to speak to you, sir, before I leave Collingborne, if that's agreeable to you.'

'Agreeable is hardly a word I'd use to describe how I feel, but—' he waved his gaunt hand in a nonchalant gesture '—I'm prepared to listen. Get on and say what you must, boy.'

'Perhaps the library would be a more suitable surrounding?' Nathaniel indicated the door close by.

The earl grunted noncommittally, but walked towards the door anyway.

Once within the library, Porchester lowered himself into one of the large winged chairs and lounged comfortably back. He eyed his son with disdain. 'Well? What is it that you want to say?'

Nathaniel still stood, not having been invited to sit. He knew his father was cantankerous with him at the best of times. He moved towards the fireplace and eyed the blackened grate before facing his father once more. 'Will you take a drink?'

The old face broke into a cynical smile. 'Is what you have to say really that bad?' When Nathaniel did not reply, he continued, 'Why not? A port might help make your words a trifle more palatable.'

Nathaniel reached for the decanter, poured two glasses and handed one to his father. 'Your good health, sir.' He raised his glass.

The earl pointedly ignored him and proceeded to sip his port.

Despite his father's blatantly hostile manner, Nathaniel knew he had to try. The ill feeling between them had festered unchecked for too long, and was spilling over to affect the rest of the family. He knew that it had hurt his mother and that was something he bitterly regretted. But with her death it was too late for recriminations on that score. Her going had taken its toll on the earl. Porchester had aged in the last years. For the first time Nathaniel saw in him a frailty, a weak old man where before there was only strength and vitality. And it shocked him. They had always argued, his mother blaming it on the similarity in their temperaments. Nathaniel thought otherwise. The matter with Kitty Wakefield had only brought things to a head. He could not go away to sea without at least one more attempt at a reconciliation.

'Is it money you're after or do you find that you need my influence with the Admiralty after all?' Porchester's insult was cutting in the extreme.

The corner of Nathaniel's mouth twitched and the colour drained from beneath his tanned cheeks. He controlled his response with commendable restraint. 'Neither. I wish to have an end to this disagreement. The…incident…with Kitty Wakefield happened a long time ago and she's since married. I'm sorry that it has led us to where we're at now.'

The earl looked at him, a hard gleam in his eyes. 'You weren't sorry then, as I recall, seducing a young innocent girl and then refusing to marry her!'

'Kitty Wakefield was no innocent, whatever her father led you to believe. She engineered the situation to her own ends, thinking to force a marriage.'

The earl gave a cynical snort and took a large gulp of port. 'So you claim. Where's your sense of honour? If you didn't want to wed the girl, you should have controlled your appetite.'

The glass stem slowly rotated within his fingers and he let out a gentle expulsion of breath. 'If you won't forgive me on my own account, won't you at least agree to some kind of reconciliation for my mother's sake?'

The Earl of Porchester became suddenly animated. His previously slouched body straightened and he leaned forward in his chair. 'Don't dare to utter her name. It was the scandal associated with your debauchery and gambling that drove her to the grave!' He shouted the words, then collapsed back against the chair. His voice became barely more than a whisper. 'You broke her heart, lad, and that is something for which I'll never forgive you.'

The muscle twitched again in Nathaniel's jaw and his eyes hardened. 'That's unworthy of you, sir.'

'Unworthy!' the old man roared. He struggled upright, leaning heavily upon the ebony stick beneath his white-knuckled fingers. 'That's a word descriptive of yourself, boy! How dare you? Get out and don't come back here until you've changed your ways. You'd do well to take a leaf out of Henry's book. He's not out chasing women, drinking and gambling. Thank God that at least one of my sons can face up to responsibility. He knows his duty, has settled down and is filling his nursery. It's about time you grew up enough to do the same.'

The accusation was unfair. The earl's estimation of his character was sadly misinformed, but Nathaniel knew that any protestations would fall on deaf ears. The discussion was at an end and he had succeeded only in making the matter worse. He should have let the words go unanswered, but he could not. Such was the hurt that he stuffed it away and hid it beneath a veneer of irony. 'There's hardly a proliferation of suitable ladies available to court upon the high seas, and, as that's where I'll be spending most of my time, it's unlikely that I'll be able to meet with your suggestion. I'm sorry to disappoint you yet again.'

'It's nothing other than I've come to expect,' came the reply.

They finished their drinks in silence before Nathaniel took his leave.

Chapter Three

Georgiana urged the mare to a canter and looked around for her groom. The news that Lady Farleigh had gone to Collingborne and was not due to return for at least two months had come as a severe disappointment. It felt as if yet another door had slammed firmly shut in Georgiana's face, for if there was anyone who could help her out of her present predicament it was Mirabelle Farleigh.

The interview with her stepfather the previous day had left her shocked and disillusioned. The faint nausea of betrayal lingered with her still. Never could she have entertained the notion that he would have used her so, even if he was labouring under the misapprehension that he was doing what was best. She'd been so sure of his understanding, so confident of his support. All of those beliefs had shattered like the fragile illusions that they were. Her stepfather had clearly misread Walter Praxton's character to have agreed to such a devious plan. She swallowed down the pain as she recalled his zealous principles in which he had instructed them all. His actions made a mockery of them. She did not doubt for one minute that he would make good on his threat. He had made it clear what would happen if she made any appeal to Mama. And, if she refused Mr Praxton, her life was effectively over—her papa's influence would see to that. She would be an example to Prudence so that he would never have to deal with such insurgent behaviour from her little stepsister, or from Francis or Theo for that matter. The dapple-grey mare shied away from the street hawkers' carts, forcing Georgiana to leave her troubled thoughts and concentrate on Main Street and its normal chaos. It was not long before they reached Tythecock Crescent and home.

Immediately that she entered the house Harry, the youngest footman, directed her to her father's study.

'Where have you been?' Her stepfather was standing by the window and had obviously witnessed her return.

She smoothed the midnight-blue riding habit beneath her fingers and tried to appear calm. 'I called on Lady Farleigh. She asked if I would visit and I wanted to thank her for her kind hospitality.' Georgiana was just about to explain that the lady had not been present when Mr Raithwaite interrupted.

'I hardly think such a trip is in order. If you remember correctly, my dear, you left Lady Farleigh with rather a tawdry view of your reputation and it wouldn't do to remind her of that until we've remedied the affair. Once you're married then I've no objection to your seeing her, and I don't suppose that Mr Praxton will have either.' He touched his hands together as if he were about to pray, moving them until the tips of his fingers rested against his grizzled grey beard.

What would he say if he knew the extent of that which she had confided in Mirabelle? Georgiana looked directly at her stepfather, unaware that distaste and pity were displayed so clearly on her face.

Edward Raithwaite saw the emotions and they stirred nothing but contempt and frustration. 'In fact, it would be better if you remained within this house until the day of the wedding. We don't want to encourage any idle chatter, now, do we?'

'I'm to be a prisoner in my own home?' Georgiana could not prevent the words' escape.

'Let's just say confined for your protection, and in *my* home, Georgiana.'

She glowered at him, but said nothing.

'The wedding will take place in two weeks' time at All Hallows Church. Your mother has arranged for a mantua-maker to attend you here tomorrow to prepare your trousseau.' He looked away and picked distractedly at the nail on his left thumb. 'That will be all, at present.'

And with that summary dismissal Georgiana made her way to her room.

The moon was high in the night sky and still Georgiana lay rigid upon the bed. Thoughts of her stepfather's and Walter Praxton's treachery whirled in her brain, ceaseless in their battery, until her head felt as if it would burst. Such a tirade would not help her situation. She must stop. Think. Not the same angry thoughts of injustice and self-pity, but those of the options that lay before her. What options? Marry Mr Praxton and ally herself with the very devil, or have her sanity questioned and be sent to the Bethlehem Royal Hospital in London? Neither choice was to Georgiana's liking. She calmed herself and set to more productive thinking. Why had Papa confined her to the house? What was it that he was so afraid of? And quite suddenly she knew the answer to the question—a runaway stepdaughter. With the realisation came the seed of an idea that might just prove her salvation.

Within five minutes she was standing alone inside the laundry room, her bare feet cold against the stone-flagged floor, the candle in her hand sending ghostly shadows to dance upon the whitewashed walls. It did not take long to locate what she was looking for and, stuffing her prize inside the wrapper of her dressing gown, she crept back up to her bedroom. After her booty had been carefully stowed under the bed, she climbed once more beneath the covers, blew out the candle and fell straight to sleep. A smile curved upon her lips and her dreams were filled with her plan to foil Papa's curfew and his arrangement for marriage.

During the subsequent days, it appeared that Georgiana was content to pass her time in harmless activity, and all within the confines of the house in Tythecock Crescent. She amused her youngest siblings Prudence and Theo and spent some considerable time conversing with her stepbrother Francis who, at fourteen, had been summoned home from school to attend the wedding. Surprisingly Francis's bored manner, while still managing to insult his sister at any given opportunity, did not seem to annoy Georgiana, who was the very model of a well-bred young lady.

Mrs Raithwaite was much impressed by this novel behaviour, attributing it to Mr Raithwaite's firm stance. It seemed that her daughter had at last overcome her initial reservations to an alliance with Mr Praxton. Not that Clara Raithwaite had an inkling of comprehension as to just why Georgiana had taken such an apparently unprovoked dislike for that perfectly respectable gentleman. He seemed to Clara a most handsome fellow with commendable prospects. *And* he had so far managed to ignore Georgiana's stubborn tendencies.

Mrs Raithwaite's delight abounded when her daughter entered a conversation regarding Madame Chantel and her wedding dress. Quite clearly Georgiana had resigned herself to the marriage and the Raithwaite household could at last breathe easy. They, therefore, were most understanding when two days later Georgiana complained of the headache and was forced to retire early to bed. Mrs Raithwaite ascribed it to a combination of excitement and nerves, which she proclaimed were perfectly normal in any young lady about to be married. And when Georgiana hugged her mother and told her that she loved her and hoped she would be forgiven for being such a troublesome daughter, Mrs Raithwaite knew she was right. For once, Clara Raithwaite's diagnosis of her eldest daughter's emotional state was accurate.

Georgiana had forced herself to lie still beneath the bedcovers, feigning sleep when her mother came in to check on her. Only once the door had closed and her mother's footsteps receded along the passageway did she throw back the covers and set about her activity. With all the precision of the best-planned ventures, Georgiana moved without sound, aided only by the occasional shaft of moonlight stealing through her window. Her actions held a certain deliberation, a calm efficiency rather than a frenzied rushing.

From beneath the bed she retrieved her looted goods and set about stripping off her night attire, never pausing even for one minute. Time was of the essence and there was none to spare. With one fell snip of the scissors, purloined from Mrs Andrew's kitchen, her long braid of hair had been removed. Georgiana suppressed a sigh. This was not the time for sentimentality. At last she had finished and raised the hand mirror from the dressing table to survey the final result. An approving smile beamed back at her, and deepened to become a most unladylike grin. The effect was really rather good, better even than she had anticipated. Now all she had to do was hope that the coachman and postboys would not see through the disguise.

She loosed the few paltry coins that she could call her own upon the bed and, gathering them up, tucked them carefully into her pocket. The rest of her meagre provisions were stowed within a rather shabby bag that she'd managed to acquire from one of the footmen. Everything was in place. It was time to go.

She could only hope that Mama would forgive her. It wasn't as if she was just running away. No. She'd never been a coward and didn't mean to start now. It was advice and help that she needed, and Lady Farleigh had offered both. The trouble was that Mirabelle Farleigh had gone to Collingborne. And so it was to precisely that same destination that Georgiana intended to travel. Fleetingly she remembered Nathaniel Hawke's concern. *Who are you afraid of? If Mr Praxton has done aught that he should not have...* Would it have come to this if she'd told him the truth? Too late for such thoughts. One last look around her bedroom, then she turned, and slowly walked towards the window.

If a casual observer had happened to glance in the direction of Number 42 Tythecock Crescent at that particular time, a most peculiar sight would have greeted his eyes. A young lad climbed out of the ground-floor window, a small bag of goods clutched within his hands. From the boy's fast and furtive manner it could be surmised that he was clearly up to no good, and was acting without the knowledge of the good family Raithwaite, who occupied that fine house. Alas and alack that the moral fibre of society was so sadly lacking.

Georgiana sped out along the back yard, down Chancery Lane, meeting back up with Tythecock Crescent some hundred yards down the road. Even at this time of night the street was not quiet, and she was careful to keep her head lowered in case any one of the bodies meandering past might recognise Mr Raithwaite's daughter beneath the guise of the skinny boy. It was not far to her stepfather's coaching house, the Star and Garter, and she reached its gates within a matter of minutes. Fortunately for Georgiana, there was still room upon the mail to Gosport, and she soon found herself squashed between a burly man of indiscernible age, and a well-endowed elderly lady. Ironically, no member of the Raithwaite family had ever travelled by mail, and it was not far into the journey when Georgiana came to realise the reason. The burly man was travelling with two other men seated opposite; all three smelled as if they had not washed in some time and insisted on making loud and bawdy comments. As if that were not bad enough, the straggle-haired one opposite Georgiana spotted the young woman positioned further along and proceeded to eye her in a manner that made Georgiana feel distinctly uncomfortable, and profoundly glad that she had had the foresight to disguise herself in Francis's clothes.

'Come on, darlin', give us a smile.' The man flashed his blackened teeth at the woman who, seemingly completely unaffected, did not deign to reply.

The burly chap beside Georgiana sniggered. 'Won't even smile at some fellows that are bound for sea to keep out that tyrant Boney! It's us seamen that saves the likes of you, missy, our bravery that lets you sleep easy in your bed at night.'

'Yeh!' his companion grunted in agreement. His beady eyes narrowed and his expression became sly. 'If you won't give us a smile, darlin', maybe you'll give us one of your sweet kisses instead?'

Georgiana felt a rough elbow dig into her ribs, and a boom of laughter. 'What do you 'ave to say about it, young master, eh?'

Georgiana's heart leapt to her chest and she didn't dare to look round.

The man persisted. 'Oi, with all that fancy clobber, he thinks he's too good to talk to the likes of us. Is that it?'

'No, sir.' She forced the voice as a low rumble, and shook her head.

'Want to give that lass a kiss?'

Georgiana looked at the floor and shook her head. 'No, sir.'

The third sailor spoke up at last. 'Leave the lad alone, Jack. He's still wet behind the ears, just a young 'un. Let's get some sleep on this bloody coach while we can.'

'I was only 'avin' a laugh,' Jack protested, 'weren't I, lad?'

The journey seemed long in the extreme, although it took little more than three hours. By the time they arrived in Fareham, close by Portsmouth, Georgiana was cold, hungry and tired, having been exhausted by excitement and nerves. And she had yet to travel to Havant from where she could catch the mail in the direction of Petersfield, thus allowing her to make her way to Collingborne. To make matters worse, the first stagecoach to Havant did not leave until early the next morning. After all this she could only hope that at the end of her travels, she would not be turned away from Collingborne House and that Mirabelle Farleigh would offer her the help she so desperately needed. Pray God that it would be so.

Captain Nathaniel Hawke stood on the quarterdeck of the *Pallas* and surveyed the busy commotion on his ship. The *Pal-*

las was a frigate, a long, low sailing ship, the eyes and ears of the navy. Before the quarterdeck a chain of men were hauling spare spars, placing them down beside the rowing boats on the open deck beams. Others scoured water casks ready for refilling. Shouts sounded from those up high checking the rigging, climbing barefoot and confident, white trousers and blue jackets billowing in the strong sea breeze. The smell of fresh paint drifted to the captain's nose, as the men dangling over the bulwark on their roped seats, brushes in hands, applied the last few strokes of black across the gunport lids of the broadside. The black coloration contrasted starkly with the ochre yellow banding around the gunports themselves, setting up the smart so-called 'Nelson's Chequer'. In the distance, beyond the forecastle, the finely carved lion figurehead glinted proudly in the sunlight. 'How fares Mr Hutton with his repairs?'

'He's completed all of the gunports on the starboard broadside and is halfway through those on the larboard. Mr Longley is continuing with caulking the hull and estimates that the job will be complete by this evening.' First Lieutenant John Anderson faced his captain, resplendent in the full naval uniform that he had so recently purchased. He held himself with pride and eyed Captain Hawke with a mixture of respect and admiration. 'The men are working hard, Captain, and all should be ready in two days. We'll meet the sailing time.' There was a strength and enthusiasm in his voice.

Nathaniel turned from his view of a chaotic Portsmouth Point and faced his second-in-command. The lad had everything that it took to make a good first lieutenant except experience. And that was something that would not be long in coming if Nathaniel had his way. 'Indeed, Lieutenant, they've worked like Trojans, we all have. You're right in your estimation of the work. But it's not the repairs that threaten to postpone our departure.' He glanced away, out to where the open sea beckoned. 'We both know the real problem—our lack of manpower. We've not enough crew to properly man this ship and I cannot take her out as we currently stand. The men that we have are good and true, all came forward willingly to serve on the *Pallas* because she's widely known to be a fair and lucky ship.'

Don't be misled, sir. The men are here because Captain Nathaniel Hawke is reputed to be one of the best post captains to sail under and all that have sailed with him previously have been made rich with the prizes he captured. But the lieutenant knew better than to speak his thoughts.

Nathaniel's face had grown grim. 'But for all that, we've insufficient numbers to sail. It seems that we're forced once more to turn to Captain Bodmin to supply the extra men needed.' The knowledge curled his top lip.

Lieutenant Anderson sensed the captain's reticence in the matter. 'Most of the ships that sail from here require Captain Bodmin's services and a good proportion of their crews comprise pressed men. It's no reflection on you, Captain. Be assured of that.'

'Thank you, Mr Anderson.' He clasped his fingers together. 'It seems that we've no choice, for if we're to sail we must have men, even pressed men who've never set foot off land before and lack any seafaring skills. Not that that is what presents the biggest problem. They've no desire to be on board and so will cause any manner of trouble to illustrate the point. Little wonder when they've been forcibly deprived of their freedom. God knows, Mr Anderson, the Press Gang is very much a last resort. Better one volunteer than three pressed men.'

Both men turned and looked once more out across the crowded harbour of Portsmouth.

Georgiana was not feeling at her best as she huddled in the yard of the Red Lion. She felt as stiff as an old woman and she'd long since eaten any vestige of food contained within the bag pressed against her chest. The delicious aroma of hot mutton pies wafted from the pie seller just beyond the courtyard gates.

'George, fancy a pie?' The gruff voice surprised her.

Georgiana looked down and shook her head. 'No, thank you, sir,' she uttered in as manly a tone as she could manage. Her stomach protested with a fierce growl.

Burly Jack, as she'd taken to calling him, although not to his face, whispered to Tom, 'Lad's not the full shilling, but he's 'armless enough. Reminds me of me nephew.' He straightened up and raised his voice in Georgiana's direction. 'Come on, now, boy, don't be too proud for your own good. You must be starvin'. I 'aven't seen you eat nothin' all night.' Jack advanced, carrying three steaming pies, and thrust one towards her.

An audible rumbling erupted from Georgiana's stomach.

Tom laughed. 'Don't try tellin' us you ain't hungry. They must have heard that stomach growl in the streets of London!'

The pie loomed before Georgiana, all hot and aromatic. She felt her mouth fill with saliva and could not help but lick her lips.

'Come on, lad.'

The pie danced closer, calling to Georgiana with an allure that she had never experienced before. Her hand reached out and enclosed around the vision of temptation.

Burly Jack delivered an affectionate blow to her arm before the trio headed off towards the closest tavern.

Georgiana slumped against the wall. She bit through the

pastry until delicious gravy spurted into her mouth, so hot that she could see the wisps of steam escape into the coolness of the surrounding air. Squatting down, she leaned her back against the rough-hewn stone behind her and chewed upon the heavenly chunks of mutton. It was strange just how content-ing the simple act of filling one's empty belly could be. Gravy trickled down her chin and she lapped it back up. She was just wiping the grease from her fingers down Francis's brown woollen breeches when it happened.

Yells. Thuds. The sound of Burly Jack's voice raised in anger and fear.

Georgiana started up like a scared rabbit, peering all around. The voices came from the other side of the wall. Darting through the gate she ran round and into the narrow alleyway. 'Jack!' Her voice rang out clear and true.

In the gloom of the alley her travelling companions had been set upon by several men. There was much flying of fists and kicking of legs, but Georgiana could just see that Burly Jack was being thoroughly bested. Without pausing to consider her own position, she launched herself upon Jack's attacker, ripping at his hair and boxing his ears for all she was worth.

'Run, lad!' Jack's voice echoed in her ear. It was the last thing she heard before she was felled by a hefty blow to the back of her head. And then there was nothing.

Georgiana awoke to a giddy nauseous feeling. There was an undoubted sensation of swaying that would not still whether she opened her eyes or closed them. Not that it made any difference to what she could see within the dense black-ness of where she now found herself.

She tried to sit up, but the throbbing of her head increased so dramatically that she thought the remnants of the mutton pie would leap from her stomach.

'George, is you awake yet?' The unmistakable tone of Burly Jack's voice sounded.

'Yes, sir.' She groaned. 'Where are we? I can't see anythin'.'

A hand landed on her thigh and she let out a squeak.

'There you are, lad. Did them bastards 'urt you? Looked like they landed you a right good 'un on the 'ead.' Jack's hand moved up to her arm. She prayed it would stray no further.

'I'll mend,' she uttered, trying to quell the queasiness rising in her stomach, and struggled to a sitting position.

Jack's hand patted her arm. 'That's the spirit. Tom and Bill's 'ere too. Bastards got us all, and two others by the name of Jim and Rad.'

'The lad sounds young.' Rad's voice came out of the gloom. 'Voice ain't broken yet.'

'He *is* young, so don't be startin' nothin' with 'im or you'll 'ave me to answer to.' Burly Jack's voice had lost its soft edge.

It seemed that Georgiana had found something of a protector within the smelly dark hovel. Would he remain so if he fathomed her secret? It was not a question that she wished to test. The rocking motion seemed to be getting worse, just as her eyes had adjusted to see grey shapes within the surrounding darkness. And with it grew her nausea. 'Dear Lord!' The curse escaped her as the retching began.

'Easy, lad.' Burly Jack's voice sounded close. 'You'll get used to it soon enough and then it won't never come back. Seasickness ain't a pleasant feeling, but there ain't nothin' can be done about it.'

'Seasickness?' Georgiana questioned with a feeble tone.

'Oh, aye, lad. What d'you think them fellows wanted with us? They're the bloody Press Gang and you're aboard ship now.' Jack's words had a horrible nightmarish quality about them.

She blinked her eyes into the darkness. 'You must be wrong, sir.'

'Nope,' Jack replied with a definite cheery tone. 'You're a ship's boy on the *Pallas* now, young George, whether you like it or not. Best get used to the idea before the bosun comes to fetch us.'

Georgiana let out a load groan and dropped her head into her hands. She was once again in a diabolical situation as the result of her own foolhardy actions. But this time there would be no handsome Lord Nathaniel Hawke to jump headlong in and save her.

'You've interviewed them all, Mr Anderson. So what do we have?' Nathaniel continued in his stride towards the small group of men standing at the far end of the main deck.

Lieutenant Anderson walked briskly alongside. 'Good news, Captain Hawke, sir. There are five men, three of whom have plenty of experience at sea. I've rated them as able seamen, sir. The other two are landsmen, never set foot on a ship before, but I estimate that they'll be quick to learn. All are now registered on the *Pallas*' books.'

Nathaniel's face was grim. 'It sickens me to the pit of my stomach that I'm forced to resort to such a thing. I'd rather have them here willingly or not at all.'

'You're only following orders, Captain,' the first lieutenant pointed out. 'And I fancy that they'll soon change their minds as to a life at sea once they've sailed on the *Pallas*.'

Nathaniel remained unconvinced, but he had a job to do and he had best get on with it, no matter that having pressed men aboard his ship left a bitter taste in his mouth. 'Three able seamen, you say?'

'Oh, and there's a lad of fourteen as well. It seems that he was with the sailors when they were taken by Captain Bodmin's men. We're still short on ship's boys, so I've rated him as a third class. Mr Adams is under the impression that the boy is dim-witted; indeed, I did notice that he keeps his head down and mumbles when spoken to. But I thought…well, with the need to leave port that…' John Anderson struggled to find the words.

Nathaniel came to the rescue. 'Given the right instruction I'm sure that the boy will learn. You did right, Mr Anderson. Better that he ends up here with his friends than alone aboard another ship.' He pushed the stories of what had happened to lone youngsters on certain other ships out of his head. Not while Nathaniel Hawke had breath in his body would any such depravity take place on the *Pallas*.

The pressed men stood separately from the rest of the crew, forming a small distinct group. As Nathaniel and John Anderson approached, the group stiffened and stood to attention.

'Stand at ease, men,' Lieutenant Anderson commanded.

The men responded.

Nathaniel stood before his crew and surveyed the latest additions. 'Welcome to the *Pallas*. Some of you may not be here by your own free choice, but you're here to serve your king and country nevertheless. Our voyage may be long and difficult. Indeed, we will be exposed to many perils and threats. But as men of England I know that you will fight, as we all fight, to retain our freedom. For if our great navy does not fight, we may as well collect Bonaparte ourselves and deliver him to London's door.'

He looked into each man's eyes in turn.

'This voyage is not an easy walk. I demand your obedience, your loyalty and your diligence.'

The first two faces in the line were pale, their skin tinged with a greenish hue—the landsmen, no doubt. They were listening despite their rancid stomachs.

'In return I offer you adventure, and the chance of wealth. There are prizes out there, gentlemen, and they are ours for the taking.'

The next three were ruddy and vigorous. Two fellows of medium build and one large bear of a man. All were intent on his words.

'But with the biggest prizes come the biggest dangers. And only the best crews will win them in the end. With drilling, with perseverance, with determination, gentlemen, we can be the best of crews; we can win the best of prizes.'

He swung his arms in a wide encompassing gesture to the massed crew. 'Gentlemen, I give you the best of me, and I demand the very best of you, each and every one of you. We sailed yesterday under sealed orders. We have reached the specified longitude and latitude and I can reveal to you all that the *Pallas* will proceed to the Azores and cruise there to capture any enemy vessels encountered. The pickings will be rich indeed. What say you, men, will you give me your best?'

The deck resounded to raucous cheering. Even Burly Jack, Bill and Tom clapped one another on the back and raised their voices. Jack laughed down at Georgiana and spoke out of the corner of his mouth. 'This is much better than the poxy vessel we were bound for. We'll be rich, lad, rich!'

Nathaniel's voice sounded above the din, and an immediate hush spread. 'Then let us commence our voyage as we mean to finish it.' As the crowd dispersed, Nathaniel glanced at the boy hovering by the elbow of the large man. Lieutenant

Anderson had been accurate in his description, for the lad's gaze was trained firmly on the wooden floor, his head bent low. 'What's your name, boy?'

The boy's head bent lower, as if he wished the deck to open and swallow him up. 'George, Captain, sir.'

Nathaniel had to strain to catch the low-pitched mumble. 'And your family name?'

The small boots standing before him shuffled uncomfortably. 'Robertson, Captain, sir.'

'Well then, Master Robertson, my first command to you is that you stand up straight at all times and look whoever may be talking to you directly in the eye. Do you understand?'

'Yes, Captain, sir,' the faint reply came back.

The boy's head remained averted.

Perhaps Mr Adams had been right in his estimation of the boy's wits. Nathaniel frowned. 'Master Robertson,' he said somewhat more forcefully.

The large sailor nudged the boy and hissed between blackened teeth, 'Do as the Captain says, George. Stand up straight. Look up.' He turned back to the captain. 'Sorry, Captain, he's a bit slow, but he's a good lad.'

Nathaniel's gaze drifted back to the stooped figure.

Slowly but surely Georgiana straightened her shoulders and raised her face to look directly at Captain Hawke.

Nathaniel blinked. There was something familiar about the dirt-smeared little face that looked up at him. A memory stirred far in the recesses of his mind, but escaped capture. Surely he must be mistaken? The boy was clearly no one he had ever seen before. He tried to shrug the feeling off. And all the while George Robertson's youthful grey-blue eyes were wide with shock. 'That's how I prefer to see you at all times, Master Robertson. A seaman should be proud of himself, and as a boy aboard my ship, you've much to be proud of.' Captain Nathaniel Hawke returned to his cabin with a faint glimmer of unease that could not quite be fathomed.

Georgiana's knees set up a tremor and she pressed her hand to her mouth. She thought that her nausea had subsided with the fresh sea air of the open deck. The sight of the gentleman striding purposefully towards them brought it back in an instant. Dear Lord, but he bore an uncanny resemblance to Lord Nathaniel Hawke. It was a complete impossibility, of course, or so she told herself. Many men were tall with dark hair that glowed red in the sunlight. But as he came closer, and Georgiana was able to look upon those brown expressive eyes, fine straight nose and chiselled jaw line, she knew that her first impression had not been mistaken.

Her sudden gasp went unnoticed as Lord Nathaniel addressed the surrounding men. Shock gave way to relief. Providence, in the guise of Nathaniel Hawke, had helped her before and was about to do so again, or so it seemed. Even as her spirit leapt, the stark reality of her circumstance made itself known to her. Only two kinds of women came aboard ships, the wives of officers, and those who belonged to what she had heard termed the oldest profession in the world. Georgiana belonged to neither group. Yet the *Pallas* had sailed from Portsmouth two days since. Her position was precarious in the extreme. The very presence of an unmarried lady aboard Nathaniel Hawke's ship was likely to place him in a difficult situation. Her own reputation no longer mattered, but she had no wish to cause trouble for the man who had saved her life. There seemed to be no other alternative than to continue with her deception as the simple-minded boy. She dropped her gaze to the spotless wooden decking and played her part well, hoping all the time that Nathaniel Hawke would not recognise any trace of Miss Georgiana Raithwaite.

'Oi, dopey!' The rough-edged voice sounded across the deck. 'Have you got cabbage for brains or what?' The fat gunner's mate delivered a hefty slap to Georgiana's ear. 'Get this bloody place cleaned up before Mr Pensenby arrives. If he sees it in this state, you'll be on reduced rations again. Now get a bloody move on.'

In the two weeks that had passed since the *Pallas'* departure from Portsmouth harbour, Georgiana had managed to avoid the worst of trouble and had retained her disguise. All trace of seasickness had vanished thanks to her daily consumption of grog. It might have tasted foul, but it had settled her stomach when she thought it would never be settled again. Her hands still bore some open blisters, although most had healed to calluses upon her palms. Her hair was matted and itchy beneath the dirty black woollen cap that she permanently wore and her feet were rubbed and sore from clambering barefoot over the slippery decks. As if that were not bad enough, she seemed to be covered from head to toe in a layer of filth from her newly appointed position of gunroom servant. Heaven only knew quite how scrubbing floors and tables, washing plates and glasses, and being at the beck and call of every officer and young midshipman, as well as waiting at their dining table, could have got her into such a state! It was not an easy job, but it was infinitely preferable to that of the 'Captain of the Head', young Sam Wilson, who had the unenviable task of cleaning the lavatories at the head of the ship. Sam was only eight years old and she had taken the little lad under her wing.

She saw little of Jack and the others except at the odd meal time, when his hearty laughter allowed her to find him amidst the rows of rough wooden tables and benches set between the guns that transformed the upper deck into a mess each mealtime. As Georgiana grew accustomed to daily routine on board ship, she began to think that perhaps she might just survive the voyage in the guise of George Robertson, but she had reckoned without the interference of the second lieutenant, Cyril Pensenby.

'Lieutenant Pensenby, sir!' The gunner's mate straightened and saluted the poker-faced young gentleman who had just strolled into the room.

'Holmes.' Georgiana watched as the officer's snowy white breeches brushed inadvertently against one of the narrow wooden benches. The lieutenant glanced down and stopped dead still. He raised his eyes and looked accusingly at Georgiana, whose own gaze remained riveted to the discoloured smear that now sullied the material stretched across the gentleman's leg. 'Master Robertson,' his cultured voice lisped, 'you will scrub this room from top to bottom until it has not one grain of dust, not one smear of dirt. And when you've finished you shall scrub yourself clean in a similar fashion. There is a bathing cask up on deck. See that you make use of it. I shall return before the first dog watch to inspect the work you've undertaken. I hope for your sake, boy, that it meets with my approval.'

Georgiana stared wordlessly at the retreating figure.

The gunner's mate eased his corpulent frame on to the bench. 'Best get started, lad. The lieutenant ain't a man to be trifled with and he won't cut you no slack on account of your simple-minded ways. Gunner won't be best pleased either.'

Three hours later the gunroom was shining like a new pin. *Please don't let anyone mess it up before he sees it,* Georgiana prayed, before setting about cleaning the worst of the ingrained muck from her face and hands in a small wooden basin. Most of the dirt had been brushed out of her blue culottes and jacket before Lieutenant Pensenby returned.

He perused the gunroom down the end of his long thin nose, saying nothing, before turning his scrutiny to Georgiana herself. 'Roll up your sleeve, Robertson,' the curt voice commanded.

Georgiana did as she was told, holding one grubby arm up for inspection.

'You have not bathed.'

'Beggin' your pardon, Lieutenant, sir, but I cleaned myself just as you told me.' Georgiana tried to retrieve her arm from beneath the gentleman's fingers.

Cyril Pensenby's thumbnail scraped against her skin, releasing a layer of blackened grime. 'The evidence speaks for itself, boy.'

'No, sir, you're mistaken, sir,' Georgiana mumbled in as low a tone as she could muster.

Mr Pensenby's brows lowered and he thrust Georgiana's arm angrily away. 'Are you calling me a liar, Robertson?'

What had started as a small matter was rapidly escalating out of control. 'No, Lieutenant, sir.' She bit at her bottom lip and focused on the decking around Mr Pensenby's feet.

Pensenby turned to the gunner's mate. 'See that this boy is scrubbed clean in a cask bath. Immediately, Holmes.'

'Aye, Lieutenant Pensenby, I'll see to it personally, sir.'

Georgiana's eyes widened in terror as she realised what was about to happen. 'No!' She made to run past the two men, but fat fingers closed cruelly over her wrist and dragged her back.

'Come along, Master Robertson, ain't nothin' so very bad about havin' a bath. Let's be havin' you up on deck, lad.'

Georgiana wriggled and squirmed, but nothing, it seemed, could dislodge the gunner's mate's firm grasp. By the time they had reached the deck she could scarcely catch her breath.

'Hoist up the cask!' the gunner's mate instructed, and attempted to remove the simpleton's jacket.

Georgiana yelled for all she was worth, her voice rising higher in her panic. 'Jack! Jack!' She plunged her teeth into the fat man's hand and kicked as hard as she could at his shins.

'Ouch! You little bugger!' Holmes released the skinny arm to deliver a weighty cuff to the lad's ear.

It was the opportunity that Georgiana had been waiting for and she needed no invitation. Before the gunner's mate could recover, she legged it straight up the rigging of the main mast. She didn't dare look down, just kept on climbing up towards the topgallant mast. The wind blasted cold and icy, contriving to knock her from her precarious perch, but she clung to the ropes until her fingers hurt. Voices murmured from far below, their words lost to the wind. Her heart pounded in her chest and she watched with rising misery as the light diminished in the surrounding sky.

'What the hell is going on?' The men scattered before Captain Hawke.

Lieutenant Pensenby stepped forward. 'Ship's boy Robertson disobeyed a direct command, sir. He attacked Holmes here when he tried to effect that order.'

'And what exactly was the command, Mr Pensenby?'

Pensenby's thin face flushed. 'The boy and the gunroom were filthy, Captain. Indeed, it wasn't possible to enter the place without soiling my own uniform. As I am adverse to having such a dirty specimen serve the food upon my plate, or, indeed, to sup in unclean surroundings, I instructed that he clean both himself and the room. He complied with the room, but is most reticent to bathe himself, sir.'

Nathaniel groaned to himself. This was the last thing he needed. That half the ship's company was lacking in personal hygiene could not have escaped Pensenby's notice. Indeed, most of the men saw bathing as something undertaken only by eccentrics. But flouting of any order was not something that could be taken lightly, especially when it had been issued by the second lieutenant. 'And where is the boy now?'

All eyes looked up into the rigging.

'Ah,' the captain murmured by way of understanding. 'Fetch able seaman Grimly.'

Someone was coming up to fetch her. She dared a look and saw Jack not far below.

'What the 'ell 'ave you been doin'?' the gruff voice queried. 'Pensenby's got his dander up about you and no mistake and I ain't gonna be able to stop 'im.' Burly Jack sighed. 'Bathin' ain't exactly my delight, but couldn't you 'ave just 'ad a quick duck in and out?'

Georgiana's hands wove themselves tighter through the ropes. 'No, Jack. Don't make me go down. I won't have a bath. I can't.' The words were barely more than a hoarse whisper into the wind.

'If you don't come down with me they'll just send someone else to get you. Come on, lad, don't make it worse than it already is.'

He was right. Pensenby would never leave her be. There was nothing else for it, she would have to throw herself upon Nathaniel Hawke's mercy and hope for the best.

Chapter Four

'Master Robertson, no man or boy on this ship is exempt from the line of command. To disobey an order from an officer is an offence, and one that merits disciplinary action.' A chill wind blew hard across the deck, carrying in its wake the damp smell of rain. Darkness was closing in fast, and the lanterns were being lit. Nathaniel felt a pang of sympathy for the lad; nevertheless, it was the first direct contravention of an order and his response was likely to set a precedent amongst the men. 'Lieutenant Pensenby has instructed you to bathe and bathe you shall. See to it, Mr Holmes.'

'Aye, aye, Captain.' The boy was so pale he looked as if all the blood had left his body. Holmes quelled the thought, he had a job to do. 'You ain't got nothin' different from the rest of us, lad. Let's get on with it.'

Panic constricted Georgiana's breathing. 'No! Wait!'

Holmes's hand clamped upon her shoulder and Captain Hawke made to walk away.

'Captain Hawke, please wait, sir. I can explain.' Her usual hushed mumble was forgotten. She lashed out at the man beside her. 'Leave me be!'

It was imperative that he remain indifferent to the boy's pleading voice. Such scenes were always difficult for Nathaniel, but he could not back down. He continued towards the forecastle.

'You will not address the captain, Robertson, it is not your place to do so,' Pensenby interrupted.

Her jacket had been removed and Holmes was tugging at her culottes. Georgiana bellowed as loudly as she could, and tried hard to maintain the slight edge to her accent. 'I must speak with you, Captain, sir. Please, sir!'

Still she saw only the receding view of his deep blue coat, his shoulders squared, his golden epaulettes glinting in the lantern light.

'It concerns Farleigh Hall, sir.'

Nathaniel ceased his measured steps and swung round. Surely he had misheard? 'What did you say, boy?' He drew his brows together in perplexity and walked slowly back to where the gunner's mate held the boy in a neck lock.

'Farleigh Hall,' Georgiana managed to choke the words out.

Something was most definitely amiss. How did a simpleton third-rate ship's boy know of his brother's house? An uneasy feeling was gathering in his gut. 'Release the boy, Mr Holmes. I would hear what he has to say.'

With considerable relief Georgiana lurched forward, her hand pressed to the bruising on her throat. 'It's private, Captain, sir. I must speak with you alone, sir.'

If Nathaniel observed that his previously tongue-tied ship's boy had suddenly developed a clear and coherent manner of speech, he forbore to mention it.

Pensenby's countenance was growing tarter by the minute. 'How dare you?' he spluttered with the indignation of a man who could not quite believe what he had just heard. 'I've never seen a more audacious manner in a boy.' The second lieutenant's temper was wearing dangerously thin. 'You will be punished for this insolence.'

'Make 'im kiss the gunner's daughter,' a coarse voice added from the background.

The prospect of being bent over one of the long guns and caned on the backside was enough to make Georgiana's hair to stand on end. 'Lady Mirabelle,' she squeaked in defiance, and, 'Lord Frederick,' just for good measure.

Nathaniel's mind was decided in an instant. 'I'll interview the boy in my cabin. Have him brought down immediately.'

Georgiana's knees almost gave way with relief as Holmes dragged her along in the captain's wake.

'But…' Lieutenant Pensenby's jaw dropped.

'Thank you, Mr Pensenby. Continue with your duties.' Captain Hawke's clipped tones floated back to reach him.

The captain's cabin, positioned at the rear of the gun deck, was incredibly large in comparison with the cramped conditions endured by the rest of the crew, and furnished well, if not luxuriously. As well as a desk, captain's chair, dining table, six dining chairs and a small chest of drawers, there was a large and very fine oil painting depicting Lord Nelson's victory against the French Admiral Brueys at the Battle of the Nile. Amidst the elegance of the décor were two large eighteen-pounder long guns, shone to a brilliant black finish. Nathaniel Hawke leaned back against the desk, stretching his legs out before him. The cocked hat was removed and positioned carefully on a pile of papers to his left. An errant lock of hair swept across his forehead and his eyes glowed deep and dark.

'Well, young Robertson, tell your tale.'

Georgiana felt the tension mount within her, and quickly slipped on the torn jacket that Holmes had replaced in her hands. An extra layer of protection against what was to come. And what *was* to come? She had no notion what Captain Hawke's reaction would be. No notion at all. She licked her dry, salt-encrusted lips and began. 'Thank you for agreeing to my request for privacy. I'm sure that you'll agree to its necessity once you've heard the truth.'

'Indeed?' One winged eyebrow raised itself. 'You suddenly have a most eloquent turn of phrase, Master Robertson. The prospect of a bath seems to have overcome your tendency to the whispered mumbling of a simpleton.'

Georgiana cleared her throat and clutched her hands together. How did one go about imparting such a revelation? 'Quite,' she muttered softly.

The silence stretched between them.

Nathaniel's hands stretched flat upon the desk and he leaned forward. 'I believe that you have something to tell me.'

Such long strong fingers, so representative of the power within the man himself. An image of those fingers stroking her cheek popped into her mind and she flushed with guilty anger. How could she think such a thought, and at a time like this? A warm blush rose in her cheeks and she rapidly averted her gaze.

Nathaniel did not miss the emotions that flashed so readily across the boy's face, nor the telltale rosy stain beneath the dirt-stained cheeks. He waited, curiosity rising.

'I… You…' She paused, unable to find the words. Oh, heaven help her! Taking a deep breath, she launched into the story. 'There's no easy way to say this, Captain Hawke, so I'll strive to be brief and to the point. Please remember throughout that I…that I never intended the position in which I now find myself. Such a possibility never entered my mind.' She looked up at him suddenly, her eyes wide and clear, her voice elegant and polite. 'The fact of the matter is that I'm not who I appear to be.' She paused, her breathing coming fast and furious, almost as if she had ran the length of the ship.

'I'd gathered that much. And you're now about to do me the honour of revealing your true identity.' His tone was dry, but there was an encouraging gentleness in his eyes and Georgiana knew that Nathaniel Hawke was a fair man. The knowledge gave her the confidence she so desperately needed to continue.

'Yes.' The single word slipped softly into the silence of the cabin.

Nathaniel experienced a reflexive tensing of his muscles and an overwhelming intuitive certainty that the next words to be uttered by the ragamuffin boy standing so quietly before him would change his life for ever.

The boy's chin forced up high. The grey-blue eyes met his without flinching. The narrow chest expanded with a deep breath. 'I am Miss Georgiana Raithwaite, recently of your acquaintance at Farleigh Hall.' Still the breath held, tightly squeezed within her lungs. She waited. Waited. And never once did her gaze wander from those dark eyes that were staring back at her with an undisguised disbelief.

Silence.

The blood ran cold in Nathaniel's veins and a shiver flitted down his spine. It was not possible. The ragged boy, Miss Raithwaite. 'You cannot be Miss Raithwaite. You're a...'

Georgiana endured the roving scrutiny of his eyes without moving. 'Now you understand why I couldn't comply with Lieutenant Pensenby's command.' She raised her eyebrows wryly and bit her bottom lip.

'Hell's teeth!' Nathaniel cursed and stood upright. A horrible sinking sensation was starting within his stomach, for beneath the grubby urchin face he could see what had previously eluded him—the fine features of the young woman he had pulled from the River Borne. 'Your hair... Have you—?'

'Naturally,' replied Georgiana. 'It wouldn't have been much of a disguise otherwise.' She whipped the cap from her head to reveal her sheared and matted locks.

'Dear God!' Nathaniel could not suppress the exclamation.

'Yes, quite. It's in a horrible filthy state, as is the rest of me. How ironic that my present trouble has arisen from my refusal to bathe when that is one of the things I've longed so ardently to do these two weeks past.' She smiled then, a smile that lit up her face.

Nathaniel stared, and stared some more. Inadvertently his eyes dropped lower, as if he would see what lay beneath the torn blue jacket. 'You show no external signs of...of, um...'

'Bindings. Terribly uncomfortable things to wear, if you must know,' she said stoutly.

Captain Hawke's swarthy complexion flushed. 'Yes, quite.'

'But it wouldn't have done at all for Burly Jack or the others to have discovered otherwise.'

'Burly Jack?' Nathaniel's brows knitted.

'Able Seamen Grimly, sir.' She sighed. 'He's been looking out for me, you see, since we became acquainted on the mail-coach to Fareham.'

There was a definite pain starting behind his eyes. The tanned fingers rubbed at his forehead. 'No, Miss Raithwaite, I don't see at all. I think you had better explain all that has happened since I saw you last.' He gestured towards a wooden chair and said politely, as if they were both in the drawing room of Farleigh Hall, 'Please be seated.' He then lowered himself into the red leather captain's chair and prepared to listen.

Georgiana started to talk and, with only the occasional interruption from the captain, continued to do so for some considerable length of time.

'So let me check that I have understood you correctly, Miss Raithwaite.' He watched her with a quizzical expression. 'Following a disagreement with your father, you ran away from home, by mail, to seek refuge with a friend who lives near Portsmouth, and were mistakenly taken by the Press Gang?'

'Yes.' She folded her hands before her and tried to look composed.

He wasn't fooled for an instant. Nathaniel Hawke knew guilt when he saw it. 'And may I enquire as to the nature of your disagreement?'

Her fingers pressed to each other. 'I cannot reveal that, my lord. It regards a personal issue.'

'Such as your betrothal to Mr Praxton?' he asked softly.

Her eyes met his, then dropped to scan the mahogany surface of his desk as colour flooded her cheeks.

'Yes,' she whispered.

A small silence elapsed.

'Then I'll write to your father and at least let him know that you're safe.'

'No!' Georgiana was out of her seat and facing him with a look of pure horror. 'No, I beg of you,' she pleaded. 'If you have the smallest consideration for me at all, my lord, please do no such thing.'

He felt her distress as keenly as if it were his own. 'Very well, but if I'm to help you I must ask that you tell me the truth, all of it.'

The moment had come. She swallowed hard and squared

her shoulders. The truth, whatever it was, had affected her dearly. He watched her gather her courage, watched her sweet lips open in preparation. 'When I said that my father approved of my betrothal to Mr Praxton, I was not telling you the whole story. He…he and Mr Praxton…' It seemed that she could not find the words. 'After what happened in Hurstborne Park with Mr Praxton's…plan, Papa was so angry with me, and I with him. I just couldn't believe what he meant to do. Papa knew how I felt and still he didn't care. He was determined to have his own way, wouldn't even listen to me. In my heart I knew that I couldn't do as he bade, so…so I decided to run away.'

A horrible sensation was settling on Captain Hawke. He thought he could see exactly where Miss Raithwaite's tale was leading. And that somewhere was in the direction of a disapproving father and an elopement. There would be no friend near Portsmouth, of that he was sure, only Walter Praxton waiting at their chosen place of assignation. Damn the scoundrel! He schooled the emotion from his voice. 'Your father's response to Mr Praxton's actions in the park is understandable. No man would condone such treatment of his daughter. It's hardly surprising that he won't have you wed Praxton. The man is a knave.'

'No, you misunderstand. Mr Praxton—'

'Is no gentleman to behave as he did. I cannot think you would believe anything other. Think, Miss Raithwaite, what kind of gentleman would have encouraged you to such actions? Deserting your family, dressing as a boy, travelling across country alone, and on the mail of all things. Why, anything could have happened to you!' He raked his fingers through his hair with mounting exasperation. Hell, but did the girl have no inkling as to what sort of man Praxton was? Little idiot! The thought of Miss Raithwaite allowing Praxton liberties made his blood boil.

'Captain Hawke, you're mistaken in what you think. Mr Praxton is indeed a—'

Nathaniel knew exactly what Praxton was. He didn't want to hear the woman before him plead the wretch's case. 'I suppose you mean to tell me next that you love him and that is excuse enough.' It was a brutal statement, brutal and angry and disappointed.

Her mouth gaped open and beneath the dirt he could have sworn that her skin had drained of any last vestige of colour. She gripped the edge of his desk, leaned forward towards him and said in her most indignant voice, 'I beg your pardon, sir!'

'If you speak a trifle louder, Miss Raithwaite, you need adopt your guise no longer, for every man on the ship will have heard a woman's voice from within my cabin.'

The grey-blue eyes closed momentarily before fluttering back open. 'I'm sorry, Captain Hawke. I'm trying to tell you that your beliefs concerning Mr Praxton are quite wrong. The incident in the park was not how—'

But Nathaniel had no intention of listening to Miss Raithwaite defend the scoundrel. It was hard enough knowing that she had feelings for him. 'I do not wish to hear your thoughts on Mr Praxton. Whatever your plans were, they can be no more. We must concentrate on the situation we now find ourselves in.'

Those clear fine eyes stared at him with such wounded disbelief as to render him the cruellest tyrant on earth.

'It seems that you have made up your mind on the matter and nothing I can say will change it.'

There was a melancholy in her voice that he had not heard before. Why did he have the sudden sensation that he had just made the worst blunder of his life? Damnation, the truth was harsh, but it was kinder than letting her believe Praxton's lies. And she was right, nothing *would* make him warm to the rogue. 'The Atlantic Ocean lies between you and Mr Praxton now. You had best forget him, Miss Raithwaite. He cannot reach you here.'

When she bowed her head and did not answer, he knew that nothing he could say would affect the girl's affection for the villain. He battened down his own feelings and moved to deal with the practicalities of disguising a lady's presence on board his ship, all the while oblivious to the relief that his last comment had wrought in Miss Raithwaite.

Quite why Nathaniel was so adverse to hearing the truth about Walter Praxton escaped her. If only he had let her explain. But perhaps it was better this way, for heaven only knew what a man like Nathaniel Hawke would do if he understood exactly what Mr Praxton and her papa had been about. And that was sure only to make matters worse, for them all. Let him think the worst if it would prevent him becoming embroiled with Mr Praxton. Besides, he was right. That she had set out to seek Mirabelle's advice no longer mattered, for she was far beyond any help that lady could now offer. On a social standing, even Mr Praxton's loathsome attentions paled in contrast to the circumstance into which she had now stumbled…well, thrown herself. She was under no illusion as to exactly what she had done to her reputation just by running away. And then there was the small matter of being pressed aboard a naval frigate…as a boy.

At least her papa's evil plan had been foiled. No man, not even Mr Praxton, would wish to wed her now. Even so, she could not help but be glad at Nathaniel's words: *the Atlantic*

Ocean lies between you and Mr Praxton… He cannot reach you here. The hairs on the back of her neck prickled. Somehow, she doubted that she had heard the last of Walter Praxton.

The door opened to reveal Captain Hawke's head. 'Morris, organise that a large tub of warmed sea water be brought to my night cabin. And also a jug of warmed fresh water.'

'Aye, Captain.' As the captain's head disappeared once more the young marine sent a look of bewilderment to his opposite sentry, shrugged his shoulders and scurried off to do as he was bid.

Neither did the captain's steward or his valet blink an eyelid when he requested fresh bedding and clean clothes of a size to fit Master Robinson. But it did not take long for the news to spread far and wide aboard the *Pallas*. Indeed, in a matter of hours, both Lieutenants Anderson and Pensenby had heard the rumours.

'I cannot credit that he's treating the boy in such a way.' The tip of Mr Pensenby's long nose trembled at the very thought. 'There is no doubt some unsavoury motive at play. Robertson openly flouted my command and what does he receive in return? A flogging? Reduced rations? Crow's nest watch? Oh, no. Master Robertson is treated to a private warmed bath within the captain's own cabin. There's something very much amiss.'

John Anderson's brow furrowed. 'I'm sure that there must be some perfectly reasonable explanation for what has happened. We shouldn't jump to conclusions. No doubt the captain will inform us of anything that we should know.'

'Mark my words, Mr Anderson, only trouble will come of this. Trouble and nothing else.' His wide thin lips compressed. 'We both know the direction the men's thoughts will take.'

Lieutenant Anderson said nothing, but turned his attention once more to the log he was writing.

The water lapped warm and luxuriant against Georgiana's naked skin. She sighed and relaxed back within the captain's personal hip bath, bending her knees until her soapy head submerged beneath the surface. When the worst of the lather had been removed, she reached for the jug and poured its freshwater contents over her cropped hair. The ebony locks squeaked clean, and Georgiana marvelled at Nathaniel Hawke's generosity. Freshwater was precious; she did not know how long it would be before they would have an opportunity to replenish the supply. And yet he had not expected her hair to suffer the coarse drying effects of seawater. As she stepped dripping from the tub and wrapped the cloth around her, she looked with curiosity at the small room around her, marked so clearly as belonging to Captain Hawke. Besides the furniture she'd already noticed, there were a case of books, a small table and chair, a heavy sea chest, a basin, shaving accoutrements, a mirror fixed upon the wall…and the cot. A shiver ran down her spine and she dried herself briskly, stepping into the clean clothes that Nathaniel had provided for her.

She folded the cloth and could not resist inspecting her reflection in the mirror. A pale face with short dark hair stared back at her. There was a purple bruise to the side of her right eye and a cut upon her lip. Now that the dirt was gone, she felt naked, exposed, as if anyone who looked at her would know *who* she really was, *what* she really was. She arranged the straggle of hair as best she could using only her fingers, then stepped away with deliberate care towards the flimsy connecting door, and paused. He believed that she loved Walter Praxton, that her father had forbidden her marriage to the man. As if anything could have been further from the truth! How could he even think that she would let that rogue so much as touch her? Her gorge rose at the memory of Walter Praxton's roving hands, his greedy mouth. She swallowed it down, pushed the shame and disgust away, determined never to think of it again.

Nathaniel Hawke was a good man, a man that attracted her in a way she'd never felt before. She'd tried to tell him, wanted to shout the truth when he'd misunderstood. But she couldn't, not if she wanted to stop him challenging Mr Praxton and her papa. She was nothing to Captain Hawke save a problem, a thorn in his side, turning up at the worst of times, like a bad penny. It was bad enough that he'd already risked drowning to save her. And now here she was, on his ship, in the middle of the sea, alone, and in the guise of a boy! Little wonder that he was angry. Best to remember her place, quell such inappropriate feelings for the man and get on with surviving the consequences of her own foolish actions. With this resolution in mind, she knocked softly upon the wooden panels and passed through from Captain Hawke's night cabin to the one that he used during the day.

The man himself was sitting at his desk, a glass of brandy held loosely in his hand. Grey winter light from the large windows behind the desk contrasted against the stark outline of his broad shoulders. He appeared to be deep in thought, a distant gaze in his eyes. Georgiana's resolution wavered at the sight of him. The errant curl still dangled temptingly on his forehead and her fingers itched to smooth it back to its rightful place. She suppressed the urge, blushed that she should have thought such a thing, and sat down in the chair across from Captain Hawke.

'Thank you, sir, I feel so much better now that I'm clean. And I'll no longer be a cause of offence to Lieutenant Pensenby.' She smiled and felt suddenly shy.

Nathaniel could have groaned aloud. How could he have ever thought that the girl before him was anything other? The delicate bone structure, straight little nose and full pink lips. Her eyes twinkled blue washed with shades of grey, and her eyelashes were sooty and long. How could any man fail to see what was right in front of his very eyes? The dirt had camouflaged her well and now that it was gone he wondered if the rest of the crew would see what he did. And that wasn't all the dirt had hidden. He frowned and, reaching forward, gently clasped his fingers to her chin.

'How did you come by these marks?' His voice was gruff, belying the careful touch of his fingers as he tilted her face to view the bruising near her eye. He couldn't help but notice how white her skin was next to the brown of his hand. And soft…so very, very soft.

Her skin burned beneath his touch, and a strange light-headed feeling came over her. For some inexplicable reason she found herself unable to reply, unable even to think of anything other than his strong warm fingers that touched like a feather to her face. The pulse leapt to a frenzy in her neck, so that she was sure that he would see it. But still she could not move, frozen by her own response to the man sitting before her.

Nathaniel looked down into Miss Raithwaite's shimmering eyes and experienced an urge to pull that slender body into his arms and kiss her. And not in the least chaste or polite manner. The kissing that he had in mind was of an extremely thorough nature. He watched as her lips parted, almost as in invitation. His fingers caressed her chin, moving up to capture the smoothness of her cheek. His heart thumped loudly within his chest, he lowered his mouth towards hers and—'

A short sharp knock sounded at the door.

Brandy splashed on to the captain's desk. Georgiana jumped so high that Nathaniel's hand brushed against her breast. Even through the depth of her bindings she felt his warmth. She gasped. Blue eyes held brown in confused horror.

'Quickly, slip into the night cabin and don't make a sound,' Nathaniel whispered in her ear. His large hand covered hers, gave one brief squeeze of reassurance and was gone.

She reacted instinctively, moving quickly and quietly to the connecting door.

When Lieutenant Anderson entered, it was to find the captain engrossed in some charts, and no sign of ship's boy Robertson.

'First Lieutenant Anderson.' Nathaniel's voice was laconic and mellow, betraying nothing of the turbulent emotions simmering so recently in his breast.

'Captain Hawke, sir. I beg your pardon for the intrusion, but my hourly report is due.' The young man's face appeared a trifle flushed.

Nathaniel leaned back in his chair and surveyed his lieutenant. 'Indeed, it is, Mr Anderson. Please proceed.'

John Anderson cleared his throat and recited his list. 'All stations have been checked. The first dog watch passed without event and the first watch proper commenced. All is in order. Ernie Dobson's tooth has been extracted and he's been allocated an extra quart of grog. There's no change in the weather and we are continuing on course as per your instructions. That is all I have to report, sir.'

'Thank you, Mr Anderson. That will be all.'

But the first lieutenant stayed firmly rooted to the spot, an awkward expression plastered across his face.

'Was there something else, Mr Anderson?' Nathaniel had a fairly accurate idea of what was causing John Anderson to linger.

'No, Captain… Well, perhaps…' Mr Anderson appeared to be finding a spot upon the cabin floor of immense interest.

Nathaniel decided to put the officer out of his misery. 'Would you care for a brandy, Mr Anderson?'

The first lieutenant looked up in surprise. 'Yes, thank you, sir.'

'There's been talk of my dealings with ship's boy Robertson.' It was a statement, not a question. He passed the glass to Anderson.

'Yes, sir.' His cheeks were glowing with all the subtlety of two beacons.

Nathaniel's jaw clenched grimly. That the captain had ordered a private bath for the boy within his own cabin would be known by every man on the *Pallas* by now. He was under no illusion as to what the common interpretation of his action would be, and that was something that would have to be dispelled as quickly as possibly. Nathaniel was thinking and thinking very fast. John Anderson's green eyes had raised to his in quiet anticipation. Whatever Nathaniel told him, it could not be the truth. 'It's a delicate matter over which discretion is required. I trust that I have your complete confidence in the matter?'

'Of course, sir!' Lieutenant Anderson had drawn himself up to his full height and was regarding his captain with more than a little curiosity. He sipped at the brandy.

'The boy, Robertson, is not who he seems.'

Anderson's eyes were positively agog. 'No?'

'No.' Nathaniel's tone was conspiratorial. 'Indeed, Robertson is a pseudonym he's used to his own ends.'

John Anderson nodded triumphantly. 'I knew that all wasn't as it appeared, sir.'

'Master Robertson—we'll continue to call him that for reasons that will soon become apparent—should not be aboard the *Pallas* or any ship. Mr Anderson, the boy is my nephew.' He paused for effect. 'My brother, Viscount Farleigh, has strictly forbidden George a career at sea. The boy, naturally, wants nothing else. He has therefore run away from home to pursue his dream. He didn't, of course, anticipate a brush with Captain Bodmin's men. I don't need to impress on you, Mr Anderson, exactly what my brother's response would be should any harm come to George while he's in my care. It's bad enough that I failed to recognise the wretched boy beneath his disguise of filth and rags and halfwit trickery.' Nathaniel sighed and took a gulp of brandy. 'I suppose Henry's overprotectiveness is understandable, given that George is his oldest son and therefore ultimately heir to the earldom of Porchester.'

'Dear Lord!' Mr Anderson exclaimed with feeling.

'Puts me in a bit of a quandary and no mistake. Until I can deliver the boy back to my brother, I'll have to keep a very close eye on him. If Henry knew that his son had been sleeping in a hammock squashed amongst those of the midshipmen, he'd have a fit!'

The lieutenant saw an opportunity to solve the captain's problem. 'The boy may share my cabin, sir, and I'll see to it that he's kept safe.'

The thought of Miss Raithwaite sharing a cabin with the most personable First Lieutenant Anderson brought an uncommonly disgruntled feeling to Nathaniel Hawke. If he had not known better, he would have thought it reminiscent of jealousy. 'An admirable offer, Lieutenant, but quite unnecessary.

I mean to have the boy as my personal servant. He shall sleep within my own cabin.'

Georgiana, whose ear was pressed firmly to the wooden connecting door, almost fell against the supporting structure at Captain Hawke's words. She had to admit that the story Nathaniel had concocted at such short notice was reasonably believable; in fact, she'd been admiring the gentleman's quick wits and imagination—up until his last utterance.

Nathaniel continued, blissfully unaware of Georgiana's rising indignation at the other side of the door. 'This apparent favouritism is bound to lead to supposition by the men. And it will be all the worse if the true nature of our relationship is not known.'

Mr Anderson's sharp intake of air at Captain Hawke's remark led to an inhalation of brandy and a subsequent plethora of coughing and spluttering. 'Quite so, sir.'

'Perhaps I could rely on you to see that the men are informed, by covert means, of course. A chance remark in Mr Pensenby's ear should suffice.'

The first lieutenant smiled. 'I'll see to it right away, sir.' He finished the brandy without coughing. 'It'll be all round the ship by lunchtime tomorrow.'

Captain Hawke raised his glass in salute. 'That will do nicely, Mr Anderson, very nicely indeed.'

By the time First Lieutenant Anderson exited Captain Hawke's day cabin, Georgiana was adamant that there was no way on earth that she would share a cabin with Nathaniel Hawke. She had even rehearsed a polite refusal of his offer, for undoubtedly he thought it the gentlemanly thing to do. *Thank you, Captain Hawke. You are most kind in your offer, but I cannot comply. It would be quite unseemly behaviour for a lady.* But then, Georgiana reflected, hadn't the vast majority of her behaviour of late come under that description? She sat down on the bed, touched her left hand to the lobe of her ear and worried at it as she set about thinking what her best course of action should be. In truth, there were not a great many options available. She was still mulling over various scenarios when Captain Hawke entered. Georgiana jumped up from the bed.

'You didn't knock,' she said, and her voice sounded breathless within the small confines of the cabin.

Nathaniel's eyebrow lifted and a tiny smile tugged at the corners of his mouth. 'I didn't mean to startle you, Miss Raithwaite—or should I say George? Now that I've revealed to Mr Anderson that you are in truth my nephew, Lord George Hawke, it's advisable that we stay in our respective roles at all times. Just think what he would say if I mistakenly referred to Miss Raithwaite!' Nathaniel pulled such a comical expression that the ponderous burden of anxiety eased itself from Georgiana's shoulders and she laughed.

'Should I then call you Uncle Nathaniel?' A mischievous light shone in her eyes.

Nathaniel grinned provocatively, as he stepped forward. 'Only when we're alone.'

She was so close that he could smell the clean soapy aroma arising from her jagged riot of ebony locks. She was still laughing as she turned her face up to his. Long sooty lashes swept up to reveal those magnificent eyes. Quite suddenly the laughter had gone and an arc of tension leapt between them. Georgiana was not a small woman, but the top of her head only met with Nathaniel's shoulder. He experienced an urge to pull her into his arms. It was absurd and completely unreasonable. And no matter his father's thoughts to the contrary, Captain Hawke was too much of a gentleman to take advantage of a lady in any situation. Calmly, deliberately, he moved back and looked away, pretending to examine the books lying open upon his table. 'But as you are pretending to be my nephew, and my nephew is pretending not to be my nephew…' he twitched his brow comically '…then it should suffice to call me Captain Hawke.'

A flicker of excitement exploded in Georgiana's belly the minute she looked into those dark smouldering eyes. Eyes that seemed to enchant her will, so that she could not remain unaffected whatever her resolve. No. Sharing a cabin with this man would be positively dangerous. And as the night was drawing in they had best resolve the issue here and now. She moved the chair to the far end of the tiny cabin and sat herself down on it in a ladylike fashion.

Nathaniel tried not to notice her legs that looked to be long and shapely within the culottes.

She pressed her hands demurely together and began. 'Captain Hawke, I couldn't help but overhear your words to First Lieutenant Anderson.'

'You were eavesdropping?' He looked up with surprise.

Georgiana had the grace to blush. 'It couldn't be helped, sir. The wall is so very thin.'

Nathaniel raised a cynical brow in her direction.

'It's very clever of you to play a double bluff so that the crew think they have discovered that I'm your nephew.'

The deep dark eyes regarded her, but he did not reply.

'I'd like to thank you for helping me. I'm aware of the difficulty my presence must present to you.'

He sincerely doubted whether Miss Raithwaite fully understood the precise nature of the difficulties that she presented, and he was not about to enlighten her. 'It's nothing that cannot be surmounted.'

'Nevertheless, would it not be more sensible for me to continue as before? It would certainly be less problematic to you, and is the option that is least likely to attract attention.'

'You've underestimated Mr Pensenby's preoccupation with naval regulations. You've slighted him before the crew. Direct disobedience with no punishment. And all seemingly because you're my nephew. The matter won't sit well with my second lieutenant. Indeed, he's probably worrying himself into a frenzy over the blatant breach in protocol. The man has a nose for subterfuge. Can sniff it out at twenty paces. Why do you think I want you under my command? Reverting to your previous role would be too risky, and I cannot allow it.'

She tossed her head in exasperation, even though she knew that he spoke the truth. Pensenby had the tenacity of an elephant, he would never forget and his curiosity had been roused. The prospect of such a man discovering her real secret was too dangerous, for who knew what Pensenby would do with the knowledge, being such a stickler for conformity and, according to Nathaniel, the nephew of Rear Admiral Stanley. 'Yes. I believe you're a good judge of character.' She looked at Nathaniel shrewdly. 'Then I'm to act as your servant?'

Nathaniel gave a brief nod of the head. 'It's the best I can think of to protect you,' he said simply. 'It will keep you close to me.'

A faint blush stole over Georgiana's cheeks at his words. She cleared her throat and attempted to look nonchalant while not meeting his eye. 'What of the sleeping arrangements? I know that you don't wish me to continue in my place down in the midshipmen's berth, but…'

'Surely you must have heard my comment to Mr Anderson? You heard everything else.' His eyes held a twinkle and his lips the glimmer of a wicked smile. 'You will sleep here, Miss Raithwaite.' He gestured towards the cot taking up most of the small cabin space.

It seemed that her heart lurched to a halt within her chest before setting off again at full tilt. She stared at him, shocked, horrified at the words he had just spoken, but beneath it all crept a tiny sliver of desire. And it was this that caused Georgiana to exclaim in a tone so frosty that it could have frozen the Thames, 'I beg your pardon, Captain Hawke. I believe I must have misheard you.' All thoughts of the polite refusal she had rehearsed were forgotten.

Nathaniel's eyes glowed even more wickedly. 'Your hearing cannot be faulted, nephew George. You will sleep in my bed.' He tried hard not to laugh at the expression of fury that was forming upon Miss Raithwaite's normally sweet face.

'Captain Hawke—' she stood up quite suddenly '—no gentleman would suggest such a scandalous arrangement. You cannot honestly expect me to… I assure you that it's quite out of the question. What kind of woman do you take me for?' Miss Raithwaite's eyes flashed with the violence of the stormiest sea. With her head held high and her hands planted firmly on her hips, she presented an admirable sight.

Nathaniel's fingers touched to his breast, and he feigned a look of total astonishment, which soon turned to one of most convincing wounded insult. 'Miss Raithwaite,' he gasped. 'You cannot think…? You did not…? Heavens above, dear girl, what kind of man do you take me for?'

The hurricane dropped out of Georgiana's sails. She looked suddenly very unsure of herself.

'You will sleep in here, Miss Raithwaite, and I—I will sleep next door.' Nathaniel was modelling his manner on the pompous Mr Pensenby. 'Anything else would be most unseemly behaviour for a lady, most unseemly indeed.'

Her skin burned the fiery red of embarrassment. 'Of course… Please accept my apologies, Captain Hawke, I thought—'

'I know very well what you thought, Miss Raithwaite,' replied Nathaniel with a grin. Something of Georgiana's excruciating discomfort showed in her face and it tugged at Nathaniel's heart. A pang of guilt smote him. 'I have a confession to make.'

Georgiana's heart trembled a little. He was in earnest. She looked at the captain with escalating suspicion.

Nathaniel's grin cracked wider. 'I'm teasing you.'

Her mouth opened wide. 'Why, you… That was a most ungentlemanly thing to do!' She stepped towards him.

'I couldn't resist it. You're so very charming when you're angry.' He laughed aloud.

'You, sir, are a rogue!' announced Georgiana with force, but her eyes had calmed to a tranquil blue and her mouth turned up at the corners.

It was Nathaniel's turn to look sheepish. He held out his hands towards her. 'You're right. I shouldn't have tricked you. I do beg your pardon.'

'I shall have to think about it, Captain Hawke,' she said in her sweetest voice.

'I fear the worst, sir, it's as we thought. The hank of hair beneath her bed, the kitchen scissors within her bedroom, and the missing clothes belonging to Francis—all evidence points in one direction only. The wretched girl has brought disgrace on us all.' Edward Raithwaite pinched the skin between his eyes and crumpled back in his chair.

The man seated opposite him rose. 'If I may be so bold, Mr Raithwaite, as to suggest that some brandy is required.' When Edward Raithwaite nodded limply, the man set out two balloon glasses and dispensed the tawny liquid. Passing the measure to the older man, he sat back down before resuming the conversation. 'It's not too late to discover her direction and halt her progress, but we must not delay our action, for every minute that we wait she travels further from the security of your home, and closer to danger.'

Mr Raithwaite's heavy-lidded eyes had succumbed to the temptation to close. He sipped at the brandy without trying to open them. 'How dare she do this to me? It's just reward for the selfish pampering by her mother. Clara was always too soft with the girl. And now look where it's got us. We shall all bear the brunt of her silly action. To be the subject of such petty gossip and infamy when all I am guilty of is living my life as a decent upstanding man of business. What have I done to deserve such a daughter, when I have struggled to do nothing but my best for her?' He seemed content to wallow for a little longer in a quagmire of self-pity.

'You've done nothing sir, save to act as a father. All of your actions have been only with Miss Raithwaite's best interests at heart, even to the point of sending her to Mrs Tillyard's Academy for Young Ladies. It seems that, despite your aspirations, all that she learned was to follow her own will.'

'A stubborn and self-gratifying will at that,' added her father.

The man inclined his golden head. 'She is perhaps a trifle strong-willed, but, in the hands of the right husband, such a flaw could be remedied.' He smiled, revealing a row of perfect white teeth to offset the pretty looks of his face.

'Our plans fade to dust, Praxton. What desire have you for a woman whose reputation is tarnished? She has absconded, dressed as a boy! For all we know she's run off with a lover!' He clamped his large loose-skinned hands over his face. 'Oh, heaven help us, for we're soon to be a laughing stock throughout the town, and wherever else this story travels.'

Walter Praxton examined his nails before replying. 'All is not lost, sir, for I have it on good authority that a young boy matching your daughter's height and build was observed to take the evening mail to Gosport on the night in question. A boy that no one of the town knew, and who didn't alight from any other coach. He was quite alone amidst the travellers, no sign of any possible *lover.* I rather think—' his mouth twisted to a crooked semblance of a smile '—that the reason for Miss Raithwaite's flight was due to her determination not to become my wife.'

Mr Raithwaite's eyes opened at that. 'Surely you're mistaken, for, no matter what she thinks she feels, Georgiana would not disobey me so blatantly.'

'I doubt that your daughter views the situation in quite the same way.'

The grizzled head shook once more. 'I'll put it about that she's gone to stay with an elderly relative in Scotland. At least that may buy us some time with which to attempt to remedy this damnable mess. When I get my hands on her—'

Mr Praxton swiftly interrupted. 'The betrothal is still binding. If I can discover her location, then the situation might be resolved if I were to immediately marry Miss Raithwaite. That way she could return here as my wife, with all threat of scandal avoided. Do I have your permission to force her to a speedy exchange of vows by whatever means are required?'

'You would still wed her, after all she's done? What if she's dishonoured? A fallen woman? Would you take her even then?' Edward Raithwaite's tired eyes focused with a new clarity.

'I would take her whatever the circumstance, provided that any threat of ensuing scandal could be extinguished.'

The older man leaned forward and with a deliberate and careful manner said, 'Well, in that case, Mr Praxton, you must do whatever you deem necessary to resolve this matter satisfactorily. You have my full support.' One fleshy hand thrust forward and clasped Mr Praxton's in a firm shake. 'I wish you Godspeed, Walter, and may you save the situation for us all.'

Mr Praxton glanced back only once at Tythecock Crescent, and as he did anyone close by would have heard him utter softly, 'I will have you, Georgiana Raithwaite. One way or another, you are mine.'

Chapter Five

Captain Hawke was taking the noon sight with Lieutenants Anderson and Pensenby, and the young midshipmen. The murmuring hush of their voices lapped against his ears as, armed with their sextants, they compared measurements and subsequent calculations of the ship's latitude. Across the breadth of the forecastle he could see Jenkins, the quartermaster, at the great steering wheel, hands firm upon the burnished wood. Canvas flapped and ropes creaked as the wind moved to catch the sails. He stifled a yawn and, turning to look out across the great expanse of the cold grey water, thought of the previous night spent sitting upright in his captain's chair. Little wonder that he'd only managed to catnap through the long dark hours, and had been up on deck before the bosun had piped the hands just before dawn. In truth, he had pondered long and hard over the matter of Miss Georgiana Raithwaite.

It was unfortunate that for this trip none of the officers had brought their wives along for company. Indeed, there were no women aboard, only one hundred and eighty-five men. Nathaniel grimaced and corrected himself. One hundred and eighty-five men and one lady. A lady whose ability to place herself in quite the worst situations possible was equalled by none. To have almost drowned in the River Borne was one thing. To have run away from home, been taken by the Press Gang and worked, disguised as a boy, undetected upon his ship for two weeks was quite another. That the captain of that ship could have failed to notice such an absurd thing was preposterous.

He glanced once more at the group of young men behind him. Such enthusiasm, such commitment. If any one of them learned of Miss Raithwaite's secret, she would be well and truly ruined—if she wasn't already. And despite what his father thought, that was something Nathaniel could not let happen. The girl affected him far more than he was willing to own—her courage in the face of what for her was most definitely a disastrous situation, the transparency of emotion upon her face, those eyes that mirrored the colour of the sea before him. That he was attracted to her was obvious. He'd felt it since the moment she opened her eyes and looked up at him on the riverbank, her long hair dripping river water, her body relaxed and trusting in his arms. It had obviously been too long since he'd had a woman. A physical need, nothing more. But even as the thought formed, he knew it wasn't true. What he felt for her was much more than that, more than he was ready to admit.

Quite how Miss Raithwaite had escaped detection was nothing short of a miracle. He gripped the smooth wood of the quarterdeck rail with tense hands. It was imperative that no one should discover the true identity of Lord George Hawke or, indeed, Master George Robertson. He walked back to the small group of would-be officers without a hint of the worry that plagued his mind or the fatigue that pulled at his body.

Georgiana was helping Mr Fraser, the captain's valet, in cleansing the great man's clothes. She struggled to hold back her laughter at the reverential voice that Gordon Fraser constantly adopted when speaking of Captain Hawke.

'Now, Master Robertson,' Mr Fraser said in his lilting Scottish tones, 'it is vital that *Captain Hawke*'s shirts—' he lowered his voice as he uttered his master's name '—are treated exactly to his liking. Gather up the washing tub and follow me.' He marched off across the deck with the manner of a schoolmaster who would brook no nonsense.

Georgiana did as she was bid, scooping the wooden basin under one arm and holding three of Nathaniel's shirts in the other hand.

They stopped before a large wooden cask. 'Off with the lid and fill your basin.' Mr Fraser stood well back.

'Yes, sir.' Georgiana prised the lid off and promptly dropped both the basin and the shirts in her hurry to scramble away. 'Dear Lord!' she mumbled beneath her breath and retched.

Mr Fraser pursed his lips. The boy had to learn, even if he was the captain's nephew, perhaps even more so. 'We haven't got all day, laddie. Now, retrieve your basin and *Captain Hawke*'s shirts, and do as you're bid.'

The hard biscuit and apple eaten for luncheon were threatening to make a reappearance upon the deck. Georgiana's stomach heaved. 'What on earth…?'

'That's quite enough, Master Robertson. Stop behaving like a namby-pamby and get back over there.' He twirled at his grey moustache.

Georgiana held her nose, approached the cask, and fulfilled Mr Fraser's requirements as quickly as she could. The liquid slopping within the basin was dark brown in colour and stank to high heaven.

'Submerge the shirts and scrub around the cuffs and collar to remove any marks.' He handed her a small brush.

The thought of plunging her hands into the vile liquid brought Georgiana's stomach back up into her throat. 'Yes, Mr Fraser,' she managed to croak.

'When you're sure there are no stains left, you can start using the soap. Then give them a good rinse in sea water from the cask over there. Ring them out and then peg them on to the line fixed at the far corner. After that I'll instruct you in the care of the *captain*'s boots.' Mr Fraser was clearly used to giving orders.

The stench was unbearable and her hands were soon red raw with the scrubbing. It occurred to Georgiana that perhaps a gunroom servant hadn't been such a bad job after all. Finally the chore was done and she was just pegging the shirts on the line when Captain Hawke and the boatswain wandered by, deep in conversation. Nathaniel's eyes held hers for a moment, although he gave no other outward sign of having seen her, and in the next instant he had passed by. Irrational as it was, Georgiana felt a pang of annoyance. What did she expect him to do? Execute a tidy bow at his ship's boy? Enquire as to her health this fine afternoon? Georgiana grumped back down to Mr Fraser.

'You managed then, boy?' Mr Fraser's single jaundiced eye was trained upon her.

She stifled the words that so longed to jump off the tip of her tongue. 'Yes, Mr Fraser, sir.' The old man was kind enough for all his stern ways.

'You'll soon get used to the washing stench. Stale piss is never fragrant. And it'll have grown a mite more pungent by the time we reach our destination.'

The blood drained from Georgiana's face, leaving her powder white. 'Stale piss?' she uttered faintly.

'What else did you think it was?' retorted Mr Fraser with a snort. 'There's nothing better for shifting dirt.' He noticed his assistant's pallor. 'You've a lot yet to learn, laddie, a lot to learn.' Shaking his head, he went to fetch the revered Captain Hawke's boots and shoes.

The pillow was plump and soft and smelled of Nathaniel Hawke. Sandalwood and soap and a distinctly masculine aroma. Georgiana snuggled beneath the covers and marvelled at the luxury. No choir of snores, wheezes and coughs, no foul odours from a multitude of youthful male bodies, no scuttle of rodents. Bliss! During her two weeks in the midshipmen's berth she had failed miserably in her attempt to grow used to the narrow hammock strung so closely between those of Mr Hartley and Mr Burrows. Each night had seen her lying rigid and afraid to move, lest she fell out, until she found sleep by virtue of sheer exhaustion. The alternative of sleeping on the dampness of the deck below, amidst the spiders and the rats, was too awful to contemplate. She stretched out her spine, unmindful of her bindings, and pulled the sheet up to meet her nose. A contented sigh escaped. Such warmth, such comfort. She sighed and wriggled her legs around.

It was wonderful to be able to relax, to drop her vigilance of trying to disguise her voice, her manners and all feminine tendencies, which, she had come to realise, were too numerous to count. A space of her own. Privacy. Safety from discovery. Heaven only knew what Mama would do if she knew her situation. Swoon, no doubt. It was the first time that she'd allowed herself to think of Mama, of little Prudence and Theo. Even her stepbrother Francis with all his teasing and impudence did not seem so bad. Please God, keep them safe. She felt her eyes begin to well and took a deep breath to allay the tears that threatened to fall. Mama would be worried sick, not knowing where she was, and Papa... Papa would be livid. In her rush to escape marriage to Mr Praxton, she'd only succeeded in making things difficult for her family. There would be gossip, and worse. Denigration, castigation, direct snubs. Poor Mama. She wept silently, stifling her sobs in Nathaniel Hawke's pillow. Sleep finally found her with swollen eyelids and the taste of saline upon her lips.

It was still dark. Georgiana's eyes strained against the gloom. It seemed barely five minutes since she had laid her head on the pillow. Nathaniel's soft tread sounded from the adjoining cabin. A dull pain thrummed around her head. She groaned, dragged her fatigued body from the bed and started to dress herself. Late, she was late. What would Mr Fraser say? No time for boots.

Nathaniel sipped at the brandy and stared at the charts laid on the desk before him. It was a little after two o'clock and he still could not find sleep. The lantern light flickered as he moved to peer blindly from the windows. He had stood there some time when he heard the noise, and turned with confusion to look at the connecting door. Therein lay the reason for his insomnia. The indomitable Miss Raithwaite, who had not the slightest notion of the precarious position into which she had thrust herself. He smiled at the memory of her determined face—she certainly did not enter into anything faint-heartedly. Even as he thought it the door creaked open and Miss Raithwaite—or should he say Master Robertson?—stumbled out fully dressed. 'George?' he quizzed lightly.

'On my way to my station, Captain, sir,' she pronounced through tired lips and dragged herself towards the door. She had reverted to her 'boy's' voice even though they were alone.

Nathaniel's eyes opened wide, suddenly alert. 'George,' he said again and moved to grab at her shoulders.

Georgiana's sleep-fuddled mind could not comprehend what had happened, only that she now found herself staring up into Nathaniel Hawke's handsome face. 'Late, I'm late,' she mumbled, and tried to disengage herself.

He gathered her slender body into his arms and held her against him. She did not protest further, just laid her head against his shoulder. Nathaniel swallowed hard. She was warm and soft. The effects of the brandy swam through his brain. His hand swept across her back, moving up to touch the delicate nape of her neck. No woman had ever felt this right. He pressed a kiss to the top of her head, revelling in the sweetness of her smell and with great reluctance held her away. 'You're sleep-addled, George. It's the dead of night, and you should still be asleep.' His winged eyebrow twitched as he smiled down at her.

'But I heard the hands piped.' Her voice was sleepy and low.

Nathaniel drew his thumb gently against her cheek. The skin was still soft and white. 'Perhaps in your dream.'

Georgiana could not move. Still heavy with sleep, she felt mesmerised by the man in whose arms she stood. His voice was gentle, and there was such kindness in his eyes that it gladdened her heart. Couldn't her stepfather have desired to marry her to a man such as this? A man who was just and fair, a man who had risked his life and now jeopardised his career to save her. She sighed, as his warm hands held her from him. He would never be interested in the likes of her, even if she hadn't made such a mess of things. Not when his father was the Earl of Porchester. For all his standing, Nathaniel Hawke would always do what was right.

'Let me help you back next door.' His voice was soft in her

ear as he lifted her up fully into his arms, her bare feet brushing against his breeches.

Georgiana was surely dreaming, and it was the same stuff
that had filled all her nocturnal thoughts of late. His arms were
strong and he carried her as if she were the merest feather-
weight. She laid her head against the hard muscle of his chest
and felt the rhythmic beat of his heart. A lady would not have
done such a thing, Georgiana knew that implicitly, but still she
did nothing but revel in the warm languor that was spreading
throughout her body.

Nathaniel pushed open the connecting door, pulled back
the covers and carefully laid Miss Raithwaite upon the bed.
The strength of the feeling she invoked shocked him. She
should not have to suffer the rigors of ship life in the guise of
a fourteen-year-old boy. The sight of her washing his shirts
had worried him and he had resolved to speak to Mr Fraser
to go easy with the lad. Her head sank into the pillow and he
made to release her. It certainly would not do to linger in such
a situation.

Suddenly, without any warning whatsoever, even to herself, Georgiana succumbed to the mad impulse to wrap her
hands around Nathaniel Hawke's neck.

Nathaniel froze, the breath caught in his throat.

She thrust her fingers through his auburn locks as she had
so longed to do, trailing them down to feel the taut muscles
in his neck. 'Closer, come closer.' The words escaped as a
whisper. The dream felt very real.

Nathaniel stared down at where he knew her face to be. He
knew without seeing that her eyelids would have swept shut.
Through the darkness he felt her rise beneath him, touching
her lips to his cheek in a chaste kiss.

'Oh, God!' The blasphemy tore in a gritty hush from his

throat. Never had a man been so tempted. Her soft cheek pressed to his and his body responded instinctively. His lips turned to seek hers and, upon finding them, possessed them with a gentle insistence. Their lips writhed in a torment of ecstasy until his tongue could no longer resist the sweet allure of her mouth and raided within, seeking its hidden intimacy with an increasing fervour.

Georgiana floated in a blissful haze of delight. Her hands slid of their own accord across the broad muscle of his back, basking in the heat of his skin through the fine lawn of his shirt. More, she wanted more of this strange enchanting feeling.

The cot swayed as he clambered upon it and lay his length against her. The wool of his breeches could not disguise the feel of her legs beneath him. He fumbled with her shirt and soon felt the satin skin beneath his hand. She made an inarticulate little noise, but did not draw back. His fingers wove their sensual magic across her stomach, swirling up towards her breast, only to meet with the coarse linen wrap of her bindings. It was enough to bring Nathaniel crashing to his senses. In that single instant he realised their predicament, and stopped.

'Nathaniel?' Miss Raithwaite's sleepy whisper sounded through the darkness.

Hell's teeth, it was enough to tempt a saint! Slowly, gently, he disengaged himself from the slender soft arms surrounding him. 'You're sleep-addled. Miss Raithwaite. I must not take advantage of a lady in my care.' His teeth gritted in determination. 'Please forgive me.' And, so saying, he turned and strode briskly from the cabin, closing the door firmly behind him.

In the weeks that passed Captain Hawke took considerable care that just such a situation did not arise again. He threw himself into his work upon the *Pallas* and struggled to think of his ship's boy as George Robertson rather than Miss Raithwaite. The task proved difficult, but not impossible. His illicit actions of that night had shaken him more than he cared to admit. For in acknowledging the young woman's allure and his own inappropriate response, he felt that he had behaved as the singular debauchee his father thought him. He had embraced the role willingly for those tender few minutes, had revelled in Georgiana Raithwaite's warm caress, until he'd realised the shamefulness of what he was doing. And the thought repulsed him. He thrust it away, determined to think no more of that night. Mercifully Miss Raithwaite had made no mention of the incident, and continued to adopt her guise of the ship's boy, revealing nothing more by her outward demeanour. Perhaps the fates had been kind to him, and robbed her of the sleep-laden memory. It was a prayer uttered most fervently by Nathaniel, although he was not naïve enough to believe that it would be answered.

Georgiana had woken to a heaving frenzy of conflicting emotions. Not only did she have a very clear and precise memory of her actions of the previous night but she also had to admit to having experienced a distinct pang of disappointment when Nathaniel Hawke had behaved like the gentleman he was and refused to continue his interest. She, on the other hand, to her extreme chagrin, had behaved like a wanton and was subsequently reaping a much-deserved vengeance of guilt. It was her first kiss, the first tentative touch of a man's body. How could Miss Georgiana Raithwaite have behaved like a veritable slattern? With her fancy schooling, formidable parenting and proper Christian upbringing, she was nothing but a drab. She cringed when she thought what she had tried to do, the blatant seduction of a man who had done nothing but sought to help her. What must he have thought of her? Utter abhorrence, nothing less. Especially in view of what he thought she had been about with Mr Praxton in Hurstborne Park. Oh, Lord! She still had to face him. Confusion, fear and guilt vied in her breast.

With frank determination Georgiana pulled her fragmented emotions together, squared her shoulders and decided that she would pretend that the incident had never happened. It seemed the only way to survive the months that lay ahead. In all the days and weeks that rushed past with gathering momentum she threw herself body and soul into the role of the captain's boy. Georgiana Raithwaite no longer existed, only the juvenile George Robertson. And through the boy she learned to quell the attraction she felt for Captain Nathaniel Hawke.

'Take in all the canvas until she's bare. We'll have to try-a-hull. Have the galley fire extinguished and check that the magazines are secured.' Captain Hawke lowered the small brass spyglass from his eye and turned to face Mr Anderson. 'There's a storm brewing, and from the cloud formation I'd say it'll have its way with us if we're not careful.'

'Aye, Captain. It doesn't look good.'

'With the wind the way it is we can't tack safely into it and any other move would have us well off course, or worse. Our best option is to weather the storm until it passes.'

John Anderson nodded his head. He'd trust Nathaniel Hawke above all others. The man had an uncanny ability for choosing wisely, even if it did appear sometimes slightly questionable to those who had neither his knowledge nor his experience.

The deck heaved beneath their feet as the white-crested waves buffeted the bow of the *Pallas*. The wind howled above the roar of the waves. All around them timber groaned and creaked as the sails were retracted. Men climbed fast, loosing the ropes, securing them again when the canvases had been taken in. Spray stung at their faces, dripped from their hair, soaking their clothes and drenching the decks.

'All men to stay below other than are absolutely necessary up here. I'd say we have twenty minutes at the most before it reaches us.' Nathaniel's face was grim.

'Yes, sir.' Lieutenant Anderson watched his captain's determined stance, a shiver of apprehension snaking down his spine. 'What's so bad, sir? We've suffered storms before and faired well enough.'

He did not want to frighten the young man, but forewarned was forearmed. 'Never a storm like the one that's coming for us now. Pray to God, Mr Anderson, that it passes quickly.'

'Promise me, George, that you'll stay in my day cabin until the storm has passed.'

She could see the anxiety in that determined glare. For a moment she thought that it was true what they said—the eyes were the windows to the soul, and Nathaniel Hawke's soul was concerned by whatever he had seen sweeping down towards them across the ocean. He cared no more or no less about any man aboard the *Pallas*. Each was a member of his crew; he saw every one of them as his responsibility. 'Yes, sir. There's darning to be done and I'll keep myself busy with the linen repairs.'

Still he seemed restless and uneasy. 'Promise me,' he said, his voice quiet and insistent. Seawater dripped from dark, sodden hair to run down his cheeks.

'I'll give you no cause to worry more over me than any other man or boy aboard this ship. I promise I'll do as you command.'

Lines of tension were deeply etched into the flesh around his mouth, his coiled energy palpable within the confines of the small cabin. She longed to give him some measure of comfort, some little encouragement in the task that lay ahead. Wanted to touch her lips to his and tell him that all would be well. But George Robertson could not. She forced a smile to her mouth.

He stood still, silent, and regarded her for a minute, a single long minute, with an unreadable expression upon his face. Then turned and walked towards the door, shouting over his shoulder, 'Fraser and the others will keep you company. It's going to be a very long day and an even longer night.'

The waves grew larger as the wind set up a banshee howl. Through the windows in Nathaniel's cabin, ship's boy George Robertson watched the cold grey sea whip into a fury of froth and lashing fingers. It attacked the ship with violence as the sky darkened to a deep lifeless hue, chasing the light away. Only three bells had sounded, but already they could scarcely see within the captain's cabin. The *Pallas* pitched and rolled at the mercy of the roaring ocean, her pine structure creaking and groaning under the strain. The holed bed linen slithered to the floor undarned as Georgiana clung to the unlit candle sconce. Waves battered at the feeble glass of the windows until she thought they surely must shatter beneath the hostile assault. A single lantern swung from the ceiling, lurching and swaying with the convulsions of the ship, illuminating the captain's servants as monstrous distortions.

'How're you doin', laddie?' Mr Fraser's lilting voice enquired. He raised his head from the game of cards that he was enjoying with Bottomley, the captain's cook, and Spence, the captain's steward.

'Survivin', thank you, sir. Will the storm last long?'

The grizzled grey head concentrated upon his hand of cards. 'As long as it has a mind to last, no' a moment less.'

A wave battered the stern, sending Georgiana hurtling across the room.

'Steady, lad!' the valet exclaimed, reaching out a gnarled old hand and hoisting the boy back by the scruff of the neck.

Three books fell off Nathaniel's desk and a silver wine goblet rolled across the floor. Bottomley stopped it dead with his toe. Just when Georgiana thought that things could not possibly get any worse, a torrent of rain was released from the heavens to beat the *Pallas* into submission. A sheet of driving shards lashed the frigate without mercy and a rumble of thunder cracked loud. Somewhere across the deep darkness a tiny flicker lit up the sky, then it was gone as quickly as it had appeared. Dear Lord, nothing could hope to survive against such ferocity.

Fear twisted at Georgiana's gut. 'Where's the captain?'

'Up on deck.' Mr Fraser's single eye focused upon the boy and softened a little. 'No need to worry, laddie. The captain knows what he's doin'. Been through a hundred storms, he has, and never got caught yet.'

'But shouldn't we be helpin', sir?' The thought of any man, let alone Nathaniel Hawke, out facing the wrath of the heavens was worrying in the extreme.

Mr Fraser shook his head. 'We'd only create more hindrance than help. The captain'll send for us if he needs us. Best to just stay out the way and look after his cabin.' The boy's eyes looked huge in the whitened pallor of his face. Poor lad. 'It'll pass soon enough, laddie. Best turn your mind to other things.'

A pile of papers slid off the desk and landed with a thud

by her leg. She grabbed them and crawled along the floor to stuff them inside a drawer. Mr Fraser was right. There was nothing any of them could do about it, other than wait for the storm to pass, and pray that the *Pallas*' crew remained safe.

The thunder rolled across the sky, masking the muffled knock at the door. A drenched seaman staggered in, dripping water across the polished wooden floor. 'Man overboard,' he said through gasping breath.

'Who?' Mr Fraser's single eye widened at the news.

'Midshipmen Hartley.'

'Are we needed?' His ancient tone was clipped, determined.

'Not yet.'

And the sailor was gone.

Time dragged by. And still the storm showed no sign of abating. Georgiana hoped that Mr Hartley had been saved, but even as she turned her gaze once more to the large sea-battered windows she knew it was unlikely that anyone plunged into such a furore of indomitable wave power could survive. Drowned beneath the towering waves, or smashed like a weightless puppet against the hull. Dear God protect them all, she prayed like she never had done before, protect them all, but especially Nathaniel Hawke. Fear that he might be injured or, God forbid, die, pierced a pain through her heart. Never that, please Lord, never that. Why should she care so much for him? Was it his kindness or his strength, or the way he was just and fair? Maybe it was because he made her laugh, made her want to be with him? She laid her head against the edge of Nathaniel's desk, clinging tightly to the wooden leg with one hand, worrying at her ear lobe with the other. Whatever the answer, ship's boy George Robertson had no right to such feelings. Whether Georgiana Raithwaite did was another matter altogether.

* * *

Georgiana awoke to the stern tones of Mr Fraser and a vigorous shaking of her shoulder. 'Robertson, waken yourself now, laddie. There's plenty work to be done. It's no time to be nappin'.'

The violent heave of the frigate was no more. No batter of rain, no riot of waves, no screaming darkness. She crawled out from beneath the captain's desk and made for the windows. A calm leaden sea and colourless sky stretched endlessly ahead.

She turned to the elderly valet. 'Mr Hartley, sir?' The question had to be asked.

'They fished him out alive, if not well.'

'Thank God!'

Mr Fraser's eye narrowed. 'There'll be no takin' the Lord's name in vain on this ship.'

'And the captain?'

Fraser mellowed slightly at the anxiety-edged voice. 'In fine mettle as ever. Come on, laddie, you're gabbin' like a fishwife. You youngsters would do anythin' to avoid work. Got to keep my eye on you!' His single eye stared large and cod-like at Georgiana.

'Yes, Mr Fraser, sir.' She breathed her relief and watched while the cod eye delivered her a hearty wink.

Nathaniel was exhausted, but he knew that there was still much to be done before he could rest. Jeremiah Hutton and his assistants were already sawing up wooden spars to repair the damage done to the mizzen topgallant mast. Debris strewn across the decks was in the process of being cleared. And midshipman Hartley had apparently survived his ordeal with little more than a scratch to his arm.

Georgiana clambered upon the forecastle and surveyed the damage. 'Set to it, lad.' A basin was pressed into her hands. 'Gather up seaweed and all else, exceptin' fish, heave it over t'side. Look smart, now.' She felt a thrust in her back and the voice was gone.

Pieces of wood, shells, dead and dying fish and stinking seaweed covered the floor before her. She scanned up towards the quarterdeck for any sign of Nathaniel. The seaweed squelched cold and slimy beneath her fingers. Sam Wilson's thin body emerged ahead, gathering up the fish in his basin.

'Sammy!' she hailed.

The little lad looked round. 'George! Place ain't been the same without you.'

'It's good to see you too.' She embraced the skinny body, glad that the orphaned youngster had survived the storm unscathed. Sam Wilson worried her more than she let anyone know. 'Have you been helpin' Jack like I told you to?'

'Yeah, I'm Jack's mate. He's learning me knots for the riggin', and he don't let no one cuff me, or take me grog.' Sam gave her a gap-toothed grin.

'What happened to your teeth?' Georgiana held the lad at arm's length and inspected his small grubby face.

He trailed a dirty hand across his runny nose. 'Fell out when I was eatin' me biscuit. Jack says more'll grow.'

Georgiana smiled at the small ragamuffin before her and ruffled his matted hair. Poor little mite, thank goodness Burly Jack was looking out for him.

'Master Robertson,' a curt voice sounded. 'Much as I hate to interrupt your little reunion, there's work to be done aboard this frigate. And that means for all of us, no matter who we might happen to be.' The veiled snub hit home, causing Georgiana to blush and resume her debris collection with renewed vigour. Lieutenant Pensenby leaned back against the railing and watched the boy's progression with shrewd eyes. There was something strange about George Robertson, something very strange indeed. The way that he'd hugged ship's boy Wilson, the clear, fine-boned face. It smacked of something unnatural, even if he was the captain's nephew, or at least purported to be. Perhaps Captain Hawke was not quite the hero everyone thought. All was not as it presented itself, of that Cyril Pensenby was sure, and, one way or another, he meant to get to the bottom of the puzzle.

Captain Hawke worked solidly for the next two days, ensuring that every last speck of storm damage on the *Pallas* was repaired. He had already left the day cabin when Georgiana awoke and slipped through to pass to the station call for drill each morning, not returning until long after she had fallen asleep within the comfort of his cot. On the third day she had entered the captain's cabin with a pile of freshly pressed neckcloths to find him poring over charts with both his lieutenants. The great stern windows striped pale winter daylight across the three men. Crossing quietly to his great sea chest, that he had had moved from the night cabin, she made to stow the linen safely and retreat without notice. Their voices mumbled in conversation, but she kept her head down and her eyes averted. She had almost reached the door when Nathaniel spoke out.

'Wait behind, Robertson. I want to speak with you before you continue with your duties.'

She had no choice but to do as she was bid, hovering awkwardly near the exit while the captain finished his business with the lieutenants. Both men's gazes washed over her, but the weight of Pensenby's stare drew her attention. She glanced up to catch his regard, and the look within those small overly-curious eyes made her wary. Captain Hawke had not been wrong in his estimation of Second Lieutenant Pensenby. And the knowledge released in her a small spasm of worry.

The door closed.

'Sit down, George.'

She glanced once more at the cabin door as if to make sure Pensenby was gone, and moved to one of the chairs positioned beside the captain's desk.

'Captain Hawke,' she said quietly, inclining her head like some great lady, and composedly sat herself down.

Nathaniel watched the graceful figure before him. He cleared his throat and adjusted his neckcloth. 'I just wanted to be sure that you took no hurts from the storm.'

Georgiana bowed her head to hide the smile that leapt to her lips. Nathaniel Hawke had been worried about her after all, and the thought, inappropriate as it was, brought a gladness to her heart. 'None at all, thank you for your concern, sir. Mr Fraser looked after me most admirably.'

'It must have been a frightening experience for you, all the same.' There was a concern in his eyes that he could not entirely mask.

Georgiana shrugged her shoulders slightly in a dismissive gesture. 'Yes, but not as fearful as the thought of those of you facing the storm up on the deck. When I heard that Mr Hartley had been washed overboard...'

'His rope snapped, carrying him over. Fortunately we were able to retrieve him.'

She smiled at him. 'It seems that on this occasion luck was on your side.'

'Luck plays her part, but experience, skill, a decent ship and a good crew of men are the foremost defences against a stormy sea.' He raised his brow, and the corners of his mouth tugged up in a crooked smile. 'I sound to be singing my own praises, but that isn't my intention. Your acclaim should be for the men who did their jobs so well in the face of the storm.'

Laughter played on her lips. 'Captain Hawke, an arrogant man? Who would have thought it?'

His eyes creased with the boyish grin, but beneath it she could see the toll fatigue was taking upon him.

'There's a tiredness in your face. You're bone weary and should rest.' The thought was spoken aloud. She glanced down in embarrassment, unwilling that he should guess the truth of her feelings for him. 'Forgive me, Captain, I shouldn't have spoken.'

One long tanned finger gently tipped her chin up. He was still smiling. 'Could it be that my nephew has a thought for my welfare?'

Georgiana could not prevent the colour that flooded her cheeks. 'Yes...no...I...' then exclaimed, 'You're teasing me again, sir. I should be about my duties.' She made to pull back, but he stopped her.

'Maybe so, but not before you've answered your captain's question, ship's boy Robertson.' Nathaniel's eyes shone wickedly.

He had not removed his hand from her chin, and in truth had no compulsion to do so. What was it about the dark-haired girl before him that attracted him so? Even during the long hours of work he had found himself desiring her company, to hear her clear voice, watch the rose blush grow in her cheeks when he teased her, witness her enthusiasm for learning anything and everything she could about the ship. She had a good mind, that much was evident. A mind wasted as a third-class ship's boy. And the marriage mart of today would view it as a mind wasted on a woman. But Nathaniel did not think so.

When she looked at him her eyes were a cool, calm grey blue. 'I'm concerned for every man upon the *Pallas*, including her captain.'

'Even Mr Pensenby?' It seemed he was willing to say anything to prolong the conversation, anything to prevent her leaving. He had missed her these past days. The realisation hit him with the force of a mid-Atlantic gale.

The light in her face dimmed and a frown crept between her eyes. 'My concern is *about* Lieutenant Pensenby rather than *for* him.' Her fingers stole to worry at the lobe of her ear. 'It would seem that the second lieutenant does not quite believe our story. There's something in the way he looks at me, as if to say he knows something is amiss. Perhaps I'm just being fanciful, but it leaves me uneasy.'

'Yes.' Nathaniel looked pensive. 'My thoughts flow in a similar direction. We had best have a care where Pensenby is concerned. He has a scholar's mind for analysis and a passion for a puzzle. The sooner that his focus is trained on Bonaparte's forces, the better.'

They looked at each other, without further speech. And within each breast stirred disquiet and beneath it something else warm and joyous.

He touched his thumb to her cheek with gentle reassurance. 'Don't worry, I won't let him discover our secret, whatever it takes.'

A sense of unity blossomed between them, as if it were just the two of them together, against the world.

The severity of his gaze softened.

A knock at the door revealed Mr Fraser.

'There you are, laddie. If you're finished with the boy, I'll be off with him, Captain.'

Captain Hawke nodded his compliance. 'Go ahead, Mr Fraser.' But the dark eyes did not leave Georgiana's slender frame until she had departed his cabin.

'Mr Fraser,' he called as the grizzled head disappeared around the door.

'Aye, Captain?'

He looked at his valet meaningfully. 'Keep the boy within your sight at all times.'

Fraser's lone eye glared unblinkingly back. An unspoken understanding passed between them and he nodded. 'That I certainly will, sir.'

And he was gone, leaving Nathaniel to contemplate how best to deal with Lieutenant Pensenby.

Chapter Six

It was not long before they arrived in the warmer waters of their destination. Despite it being so late in the year the seas surrounding the Azores were clear and calm and of such a bright coloration that Georgiana never ceased to marvel at their beauty. The cold dark skies of England had been left far behind, replaced instead with a cloudless expanse of blue. Even more incredible was the temperature, for, as those novice members of the *Pallas'* crew discovered, it was pleasantly warm. Indeed, such was the sun that an awning was positioned over the quarterdeck each morning to protect the officers about their work. The men did not take such precautions from the heat, preferring instead to divest themselves of their shirts at any excuse. On first sight the exposure of masculine flesh rather shocked Georgiana, who tried to avert her eyes from such indecency. She was thus engaged one morning when she tripped over a large coil of rope, landing face down on the swabbed and holystoned deck. Mr Fraser had hauled her up, dusted her down and given her a good tongue lashing for not watching where she was going. Thereafter, Georgiana had learned to take the seminaked sights in her stride, much to Captain Hawke's disapproval.

As they travelled further south past Madeira, the sun grew stronger and the smothering heat sapped the strength of them all. Even Nathaniel wilted a little beneath the dark blue wool of his dress coat, perspiration soaking through from his shirt to his waistcoat. And as Mr Fraser put it, with the captain having such a peculiar compulsion for clean clothes and bathing, Georgiana was kept busy with the laundering. Not her most favourite of duties. Indeed, she could steadfastly avow to the truth of Mr Fraser's earlier prediction concerning the pungency of the stale urine. It was while filling her basin with the well-matured fluid that Georgiana heard the captain's voice suddenly close behind her.

'Just what do you think you're doing, Master Robertson?' he demanded in a whisper. His annoyance was plain.

Georgiana, who had been daydreaming sweet and pleasant thoughts as a diversion from the rather distasteful task at which she was employed, jumped as if she'd been scalded. This had the unfortunate effect of spilling the aromatic contents of her basin down the length of her, soaking her jacket, waistcoat, shirt and culottes. Even her feet did not escape the frothy brown deluge.

A yell wrought forth. She spun round to see Nathaniel looking at her, an expression of undisguised horror set clearly on his face. 'Captain,' she ground out through gritted teeth. 'I didn't hear your approach, sir.'

'Evidently not,' uttered the captain.

If looks could kill, Nathaniel knew without a doubt that he would have lain mortally wounded upon the deck. For Georgiana was eyeing him with an accusing look of 'it's all your fault'.

The urine dribbled down the bare flesh of her stomach and was soaking its way through her bindings. She grimaced at Nathaniel. 'You wanted to know about my actions, sir?'

'This is not your duty,' he hissed.

Georgiana opened her eyes wide and stared at him incredulously before muttering drolly, 'I beg to differ, sir, but it surely is.'

By this stage Mr Fraser was travelling towards them at a fair rate of knots for an elderly retainer, and several of the crew had noticed the boy's state.

'I'll speak to you later,' was all he managed before the valet was within earshot.

'Laddie!' Fraser bellowed. 'I turn my back for two minutes and you've landed yourself in mischief!' As he stepped closer the stench assailed his nostrils. 'In the name of…' He retreated rather quickly, his eyes watering. 'You'd best stand down wind of us, laddie, the captain'll not be wanting to smell that.'

Georgiana pressed her lips firmly together and moved to where Mr Fraser was pointing. 'I wouldn't want to inflict anythin' so horrible on the captain, sir.'

Nathaniel did not miss the murderous glint in her eye, even if Mr Fraser remained oblivious.

'Quite so, laddie, quite so.'

The baking heat of the sun caused steam to rise from Georgiana's sodden clothes, magnifying the smell acutely.

Nathaniel coughed once and Mr Fraser set about a loud and raucous choking sound.

'Have someone else finish this job, Mr Fraser, I rather think that Master Robertson is in need of a change of clothes.' A smile twitched at his face. 'Either that or we've found the perfect weapon to inflict upon our enemies.'

Guffaws sounded all around.

Georgiana's eyes darted daggers. 'Yes, sir, right away, sir,' she muttered, and made her way below, leaving behind a trail of smelly wet footprints.

* * *

'Beast!' the word escaped Georgiana as she huddled within the hip bath, washing her limbs with cold seawater. Anger had given her the strength to fetch and fill the bath herself. With the chair wedged firmly beneath the handle of the interconnecting door of her cabin—or should she say the *captain*'s cabin?—she stripped naked and balled the stinking wet clothes in the corner, ready to be rinsed once she had removed every last trace of the offensive odour from her own person. *If he thought he could just come upon her and cause such a mishap...* How she fumed. *He was rude and uncaring, the antithesis of a gentleman, and...* And he was none of these things. Georgiana plummeted off her high horse and acknowledged the truth. Nathaniel Hawke was everything to be respected in a good man. It was only her pride that was smarting, as well it might, having been soaked in the stale urine of one hundred and eighty-five burly members of the King's Navy. Ugh! She shivered at the very thought. And no matter how hard she scrubbed, it seemed that she could detect the faint whiff of that unsavoury excretion. By the time she had completed her ablutions, the tablet of soap was very small and she was once more fragrant and cleansed. Her clothes lay clean and ready to be hung out on deck. At least they would dry quickly in the warm breeze. All except her bindings, which she could not risk revealing to any other eyes. They dripped alone, a saddened state in the corner.

Georgiana looked down at her newly donned shirt and took a sharp intake of air. It would not do, it just would not do at all. Pulling on the waistcoat and jacket she inspected herself further. The problem still manifested itself in a rather obvious way. She would have to wait some time before facing the crew of the *Pallas* once more.

There was a tap at the door.

'George.' Nathaniel's voice sounded through the wooden panels.

She did not answer.

The handle shifted beneath Nathaniel's hand, but the door stuck fast. 'George,' he persevered. 'I shouldn't have laughed at you. It was an unfortunate accident. You're not hurt, are you?'

'No. I'm quite recovered from the incident, sir.'

'Open the door, I wish to speak with you.' His voice sounded a little impatient.

Georgiana's gaze scanned the empty cabin. 'I cannot.'

'Why not?' She could hear his perplexity.

She paused, thinking quickly. 'I…I'm not suitably dressed.'

'Well, put some clothes on and be quick about it.' Nathaniel Hawke could be a persistent man when it suited him.

A pool of water was collecting on the floor beneath the bindings. It would be some hours before they would be dry enough to wear again. Neither Captain Hawke, nor any other member of the crew, would believe that it took that length of time to bathe and dress. 'It will take some considerable time, sir.'

'I've letters to write. Come out when you're ready.' He listened for her reply, as his boots echoed across the wooden floor to his desk.

There was nothing else for it. She would have to tell him the truth. 'Captain Hawke, are you still there?'

'Yes.'

She pictured him sitting serenely at his desk, quill in hand, a sheet of paper in readiness before him. 'Are you quite alone, sir?'

She felt his gaze shift from the paper to the door. 'Yes. Is something the matter, George?'

A small silence.

'Yes, sir.'

The boots had risen and were making their way back over to the other side of the doorway. 'George?'

More silence.

Then, 'I cannot leave the cabin until tomorrow, sir.'

'Why ever not?'

She chewed on her lip. 'It's rather difficult to explain, sir.'

Nathaniel's apprehension was mounting by the minute. The girl must have hurt more than her pride. Worry pulled at his brow. 'Open this door at once, George.'

'I cannot.'

'If you don't, I'll take the whole damn wall down.' What the hell had happened to make her afraid to open the door? Had Pensenby accosted her? Nathaniel felt suddenly apprehensive at the thought. 'George!' The door handle rattled uselessly in his fingers. He contemplated dismantling the flimsy structure—it was, after all, designed to be removed into storage during battle situations.

Georgiana leapt up off the bed and placed her hands against the door. 'Please do not, sir. I beg of you.'

The girl was clearly distraught. He forced his voice to sound calm, reassuring. 'I cannot help you if you won't speak to me. Just open the door.' And all the while the knot of worry within his stomach expanded.

Silence.

She sighed. It was no use, her rebuttals and half-explanations were just making things worse. For all his efforts, she could hear the unease in his voice. Slowly she removed the chair and opened the door.

'Georgiana,' Nathaniel uttered with relief and stepped through the portal. Nothing seemed to be amiss. She appeared fully dressed and uninjured. He grasped her shoulders and scanned her face. 'What's wrong? Why wouldn't you open the door?'

He watched the rosy hue rise in her cheeks as she would not meet his gaze. It was quite unlike her normal behaviour. 'Georgiana,' he whispered again and pulled her into an embrace. He touched a kiss to the top of her head and soap and seawater tickled his nose. His hand slowed its caress across her back as he looked down into her eyes. 'Is it Pensenby? Has he questioned you?'

The blush deepened. 'Oh, no, nothing of that nature.' She tried to pull away, but his arms only tightened around her. She swallowed hard. 'Perhaps, it's not so much of a problem as I'd imagined if it's not apparent to you.' Easing herself away from him, she stood back and, despite the mortification she was suffering, held herself open to his perusal. 'Do you notice no change in my appearance, sir? Please be truthful.'

His brow wrinkled in puzzlement as he scrutinised her hair and face, his gaze dropping to examine her newly donned clothes. Was it his imagination, or had she, was she…? Brown eyes met blue and a dark winged eyebrow raised its enquiry. 'Take off your jacket.'

'No, indeed I will not!' Two pink spots burned brighter upon her cheeks.

At last Nathaniel experienced a glimmer of understanding of his ship's boy's strange behaviour. 'Come now, George, it's better if I see the full extent of the problem.'

Embarrassing though it was, she supposed him to be right. The jacket was quickly thrown upon the bed. 'Perhaps it's not as obvious as I'd thought. If I were to keep my jacket on—'

'It would not hide the fact that you have a most admirable figure, nephew George, a fact that would not go unnoticed by the entirety of the company.' He raised appreciative eyes to hers. 'Yes, I believe I understand your dilemma.'

She snatched the jacket back against her breast. For, once freed of its restraining bindings, Georgiana's bosom was clearly apparent and in complete defiance of her ship's boy status. The reappearance of the hitherto forgotten attribute rendered Miss Raithwaite uncomfortably self-conscious. 'Captain Hawke, if you would kindly refrain from staring,' she said.

'I do beg your pardon, nephew George,' replied Nathaniel, executing a small bow in her direction. 'But the view is uncommonly good.'

'Nathaniel Hawke!'

A broad smile spread across Nathaniel's face. 'Forgive me, George. It's quite clear you must remain cabin bound until your, um, bindings are wearable once more.'

'That,' said Georgiana with some exasperation, 'is what I've being trying to tell you.'

'I'll inform Mr Fraser that you're assisting me with my letter writing and we're not to be disturbed.'

A shiver tickled at the nape of Georgiana's neck. The prospect of remaining undisturbed in the company of Captain Hawke seemed remote indeed.

The white of the marine sentry's crossbelts and facings stood out starkly against the scarlet of his coat. He gripped his musket and looked at the second lieutenant indifferently. 'Orders is orders, Lieutenant Pensenby. If the captain says no disturbances, that's what he means.'

'I beg your pardon!' Cyril Pensenby was annoyed to find the captain could not be interrupted. 'I'm quite sure that the order did not include Lieutenant Anderson or myself, and—' he puffed his chest out in self-importance '—given the importance of my news, he will want to know.'

The sentry looked unimpressed.

'Has he someone in there with him?' Pensenby snapped.

The marine's shoulders shrugged, and he scratched at his head beneath the brim of his tall black hat. 'Only the servant boy Robertson. But it makes no difference to my orders, sir.'

Cyril Pensenby's face took on a sharpened expression. 'Indeed. Well, I'm afraid I must override your orders and insist upon seeing the captain. There's no time to waste, man.' Without further ado, Lieutenant Pensenby rushed past the marine and straight into Captain Hawke's cabin.

Everything around the cabin seemed perfectly in order. In the middle of the room the polished mahogany of the cleared dining table glinted in the sunlight. Six ornate chairs were tucked beneath it, awaiting the time it would be set for dinner. The desk was positioned closer to the windows lining the back wall of the cabin, its surface littered with papers and charts. Three pens lay beside the inkwell, a small sharpening knife in front of them. The red leather captain's chair behind the desk was empty. Nathaniel was standing, arms behind his back, peering out of the stern windows while he dictated a letter. Ship's boy Robertson was seated at the near side of the desk, neatly transcribing the captain's words on to paper. Both faces shot round to stare at him.

The marine stumbled in at Pensenby's back, musket raised towards the lieutenant. 'I told him you wasn't to be disturbed, Captain, but he wouldn't listen.'

'Mr Pensenby?' Captain Hawke turned a glacial eye upon his subordinate and moved swiftly to shield Georgiana from the men's view.

Georgiana's hand surreptitiously stole to cover the front of her neatly buttoned jacket as she shifted in her seat to present both the second lieutenant and marine with a fine view of her back.

'Forgive me, Captain Hawke,' Pensenby looked over the captain's shoulder at the rear of the boy's head. 'I thought you would wish to know that the look-out has sighted two French frigates heading in our direction.'

'Very well, Lieutenant.' Nathaniel hid the shock well. 'I'll join both Lieutenant Anderson and yourself on the quarter-deck shortly. That will be all.'

He waited until both men had left the room before turning to Georgiana. She looked so young, so vulnerable. He ignored the urge to take her in his arms, protect her for ever. 'Lock yourself in the night cabin—' a key passed between them '—and open the door for no one except myself. I'll instruct that it should be left intact when we ready the guns. Do you understand?' He wondered at the degree of concern he felt for her. If anything happened to her, he would never forgive himself.

A brief nod before she touched her hand to his arm. 'Be careful.'

They looked into each other's eyes before Nathaniel swept a feather kiss to her lips and was gone.

Through the magnification of the spyglass he could see that they were both large frigates, loading forty guns apiece, with the French tricolour fluttering boldly at the stern and a pennant at the topmast. He glanced at Pensenby, saw the shadow of fear in his small shrewd eyes. The stiff northwesterly wind would lead them directly to the *Pallas,* of that there could be no mistake.

'They'll be within range in approximately one hour, sir.' Lieutenant Anderson was pale, but his blue eyes glittered with excitement.

Nathaniel knew what he must do. 'Let out each canvas in full, we move with top speed in a southeasterly direction.'

'But that would take us towards Santa Cruz and the Canary Islands, both of which are held by Spain.' Lieutenant Pensenby frowned his disapproval.

'Indeed, it will, Mr Pensenby. It's what they'll least expect. Before reaching Santa Cruz, we'll turn and head out towards the mid-Atlantic, before sailing back up to the Azores.'

John Anderson was looking somewhat crestfallen. 'We are to run?' In his mind's eye he was already valiantly engaged in the dramatic glory of battle, annihilating the French ships, and all for the sake of King and country.

Nathaniel saw the slumped shoulders and read the reason correctly. 'In a straight confrontation we don't stand a chance against them. They each carry forty guns to our thirty-two, both are made of oak to our pine. The *Pallas* simply cannot withstand the pounding she would receive. Hit for hit we would suffer vastly more damage than they, not to mention the injury to the men from the splinters. They would have us down in a matter of minutes.'

'Then all is lost and we should strike our flag,' said Lieutenant Anderson miserably.

'Quite the contrary, Mr Anderson. We must look to our advantages and make the best use of them.'

Pensenby piped up, 'But you said that the *Pallas* is no match for them in battle.'

Nathaniel closed the spyglass with a snap. 'No, Mr Pensenby, that is only the case in direct confrontation. There are many other types of battle.'

'But we're to run.' John Anderson looked puzzled.

'For now, until the conditions favour us rather than our enemy.' Both men regarded him in silence. 'The *Pallas* is smaller, and at only 667 tonnes, significantly faster. She should easily outrun them. Then it's simply a matter of waiting until the timing is right.'

Lieutenant Pensenby seemed reassured by this. He was not a man suited to the bloody physicality of war, and the prospect of escaping what would undoubtedly prove to be a crashing defeat beckoned appealingly.

Captain Hawke strode across the quarterdeck to shout orders to the ship's master. He paused momentarily, looked back over his shoulder, and said, 'Rest assured that I'm not Byng, Mr Anderson.'

John Anderson thought of Admiral Byng who had been executed for failing to engage the Spanish Fleet with sufficient vigour. No, he did not doubt Captain Hawke's courage. He would do better to watch and learn.

With the sails set fully to capture the wind the *Pallas* skimmed across the surface of the water with a deftness of speed that could not hope to be matched by her bigger, bulkier opponents. Heading further south into Spanish waters, they had lost sight of the two large French frigates before Nathaniel gave the order to change direction.

Georgiana could feel from the rolling motion that the ship was fairly flying across the waves, and concluded with relief that they were fleeing from the French. Although she did not know the size or manner of the enemy, common sense warned her that two against one did not offer good odds of a favourable result. This, coupled with what she had learned: the *Pallas* was experimental in design, being unusually small for a frigate and built entirely of lightweight pine rather than sturdy English oak. It did not take a genius to surmise that any big gun fire would tear the ship apart.

Although Georgiana had no direct knowledge of exactly what naval battle involved, she had spent many an evening listening to Burly Jack's reminiscences, tales of glory and honour, descriptions of blood and gore, death and decay. She shivered and drew her jacket closer around her. Nathaniel Hawke could be the best damn naval captain in the world, but, outnumbered and disadvantaged by his ship, there was little doubt as to the outcome of any encounter. And the thought of it brought a shiver to her soul. If she were to lose him now… She bit at her lip and wrung her hands together. She knew what would happen if the French were to catch up with them. For the second time in Georgiana's life she was sailing dangerously close to a watery grave, poised to topple. She dropped to her knees and prayed for a gale that would spirit the *Pallas* with wings, far, far away from the long guns of the French.

A dense sea fog shrouded the *Pallas*, as she swept slowly, steadily on, cutting a path through the vast Atlantic Ocean, blind but for her trust in her captain's charts and compass. Silently stalking her prey through the muffled cloud that enveloped her. All calls had been stifled, all pipes quelled. She floated as a ghost ship ever closer to her quarry, ears straining, guns readied. Then they heard it, an eerie shout through the gloomy miasma. Fingers moved to cock their muskets, hands to quietly draw their swords. Captain Hawke whispered his orders and the *Pallas* responded mutely, slipping into position. A bell sounded close by, its clang deadened by the blanket of fog. Nathaniel waited. Waited. Biding his time.

Breath by breath. Second by second. He only hoped his calculations were correct, there would be no room for error. One
chance, and one chance alone, to take the prize or be damned
in the process.

Even as his hand clenched, poised to give the final command, his mind flitted to the girl locked below in his cabin.
Like a moth to a flame he was drawn to her. Could no longer
deny his compulsion. Was glad even that she was here on his
ship, in his care, for all the danger that it brought. He knew
he was a scoundrel to think such a thing. Hadn't he learned
his lesson with Kitty Wakefield? He had no right to gamble
with Georgiana's life, none but the knowledge of her likely
fate at the hands of a French captain, or, even worse, a French
crew. That was if she survived the wrecking of the *Pallas*.
They were all supposedly governed by the gentlemanly rules
of warfare. But Nathaniel knew that these were employed as
and when it suited. Georgiana would stand little chance
against either the Atlantic Ocean or their French opponents,
and the thought lent strength to his resolve. There could be
no failure. Not for her. Not for any of them. He could only
hope that the *Pallas* would live up to her name—the Greek
goddess of victory. With a steady hand and a courageous
heart, Captain Hawke gave the order.

The full force of four carronades on the *Pallas*' forecastle
blasted at close range upon the hapless and unsuspecting
French frigate *Ville-de-Milan*, inflicting substantial damage
to the hull. In the lull that followed Captain Hawke personally led the small boarding party to secure the ship. In a matter of minutes the task had been completed. Nathaniel
returned to the *Pallas*, ready to engage the second frigate positioned close by. The yells of her crew alerted him as to her

precise position and he swung the *Pallas* round to hide her bow. The French guns fired before the manoeuvre was complete, shattering the foremast and splintering the bow. The *Pallas'* carronades roared again, delivering their massive twenty-four-pound round shot with a snarling ferocity. The *Coruna* slipped behind the *Ville-de-Milan*, but Nathaniel had anticipated the move and was already leading his men across the barren boards of the first frigate to reach the second. Nothing could stop him, Georgiana would be safe and the prize his.

Georgiana shivered at the unnatural hush that surrounded her. No voices, no banging, no footsteps, no pipes, no bells. Only the gentle lap of water and the weary creaking of timber. Foreboding prickled at the nape of her neck and she was aware of a tight smothering tension. She sat rigidly in the small chair within the night cabin and waited. Sweat trickled in slow rivulets down her back. Fingers grew cold and numb. Silence. Suddenly an enormous explosion ricocheted around her, the blast echoing in her ears. Even locked below within the tiny cabin, the unmistakable odour of gunpowder pervaded. She leapt up from her seat. The *Pallas'* guns were firing. Nathaniel must be cornered, under attack. Dear Lord! The ship shuddered violently, landing her forcefully to the floor. Men's screams, voices shouting. Georgiana struggled to her feet. Fear rippled through her, but it would not stop her. She could no longer stay hidden and safe while the rest of the crew faced death and capture. Ship's boy Sam Wilson needed her, able seaman Jack Grimly needed her, and then there were the others. And the most important name of all held close to her heart—Nathaniel Hawke. She would do what she must to help those that she had come to think upon as friends. For Nathaniel she would lay down her life. Without further ado she slid the key into the lock and turned the handle.

Scenes of mayhem greeted Georgiana as she ran along the gun deck. Surprisingly the long guns were run in and silent, gun teams at the ready. Neither was the usual screen of pungent blue smoke hanging in the air, but she scarcely had time to ponder upon it. Two massive holes gaped on both the starboard and larboard sides where a round shot had ripped its way through and fortunately departed again. Not so fortunate was the devastation it had reaped on its route. Part of the capstan had been destroyed and enormous splinters of wood lay all around. Worst still, Georgiana could see the surgeon tending a blood-soaked figure on the floor. Several other men slumped nearby, their faces ashen, their clothing ripped and red-stained. Blood pooled invisibly upon decks painted red for just such a purpose. She ran to the surgeon's mate kneeling over a prone body.

'Mr Murthly, can I assist you, sir?'

Robert Murthly, a sturdy young man with untidy red hair, looked up at the boy. 'Captain wouldn't be best pleased to find you here, Robertson—or should I say *Lord* George? Shouldn't have thought you'd have wanted to dirty those fine letter-writing hands of yours.'

The gossipmongers had been busy. She looked beneath the sneer on the surgeon's mate's face and saw fear and fatigue. Little wonder he despised her, thinking her a pampered brat to be coddled in the captain's cabin while the rest of the ship risked their lives. Surreptitiously she fastened her jacket, and hoped that the surrounding chaos would draw Murthly's full attention. With so much blood and carnage she doubted that any man would have the time to notice the subtle change in Lord George Hawke's appearance. Besides, the crew were about to learn there was a whole lot more to the captain's nephew than they supposed. 'I'm here to help, sir, just tell me what to do.' Her voice was harsh and gritty, its tone as low as she could manage.

The surgeon's mate wiped the sweat from his brow with bloodied fingers and regarded her with deliberate consideration. Most of the men were busy securing the French frigates, and the gun crews were not permitted to leave their stations. An extra pair of hands, even aristocratic ones, would come in useful.

'Murthly!' bellowed the surgeon. 'Have a table shifted over here and quickly.' He gestured to the mess tables that interspersed the long line of guns. 'This man won't make it below, losing too much blood. We'll have to operate here. Run and fetch my instruments.'

Murthly looked at Georgiana. 'Move the table like he says.' Then the squat figure was off and running.

Georgiana, helped by one of the nearby powder boys, dragged the rough wooden structure that passed for a table across to the surgeon.

The surgeon scarcely looked at her, just dumped the haemorrhaging body down on to the surface that had so recently served up a dinner of salted meat and biscuit.

The seaman's face was chalk-white and smeared with sweat, his lips trembling as he tried to suppress the moans of pain. She skimmed down and saw the ragged stump where what had been his hand hung. His breathing came fast and shallow and his pupils shrunk to pinpricks. No time for rum, nor for the opiates which would have deadened his agony.

Nimble fingers loosed the belt from her waist and looped it around just below the sailor's slack elbow. She tightened the tourniquet and held the injured arm aloft. Her other hand touched to the man's brow, its cool fingers wiping the sweat from his eyes.

The surgeon looked at her then, a suspicious expression of enquiry on his face.

She said nothing, just focused on the injured man lying so helplessly before her.

Murthly's feet clattered back along the gun deck. He threw open the wooden box that he carried and handed the surgeon a large and wicked-looking knife. 'Tourniquet already in place,' he observed, and saw the surgeon's eyes flit to the captain's nephew.

'Yes,' he said drily. 'Speed is our saviour,' he proclaimed, 'let's not waste any more time.' He paused before the blade contacted the bloodied pulp of reddened tissue and addressed Georgiana. 'See what you can do for the others. There are clean linen strips within the box.'

She did as she was bid, using the knowledge she had gleaned from her furtive reading of Mr Hunter's *A Treatise on the Blood, Inflammation, and Gunshot Wounds*. A fascinating book, if not one of which her stepfather would have approved for either her or Francis. Thankfully her stepbrother's secret medical ambition had led him to lodge the book safely beneath his bed. When the last of the men had been transferred to the sick berth down on the lower deck, Georgiana slipped away to discover what had become of Nathaniel. She had just made her way up the companion ladder when the answer to her question appeared most suddenly, for, as she stepped from the last rung up on to the uppermost deck, she practically collided with Captain Hawke.

'George!' The word escaped unbidden, as his hands closed around her upper arms. His gaze swept over her, taking in the dried blood streaking her face, the pale fragility of the skin beneath and the dark stained clothing, and a pulse of horror beat in his breast. Behind him Lieutenant Anderson cleared his throat, and with a start he came crashing back down to the reality of the situation. Not only had Georgiana blatantly disobeyed his order, but she was now risking her secret in an awkward situation. Perdition, but the girl seemed utterly determined to destroy her own reputation despite all his efforts. His eyes darkened. 'Get back down below, Robertson,' he barked.

Georgiana blinked, the breath caught in her throat. He was safe, unhurt. Her heart leapt at the sight of him. Thank God. But even as she relaxed with relief she saw the change wash over his face. And the tide that it brought with it was not one of love or even affection, but one of blazing fury. 'Nathan…' She remembered herself in time. 'Captain Hawke,' she amended, deepening her voice.

'That is an order.' His words were hard and angry, a stranger to her ear. Just as she turned to retreat she caught sight of the two smartly dressed French captains standing proudly behind him, their intense, dark eyes trained on Nathaniel. For one awful minute she froze, suddenly aware of how close she'd come to betraying herself. Wandering about the ship without the protection of her bindings, almost calling the captain by his given name, and all in full view of not only their own men, but also the French!

It was Nathaniel who recovered first, releasing his rather overtly intimate grasp on his ship's boy's shoulder. The breath had stilled in his throat, alarm bells ringing in his head. But the face he presented to the captives was calm and self-assured. 'Lieutenant Pensenby will escort you both to your quarters. Those of your men taken aboard will be held below, the remainder will be well treated upon your own ships. Please make your needs known to Mr Pensenby. I shall endeavour to call upon you in a short while.'

Only when his prisoners had been removed from earshot did Captain Hawke turn to his ship's boy. 'I'll have the key, if you please.' The handsome features appeared completely devoid of emotion. He did not trust himself to reveal a hint of the torrent that raged within him.

'Yes, sir.' From within her pocket she produced the cabin door key and held it to him.

He grasped it, taking care great care not to brush against her still bloodstained fingers. The dark eyes remained carefully shuttered as he turned away. A muscle twitched in the firm line of his jaw. 'Lieutenant Anderson, escort my nephew to my night cabin. See to it that the door is locked, from the outside, and return the key to me.'

Georgiana's turbulent blue eyes swung to meet his, but his gaze remained fixed hard and uncompromisingly ahead.

'I'll be in the sick berth with the surgeon, Mr Anderson.' With that the tall figure climbed down the companion ladder and strode off to check upon the injuries his men had sustained.

A cold breeze raked across the deck, rippling the British flag above. And below John Anderson moved quietly to take hold of the boy's arm.

Walter Praxton lifted the tankard before him and sipped at the ale. The Crown was quiet on account of the Impress Service's activity in the area. Only once the *Leander* had sailed would the men return from the surrounding villages. A warm fire blazed in the hearth, lightening the grey misery of the cold December day. He barely noticed the slant of winter rain that pattered against the mullioned glass windows, so intent was he on the small weasely man seated opposite.

Bob Blakely was five foot in height, of skinny build with hair the colour of the rats that meandered leisurely through the streets of Portsmouth. A short ragged moustache perched upon his upper lip, and a peppering of stubble added to the impression that washing did not constitute one of Mr Blakely's favourite pastimes. He sucked on a long pipe and regarded the rich gent with small glassy eyes.

'Like I said, Mr Praxton, sir, me contact saw the boy you're after pressed aboard a frigate that was then in dock. They don't normally take boys, but he wasn't alone, was he?'

Walter Praxton raised an enquiring brow that did not so much as crease the perfection of his handsome face.

'Was with them three seamen from on the mail. It was them that the Press Gang was after. Expect they took the lad 'cos he was there in the wrong place at the wrong time, so to speak.'

'Which frigate?' The ale tasted smooth and mellow to Mr Praxton's jaded pallet.

A grubby hand displaced the runny discharge seeping from his nose before Bob Blakely saw fit to continue. He swigged at the ale, smacking his thin chapped lips as the last of it slid like nectar down his throat. 'Could do with another of those.' He eyed Mr Praxton hopefully.

As the ever-parched Bob had proved himself efficient in obtaining the information that he was so eager to learn, Walter averted his eyes from the black grimy fingernails cradling the empty tankard and gestured for the serving woman to fetch another jug of ale. 'We wouldn't want you going thirsty. Drink up, my good man. Remember the payment we've arranged.'

Bob Blakely tapped his nose and gave the rich man a sly wink. 'You're a gentleman, Mr Praxton, and if I don't have the info that you're after, me name's not Bob Blakely.'

Walter stifled a retort and forced a smile to his face.

'Was the *Pallas*, as sailin' under Captain Hawke, sir. Left here start of last month, but under sealed orders. No one knows her destination, but me *friend*—' he stressed the word most forcibly '—in a certain place, heard tell that she's due back before Christmas. Ain't that 'andy. Not long to wait for that boy of yours, if he's still alive, that is.'

In a furtive gesture Praxton slid three guinea pieces to the man and bid him good day. Pulling his hat low and turning up the collar of his great brown coat, he braced himself to face the onslaught of the hostile English weather.

'Nice doin' business with you, gov,' came the contented reply, and Bob Blakely settled down to the comfort of another night within the snug warmth of the tavern.

Chapter Seven

It was the aspect of war that Nathaniel hated. The price to be paid for victory and defeat alike. Admiralty might issue the orders, but it was not the old men in their elaborate uniforms that met the round shot, or took the splinters. They did not shield the ship with their bodies, or run with valour into a fracas of whirling cutlass and musket. Men that had been pressed to the service against their will, men who risked all in the hope of sharing in the prize, a financial salve to the poverty that afflicted their lives—it was a tragic necessity of war, and it never failed to cut Nathaniel to the quick. His ship, his men, his responsibility. And just as he rejoiced in their victory, so he suffered with their loss. Each death remained scored within his mind, each fallen seaman rendered immortal by Captain Hawke. Compassion. It was his biggest strength, winning the men to his cause, buying their loyalty for a lifetime…and also his gaping weakness, to feel for ever their torment.

He touched the sailor's shoulder. 'Well done, lad. Bravely fought. How fares your leg?'

'It'll mend, Captain. Now that t'surgeon's had his way, splinter's out. Says I should keep t'leg, and gain a limp.'

'No shame in that, Brown. There's always a place aboard my ship for a willing seaman, limping or not.' The captain moved on to the midshipman whose face had been sliced open by a flying splinter. 'Mr Hartley.'

The young gentleman nodded his head, the jagged stitching on his cheek already turning a purple coloration.

'You did a good job, Hartley. We've taken the day and the prize is rich indeed. A small scar won't do your future within His Majesty's Navy any harm. Your courage has been noted.'

Mr Hartley's smile pulled at the weeping wound. 'Thank you, Captain, but I fancy my young lady won't see it that way.'

'I have it on the best authority,' retaliated Nathaniel, his dark eyes lightening, 'that ladies see such marks as a badge of bravery. I'm sure it will do your reputation no harm at all.'

Captain and midshipman laughed together before Nathaniel moved on to visit the rest of his men.

'Captain Hawke.' The surgeon hurried over to him and walked some way along the deck beside him before raising the subject foremost in his mind. 'Ship's boy Robertson, sir, seems to have a wealth of medical knowledge. With whom did he study?'

Nathaniel looked at the surgeon in surprise. 'I don't know what you mean, Mr Belmont.'

The surgeon blinked back at him. 'Your neph— I mean, the boy, clearly has treated wounds before. Such knowledge is not come by easily. He must have experience of working in the surgical field. I wondered whom it was he assisted? Some of the techniques he employed were specialised to say the least. Almost as if they came straight from the pages of one of John Hunter's medical texts.'

A vision of a blood-soaked Georgiana drifted into Nathaniel's mind. So that was where the blood had come from. 'Am I to understand that the boy helped in the treatment of the wounded?'

'Why, yes. Robertson was a marvel. Young Richardson would have bled to death without his quick thinking. Foot completely severed, you know. The boy's got a feel for surgery, Captain, and it would be a shame to see it wasted. I'd be happy to have him help down here.'

Georgiana Raithwaite had quit the security of his cabin amidst the pounding fury of battle to help tend the wounded! Nathaniel reeled. The girl was incredible, infuriatingly disobedient, without a thought for her own safety, or indeed the discovery of her secret, but incredible all the same. He knew that he would have defied the First Lord of the Admiralty himself had he been ordered to lie useless within a cabin when all around a battle was sounding. A sigh escaped his lips. They were not so very dissimilar after all, the captain and his ship's boy. Even if that slim dark-haired waif was hellbent on ruining her reputation. With a heavy heart he made his way steadily towards the cabin that housed the woman in question.

Georgiana was sitting in the wooden chair, reading by the light of the flickering lantern. Or that at least looked to be what she was doing, by virtue of the book balanced carefully before her. She did not move upon Nathaniel's entry to the cabin, only glanced up at him with questioning eyes.

Somehow she had managed to cleanse the blood from her hands that were folded neatly before her. The same could not be said for the rest of her uniform. The darkened jacket had been hung over the back of the chair, leaving him a clear view of a blood-splattered shirt and the shapely figure it failed to conceal.

Two voices spoke at once. One mellow and deeply masculine, the other clear and soft. 'I'm sorry.'

They stared at each other in surprise.

'I should not have treated you so, Georgiana.' His lips shaped a wry smile, finding the motion unexpectedly easy despite all that had happened, in view of what he knew he must do.

The angular line of his jaw, those firm full lips, and black winged brows all held an indefinable tension, and in his eyes lurked fatigue tumbled with relief. Such responsibility of command demanded a high price. That he paid it in full was clear to see. She had not anticipated his apology. Indeed, from the carefully controlled, impassive countenance he had last presented she could have sworn he would give her a thorough verbal lashing. 'Perhaps, sir, your anger was understandable given that I appeared before you at the most inopportune of moments, and in complete defiance of your orders. My only defence is that I was concerned for your welfare, if you'd taken an injury in the attack. I'm afraid that I acted without proper thought or consideration.' Her nose wrinkled up and her eyes squeezed shut at the memory conjured by the confession. 'Indeed, I almost called you by your given name. Most unseemly for a ship's boy to his captain.'

'A floggable offence,' Nathaniel assured her with mock severity.

When she opened her eyes it was to see a bemused expression.

The thought of Georgiana Raithwaite being concerned for his safety was really a rather pleasant one. 'I'm touched by your concern, Miss Raithwaite, and can assure you that I'm quite unhurt.' He made as if to reach his hand to her face, but checked the motion just as it began. Best wait to discover her response first.

A rosy glow spread over her cheeks. 'Yes. For that at least we must be thankful.'

'And what of you? The shock of seeing you appear

drenched in blood did me more damage than the *Coruna*'s guns!' More damage than he was willing to admit even to himself. 'I thought for one horrible moment that you'd been injured.' A little line of worry creased between his eyes.

It was really rather endearing, or so Georgiana thought. 'Not me, sir,' she said.

'What were you up to, to become so blood-soaked?' The dark eyes narrowed suspiciously. 'Mr Belmont has some strange notion that you're accustomed to assisting in surgical procedures. He requested your transference to the sick berth!'

Miss Raithwaite looked suddenly a picture of pious innocence. 'I cannot think why.'

'And the blood?' He indicated her attire.

She sighed. 'I couldn't just sit here and listen to their screams, Captain Hawke. I heard the guns and didn't know what was happening. At first I thought that we were under attack. Those men… Such hurts as I've never seen the like of. Oh, Nathaniel…' She closed her eyes as if to block the memory. 'There was so little I could do for them.'

His fingers touched lightly to her shoulder, unable to bear her distress, wanting to pull her into his arms and protect her from the world. 'Mr Belmont tells quite a different story, and so, I gather, would the men that you helped. We've lost none. All survived.' Gently he pulled her upright, looking down into her face. 'There's another matter that we must discuss, Georgiana.' A matter of honour, a matter of doing what was right even when his father thought that he was all wrong.

The deliberate use of her given name sent a delicious little shiver through her body, but something in his tone forewarned her of the gravity of his intent.

'Truly I didn't know that the Frenchmen were aboard,' she explained. 'Moreover, the blame for my foolish actions rests entirely with me, for it was I who directly disobeyed your command and I who presented myself in full view of your captives. Now I fear that I may have jeopardised my position.'

The girl had unwittingly stumbled directly upon the heart of the problem. A rumble of apprehension rattled through him. Somehow he doubted that his forthcoming proposal would meet with such sweet compliance. It was, after all, Walter Praxton that she loved, not himself.

'Georgiana, the presence of the French captains has served to highlight the risk we're running. It will only take one man to see through your disguise and we're done for.' He could be nothing other than frank in his explanation. Miss Raithwaite needed to face the truth.

Georgiana's fingers found her ear lobe and started to fidget. 'But we've been safe until now.'

'Yes. Lady Luck's been on our side, but she won't be for ever.' Nathaniel's voice was grim. He saw the anxiety in her eyes and misinterpreted its cause. 'Don't be distressed, Miss Raithwaite, for I swear that no harm will come to you. You're an innocent in all of this…debacle, and…'

The smooth brow crinkled in bafflement. *Innocent?* What was the man talking about? She was the singular cause of all that had happened.

'Through no fault of your own, you've been placed in a compromising—no, ruinous situation.'

No fault of her own? Georgiana's sooty long lashes batted in astonishment. Who was it, then, that had cut her hair, dressed her in Francis's clothes and forced her upon the mail to Fareham? Didn't he realise that it was all her own fault? 'Captain Hawke.' She held her hand up to still his flow, gentlemanly and eloquent though it was. 'I fear that you're ascribing an innocence to me that's quite unwarranted.'

Nathaniel, who had been on the point of delivering his *fait accompli*, stalled, regarding her with an expression of shock. Had Walter Praxton then stolen more than a few kisses that day in Hurstborne Park? It was like a kick to the gut. He hesitated over the words to express himself. 'You…you're no longer an innocent? Are you trying to tell me that you've… that you and Mr Praxton—?'

'Dear God, no!' Georgiana's face flushed scarlet. 'However could you think such a thing?' She made to step back from his looming figure, caught her legs against the chair and stumbled. In an instant his arms enveloped her, saving her from the fall, pulling her upright and against the length of his muscular body. He held her, a peculiar expression of relief on his face, before setting her back on her feet and retreating to the far end of the cabin.

'Then what do you mean, Miss Raithwaite?' Everything about him was static and still, the calm before the storm.

Exasperation and embarrassment lent an edge to Georgiana's retort. Why was it that each time she tried to remedy a situation she only succeeded in making it worse? 'I'm merely trying to tell you, Captain Hawke, that we are in this ridiculous situation because of my actions and my actions alone. *I* ran away from home. *I* disguised myself as a boy, and I didn't exactly hide myself from the officers of the Impress Service. No sir, I cannot, in good conscience, stand here while you describe me as the innocent victim. The terrible truth is that the fault is mine.' She turned stormy eyes to his, raised her voice in impassioned plea. 'Please believe me when I say that I had no thought that matters would unfold as they did. I didn't mean to ruin you, Nathaniel.'

He stepped towards her boldly, disbelieving. '*You* have ruined *me*?'

She shook her head and lowered her eyes. 'I'm sorry sir, that you've suffered when your only crime has been to help me.'

'Georgiana…' his voice gentled and he was so close she could feel his breath upon her hair '…you seem to be under a mis—'

'No, Nathaniel. Don't make excuses for me. My reputation is ruined. I know that.' She raised her head and looked him directly in the eye. 'I'm prepared to live with the consequences of my actions. But please believe me when I say that I didn't mean to risk your position, sir.'

He watched her intently. 'You've no idea of how your life would be affected if you were found aboard this ship, unchaperoned amidst all these men. A ruined reputation is easily said. It's not so easy, Georgiana, to live with. To be ostracised by society, shunned by respectable women and subjected to the worst kind of attention from those who would call themselves gentlemen.'

'I will bear it.'

She felt his forefinger touch her chin, tilting her face up to his. 'You need not. There is another way.'

The muscles tensed beneath his fingertip. 'Not for me, there isn't.'

He could see the stubborn determination in those clear grey-blue eyes, knew that she would never accept him for her own sake. Nathaniel had no intention of allowing her wilful pride to condemn the rest of her life. And in that moment he knew just the ploy to use. If Georgiana thought her presence a threat to his career, then who was he to correct the misunderstanding? 'There's only one thing that we can do, given the circumstances. I know that you don't want to, but it's with both our welfares in mind that I ask it.'

The breath stilled in Georgiana's throat. Everything

stopped, or so it seemed, except the loud rhythmic thud of her heart.

Rich dark eyes held hers with a burning intensity. His fingers moved softly to caress her cheek. 'Will you do me the honour of accepting my name in marriage?'

In that split second Georgiana's world turned upside down. He wanted her for his wife? She felt suddenly light-headed. 'M-marriage?' she uttered faintly.

'Indeed.' His breath was warm upon her face. His eyes watchful, waiting.

She was conscious of the gentleness of the long fingers that had stilled upon her skin, of the sheer strength of the man, and his determination to do what he thought was right. 'Would it set matters right with the Admiralty?' They stood so close yet without touching, save for the featherprint of his fingers on her cheek. Across that small space the heat of his masculinity scorched the full length of her body, pulling her like a magnet. 'I mean—' she glanced away '—how could you be saved simply by marrying me?'

'Saved by marriage.' The words were soft, whispered almost as if he were thinking them aloud. His fingers moved to stroke her silken ebony locks.

She stood entranced, unable to move.

'To have a woman steal unknowingly upon a ship, disguised as a boy, and subsequently employ her as a ship's boy, having her sleep each night within one's own cabin is enough to condemn any captain. But if that same captain were to wed his betrothed in a distant British base, and transport that lady back to England as his wife, then that is an entirely different matter. It would, of course, be frowned upon, a slap on the wrist and all that. Nothing more. My captaincy would be safe.'

The explanation made sense. 'I see,' she replied a little

breathlessly. The proximity of Nathaniel Hawke's large and manly body seemed to be having rather a strange effect upon her. She struggled to retain a modicum of her common sense before it all deserted her.

His deep melodic voice sounded again. 'I wouldn't be the only one to benefit from a matrimonial arrangement. When I thought to wed you, Georgiana, it was not only the salvation of my own reputation that I had in mind.'

'No?' What, then, did he have in mind? Some measure of the same affection that she felt for him?

'A good marriage would remedy any blight on your reputation.' He smoothed her hair behind her ear, his fingers slipping down to capture the soft lobe that she worried so frequently at. 'I know that I'm not your choice, Georgiana.' He thought fleetingly, and with considerable discontent, of Walter Praxton. 'But I would endeavour to make a good husband.'

The shimmering grey-green lights within her eyes dimmed, and she looked away to hide her disappointment. It was clear that her fondness was not returned.

When she still did not answer, he prompted, 'So, Miss Raithwaite, will you consent to marry me?'

'To save us both?' she questioned in a small flat voice, so unlike her own.

'That's certainly one way of putting it.'

She raised her chin a notch. 'Then, sir, my answer must be yes.'

But the bleakness in her eyes did not escape Nathaniel's notice.

Since the prisoners had come aboard Nathaniel had confined Georgiana to the night cabin. Soon they would reach the British station at Gibraltar, where he meant to deposit the

Ville-de-Milan and *Coruna*, and both their crews. Such a net of prizes would at least secure a decent financial recompense for them all. And he would see to it personally that his men were amply rewarded. Only when his precious French cargo had been unloaded would he be truly at ease. Nathaniel dared take no chances when it came to Georgiana. She would not be safe until they were married.

Married. He still did not fully understand how it had come to this. A mixture of honour and guilt and determination to prove his father wrong. But he had to admit that the prospect of marrying Georgiana was not altogether unattractive. Indeed, the more he thought on it, he could see that it would have a significant number of positive advantages. The girl was intelligent, and could engage him in interesting conversation more than any other female he knew. And, although she was shy, she was certainly in possession of a wicked sense of humour. For all her youth she seemed to have a certain maturity of spirit that appealed to him. Not to mention her attributes of a more physical nature. There had been a tension between them since first he'd pulled her from the River Borne, a thread of attraction that bound him to her in ways he could not hope to understand. He wanted her, all of her, from the ripple of her laughter to the endearing way she worried at her ear lobe, from her strength of courage to the fire in her eyes. Yes, indeed, marriage to Miss Raithwaite would be no bad thing.

Captain Hawke was definitely in a good mood. First there was the humming, followed by the marked spring in his step and his uncommon lightness of spirit. Lieutenant Anderson eyed him with mounting suspicion.

'Does Master Robertson show no sign yet of a possible recovery?' the first lieutenant enquired with concern.

Captain Hawke appeared supremely unaffected by his nephew's unfortunate condition. 'No, none whatsoever, Mr Anderson. Such a pity.' He leafed through the pages of the book before him. 'Have you spoken to the purser yet? I want to be sure that we've adequate provisions for our journey back to England. Plenty of lemons and vegetables. I don't want the men succumbing to scurvy. Perhaps some extra live-stock to bring a bit of relief from the salted beef.'

'All is in order with Mr Tufton. He's produced his lists of provisions to procure and all his records are up to date and accurate. May I be so bold as to suggest that you speak to the surgeon?' John Anderson shuffled his boots together rather uneasily.

'Regarding the food rations?' A perplexed look crossed Captain Hawke's face. 'Shouldn't think he's got too much to say on the matter, as long as the men are reasonably well fed.'

The lieutenant examined a spot on the toe of his boot. 'No, sir. I was thinking more for the boy. He's been unwell for some days now.'

'Oh,' replied his commanding officer, in rather hearty tones, 'no need for that. Running a bit of fever. Nothing serious enough to bother Mr Belmont with. Now, as to those repairs on the gun deck…' and the captain continued in his chipper tone.

A knock sounded at the door.

'Enter.'

'Ah, Captain Hawke. I was just wondering whether young Robertson is feeling any better?'

Nathaniel barely raised his eyes. 'No improvement yet, Mr Fraser. You'll be the first to know if there's any change.'

The elderly valet's head shook in disbelief. 'Poor wee lad-die. Sick to the bottom of his stomach. And him being such a help to Mr Belmont on the gun deck an' all.'

'Sickness, you say, as well as the fever?' the lieutenant piped up.

The pale eye widened. 'Has the lad a fever on top of the terrible vomiting? You never said so, sir.' Mr Fraser was looking accusingly at the captain.

When Nathaniel raised his head it was to find one and a half pairs of worried eyes trained upon him. Heavens above. What was their sudden fascination with George Robertson? 'Mr Anderson,' he said through gritted teeth, 'Mr Fraser, Master Robertson has a slight fever and a little sickness. It is nothing to overly concern yourselves with. The boy is fine.'

By the time Nathaniel was *en route* to visit Mr Tufton, the purser, his good mood was wearing a trifle thin. Not only had he been visited by both the surgeon and his mate, to enquire as to the rumour they had heard concerning ship's boy Robertson and his failing health, but Lieutenant Pensenby, yes, Cyril Pensenby, had accosted him on the quarterdeck to ask of the boy's welfare. Had his whole crew become obsessed with George Robertson? What the hell was going on?

It was a large captain of somewhat surly disposition that finally reached the orlop deck and the purser's store. 'Mr Tufton,' he began.

The purser, a short, extremely round man, was squashed within the dimly lit, caged store, directly between the sacks of flour and oatmeal and the small wooden casks of suet and butter. 'Captain Hawke. Am I pleased to see you, sir. Couldn't help wondering how the young lad Robertson was faring. Heard he's been a bit poorly of late.' An aroma of dried fish and vinegar filled the air as Mr Tufton moved forward.

The captain turned a jaundiced eye on him. 'I've suddenly

remembered a most pressing appointment elsewhere. I bid you good day, Mr Tufton.'

He had almost made it back safely to his day cabin, striding past the numerous bodies busy in cleaning and checking the great long guns, when a gruff voice assailed him. 'Captain Hawke, beggin' your pardon, sir. It's about the lad, George. Has the swelling spread? Will he lose the leg?'

Nathaniel stared wordlessly at the huge figure of Burly Jack, before managing to mutter, 'The leg?'

'Aye, sir, the bad leg, like, what's got the swellin'.' The big man wrung his hands together. 'He's a good lad, even if he is your nephew, sir.' He winked broadly, 'But I'll mention nothin' of that to the others.'

Captain Hawke decided to accept this comment in the vein in which it was offered. 'His legs are quite uninjured, although he does have a mild fever and sickness, nothing serious. Why are you so concerned about him?'

Able seaman Grimly looked the captain level in the eye. 'Lad got lifted by the Press Gang when he was trying to help me. George charged in when they set about me. He didn't care nothin' for his own safety. Like I say, he's a good lad, a loyal lad.'

It was a very pensive Nathaniel Hawke that returned to his cabin.

Georgiana sat alone in the night cabin. The book sagged heavily in her hands. She closed it with a snap before standing to stretch out her back. It had been some days since she had agreed to become Nathaniel Hawke's wife, yet her feelings on the matter had not changed. He was kind, courageous and caring. Never one to shirk responsibility he would do what he knew to be the right thing, in spite of every adversity. He made her laugh, never spoke to her in the condescending manner of which her papa and Mr Praxton were so fond, and was possibly the most attractive man she had ever set eyes upon. Quite simply, she loved him. She'd known it from the moment the French guns had fired. It was strange how the risk of death brought a clarity to one's feelings. Indeed, had she not secretly wished to marry such a man as he, even at their first acquaintance in Farleigh Hall? That meeting now seemed a memory from the long distant past, so much had happened in the interceding weeks. Too much. Now her wish had been granted and she was to marry Captain Hawke. Betrothed to such a man, a glorious man, who gladdened her heart and warmed the blood in her veins. She sighed and wriggled her arms in an attempt to regain sensation in her numbed fingers.

The prospect of her forthcoming nuptials curiously saddened her, for he had left her with no illusions as to the reason for the wedding. It was nothing more than a means to salvage both their reputations. At least he'd had the decency to be honest with her, even if that honesty had wrecked those daydreams of which she had grown so fond—Nathaniel declaring his undying love, whispering sweet words in her ear, kissing her fully on the lips… She clamped the thoughts down, labelled them as childish and silly and unrealistic. He was kind to her, and undoubtedly concerned for her welfare. But it was quite clear that he did not experience the same battery of overwhelming emotions that afflicted her on his mere touch. The thought of his kiss was enough to bring a gentle glow to her cheeks, and the memory of that one stolen night when she'd… Blazing heat engulfed her body. Yet he'd never even alluded to the incident. Burly Jack's words echoed in her mind: *When a man's been at sea long enough he ain't too fussy over women, George. Anythin' will do, as long as she's willin'.* It was not a pleasant realisation.

* * *

When Nathaniel entered the cabin, it was to find a rather pale-faced ship's boy sitting glumly on his cot. 'Dinner will be here shortly.' It had become their usual custom to eat together at his table, waiting until Bottomley, the captain's personal cook, had departed before Georgiana emerged from the night cabin. Let his officers think it strange that their captain no longer invited them to the splendour of his dinner table once or twice a week. His concern rested more with the woman before him. 'Have you a little more appetite than last night?'

With Georgiana shut away from the world, the sun-kissed pale golden hue on her face had begun to fade. She was naturally of a white complexion, but within the dim light of the night cabin the pallor of her fragile skin seemed exaggerated and a little unhealthy. 'I'm afraid that my idleness has sapped my hunger.' She saw the worry ignite in Nathaniel's dark eyes and sought to reassure him. 'But I'm sure that your cook's excellent skills will tempt my appetite.' A smile lit up her face. 'You're spoiling me with all this good food. I should be dining on hard biscuit and salted beef stew like the others.'

Nathaniel crooked an eyebrow. 'Imagine the outrage if it became known that Captain Hawke had offered his betrothed a diet consisting of weevil-clogged biscuit and salted beef. Why, I should be barred from entry to all the fashionable places!' He held a limp-wristed hand to his brow as if he were London's greatest fop.

'You're teasing me again!' She laughed, then, holding herself with regal dignity, affected to fan herself in the manner of a lady at a high-season assembly. 'La, Captain Hawke,' she said in her best imitation of the flirtatious tones she had heard those same ladies employ, 'do you not know the latest *on dit?*

Why, weevilly biscuit and salted beef are quite the rage in all the most fashionable establishments!' Her long raven lashes batted seductively and she delivered him a most artful look through them.

If the marine posted outside the captain's day cabin thought anything unusual in the peels of laughter that emanated from within, he was wise enough not to comment upon it. The most he allowed himself was a little sidelong glance at his fellow sentry.

Only when Bottomley had delivered the dishes did Georgiana emerge from the tiny room that had become her prison. The table had been covered with a pristine white tablecloth and laid with a finely decorated dinner service and plain silver cutlery. The flickering light from the branched candlestick centrepiece reflected in the silver serving dishes, casting a warm glow around the cabin. Chicken cutlets, a leg of mutton, gravy soup, puréed potatoes, fried potatoes and even a seed cake. Nathaniel had brought his own provisions as well as those for his officers. The food was indeed tasty but, in truth, she had no appetite despite Nathaniel's obvious efforts to cajole her.

'Perhaps a little wine?' Nathaniel made to fill her glass from the heavy crystal decanter.

Normally she declined, knowing that her papa had never allowed such a thing. Indeed, she'd not grown used to the daily ration of a gallon of beer and the strange-tasting grog in all the time that she'd been aboard the ship. She drank what she could, but Georgiana's generosity with sharing her ration had soon made her popular amongst her shipmates. But strangely tonight, in a daring gesture of defiance, she accepted the captain's offer. 'Yes, thank you, sir, that would be very nice.' She sipped the wine delicately, wondering what her stepfather had caused such a fuss about. The contents of her glass were not particularly pleasant and had, in fact, a slightly sour taste, not that she would admit as much to Nathaniel.

Captain Hawke lounged back in his chair, watching Georgiana with an unreadable expression upon his face. After a little silence he said quietly, 'Are you going to tell me what's making you so miserable?' He took a small sip from his own glass.

His question was so unexpected that Georgiana inhaled the mouthful of wine she was in the process of swallowing, and then proceeded to cough and splutter its remains down the front of her white linen shirt and waistcoat. One warm large hand clapped her heartily upon the back. By the time the coughing had subsided enough for her to speak, Georgiana had regained some measure of composure. 'Miserable? Whatever makes you think that I'm miserable?' she queried in a still-croaky voice.

Nathaniel fixed her with a knowing stare. 'I've seen men face flogging around the fleet with a cheerier countenance. Come, tell me what ails you.' His hand squeezed her shoulder reassuringly.

Still seated, she glanced up at the concern clearly writ upon his face. She wanted to say, *I'm betrothed to a man that I've come to love, and he would marry me only because I've pushed him to such a dire situation that he has no other option to escape complete ruination of his beloved career. And, because I've done such a terrible thing, I fear that he'll grow to hate me.* But all she actually managed was, 'I fear you're mistaken, sir. I'm only a little anxious over your position if my identity was to be discovered.'

'You mustn't worry, Georgiana.' He stroked the errant

lock of hair from her brow. 'It will all be over soon. Hold fast until then.'

Georgiana's spine tingled with the closeness of his presence behind her. And the warmth radiating from his light touch on her shoulder had ignited a spark of inexplicable excitement within her. In a few days she would be his wife. His wife, no less. And the knowledge set the pulse racing in her neck. She tried to concentrate on what she was saying. 'How do you propose to effect this replacement of George Robertson? Won't anyone notice that I'm gone?' She took what could only be described as a swig of wine.

'Notice? Georgiana, you've been hidden next door too long. Every blasted man on this ship has expressed a profound interest in your state of health!' Nathaniel placed his other hand on her opposite shoulder and began to massage the taut muscles beneath.

A slow warm delicious sensation had started within the core of Georgiana's body. She allowed the magical motion that his hands were weaving to continue, even though every shred of common sense warned her otherwise. Burly Jack's words slipped far from recall. 'Really?' Her blue eyes opened wide.

'Yes, really,' retorted her captain. 'Can't be working them hard enough if they've time to dwell on the welfare of m'ship's boy.' He tried, and failed, to sound strict.

One small hand touched to where his were still so busily working on her shoulders. 'You don't suppose that they have an inclination that I'm not a boy, do you?' Another gulp of wine descended.

'Most certainly not.' A butterfly kiss flitted to the crown of her head. 'They're steadfastly convinced that you're my nephew. It seems that they regard the dratted boy with some affection.' The long tanned fingers paused in their ministrations. 'I can't think why!' he added with an impudent glimmer. 'Can you?' Glossy dark locks parted to reveal the soft white flesh at the nape of her neck. His thumb moved to caress it in a slow sensual circle.

She sat rooted to the spot, unable to move. Touched as if by Midas to cold static metal, except the blood pounding through her veins and the rampant heat rising through her body proved she had not turned to gold. 'Nathaniel,' she whispered slowly, 'I don't think that you should be doing that.'

'Doing what?' he enquired with a tone that belied innocence.

Her words were hushed and breathy. 'Your fingers, touching… touching my neck.'

'Yes,' he said solemnly, 'you're quite right. I shouldn't be doing this with my fingers.' And he bent lower until his mouth met her neck.

'Oh!' exclaimed Georgiana in a soft moan. 'I…I didn't mean…' Words ceased as he nuzzled the tender skin with the full force of his lips.

She melted beneath the flame of his touch, a silky smooth sensation washing over her, dragging her down into a spiral of leaping desire.

'Georgiana…' Her name escaped his lips as he pulled her gently up from the chair. She felt the warmth of him against her. 'Sweet Georgiana.' His hands slid over her shoulders, down over the coarse linen of her shirt, and down further still to close around her buttocks.

'Nathaniel,' she gasped, 'we must not…' Her thoughts struggled out from beneath the feathery down of his embrace.

He moved his hands in a sensual massage, sliding his fingers against her hips, stroking with an increasing intensity.

'Nathaniel…' A yawning need was growing within her. Every caress, every touch, banked the fire higher until she thought she would expire for want of his hands upon her skin, for his lips to claim hers.

His mouth nibbled the soft lobe of her ear as his fingers found passage beneath her shirt, basking on the smooth satin of her back. 'Georgiana!' His words were low and husky, stirring her blood to run faster, wilder.

Her skin tingled beneath his touch, ached for more. The long tanned fingers fluttered against her stomach, then traced a path higher, to splay against the coiled linen strips that hid her breasts. Even through the thickness of the bindings her nipples tightened. She arched, driving herself against his palms, clutching his hands harder to the coarse wound cloth. His tongue lapped against her neck, sucking the sweet nectar of her skin. At last his fingers found the knotted end of linen strip. She reached her searing lips to his—

A knock sounded against the door.

Georgiana's heart lurched in her chest.

'Wait where you are,' Nathaniel ordered loudly.

A voice floated through the wooden panelling, sounding suspiciously like Lieutenant Anderson's dulcet tones. 'The prisoners are requesting your presence, sir.'

Nathaniel stared down at her, his eyes darkened to a smouldering black, the starkness of reality intruding on their passion. His breath came harsh and ragged and the glisten of sweat showed upon his skin.

Georgiana tensed in his arms as the lieutenant's voice delivered her back down to earth. The sparks extinguished within her flashing eyes and her cheeks glowed hot and pink. She could still feel the warm press of Nathaniel's hands in a place they most certainly should not be. She glanced up at him, suddenly afraid.

'Lieutenant Anderson?'

'Yes, sir.'

'Make them wait. I shall be along presently.'

The footsteps receded.

She relaxed in his strong arms, daring to breathe again. 'Nathaniel, we should not have…' Her face burned scarlet.

'The fault is mine. *I* should not have. But you're a very tempting woman and—' he crooked a smile '—we're soon to be married. I'm very much looking forward to that day.' He raised one dark winged eyebrow, and delivered a chaste kiss to her forehead. 'Until then I shouldn't take advantage of you. Please—' he touched a kiss to the rosy swell of her lips '—forgive me.' Finally, and with some considerable reluctance, he prised his hands from her body, fixed her shirt neatly back into place and escorted her back to the night cabin. 'Hold fast, sweetheart, just a few more days to wait.' He executed a bow, hastily donned his undress coat and strode from the cabin.

Chapter Eight

How could a girl of one and twenty survive undiscovered amidst a crew of seafaring men? For the umpteenth time Walter Praxton pondered the conundrum, returning again to his ultimate conclusion that it was impossible. That led him to extrapolate two possible scenarios. Firstly, that on the remote chance she had managed to hide her fair sex, she was likely to have expired from the hardship of life at sea. Secondly, and perhaps even worse, if it was known that she was a woman, then what men in the confines of a ship at sea would not rejoice in the comfort that her body offered? Mr Praxton allowed himself the indulgence of remembering just how very appealing Georgiana Raithwaite's soft curves were, her slim body pressed to his. No matter that she had spurned his kisses, had thrust herself from him. Even the memory of that heaving bosom, those flashing eyes, drove him instantly to a state of arousal.

What would he do if she had been badly used, had fallen, as Edward Raithwaite so aptly put it? Would he still want her then? But Walter Praxton knew the answer before even the question had formed in his mind. Her image obsessed him, goaded him. The one woman who seemed immune to his handsome looks. The one, alone, who had not succumbed to the enticement of his charm. How ironic that it was she above all others that he wanted. More than wanted, for want did not come near to describing the utter determination that burned in Walter Praxton's breast. He would have Georgiana Raithwaite if it was the last thing he did.

Georgiana lay alone on the bed, reliving her shocking conduct of earlier that same evening. Now that Nathaniel was no longer present she was able to think clearly and with a good deal of sense. She could not deny that their encounter had been more than pleasurable. Indeed, it had left her with a most unladylike appetite for more. Her eyelids shuttered and she pressed her palms to her forehead. Dear Lord, was it really the prim and proper Miss Raithwaite who had encouraged Nathaniel Hawke in his…his…? The word would not form upon her tongue. The same Miss Raithwaite who'd readily thrown herself into a fast-flowing river to escape similar attentions from Mr Praxton. It seemed that common sense was long forgotten when Nathaniel turned his charm on her. And therein lay the problem. She could not blame the man, for she knew with absolute certainty that had she repulsed him at any point he would not have pressed her, would have behaved as the perfect gentleman. Not only had she failed to deter his actions in any way, but had positively encouraged him. When Lieutenant Anderson's interruption had sounded, it was not relief that had flooded her senses, but disappointment.

Mama had once alluded to wanton women who, without a shred of decency, undertook illicit and intimate relations with men. How horrified she would be to realise that her own daughter was now of that ilk. And Papa? Why, he would beat her senseless and disown her if he ever discovered that truth. Georgiana felt guilty at what she had done, and afraid of the powerful emotions that seemed to have the ability to turn her into a pathetic heap of quivering jelly. So much for all that she'd learned!

Nathaniel Hawke was a good man, a man of honour, and a man who had been some months at sea without the company of women. She had no idea how he amused himself back on land, no idea if he kept a mistress, or had affairs. No doubt he did, didn't all gentlemen? His affection seemed real enough when he kissed or even touched her. Surely the hoarse desire gravelled through his voice could not be feigned? Yes, he wanted her—even through all her naïvety she understood that. But now, beneath the cool light of her calm analysis, she realised that any man starved of women for such a time might behave in the same manner. Jack was right. *Anyone'll do, as long as she's willin'*, and hadn't she proven herself to be more than willing?

Anger clenched at her teeth, compressed the fullness of her bruised lips. He'd called her a very tempting woman—wasn't that proof that the nature of his affections lay with a woman, any woman, rather than Georgiana herself? Tears welled in her eyes, and she blinked them back furiously. She would not cry. Never. She had plunged herself into this ridiculous situation, and therefore she would deal with it the best she could. Rallying her courage, she held her chin high and carefully, calmly weighed up the evidence.

Her history proved that such wantonness had never previously assailed her. Indeed, she'd found Walter Praxton's kisses repugnant. Coupled with this was the fact that she'd drunk two whole glasses of wine, ignorant of their possible effect. Perhaps an excess of such a beverage could produce unladylike behaviour. Her head did feel rather light and fluffy since consuming the sour liquid. Finally, she had been virtually imprisoned within the tiny night cabin for days, and could not such a confinement result in a type of brain madness that might explain the strange effects Nathaniel Hawke was having upon her person? Yes, indeed, the evidence was strong and glaringly obvious. Georgiana felt rather less guilty and a little more woolly-headed. Now that she thought about it, the ship seemed to be rocking in a dizzy, uneven manner. It was shortly after this observation that the brilliant idea made itself known to Georgiana. Brilliant was perhaps not the word that Nathaniel Hawke would have chosen to describe it.

The moon was full and high in the night sky when Georgiana stole silently from Nathaniel's cabin.

'Feeling better, Robertson?' the marine sentry enquired.

She pulled the hat lower over her head. 'Yes, thank you, sir, a bit. The captain thought some fresh air might help.'

'Does he know that you're up and about?' Suspicion creased the marine's brow.

'Yes, sir,' she lied in her deepest mumbling voice. 'Bade me not be out too long, sir.' She prayed that Nathaniel's business on the lower deck would keep him occupied for some time.

The sentry did not appear entirely convinced, but before he could question her further Georgiana had disappeared in a swift flurry of steps. She made for the uppermost deck, keeping to the shadows, avoiding those of the watch. Silver moonlight glistened over the water, lighting its gentle undulation. All was quiet save for the tranquil lap of waves against the hull. Water slapping softly on wood. And best of all was the subtle night breeze, fresh and clear. It nipped at her cheeks, chased the foggy clouds from her head and soothed the worry

from her shoulders. She drank in the sight of the beautiful nocturnal seascape, tasted salt upon her lips, felt the wind rake
her skin, smelled what had become a welcome and familiar
scent. Carefully and methodically she impressed the scene
upon her memory. *If I lose all else, I'll remember what's before me for the rest of my life. For it is of such captivating clarity as to remind me how fortunate I am to live to witness it.*
The thought lingered even as she made her way back down
to the cabin. For although the freshness of the air had cleared
the stuffy confusion from her head, it had brought with it the
realisation that she was jeopardising Nathaniel's plans. And
that was something she did not want to risk.

The days passed quickly and the comfortable companion-
ship between Captain Hawke and his erstwhile ship's boy
grew, but it was not long before Nathaniel eventually brought
the *Pallas,* the *Ville-de-Milan* and the *Coruna* to dock within
the harbour at the great Rock of Gibraltar.

Four boats rowed ashore from the frigate. The launch and
two cutters carried the French seamen, as well as the bosun,
his assistant and several marines. The crew left imprisoned
upon the French frigates would be transported in their own
vessels. Captain Hawke and his landing party travelled in the
pinnace and consisted of Lieutenant Anderson, four marines,
two midshipmen, the surgeon, the purser, both French captains and, of course, Captain Hawke's ailing servant George
Robertson.

'You look a little better, Master Robertson. Do you feel
somewhat recovered?' Lieutenant Anderson enquired as the
pinnace was rowed towards the shore.

Georgiana tugged nervously at her ear. 'Yes, sir, much better, thank you, sir.' Then, following a rather black look from Nathaniel, hastily amended the report upon her health. 'That is, except for the headache, sir.' She averted her eyes to the shoreline.

Mr Belmont leaned forward, his perceptive surgeon's eye peering at her face before turning to address the captain. 'Captain Hawke, I don't profess to be a physician, but I have some little knowledge that may help the boy's condition. Perhaps, if I could examine him when we return to the ship? I know that you did not previously deem it necessary, but the sickness has persisted for quite some time.'

Nathaniel nodded briefly as if the subject was of little consequence. 'Of course, Mr Belmont, do as you see fit. Mr Tufton, use the launch to transport the provisions back to the *Pallas*; my business ashore will take some time and I'll return with the pinnace later.'

'Aye, sir,' replied the purser.

Rear Admiral Tyler was only too happy to welcome Captain Hawke and his party to the station on Gibraltar—his joviality perhaps due, in part, to his profound love of receiving captured vessels. With the necessary documents completed, Admiral Tyler was keen to invite Nathaniel and his officers to a celebratory dinner the following evening.

The main town, or city as it was termed on the Rock, was bright and busy. Despite the advancement of the year, the sun was shining and the temperatures mild. In the background loomed the dominating huge stark purple grey of the rocky terrain. Within the city matters were less severe. Both men and women in colourful clothing called from behind their street stalls set out in the commodious market place. Small flat-roofed houses crowded from the sea wall up the steep elevation towards the Rock, their walls whitewashed and clean, splashed with the vibrant reds and pinks of the strong-smelling flowers that clambered upon them. Mules, laden with large cylindrical bags, trotted in small troops to and from the harbour, competing with the rumble of the wooden carts. Colonel Drinkwater's fine library stood proud in its newly completed building, proclaiming the cultured interests of the Gibraltarians. In the distance, at the northern extremity of the hillside, were the ruins of a Moorish castle. In the centre of the city was Commercial Square, across which more pedlars displayed their wares. But the most astounding sight that met the officers of the *Pallas* was two small Barbary apes lounging at the edge of the city, nibbling on a large pile of bread and fruit. Mr Belmont and Lieutenant Anderson were quite taken with the creatures, so much so that they set to sketching the scene before them. Thus it was that Nathaniel found himself able to slip discreetly away, accompanied only by his ship's boy.

Through the narrow back streets they wove, following the directions that the man had relayed to Nathaniel. Georgiana grinned as she thought of the wary suspicion on the fellow's face. But then it wasn't every day that he was accosted by a captain of His Majesty's Navy asking where he might find a lady's dressmaker.

'Keep up, George, we haven't got all day.' Nathaniel reached an arm round to catch the rather out-of-breath ship's boy straggling behind.

She had been taking too much of an interest in her surroundings. 'My legs aren't as long as yours,' she grumbled.

'And my eyes aren't so big as yours,' came the droll reply.

She had just rallied a spurt of energy to keep up with the

tall figure along Waterport Street when he turned down an alleyway and came to an abrupt halt. Georgiana panted mercifully at the rear.

'Here we are, Master Robertson. Let's just hope that Mrs Howard is prepared to help us.'

Mrs Evelina Howard was a lady of large proportions with kind grey eyes and the most artfully *coiffured* grey hair. Originally from Brighton, she had arrived on the Rock some ten years ago, as the wife of an elderly naval officer. Since being widowed, she had established a small dressmaking service to cater to the ladies of Gibraltar, a business that had proved lucrative in the extreme. If the sudden appearance of a tall darkhaired naval officer with a boy by his side startled Mrs Howard, she was too polite to show it. She observed the golden epaulettes on both his shoulders, the gold-edged lapels and collar, and the embroidery upon the cuffs and pocket flaps of the smart dark dress coat.

'Good day, Captain. How may I help you?' She eyed him serenely, wondering as to the woman who had obviously prompted his visit to her establishment. Wife or mistress? Mrs Howard speculated that the man before her would never lack for the attention of female admirers.

Nathaniel bowed. 'Captain Nathaniel Hawke, of His Majesty's Navy, at your service, ma'am.'

The grey head inclined graciously.

'Mrs Howard,' he began, 'it's on a matter of some delicacy that I seek your help. A matter that demands the utmost discretion and for which, if you are prepared to assist, I will recompense you most generously.'

Mrs Howard felt a quiver of curiosity. 'You intrigue me, Captain Hawke. Are you asking me to undertake something illegal, immoral, or both?' Everything about her bespoke a calm still.

'Neither, madam. My request is, however, unusual and, were it to become widely known, would prove injurious to the lady concerned. It is somewhat urgent.' He had not moved and yet the sheer height and power of his frame dominated the surroundings.

She walked to the door and turned the key within the lock. 'Then you had better tell me, Captain, with all speed.' Rustling back across the room, she faced him and waited composedly for the story to unfold.

For just a moment, one single moment, Evelina Howard's usual aplomb deserted her as she stared slack-jawed at the boy. The serene grey eyes flicked back to Captain Hawke questioningly.

'Miss Raithwaite is both a lady and my betrothed,' he said firmly, irrefutably.

Mrs Howard smoothed her hands over her skirts. 'Of course.' And, when she looked up, there was nothing upon her countenance to betray the shock. 'Then you had best be about your business, sir, and leave the lady to me.' She did not miss the fleeting touch of his hand to the boy's, or the concerned reassurance he muttered in his ear before he departed.

'So, Miss Raithwaite, I think we had better begin with a bath.'

'But that's not—'

The older woman's voice interrupted. 'You smell of ships and the sea. Perhaps not the most desirable of fragrances for a young lady. Blunt words, but pray do not take them unkindly. We've much to do if we're to fulfil Captain Hawke's requirements.'

And so the day progressed and did not end until Georgiana had been scrubbed, rinsed, perfumed, poked and pinned into an endless variety of costumes. The transformation had now entered its final stages.

'It would be indelicate of me to enquire as to how you came to be in your present circumstance, miss, and therefore I won't. But I couldn't live comfortably with my conscience if I didn't offer you my help to escape a situation that may not be of your making.' The capable fingers coaxed ebony curls to frame Georgiana's face.

Georgiana looked up into the kind eyes that held hers in the mirror. 'Thank you, ma'am, for your concern. I fear that my appearance had misled you, for my fate is entirely of my own making.' She looked away, blinking, unable to say what would follow next. *As, I'm most ashamed to admit, is Captain Hawke's.*

'*Entirely* of your own making?' queried Evelina. 'In my experience, no lady's fate ever is. Women have so little say in the shaping of their lives, bound as they are by the constraints of their fathers and husbands.' When the girl did not reply, the modiste continued, 'When is the wedding?'

A blush spread across Georgiana's complexion. 'I'm not sure of the precise date.'

Mrs Howard regarded her with a knowing look, but said nothing.

'It's not what you think,' she protested. 'Captain Hawke has not ruined me!'

The pale eyebrows raised a notch and lowered demurely. 'Then it's a love match?'

'Yes...no...I cannot...'

'Do you love him?' Evelina asked quietly.

Georgiana's head drooped. 'Yes.'

'But you fear he doesn't love you?'

The ebony curls shook beneath her fingers. 'No. I know he doesn't.'

Mrs Howard moved round to take the girl's hands. 'From what I've seen, Miss Raithwaite, I believe you're very much mistaken. Captain Hawke most definitely had the look of a man in love.'

Georgiana sighed. 'Dear Mrs Howard, I know you're trying to help me, but you wouldn't if you knew what I'd done.'

The matronly lady patted the small hands within hers. 'Surely it cannot be so very bad?'

'Oh, but, ma'am, I very much fear that it is.' Georgiana said solemnly.

'Do you wish to tell me about it?'

Stormy blue eyes met peaceful grey. 'Yes, I believe I do.'

The sun had dropped low in the sky when Nathaniel Hawke returned to the modiste's establishment to collect Georgiana. He soon found himself ushered through to a small parlour.

'Captain Hawke.'

'Your servant, Mrs Howard.' Nathaniel bowed, his eyes scanning the room for a sign of Georgiana.

The plump pleasant face smiled. 'You are no doubt keen to make the acquaintance of Miss Raithwaite once more.'

'Yes, indeed.' Nathaniel tried to quell his rising impatience.

Mrs Howard sat down on a pink scalloped chair and fussed with making herself comfortable before facing her visitor once more. 'Forgive me, Captain Hawke. Won't you take a seat?'

Nathaniel did as she directed.

'Do you plan to stay long in our little town, sir?'

'No, no more than a se'nnight.'

The cool grey eyes watched him.

'We return to England, having fulfilled our duty, ma'am.' He glanced towards the closed door and back at Mrs Howard.

The Captain's Lady

'Something at which I understand you're quite adept, Captain.'

Nathaniel's gaze swung to hers. The skin prickled at the nape of his neck. 'As is any naval officer, ma'am.'

Silence.

Evelina Howard spoke quietly. 'No, Captain Hawke, I don't believe that every officer would have acted as you have done.'

His heart set up a gallop, a tiny muscle flickered in his cheek. 'Please be direct, madam. Of what do you speak?' Precisely what had Georgiana told the woman, and where was his betrothed? His fingers resisted the urge to drum on the arm of the chair.

'Why, of Miss Raithwaite, of course.' She smiled at the frown descending upon his brow. 'You were quite right in what you told me, sir. Miss Raithwaite is a lady…a young and naïve lady.' She waited for the captain's response.

His eyes darkened. 'She is also the lady promised to be my wife before we leave this place.' He paused. 'You'll be well paid for your silence, Mrs Howard. Don't seek to destroy her reputation by a careless word.' His gaze narrowed. 'Where is Miss Raithwaite? She should be ready to join me by this hour.'

Satisfied by his response, Evelina raised herself and walked to the doorway. 'Miss Raithwaite!' Her voice raised just enough to carry upstairs. She turned to face Nathaniel once more. 'I thought it prudent to allow the servants the day off. They do so love to gossip, and we wouldn't want today's events to be discussed around the Rock.'

Any response Nathaniel might have uttered was forgotten as he gaped at the figure moving into the room. Dear God, he'd forgotten just what she looked like as a woman. Leaping to his feet he stepped towards her, noting the pink tinge in her cheeks and the embarrassed little smile playing upon those voluptuous lips. 'Georgiana!'

Mrs Howard watched as Captain Hawke stared at the young woman who stood rather self-consciously before them. The girl's face illuminated with a radiant smile as she moved to throw herself into the captain's arms.

'Hmph…hmm!' Mrs Howard developed a sudden irritation in her throat, respectfully reminding the love-struck couple that they were not alone.

'Oh!' Georgiana remembered herself just in time, skidded to a halt on Mrs Howard's best rug and managed to stutter, 'Captain Hawke!'

'Miss Raithwaite!' gasped the erstwhile supremely confident captain. He looked, thought Mrs Howard, a little shaken.

They stared at one another, a palpable flow of attraction between them.

Evelina Howard's mouth curved into a smug smile. She clearly had not been mistaken in her first appraisal of Captain Hawke's feelings for the girl. Why, he was looking at her with such tenderness it would have moved Mrs Howard to tears, if she had been of such a silly disposition. One small dry cough echoed in the room. 'So, Captain Hawke, do you find Miss Raithwaite's appearance satisfactory?'

Nathaniel recovered himself, dragged his eyes from the vision of loveliness before him and addressed the dressmaker. 'Indeed, Mrs Howard, it's much more than satisfactory. Let's discuss payment before Miss Raithwaite and I leave.' He removed a purse from his pocket.

Mrs Howard gestured Georgiana to be seated. 'Where do you intend to stay this evening?' A closed expression had descended upon her face.

'Miss Raithwaite will be safely lodged at an inn.'

Her eyebrows raised. 'Alone and unchaperoned?'

An uneasiness stole over Nathaniel. 'Yes,' he replied harshly. 'We have little choice.'

'That, Captain Hawke, is where you're mistaken. May I be so bold as to make a suggestion that could prove mutually beneficial to us all?'

Thus it was, having discussed the matter in detail, that Nathaniel returned to the *Pallas* without his ship's boy George Robertson. Tomorrow would see the introduction of his betrothed, Miss Georgiana Raithwaite, to Gibraltarian naval society, and all under the chaperonage of the highly respectable Mrs Howard.

The next evening when Nathaniel called upon Mrs Howard's establishment, it was to discover two immaculately attired ladies patiently awaiting him in the parlour. Georgiana's skin glowed with an opalescent sheen beneath the pale aquamarine of her shot-silk gown. The satin ribbon sash around the high waist served only to draw attention to the gentle curve of her bosom above. The neckline was plain with a low, but not indecent, décolletage. Matching long gloves and a finely worked shawl completed the ensemble. Small curls of dark glossy hair kissed the edges of her face and a beaded bandeau triumphed as her crowning glory.

His eyes swept over her as if seeing her for the first time, feasting upon each detail.

'Miss Raithwaite, you take my breath away,' he said at last, before turning politely to Mrs Howard to compliment her own silver-grey outfit.

Elation glowed in those calm grey eyes. 'I do not think that we have to fear that your officers will recognise George Robertson,' she said.

'No, indeed, Mrs Howard, you've worked a miracle,' conceded Nathaniel.

Georgiana smiled up at the tall dark captain smartly clothed in his full dress uniform. In truth, she thought she had never seen him look so devilishly dashing, and longed to press a kiss to the stark line of his jaw. 'Mrs Howard has been a wonder. Even I was surprised when I looked in the mirror.'

'We had best leave, for it wouldn't do to be late for Admiral Tyler's party. I have taken the liberty of hiring a carriage to transport us the short distance to the admiral's house.' Nathaniel gestured towards the door. 'Ladies.'

Admiral Tyler was a jovial bluff sort of fellow, who had grown rather rotund with the comfortable ease of life in Gibraltar. His wife, a little pudding of a woman, buzzed around him like an industrious bee. The old admiral's eyes lit up on sighting the young lady following in Captain Hawke's wake.

'Sir, may I present my betrothed, Miss Raithwaite, and of course her chaperon, Mrs Howard, with whom, I'm sure, you're already acquainted.'

Before her husband could reply, Lady Tyler ejected a nervous titter. 'But of course, dear Mrs Howard, quite the best modiste on the Rock. I do so rave about her designs. Always such a pleasure to meet with you.' She lavished a huge smile on Evelina and turned her attentions to the young woman at her side. 'Miss Raithwaite, what a positive delight.'

Georgiana, knowing herself to have been suddenly thrust into the spotlight, anchored down her quivering apprehension and managed her devoirs with a surprising calm confidence. It seemed that Lady Tyler could have rivalled Mirabelle Farleigh when it came to the chatterbox stakes. For, once Lady Tyler started to talk, she apparently found it difficult to stop.

Not that Georgiana complained—it was much safer to allow their hostess to draw the focus of attention away from her own nervous self.

'How did you come to arrive without my notice? Mrs Howard has kept you hidden all to herself. For that I must chastise her most thoroughly.' A plump white hand reached forward and tapped an elaborate turquoise-coloured fan upon Mrs Howard's substantial arm. The modiste bore such patronage with a steadfast spirit, betraying not one inkling of her true opinion on Admiral Tyler's feather-brained wife. 'And, Captain Hawke, such a fine young captain. Haven't I always said that the navy needs just such men?' she cooed up at him, batting her lashes in an unbecoming flirtatious manner, which she managed to employ when in the company of any man of good breeding.

Nathaniel suffered her attentions admirably well, so much so that the falsetto of her laughter soon penetrated every nook and cranny of the drawing room.

'La, Captain Hawke, I declare you are a gentleman of hidden talents. To land so magnificent a prize, and with such little effort.'

His eyes fleetingly sought Georgiana across the crowded room. She shone, outstanding amidst the ladies of Gibraltar, and his heart swelled with tenderness and possessive pride.

Lady Tyler's shrill laugh raked across his musings, dragging him back to face her. 'You naughty man, that was not the prize of which I spoke, as well you know.' She delivered him a teasing tap of her fan.

'Indeed, but Miss Raithwaite is a prize above all,' he responded gallantly.

Lady Tyler shrieked even louder. 'That's quite the most romantic speech I've heard.'

The admiral joined them, intent on relieving Captain Hawke of his wife's presence. There was only so much that any one man could be expected to suffer.

'Ronald, dear—' she beamed '—I was just commenting on how very romantic Captain Hawke is concerning his betrothed.'

'Quite so, quite so. Couldn't help noticing that Lieutenant Pensenby is looking rather down in the mouth over in the corner. See if you can't coax him along, Jane.' He turned to Nathaniel, one large veined hand patting Lady Tyler's consolingly, 'M'wife's the best hostess on the Rock. Got something of a reputation to uphold within our little society.'

Jane Tyler screeched appreciatively.

'Off you go, m'dear.' He surreptitiously gestured towards Pensenby, and Lady Tyler headed off in the direction of the unsuspecting lieutenant. 'A damned fine accomplishment, Captain Hawke, well done, m'boy. That's what I like to see.'

'Thank you, Admiral Tyler.'

Ronald Tyler swirled the wine in his glass and looked towards Georgiana Raithwaite, who was now engaged in a conversation with Lieutenant Anderson and Mrs Howard. 'Fine filly of a gel,' he exclaimed. 'No wonder you've stored her quietly with the charming Mrs Howard. Too many ships in port to take any chances, what?'

Nathaniel saw the opportunity beckon before his eyes. 'Indeed. I wished to seek your advice on a related matter, sir.'

Admiral Tyler puffed out his chest and pretended not to be flattered. 'What is it that you need to know, young Hawke?' The admiral had adopted a distinctly paternal attitude to the man before him. For all his bravado, he recognised a good sea captain when he saw one.

Nathaniel met his enquiring gaze directly. 'I have a mind to marry Miss Raithwaite before we set sail for England once more. But the *Pallas* cannot linger here—we must reach Portsmouth before Christmas.'

'Say no more, say no more, Captain.' The admiral tapped the side of his nose in a sly fashion. 'No need to tell me how deuced an uncomfortable journey it would make, confined to ship with Miss Raithwaite when the lady is not yet your wife.' A suggestive wink issued from the wrinkled eye. 'Leave it to me, Hawke. I'll have a word with the chaplain, Mr Hughes. The licence will be ready and waiting before the week is out. Of course, you'll allow Lady Tyler to arrange the wedding in the King's Chapel, and the breakfast here in Belstone House. She would stop speaking to me if it were any other way. Come to think of it, that might not be such a bad thing!' He chortled and emptied the contents of his glass down his throat, none the wiser that Nathaniel Hawke knew exactly the difficulties of just such a journey with his young lady.

At the other end of the elaborate drawing room Georgiana was fencing Lieutenant Anderson's polite enquiries. 'Yes, thank you, Lieutenant Anderson, I am enjoying my visit to Gibraltar very much. The climate is so much milder, and drier than England's.'

John Anderson was having difficulty in drawing his eyes away from the enchanting young woman before him. 'Please don't think me bold, but I have the strangest notion that I've seen you before. But I'm quite sure that we've never been introduced, for I wouldn't have forgotten you.' A hint of pink crept into his cheeks.

'Perhaps I remind you of someone.' Georgiana's heart fluttered fast and furious.

'A *lady* of your acquaintance in England?' added Mrs Howard emphatically.

Lieutenant Anderson puzzled over the matter a moment longer. 'That must be the explanation, but memory fails me for the minute.' Suddenly memory was no longer a consideration, for Georgiana bestowed her most dazzling smile upon him.

'I would be most grateful if you were kind enough to explain exactly how you captured your prizes.'

John Anderson's cheeks flushed deeper. 'It was all Captain Hawke's doing, Miss Raithwaite.'

But Georgiana had no intention of allowing the first lieutenant to return to his musing of why he found her face familiar. 'I'm quite sure that he didn't perform such a task entirely alone. Won't you tell me an account of the ship's adventures?'

'Of course, miss, if you'd truly like to hear.' Lieutenant Anderson would not have refused the delectable Miss Raithwaite anything that she desired, and was soon in his element, describing the method by which the two French frigates were taken.

Nathaniel had the honour not only of taking Lady Tyler in to dinner, but also the delightful prospect of sitting beside her for the duration of the meal.

Georgiana was seated farther down the table between the vying attentions of Lieutenants Anderson and Pensenby.

One fleeting conspiratorial glance passed the length of the table between the grey-blue eyes and the deep brown, then was gone.

'Captain Hawke didn't mention your rendezvous here. I had supposed the presence of the *Pallas* within these waters to be solely because of her prizes.' Cyril Pensenby was attacking the roast beef with increasing vigour. He raised inquisitive eyes to hers.

Mrs Howard made her presence known. 'Miss Raithwaite's

trip had long been planned. She's enjoyed a most interesting visit in the weeks since her arrival.'

'Indeed, I wasn't suggesting anything to the contrary.' Although the girl seated by his left side was not what he considered a beauty, he had to admit that she possessed a certain inexplicable quality of attraction. A dewy fresh complexion and lips shaped to tempt a kiss from a man of stone. But that wasn't what held Cyril Pensenby's attention at the minute. His gaze fastened firmly upon her *décolletage*, on the glinting jet beads surrounding her neck, and lower to the swell of her bosom. It was evident that he had been too long from port. 'I can quite understand Captain Hawke's desire to collect you and take you back to England.' The remark was addressed to the curve below Georgiana's neckline.

'Are you one of the Pensenbys of York?' enquired Mrs Howard, determined to draw the man's attention from her charge.

With some reluctance Lieutenant Pensenby remembered his manners and entered into conversation with the formidable woman, leaving Miss Raithwaite to be monopolised by Mr Anderson.

At last the evening was done and Georgiana was making her way to the safety of the carriage, Nathaniel's reassuring presence close by. For all that she had enjoyed the dangerous game they played, she could not be sorry that the night was at a close. It was more of a strain than actually pretending to be George Robertson! She was just poised to climb into the carriage behind Mrs Howard when the hushed tones of Lieutenant Anderson sounded.

'Please excuse me, Captain Hawke, I wondered if I might speak with you before you return the ladies to their residence?'

Nathaniel was not best pleased by John Anderson's interruption, especially as he was desperate to gain some time with Georgiana, something that had so far evaded him throughout the evening. 'Mr Anderson?' He turned a glacial eye upon the officer.

'It's Master Robertson, sir, I'm concerned for—' The lieutenant halted abruptly as Miss Raithwaite missed her footing on the steps.

With a lightning reflex Nathaniel's arms were around her, lifting her up and against him, concerned eyes scanning her face. 'Georgiana!' he whispered, a look of intense urgency tensing his jaw.

'It's nothing. I'm a little tired and careless, and somehow missed my footing. No damage done.' She blushed profusely, aware of both the close heat of his body and Lieutenant Anderson's fixed interest. To make matters worse, Admiral and Lady Tyler had noticed the rumpus and were making their way steadily to the epicentre of the commotion.

Mrs Howard hurriedly removed Georgiana from Captain Hawke's arms, guided her into the seat, and fixed her firmly into position by means of a blanket across the knees.

The strain of Lady Tyler's high voice carried to the carriage. 'So romantic, so in love!'

Georgiana blushed the colour of port wine. Captain Hawke clambered aboard, bid his lieutenant meet him at the pinnace in half an hour, and escaped into the blackness of the night.

Chapter Nine

Georgiana sat at one end of Evelina Howard's parlour. Nathaniel sat at the other. The clock on the mantel sounded its slow and steady rhythm in measured ticks.

Mrs Howard stood beside the doorframe. 'All that chatter has rendered me quite thirsty.'

It occurred to Georgiana that no one could possibly describe Mrs Howard's articulate conversation as chatter. No, chatter was a word that could only be ascribed to the likes of Lady Tyler and Mirabelle Farleigh, although she had rapidly revised her opinion on any similarities existing between those two women.

'I'm sure, Georgiana, that you would benefit from a dish of tea. Captain Hawke, may I offer you some refreshment?' Her serenity spread like ripples in the room.

'Yes, thank you, tea would be most acceptable.'

The soft rustle of grey silk and they were alone, separated by space and Mrs Howard's elegant furnishings. Each gaze fixed on the other, intense brown deepening to a dangerous dark smoulder, stormy blue lit with sparks of the translucent silver of the sea.

Nathaniel broke the silence first. 'Well done, Georgiana, you were wonderful tonight. I'm quite sure that nobody suspected in the slightest. You weren't too uncomfortable I hope?'

'No.' The long ebony ringlets of the hairpiece tickled the skin of her neck. 'Indeed not. It was really rather exciting, apart from Lieutenant Anderson's insistence that my face was familiar.' A grin spread across her cheeks. 'And, of course, his overt reference to George Robertson. I must confess to being surprised at that, and at the most inopportune of moments! Your officers and Admiral Tyler will pity you that you're promised to the most clumsy-footed of women, not knowing that I've yet to find my land legs!'

Nathaniel laughed, flashing white teeth against the subtle blue shadow of his jaw. 'I promise you, it's not pity that they feel!'

'Whatever do you mean, sir?' she countered, rising from her chair, hands on hips.

'You know very well and I don't mean to make your head swell with too many comments on the extent of your beauty.' His eyes glinted dangerously and his mouth had moved to a lopsided grin.

The sight of his powerful athletic figure encased in the magnificent full dress uniform was impressive. Georgiana tried not to stare. 'You're teasing me again, you wretch.'

He moved playfully towards her. 'That's a fine way to address the captain of your ship, and your betrothed—a wretch, indeed! I should have you strung up and flogged for the very mention of the word.' Reaching her, he pulled her to him with mock severity. He knew it was a mistake from the minute that his fingers wrapped around the bare skin of her arms, between the end of her short puff sleeves and the start of her long silken gloves. So soft and smooth, so warm and inviting.

A harsh intake of air. He was so close that she could smell

his scent—soap and sandalwood, and something unique and masculine. The skin on her arms burned beneath the touch of his fingers and a pulse leapt in her throat. The dark smoulder-ing eyes were filled with tenderness and a look that Georgiana knew now to be desire. She wondered if her own face betrayed her rising emotions as clearly as his, for then Nathaniel would not mistake what he saw there. Her hands moved of their own accord to gently cup the roughened skin of his face, tracing the outline of his jaw with infinitesimal care.

'Georgiana!' he breathed, and the name was pained on his lips. 'My own sweet Georgiana.' His hands slid round to the soft silk of her back, gliding over the curve of her hips. His head turned to capture her gloved fingers to his mouth, nib-bling on their tips, lapping against them with his tongue.

At last she could bear it no longer and, rising onto the points of her toes, replaced her fingers with her lips, meeting his tongue with her own until they arced in a sensual light-ning of passion.

China chinked on china and the thud of Mrs Howard's sud-denly heavy footsteps sounded outside the parlour. Nathaniel thrust his betrothed back down into her chair and, by the time their hostess entered the room, was examining a small porce-lain vase on the mantelpiece. Silence echoed loudly.

'Your tea, Miss Raithwaite.' Mrs Howard passed the deli-cate dish and saucer to an extremely red-faced and breathless Georgiana. Amazingly Mrs Howard appeared to notice no change in her charge's appearance and busied herself with supplying the same beverage to Nathaniel. 'Captain Hawke,' she said politely. The steady silver gaze slid to his, and Nathaniel inclined his head in a silent salutation.

The deep mellow voice sounded within the room, his words halting Georgiana's sip of tea midflow. 'Miss Raithwaite and I were just discussing Admiral Tyler's kind offer to hold our wedding breakfast in Belstone House. I'm hopeful that everything shall be in place to allow our marriage before the week is out.'

It was Mrs Howard's turn to acknowledge his response, which she did most amiably with a smile and a nod of her immaculate head. 'That,' she said smoothly, 'is something I'm very relieved to hear.'

Georgiana squirmed within her seat, acutely aware of the unrefined hurry of her forthcoming nuptials, and the magnitude of the obligation she had thrust upon Nathaniel Hawke. Whether he wanted to or not, he could not reasonably do anything other than wed her. She reminded herself that he was taking such drastic action to save his own reputation as well as her own, but what if… A shadow of cold wheedled its way through the warmth that blazed within Georgiana's breast. It was a matter that deserved nothing less than the foremost consideration. She looked up to find herself the focus of both Nathaniel and Mrs Howard, and realised that she had paid no heed whatsoever to the conversation. 'Please forgive me, I was wool-gathering.'

'So it's settled, then,' concluded Mrs Howard. 'We look forward to seeing you tomorrow, Captain Hawke. Until then we'll bid you good-night.'

Captain Hawke took his leave as the most gracious of gentlemen, entrusting his precious prize to the safe care of the dressmaker.

'Sir, I wondered if I might be so bold as to enquire of Master Robertson's condition?' Lieutenant Anderson spoke in a quiet voice, but not of sufficiently low volume to prevent the remainder of the boat from pricking up their ears. He was seated beside the captain as the pinnace rowed back out to the *Pallas*. The gentle murmur of conversation died out. Only the sweep of the oars through the water sounded in the warm night air.

Nathaniel resisted the urge to ask just what damn business it was of Anderson's and answered as if it were not a matter of concern at all. 'Oh, the boy has taken a turn for the worse, I'm afraid. Presently he's lodged with an acquaintance of mine in the town and will be attended by a physician tomorrow.'

'I cannot help but overhear your words, Captain,' exclaimed the surgeon, who had in truth been straining to listen from his position at the other side of the small wooden boat. 'Allow me to offer my services, humble though they are. I'll happily attend the boy tomorrow and assist the local physician in any way that I can.'

'Thank you, Mr Belmont, but that won't be necessary.' Captain Hawke made to turn the talk to another subject, an aim that was to be thwarted by the tenacious interest of his officers.

Mr Pensenby spoke up. 'Sir, I saw the like of Robertson's symptoms when I was in the East Indies. Sweating, fever, pains within the stomach and a terrible sickness. Not a pretty sight, and many of the afflicted men did not recover. Ran rampant amidst the crew, lost a third of the men. Still, it's unlikely to be the same thing, different part of the world and all that.'

Nathaniel suppressed a smile. Cyril Pensenby may well just have handed him the very excuse to leave poor George Robertson behind on Gibraltar. 'Let's leave it to the expert and pray that such a plague is never visited upon the *Pallas*.'

'Amen to that,' came the unanimous response.

Alone in the cosy bed in the largest of Mrs Howard's visitor bedrooms, Georgiana lay wide awake. For all her fatigue, sleep was proving elusive, in part due to the lack of the habitual rhythmic roll of the *Pallas* to which she had grown so accustomed. But that was not all. For the tiny seed of a thought revealed to her prior to Nathaniel's departure had taken hold and germinated. And with it she knew a method that would release Captain Hawke from the prospect of an enforced marriage. A cold and hard knowledge that would not let her sleep, relentlessly straying into her mind each time she drove its discomfort to the dark and distant recesses.

It was twenty minutes after two o'clock when Georgiana decided that a dish of tea was required to remedy the situation.

The house was quiet and lit only with the silver beams of a full moon flooding through the unmasked windows of the landing and lower rooms. Bare feet tiptoed step by step downstairs and on to the cold stone floor of the kitchen. Breathing her good fortune that none of Mrs Howard's maids actually lived in, she had just set the kettle of water to boil when she was interrupted by a soft padding and a gentle voice.

'Georgiana, whatever is the matter? What are you doing down here at this time of night?'

She wrapped the dressing gown tightly across her chest, trying to warm herself against the nocturnal chill. 'I'm sorry if I woke you, Mrs Howard. I couldn't sleep and thought some tea might help. Would you like some?'

'Perhaps a small dish.' Mrs Howard's grey hair was plaited tidily into a braid that swept far down her back. She paused, before adding, 'And you will, of course, tell me what it is that is troubling you, my dear.' No one would ever think of disobeying the quiet command intrinsic in that voice.

An ear lobe suffered several pulverising squeezes between

thumb and forefinger before Georgiana could find the words to answer. 'It's Captain Hawke and our forthcoming marriage.' She glanced rapidly at Mrs Howard before resuming her watch on the kettle.

'A watched pot never boils,' quoted the modiste. 'Georgiana, come and sit at the table with me.' Grey eyes observed the girl's cold bare feet. 'On second thoughts, run and fetch your slippers, my dear, before we continue, or you're bound to catch your death of cold.' A clucking, tutting noise filled the kitchen as Georgiana rose to do as she was bid, and eventually they were settled comfortably with their tea.

The steam rose from the dish as Georgiana sipped gingerly.

'Now,' said Mrs Howard, 'you were about to tell me precisely the nature of your concerns with marrying Captain Hawke.' She drank her tea and waited with her usual patience.

Georgiana fiddled with her ear. She sipped some tea. And adjusted her slippers. And her dressing gown. 'Well…it's just that…oh, it sounds so feeble when it comes to transfer thought to spoken word!'

'I'm sure that it's no such thing,' said Mrs Howard reassuringly. 'Perhaps you are worried as to the nature of your wifely duties? You are far from home, and your mama, but have no concerns, my dear, for I'll tell you all that you need to know. And they're nothing to worry about. Indeed, you are likely to find them really quite pleasurable.'

A furiously blushing Georgiana gulped the rest of her tea, hot though it was, and tried not to think of what Mrs Howard was alluding to. Unfortunately the memory of intimacies shared with the captain came flooding back all too readily. She cleared her throat. 'Thank you, ma'am, for offering such advice, but that isn't the cause of my quandary.'

'Do you find the thought of wedding Captain Hawke distasteful?' The modiste asked the question even though she had witnessed its answer with her own eyes.

'No, indeed, there is no other man whom I'd rather marry.'

'You said that you love him, and you really do, don't you? Any fool with eyes in his head can see that.'

'Yes,' she said simply.

Mrs Howard took Georgiana's hand between her own. 'Then, tell me, dear girl, precisely what is the problem?'

'I don't want him to sacrifice himself by making a marriage that's not of his own free will. He will wed me to save both our reputations. Can you imagine what would be thought of Captain Hawke if the truth were to emerge? A woman creeps aboard his ship, serves as a ship's boy, before being transferred to the position of captain's boy, sleeps within his own night cabin, while the captain lies to the crew that the lad is his nephew! Through my folly, and nothing of Captain Hawke's fault, I've placed him in a position that could ruin his career, something that he's worked long and hard to attain. I've forced him to a marriage. Nathaniel Hawke doesn't love me, and I fear that eventually he'll grow to hate me.' She turned saddened eyes to Mrs Howard. 'How can I marry him, knowing all that I do?'

The older woman was quiet for a little. 'I take it that Captain Hawke himself told you of the threat to his captaincy?'

'Nathaniel only confirmed what I already knew. It's the reason I agreed to marry him.'

'I see,' said Mrs Howard. 'Not because your own reputation is ruined and you love him?'

Georgiana darted a startled look at her chaperon. 'Nathaniel is of the aristocracy. My father's an inn-owner. I bring no dowry, no contacts, nothing that could be of any use to a man like Nathaniel, nothing except Georgiana Raithwaite. I would never agree to wed him to save myself.'

Evelina Howard smiled. 'But you'll do so to save him?'

'Of course.'

'Would you believe me if I told you that Captain Hawke holds you in very great affection?'

The girl slowly shook her head.

'I'd wager that you've misjudged his true feelings. Many gentlemen can be a little reticent to convey their romantic sensibilities. It doesn't follow that they don't care. Besides, you're forgetting, I've seen the way that he looks at you!' She raised one perfectly shaped eyebrow and turned up the corners of her mouth.

'I'm afraid you're mistaken, ma'am.' Georgiana sighed. 'Although it pains me to admit the truth, I must. Captain Hawke is not indifferent to me. Indeed, I do believe he actually feels some element of—' she paused, blushed, and completed her sentence '—of desire for me. But living amidst one hundred and eighty-five men these past weeks has certainly been educational. For I've learned that when a man is at sea for any length of time, confined with other men, and away from women, he's liable to desire the company of any woman. And I stress the word *any*.'

Mrs Howard fixed a determined look upon her young charge. 'Georgiana Raithwaite, I dread to think what manner of education you've been exposed to. Suffice it to say that men do have certain, shall we say, appetites, but if Captain Hawke was of such a mind he would have taken advantage of you long before the *Pallas* docked in Gibraltar. And as you've assured me that the captain has not…ruined you, then we can be confident that it's not his carnal appetites that are driving him to marry you.' She did not add that a man with the looks and position of Nathaniel Hawke would have no difficulty finding any number of women within the port to satisfy those needs.

'No,' agreed Georgiana, 'it's his sense of honour and the fact that his back is against the wall that propel him.' She shook her head. 'There's no way to postpone the wedding and save face, so I thought that perhaps after the ceremony I could stay here with you while Nathaniel sails for England. He could then obtain an annulment, leaving him free to marry as he wills. I, of course, would wait some time before returning.'

Evelina Howard carefully placed the fine porcelain dish upon the saucer. 'To resume your place in the bosom of your family? To stand once more within the marriage mart, and wed a man other than Captain Hawke?'

'No, I could never do that! I'll stay in Portsmouth and become a paid companion.'

'You think to have it all worked out,' said Mrs Howard smoothly. 'But—' she raised her cool grey eyes to Georgiana's '—you've omitted to consider one vital fact.'

Georgiana's brow furrowed.

'I leave Gibraltar for England after your wedding. I've a notion to return to my roots, and Captain Hawke has been kind enough to offer me transport upon his ship. We shall make the journey together, my dear, and arrive in Portsmouth before Christmas.'

'But…'

Mrs Howard's firm hand patted Georgiana's. 'Life as a poor miserable spinster at the beck and call of arrogant old women, or marriage to Nathaniel Hawke—I wouldn't have thought the choice a difficult one. The man loves you, Georgiana, as you love him. Be happy with the chance that fate has dealt you, take the risk, and you'll see that I'm right.' She rose and, leaving the empty dishes still upon the wooden table, moved slowly across the moonlit room. 'Now, I, at least, am for bed, and so too should you be.'

With Mrs Howard's words echoing in her mind, it was some time before Georgiana finally found sleep.

Walter Praxton tutted at his fingers stained with ink from the quill held tightly between them. He scrubbed at them with his handkerchief before continuing with his carefully constructed text.

Portsmouth
December, 1804

My dear Mr Raithwaite

I write to apprise you of the latest knowledge that I have ascertained concerning your daughter. It is with a degree of trepidation that I reveal that Miss Raithwaite conspired to travel to the town of Fareham, unaccompanied upon the mail and dressed in the attire that we previously discovered. However, I am afraid to report that upon reaching her destination, she was pressed into service as a boy upon a naval frigate, which has since left dock. I cannot be certain as to the fate she has suffered upon her journey, but reassure you once again that, if there is any way that the situation can be resolved, I will endeavour, with every ounce of my being, to bring that about. I understand your distress in the matter and can only implore you to hold fast in your resolve until my return to Andover. Although your heart is breaking with sadness, I know that your concerns must now lie with the prevention of any ensuing scandal. Therefore, take some small crumb of comfort in my promise that I will return with Miss Raithwaite as my wife or not at all.

The ship she was stowed upon is due to return to this port in the next weeks. Thus, the truth will soon become apparent, and our waiting is nigh at an end. I have a man watching the port at all hours of the day and night, so fear not that the girl will elude us for a second time. No matter the expenditure, I am committed to my duty, and remind you of the freedom that you granted me when last we spoke.

When next you see me, I am confident that it will be in the capacity of your son. Miss Raithwaite shall learn the error of her ways if she has not already done so.

For now I bid you adieu.

Your faithful servant,

Walter Praxton

The week had passed almost as a blur for Nathaniel, caught as he was between completing the preparations for his wedding and ensuring that all on the *Pallas* was in order prior to the commencement of her return journey to England. On top of this he was required to fashion and reveal a clever tale to account for the sudden disappearance of Master George Robertson, a task that was proving rather more difficult than his initial estimation because of the overt interest his crew seemed to have taken in the matter. Indeed, he had barely had time to visit his betrothed. Wednesday had seen a rushed affair when he'd called at Mrs Howard's to inform the ladies that the ceremony would take place two days hence. Georgiana had expressed a wish to converse with him, seemingly at length, but, due to a pressing appointment with Rear Admiral Tyler, Nathaniel had been unable to comply. Thus it was that he found himself on Friday morning waiting with a growing sense of pleasurable anticipation for the arrival of his bride before the altar in the King's Chapel.

Lieutenant Anderson smiled nervously as his second by his side. Around the splendid interior Lady Tyler had organised the hanging of garlands of small white flowers, artfully inter-spersed between vivid green foliage swags on the ends of the pews. The chaplain hovered nearby, looking unwell, but in-sisting that he was able enough to perform the marriage cer-emony. On one side of the church a clutch of finely attired ladies and their smart naval husbands, Admiral Tyler's offi-cers, were seated on the heavy wooden pews. On the other, the officers of the *Pallas* sat rigidly upright. It appeared that Miss Raithwaite's preference for punctuality might, on this occasion, have failed. No doubt putting the finishing touches to her wedding gown, or some such matter. Or so Nathaniel thought. Not for one minute did he consider that the object of his affection's delay could be due to another reason all to-gether—that perhaps the strong-willed Miss Raithwaite was suffering a late resurgence of conscience.

'I cannot marry him,' avowed Georgiana with surprising force. 'He must not make such a monumental self-sacrifice.' She sat herself down abruptly in the parlour chair, oblivious to the crushing of the delicate pale pink silk of her train. The tiny rosebuds and pink pearls clustered around the neckline heaved dramatically with the agitated thrust of her bosom. 'No, it won't do at all.' Her fingers seized upon her ear lobe setting the single pink pearl earring dipping and diving in a veritable frenzy of motion.

Mrs Howard, far from lapsing into hysterics at the sudden change of mind in her charge and the rapid ticking of the clock, calmly faced Miss Raithwaite with a steely eye. 'No, indeed, it won't,' she said, swaying the intricacies of her clas-sically styled hair with a delicate shake of the head. 'Of course you must not marry him if you feel that it would be a mistake to do so.'

Georgiana glanced up, somewhat surprised at the modiste's agreement. She had expected at least some semblance of persuasion.

'Captain Hawke will already be present and waiting in King's Chapel. Shall I send a maid along to inform him by way of Admiral Tyler that you're jilting him at the altar?' Her voice was silky smooth, her eyes flashing the colour of sword blades. 'Don't concern yourself that he'll suffer overly much from the pity of his own officers—oh, and, of course, Admiral and Lady Tyler, and the rest of Gibraltarian society. He's a strong man, and one who is, after all, due to sail tomorrow morning.'

Georgiana opened her mouth to argue, but promptly closed it again when Mrs Howard returned, 'No, Miss Raithwaite. Kindly do me the honour of allowing me to finish what I have to say.' And so she continued. 'The scandal shall be short-lived. And I'm sure that his honour will still guarantee you a passage home aboard the *Pallas,* so there's no need for you to worry on that score either. Perhaps the journey within such confinement will give you time to explain to the captain how your treatment of him is a fitting reward for all that he's done. Risking his very position within His Majesty's Navy for a woman, only to have her jilt him, and in such a very public way. No, you're quite right, Georgiana, one's conscience must always be clear, no matter the consequences suffered by others in its purging.' She rose in one fluid movement and made to ring the bell. 'I'll dispatch the maid immediately. No point in prolonging Captain Hawke's ordeal.'

'No!' Georgiana cried. 'Your words have shown my thoughts as shallow and petty. I've been absorbed with myself, never thinking of the harm I may do Captain Hawke with my childish notions. Mrs Howard, please forgive my foolishness. My mind has been quite overcome with selfish emotion.'

Mrs Howard reached for Georgiana's hands. 'It's common for young ladies to experience such doubts just before their marriage. Cast them away, hold your head high, and with a stoic countenance do what you must to complete what this day has started.'

'Thank you.' Georgiana's voice was small, her heart suitably chastened, as she accepted Mrs Howard's embrace. 'Mrs Howard, I do believe we have a wedding to attend.'

And with that the ladies made ready to depart the modiste's establishment for the very last time.

Nathaniel's hands were growing somewhat clammy and a gnawing feeling of unease had developed within his stomach. It appeared that Miss Raithwaite's outfit must be in need of complete restyling or something else was very much wrong. John Anderson was shifting his weight between both feet, small beads of perspiration collecting upon his upper lip and brow. He pulled nervously at his neckcloth before glancing for the umpteenth time at his commanding officer. A murmur of disquiet had set up within the party as they sat bathed in the colourful light from the great stained glass window. Nathaniel had just made up his mind to send a messenger to Mrs Howard's residence when he spotted the lady herself.

Georgiana looked splendid in a pseudo-Greek classical gown of the palest pink coloration. With her dark hair swept up and adorned with a bandeau of pink rosebuds, she looked nothing but beautiful. Her ivory skin seemed to have been carved from alabaster and the single row of fine seed pearls fastened around her neck mirrored those sewn so painstakingly around the neckline of her dress and upon the three-quarter-length gloves that covered her arms.

She looked down the aisle and saw Nathaniel's tall tense

figure. Even as her eyes rested upon him he turned and looked at her. In that single moment time stopped for Georgiana. For her, there was no one else in the church. Even across the vast distance of the aisle she could see the relief in his eyes, and she cringed that she alone had set such a worry there. Had she really contemplated jilting the man? Surely only madness could have prompted such an idea? For Georgiana knew without a doubt that she could wish for nothing more than to be the wife of Nathaniel Hawke. She loved him, it was as simple as that. Her silly fears and idle threats had centred around depriving herself of that which she most desired. Yet Evelina Howard had forced her to see that, in denying herself, not she, but the very man that she cared most for would reap the cruellest of punishments. A shudder rippled down her spine at the thought of what she had almost done in the folly of her anxiety. Now, here, in this church, in his presence, she felt no fear, no worry, no imaginations of the future or gloomy speculation of what it would mean for them both. There was nothing. Only Nathaniel Hawke. And the woman that loved him. She took Admiral Tyler's arm, smiled, and walked slowly, steadily towards the one person that she wanted most in the world.

Captain Hawke's eyes swept down over the woman seated by his side and felt a swell of possessive pride. His wife. His sweet Georgiana. And not for the first time wished that the wedding breakfast might soon be over so that he could speak with her, and more. She was smiling, a picture of youthful vivacity, captivating, polite, everything a man could wish his wife to present to society. Quite deliberately he moved his thigh beneath the table to brush against hers. Watched with pleasure when those sea-blue eyes met his with surprised delight. A secret smile meant only for him. And he revelled in it, the desire to hold her to him, to protect her from any hurt, growing strong and deep within him.

Georgiana conversed admirably with all present at the table, the very picture of the happy bride. She had remembered to apologise for the tardiness of her arrival, a matter that was waved inconsequentially away by a magnanimous Admiral Tyler and his lady wife. Lady Tyler seemed in such high spirits, spouting forth maxims of romance and love at such regular intervals as to suppose that she herself might have been the bride. Amid responding graciously to her hostess and exchanging pleasantries with Lieutenant Pensenby, Georgiana still found time to watch the man beside her, the man who was now legally, and in the eyes of the Church, her husband. The dark dangerous eyes frequently swept in her direction, and in them was such indisputable affection that the breath almost caught in her throat. Perhaps Mrs Howard had been right, and Nathaniel Hawke had a care for her after all. For surely there could be no mistaking the message so clear in his gaze? Excitement fluttered in her chest, and when the strong warmth of his thigh brushed hers she felt the blood rise to her face and smiled up at him. A promise between them sealed. Secret, honourable, binding, for ever.

Georgiana pushed the curtains further back to uncover the window from which she had been examining the view of the town below. Beyond the streets of illuminated houses a smoky sky smudged with the onset of night, the horizon highlighted in a golden glow that deepened finally to a rich burnished red. Waves lapped gently upon a tranquil darkening ocean, and the topmasts of the *Pallas* were silhouetted in the distance.

'It'll be a fine day tomorrow, just right for us to set sail. When I was young my nurse taught me a saying: "Red sky at night, shepherds' delight; red sky in the morning, shepherds' warning." Look at the sunset, it's beautiful.'

Nathaniel came to stand behind his wife. 'But not as beautiful as you,' he murmured against the shell of her ear. His arms enclosed around her waist, feeling the soft silk of her gown and the warmth of the woman beneath. His lips nibbled insistently at her ear lobe.

She sighed and relaxed against him. 'It was kind of Admiral and Lady Tyler to let us spend the night here.' The thought of them both squashed within the cot in Nathaniel's night cabin with the entirety of the crew knowing full well what they were about brought a blush to her cheeks. 'I can scarcely believe that we're married now. It seems so strange to bid farewell to both Master Robertson and Miss Raithwaite. I'm fast running out of personas!'

He heard the laughter in her voice. 'That's just as well,' he replied, 'for you'll be no other than Georgiana, Lady Hawke. You had best grow to like it, as I don't intend to let you use any other.' He chuckled and pressed his lips to her neck. The subtle aroma of roses tickled his nose, and he inhaled against the soft white skin. 'You smell rather different to George Robertson. Did I ever tell you that my nephew-cum-ship's boy, emitted the most robust odour of the sea? Indeed, on laundry days it was wise to stay upwind of the boy!' Mirth creased his eyes.

'Oh, you exasperating man!' Georgiana exclaimed and swatted the muscular arms encircling her waist. 'I didn't smell any worse than the rest of the crew, and well you know it!'

'Even on a laundry day?' he teased.

She wriggled round to face him. 'And whose clothes was I commanded to scrub in that foul-smelling fluid? I'll be happy never to see that barrel ever again!'

He dropped a kiss to the top of her carefully arranged curls. 'And neither you shall. The captain's wife will find her journey to England somewhat different to that of poor George Robertson, that I promise you. Indeed, I'm quite looking forward to resuming the comfort of the cot in my night cabin.' One dark eyebrow angled dangerously.

A delicate hue of tender pink suffused her cheeks at his mention of the intimacies that lay ahead. 'You're quite incorrigible, Captain Hawke.'

'What's all this *Captain Hawke*? Next thing you'll be saluting me! We're married now, you must call me Nathaniel, as I will call you sweet Georgiana.'

She snuggled in closer to him, laying her cheek against the hard muscle of his chest. 'Nathaniel,' she breathed, listening to the thud of his heart, 'you're so kind to me, even after all the trouble I've dealt you. I must confess I feel guilty that I've forced you to this marriage against your will. Can you ever forgive me?' She stood quite still, not daring to move her face or meet his gaze, just waiting, waiting, for his answer.

Nathaniel gently held her from him and stared down into her face. His voice was soft and melodic. 'What makes you think that I didn't want to marry you?'

'Why, given the foolish position in which I'd placed us both, marriage was the only way for you to save my reputation, and protect yourself from a possible court martial. I know you to be a man of honour. Twice you've saved me from death or worse, without thought for your own situation. And for your pains you're rewarded with the burden of an unwanted wife.' Eyes the colour of the Atlantic on a wild day regarded him solemnly, huge within the pallor of her face. Tension racked her shoulders and the swell of her bosom raised and lowered with a steady control.

His dark head gently lowered to hers, moving until the tips of their noses just touched. And once there he gently rubbed against her. 'Georgiana, I know that you didn't plan to land upon the *Pallas*. It's true that your presence aboard the ship presented us both with difficulties, and that neither of us had anticipated such a situation arising. Believe me when I tell you that this marriage is very much of my making. As a gentleman I was honour-bound to wed you, but as Nathaniel Hawke—' his lips moved softly to brush hers '—I *wanted* you as my wife.'

'But…' Georgiana regarded him in bewilderment, afraid to allow herself to believe what she thought he might be saying.

'No buts, sweetheart, never any buts. In the time I've come to know you, I'm persuaded that no other lady could fulfil that role quite so well. So, you see, if anyone should feel remorse it should be me, for it was I who took advantage of a young and innocent lady within my care.' Warm breath tickled upon her skin as he traced the line of her jaw with a myriad of butterfly kisses.

The magical allure of his mouth's motions served to render her a trifle light-headed, but she could not let him take the blame so gallantly for something that she herself had encouraged. Indeed, had she not dreamt of his kisses from their very first encounter? 'Nathaniel.' His name sounded silky smooth to the roll of her tongue. 'You did nothing that I didn't want, took nothing that I didn't give freely. And know this—' her palms pressed against the strength of his body '—I would have given you much more than you took.'

A small rumble started from deep in his throat, and his mouth captured hers with an insistent passion. Lips sliding together, moist, hot, in desperation. 'Georgiana,' he whispered.

His kisses enlivened her, emboldened her beyond a level

she had reached before, goaded her to tell him the truth she had sworn never to reveal. 'Indeed, that night, that single night, when you lay upon me in the cot and kissed me, I didn't want you to leave, only to stay the whole night beneath the covers in my arms.' She felt wanton, giddy, but strangely unashamed. 'Are you shocked and disgusted with me?'

'Never!' he murmured against the soft lobe of her ear as he feasted on its tender flesh. 'You don't know what it is you would have asked.'

She twisted against him, moving her lips to press a line of small hot kisses against his throat. 'Not then, but I do now. Mrs Howard has warned me of my wifely duties.'

His voice guttered low, a hoarse whisper and no more. 'It's no duty, in truth I'll force nothing of you. Given freely or not at all.'

Slender fingers touched to the roughness of his chin, pulling it lower, so that she could look directly into those burning brown eyes. 'You're a good man, Nathaniel Hawke. I've known it since you plucked me from the Borne. I'm yours, I'll always be yours.'

His lips caressed her cheek, moving to claim the tender-shaped form of her mouth. She opened to his touch, meeting the entry of his tongue with her own. Sensation flickering down her spine, sparks of desire rising from the banking heat growing within. Those long tanned fingers traced magic upon her skin, leaving in their wake a path of awakened sensitivity. For all the time that Mrs Howard had taken to fit the elegant rosebud wedding gown to Georgiana, Nathaniel Hawke removed it deftly and with the speed of a sailor retracting the sails in the path of a burgeoning storm. The petticoats and stays were laid carefully upon the chair, leaving her female form clearly visible beneath the sheer material of her shift.

'Georgiana!' The word sounded guttural in his harsh expiration of breath. And when his hands reached out to touch her she could feel the tremble within them. He pulled her to him, his strong fingers sweeping the length of her back to cup her buttocks.

The neckcloth tugged once beneath her hands before she tossed it to the floor and returned to pull at his shirt. In a flurry of impatience he disrobed all except his fine midnight-blue breeches, which, mindful of his new wife's innocence, he determined to retain so as to save her from any fright. He had reckoned without Georgiana's blossoming passion. As he kissed her, her back arched against the poster of the bed and he felt her fingers move to the fastening on his breeches. 'Take them off.' Her voice was low and throaty with escalating desire.

Nathaniel did not need to be told twice. He watched her eyes as they dropped lower. 'Don't be afraid,' he whispered. Strong fingers slipped the fine woven shift to pool upon the Oriental rug, touching where he had ever longed to trace. Along the smooth flesh of her stomach, sweeping over the rounded curves of her hips.

The peaks of her finely formed breasts teased against the dark hair matting of his chest, causing her to gasp in an agony of spiralling need. His taut manhood probed her belly, and she wriggled against him. She felt his intake of breath before she heard it. And his strong arms moved to sweep her up on to the bed. He knelt over her, licking kisses down her neck, moving ever closer to her breasts until at last his wet tongue flicked against the rosy peaks. Georgiana's thighs burned hot and hard, even while her insides elicited a curious melting sensation. Her fingers wove between his dark glossy curls, his hair sleek and glossy to her touch. Soap and sandalwood and something that caused her to cry out his name. He slid lower, kissing the silky hidden skin of her thighs, his breath scorching other hidden places until she trembled from the need rising within her, knowing nothing but her love for the man above her and the rising pleas of her body. At last he moved away, his lips skimming her before he uttered his warning, pausing even in the depths of his passion to reassure her. With one thrust she was his, the pain dispersed by the gentle words in her ear and the soft touch of his thumb teasing her lips. He lay quite still until she eased around him and only then did he reveal to her the age-old game that escalated in such a fountain of pleasure for both its players.

Georgiana lay sated and content. Nathaniel's arms curled around her, the light touch of his sleeping breath rhythmic upon her shoulder. This night had changed her for ever, for she knew with irrefutable certainty that she loved the man beside her, the man who was now her husband. And for all that he had not uttered the words, she had seen in his eyes, his deep dark eyes, that she had captured a place close to his heart.

Chapter Ten

Georgiana was doing her best to alleviate Mrs Howard's sea-sickness. The poor woman had been unable to retain one morsel of food within her stomach since leaving the port at Gibraltar. Indeed, they had been only thirty minutes into the journey when her normally creamy complexion paled. By the Saturday afternoon her skin had taken on a greenish tinge and had stayed that way ever since. None of Georgiana's ministrations seemed to make the slightest difference and even Nathaniel declared he had never seen such a bad case. Such was the lady's malady that Georgiana was unable to leave her, spending the night-times in a hammock strung close by Mrs Howard's narrow cot in the first lieutenant's cabin. John Anderson had gallantly offered to share with Cyril Pensenby since the ladies had come aboard. The small room was crushed enough with only Georgiana and Mrs Howard in it. Heaven only knew how Lieutenants Anderson and Pensenby were coping. The hammock reminded Georgiana of her time amidst the midshipmen and ship's boys, with only fourteen inches separating each man, or boy for that matter. But she did have to admit that, even when sleeping in a hammock, the captain's wife commanded softer, warmer bedding than that of any ship's boy. Her mind flitted briefly to young Sam Wilson.

She rubbed a small spot of tension on her forehead and allowed Nathaniel to massage her shoulders.

'You must not take it all upon yourself, my sweet, you're wearing yourself out. Much more of this and *you* shall be ill. Take a break, she'll be safe alone for one night.' Nathaniel pressed a tender kiss to the nape of his wife's neck and slid his arms down to capture her waist. Even as he made the suggestion he knew that Georgiana would never default in her duty to Mrs Howard, determined in the knowledge that she owed the modiste so much. They both did. But fatigue showed clearly on Georgiana's wan features, from the shadows beneath her lacklustre eyes to the faint droop in her normally erect shoulders. 'I'm worried about you,' he uttered against the softness of her skin.

'Well, you mustn't be,' came the reply. 'Save your worry for Mrs Howard, for I fear that if she doesn't improve she'll be gravely ill, or much worse, by the time we arrive back in Portsmouth.' Georgiana stood on her toes and kissed that full firm mouth.

'In that case we had best have Belmont examine her.'

Where her lips had lingered she now traced a delicate finger. 'Mrs Howard will not like it,' she argued. 'She could scarcely endure the glance of his eye upon her.'

'Captain's orders,' pronounced Nathaniel in a masterful tone. 'It is for the lady's own good. And we shouldn't risk her health for the sake of her sensibilities. If you are present during the examination, I think her reputation will withstand it!'

Georgiana nodded. 'You're right, but she won't like it.' And, so saying, she dragged her tired body off to prepare Evelina Howard for the arrival of Mr Belmont.

* * *

Mrs Howard fared no better despite suffering the indignity of a physical examination under the surgeon's hands. In her weakened state it was all she could do to force a little water down, and she knew that it would not be long before that small luxury would grow stale and slimy. Thus, she finally succumbed to Georgiana's suggestion to try a little grog, which, surprisingly and much to her chagrin, proved to be the tonic that settled her stomach like no other. Although she was still of a nauseous disposition and kept to her cabin, the utter wretchedness of her situation eased, allowing Georgiana a little time to herself. It was therefore at the earliest opportunity that the captain's wife sought out the company of ship's boy Sam Wilson down in a darkened corner of the gunroom.

The boy was staring at her rather uneasily. What did the captain's lady want with him? Scared that he had said or done something to insult her exulted person, he said nothing, waiting for her to reveal what she wanted with such a lowly being as himself.

'Master Wilson, Sam,' she began. 'I wished to enquire as to your welfare. Is the food to your liking? Are the slops you wear warm enough against the increasing cold?'

Sam stared at her as if she'd grown two heads. Why did Lady Hawke care about as poor a boy as him? 'Yes, thank you, m'lady.' He bowed his head.

The lad was plumper than when he'd left Portsmouth, an observation that brought the hint of a smile to Georgiana's face. 'You must tell me if you're unhappy, do you promise?'

'Yes, m'lady,' he said slowly, still puzzled. She smelled sweet like flowers in summer, and glossy black ringlets peeped from beneath her fancy bonnet. Even in the faint light filtering through from the gratings in the deck above he could see that her skin was white and smooth. He thought it would feel soft to touch, but did not dare to even move towards her.

'Are the others kind to you?' she asked.

As if he could say nothing else he repeated the same words.

'And have you not a best friend aboard the *Pallas*, one who helps you, and looks out for you?'

The little lad nodded vigorously, apparently forgetting his shy reserve. 'Oh, yes,' he replied. 'I'm mate to the best sailor on this ship, able seaman Grimly, m'lady.'

She smiled at that.

'That's on account of George being taken poorly like. He was my friend before Jack.'

The name sounded slowly into a question. 'George?'

'George Robertson, m'lady. Jack said he got taken on as captain's boy 'cos he was the captain's nephew. He got sick and we left him behind. He was a good friend to me.' Sam's voice had taken on a wistful quality.

Georgiana placed her hand stoutly on the boy's shoulder. 'Don't worry, George will get better and come home to England. I'm sure he much prefers the sunshine of Gibraltar to the stormy skies that lie ahead.'

'That's what Jack said. But he didn't look too happy about it. I heard 'em talkin, when they didn't know I was listenin'.'

'And what did they say?' A horrible suspicion was forming deep within Georgiana's gut. She tried to keep her voice light as if Sam's answer wasn't so very important.

Sam wiped his nose on the back of his sleeve and leaned forward conspiratorially as he'd seen men do when they said anything of any importance that they did not want all and sundry to hear. 'That the captain had no choice, that George would have spread the disease to us all.'

Relief swamped her and the tight coil of gathering tension sprang loose.

He sniffed again. 'But they all said that the captain didn't care a stink about George once he met you, m'lady. Never even called to see him, or let Mr Belmont treat him once. Right sore they are about that.' It did not occur to young Sam that a lady might take insult at learning such a rumour regarding both her husband and herself.

Foreboding was a fine thing, especially once you'd let yourself be lulled into a false sense of comfort. 'Thank you for telling me, Sam.' She thought quickly. Discontentment below decks was the last thing Nathaniel needed right now. She wetted her lips and offered as best an explanation as she could think of. 'Captain Hawke couldn't visit George for fear of bringing the disease back to the *Pallas*. But I've seen with my own eyes his concern for the boy. He sent for word of his condition every day and was greatly worried about him. He didn't want to cause panic amidst the crew, so was careful not to speak of it.' Without thinking she pressed her arm around the boy's thin shoulders, looking down kindly into his face. Poor little lad, he was scarcely older than Prudence and Theo. 'And now you alone have the truth of it, Sam, and the next time you hear the men discussing the matter, you'll be able to set them right.'

He nodded sagely, liking the feel of the lady's soft arm around him. 'Yes, m'lady,' he said and saluted.

Georgiana pressed a small kiss to his forehead while he stared up at her with great round eyes. 'Now I'd best return to my work, Master Wilson.' And she walked away, leaving young Sam basking in the glory of her rose-scented fragrance and intrigued by the discovery that even the captain's wife worked.

* * *

Seated within the captain's cabin, Evelina Howard managed a small crooked smile when Georgiana relayed what she had learned from young Sam Wilson. Still pale, she was at least contriving to keep down the breakfast she had eaten. 'It seems that ship's boy Robertson made quite an impression with the crew. They must be an unusual lot if they show such concern over the boy.'

Captain Hawke attempted an explanation. 'It's not so much that they cared overly for George, rather it's more a matter of loyalty and of fair treatment, Mrs Howard. The men are as one family when this ship is at sea. The welfare of each depends on the co-operation of all. Each man must do his job and do it well, so that we all survive. The captain is no exception to that truth. His decisions are difficult to make, sometimes requiring the sacrifice of one for the benefit of many. Life at sea is harsh, they all know that. I had thought they'd understand that a boy suffering with what looked to be yellow fever couldn't possibly take his place aboard the *Pallas,* even if he were the captain's nephew. To do so would be to place the entire crew at risk. Besides, Gibraltar is the best place for him as the Rock suffered a pestilence not four months since, and the hospital will know well how to treat him.' Nathaniel looked stern, unbending.

Georgiana looked up into her husband's face with its angular dark brows pulled low over the burnt umber of his eyes. It seemed that with each passing day she loved him more. 'Perhaps their disgruntlement stems not so much from the fact that the boy was left behind, but more from the secretive aura that surrounded the affair. Mr Belmont was never permitted to examine him, and you never spoke with them to inform them of the situation.'

'To reveal my suspicions that he carried yellow fever would have caused panic on this ship. Mr Belmont, as a surgeon with little training in the skills of a physician, would have been quite unable to treat the boy, and such a visit would only have served to expose him to the possible contagion.' Captain Hawke's hands were clasped behind his back, allowing the ladies a full frontal view of the fine white shirt, neatly tied neckcloth and white embroidered ivory waistcoat. 'I'll have a subtle word with Anderson, that should do the trick.'

A small laugh emitted from Mrs Howard. 'I declare that I've not had so much entertainment in many a month. You two would do justice to one of Mr Shakespeare's plays!'

Husband and wife turned to look at her, expressions of puzzlement upon their faces.

'I merely meant that to hear you converse, one might be mistaken in feeling some element of sympathy for that poor boy left behind on Gibraltar. A boy who does not exist,' Mrs Howard explained.

'I feel as if he did,' said Georgiana. 'The friends that I made, the way that people treated me… It gave me a glimpse of a life outside my own, of a life that I could never possibly have hoped to understand. It was a valuable experience that I'll never forget.'

The silver eyes glowed with compassion and Mrs Howard pressed a large hand to Georgiana's. 'I didn't mean to distress you, my dear.'

A smile lit Georgiana's face. 'You must think nothing of it, ma'am, as I'm not at all distressed. I'm grateful that I've seen life from another's perspective.'

'There's a very good reason why we must continue to refer to George in such terms. It would be too easy to forget ourselves and speak otherwise in the company of the men or the officers.

The last thing we need is for an incriminating comment to be carelessly overheard. And there's always the risk that someone will see a resemblance between Georgiana and George. No, the sooner we reach Portsmouth the easier I'll rest.'

Captain Hawke's last comment left the little party feeling somewhat perturbed. The man himself strode off to communicate with his lieutenants. Mrs Howard retired to her cabin with the headache. And Georgiana suppressed the glacial feeling that someone had just walked over her grave.

It was just three days later that Georgiana had very good reason to recall the words of concern that her husband had uttered.

Surprisingly the day was dry, the absence of rain corresponding to a marked decrease in the temperature. The air fairly crackled with cold across a clear blue sky. Although the sun had not yet made an appearance the light was bright, a welcome change from the dismal murky skies that had recently plagued them. Ice had formed upon the rigging and on the casks, rendering the simplest of jobs difficult, not helped by the fact that the cold had forced the men to squeeze their callused feet into shoes that slipped so easily upon the deck. Despite donning as many items of clothing as they could, they were pained by the extreme bite in the air. Fingers and toes burned red raw, and breath caught as smoke shuddered from chilled lungs.

Given that the sea had calmed its white frothed swell a little, Georgiana and Mrs Howard decided to take some fresh air by a short walk along the quarterdeck. Evelina's demeanour had markedly improved since taking her daily ration of grog—not that she would have admitted to drinking such a thing to any other living person. Indeed, it was only by explaining that the medicinal properties were most probably due to the lime juice rather than the water, the sugar, or, heaven forbid, the rum, that Georgiana had persuaded the lady to continue with her consumption. The cold nipped two patches of pink to her cheeks, endowing her with the most healthy appearance since the *Pallas* had left Gibraltar. As there had been insufficient time to prepare an entire wardrobe, Georgiana had few warm clothes in her possession. She was dressed, therefore, in a sturdy walking dress of a bottle green with a cashmere shawl wrapped snugly around her shoulders. The cream bonnet, with dark green ribbons, tied firmly to her head, and matching gloves offered little protection against the ferocity of the temperature, but as the ladies did not intend to dally long upon the open deck Lady Hawke was not too disconcerted by the rasping cold.

The view was spectacular, all yawning clear sky above and icy swirling water below. Gulls hovered on air currents unmindful of the chill and the sun emerged to light the pale white blue of the waves. Georgiana and Mrs Howard were just making their way back across the main deck to retreat towards their cabins when they heard the shout.

'Man overboard!'

Georgiana's heart set up a patter, the wintry freeze seeping from her skin through to the pit of her stomach. Images of the cold blue ocean leapt in her mind. No man could survive immersion in that. Her eyes met Mrs Howard's horrified stare. She stopped, paused for a heartbeat, and then without having exchanged as much as a single word the two women turned and ran to where they could see a small crowd amassing. Nathaniel was there before them, his cheeks ruddy from the bite of the weather.

'Bare the masts and lower the cutter!' he yelled.

Beyond the polished outer rail, out amidst the silver blue

swell of water, a small figure bobbed, tiny arms flailing, the faint strains of a voice carried away by the wind.

Forward progress halted. The *Pallas* bobbed on the undulating waves as the boat was lowered to meet the bitter waters. Men had gathered, watching, praying, while Jack Grimly and Billy Todd rowed closer to where the figure had disappeared. Tension tightened, time ticked by, the deck of the *Pallas* so quiet as to hear a pin drop. Against the silence a roar went up, cheering, men slapping one another on the back. A limp figure pulled from the icy depths, hoisted back aboard.

Georgiana felt Nathaniel close behind her. His strong voice sounded quietly in her ear. 'Go below, Georgiana. This may not be a pretty sight.'

She turned her head to where he had been, but he was gone, striding across the deck to meet Jack Grimly and his sodden parcel.

Georgiana's insides turned to ice, her husband's warning forgotten in an instant. Nausea quickened in her gut, for across the distance she could clearly see the small thin body, the sandy hair flat and dark with water, and the white pinched features.

'Sam!' The name erupted loud and distraught from her lips, but she had no notion that she had spoken, running as she was to close the space between them.

He did not move, his face a carved effigy, white, waxen, his mouth edged with a gild of blue. Water trickled down the elfin chin as Nathaniel rolled him to his side and back again, touching his fingers to the stalk of a neck, shaking his own dark head as he did so. He rose and spoke quietly to able seaman Grimly.

'No! No!' she whispered. Her frozen fingers tugged at the ivory shawl, wrapped the cloth around the boy. She pulled the chilled wet body to hers, giving her warmth, taking his cold. Against her cheek, where his breath should have been, was stillness. 'Turn him upside down, quickly!' She glanced around her for a man large enough to do so. They watched her quietly with pained eyes. 'What are you waiting for?' she yelled.

Nathaniel stepped forward and took the body from her tender grasp. He moved to hand the boy to Jack.

'Nathaniel!' Her voice was urgent, high-pitched, panicked. 'Please!'

'It's too late, Georgiana. His heart doesn't beat nor does he breathe.' His voice was solemn, quiet in tone. He made to take his wife's arm, but she resisted.

'Please, Nathaniel,' she whispered. 'Please try. I've read of a man pulled from beneath an ice sheet who appeared to be dead; within the hour he had recovered enough to speak. What have we to lose?'

The men were watching him, compassion in their eyes. The boy was dead. The captain's wife grasping at straws, unable to face the fact, her softness serving only to highlight the tragedy of the situation. An ordinary seaman sniffed aloud, the bosun's mate cleared his throat, and tears trickled from Jack Grimly's roughened cheeks down on to the bundle within his arms. It heartened them to know that a fine lady could care so much for a dirty ship's boy whom she barely knew. They waited to see what the captain would do.

'Turn the boy upside down. Hold him by the ankles,' instructed Captain Hawke. He then delivered two hearty wallops to the boy's back. The figure dangled limp and unresponsive. Jack lowered him to the deck.

Mr Belmont raked a path through the crowd, dropped to his knees and examined the boy. Shocked eyes locked with the captain's. 'A heartbeat, albeit a faint one, but a heartbeat at that. And he breathes.'

A murmur sounded through the surrounding men.

'Thank God!' uttered Georgiana, and promptly knelt beside the surgeon, holding her hands around the thin flaccid shoulders, peering down into the deathly white face. The warmth of her breath whispered against the cold wet skin.

The eyelids flickered, a feeble splutter sounded.

'Sam, you're safe now. Mr Belmont will look after you and make you better.'

His clear tawny eyes opened, 'George.' The word was weak, gravel upon his injured throat. 'George,' he said a little more strongly, unable to move his numbed exhausted body. The curve of a smile played upon his pale lips and his eyes shuttered once more.

Georgiana smiled back and, removing her sodden glove, touched her palm to cup the boy's cheek. 'Sleep now, Sam, all will be well.'

It was not until she turned to Mr Belmont and saw the strange expression upon his face that she realised exactly what had just happened. The surgeon said nothing, just stared, eyes fast upon her, looking and looking as if he would peel back her very skin to find what was beneath. A quiver of fear darted in her chest and she raised her gaze to the men surrounding them, eyes scanning faces that for the main showed only relief and joy. But not Jack Grimly. The sailor was regarding her with a combination of disbelief and horror. Silent. Static. All of a sudden she felt chilled to the marrow, a terrible cold that seeped through, freezing, pervasive. She could not move. The breath caught in her throat. Blood pounded in her head. Dear Lord, what had she done? All of her fear and dread welled up, bursting forth in a surge of riotous emotion that threatened to overwhelm her. But the fear was not for herself, and neither was the dread. Only one person mattered.

And if she was not very much mistaken she had just thrown that man's reputation to the wind. She stumbled to her feet, only to find a pair of strong arms engulf her. Deep dark eyes met hers momentarily before he pronounced in a voice that would tolerate no defiance, 'The lad is babbling. Take him below, Mr Belmont, and see that he gets the best of care. For I had not thought that any man, let alone a boy, could beat the sea today.'

The crowd dispersed, the surgeon directing able seaman Grimly to carry young Sam. Jack looked directly into Georgiana's eyes and then was gone.

The green velvet of her dress hung heavy with frozen seawater, dragging her down to meet the dark-stained planking. Her head ached, a searing pain. Her eyes closed against it. She heard Mrs Howard's words, but they made no sense, just sounds buzzing distantly in her ears. It was so cold, so very cold. And to her added mortification she felt her knees buckle before someone somewhere lifted her up and she knew no more.

Captain Hawke touched a hand to the boy's brow and spoke quietly. 'Will he live?'

The surgeon wiped his hands upon the cloth and moved to spread another blanket over the small form. 'No reason why he shouldn't.' Mr Belmont's eyes met the captain's and looked away again. 'With his hammock strung close to the galley fire he's as warm and dry as he's going to get aboard this ship. He's young and a hardy little thing.'

'Good. I don't want to lose the lad.' Nathaniel made to walk away.

'Is Lady Hawke recovered, sir? She seemed to have suffered a little in her bid to help the boy.' All the while Belmont's eyes did not leave Sam Wilson.

Nathaniel held himself taut, just waiting for the man to say what he knew he would. From the minute that the boy had uttered George's name to the sudden realisation dawning in the surgeon's eyes, he knew. Now he must do what little he could to salvage the situation. Let them say what they would—he was still the captain of the *Pallas,* and, as his wife, Georgiana still deserved their respect. And so he waited for what was to come.

'Captain—' Mr Belmont's voice sounded clear and loud enough for the men working around them to hear '—it's very common in cases of exposure to extreme temperatures for the patient to become dazed and confused. The boy is likely to confuse names, faces, people, but hopefully the effect will soon be remedied.' His gaze held Nathaniel's with a profound intensity. A silent promise, an affirmation of allegiance.

Nathaniel bowed his head in a small gesture of acknowledgement. 'Thank you, Mr Belmont,' was all he said, but those few words contained a wealth of gratitude and respect. They looked at one another a moment longer before the captain walked away to be about his business. He almost made it past the long guns with their open ports when a voice stopped him.

'Captain Hawke, may I speak with you, sir?' Lieutenant Pensenby appeared by his side.

Nathaniel gritted his teeth and waited for the second lieutenant to say the words.

Pensenby's voice lowered in volume. 'In confidence, sir.'

The two men climbed up and headed to the forecastle out of earshot of the crew.

'I saw what happened over there, heard what the boy said to Lady Hawke.' Pensenby's long face was gaunt in its austerity.

Nathaniel watched him carefully. 'What do you mean to do about it?'

The slight hint of colour rose in Lieutenant Pensenby's pale thin cheeks.

Seagull cries sounded overhead, the murmur of men below, creak of timber, lap of waves. Pensenby said nothing.

Nathaniel would not ask the question again. The wind ruffled through his hair, nipping at his face, but it was neither the wind nor the falling temperatures that drew the shiver down his spine.

When Pensenby eventually spoke there was an unusual stillness about him and his shrewd sharp gaze rested not on Captain Hawke, but far out to sea. 'I know what you think of me, sir. That I hold my position only because of who my uncle is.'

'I choose my own crew, Pensenby, you know that. Whatever Admiral Stanley might have done for you, he didn't secure your place aboard the *Pallas,* your own merit did that.' His gaze shifted to where Pensenby's lay.

'For the first time in my career,' replied the second lieutenant.

'But not the last.'

'We shall see.' The narrow lips pressed firm. 'It wasn't me that I came to speak of.'

'No,' said Nathaniel quietly.

Pensenby didn't turn his head, didn't even move his eyes from their distant focus. His words were slow, stilted. 'I knew from the first that there was something about George Robertson, something that wasn't right, but I never took him for a woman. Indeed, I must confess, Captain, to having thought the worst…about yourself, sir.' He looked at him then, with direct and bold eyes. 'It's a blessed relief to learn that my suspicions were wrong.'

'Indeed, it is,' said Nathaniel wryly.

'I wanted to tell you that you need not worry over the matter. Lady Hawke's reputation is quite safe. Most of the men will not have noticed, and I'll ensure that those who did never speak of it.' One bony hand extended. 'You have my word, Captain.'

A firm handshake, and Pensenby was gone.

Darkness had closed in upon the sky before Nathaniel returned to his cabin. Everything lay just as he'd left it that morning. Charts neatly stacked in a tidy pile, the log book, his quills… But everything had changed in the hours since. He found his way to the thin wooden door that led to the night cabin and knocked.

The room within was dark, the lantern unlit, the only light spilling in from the adjacent cabin. He could see her slender form seated upon the small wooden chair, her head held upright, her shoulders squared. She rose in a graceful motion, her figure too far recessed in the darkness to see her features. There was silence and the trace of summer roses. One strong long-fingered hand snaked forward and, enclosing her wrist, gently pulled her forward. The faint edges of the warm yellow lantern light glowed upon her face, revealing eyes that were trained steadily on his own. Standing there within the darkness, he felt the fatigue wash over him, pulling at his muscles, dragging at his mind. He leaned down to rest his cheek on the top of her head, inhaling the sweet fragrance of her hair, as his arms wound around the softness of her body.

'Georgiana,' he whispered into the silence, and the word dripped heavy and tired.

He seemed so weary, exhausted with disappointment. She closed her eyes tight to stop the fall of the tears that welled too readily. Little wonder that he was so saddened when she had just unwittingly undone all of his hard work. His cheek was warm and light upon her hair, as if even now he sought to hold the full weight of the burden from her. She turned her face up to his, noting the dark play of shadows. 'I'm so sorry,' she said. 'I thought only of the boy, nothing else.'

Still he said nothing, only holding her close, their two bodies merging as one within the amber flickering shaft.

And now that he was here, at last, she wanted to tell him that she would rather have ripped her heart from her breast than hurt him in any way, that yet again, through her own folly, some aspect of his life was at risk, that he deserved so much better—all the thoughts that had flooded through her head since that fateful moment. But those words would not come, tucked tight and deep inside. Instead, she found herself chattering on with all the indiscretion of Lady Tyler.

'He's only eight years old. Eight. Lived in Portsmouth all of his short life. His father was a man of the navy, died at sea six months since. Mother's a widow. Fond of the gin. Six little sisters. Sam thought to follow in his father's footsteps. That's why he joined the navy, that and the fact that his mother couldn't afford to feed him. God knows what will happen to all those little girls.' She paused as if to ponder on the question. 'When I saw him there, so pale and lifeless, I thought I couldn't bear it. Such injustice. How did he come to fall overboard? What was he doing?'

Nathaniel's deep voice rumbled low beside her ear. 'Helping the men to clear ice from the lower rigging. It seems that his shoes slipped on the ice, and unfortunately the safety rope around his waist came loose.'

She shook her head slowly. 'I didn't think any further than to save him. That life would breathe again in his frail little body, and when Mr Belmont said he was alive, I rejoiced. That small dear face. I didn't even notice that he'd called me George. Only saw his smile and was glad.' Her hands crept up to grip the top of his arms. 'Why should anyone take note of Sam's words? He was cold and shocked. Surely no one will take that one slip of the tongue seriously? He's just a child.' Her stormy dark eyes were pleading, her fingers biting. But even as she said it she knew what she'd seen in the surgeon's face, and Jack Grimly's.

'No one took Sam's mistake seriously, Georgiana. But by saying what he did, he exposed that inconceivable thought for the merest fraction of a second, and that, I'm afraid, was long enough to do the damage. Any association between the image you present now and that of George Robertson would be enough to alert those who'd dealt closely with my servant. The suggestion alone was our undoing.'

'Do they all know?' She clung to him, felt his muscles tense beneath her hands.

His long fingers slid to her shoulders to where her skin was bare and cold. 'It's too early to say. Mr Belmont does, but he won't speak of it. Of the others I'd guess Mr Anderson and Mr Fraser to have realised. Cyril Pensenby most definitely so. The men are an unknown entity. Only those close enough would actually have heard Sam's words.' He omitted to mention that gossip would soon inform those who had not. 'But it seems that you have something of a champion in my second lieutenant.'

'Lieutenant Pensenby?'

'The very one. He means to silence the men and protect your reputation.'

'Pensenby! I can hardly believe it.' Her eyes opened wide and round. 'But what of his uncle? Won't he tell Admiral Stanley?' She couldn't bear to think what that would mean for Nathaniel.

'No, Georgiana, I don't believe he will.'

Even if Nathaniel was right, gossip had a way of reaching those that it should not. 'Jack Grimly knows. He gave me such a strange look before he took Sam away. It was as if I'd betrayed him, which of course I did. I lied to him, to them all. It's not something of which I'm proud.' A shiver rippled down her spine.

Nathaniel wrapped his arms around her. 'You're cold, let me warm you.'

'I've ruined you after all,' she whispered so quietly that the words almost missed her husband's hearing.

'No, never that. Let's just wait and see what emerges. Fate has a strange way of contriving the outcome she always intended. Don't worry, Georgiana. You're my wife now, and that's enough to protect you.' He kissed her forehead, smoothing the worry furrow with the sweep of his thumb.

Her eyes held his, as dark a blue as ever he'd seen them. 'But what of Captain Hawke?' she asked. 'Is marriage enough to protect him?'

'Of course.' He swept her up into his arms, and laid her gently in the cot. And throughout the night, long and cold, he held her as if he would never let her go.

If Georgiana had thought the revelation to have earned the crew's condemnation, she was to be pleasantly surprised. The following day she could sense no discernible difference in the men's treatment of her but, even so, she was not foolish enough to indulge in the belief that they did not know. There were no whispers following in her wake, no utterances of George Robertson's name in her hearing, no stares, no cat calls. Even when she braved the elements to appear upon the forecastle in her woefully inadequate plain blue dress and matching pelisse, the men did not stare, only nodded their usual greeting in her direction. Nathaniel, who had been scanning the horizon with his spyglass, chided her for her presence.

'Georgiana, you'll catch your death up here, go below at once. Even Mrs Howard has had the sense to stay within her cabin.' A frown marred the strong angular face.

The weather was his excuse, of course. She knew that. Knew that he thought her appearance following yesterday's revelations to be foolish in the extreme. But she had to see for herself the damage she had caused, and for that small task she would have walked quite willingly into the very jaws of hell. He was regarding her with an expression of displeasure, his dark brows brooding and low. A shiver stole through her. It seemed that an icy coldness had beset her since Sam's unwitting utterance, and she could find no warmth to thaw it. Nathaniel might say that he did not blame her, but he was too honourable a man, too kind a man, to do such a thing. For, despite the words he shaped to comfort her, Georgiana was aware of the change within him. A wariness, a fatigue that had not been there before. The blame lay quite firmly with herself, she needed no other soul to tell her that. Her husband— the very words brought a sear to her heart—was right in his dictate to wait and see. It was quite naturally the sensible course to take. But the lack of action, amid the stretch of time ahead, wound Georgiana's nerves taut as cheese wires around a block. Waiting was not an activity at which Miss Raithwaite had ever excelled. She was a woman used to striking while the iron was hot. It had always been her way, much to the irritation of her papa.

She did not speak, merely turned and retreated from his domain, walking briskly down towards the hatch that led to the gun deck, a new determination in her step. Georgiana Raithwaite had not been content to sit back and meekly accept her stepfather's injustice. And neither would Georgiana Hawke. She loved Nathaniel, of that she was certain, and if she had gone to such ridiculous lengths in an attempt to thwart Walter Praxton, what more would she do to save the man that she loved? No matter the cost, no matter the sacrifice, Captain Hawke would not suffer the humiliation of a court martial, nor would he lose the *Pallas*, which he so loved. Georgiana would see to that.

Unaware of the burgeoning resolve within his wife's breast, Nathaniel was navigating the ship through worsening weather, creeping ever closer to their destination. With two further injuries from accidents in the rigging, the stormy seas, dark skies and pressing time, Nathaniel worked hour after hour, intent on making it home safely in time for Christmas. The torrential rain and lashing winds had delayed their progress, and although they had made up a little time during the subsequent cold snap, he could be nothing less than vigilant to meet his goal. For despite the short duration of their trip his men were tired, wrung out by the ferocity of the weather. The capture of their prizes seemed a long distant thing, and Nathaniel was keen to press the prize agent so that the men received their payments promptly.

They were good men, loyal to the last. Hadn't the incident with young Sam Wilson proven that? For all his denials to Georgiana, the matter did worry at him. It would be an impossible task to silence a whole crew, and the exact manner of their courtship would make interesting telling throughout the taverns on the cold winter nights ahead. Georgiana was his wife now. The damage had been limited. But that didn't mean he was about to stand back and allow any aspersions to be cast her way. Come hell or high water, he would do what he could to protect her.

Chapter Eleven

It was late in the day when Georgiana finally found an opportunity to converse with Jack Grimly alone. The orlop deck was deserted and in shadowy darkness as she silently dogged his footsteps along to the tools store. The smell of stale dampness hung heavy in the air. Just as his fingers reached towards the storeroom door she spoke. 'Mr Grimly, I wondered if you might spare me a few minutes of your time.'

His large body started and his head swung round in alacrity. 'Bloody 'ell! You nigh on gave me a right turn!' Then, recovering himself, he added, 'Beggin' your pardon, *Lady* 'awke, I've no wish to offend your ears with such language.' Without waiting for a reply he moved to wrench the door open.

'Mr Grimly.'

Jack's hugely broad back presented itself. He made no sign as to having heard.

'Jack!' The word was like a sigh on Georgiana's lips. 'Please. Won't you even listen to me?'

He turned and faced her then. 'If the captain's wife commands my attention, who am I to disobey?' His gaze was cold and hard, his tone no better.

What right had she to feel aggrieved at the contempt in his eyes? She'd taken what he had offered in good faith and given back nothing but dishonesty. No wonder she now suffered under his condemnation. 'Jack, I'm sorry that I lied to you. I'm sorry that I pretended to be someone that I wasn't.'

'Not 'alf as sorry as I am.'

She forced herself to look him directly in the eye. 'You trusted me and I betrayed you. I know that nothing can excuse such behaviour. I deserve your contempt in full, but Captain Hawke does not.'

Jack stood silent, waiting, a shadowed figure behind the flicker of his single lantern.

Taking a deep breath, she steeled herself to the task. 'I have no excuses. All that I can offer is my trust in return for the trust that you once had in me.'

She saw the cynicism, heard the utterance, 'Your *trust*?'

Refusing to give up, she stumbled on. 'When we met on the mail coach, I was fleeing my home. It seemed safer, at the time, to dress myself as a boy. I thought it would attract less attention and let me reach my destination unhindered.'

'Your destination?' he mocked. 'Running off with a lover, most like.'

'No!' Georgiana's denial was swift and determined. 'There was a lady who offered to help me…' The sentence trailed off unfinished. 'It doesn't matter now. All that I'm trying to say is that I had no notion that I would end up aboard this ship. It was never my intention to involve you, or Captain Hawke, or anyone else for that matter, in my harebrained scheme. But…well…somehow it happened.'

Something of the frostiness thawed from Jack's manner. 'Not *somehow*. You ruddy well jumped on that Press Gang Officer's back and tried to box his ears!'

'Only because he was punching you while you lay on the ground!' Her indignation was clear. 'What did you expect me to do, just let the two of them half-kill you?'

'Yes!' he shouted back, then shook his head and gentled his voice. 'It was bad enough when I thought it was a soft-brained lad who'd come to my rescue, never mind a slip of a *girl*!'

'Well, I don't see what difference it makes.'

Jack's eyes rolled firmly up into his skull before reappearing. 'You bleedin' well wouldn't!'

A rat scuttled by Georgiana's foot, but she resolutely held her ground. 'Regardless of that, once I found myself to be on the *Pallas* we had sailed and were out at sea. I couldn't just suddenly say, *"Please can you turn the ship around on account of my mistakenly being on board,"* especially when I saw who was captaining her. There seemed nothing else for it but to keep up the pretence.'

Jack's brow lowered suspiciously. 'What do you mean, *especially when you saw the captain*?'

Georgiana sighed and looked down into the darkness surrounding Jack's feet. 'Captain Hawke was not unknown to me. He'd already saved me when I ju…fell into a river.'

'God in heaven! What kind of lady are you? Running away from home, attacking officers of the Press Gang, nearly drowning?'

'I know that it doesn't sound good, but—'

'That's putting it mildly!'

'Urgent situations call for urgent actions.'

He looked at her soberly. 'Like the one where you shinned up the mast rather than 'ave a bath?'

'Yes,' she said simply, then added, 'I must admit that the sight of the cask bath being hauled up from the water was not a pleasant one.'

One bushy brown eyebrow raised. 'No, 'appen it wasn't.'

'My presence on board places Captain Hawke in a very difficult situation. He's never acted as anything other than a gentleman. Indeed, he even married me to try and repair the damage I've caused.' Her teeth gritted to prevent the waver in her voice. 'Hate me if you must, Jack, but please spare Nathaniel. He's paid enough because of my foolishness. Please don't push the cost any higher. There's nothing else that I can—'

One large hand moved to touch her arm. 'Lady 'awke—' he began.

Her eyes glittered brightly in the candlelight. 'My name is Georgiana, George to my friends.'

The silence stretched between them.

'You've 'ad a wasted journey.'

She stared disbelievingly into the big man's face. Not Burly Jack. He had a heart of gold, didn't he? 'Jack?' she queried quietly.

A soft chuckle sounded in the gloom. 'Why would you think that I'd let anything 'appen to Captain Hawke…or his wife? He's a good captain and there ain't too many of them around. Besides, Pensenby's already spoken to them that 'eard what young Sam said.'

Georgiana chewed at her lower lip. 'Lieutenant Pensenby?'

'He threatened to have us flogged around the fleet if we so much as made a whisper of it. Thought you'd know'd us better than that, George!'

The blue bonnet dipped low as the tears sprang to Georgiana's eyes. She tried to speak, but the only words that sounded were, 'Burly Jack Grimly, you are a very fine man!' And she hurled herself at the big man to embrace him in a bear hug.

Jack patted her arm affectionately before gently disengaging himself. 'Here, you'll have me in trouble for manhandling the captain's wife!'

Georgiana ignored his protests and, standing on her tiptoes, pulled his head lower to plant a small kiss on his roughened cheek. 'Thank you, Jack.'

The big man blushed crimson. 'Bleedin' 'ell, George, it's the least I can do when I'm the bloody reason you got pressed in the first place!'

Laughter filled the air, before Georgiana hurried up two decks to slip unnoticed back into the captain's cabin.

Walter Praxton sipped at his ale within the comfort of the inn, not even bothering to keep his eye on the window. Not that such an observation would have proved to be of much assistance in his plan, for the small glass panels were so steamed up that the dim light of day could scarcely penetrate the mist of condensation. Blakely would alert him as to when the *Pallas* came into the dockyard—that was, if he wanted the gold guineas that lay within the finely fashioned pockets of Praxton's forest-green coat—and Walter knew that the little man would do anything that he asked as long as the price was high enough. As if summoned by the mere act of thinking about him, the weasel-faced Bob Blakely appeared.

'Mr Praxton, sir, it's the *Pallas,* she's arrived. Best come quickly, for I don't fancy that they'll hang about for long in this weather.' Rain battered against the steamy windows just to highlight Blakely's point.

Shrugging into his many-caped great coat, Mr Praxton accompanied the sodden Blakely through the door. The streets were a muddied mess, puddles pooling to overflow into miniature rivulets. Walter's expensive leather boots strode through them all the same, splattering a pattern of mud speckles around the lower periphery of his overcoat. The stench of wet wool and filth drifted from his companion and a look of disdain flitted across his face. It was gone in an instant. Walter Praxton wasn't fool enough to upset the small smelly man. Blakely, after all, was still of potential use.

By the time they reached the allotted spot, the *Pallas* was neatly and securely anchored. A small group of men huddled as a welcome party, wet and windblown. An orderly rabble of crew started to clamber out of the first boat, a trail of rain-drenched bodies rapidly forming a crowd within the dockyard. The carts and waiting carriers and cabs poised themselves to receive their customers. Officer's sea chests were large and weighty, something that no man wished to carry far on a day like this. The boys and seamen lugged the wooden chests to the waiting recipients and, with a rapid salute, and a shake of the hand in some cases, were off.

Praxton's pale blue eyes narrowed as he scanned each figure leaving the ship. He had seen several boys, none of whom could possibly have been Georgiana. Was Blakely's information flawed? He pondered exactly what he would do if that proved to be the case. The little man's life wouldn't be worth living once Walter had finished with him. The thought spread a malicious grin across his handsome face. Never once did the narrow eyes waver from their cause, trained so obsessively on the emerging crew. A tall, well-built man came into view. Dressed smartly in a boat cloak and with his cocked hat catching the worst of the downpour, he held himself with supreme ease and self-confidence. Praxton did not doubt for a minute the man's identity, for it was abundantly clear from his demeanour that this was none other than Nathaniel Hawke, the captain of the frigate. Walter frowned— where the hell was

Georgiana? If Blakely had played him false… All thought broke off thereafter as Walter Praxton's jaw gaped, slack and open. He stared as if he could not believe what lay before his very eyes. There could be no mistake. For there, walking behind Captain Hawke, was Georgiana Raithwaite, and not dressed in the guise of some ship's boy either. From where he stood he could see that she wore a dark green walking dress that matched the colour of his own stylishly tailored coat. Around her shoulders was draped a pale woollen shawl, which seemed to be absorbing the English rain with the voracious capacity of a sponge. From beneath her bonnet peeped damp ebony ringlets that were fast losing the shape of the curl. The captain turned to her, offering his arm. Beside her walked a taller woman, dressed smartly as a lady in a walking dress and cape of dove grey. The rain was gradually darkening her attire to a deep smoky charcoal.

Walter watched as Georgiana willingly took the proffered arm, smiling up into the man's rugged face. Bitter gall rose in his throat; he felt a band of tension constrict his chest and the overwhelming urge to run Captain Hawke through with the blade of his sword.

Blakely was prattling on in the background. 'Don't see the lad, gov. Not one that meets your description. Maybe he didn't make it. Like I said, it ain't an easy life out there.'

Mr Praxton ignored him, all his attention focused on the object of his desire. It was one thing to say that he would take her no matter her sullied state, and quite another to witness her play the part of another man's mistress. His teeth ground together and his lips narrowed to a thin hard line. An image of her naked white body writhing beneath the tall, powerful man at her side arose unbidden to torture his mind. He clenched his knuckles and held his breath.

'You all right, gov? Lookin' a bit pale about the gills there, Mr Praxton.'

The narrow light eyes were focused far away.

'Mr Praxton, sir,' Bob persisted, rightly concerned that his payment wouldn't be forthcoming if the gent decided to take a flaky turn.

Walter Praxton forced the wash of imaginings away, and turned to the odorous Blakely. 'The woman on the captain's arm, find out who she is,' he hissed. A cold and malevolent light sparkled in his eyes. When Blakely did not move, he snapped derisively, 'Now!'

A few minutes passed in the blissful absence of Blakely's stench, watching the captain hand both women up into a waiting hansom cab. Hawke's tall frame issued instructions to the driver before setting the ladies on their way and tracing his steps back to the ship's master and the dockyard office.

Mr Praxton began to walk in long loping strides towards the few remaining vacant cabs.

Blakely caught at his arm as he threaded his way through the thinning crowd. 'Mr Praxton, the lady is the captain's wife. It's Lady Hawke.'

A chill of pure malice traversed Praxton's heart. Hawke had not only taken her to his bed, but had married the girl! All of his dreams, all that work, all that time, destroyed by Blakely's few words. Rage erupted within his chest, but he battened it down. No one made a fool of Walter Praxton, not even the woman that he had wanted for as long as he could remember. 'Find out all you can of Captain Hawke,' he barked at Blakely, 'and meet me tonight in the Crown.' And with that he was off, his leather riding boots kicking up a pattern across the mud.

* * *

Georgiana regarded Nathaniel's town house with a little apprehension. Not because it was small and somewhat spartanly furnished, or that the few servants had yet to remove their eyes from her. Rather, it was the knowledge that this place would see the start of her life properly as Captain Hawke's wife. While aboard the *Pallas,* everything had been so much more contained, a small world of its own. Now that she was back on *terra firma*, all her problems loomed large and oppressive. No more thinking, no more planning. Here in England she would have to act or leave Nathaniel to face the deplorable consequences of her mistakes.

Mr Fraser had accompanied them from the dockyard to the house located within St Mary's Street in Portsmouth. The elderly retainer set about chasing the gawking servants to light the fires and make the rooms ready. All this involved was a change of bedding as the house was maintained in a type of semi-ready alert, not knowing when the master was due to return. With only three bedrooms and one of these in use by the rather crotchety housekeeper, Mrs Posset, Georgiana found her few belongings delivered directly to Nathaniel's room.

Mrs Posset, a small apple-shaped woman of indiscriminate years, eyed Georgiana with obvious suspicion. No amount of reassurance from Mr Fraser seemed to alleviate the coldness from her glare. It was clear that she regarded herself as some kind of defender of her employer, and had cast Georgiana in the role of the wily strumpet who had hoodwinked a naïve milord into marriage. Not so very far from the truth, thought the new Lady Hawke rather grimly, although she would not go quite as far as to describe herself in such strong terms. The housekeeper was not so condemnatory in her attitude to Mrs Howard, sensing in that lady one who would come up trumps in any altercation into which she was drawn. Besides, Mrs

Posset reassured herself, the woman was far too old to present any real threat to milord. Not that this excused her for any part she may have played in assisting the scheming young lady, if one could call the trollop so, by her side.

Thus it was that when Nathaniel returned later that afternoon to the house in St Mary's Street, he found a rather gloomy state of affairs and Mrs Posset with a face like an angry terrier.

'The house is to your liking?' he ventured, unsure of how to deal with the new-found tension.

'Quite impeccable,' replied Mrs Howard with the utmost politeness of manner. What she did not say was that she was only suffering to stay in such an abode to protect Georgiana from the worst of Mrs Posset's sniping.

Georgiana nodded and curved her lips to a smile. 'Yes, it's a fine residence,' she managed.

But Nathaniel did not miss the bleakness in her eyes, nor their stormy grey palette, that he knew from past experience to be indicative that she was in low spirits.

The evening progressed without improvement, from the dinner that was served under the direction of the rather steely-eyed Mrs Posset to Mrs Howard's early retirement due to the headache. Indeed, he could have sworn he saw the housekeeper positively glower when Georgiana announced her intention to do likewise. But Nathaniel had little time to ponder as to what lay at the root of the glumness of the ladies' mood. He supposed it to be due to fatigue, nothing more. Life at sea was hard enough for a man. The toll it had exerted upon the two women was bound to make itself known. And, besides, there was a much more pressing matter monopolising Captain Hawke's attention.

* * *

An uneasiness lay heavy across Nathaniel's soul. Tomorrow they would travel to Collingborne, a place he knew that he was not welcome. Georgiana was his wife now, come what may, and, as such, it was time she was presented to his family. The earl had told him to take a wife, and so he had. But he was under no illusion as to what his father's response to Georgiana would be. When it came to Nathaniel the earl knew only one manner of behaviour, and Georgiana would not change that. Scornful bitterness. Nothing more, and nothing less. He did not doubt that his wife would be subjected to the same. And he had yet to utter a word of warning to the woman lying upstairs within his bed. He gulped at the brandy, allowing himself the short respite that its fiery deluge offered. How exactly did one go about informing one's wife that she was married to the black sheep of the family? That his father could not stand the very sight of him—indeed, that he blamed Nathaniel for the death of the countess? With slow measured steps Nathaniel made his way to the bedroom.

Georgiana lay quite still, rolled upon her left side within the small bed, the blankets pulled high to cover her chin. She did not look round when she heard her husband enter the room. She did not need to, for the crackling fire within the grate cast the flicker of his shadow clearly upon the wall. She watched while the shadowman disrobed, folding each newly stripped article upon the storage chest at the bottom of the bed. Even in the dark silhouette upon the painted surface she could see the athletic strength in his finely toned body. Her mouth felt suddenly dry. She could hear the soft tread of his footsteps across the rugs, the rustle of his clothes as they left his limbs. The mattress tipped as his weight settled upon it and her heart tripped fast into a canter of beats. He moved to mirror the curve of her body, curling around her as if they were two spoons laid one on the other. The essence of sandalwood and soap drifted to her nose. Her heart careered to a blatant gallop and she tried to swallow down her arid throat. The touch of his naked skin seared through the flimsy cotton of her nightgown, asserting his claim over her, proclaiming their intimacy.

'Georgiana.' The hush of his words caressed her shoulder. His right hand meandered over, brushing her breasts as it traced a path to the flat plane of her stomach.

The gasp escaped her spontaneously, ejaculating into the silence of the room.

'Are you asleep?' he asked, although he must have known from the sound and the tremble of her body beneath his enquiring hand that she was not.

She wriggled round to face him, her eyes smouldering a deep dark blue in the warm glow of the fire.

His fingers slipped round to linger against her firm rounded buttocks. 'It has been a long day, sweetheart, and I know that you're tired.' Shapely lips nuzzled affectionately against her forehead.

Georgiana's body felt enlivened, as if the heavy mantle of fatigue had dropped from her shoulders. Stirrings fluttered low in her belly and a surge of excitement coursed through her veins. She raised her lips to his. 'Not that tired,' she murmured as she plucked one sweet kiss.

A dark winged eyebrow flickered, but he did not move to take her. 'Patience, sweetheart.'

Georgiana wriggled with a growing enthusiasm. This time he smiled, but when his hand moved to stroke the softness of her short feathered hair she saw that his expression was not one of desire. His jaw was stiff with tension and his dark eyes serious. Her reaction died in an instant, torn apart by a sudden trepidation. Surely the Admiralty could not know so soon? She raised herself up on one elbow and stared at him with worried eyes.

'Nathaniel?' And in that one word was the question she did not dare to ask. 'They cannot know already. We only docked today. How can they know?' It was sooner than she'd expected, too soon.

'Hush, petal.' He suppressed a pang of guilt over the white lies, knowing exactly to what she was referring. A callused thumb touched to the soft pink cushion of her mouth. 'Georgiana, there's nothing to fear from the Admiralty. Not now, not ever.' He was still looking at her, aware of the tension. 'There's another matter of which we must speak. You should be prepared for what lies ahead.'

She said nothing, just delivered a slight nod of the head and waited for her husband to find the words. The lines deepened around his mouth and a furrow etched vertically between his dark angled eyebrows. Georgiana braced herself for what was to come. A horrible possibility made itself known to her: what if he meant to put her aside after all? Was that why he was looking like a man about to face the firing squad? A sudden ball of nausea heaved in her stomach. She swallowed it down, and waited with as much courage as she could muster to her cause.

The dark eyes shuttered. 'Tomorrow we travel to Collingborne House, the seat of my father, the Earl of Porchester.'

'And he won't be best pleased that you've married the daughter of a glorified innkeeper, even if he doesn't know the rest of the truth. You don't need to tell me, Nathaniel. I never expected anything else.'

A grimace twisted upon Nathaniel's full lips. 'Nothing

concerning me would ever please my father, so don't think that the reaction he may present is in any way connected to you.'

From the tautness of his musculature, she knew that he had touched upon a subject that pained his heart. In all that had happened, through all their trials, she had never seen him so patently distressed. 'I sense there's ill feeling between you and the earl. What has caused such a rift between you?' she asked as gently as she could.

He did not want to tell her. That wasn't supposed to be a part of this conversation. Just a warning, so that she would know what to expect before she arrived at the country house and witnessed the situation for herself. Yet he could not deny her the knowledge, felt that she had a right to know. If he did not tell her, she would only hear the story from another, and what guarantee had he that that person would not bias the truth?

She saw the light sheen of sweat upon his upper lip, felt his indecision. He sighed and then started to speak in his quiet and melodic tones.

'It all happened so long ago. Nine years to be precise. I was twenty and as foolish as any young man of that age. There was a house party that Henry and I attended. He hadn't met Mirabelle at that time and wasn't quite as long-jowled as he is now. On the final night our host held a ball in honour of his daughter, a girl of nineteen with a reputation for being a little fast.' He paused and shifted his gaze, his brow marring at the memory. 'I danced with her, and then she asked me to walk with her through the gardens. Said she was too hot in the ballroom. I should have declined, but I didn't. Once we were out of sight she made her intentions very clear. And I, fool that I was, responded to them. All the worse, for I knew what was being said of her.'

Georgiana said nothing, but it seemed that a heavy hand levered upon her heart.

'I don't wish to cause you pain, Georgiana, but it's better that you know the truth. There should be no secrets between us.' Brown eyes held blue with a stark intensity, and again the flutter of guilt brushed against him.

'Of course,' she murmured.

'I was kissing her when her father came upon us. Needless to say, you can fathom his response to discovering the situation. He demanded that I wed her, and I refused. She'd set out deliberately to entrap me. And it seemed rather strange that her father decided to walk through his orange house alone, at that time of night, when he was supposed to be hosting a ball. I later learned that the very same circumstance had taken place with another young gentlemen, who happened to be heir to an earldom. Dropped their sights a little when they selected me. Probably thought that my father would see to it that I married the girl. And he damn near did.' His breathing came fast and shallow, the sheen intensifying on his brow. He swallowed hard, more of a gulp, and waited for his wife's response.

'What happened?' Her voice was low and husky, her eyes overly bright.

'I explained the whole thing to my father and refused to marry the girl. I was labouring under the mistaken illusion that he would support me. Instead, he chose to believe the lies of a mere acquaintance over his own son.'

Georgiana understood the bitterness all too well.

'It wasn't as if I bedded her, excuse my blunt turn of phrase,' he uttered aside. 'But my father's a man to whom duty and honour are everything. He would have none of it. Called me a coward and worse. Said I was a disgrace to the family name and that he'd ensure that I received not one penny in inheritance if I didn't marry the girl. Well, I refused his instruction.'

Georgiana knew that feeling too, but kept quiet.

'I removed myself from Collingborne and joined His Majesty's Navy. The old man cut off my allowance and cursed me to the ends of the earth. We didn't speak for years.'

Georgiana's hand moved to cup his cheek. 'Oh, Nathaniel,' she uttered.

'That's not the worst of it. The rift between us caused my mother immense distress. She loved us both and was caught in the middle. She couldn't disobey him, but neither could she fully desert me. I still have all of her letters. Three years ago she became ill, a wasting disease that sapped her strength and eventually her life. With the little time she had left she tried to mend the breach between us. But I was chasing Villeneuve in a frenzy of skirmishes throughout that summer and by the time I received word it was too late. My mother died thinking that she'd failed in her bid, that I'd ignored her letters. My father blamed me for her death. Said that I'd driven her to it with my scurrilous actions. Since then he can barely stand to look at me, let alone exchange a word.'

It was a heavy and unfair burden that he carried. Through the bitterness of his words and the sadness of his story Georgiana at last gleaned an understanding of what it was that drove Nathaniel so hard. Little wonder that he sought to rise through the ranks, to make something of himself in the navy. He possessed a steadfast determination to prove that he was not the unworthy cause his father clearly thought him. Nine years of a father's hatred was a lot for any man to bear. That, and an unreasonable guilt for his mother's death.

Her eyes bound to his. 'Then why do we travel to Collingborne? We could just stay here and celebrate Christmas.' She quelled the sudden image of the hatchet-faced Mrs Posset. The price was a small one to pay for her husband's peace of mind.

'No.' He shook his head in one clear defiant gesture. 'You're my wife, Georgiana, and I want my family to acknowledge you. I needn't tell you that my father won't approve of you, disapproving so adamantly as he does of me. But I'm not ashamed of you, and I don't mean to hide out with you here as if I am.' His lips were firm in their resolve, his jaw line rigid. It was not a confrontation from which Nathaniel meant to back down.

She pressed small soft kisses to the fullness of his mouth, watched the tension melt away. 'Then we'll go to Collingborne,' she whispered lightly between kisses. And when his hand strayed to caress the low hollow of her back, and his eyes darkened to a dusky simmer, she knew that the image of his father was fading from his mind. With slow deliberate boldness she leaned against his shoulders, pushing him down against the crisply laundered sheet. He showed no resistance, following where she would lead. She rolled so that the full length of her body lay on top of him, a bed of firm muscle and long limbs. Even as she lay there, calm and still, she felt his interest stir against her. A small wicked smile curved upon her mouth. Before this night was out, Nathaniel Hawke would have no further thought of his father, of that she was quite determined.

Without further warning she rose to a kneeling position, straddling his thighs in a most indecent fashion. If Mrs Posset thought her a strumpet… Her smile deepened at the disapproval her current posture would have caused the housekeeper. Teasing her fingers through the coarse dark hair across the breadth of his chest, she balanced a tip against each darkened nipple. He was watching her through eyes filled with dark and dangerous passion. An intensity of expression, a spring coiled tight and strong. Her hands slid lower to explore the defined ripples down his stomach and abdomen.

He tensed beneath her and reached for her, murmuring her name with something akin to a growl. But before he could touch her she caught his hands, pressed them down to the soft rumple of the pillow above his head. When he would have moved she shook her head and stayed him with a kiss to the tautness of his stomach. He groaned and moved beneath her, eyes closed against temptation. She waited until his gaze found hers once more, then with a languorous grace peeled the nightgown from her body. It dripped slowly to the floor in a white frothy pool. She saw his eyes widen, watched her name shape upon his mouth. Slowly, surely, she moved to lower herself against the burning hardness of his masculinity. Nathaniel did not think of the earl then, or later that same night when they lay entwined together in sated contentment.

A white dusting of frost glittered in the bright morning sunshine, casting a magical feel to the landscape. The ice-clad streets and smoke-billowing houses of Portsmouth had been left far behind as Walter Praxton urged his mount on at a relaxed pace. The winter chill nipped, rouging his cheeks a ruddy red. Next to the golden curls flowing down from beneath his hat he had taken on the appearance of a beautiful cherubim, his clear light blue eyes adding the final touch to the splendid angelic visage. It was an image that had gained Mr Praxton almost everything he had ever desired in life. Almost. For the one thing that he wanted most in the world did not seem to notice the charm that had the other ladies in a flutter. Indeed, three ladies had actually been known to swoon, such was the young man's impact on members of the fairer sex. Alas, Georgiana Raithwaite was not one of them.

Undoubtedly her appreciation of the finer things in life had been somewhat tarnished by her experiences at Mrs Tillyard's

Academy. Or so Mr Praxton concluded, for what other reason could there be for her adamant refusal of him? If he had not known better, he would have sworn that the girl bore a downright dislike for his person, when he had presented himself to her in nothing other than a charming and generous light. No, the wretched Mrs Tillyard could only be to blame.

He watched the progress of the plain black travelling coach in the distance. Therein was housed the woman who haunted his dreams, alongside her husband. He could scarcely bring himself to utter the word, such was his contempt for the man. But not for much longer. For Walter Praxton had not lain idle. Indeed, he had not slept much of the previous night under the weight of his industrious scheming. He had lost her once, but the matter would soon be rectified. He just had to bide his time. Gloved fingers pulled the brim of the hat lower over his eyes to shield the glare of the sun. And such was his focus that he no longer noticed the cold stiffness in his knees or the numbness in his fingers and toes.

Georgiana felt the warm press of Nathaniel's thigh next to hers and tried to pretend that she did not feel a sear of excitement quiver through her. Immediately opposite, in the small quarters of the hired coach, Mrs Howard sat, back straight, immaculately clothed, her eyes closed. Even while dozing, Mrs Howard managed to exude an air of serene sophistication. Georgiana, who was anything but relaxed, wondered if anything ever succeeded in rattling the modiste. Not for the first time did she covet just a little of that lady's decorum. Seated beside the elegant figure was Nathaniel's valet, Mr Fraser, who, with rather less delicacy, was lounging quite happily in the corner, making a sound like the workings of one of the great wood saws Georgiana had observed aboard the *Pallas*.

Nathaniel's eyebrow raised and he cast a jaundiced eye towards his valet. 'It's thanks to Mr Fraser here that I've learned to sleep soundly through the liveliest of gun practices at sea. One becomes inured to the sound of his snoring after a while. When we first knew one another, I made him sleep at the other end of the ship!'

Georgiana laughed. 'Poor Mr Fraser. But it is a snore to outdo all others. How Mrs Howard can sleep with such a racket sounding I'll never know. I think I begin to understand why there isn't a Mrs Fraser.' She pulled Nathaniel's boat cloak more firmly around her and rubbed her fingers together. 'Indeed, I suddenly realise how fortunate I am that you do not snore nearly so loud.'

'Madam, I rebut your suggestion that I snore at all,' he said solemnly, only the quirk of the muscle in his cheek giving lie to the austerity in his voice.

'Nathaniel Hawke, you could rival the noise of an eighteen-pounder long gun on a bad night!' she exclaimed saucily.

He moved to capture her hands. 'Minx! Quite obviously I'm not tiring you out enough in bed if you imagine you hear such things in the night!' As his fingers closed around hers, he frowned. 'But you're freezing!' He rubbed her hands within his own, adding warmth with his breath. 'Come here, you'll be warmer on my knee, sweetheart.'

Before she could say otherwise, a pair of strong arms had pulled her deftly on to him, and her mouth had been robbed of one lusty kiss. 'Nathaniel!' she uttered in a furious whisper, her cheeks suddenly a picture of pretty pinkness. 'We're not alone, it's broad daylight and we're halfway across the countryside in a travelling coach!' The horrified scandal in her expression drew the devil in him.

'So?' he asked. His dark eyes opened wide and innocent,

even as a wicked grin plucked at his sensual firm lips. 'I know a method for warming you most thoroughly, lady wife.' Long, lean fingers meandered over her arm in a tantalising fashion, drawing a gasp from Georgiana.

Mr Fraser chose that precise moment to stir within his sleep, mumbling in a blatant Scottish lilt, 'You can't be leaving wearing *that* neckcloth!' It was clear that Captain Hawke's rather relaxed attitude to his attire was the substance of Mr Fraser's nightmares.

Georgiana and Nathaniel exchanged conspiratorial glances, suppressed a chuckle, and reverted to a more respectable seating arrangement. And just in time as Mrs Howard shortly awoke feeling much refreshed from her short nap.

It was early afternoon when Mr Praxton stood within the woodland surrounding the grounds of Collingborne House. The trees were dark and barren, their gnarled and twisted shapes softened by the deep green gloss of the interspersed holly bushes and their abundance of rich red berries. Black birds and mistle thrushes scurried in the surrounding shrubbery, pecking at the remains of autumnal wind-fallen apples. High in an oak tree a robin sounded its familiar call. But Walter Praxton was blind and deaf to the beauty that surrounded him, his eyes and ears trained only on the scene occurring some distance away on the steps of the great country mansion.

Chapter Twelve

Collingborne House was more splendid than anything Georgiana had ever seen before, but its air of grand opulence could not hide the aura of sadness. With its red-coloured stone and white-bordered windows, the house was a bright jewel within the winter-darkened landscape. On arrival they had been ushered into a sun-filled drawing room while, beneath their polite façade, the servants ran around in a frenzy, informing the earl of his unexpected visitors and readying the bedrooms. It was not long before a familiar voice sounded from the doorway.

'Georgiana!' Mirabelle Farleigh, complete with baby in arms, paused by the door before rushing forward in a heady cloud of lavender-perfumed scent. 'What are you doing here? And Nathaniel? This is a surprise!' She eyed Mrs Howard with undisguised curiosity but in the most friendly of manners. Reaching forward, she clasped one of Georgiana's hands that was peeping out from beneath the swathes of Nathaniel's great boat cloak. 'My word, but you're cold, dear thing. Come and warm yourselves at the fire.' She gestured towards the yellow flames blazing within the grate. 'Don't be shy,' she added, her eyes seeking those of Mrs Howard. Baby Richard gurgled his own welcome and pointed one tiny finger at Georgiana.

'Mirabelle,' said Nathaniel, 'allow me to introduce Georgiana—' he paused '—my wife, and her companion, Mrs Howard.'

For the first time since Lady Farleigh had entered the room silence reigned supreme. Even baby Richard stopped slavering against his mother's arm. The petite flaxen-haired woman stumbled back to sit hastily on the sofa. Periwinkle-blue eyes stared like two large pennies and the perfectly formed mouth gaped round as if expressing a continuous 'O'. 'W…wife?' she managed to stutter. And then the best of her breeding declared that Mrs Howard was most welcome at Collingborne and that she, herself, could not have wished for a more amiable sister. Reaching up to embrace Georgiana, she declared it was the best Christmas present she could have asked for. 'Oh just think how delighted Henry will be! And Freddie! This is truly going to be a Christmas to remember!'

Nathaniel smiled wryly, convinced that the word *delight* would probably not describe his brothers' feelings when they learned that Georgiana was his wife. But Mirabelle was right about one thing—this certainly would not be a Christmas to forget. And just at that point a scuttle of little feet outside the door announced the small sturdy frame of Charlie.

'Unc Nath!' he yelled from the doorway and scampered across the drawing room to tangle himself around his uncle's long legs.

Laughing aloud, Nathaniel scooped the boy up high and kissed his chubby pink cheek. 'And this is your Aunt Georgiana come to visit you for Christmas.' Holding Charlie in his arms, he turned to face Georgiana, seeing the soft gentleness in his wife's face as she looked at the child.

Charlie feigned shyness for a minute, then touched a small sticky hand to Georgiana's arm. 'Ant George,' he said with the utmost politeness and smiled.

Dark eyes met grey blue, and crinkled. 'Out of the mouths of babes,' Nathaniel said, and passed a protective arm around Georgiana's waist.

'You sly dog!' Freddie proclaimed with his usual abandon. His long legs were stretched out before him as he lounged back in the winged chair. 'Telling me that Miss Raithwaite was highly unsuitable for marriage, then snapping her up for yourself.'

Henry stood by the library window, staring out at the frost-kissed lawns, a surly expression upon his face. 'Her father owns coaching inns in Andover, Winchester and Newbury. Hardly a lineage to boast of. I didn't think you'd stoop so low to spite Father. '

The hand laid so casually upon the padded arm of Nathaniel's chair curled to form a tight fist. 'Her parentage is nothing worse than mine.' He stared at Viscount Farleigh's profile, partially silhouetted against the brightness of the window. 'Believe me when I say that I'd never allow our father to influence my choice of bride.'

'No,' Henry drawled slowly. 'But you must admit, Nathaniel, that the girl is an odd choice given your situation. Father has sworn that you'll receive not one penny from him, and neither will he sponsor your naval career. If she were an heiress, I could perhaps understand it, but one could hardly describe her as that.'

Nathaniel savoured the brandy, trying desperately to control the anger banking in his chest. 'There are reasons other than money or advancement for a marriage. Georgiana's my

wife whether you like it or not. We'll not beg for your bless-
ing.' He was seated within the great winged chair opposite
Freddie and turned slightly towards the windows. For all his
apparently relaxed posture there was a tight whiteness around
his mouth and a dark gleam in his eyes. He had known it
would not be easy, and the worst was yet to come.

'Well, I say she's jolly fine,' exclaimed Freddie, his face
lighting up at the memory of the delightful Miss Raithwaite.
'Would have expressed an interest myself if someone hadn't
put me off the scent.' He nodded and sipped at the brandy.
'Don't be such a stuff, Henry, give the girl a chance. You
haven't even spoken to her. Besides, Mirabelle likes her and
will vouch for her.'

Nathaniel hoped for the life of him that neither Freddie nor
Mirabelle would see fit to make any mention of Mr Praxton.

Henry turned a gimlet eye to his youngest brother.
'Mirabelle likes everyone. She's forever taking in waifs and
strays and involving herself in charitable works. I cannot help
but think that that is where Miss Raithwaite should have
stayed—as a good cause, and nothing more. Indeed, Mirabelle
spoke to me of the girl. Just because you saved her from
drowning doesn't mean you're obliged to wed her, for goodness' sake!'

Freddie refilled the glasses, deliberately ignoring Henry's
refusal. 'Whatever you say, Henry, you can't deny that Georgiana Raithwaite's a damned attractive woman. Nathaniel
hasn't got ice in his veins, you know. What's he supposed to
do after being stuck away at sea for all those months? Got to
get himself a wife at some time!'

'I am not contesting that point,' Henry said with affected
pomposity. 'Say what you will, she's the daughter of an innkeeper and that alone makes her unsuitable to be married to

any member of this family. She's nothing but a mercenary Miss. Hell's teeth, Nathaniel, if you wanted her, why didn't you just bed her? We could have paid her off easily enough then. You weren't so reticent with Kitty Wakefield.'

The words were scarcely out of his mouth when Nathaniel was before him, his face white and bloodless. 'Cease this talk, Henry. I won't just stand by and let you insult my wife. Take back your words or I'll forget that we're brothers.' The rage that kindled in Nathaniel was akin to nothing he had ever experienced before. It was as if a red haze had descended before his eyes. His throat constricted and he swallowed hard, his fists bunched dangerously by his sides. 'Take them back.' His voice was low pitched, heavy with intent.

Henry stood resolutely silent. Then uttered, 'I will not. I speak nothing but the truth.'

'Nathaniel!' Freddie leapt to his feet, but it was too late.

'Then I have nothing more to say to you, Henry. You're no longer my brother.'

Freddie squeezed between his brothers, his hands pushing against Nathaniel's chest. 'This is absurd. What the hell are the two of you doing?'

'Defending my wife's honour,' said Nathaniel in a steady tone. 'I'll have nothing more to do with Henry until he apologises.' And the rage that consumed his body knew he would never back down from what he had begun.

Brother stared at brother, each silent in the knowledge of what had come between them.

'So be it,' said Henry and removed himself from the library.

A thoroughly chilled Mr Praxton was just about to find his way to the local village inn when he spotted Nathaniel Hawke cantering down the gravel driveway. Even across the distance that divided them Praxton could see the tension that beset the other man's body. So matters within the great house had not got off to a good start. A sneer played across his lips. Trouble within the Hawke family could only bode well for his own cause. Perhaps the earl was having difficulty accepting the facts about his new daughter. He wondered as to exactly which aspect of Georgiana's scandalous behaviour had upset the aristocrat most. Was it her running away on the mail, disguising herself as a boy, or being press-ganged aboard his son's ship? He had to admit that the choice was really rather superb. Especially in the light of the fact that Georgiana's parentage alone was enough to render her unacceptable to any of them. Matters were possibly not as dismal as he had painted them. Information on the Hawke family could only prove useful to his cause. With that in mind, he retired from the fading daylight towards the village of Collingborne. Georgiana was slipping closer towards his grasp, even if the woman did not realise it herself. And the thought of what he would do to her when he caught her fired the chill from his body.

'You did what?' Georgiana sat up, the covers of the great four-poster bed falling to her waist. The hour was late and she had almost been asleep when she heard her husband enter the room. Now her head danced dizzily as she struggled to comprehend the enormity of what he was telling her.

Nathaniel threw his finely cut coat on to the chair beside the tallboy in the corner, and stripped off his neckcloth. Even galloping the gelding full speed across country had not blunted the edge of his fury. 'No one will cast such a slur on your character and think to get away with it, even if he is my brother. Henry shall take back his vile words or I'll disown him as my brother.'

She clasped her hands to her cheeks in horror. Surely this could not really be happening? A serious quarrel with Henry and all over her honour, her damned supposed honour. 'Nathaniel, please, stop, think what you're doing.' She clambered out of the bed and stood facing him clad only in the voluminous swirl of her white cotton nightgown.

'I know exactly what I'm doing,' he said between firm set lips.

She could see by the stubborn tilt of his jaw that he wasn't going to be easy to reason with, but she had to try. Heaven only knew just how much she would. 'What did you expect when you brought me here?' she demanded, elbows akimbo. 'That they would welcome me with open arms? We both knew what this visit was to be about. I thought that we'd prepared ourselves to meet what we would find.'

He threw his shirt aside and sat down on the bed to strip off his boots, the muscles in his back rippling from his exertions. 'My father's insults are to be expected. That he has not deigned to grace us with his presence is exactly the welcome I expected. But what I'm not prepared to accept is Henry's condemnation of you.' His eyes glittered dark and dangerous as if he were recalling events from earlier in the day.

'Put yourself in his shoes. He's your older brother, Porchester's heir. It's only natural that he feels the weight of family responsibility heavy on his shoulders. He's only doing what he thinks best for you. How would you feel if matters were reversed and Henry had taken an unsuitable woman to wife? You would speak out, wouldn't you?'

'That's not the point, Georgiana,' he argued. 'The matter is not reversed and I won't allow him to speak of you in that way.' How could he explain to her the anger that stuck like a bone in his throat, when he did not understand it himself? Her words were sensible, the same advice as he would give to any other, and yet he could not swallow them, for all he knew that he should.

When he did not answer, just began to remove his stockings, she flounced round the other side of the room to face him once more. 'He's your brother. Would you lose him over a silly argument?'

'Georgiana, let it be. Henry knows how to resolve the matter.'

'And what of you?' she said with gritty determination. 'You would throw away all that is between you, alienate yourself from your brother as well as your father, and at Christmas?'

He shrugged his shoulders with false bravado. 'If that's the price, then I'll pay it. Regardless of what people think, I have some sense of honour.'

She clutched at his shoulders, her fingers biting hard, pulling the full weight of his attention to her. 'Then hear me, Nathaniel Hawke, and hear me well. I won't allow you to lose Henry over such a pettiness. It's my honour he's insulted and therefore I'll have the say of any action taken to defend it.' Grey lights flashed boldly in her eyes as she leaned closer to him, her face barely inches from his. 'When I cut off my hair and dressed in my stepbrother's clothes I decried my honour. When I ran away to Fareham in the company of strangers I decried my honour. When I served under false pretences aboard the *Pallas* I decried my honour. And, worst of all, when I forced you to face ruination or marriage, what did I do to the little honour I had left? I'm not so high in the instep that I cannot suffer whatever words your family may choose to throw at me. And if I can suffer it, so can you.'

'Georgiana—' he started to interrupt but she would have none of it.

'No, Nathaniel, hear me out. You would deprive yourself

not only of Henry, but of Mirabelle and the children too. And what of Freddie? Where will he stand with his loyalties divided? You would tear this family apart.' She saw the pain appear in his eyes. Her hands moved up to take his face between her palms. 'And what would that knowledge do to you? I don't want to lose the husband that I love.'

The last word echoed in the stillness between them. Their faces were so close that the warmth of their breath met and mingled. She saw the darkness clear from his eyes, watched them open wide and clear. 'You love me?' It was a mere whisper on a breath, but Georgiana knew what he asked.

'I've always loved you, Nathaniel Hawke, from that first day upon the river bank when you saved my life.'

He stared at her as if he could not believe the words that had just fallen from her mouth. Stared at her as if he thought never to look upon her again. His arms moved to hold her to him so that she could feel the thud of his heart against her own. Lip to lip, breast to breast, hip to hip, they lay still and heavy, each breathing the scent of the other. And all the while those dark eyes held hers, never flinching nor fading in the intensity of their focus. Silence surrounded them save for the haunting rattle of the wind against the windowpanes. When at last he moved to take her it was as if it was the first time. Such tenderness, such passion, and yet with so much more. Even as he moved over her Georgiana knew the difference. For this was a union not just of bodies but also of souls. A merging of hearts for ever. The knowledge pushed the experience into the realm of the extraordinary. It seemed that they floated clear of the bed, of the great house itself, melting together in a liquid pool of ecstasy that surpassed ordinary mortal experience. Even when Georgiana curled sleeping around him, Nathaniel knew that everything had changed. A world of dif-

ference sparked from one small innocuous word. Love. She
had said it. Had spoken the truth. And in the darkness of their
bedroom and the nocturnal hush of Collingborne House he lay
brooding upon exactly what that meant. Truly, nothing would
ever be the same again.

It was the day before Christmas Eve and both Nathaniel
and Henry were still proving to be wilfully stubborn when it
came to the matter of Georgiana. Henry, in his position of the
older and wiser sibling, would not soften in his condemnation for all of Mirabelle's tears, tantrums and pleadings. Neither would Nathaniel withdraw his stubborn ultimatum. After
that night, when she had believed him to have understood all
that she had tried so hard to express, Georgiana was left lonely
and confused. The man she loved seemed strangely distant,
removed to a place she could not reach. That he fully intended to lose Henry over the foolish notion of her honour
only fired the pain that ravaged her breast. What matter that
she loved him, had bared her heart and soul, only to have it
cast firmly back in her face? He did not love her, that much
was clear. Indeed, had he not since taken pains to avoid her,
creeping late into bed when he knew her to be asleep, and rising early in the morning?

As soon as she entered the breakfast room Henry, Lord Farleigh, departed, turning his back to meet her in a direct cut.

Mrs Howard rose swiftly from the table. 'We were beginning to worry that you'd overslept. Come and help yourself
to breakfast. The choice is quite superb.'

Georgiana's normally robust appetite suddenly shrivelled
to the size of a small dried pea. 'I'm not hungry, some coffee
will suffice.'

'Nonsense,' replied Mrs Howard. The lady proceeded to

create an assortment of devilled kidneys, eggs and bread rolls upon a plate and placed it before Georgiana. 'Take my word for it, my dear, you'll feel much better for eating.'

Georgiana's gaze met those of Mirabelle Farleigh. The small woman smiled, but it did not hide the ashen hue of her complexion or the dark shadows that smudged beneath her red-rimmed eyes. 'It isn't your fault, Georgiana. They're both as bad as each other. Henry shouldn't have said the things that he did. I'm sorry that it's come to this.'

'No, Mirabelle. It's I who should apologise. Lord Farleigh seeks only what is best for his family. His younger brother has been married in haste to a woman who cannot be described, by any stretch of the imagination, as a good match. I fully understand his feelings on the matter.' Georgiana prodded a piece of kidney with her fork.

Mirabelle pushed back a lock of hair that had escaped to sweep over her cheek. 'You're a good woman, Georgiana, and my husband's more the fool for his blindness. For all that I love him, I've never seen him so stubborn and unyielding.' She pressed the lace of her handkerchief to her mouth. 'Please excuse me, Georgiana, Mrs Howard.' A rustle of skirts and she was gone.

'Stop playing with your breakfast, Georgiana. Starving yourself shall not assist any aspect of the matter.' The silver eyes regarded her calmly, sensibly, loosening the tension within the room.

'You're right as ever, Mrs Howard,' said Georgiana. She chewed on the food thoughtfully, pondering the situation with cool composure for the first time.

Neither woman spoke, each reassured and comfortable in the other's presence. After some time, when Georgiana had scraped her plate clean and was sipping on her second cup of coffee, she asked, 'What's your opinion, ma'am? What should we do?'

Mrs Howard folded her long manicured fingers before answering. 'It's not my place to comment.'

Georgiana looked up at her, disappointment on her face.

'Georgiana,' the older woman sighed, 'I shouldn't, but…' One slow blink of the silver eyes and she continued, 'You must do whatever it takes to ensure that the disagreement is resolved. And now, please excuse me, my dear. I've already said too much.' So saying, Evelina removed herself swiftly and gracefully from the breakfast room.

Georgiana sat alone, bathed in a ray of pale winter sunshine. Mrs Howard had not told her anything other than she already knew herself. Yes, her heart was raw from Nathaniel's rejection. But a family was at stake here. Wallowing in self-pity would not prevent Nathaniel's self-imposed isolation. Whatever the outcome, the Hawkes would be destroyed, and Georgiana knew quite calmly, quite clearly, that the fault would lie with her own self. If only she had not run away, if only she had not ended up aboard the *Pallas,* if only she had not married Nathaniel… There were so many *if onlys*. On board the frigate, before they had ever come to this place, she would have staked her very life that Nathaniel could never have behaved in this way. To risk all that was dear to him, and over her. She could not stop him, just as Mirabelle could not stop Henry. The more that Georgiana thought, the more she came to realise that there was only one person who had the power to do such a thing. One man who could prevent the downward spiral of events. She squared her shoulders, took a deep breath, and determined that this was one occasion that would never merit an *if only*.

* * *

The Earl of Porchester looked up from his desk at the woman standing so doggedly before him. With her clear pale skin and short dark hair, she could hardly be described as beautiful, but there was something magnetic about her, the arrangement of her features, and those eyes. Porchester felt it, just as clearly as his sons had before him. It was, no doubt, an attribute she used to good effect—to catch a husband beyond her class, beyond her means. If she thought to manipulate him so easily, she was in for a surprise. He knew that he had been inordinately rude in refusing to meet her, and that nothing excused his appalling breach of manners. A wave of disquiet swept over him at the thought. He brushed it carelessly away. 'I did not request your presence, madam.'

'No.' Her voice was quiet but steady.

He watched her from beneath his dark hooded eyes, waited for her discomfort to grow before gesturing in the direction of the worn leather chairs by the fireplace. 'Sit down.' It was not an invitation. He moved around from behind the barrier of the desk.

'Thank you, my lord.' Georgiana settled herself into the chair and watched while the earl took the other. She noted that he was almost as tall as Nathaniel and, even if the years had not left him unmarked, he still had an impressive stature. Although his hair had turned to a distinguished silver, he did not appear old—it merely lent him an air of sophistication. For a man busy about work within his study he was dressed immaculately in a black superfine coat, under which a silver-grey waistcoat and pristine white shirt could be seen. With his black breeches and silver buckled shoes he presented a formidable image. A lavender neckcloth completed the elegant attire. She felt more than a little intimidated by the Earl of Porchester. Her gaze flickered nervously to his face, and she almost gasped aloud at what it found there. For Lord Porchester was possessed of the same expressive eyes as each of his sons and he was watching her with a cold disdain. Even the knowledge of his hostility to her husband, and therefore, by association, to herself, had not prepared her for the severity of the earl's presence. The power of speech appeared to have deserted Georgiana as she stared overawed at the man seated opposite. A vision of Nathaniel came to her aid and she forced herself onwards, and upwards.

'Please forgive my interruption, sir. I'm sorry to disturb you when you're clearly busy, but I wondered if you might spare me a few minutes of your time.' The sides of her throat were in danger of sticking together such was their aridity, and her stomach was starting to rebel against the devilled kidneys. It growled loudly in the pause after her words. A hint of colour suffused her pale cheeks and she muttered, 'Oh, please do excuse me, my lord.'

The harshness in Lord Porchester's dark eyes did not even waver, just remained trained on the woman seated before him. 'What do you want?' he asked with uncivil bluntness. 'Other than what you've already acquired for yourself.'

She felt the colour deepen in her cheeks at the insult. 'I ask only that you'll listen to my request.'

'Asking for more already?'

The muscle in her jaw twitched before she schooled it to remain impassive. 'I'm not here for myself. You will think what you want of me. I cannot change that, nor am I about to try.'

A dark eyebrow raised in response. 'Then I ask you again, what do you want?'

She swallowed hard. 'Nathaniel and Lord Farleigh have argued.'

He waited.

She swallowed again and tried to make him understand. 'It's serious. They won't speak to one another and neither is prepared to back down.'

'Over what have they disagreed?' The expression on his face was closed, but the tone of his voice suggested that he already knew.

'Over myself.' Her hands clasped firmly together. 'Nathaniel has taken exception to Lord Farleigh's opinion.'

'And what exactly is Henry's opinion?' Just how much was she prepared to reveal?

Georgiana steeled herself to say what must be said. There could be no evasion, no hiding from the truth. 'He doesn't approve of me, sir. He believes that I married Nathaniel to further my own ends.'

The earl smiled, and the slow ironic curve of his mouth was more chilling than his frown. And still those dark eyes looked coldly on. 'It's nothing less than the truth.'

The silence stretched between them.

'Nothing I say will persuade you otherwise. I'm not here to plead my case. In fact, I deserve your condemnation more than you can know. But I won't stand by and see brother against brother, or watch the destruction of my husband's family. Whatever you think of him, Nathaniel deserves better than that.' Her fingers strayed surreptitiously to worry at her ear.

The dark eyes widened, and watched as Georgiana unwittingly mirrored the habit of the earl's late wife. It was an action that had ever betrayed concentration or anxiety in his beloved countess. And in that single motion, time stripped away so that he could see Mary, bright, alive, smiling, before the pain, before the dark finality, before the bitter years of misery. When he looked again, there was only the frightened girl

wearing her defiant courage like a badge. 'Nathaniel has exactly what he deserves,' he said, but there was a huskiness to
his voice that had not been there before.

'No.'

Their gazes locked.

'You're wrong about him. Your son, my lord, is an honourable man. Whatever else he is, never doubt that.'

A mirthless laugh escaped the old man. 'You plead his case
well. He will be pleased.'

'He doesn't know that I'm here.'

The clock ticked loudly upon the mantel.

She tried again. 'Nathaniel is a good man. He's sacrificed
much in the name of honour and duty.'

Another pause.

'I'm listening,' he said, and Georgiana knew it to be the
best chance she would get. To reveal the extent of her husband's sacrifices would be to declare the scandalous truth
about herself. If Lord Farleigh disapproved of her because she
was an innkeeper's daughter, she could only imagine the family's reaction when they learned the rest. She would have to
leave, of course. For that, Lord Por-chester would know that
for all these years he had been wrong about his son. The price
was high, but she knew she could do nothing other than pay
it, and willingly so. So she raised her chin and straightened
her back. 'There's much to tell,' she said quietly, 'and I'd have
you know it all, my lord.' With a calm determination she proceeded to do just that, neither omitting details nor embellish-
ing facts. And all the while the Earl of Porchester listened in
studied silence.

'So now you know, my lord, how honourable a man
Nathaniel Hawke is.' She sat caught in her memories, know-

ing, whatever the future held, she would never stop loving Nathaniel. Slowly she forced herself back to the present. 'Will you speak to him, make him see that this quarrel is utter folly?'

Those hooded dark eyes were regarding her intensely, and still he had neither moved nor spoken. 'It was ever my intent,' he said slowly.

'But you…I thought—' Georgiana broke off.

'Then you thought wrong.'

The grey-blue gaze shuttered and she bit down hard on her bottom lip to stop the tremor.

'Why have you told me this?'

She blinked in confusion. 'So that Nathaniel won't lose his family.'

'And for that you are prepared to give him up yourself?'

The question hung in the air between them.

'Yes.' The blood drained from her face. She knew what he was asking, what she'd known he would demand even before she'd told her story.

He leaned forward in his chair. 'Why?'

'Because I love him,' she whispered.

'Thank you, Georgiana,' was all he said as he released her to go. But the earl did not move from the chair in which she left him, and his thoughts lingered still on the man who had married to save a woman from utter ruin.

Walter Praxton blew misty winter breath upon his chilled fingers in an attempt to warm them. He did not dare to light a fire within the small woodsman's hut he had stumbled upon for fear that his presence would be noticed. Each night was spent comfortably ensconced in the snug warmth of the Fox and Hounds Inn within the village of Collingborne, each day in the tireless surveillance of the woman who haunted him incessantly. Whether in waking or sleeping he could think of little else, watching her as he did, hour by hour, with the aid of his spyglass.

The fact that Captain Hawke did not appear to spend any time in Georgiana's company heartened him. Obviously he had married her from some misplaced sense of honour. Walter did not allow his mind to wander to those activities that occurred during the long dark evenings when he was safely stowed within the inn. Those thoughts were liable to induce in him a fury that surpassed any he had previously known. Besides, he had already laid his plan, and tomorrow would see the start of it.

He knew the route across the fields and woodland that Captain Hawke had taken these past four mornings. The sight of the man upon the grey gelding instilled in him nothing but a jealous loathing. That he could call himself Georgiana's husband, that he was the one who had no doubt had full possession of her body. There was really nothing else that Walter could do, or so he had told himself just half an hour earlier as he tied the thin rope across the path. His selection of location was superb, the rope being positioned just after a sharp bend in the woodland track. The trap would not be seen until it was too late. Walter's pale eyes glittered at the very thought, before raising the spyglass once more to resume his vigil. The sight that met his eye brought a sneer to his face and set him off at a gallop down the hill towards Collingborne House.

The winter sun had sunk low in a pink-kissed sky but still sheathed the garden in its dazzling beauty. Frost-stiffened grass crunched beneath Georgiana's feet as she made her way down to the holly bushes, and her breath clouded as smoke in the crisp cold air. Following her discourse with the earl that morning, she worried precisely as to when she should leave and what Nathaniel would have to say when he realised just what she had done. Unable to reveal her fears to either Mrs Howard or Lady Farleigh, Georgiana had left the two ladies contentedly playing cards within the stuffy heat of the blue drawing room. She revelled in the sharp nip in the air, felt it clear her head a little. A short walk in the gardens to gather her senses together was all that was required. She had already packed the few items of her wardrobe. Before her she heard the startled warning call of a blackbird, then saw its small dark shape flutter up inside a large and seemingly dense holly bush. She rubbed her fingers to the dark spiky gloss of its leaves. Such a fountain of colour amidst the drab bare browns of Yuletide. A soft tread on grass, warm breath against the back of her neck, and a presence so close as to all but touch her.

'Georgiana.' The whisper sounded at her ear, so unmistakable that it caused a cold prickle across her skin and sent a shiver down her spine.

She spun round and looked up into the cruel handsome face she had never thought to see again. 'Mr Praxton!' she gasped, feeling a horrible tightening sensation within her chest. Her fingers crushed the enclosed holly leaf, puncturing her skin so that it bled, but she was aware of nothing save the pale blue eyes trained on hers.

'Did you think that I had abandoned you, my sweet?'

Spiny leaves needled her back as she tried to increase the distance between them.

'Never think that I would not fulfil my duty to my betrothed.' He stepped closer so that their bodies were touching.

Georgiana felt the stirring of panic in her breast. 'Sir, my circumstances have since changed. I'm now another man's wife. Please leave before my husband arrives.' She struggled to step aside.

Walter Praxton's hands grabbed her upper arms in a vice-like grip. 'Your precious husband is drinking himself into a stupor in the library and doubtless plans to stay there for the remainder of the day. No, Georgiana—' and his voice was cold and hard '—Captain Hawke is merely a temporary aberration in your life. You had no right to wed him when you belong to me, even if you were a ship's boy on the *Pallas*.'

'Dear God, no,' she cried, feeling her legs tremble beneath her.

He smiled down at her, and in it she saw the measure of his madness. 'There is nothing I don't know, my dear, but through it all I'll still have you.'

Her mouth opened to scream, but met with a sharp blow from Walter's fist. Then there was nothing but a gathering nausea and a rolling darkness.

Chapter Thirteen

Nathaniel watched as the yellow flames engulfed the log, sending small sparks and spits cascading over the hearth. The room was pleasantly warm and the brandy had numbed the raw edge of his emotions. But still he could not make sense of the riot of thoughts rampaging through his head. He did not want to hurt Henry, never would have imagined himself doing so, not in a thousand years. There was a part of him that looked clearly at the mayhem unfolding and told himself not to behave in such a ridiculous fashion. It was the part of himself to whom he had always listened, refusing to allow his feelings affect his judgements or decisions. For once he had turned a deaf ear to its advice. Unaccountable it may be, unfathomable even, but he knew that he would never let anyone, no matter who they might be, hurt Georgiana. He did not understand the depth of his feelings, just knew that he needed her and would never let her go.

Since her admission the other night he had deliberately avoided her, for her pleas could stir his heart like no other, and he was adamant that he would not let Henry off so lightly. Georgiana deserved comfort, understanding and respect for all that she had suffered, not condemnation. And Nathaniel meant to see that she would be treated with all three. His family could take umbrage with *him*, not his wife. Her words replayed in his mind, '...*the husband that I love*', and he smiled. Damnation, how he missed her. What must she be thinking of his neglect? That he did not care for her? Never that. The thought of her suffering stirred pain in his heart. He set the brandy glass down carefully upon the table. He would go to her, explain all, beg her forgiveness. It was with a renewed vigour in his step that Nathaniel ascended the sweeping staircase.

The first things that he saw were her bags packed neatly in a small pile beside the door. His heart lurched cold as he drew his own conclusions. Within fifteen minutes he had ascertained that she was not present within the entirety of the house and was treading back up the stairs when he heard the study door open and his father's voice.

'Nathaniel.'

He paused mid-flight and turned to face the earl. 'Sir, I don't doubt that which you wish to discuss, but I've more pressing matters on my mind at this minute.' He made to turn away but was prevented doing so by the command in the tone.

'Nathaniel!'

He could not ignore it. His head nodded once and he followed the old man into the study.

'Drink?' his father asked, lifting the brandy decanter from a small round table placed close to the wall.

'No, thank you, sir, I have imbibed too much this day as it is.'

They stood facing one another, tense, waiting, and from each face the same eyes looked out.

At last Nathaniel spoke. 'I know you've called me here over my quarrel with Henry, but I cannot...will not, allow him to cast aspersions on Georgiana's character. Contrary to his opinion, and no doubt yours, she did not seek to trap me into marriage, and neither is she some kind of trollop. She's my wife and I—'

Lord Porchester interrupted. 'Save your breath. I know full well what Georgiana is.'

The gasp of incredulity that escaped Nathaniel echoed round the room. 'You go too far, sir.' He stepped forward, the closing distance between them much more of a threat than his words could ever be. 'I can bear your censure, even your contempt, but I won't let you say one word against Georgiana.'

Father looked at son. Son looked at father. Tension quivered tight and dangerous.

And then one corner of the earl's mouth raised to form a sarcastic smile. A dark brow lifted mockingly. 'You love her?'

No reply save the flare of Nathaniel's nostrils.

The earl barked a hollow laugh before the slight grimace of pain flickered across the elderly features and then was gone, masked once more behind the imperial stare. 'Sit down, for God's sake.' The utterance was little more than a tired sigh.

Nathaniel's gaze flitted once to the door before he moved to the chair.

The curve of a balloon glass was pressed into his hand, and his father sat down in the twin chair at the opposite side of the fireplace.

'This nonsense with Henry—I want it stopped—now.' Lord Porchester took a swig of brandy.

'Do you even know what the argument is over?'

Another sip of the amber liquid. 'It isn't worth losing a brother over a woman, Nathaniel.'

'But a son is a different matter entirely.'

They both knew to what he was referring.

'You judge me harshly, son.'

'As you judge me, sir.'

The flames crackled in the fireplace. The curtains rippled in the draft.

'You'll have your apology, I'll see to it. And that will be an end to the matter for both you and Henry.'

Nathaniel leaned forward. 'Why do you care? I'd have thought the fact that Henry and I are at each other's throats to have suited you.'

A soft snort of disgust issued from the chair opposite. Nothing else.

Nathaniel rose to his feet, placing the untouched brandy on the occasional table. 'Please excuse me, sir. I must find my wife.'

Porchester's eyes stared into the dancing flames, remembering the girl who had ventured here like Daniel into the lion's den. Remembering her courage and dignity, and that same betraying gesture so like Mary's across the years. God, it still hurt, hurt like hell…to lose a woman that you loved. A ragged sigh shuddered through his frame.

'Sir?'

Control resumed, vulnerability fled. 'Why didn't you tell me?'

'Tell you?'

'About Georgiana, about what happened aboard the *Pallas*.'

Nathaniel froze where he stood, his gaze widening momentarily. 'I don't know what you mean.' But the words were stiffly formed through rigid lips.

Lord Porchester looked directly at him. 'I'm sure that you do. It isn't every day that you marry your ship's boy.'

His son's lips parted.

But Porchester was there first. 'Maybe I have judged you too harshly. The girl was right.' The brandy glass touched to his mouth. 'Georgiana…' He savoured the name.

'How do you—?'

'She came to see me.'

'Georgiana?'

'She might be trade, but you're right, she doesn't deserve Henry's condemnation. As I said, I know exactly what Georgiana is, nothing but courageous.'

Shock registered on Nathaniel's face. And then the dark eyes narrowed to a cool calculating focus. 'The bags…she's packed her bags. I thought…' Long tanned fingers raked through the mahogany locks. 'You told her to leave.' The accusation was little more than a whisper. His voice raised, 'Didn't you?'

'I told her nothing,' came the tart reply.

'You would have me lose the woman that I love. And why? Because she doesn't meet your standards?' Nathaniel stared down at the man he called father. 'Because she isn't Kitty Wakefield?'

But the earl heard nothing past those few words, '…*lose the woman that I love*.' The glass slipped from his limp fingers to smash against the hearth. Blood drained from his cheeks, leaving a pallor that hid nothing of the toll exerted by heartbreak and bitterness. 'Don't say that. Never say that,' and the voice that whispered was that of an old man.

Nathaniel leaned low and looked into the haunted face. 'Father?'

The eyes that raised to his were, for once, neither mocking nor cold. 'I never realised… I didn't think…' The silver grey head shook once as if to clear the weakness of the thoughts. When he spoke again it was with the strength Nathaniel had always known. 'If her bags are still here, then so is she. It isn't too late, Nathaniel.'

The words hung between them. A two-fold meaning. One message. Hope.

'I've searched the house, there's nothing to be found.'

'Then we'll search again,' said Porchester and rose to stand by his son.

'Whatever is the matter? You look positively dreadful.' Mirabelle placed her cards on the table and rushed to Nathaniel's side. She clung to him and eyed the earl with undisguised ill ease.

Nathaniel's face was unusually pale, exaggerating the dark glitter of his eyes and the stark mahogany hairline. He took her hands in his, speaking with an urgency that Mirabelle had not heard him use before. 'Have you seen Georgiana?'

As Mirabelle's curls shook in denial, Mrs Howard stepped forward. 'She left our company some half an hour since. I couldn't help but notice that she seemed a little preoccupied with her thoughts, as if she had much to think about.'

'She's not in her room or visiting the children in the nursery. Indeed, I've searched the whole house and she's nowhere to be found.' Nathaniel could not hide his escalating concern. He did not mention the pile of baggage arranged so neatly upstairs, or what had passed between her and his father.

Mrs Howard's expression softened. Nathaniel Hawke's feelings concerning the girl could not have been clearer had he proclaimed them from the steeple tops. And whatever his reasons for avoiding Georgiana's company these past days, it was not a cooling of his ardour. Not much escaped the vigilant attention of Evelina Howard. Her gaze moved to the earl and rested a moment before gliding back to his son. 'Perhaps Georgiana has decided to walk in the gardens. On a pleasant afternoon like this it would be the perfect setting in which to order her thoughts.'

She had scarcely completed her words when Nathaniel had gone, whirling through the door as a large dark blur.

The earl cleared his throat. 'Pray forgive my son, ma'am, he is anxious to locate Georgiana's whereabouts.' He watched the serene silver-eyed woman before him incline her head in mute agreement. 'Indeed, I must also ask your forgiveness for the tardiness of my introduction. You must be Mrs Howard.'

Mirabelle watched the discourse between Evelina Howard and the Earl of Porchester with surprise. Lord Porchester was being positively polite—and did her eyes deceive her, or was that the subtle hint of a blush creeping upon Mrs Howard's cheeks? Well, well, well, who would have thought such a thing? Mirabelle was just warming to her train of thought when the door burst open to reveal Nathaniel, with Frederick by his side.

'She's not in the gardens nor any place that I can think.' His voice was grim. 'We must find her before darkness falls.' Not one person within the room could fail to see the harsh control with which Nathaniel Hawke reined in his emotions. He turned to address his father. 'Sir, if you would be so good as to undertake a second search of the gardens and stables, Freddie and I will ride to the village in case she's walked out that way.' As Porchester gave a brief nod, a strong voice sounded from the doorway.

'No. I'll go with Freddie. You stay here.' Henry walked into the room. 'Father has spoken to me and it seems that I owe Georgiana an apology. Evidently I've been mistaken in my opinions, and I mean to tell her so.' The pain in his brother's eyes betrayed that he loved the girl, and, if what his father had said was true, Henry knew that he had been unfair in his treatment of Georgiana.

Brother stared at brother, and the silence ticked by before Nathaniel firmly clasped Henry's hand. 'Thank you,' was all he said, before the men of the Hawke family moved rapidly to action.

Georgiana came round to find herself lying on her side upon a narrow bed. Memories of Walter Praxton's leering face lurched her with a shudder back to the present. She did not move or even attempt to open her eyes, just tried to gauge her state and if the vision of her nightmare was still present. A coarse rope secured her arms behind her back and her ankles together. Although her bindings were not unreasonably tight, her limbs had grown stiff and uncomfortable from their restrictions. She was aware of a painful tenderness around her jaw and the left-hand side of her lower lip felt stung and swollen. Despite the grey blanket draped over her body the air was chilled, seeping a dampness through to her bones. All around the woody smell of decaying forestry filled her nose. Within the stillness of her surroundings she heard the cawing of crows, and the squeak and scrabbling of something else she preferred not to think of. She suppressed a shiver and slowly opened her eyes.

The hut was small and wooden, obviously the temporary abode of some shepherd or woodsman. Apart from the small truckle bed, the only other furniture comprised a stool and a wooden crate upturned to form a table. Strips of wood and sacking had been nailed securely over the single tiny window, possibly to keep out the worst of the cold or to hide the flickering illumination of the candle lantern placed on the table. On the bare wooden floor sat a saddlebag, a tankard and a bottle of wine. Clearly Mr Praxton had made liberal use of the hut, but how long had he been here, watching her? She dared not guess, only gave thanks that he was not present at this minute. Her gratitude was to be short-lived, for just as she struggled to a sitting position and strained against her bindings the gentleman reappeared.

'Ah, my dove, you're awakened once more.' He touched a hand to her bruised face, frowning as she flinched. 'Forgive my rather brutish treatment, I could not allow you to alert anyone to our plans.' His fingers slid round to cup the back of her neck, and he crouched low to look into her eyes.

Georgiana's fear squirmed inside, but she thrust it down out of sight and forced herself to face Walter Praxton with a convincing façade of calm. 'Mr Praxton, I've already told you that I'm married. Whatever plans you once had, can be no more. Cease this game now, let me go free, and I won't speak of the matter.' The firmness in her voice betrayed no trace of a tremor.

Praxton's frown vanished, replaced instead by a smirk. 'Do you think to fool me so easily? I haven't spent these last months tracing you to give you up to any man, least of all Hawke.' He leaned closer, until she could feel the warmth of his breath upon her skin. 'He only married you because his honour gave him no other option. You must be aware by now that he doesn't care for you.' Then added silkily, 'Not as I do.' The pale eyes looked deep into hers as his lips moved to claim her mouth.

'No!' Georgiana shrank back. 'No,' she said, with a little more control. 'You're wrong.' Her heart hammered within her chest and the blood pounded in her temples.

A suspicion was forming in Walter's mind, too horrible for him to fully contemplate. Surely Georgiana did not actually hold any affection for the man she called husband? He remembered her face smiling up at the captain's in Portsmouth dockyard. His fingers tightened, drawing a gasp from the woman before him. If that was her game, Walter would use it to his advantage. 'So you seek to bind a man who doesn't want you, to ruin his life, destroy his standing within his family.

You're promised to me, and always have been. What of my reputation? What of my feelings in the matter?' He paused, to allow his words to hit their target. 'You are selfish in the extreme, Georgiana. What cares have you for anyone other than yourself? Not your family whom you left to face your disgrace, nor your betrothed, not even the man that you call husband.'

Georgiana's throat tightened. Every word that dripped from Walter Praxton's tongue played on the worst of her fears. She *was* selfish and thoughtless. She *had* treated them all abysmally. He only spoke the truth. She stared at him, voiceless, not knowing that her eyes betrayed all.

Walter loosed his grip on Georgiana's neck, knowing her resolve to be perilously close to crumbling. 'Let me save us all,' he whispered, his eyes softening.

Thoughts whirled in Georgiana's confused mind. She had forced Nathaniel into marriage, had inadvertently set brother against brother, and was about to be banished from Collingborne. What's more, since she had bared her heart, her husband had taken definite steps to avoid spending time in her company. But she loved him, damn it! She looked into the pale eyes before her and saw the malice and cruelty simmering below the surface. Lust and obsession stared blatantly back. Even as she struggled to hide her revulsion at the fingers caressing her shoulders, she knew she could never give herself to any man other than Nathaniel, and especially not Walter Praxton.

'Mr Praxton, thank you for your kind offer of help, but I'm afraid that I cannot accept it. I will return to my family and cast myself upon their mercy.' She felt the pressure of his fingers grow until it became almost unbearable, gnawing into her skin. A hiss sounded close to her ear.

'And I'm afraid that I cannot allow you to refuse,' he breathed, and pressed his hot avaricious mouth to hers.

Nathaniel knew that what his brothers had to say did not bode well before they even opened their mouths. Henry's expression was stern and forbidding, a sure sign that he was worried. Freddie looked unusually thoughtful.

'I take it you found no sign of her?' Nathaniel had not yet removed his caped great coat or gloves.

Henry shook his head. 'Nothing.' He watched the strain tighten his brother's face, pinching the lips white even beneath the yellow light of the candles. 'Why didn't you simply tell me that you love her?' It was a question uttered quietly, but all eyes in the room trained on Nathaniel for his answer.

Dark eyes glittered within the pallor of his face. The clock on the mantel punctuated the silence in staccato strokes. 'Because I didn't realise it myself until today,' he growled. Long fingers threaded themselves through the deep dark brown of his hair, thrusting the unruly waves back from his face. He started to speak, then stopped, cleared the emotion from his throat, and resumed once more. 'It would seem that Mrs Howard was correct. One of the maids saw Georgiana leaving the house wearing her cloak, and there were signs that someone had walked across the lawns to reach the shrubbery at the front of the house. It's dark outside and the temperature is dropping. Georgiana should have returned long since.'

'She must have met with an accident,' piped up Mirabelle. 'Perhaps she's twisted her ankle and cannot get back from where she has fallen.'

The earl spoke up. 'Nathaniel and I have scoured the grounds. She's not to be found.'

'Then maybe she walked farther than you searched.' Mirabelle would not allow herself to think the worst.

A calm voice spoke. 'Captain Hawke, may I be so bold as to suggest that you check Georgiana's wardrobe.'

'There's nothing missing,' replied Nathaniel rather tersely and moved towards the door, before pausing to address his father. 'You don't think…?'

'No, not without her bags.'

More to alleviate the awkward silence that followed his father's words than anything else, Freddie spoke up. 'Rather peculiar coincidence in the village. That chap Praxton, who visited with Georgiana's father at Farleigh Hall, has been staying in Collingborne of late.' Nathaniel paused mid-stride, but Freddie rambled on, oblivious to the spasm of tension that seized his brother's body. 'Spoke to the landlord of the Fox and Hounds. Praxton's been a good customer. Apparently has business in the area. Fancy him turning up in this neck of the woods. Strange.' He was just starting to give the matter the full weight of his consideration when he glanced up to see an unfathomable expression cross Nathaniel's face.

'Walter Praxton!' he exclaimed harshly. 'His presence might well explain the situation!' It seemed that a knife twisted in his heart, and the breath knocked from his lungs. 'Georgiana was betrothed to Praxton before she wed me.' The words scraped raw his already bleeding heart, but he refused to let his family see just how deeply the wound had pierced. 'Even now her travelling bags lie packed and ready in her bedroom,' he uttered by way of explanation.

'Ah,' said Henry softly. 'You think she has deserted you.'

Evelina Howard shook her head in denial and stepped forward to speak. 'Captain Hawke, surely you could never believe such a thing?' And for the first time Nathaniel saw a flicker of worry cloud the woman's eyes.

'Run off with Praxton?' queried a confused Freddie.

A peel of ironic laughter sounded within the room. Five pairs of eyes riveted to the source—Mirabelle Farleigh. The small woman leapt to her feet, ringlets shaking, mouth wide and incredulous.

'Mirabelle!' Henry's voice sounded stern. He moved towards her, saying to the others as he did, 'She's overwrought and has become hysterical.' His hand closed gently over her arm but she threw it off with, what her husband thought to be, surprising force.

'I most certainly am not.' She pulled away from Henry and towards Nathaniel, who was trying and failing miserably to disguise the fact that he looked like a man who believed the bottom to have just dropped from his world. 'Men!' she snorted. 'Sometimes they've not one ounce of sense in those great oversized bodies of theirs!'

Mrs Howard was smiling and even the earl had reverted to a marginally more relaxed stance.

'Mirabelle, contain yourself!' commanded her husband with growing exasperation.

Lady Farleigh paid no regard whatsoever to Henry, who was trying to coax her away from his brother. She planted herself like a small rock before her brother by marriage. 'Nathaniel,' she said, 'remember when you saved Georgiana from drowning in the Borne?' She did not wait for his answer. 'Did you suppose that she slipped and fell? Of course you did. Well,' the lady concluded, 'you were wrong. She jumped into the river rather than submit to Mr Praxton's advances upon the river bank.'

Nathaniel's brows lowered and he stared at Mirabelle in confusion.

'Precisely why did you suppose that any woman would run away from home, alone, and by mail coach? Oh, and end up pretending to be a boy aboard your ship?'

The dark eyes shifted accusingly to his father. 'Does everyone know the entirety of the story?'

'Don't seek to change the subject,' instructed Mirabelle. Henry's hand tightened around her arm. 'Georgiana did all of these things to escape Walter Praxton.'

'But—'

Mirabelle gave him little chance to speak. 'Yes, she was betrothed to the man, but it was most certainly against her will. Her father intended to force the wedding, leaving Georgiana few options. When she fled, she was intent on making her way here to Collingborne.' She looked round at the earl. 'She wanted my help, and would have had it had it not been for the Impress Service.'

'I say, Georgiana's a bit of a dark horse all right!' Freddie had perked up substantially at the revelations. Even the quelling look pressed upon him by his father failed to staunch the flow of admiration. He whistled and exclaimed, 'What a girl!'

When Nathaniel still had not spoken, Mirabelle rounded on him. 'And aside from all of that, Nathaniel Hawke, how could you think she would run off with anyone else when it's as plain as the nose on your face that she's head over heels in love with you!'

Nathaniel's face drained of any last vestige of colour.

'And what's wrong with that?' demanded Mirabelle on seeing the haunted look flit across his countenance.

'Nothing at all, aside from the fact that, from what you say, it's growing increasingly probable that Georgiana has been abducted by Praxton.'

* * *

Georgiana choked as Walter attempted to pour half a tankard of wine down her throat. The cold liquid splashed over her mouth, cascading down her chin and neck to stain her gown dark wet. The rough fingers that had prised open her bruised mouth moved rapidly away as she set up a chorus of coughs and splutters. By the time she had regained her breath her cheeks were as red as the wine that stained them.

'Come, now, Georgiana, don't resist so. The wine will warm you against the night chill, and—' he paused and looked at her, desire clear in his eyes '—help you to relax. It will make things a deal easier for you.'

'I don't want it,' she spat at him.

A wicked leer struck his face. 'You're then as eager for me as I am for you? Come, sweet dove, let Walter warm you.' His hands slid over her shoulders, travelling slowly down to skim her breasts, outlined starkly by the clinging wet fabric of her dress. 'But first we must get you out of these wet clothes.'

Dear Lord help her! Praxton meant to ravish her here, a scant two miles from the house that contained her husband. Nathaniel! Nathaniel! She wanted to cry his name aloud, but knew that to do so would only incense Walter further. His fingers loitered by her nipples, causing the gall to rise in her throat. A thick wet tongue snaked across her lips, trying to breach the fortress of her mouth. For a moment she thought she would wretch from the sickening assault, but managed to pull herself away from his lips. 'No! Stop! Mr Praxton, we must…' The words faltered as he reached round to her back and started to unfasten the buttons of her gown. 'No!' she exclaimed as she tried to remove herself from his grasp. But there was nowhere to go and, with her hands and feet still bound, there seemed little to help her evade his attentions.

Cold air prickled the skin beneath the thinness of her shift following the trail of Walter Praxton's fingers. 'Mr Praxton, stop this madness at once!' she pleaded.

'You don't know how long I've waited for this night. How much I've wanted to plunder your soft white body.' His breathing had grown somewhat laboured and uneven.

'If you have any regard left for me whatsoever, do not use me like this. Please.' She relaxed a little as he stepped away, thinking to have found some vestige of honourable behaviour within him. But she was much mistaken. As Walter Praxton peeled off his finely fashioned coat and loosed his neckcloth, she saw the manic gleam within his ice-pale eyes and knew that all was lost. He would not stop until he had what he wanted. And the thought of exactly what it was that he wanted brought a black desolation to her soul. From deep within she drew a tiny spark of courage and fanned it with thoughts of all that Nathaniel had done to save both her reputation and her life. The flame burned brighter. She saw the bulge within Walter's breeches, watched while his fingers moved to unfasten them, gulped as he moved towards her.

'You always were a cowardly bully, Mr Praxton. Did you never wonder why I would do anything rather than marry you?'

Walter Praxton stopped in his tracks, a frown of annoyance darkening his golden looks. 'Mutinous thoughts planted in your head by that blasted Mrs Tillyard. Even your stepfather admits his folly in sending you to her. Of course, he was never strict enough with you, always gave in to the wants of that foolish mother of yours. I won't make the same mistake.'

She held his gaze. 'You seek to inflict your will on others through the use of violence and intimidation and money. Without those three bedfellows you would have nothing!'

'I'm a successful businessman, Georgiana, rich, good looking, all in all a highly desirable catch. It seems that it's only you that cannot see what's before your very eyes. Just think, you'll be the envy of young ladies all across Hampshire when they learn that you're my wife.' He was at her side, tugging down the arms and bodice of her dress until only the rose-stained damp shift stretched across her breasts veiled her body from his gaze.

'You're mad if you think that I'll ever wed you. I'm wife to Nathaniel Hawke and there'll be no place you can hide when he discovers that you've defiled me.' She flung the words at him, knowing that, whether Nathaniel loved her or not, he would always see justice done.

He laughed, an evil sound that rasped at her taut nerves. 'Defile? I promise to have done a damn sight more than that before this time tomorrow.' His hands groped at her breasts, kneading them painfully beneath his cruel fingers.

She refused to cower, had done with pleading. Her eyes met his forcefully, without fear. 'Do what you will, but know that I feel nothing for you, neither love nor hate, just the grey emptiness of nothing, which is exactly your worth. All my love lies with my husband and, whether you rape me, or beat me, or kill me, you'll never change that.'

One hand wrapped itself painfully in the dark silky ebony of her hair, pulling her up until their faces were so close that they shared the same breath. 'You have been a brave wife to him.' A smirk played across his lips, the candlelight glinting in his golden hair. 'But will you be so brave a widow?'

It seemed that her heart had ceased to beat. She gasped air into her constricting lungs. 'No!' she shrieked. 'You are no threat to Nathaniel. He's more of a man than you'll ever be!'

The blow landed hard against her temple, stunning her wits, collapsing her body. 'Bitch!' he cursed. 'How little you know.' He saw the storm clouds gather in her eyes. 'What

would you give to save his life? Yourself? Would you beg me?'
His mouth moved to a smile and his fingers danced around
the neckline of her sodden shift.

What it was that drew Nathaniel towards the far side of
Beacon Hill he could never be sure, but the growing sense that
Georgiana called him urged him on. Through the blackness
of the night the candle lantern illuminated little, but as the
heavens smiled on him the thick cover of clouds rolled back
to reveal a huge opalescent moon. Silver light bathed the
countryside so that the small group of riders made good
progress. The earl wanted to split up, make a sweeping check
of up to old Tom's farm in one direction and John Appleton's
in the other. But Nathaniel was steadfast in his refusal, adamant in his determination that they search Beacon Hill before
all else. Then he saw it. The faint hint of light emanating from
the woodsman's hut within the copse of trees. And even before they had spurred their horses a fraction closer, he knew
that Georgiana was within.

They dismounted and left their horses, creeping quietly forward through the frozen brush until they reached their target.
Through the somewhat battered looking wooden door the
murmur of voices could be heard, a man's laugh, mocking and
loud, a woman's denial, vehement, disgusted. Nathaniel did
not wait to hear any more. The door gave way beneath the ferocity of the combined weight of his and Henry's kicks. The
sight that met his eyes ignited in Nathaniel a fury and fear that
escalated beyond all control.

Walter Praxton was kneeling upon the bed, golden hair
glowing in the candlelight, shirtless, in the process of loosing the fastenings on his breeches. Beneath him lay Georgiana, her face white and pinched, her gown ripped open, a

thin stained shift moulded to her breasts. For the merest fraction of a second Nathaniel paused to assess the scene, then moved in a fluid motion to deliver first one resounding blow and then another to Praxton. The younger man pitched to the floor, limp and helpless beneath the weight of Nathaniel's towering rage. Dark eyes glowered with implacable anger and he would have pressed his assault further had it not been for her whisper.

'Nathaniel?' Her voice was small, strained, as if she could not be sure that the man before her eyes was a mirage of her own making or of flesh and blood. All thoughts of Praxton were forgotten as he reached down, cradling her in his arms.

'Dear Lord, what has he done to you?' he uttered hoarsely, scanning the darkening bruises on her face and the ripped bodice.

She smiled then, and it banished the horror from her expression. 'You came in time,' was all she said, and a solitary tear trickled down her cheek.

He clutched her to him as if he would never let her go, touched his lips gently to her cheek, her forehead, her chin. 'Thank God you've taken no more hurts. I'd never have forgiven myself if…' He could not continue. Clearing his throat, he stood up and, shrugging off his coat, wrapped it around his wife's trembling body, before freeing her bound hands and feet. 'You're safe now and we must get you home.'

'What of him?' Henry's toe touched to Praxton's still-limp body.

'Strap him across his horse. We'll keep him at Collingborne until the High Constable can be notified.'

Nathaniel clambered upon his gelding and was in the process of lifting Georgiana up from his father's arms when it happened. Just as Henry and Freddie were placing Walter

Praxton's body across his own saddle, the wretched man suddenly roused from his feigned faint, delivered Henry a solid kick in the chest, and made off at a furious gallop. Nathaniel's brothers made to follow.

'No!' he yelled. 'Let him go for now.'

Freddie turned incredulous eyes upon him. 'You would let that villain escape?'

'It's dark and freezing. He'll not get far dressed as he is. We'll find him a damn sight easier by daylight. And besides, Georgiana has suffered enough this night. We should take her back to Collingborne now.'

With great reluctance Freddie was forced to concede that his brother was most probably right.

The next morning Georgiana awoke, snuggled warm beneath the covers of the four-poster bed in the rose room within Collingborne House. Apart from a tenderness around her face and head she had sustained no other hurts from her ordeal with Walter Praxton. The image of Nathaniel bursting through the door to save her from Praxton's evil intent would stay with her for ever. She knew then that she could never leave him, despite all the trouble she had brought upon him. He would have to cast her out himself if he wanted her to go. And whatever he may have said, or more for that matter left unsaid, she knew from the look upon his face when he'd held her to him within that cold dismal hut that he would never do that. Tenderness, relief, guilt, concern, desire, and something else that she feared to name, lest she be mistaken. The thought brought a smile to her face, nipping at her bruised lip, and she cast a probing hand over the sheet in the direction of where her husband had lain all the night through. It met with the emptiness of cooled sheeting, nothing else. She sat up abruptly, alarmed at the prospect he had gone.

'Georgiana!' A deep melodic voice sounded from the other side of the room. His tall dark figure turned from the bright white light of the window and moved towards her, but not before she had scrambled from the bed to stand before him, she in her voluminous white nightgown, he fully attired in the smartest of clothes.

'It's Christmas Eve.'

He could hear the consternation in her tone. Little wonder following her ordeal at that rogue's hands. How would she take the news? he wondered. At least she would never have to worry again in the future. 'Yes,' he agreed quietly.

Her hands grasped his arms, and she stretched up on her tiptoes to look into his face. Eyes the colour of a winter Atlantic scanned his, imploringly.

'Georgiana?'

She felt the muscles contract beneath her fingers, knew the strength contained in those arms.

'What's wrong? There's nothing more to fear. Praxton is dead. We found his body this morning out by Parson's Gully. It seems that he knew I rode out that way each day and had set a trap for me across the path. We found the same rope in one of his saddlebags. No doubt he planned to make it look like an accident and then miraculously be on hand to comfort the grieving widow. In the darkness Praxton couldn't see and plunged straight into it. His neck was broken in the fall.' He moved one arm to curl around her waist, while the other hand stroked enticing circles upon her back.

Her eyes widened momentarily and she shuddered. 'Killed by his own treachery,' she said softly.

'Georgiana.'

She shook her head. 'It isn't that.' She loosed her hand to

pull at her ear lobe, her gaze dropping to meet level with the breadth of his chest.

'I've written to your father informing him of our marriage and Praxton's death. I know that he tried to forcibly wed you to that scoundrel and so you need not see him again.'

'You're very kind to me, Nathaniel Hawke. But I shall not fear to visit my family with my husband by my side.'

The cloud of worry still lurked in her eyes. 'What is it, Georgiana?' He touched a finger gingerly to her cheek to raise her eyes once more to his.

'Henry. I know he was there at the woodsman's hut. But you and he… Your disagreement…'

Nathaniel stared at her as if she had run mad, then suddenly smiled. He pressed a tiny kiss to the tip of her nose and laughed. 'Is resolved, sweetheart. I should have told you last night, but there were other more pressing matters on my mind.' The twinkle in his eye brought a blush to Georgiana's cheeks. 'Henry has apologised unreservedly for his behaviour, and is desperate to beg your forgiveness.'

'But—'

'You might say family relations have never been so good.' Nathaniel traced the delicate outline of her face. Her eyes flicked towards where she had placed her travelling bags, only to find they had disappeared.

Nathaniel plucked a kiss from one eyebrow, then the other. 'I took the liberty of instructing the maid to unpack your things.'

'But your father—'

'My father is awaiting your arrival downstairs with great impatience.'

A little line of worry wrinkled between her eyes.

Nathaniel's thumb soon soothed it smooth. 'He wants you to stay. As I do, minx.'

Georgiana smiled at that.

'When I realised that Praxton had abducted you, it was the worst moment of my life. Finding you before he could inflict any more harm on you was the best.'

'Nathaniel,' she whispered, but he stilled her lips with the featherlight touch of a finger.

'No. I want you to know this first. These past days I've been a fool, avoiding your company, arguing with Henry, and all because I refused to face what was there before my very eyes. I love you, Georgiana. Always have done and always will. I was just too damned stupid to realise it until it was almost too late. Can you forgive me?' Deep dark eyes held hers with impassioned plea.

She reached up her lips so that they hovered just beneath his. 'What is there to forgive? You've saved both my life and reputation three times. I'm yours, Captain Hawke, whether you want me or not.' Her mouth slid to a wry grin. 'You'll have no more chances to rid yourself of me.'

His hands slid to her buttocks, gripping her to him so that they moulded together. 'Lady Hawke, you'll have no more bids to escape me, captain's orders!' A dark eyebrow winged high as he nuzzled his mouth to her neck.

Georgiana claimed his lips with hers, all bruises forgotten in the mounting passion. And when their tongues arced together in tantalising seduction, Nathaniel knew that it would be quite some time before they left the safe haven of their bedroom.

Henry was becoming positively worried. 'Perhaps she's taken a greater hurt than we knew. Look at the time and she still hasn't woken. Nathaniel's been up there for at least an hour. Maybe I should go up and investigate the matter.'

'I'm sure that Georgiana will join us as soon as she is able.'

Mirabelle touched but one light hand to the viscount's sleeve; it was enough to bring him seated back down by her side.

Freddie smiled knowingly. 'You mean as soon as Nathaniel lets her out of bed,' he added with a wicked gleam in his dark eyes.

'Freddie!' admonished Lord Porchester. 'There are ladies present!'

Mirabelle smiled broadly in her husband's direction.

Freddie coughed and looked at Mrs Howard.

Mrs Howard's expression remained demure as she sipped her madeira and watched the snowflakes drift gently past the drawing room window. 'To Nathaniel and Georgiana, may their lives be blessed with health and happiness.'

Voices raised in hearty agreement.

And the snow conspired to wrap Collingborne House in a thick white blanket of love.

Mistaken Mistress

Chapter One

May 1815

'*K*athryn, my sweet dove, you're the only woman for me. Say that you'll be my wife, I beg of you!' Lord Ravensmede plucked her svelte figure into his arms and placed an ardent kiss of love upon her perfect pouting lips. His glossy dark hair mixed with the rich red-brown ringlets dancing temptingly at the sides of her beautiful face. He moved back to stare into her eyes, eyes that were of a serene silver coloration and not at all a bland grey. 'I love you, Kathryn Marchant!' he declared with passion and kissed her again, mindful not to spoil the arrangement of her new and highly fashionable lemon silk dress.

'Kathryn, Kathryn! Stop wool-gathering and attend to me at once! Are you deaf that you cannot hear me calling you?' Lottie stared at her cousin with narrowed eyes. 'For heaven's sake,' she whispered loudly, 'you're here to assist me, not gawk around like an imbecile.' Her voice resumed its normal tone and with one white and perfectly manicured hand she gestured vaguely in the direction of the floor. 'The hem of my dress has caught on the buckle of Miss Dawson's slipper. Disengage it before any damage is done.'

As Kathryn stooped to free the offending article, which

proved to be more difficult than anticipated, she listened to Lottie's conversation. *Dear Lord*, she thought. *The pair of them are as vainly empty-headed as ever!* Then had the grace to blush when she remembered the content of her own sweet daydream.

'Jane, I declare they're both prodigiously handsome. I couldn't pick which man is the better of the two.'

'Well, they're rakes, both of them. My mama has warned me to stay clear of their sort.'

'Tush, Jane, you're such a ninnyhammer at times. They may be rakes, but they're titled and wealthy to boot…and so devilishly good looking. Would your mama say no to you landing a lord?'

'They're looking over here, Lottie.'

'No!'

'Yes, indeed, it's true.'

'Look away, quickly! Don't let them see that we've noticed them.'

Not only did Miss Dawson avert her head but, in a moment of preoccupation, which can only be supposed to have resulted from her excitement over the gentlemen in question, she also stepped back.

Kathryn gasped as Miss Dawson's large foot inadvertently trod on her fingers. The good that resulted from this was that Lottie's dress was freed in an instant. The bad, aside from Kathryn's bruised digits, was that a small tear appeared in the hem.

'Dear Lord, I don't believe it! My dress is ruined. This is the first time I've worn it and, thanks to Kathryn, it's ruined. I may as well go home this instant.' Tears pricked at Lottie's blue eyes, rendering them brighter and bluer, if that were at all possible. The tiniest flush of pink crept into her cheeks, completing, in Kathryn's mind at least, the perfection of her beauty.

'No, dear Lottie. It's scarcely noticeable. A small stitch will soon have that remedied,' Miss Dawson soothed her friend.

Lottie's pale eyebrows arched in irritation as she peered down at Kathryn, who was trying her best to conceal the damage. 'You did that on purpose, just to ruin my evening!'

Then she turned to Miss Dawson once more. 'Kathryn's such a spiteful cat. You'd think she'd be grateful, wouldn't you? Saved from destitution by the kindness of *my* family.'

Miss Dawson's eyes opened wider. She tried to speak. 'Lottie—'

But Lottie was in full rant as she warmed to one of her favourite subjects. 'And what does she give in return? Humble gratitude? Most certainly not.'

Miss Dawson tried again. 'Lott—'

'If you would be so kind as to let me finish, Jane. As I was saying, all she gives is jealousy and stupidity!'

'Indeed, life can be so tedious sometimes, Miss Marchant, don't you think?'

The deep masculine drawl caused Lottie to jump. She turned startled eyes in the direction from which it had sounded. Her expression of spiteful fury transformed instantly to one of demure innocence. 'Lord Ravensmede,' she uttered faintly. And looking beyond the breadth of his shoulder, 'Lord Cadmount.' Belatedly, and with a countenance that had stained ruddy, she made her devoirs.

Kathryn looked up from her knees and saw Lord Ravensmede so very far above her. *Not like this. Please, don't let him see me like this!* She swallowed her embarrassment and rose swiftly to her feet, allowing the two quizzical glances to wash over her. The thumping of her heart was so loud that she feared the whole ballroom would hear it. On either side of her were the taller forms of Miss Dawson and Cousin Lottie in all their finery. And not three feet in front stood the subject of her daydreams—the Viscount of Ravensmede. This time there was no lemon silk dress for Kathryn, no pretty dancing ringlets. The reality of their meeting stood in stark contrast to her dream. Still, she mustered a stiff little smile.

Ravensmede's gaze did not linger, returning instead to Lottie, who was frantically fanning herself to remove the scalded heat from her cheeks. She batted her eyelashes, looked coy, and did not offer to introduce her cousin. Neither did his lordship request an introduction. Indeed, he had looked at her, in Kathryn's own view, as if she were no more than a crumb upon the floor.

Attraction retreated. Indignation rallied. Anger advanced. Quite clearly Lord Ravensmede's handsome looks were not matched by a handsome temperament. Why, he was possibly one of the rudest men Kathryn had ever met. And then it dawned on her exactly why Lottie had made no introduction. Lord Ravensmede thought her a servant, and Lottie, dear Cousin Lottie, wanted it to appear so to excuse the chastisement he had interrupted. Two fiery patches erupted on Kathryn's cheeks. She might be an orphan, and poor. She might live under the name of companion and work as a servant. But through all her shabby misery she still had her good name, and that knowledge lent her courage. Might well they talk of a breach of manners! She set a stubborn tilt to her jaw and in a frosty tone uttered their given names. 'Lottie, Jane, gentlemen—' she eyed Lord Ravensmede with special dislike '—please do excuse me.' She saw the arrogant arch of his eyebrow. With a degree of satisfaction and her head held high, she turned on her heel and walked away.

Ravensmede noticed her then, the small sparrow of a girl with her ancient grey gown and her ruffled dignity. The look that she shot him from those stunning silver eyes was not one the Viscount was used to seeing in women: disapproval, dislike and disappointment all wrapped up into one. A spark of interest ignited. Ravensmede followed the retreat of the girl's straight back until she disappeared into the crowd. Even then, he continued to trace her steady progress weaving through the crush of guests until he heard Cadmount say with the glimmer of a laugh, 'One just can't get the staff these days.'

He watched while Miss Dawson creased with embarrassment and glanced nervously at Miss Marchant, whose bland prettiness seemed only mildly perturbed. Neither replied. Ravensmede tucked the matter away for later consideration and idled away a little more of his time before announcing, 'Ladies, please excuse me. I have a rather pressing engagement.' Then he headed off on the real purpose behind his attendance at so dull an affair as Lady Finlay's ball.

Kathryn had almost made it out of the ballroom when she was halted by a woman's haughty voice.

'Just where do you think you're going?' Aunt Anna loomed behind her, reticule in hand, resplendent in a cream-and-rose creation.

'The ladies' retiring room.' Kathryn forced a politeness to the words that she did not feel. It was the only way of dealing with Aunt Anna. Every other means only worsened the situation. That she was reliant on her aunt and uncle's charity for the roof over her head and the food in her belly was something that she never forgot. Neither, for that matter, did they.

'You've left Lottie alone?' The question was in her aunt's usual imperious tone. Kathryn could have sworn that it was edged with accusation.

'No. She's with Miss Dawson.' Kathryn looked at her tall well-dressed relative and waited. She omitted to mention the conditions under which she had abandoned the younger women. No doubt Aunt Anna would find out soon enough.

Mrs Marchant frowned, as was her habit when addressing her niece, and averted her gaze. 'Then you had best be quick about your business. You're here as Lottie's companion, try to remember that. My patience wears thin with reminding you.'

Still Kathryn stood, betraying nothing, her face a mask of polite indifference.

'Well, what are you waiting for? Get on with it.' Mrs Marchant waved her hand in a dismissive gesture.

Kathryn turned and walked away.

She sighed and rubbed at her brow to ease the knot of tension. In truth Kathryn had no need to visit the retiring room; it was merely an excuse to avoid the loathsome Lottie. No matter the cost, Kathryn knew that she needed some little time away from the spoiled spite of her cousin and the arrogant disregard of Lord Ravensmede. She'd already done quite enough damage on the Lottie front, the repercussions of which would no doubt be reaped in the very near future. And as for Lord Ravensmede...

Walking as briskly as she could, she passed unnoticed through the throng of hot, perfumed bodies and escaped into the hall. Quite where she was going she did not know—anywhere would do as long as it gave her the respite she sought. Just five minutes to cool the splurge of temper that had risen too readily. Over the past three years she had learned to school such reactions, to bear all with a stoic countenance. It was better, after all, to show nothing. And now, despite all of that practice, she had almost lost her temper.

Five minutes. It surely wasn't too much to ask. Five paltry minutes, and then she'd turn her feet around and return to face it all once more, as if she had never been away. No one need notice. Indeed, no one ever did notice plain Kathryn Marchant, which is why Aunt Anna and Uncle Henry had agreed to have her to live with them after her papa's death. She was the perfect backdrop against which to exhibit their own sweet Lottie, and, of course, it saved on the expense of employing another servant. It was something that Kathryn had firmly resolved not to dwell upon, as such thoughts could do nothing except produce a bitterness that was unworthy of all that her dear departed mama and papa had instilled in her.

The hallway had become a corridor, which continued through a set of doors towards the rear of Lady Finlay's large mansion house. Not another soul was to be seen. Evidently Lady Finlay had the servants engaged elsewhere and no other guest would be so rude or so bold as to wander so freely. The corridor became a gallery and Kathryn paused to examine the paintings that lined the walls. Faces, some faintly reminiscent of the elderly Lord Finlay, peered down at her. Just as she was examining a lofty-looking young man's features, footsteps sounded in the distance.

Lord above, she could not be found here! Why, just imagine Aunt Anna's reaction to the news that her niece had taken it upon herself to inspect her ladyship's family portraits. Glancing around in panic, she spied a single door at the end of the gallery, just at the point where the corridor turned and led away to the right. The footsteps grew louder.

Kathryn did not wait to hear any more. Within the blink of an eye she ran towards the door, and, finding it to be unlocked, whipped into the room beyond. Just in time, for the footsteps, large and plodding, passed her hiding place and continued off into the distance. She heaved a sigh of relief and turned to look at the place in which she now stood.

It appeared to be a large room with a few items of dustsheet-covered furniture clustered around its periphery. There were no candles burning and no fire within the blackened grate. Yet the centre of the room was bathed in a silver light that flooded in through a pair of glass doors. The magical illumination drew Kathryn like a moth. Lottie and Aunt Anna were no more. All else was forgotten as the moonlight lulled her under its spell. Through the panes of glass she could see the deep darkness of the night sky studded with the glitter of distant stars. But the moon itself was what held her attention—huge and white, a glowing orb amidst the darkness. Kathryn stared with increasing fascination. Such a feeling of peace. Within the silent silver room anger ebbed, indignation crumbled.

There had been nothing unusual in Lottie's behaviour; Kathryn had long since grown used to her cousin's high-handed ways. What was it, then, that had instigated her outburst? The question perhaps should have been *who* rather than *what*. And the answer, to Kathryn's chagrin, was patently obvious: Lord Ravensmede.

It was one thing to escape the reality of her life by daydreaming, but quite another when those dreams involved a particular nobleman. Unfortunately, she had been thus affected since first seeing the arrogant man across the floor at Almack's Assembly

Rooms a month ago. It was just an imagining, a game that she played inside her head, nothing more. Harmless, or at least it had been until now. But she had reckoned without this evening. She knew that no man of quality would look twice at such a plain penniless creature as herself. Witnessing the obvious disdain in which Lord Ravensmede held her was humiliating, as if the cloth had been torn from the mirror and she had been forced to stand exposed before it. Kathryn's life did not make for a pretty picture.

She thought of the past eight years, of the deaths of her parents and her sister. Nothing of Aunt Anna's dislike or Lottie's tantrums could compare with the pain that those losses had wrought. At first she had thought it intolerable, but as the weeks became months, and the months, years, Kathryn had learned to live with the ache buried deep in her heart. She could take whatever Aunt Anna wished to throw at her. Wasn't that what daydreams were for? To make life bearable? To make one impervious to hurt? Lord Ravensmede could not be allowed to change that. His behaviour was an abomination of all that was gentlemanly. He was as arrogant a scoundrel as his reputation told. For certain his place in her dreams was now forfeit. She would not think of him again. Most definitely not. And all the while the cool silver light stroked her with its comforting caress.

Kathryn could never be sure of what it was that made her suddenly draw back into the darkness of the shadows, but barely had she done so when the door creaked open and a large figure slipped inside. The door closed with a quiet click.

'Amanda?' The whisper was clearly that of a man.

She stood quiet and motionless, hoping to hide her presence from the stranger.

The soft tread of his footsteps sounded against the floor.

Her back hugged the floral-print wallpaper. *Please stay where you are and come no further.*

'Amanda?' the voice whispered again and a figure advanced into the moonlight.

The breath caught in Kathryn's throat as the light illuminated his face. *Dear Lord, no! It cannot be*. As if summoned by her thoughts, there stood the stark figure of the Viscount of Ravensmede.

His head lifted, as a hound that scents the hare, and it seemed that he could see through the darkness to look right at her.

Do not see me. Pray, do not know that I'm here. Kathryn tried to quieten her ragged breathing.

'Amanda, what game are you playing? Have you forgotten our little arrangement?' He walked slowly, determinedly towards her.

A meeting with his inamorata, except that it isn't Amanda, whomever she may be, who is here. She swallowed hard, and heard the smile in his voice.

'Very well, we'll proceed as you prefer. I must agree that it is a rather entertaining novelty…for now.'

There is nothing else for it; I will have to own my identity. Kathryn was just about to step forward when his fingers touched to her wrist. A short sharp intake of breath. She made to warn him of his mistake, only to find herself in the Viscount's arms and her would-be protestations silenced by the warm touch of his lips. She stiffened and tried to pull away.

But Lord Ravensmede clearly had other ideas. His hands stroked sensuously against her back, imprisoning her with their caress. His heat burned through the fabric of her bodice.

She pushed hard against his chest, her fingers all too aware of the unyielding muscle beneath. Panic gripped her. She struggled. Opened her mouth to scream.

Slowly, deliberately, he intensified the kiss, his tongue tracing a spell against her lips before it probed within.

Something fluttered deep within her, and all her good intentions disappeared in a warm fuzzy haze. Kathryn moaned and gave up all semblance of resistance as reality and daydream merged within the passion of the moment.

She didn't understand what was happening to her. Knew that

her behaviour was reprehensible. But her blood surged wild and strong, and the sensations assailing her would not be denied. Taste of nectar on her tongue. Touch of lips that slid against hers—demanding, enticing. Smell of clean masculinity mixed with the subtle undertones of bergamot. Even when every rational thought screamed out that she should stop she could not. Common sense fled. Kathryn answered the call of Lord Ravensmede's body. She relaxed into his arms, her rigidity shed like a cloak upon the floor. So warm, so comfortable. She sighed and nestled closer. For that one brief moment in time Kathryn was the woman of her dreams, neither poor nor dowdy, but desirable and loved. Dewy breath caressed her cheek. A soft whisper tickled her ear.

'Amanda.' The name rolled lazily off his tongue.

Kathryn descended back down to earth with a crash, all her dreams shattered in an instant. *What am I doing letting him kiss me? It's not Kathryn Marchant that he holds so tenderly, but another woman altogether. If he knew the truth...* 'No!' Her whisper was loud and urgent. She thrust herself back from him.

'What the...?' His puzzlement was palpable.

'No!' she said again, louder this time and with quiet determination. She tried to move away. But she had reckoned without Lord Ravensmede.

He stepped closer, backing her up against the wall. 'What's wrong? Was the diamond bracelet not to your liking?' One large thumb drizzled slowly down her cheek to brush against the soft cushion of her mouth. 'Come, Amanda, we're both hardened players of this game.'

Kathryn's heart thundered in her chest, her pulse leaping at her throat. Her whisper was loud against the hiss of silence. 'You're mistaken, my lord. I am not...'

Ravensmede halted her words with an ardent kiss. 'Am I then mistaken in that? Or in the fact that your kisses are the sweetest I've ever tasted?' His hands slid over her shoulders as he pulled her to him. 'Trembling like a virgin, Mrs White? Did

I not know just how determinedly you had courted my attention, your timidity might be believable.' He made to kiss her again, but was thwarted by Kathryn's wriggles and succeeded only in planting a chaste kiss upon the tip of her nose.

The time for speaking was past. Kathryn knew she had but one opportunity for escape and she created it with a sudden exclamation. 'My lord, there's someone at the window!' When Ravensmede turned to look over his shoulder, she bolted and ran for the door. Blood pounded in her temples and her breath shortened. Movement sounded behind her, but she did not look back, just kept running. Her fingers reached forward, the tips touching to the cool brass of the doorknob before their contact was severed. A strong arm wound around her waist and yanked her back against a wall of solid muscle.

'What the hell is this about, Amanda? You've been flirting with me for months, practically begging me to visit your bed, and when finally I agree you flee as if the very devil is on your heels. Let's resolve this matter once and for all, madam.' He waited with patience, but did not loosen his grip.

A thousand thoughts whirled through Kathryn's brain. Plans to escape, words of excuse, fear and panic, but through them all she knew her time had come. There was no alternative other than to let him see the truth and await his reaction. Dear Lord, if there was any other way! She steeled herself to the task, to the revulsion and anger she knew that she would see in his face. There could be no further prevarication. She ceased her struggle.

'An explanation, please, if you would be so good, Mrs White.'

'I did not mean for this to happen, my lord.'

She allowed Lord Ravensmede to turn her in his arms, knowing full well it would be the last time ever she would feel his touch. The shadow had lightened a little, but as she looked up she could see nothing more than the dark outline of his face, and was thankful that it was so. 'I am not Mrs White,' she said simply.

Silence stretched between them.

Abruptly he pulled her across the room to stand before the glass doors. Moonlight captured his stunned features, proclaiming the perfection of each contour, every plane. Dark eyes glittered incredulously, raking every fibre of her being until she thought she could stand his silent scrutiny no more. She stood stiff and erect, her pride holding all else in check.

'I am Miss Kathryn Marchant, the cousin of Miss Lottie Marchant.'

No reply, just the soft sound of his breathing, and the continued pressure of his hands around her upper arms.

A tremble set up in her legs. 'I only sought some…somewhere where I could be alone.' The words were stilted, awkward. 'I did not know that…that the room was to be used by another…others,' she corrected.

Still he did not speak.

'What has occurred here has been a mistake. I beg that you'll speak of it to no one. If my aunt was to hear…' She could not finish what she had started.

His voice rumbled low, little more than a whisper. 'Why did you not speak earlier? Inform me of my…error?'

A hot blush flooded her cheeks. 'I tried—'

He raised an eyebrow. 'Not very convincingly.'

'I could not, my lord.'

'Could not, or would not, Miss Marchant?'

She quailed beneath the intensity of his stare.

'You play a very foolish game…a downright dangerous game.'

The touch of his fingers burned where they contacted the bare skin of her arms.

'Don't tell me you have not heard of my reputation?' he mocked, then glanced away as if there was something he could not quite fathom. When his gaze slid back to hers there was something in it that caused her heart to race even faster.

She did not answer. Aridity threatened to close her throat. When finally her words came they were nothing but a hoarse whisper. 'Please excuse me, my lord, I must return to my cousin.'

'Really?' There was a lazy drawl in Ravensmede's voice that did not match the glint in his eye.

'Indeed, my lord.'

His lordship showed not the slightest inclination to withdraw his hands.

Beneath the magical glow of the moonlight her skin was pale and smooth as alabaster. Her hair was still pinned back, but some of the curls had escaped to dangle enticingly against her cheek and throat. One finger lifted a curl from her cheek, then slid down to trace the delicate line of her jaw. His gaze followed where his finger led, then meandered back to her eyes that appeared opalescent in the moonlight. Fringed with long dark lashes, glittering with unshed moisture, her eyes were quite simply beautiful. And contained in the stare that she returned him Ravensmede could see shock and guilt…and passion. She was playing with fire. Already the heat within him kindled.

'Miss Marchant, someone should teach you…' deliberately he leaned down and allowed his breath to caress her ear '…the perils…' his lips hovered by the side of her face, so close yet not touching '…of allowing yourself…' he closed the last small space that divided them until he felt his thighs brush against her skirts '…to be kissed by a rake.' Her clean feminine fragrance filled his nose. Where their legs touched he could feel the slight tremor running through her. He watched her eyes widen, but she did not try to pull away. 'Shall I, Kathryn?' he exhaled the question in a soft breath. He looked at her a moment longer, then gently, insistently, covered her mouth with his, massaging her lips in a slow, sensual motion.

She tasted sweet and innocent…and completely alluring. Desire leapt. Their first kisses had not lied. He wanted nothing more than to deepen the kiss, to drink in every last drop of her. Attraction scorched as hot as if he were the greenest of lads. He wanted to reach in and touch her as she had touched him. Temptation loomed large. And Nicholas Maybury, Viscount of Ravensmede, had never been a man to deny himself.

'By the heavens, Ravensmede! You arrange an assignation with me then fill my place with another before I arrive!' A woman's shrill voice shrieked at full volume from the doorway. 'You, sir, are a damnable scoundrel!'

He felt the girl jump within his arms, heard her sudden shocked gasp. It was with a great degree of reticence that he removed his embrace. 'Mrs White, how very good of you to join us,' he said.

The voluptuous young widow's eyes slid towards Miss Marchant and narrowed further.

He sensed rather than saw the girl's withdrawal. 'Miss Marchant and I were just admiring the night sky.'

A derisive snort sounded from the beauty. She stepped fully into the room, leaving the door gaping wide behind her. 'I know full well exactly what you and…Miss Marchant…were doing and it had nothing to do with the stars! Don't take me for a fool, Ravensmede!'

'I must insist that you're mistaken, my dear Mrs White.' He moved to stand between the two women, shielding Kathryn from the other's view. Mrs White's abundant bosom expanded before his very eyes, rising and falling with alarming speed. There was about her face a slyness that he had not observed before. He wondered that he ever could have mistaken one woman for the other, for in the clear moonlight there was certainly nothing of a similarity between them. Amanda White was tall with a curvaceous figure. Kathryn Marchant was not. And yet it was the smaller, slimmer woman in the unfashionable plain gown that he wanted; the woman whose eyes were cool silver, and whose lips were hot with untapped passion.

'I know what I saw, sir,' Mrs White said harshly. 'Miss Marchant, indeed.' Her head bobbed to look down upon Kathryn's pale face. 'My, how your standards have dropped if you have taken up with such a plain little specimen. You know, of course, that she's nothing but a poor companion.' Her pretty face hardened into malice as she stared. 'But then gentlemen will be gentlemen and have *whatever* they can from *whoever* will give it. It signifies nothing other than the perfidy of men in general. You, my lord, are no exception to the rule.'

Kathryn skirted Lord Ravensmede's large frame and made for the door, but not before Mrs White had moved to block her exit.

'You're a trifle late in leaving, Miss Marchant. In fact, you never should have arrived. Scuttle back to your aunt, I'm sure she'll be very interested in this evening's activities.' The widow laughed, a cruel and petty sound.

Through the dimness Ravensmede could see Kathryn's face, white as a ghost, her eyes huge and round, staring with a horror that even her controlled façade could not disguise. Such vulnerability, such innocence. In one fleeting moment her life had been ruined...and he was not without blame in the matter. It was one thing to have a little fun, quite another to allow the woman to suffer. He knew what would happen if Mrs White's gossip was allowed to spread. Guilt flickered. It was not a familiar feeling for Lord Ravensmede, and it led to contrariness.

'Miss Marchant,' he said with more asperity in his tone than was necessary, 'return to your family.' It sounded cold and imperious even to his own ear. She walked towards the door as if heading to her own execution. 'We shall continue our study in astronomy another time.' And he meant it. Kathryn Marchant's kisses had shattered the monotony of his boredom and awakened a long-forgotten part of him. Ravensmede had no intention of just letting her walk out of his life. But first, and more importantly, he had to deal with Amanda White. He waited until he heard the soft click of the closing door.

'Mrs White, I apologise for the misunderstanding this evening. The situation, as I said, was one of complete innocence, even if it may have appeared otherwise.'

The widow said nothing, just looked at him with her heavy-lidded eyes and an expression of smug irritation.

Rose-scented perfume wafted to greet his nostrils. Overstated, cloying, like its wearer. Strangely he had not noticed it before. 'You're a woman of some standing—' that was certainly one way of putting it '—with a compassionate nature.' There was nothing of those traits in the look she returned him, but Amanda White was above all a vain woman, and it was to this weakness that Ravensmede played. 'I know that when I ask that you make no mention of this affair, you will indulge my request.'

'Of course, Lord Ravensmede. Your request is my pleasure.' Her pale eyes glittered coldly; a veil of insincerity covered her. She stepped closer, arranging her posture to exemplify the voluptuous curves of her figure. Rosebud lips parted as if in invitation. 'But, first, have we not unfinished business to attend to?'

Lord Ravensmede looked at the woman before him, at the artfully arranged hair, and the costly silver-and-blue dress. Her generous bosom swelled, tempting, teasing in design. And then her cruel derisive words to Kathryn Marchant rang clearly in his mind, dampening any interest he may have had. Revulsion rippled down his spine.

'I'm afraid that that can no longer be the case.'

The pale eyes narrowed.

'This evening's…incident…has no bearing on the matter. Circumstances have changed.'

The pouting lips narrowed to a thin line.

'You're welcome to retain the gift that I sent.'

'Of course.'

Ravensmede said nothing, just allowed the silence to stretch to discomfort, and watched the widow's anger and irritation grow.

Mrs White's gaze broke first. 'If that is all, Lord Ravensmede, I shall bid you good evening. There is suddenly a matter that I simply must discuss with the ladies.' She turned to leave.

'Not quite all, Mrs White.'

Her movement checked. Hope leapt. 'My lord?'

Ravensmede could hear the deliberate reversion in her tone: from shrill annoyance to husky enticement. The ghost of a curve touched at his lips. 'Gossip is such a vulgar pastime, don't you think?'

She hesitated. 'I cannot agree, sir.' There was a furtiveness to her expression.

'Allow me to persuade you otherwise—a banker's draft for two thousand guineas to be delivered to your address tomorrow morning in exchange for your silence.'

Two thousand guineas! Mrs White's eyes bulged. And then she recovered herself. 'I might consider it…' she sniffed '…if the sum were perhaps three thousand.'

Ravensmede's smiled a chilling smile. It was enough to make the hairs on the back of Amanda White's pretty white neck stand on end. 'Two thousand guineas,' he said, 'take it or leave it. Make your choice before the offer is withdrawn.' He stepped towards her. 'And should you choose wrongly, Mrs White, let's just say you may find your own reputation a little the worse for wear.'

'Are you threatening me?'

'Would I do such a thing?' He raised an arrogant eyebrow as if the very suggestion amused him. 'I'm merely illustrating the rule of cause and effect. Gossip about Kathryn Marchant and you'll not find a welcome at any decent house in London.'

Anger flashed in her eyes. 'Don't be ridiculous! You know nothing, Ravensmede, nothing that you could use against me.'

He shrugged his shoulders in a nonchalant manner. 'Perhaps, but everyone has something to hide, a secret. Consider yours very carefully. For should I have reason, I would discover it.'

'You could not!' she exclaimed, but there was a definite echo of fear in her voice.

'My wealth and power are considerable. And everybody has a price. You of all people should know that, Amanda.'

She paled and took a few steps back.

He slipped his watch from his pocket and glanced down at the face. 'Time's up, Mrs White. What is it to be?'

She cleared her throat. 'I'll accept the money.'

'Bravo.' He looked at her a little longer with that same lazy expression. 'Might I be so bold as to suggest that you would benefit from a sojourn in the country. A few weeks away from the heat of the town…'

'I'll think about it,' she ground out from between gritted teeth.

'Please do,' he said as if they were having the politest of conversations.

They stared at one another with barely concealed dislike across the small distance.

'Good evening, my lord.'

She turned and was gone, leaving Ravensmede to ponder on what he had just done to one of London's most coveted women…and all for the sake of Miss Kathryn Marchant.

Chapter Two

Kathryn sat composedly watching her cousin being whirled around the dance floor by a young gentleman whose features bore a startling resemblance to a horse. On the other side of Lottie's empty chair Mrs Marchant was chatting to Mrs Brown, the tinkle of her laughter ringing out into the ballroom.

Kathryn concentrated on the music and tried to disguise her mounting worry. As the minutes ticked slowly by without a sign of either Lord Ravensmede or Mrs White, she began to hope that they had left the ball. But that would mean only one thing, and, despite everything, it was not a pleasing thought. She heard again the echo of his parting words: *We shall continue our study in astronomy another time*. Surely he did not think… But hadn't she given him every reason to believe so? So caught up in her remembrances was she that she did not at first notice the arrival of the beautiful woman accompanying Lady Spey. Only the overpowering scent of roses alerted her.

'Mrs Marchant, may I present Mrs White, who is a friend of mine.'

Kathryn senses reeled. *No!*

'Mrs Marchant!' the husky voice gushed. 'How very pleased I am to meet you. I've heard only good things about you.'

'Mrs White, the pleasure is mine.' Mrs Marchant puffed out her chest in a self-important manner.

The widow turned to view Kathryn. 'And this must be your—'

'Niece,' supplied Mrs Marchant in a rush.

'Ah,' Mrs White uttered softly, 'this must then be Miss Kathryn Marchant.' She sauntered closer and inclined a regal head. And never once did her pale ice eyes leave Kathryn's face. 'Such a delight.'

'Mrs White.' Kathryn bobbed a curtsy and forced her face to a mask of politeness. For the briefest of moments her eyes met the scrutiny, and held. Amanda White's sly smile widened.

'Please say that you won't object to my being seated with you, my dear Mrs Marchant.' It was not so much a question as an assumption. Amanda sat down with a show of elegance and proceeded to monopolise Mrs Marchant.

Kathryn sat rigid. Perspiration prickled beneath her arms. The length of her back had adhered to the grey silk of her dress. Even her palms were cold and clammy. And still she waited, while Mrs White played her cat-and-mouse game. Each time those pale eyes slanted her way, each time that husky voice lowered conspiratorially to utter, *My dear Mrs Marchant*, Kathryn's heart lurched. Every nerve in her body was stretched taut, vibrating with expectation.

'But Kathryn—' the widow broke off to pat Kathryn's cold white hand '—you don't mind if I call you that, do you?' and without waiting for an answer rushed on, 'You look so pale. Are you ill?'

Kathryn licked the dryness from her lips. 'I'm quite well, thank you.' And all the while she wanted to scream, *Tell her, if that's what you mean to do, and be done with it*.

But Mrs White had no intention of ending her game, not when her humiliation still burned so painfully. Ravensmede might have bought her silence, but Kathryn was ignorant of the fact. The widow fully intended to exact a measure of revenge upon the girl for the remainder of the evening. A slow, delicious torture, and one that would not leave Ravensmede unaffected. Amanda White relished the prospect. She drew Kathryn a malevolent smile and turned her attention back to Anna Marchant.

Kathryn's overstretched nerves began to fray.

'That woman has the cheek of the devil.'

Cadmount followed Ravensmede's focus and smiled lazily. 'The Winsome Widow White, I perceive. I thought you and the lady had reached an arrangement?'

Lord Ravensmede bestowed a withering look upon his friend. 'Not the kind of arrangement that you think. Matters have altered.'

'What are you not telling of the Winsome Widow?' Cadmount studied his friend for a moment. When no answer was forthcoming, he added, 'Or rather, should I ask which new face has captured your interest?'

Ravensmede lifted one haughty eyebrow.

'I know you too well, my friend.' Cadmount chuckled. 'You don't fool me for an instant.'

'Perhaps.'

'Come on, let's head to Brooks's. I've a mind to enjoy a turn at the tables and a drink or two. This place is so full of blasted chits and tabbies as to wear a man's soul.'

Ravensmede smiled at that, but his eyes soon drifted back to where Kathryn Marchant sat drained and rigid. Her chestnut hair was scraped back in a chignon from which the escaped curls still hung defiantly. Despite the pallor of her cheeks her back was straight and her head held up. She was afraid, but she was fighting it with courage. And courage was something that Lord Ravensmede had ever respected.

He thought of the harangue he had interrupted between pampered Miss Lottie Marchant and her cousin; thought too of how hard Lottie had tried to portray Kathryn as her servant. He remembered the feel of Kathryn's lips beneath his, and how slender her body was within his arms. Just the memory brought a stirring in his nether regions. Finally he allowed his thoughts to turn to Amanda White. The widow was no fool; she was unlikely to jeopardise the little agreement they had just reached. But a warning shot wouldn't go amiss. As he stood there, beneath the bright glow of the chandeliers, surrounded by the crowd and the melodic strains of the band, he knew just what to do.

Cadmount's perceptive gaze lit upon Kathryn. He decided to test his theory. 'Drab little chit.'

Ravensmede glanced up.

'Miss Marchant's cousin. The one she would have us believe is her servant.'

Ravensmede donned a slightly amused expression. 'Only to those with a less discerning eye. The only drab thing about Miss Kathryn Marchant is her dress. Clothing is easily replaced.'

'It's like that, then? I'm impressed. One would hardly have guessed it from the look she gave you earlier this evening. Were you a military man, you would surely have made Commander-in-Chief for your ability to claim victory from the most hopeless of situations.' Cadmount widened his eyes in feigned surprise and tried not to appear smug.

Ravensmede resumed his watch. 'You're making assumptions, dear boy.'

'Afraid it's what I must do if you won't spill the beans, old man.' Cadmount looked at the awkward little group. Their tension was palpable even across the room. 'It's rather interesting that the Winsome Widow is so friendly with Mrs Marchant. Didn't think they'd get on. Wonder what she's up to?'

'Baiting Miss Marchant, I should guess.' As if to confirm Ravensmede's words, Mrs White's gaze flitted to meet his. The widow looked pointedly at Miss Marchant, then back to the Viscount before delivering a nasty smile.

None of it was missed by Cadmount. 'Now what could the very respectable Miss Marchant have done to so upset the widow?' he mused, and looked speculatively at his friend.

The flicker of a smile crossed the Viscount's face. He said nothing.

'Care to enlighten me?'

'No.' Ravensmede didn't even look round. 'What do you know of her?'

'The Winsome Widow?' Cadmount's forehead wrinkled in mock puzzlement.

One dark brow raised in sarcastic denial. 'I was referring to Miss Marchant, as well you know.'

Cadmount scratched at the dark blond of his curls, sniffed knowingly and reeled off the information. 'Family lost their money in some confounded investment venture that went awry. Poor as church mice. Father shot himself little over three years past, the mother and sister died about eight or nine years ago; Miss Marchant must have been little more than a child at the time. Henry Marchant is the father's brother. The girl's lived with his family ever since. Have it from the best sources that she's little more than a domestic in that household. Anna Marchant doesn't take to her too well. That's as much as I know.'

'Caddie, I'm the one who's impressed. Should you wish to purchase another commission, consider military intelligence. Undoubtedly you'd go far.'

They laughed.

Then Cadmount said knowingly, 'So Brooks's will have to wait?'

'For now.'

Cadmount picked distractedly at his nails and deliberately yawned. 'Shouldn't take too long, damned chit looks as if she's about to keel over any minute now.'

The corner of Ravensmede's mouth twitched. 'Not if I have anything to do with it. How are your dance steps these days?'

They shared a look of mutual understanding. No need for further explanation between old friends.

'It'll cost you a bottle of your finest brandy.'

'Done!'

'You do know that you'll be delivering a monumental snub to the widow, don't you? I mean, the whole town is aware that she's been chasing you for months and what do you do? Head straight in the direction of the good lady and ask the plainest chit in the room, who just happens to be sitting by her side, to waltz. No denying that it don't look too good for Mrs White.'

'How very perceptive of you, Caddie,' drawled Ravensmede. 'Mrs White will soon learn the wisdom of good advice, and her departure from London might suddenly seem rather more urgent.'

The pair set off at a sedentary saunter in their deep-blue fitted tail-coats.

'Now to really set the cat amidst the pigeons!' Cadmount said under his breath. 'I hope the chit's worth it, my friend, I sincerely do.'

'It's so unusual to meet a young lady with an interest in astronomy, don't you agree?' Mrs White's voice grated against Kathryn's ear. 'I was just telling your aunt, it's such a curious trait to observe in a female.'

Kathryn gritted her teeth and looked round. The widow was enjoying herself immensely. Beyond the gleam of Amanda White's dark curls Aunt Anna's face was scowling in perplexity. It was time that things came to a head. Temptation beckoned. 'Perhaps, but I understand it to be a most enjoyable pastime.' She was relieved to hear that her voice held no trace of fear. Indeed it was positively calm. The words acted, as Kathryn knew they would, as a burr to Mrs White.

The lady's face contorted to a sour grimace before she recollected herself. 'For those of a certain set. Hardly a fitting activity for a young lady. Wouldn't you say, Mrs Marchant?'

Aunt Anna might not have understood to what Mrs White was alluding, but she definitely detected an underlying current of dislike aimed at her niece. She smiled and shifted a little closer to the widow. 'Completely, Mrs White. Please do call me Anna.'

'Thank you, Anna. And you must call me Amanda.'

The two women smiled in unity.

'There is a rather delicate matter which I'm not fully at liberty to discuss.' Mrs White held her fan over her mouth. 'You must think me foolish not to know how to proceed, but, with your valuable experience of raising such a beautiful daughter, and then your great kindness in inviting your niece into your home as a member of your family, there's no one better I can think to ask.'

Anna Marchant patted her hair and tried not to look superior. 'I've always tried to set an example. Lottie has just to make a match and my job will be complete.'

'Miss Marchant…that is, Miss *Lottie* Marchant, will have no lack of interest from *suitable* gentlemen.' Mrs White shot a glance at Kathryn. 'She's a credit to her mother,' she said. 'Which is why I must ask for your help on behalf of a friend whose charge has just been discovered to have behaved in a most improper manner with a gentleman. I declare the guardian to be quite distraught.'

'Is the girl known to me?' Mrs Marchant's curiosity got the better of her.

Mrs White nodded her beautiful ebony head. 'Most definitely. But do not press me to tell you. I'm sworn to secrecy.' She batted her fan, then added, 'It does so prey upon my mind. I'm in such a quandary as to what to do for the best. Will you trust me as I trust you, dearest Anna?'

'Of course, Amanda.'

'In that case I feel I may speak of it to you.'

Ruined. Cast out, penniless and in shame. There would be little hope for the future. Kathryn waited for the life-changing words. Stared at the floor, wishing it would open up and swallow her whole, and waited. Waited, and waited some more. And then she heard them.

'Miss Marchant, may I enquire whether your card is marked for this dance?' The deep timbre of the voice sent a shiver down Kathryn's spine. She looked up into the moss green eyes of Lord Ravensmede.

'I'm afraid I don't have a dance card. I'm here as a companion to my cousin.'

'Then I'll take it that you're free to accompany me on to the floor.' And with that he took one of her hands in his and pulled. Glancing over at the two older women, he inclined his head. 'Always a pleasure, ladies.'

Kathryn had only the briefest moment to revel in the slack-jawed gawking expressions of her aunt and Mrs White before she found herself clamped firmly in Lord Ravensmede's arms and waltzing across to the other side of the room. It all happened with such speed that she did not know whether to laugh or cry. The former won.

Lord Ravensmede raised a wry eyebrow. 'My dancing is a source of amusement?'

'Not at all.' The vestige of a smile remained upon her face. 'I was merely thinking that your timing is impeccable, my lord. Mrs White is on the brink of revealing all to my aunt. The question is whether she'll await my return before she delivers her denouement.'

'I fancy that Mrs White may have suffered a change of heart,' he said softly and glanced directly down into her eyes.

Kathryn suddenly felt acutely conscious of the touch of one of his hands upon her waist and the other encompassing the fingers of her right hand. 'I can only hope that you're right, my lord.'

His head gestured subtly in the direction of a couple some distance away.

'Mrs White and Lord Cadmount! How very clever. But you only defer the inevitable, my lord. That lady won't be quieted for long.' For someone so perilously close to doom she felt rather light-hearted.

He was still looking at her in that strange way. 'Are you quite recovered?'

A warmth swept into her cheeks and her voice became a

little gruff. 'Yes, thank you. I'm concerned only that…' She paused, and glanced towards Amanda White.

'That Mrs White will seek to destroy your reputation?'

'Yes.'

His hand gently squeezed her fingers. 'You have nothing to worry about.'

'I think, my lord, that you underestimate just how much I've heated Mrs White's ire; it will be a long time in the cooling.'

'I underestimate nothing,' he said softly. 'As I said, you need not worry. I shall see that Mrs White holds her tongue.'

Kathryn's heart kicked to a gallop. 'And how do you propose to do that, my lord?'

He smiled a devastatingly wicked smile.

Kathryn did not remain unaffected; the pulse leapt to a fury in her neck, she missed a step, and almost trod on Lord Ravensmede's toes.

His smile deepened.

Kathryn grew even more flustered. 'I'm sorry, but it's a long time since I've danced.' Her cheeks grew warm and pink. 'I didn't mean to embarrass you by my mistake.' And then she realised just how her words could equally well apply to her earlier misdemeanour in the moonlit room, and her blush intensified.

There was a twinkle in his eye. 'I assure you that I'm not in the least embarrassed.'

She looked away. The music filled the small silence between them.

'Do you enjoy waltzing, Miss Marchant?'

Her eyes flitted back to find his gaze upon her. At least the conversation had turned to safer ground, or so she thought. 'Yes, very much so, my lord.'

'Good. Then we'll waltz the next time we meet.'

Their eyes met, and held. 'I did not mean…' Kathryn's words trailed off unfinished. 'There's really no need. My aunt would not approve.' Her teeth nipped at her bottom lip.

Lord Ravensmede gave a short dry laugh. 'And you, of course, would never do anything of which your relative would not approve?'

The colour staining her cheeks deepened. She knew exactly to what he was referring.

'Then it's settled.'

The regulatory inches between them seemed to shrink. 'I don't think that…' She swallowed hard.

Lord Ravensmede's focus did not waver for a moment.

Kathryn's words of refusal remained unspoken. The final bars of 'Ach! Du lieber Augustine' sounded and she noticed the stares and whispers behind fans. Hardly surprising given that the heir to the Earl of Maybury had just danced with a woman little better than a servant, and it was the waltz of all dances. Despite the attention, and her shabby clothes, and worst of all the prospect of what awaited her back at the seats, Kathryn felt neither shame nor embarrassment, nor even apprehension. She smiled at his lordship, thanked him and allowed him to lead her back to her grim-faced relatives.

Mrs White seemed to have disappeared. So too had Lord Cadmount. And it wasn't long before Ravensmede followed suit. Only Aunt Anna and Lottie remained to scowl their disbelief at Kathryn.

'Whatever have you done to make Lord Ravensmede dance with you?' Lottie was incredulous. 'It's quite unheard of, a man of his calibre dancing with someone like you.' Her lower lip pouted to a petted curl. 'It should have been me that he asked.' She ground her slipper against the floor. 'Say it's so, Mama, say it.'

'Of course, my dearest.' Aunt Anna shot a foul look at her niece. 'It was probably the result of some wager or joke at Kathryn's expense.'

Kathryn said nothing. At least their preoccupation with Lottie told her one thing: that Mrs White had not made her revelation…yet. She supposed she ought to smooth things over or life in the Marchant household would be miserable for the rest of the week…as if it were ever anything other. A smile tickled the edges of her mouth. 'Lottie, I'm sure that his lordship approached us with the intention of asking you to dance. As you were already on the floor with Mr Richardson, he asked me, but only out of courtesy.'

Lottie's eyes flashed a hard, bright blue. 'I wasn't dancing when he returned you to us. Why did he not ask me then?'

'He had an urgent appointment, or so he told me upon the dance floor.' Beneath Kathryn's demurely folded hands her fingers were firmly crossed. 'Otherwise I'm sure he would have sought you as partner for this quadrille.'

Lottie appeared temporarily placated, but had seemingly developed the most frightful headache.

For this reason, or so it was said, the Marchant ladies bid a hasty departure from Lady Finlay's ball.

From where she stood, Kathryn could see almost the whole of the drawing room in the house in Green Street, as well as herself, reflected in the large gilt overmantel mirror. She was a drab grey figure against the yellow painted walls. The room seemed loud and gaudy, even beneath the subdued lighting of the candles flickering in the drop-crystal chandelier and ormolu cherubim wall sconces. A large group portrait of Mr and Mrs Marchant with Lottie seated demurely between them hung proudly between the two large Palladian windows opposite the fireplace. It had been painted two months previously by Mr Jackson. Kathryn's gaze alighted briefly on the cosy Marchant family captured on canvas before moving on to the lavish sets of curtains. Fringed and tasselled gold-and-yellow damask curtains festooned either side of each window. Not one of them was closed. A thin blind of cream material had been pulled down to create the illusion of privacy. Kathryn could feel the press of the sofa at the back of her knees. Its cream covering decorated with mulberry-coloured roses seemed too cheerful for a house that was so lacking in that sentiment. She shifted her feet uneasily, and was thankful for the cushion of the gold-and-burgundy patterned Oriental rug through her thin worn slippers.

'It has been one of the worst evenings of my entire life,' sobbed Lottie and flung herself into the nearest chair. 'And the blame rests entirely with Kathryn!'

'Now, now, Lottie,' cajoled her mother. 'I have told you already. Lord Ravensmede cannot possibly be interested in your cousin. I dare say it's all part of some jest the gentlemen were playing.'

'It d-didn't look like a jest.' Lottie's eyes were red and swollen from the sobbing and the feigned headache was fast becoming a reality. 'No one would have realised that it w-was.'

'Of course they did, my angel.' Mrs Marchant touched a gentle hand to Lottie's wet cheek. 'If you don't cease this weeping, your looks will be quite spoiled for tomorrow and then what will Mr Dalton say when he calls to collect you for your carriage ride?'

A suitably mollified Lottie turned to Kathryn and sniffed. 'Mama is right. You're such a spiteful cat that it serves you right that you are long on the shelf. When did a gentleman ever call for you to take you driving in the park? Never! And they never will because you look positively ghastly, and everyone hates you!'

Kathryn should have let the comments go; they were not worthy of a reply. But she did not. Although she had long since reconciled herself to a life with neither husband nor children, it still hurt to have the fact rubbed in her face. So for the third time that night Kathryn succumbed to impulse. 'And you, Lottie, are behaving little better than a spoiled and pampered brat,' she said wearily.

Lottie set up a wail. 'Mama, but hear what she's saying to me! Will you let her get away with such insolence?'

'Kathryn Marchant!' exclaimed Mrs Marchant. 'Close your mouth this instant! Do not dare to presume that you can insult Lottie before my very eyes! Haven't you caused enough damage for one night?'

'Aunt Anna—'

'Be quiet!' said Mrs Marchant. 'It's my job to instruct you in the ways of polite society as your papa would have wanted, Kathryn. It would be remiss of me not to do so.' The pink feathers in her bandeau quivered as she shook her head with mock sorrow. 'It's for your own good.' The feathers positively swayed in delight. 'As a punishment, all social outings shall be forbidden.' She looked for a response on Kathryn's face.

Kathryn gave none.

'In addition you'll have no dinner for a fortnight.'

Still no hint of emotion registered on Kathryn's face.

'And…you shall assist cook in the kitchen for the same duration. Mrs Moultrie will, of course, be under strict instructions that dinner is prohibited to you.' She smiled at the ingenuity of her little plan.

'As you wish, Aunt.' Still her gaze held steady.

'When not required by Mrs Moultrie you shall help with the laundry. That, at least, might teach you to know your place. You are here to help Lottie, not attempt to spoil her evening in a fit of jealous spite. Such malice cannot be allowed to go unchecked.'

Kathryn's eyes flickered to some point in the distance, knowing full well the game that her aunt played. What matter if Aunt Anna punished her a thousand times, as long as Lord Ravensmede and Mrs White held their tongues? It was not a hope in which she trusted.

'And you will apologise to Lottie for the foulness of your tongue.'

'She was unkind in her words to me,' said Kathryn.

'She is upset. And little wonder! This season is about making a match for Charlotte, not about you making an exhibition of yourself by dancing with the most libidinous nobleman you can find!'

Lottie looked smugly on.

'I did not—'

'And the waltz of all dances! For heaven's sake, girl, if you have not a care for your own reputation then at least have some consideration for your cousin. Through the goodness of his heart Mr Marchant has taken you into his home, fed and clothed you. And what thanks do you give him? None save to plague his own daughter with spite.'

'No, that isn't true. I merely—'

'You merely tried to steal a better match for yourself. Did you think to catch yourself a viscount, miss?'

Kathryn frowned her indignation. 'Of course not!'

'I have tried my best to see that you dress demurely and behave in a modest and sober manner, but bad blood will out.'

'What do you mean?'

'I mean, my dear, that your mother was the exactly the same: wanton.'

The word seemed to echo between them. The blood drained from Kathryn's face. 'You go too far, Aunt. My mother was not wanton. How can you cast such an unfair slur upon her name?'

'Why else did she run off with Robert Marchant? She was little better than a bitch in heat. It was hardly surprising that her family disowned her!'

'Take that back! You know nothing of my mother. She was a good and kind woman. She eloped with my father because they were in love.'

'Of course that's what she would have told you,' Anna Marchant sneered.

'My mother spoke the truth, unlike you. I won't believe your lies!'

The older woman's eyes narrowed with malevolent intent. 'You are a foul little trollop just as she was.' She advanced quickly and captured Kathryn's upper arms in a cruel grip. 'But if you think that I will allow you to ruin things for Lottie, then you're sadly mistaken.' Her fingers tightened, biting into Kathryn's flesh. 'I tolerate you here as Lottie's companion, nothing more.' The vice-like grip began to shake Kathryn. 'Start behaving with a modicum of decorum and modesty if you don't want to find yourself out on the street. How long do you think you'd last out there?' screeched her aunt. 'You'd be in a bordello or have your throat slit before a single day was out.' The rough shaking intensified.

'Take your hands off me!'

With no warning whatsoever Kathryn found herself thrust down against the sofa. 'Oh, I haven't even started with you, miss,' said Anna Marchant in a voice that chilled Kathryn to the bone.

A week later the Viscount of Ravensmede still had not forgotten Kathryn Marchant. Indeed, she was the topic of his conversation with Cadmount, and not for the first time.

'The girl's avoiding me. Why else have we seen Mrs Marchant and Miss Lottie Marchant, but no sign of Kathryn? I have endured three balls, an evening at Almack's and two routs! Imagine what this is doing to my reputation.' Ravensmede's long legs stretched out before him as he lounged back in the wing chair.

'And mine.' Cadmount loosened his neckcloth and, in a flippant gesture, dropped it over the side of his chair. 'Sir,' he slurred, 'you obviously haven't looked in the betting book in Brooks's of late.'

One dark eyebrow quirked. 'Enlighten me, Cadmount.' Despite the languor of his manner, there was a darkening of his eye and a quickening of his heart. Surely Amanda White had not reneged on their agreement so soon? Two thousand guineas should have silenced her for good. Money well spent…if she stayed silent. And she shouldn't even still be in London. He carefully refilled each glass and sat back, waiting.

'A fine drop of brandy, I do declare.' Cadmount's lips smacked with pleasure. 'I'd dance all night with the Winsome Widow for a case of this. Are you sure it was just the one bottle you promised me?'

A green gimlet eye stared back at him. 'The betting book?'

Cadmount took another gulp of brandy. 'Yes, the betting

book.' He stopped and rubbed his fingers over the golden stubble upon his chin. 'Should shave more often. Wingham says the ladies prefer a smoother approach.' He guffawed at his own joke.

'Hell's teeth, man, spit it out! What does the damnable book say about Kathryn Marchant?' For once, Ravensmede's usual aplomb had deserted him.

Cadmount blinked in confusion. ''Bout the chit…why, nothing.' He took another a drink and then looked knowledgeable all at once. Tapping the side of his nose, he leaned forward to his friend and said, 'Say no more, old man, understand it perfectly. Li'l Kathryn is your ladybird.' One wavering forefinger pressed to his lips. 'Sshh! Won't say a word.'

The amber liquid swirled around Ravensmede's balloon glass. 'Sorry to disappoint you, but there's no such understanding between Miss Marchant and myself.'

'Absolutely not.' An enormous grin erupted on Cadmount's face.

Ravensmede smiled in return. 'You are the most infuriating man when you're in your cups.

Cadmount's grin deepened, and he hiccuped.

'Brooks's betting book—what does it say with regard to me?' There was no hint in Lord Ravensmede's voice that he had drunk the same quantity of brandy as his friend.

A smile. 'That you'll be wed before the summer is out.'

Ravensmede laughed as a wave of relief swept through him. 'They think I'm on the hunt for a bride because of my attendance at Almack's? Seeking some precious chit just out of the schoolroom? I think not. You know me better than that, Caddie.'

'Indeed I do, sir,' avowed Lord Cadmount. 'Thirty-two years old, heir to an earldom, no wife, no nursery, old man breathing down your neck. Thank God I'm only a younger son. No such pressure.'

'Are you always this philosophical when you're foxed?' Ravensmede demanded somewhat sourly.

'Always.' Another gulp of brandy. 'If Kathryn Marchant's

not your girl, then why have we been trailing round one blasted place after the other in search of the little lady, and all the while missing out on the finer things in life? Beats me why you're behaving like a green lad over her. She's not your type at all!' Even the worse for several glasses of brandy, Archibald Cadmount knew exactly how to nettle Ravensmede.

In return, Ravensmede slowly and deliberately set his glass aside. 'You're quite right in thinking that I would like to make Miss Marchant my mistress.' He recollected vividly those soft supple lips beneath his, the gentle swell of her hips, and the sound of her wicked chuckle of laughter when he plucked her from beneath Amanda White's nose. 'However, she's an innocent and,' he added drolly, 'I haven't stooped quite so low as to start deflowering virgins.'

'You could always make an exception in her case.'

Silence followed the scandalous suggestion.

Cadmount waited to see if things were bad enough for Ravensmede to take the bait.

'Perhaps…' Ravensmede's eyes flicked shut. A vision of Kathryn Marchant's pale face arose. His mind meandered to imaginings of just how soft and white her skin would be beneath that hideous grey dress. Temptation loomed large. He quelled it with impatience. 'But then again, maybe not. She's made her feelings quite clear: a no-show at any of her cousin's outings this week. I've never forced a woman, and I don't intend to start now.'

'Glad to hear it, old man. Had you made an arrangement with her?'

Ravensmede thought of his promise to dance with Miss Marchant, and of her conspicuous absence from her cousin's side. 'Of sorts.'

Cadmount looked impressed. 'By Jove, this must be a first. A lady that turns you down. She won't have you. Hah! Well, it's about bloody time!' A snort of merriment resounded throughout the library. His eyes closed, but not before they had alighted on Lord Ravensmede's wry smile.

The clock ticked upon the mantel. Logs crackled within the grate.

A flicker of Cadmount's heavy-lidded eyes. 'Are you for Lady Campbell's gathering tonight?'

'I think not. I've other fish to fry.'

This time Cadmount's eyes remained shut and within a few minutes the soft sound of a snore was upon his lips. Ravensmede rose without a noise and left the library.

A sleepy whisper murmured behind him, 'Chit might as well as thrown down the gauntlet. Twenty guineas he'll have her in his bed before the month is out, whatever the right or wrong of it.'

But had Archibald Cadmount known Miss Kathryn Marchant, he would have wagered very differently.

Chapter Three

The street was thronging with bodies as Kathryn wove a path through the crowds. Although the afternoon was well advanced, the street vendors were still plying their trade, which was fortuitous, as it was on an errand of procurement that she was employed. Despite the dusty heat and the overpowering smells arising from the pigs and piles of rotting rubbish nearby, she was glad to be free of the house in Green Street, no matter how short the duration. The week had passed slowly, with Aunt Anna and Lottie taking delight in meting out Kathryn's punishment. No doubt it somehow acted to salve the snub that Lottie felt Ravensmede had dealt her at the ball. Kathryn had endured without complaint, and indeed had striven to appear positively cheerful. There was nothing like it for irritating Lottie, or Aunt Anna for that matter. Little did they know how she enjoyed her brief excursions from the house. It was only twenty minutes since Lottie, on overhearing that there were no potatoes left, had demanded a dish of potato pudding for dinner. Upon Lottie's insistence, Kathryn had been dispatched to fetch some more. It was supposed to be a degrading experience, and one that would teach her a lesson.

A while later, and overhead the dazzling sun still shone down from a cloudless blue sky. A soft humming sounded from Kathryn's lips as the notes of the music danced through her head. Her feet neatly avoided a pile of fresh horse manure and, as the tempo increased, she skipped over the stream of bloodied water running down from a nearby butcher's shop. *The noisy street had vanished. A cooling breeze fanned her face as she breathed in the fresh country air. She was beautifully composed as the gentleman swept her into his arms and they began to glide with effortless grace across the neat lawns of the country mansion. One two three, one two three, she counted the beats as her delicately embroidered slippers scarcely touched the ground. Lord Ravensmede was smiling, his green eyes twinkling in the sunlight... Ravensmede!* Kathryn banished the thought and the noisy bustle of London reappeared. She adjusted the sack of potatoes balanced on her hip and continued her steady pace.

Ahead she could see the golden glint of the railings surrounding St James's Park. The green grass and the cool sparkle of the canal beckoned enticingly. It wouldn't take long, just to shelter beneath the cool dapple shade of the trees, to feel some little sense of space. Without a moment's hesitation her dusty feet padded up the street and into the park. Carriages containing fine ladies rolled by. Smartly dressed gentlemen astride their horses trotted past. The grass was fresh and springy beneath Kathryn's shoes. Ahead the air rippled with a heat haze.

She had just paused to watch two swans upon the water when a small family group passed close by. A familiar voice caught her attention. Glancing round, she saw, with some consternation, Miss Dawson walking arm in arm with her younger sister. Kathryn became suddenly all too aware of her situation. There could be no hiding the large and conspicuous sack of potatoes, and Miss Dawson was sure to mention any such meeting to Lottie. And then Lottie would know exactly what Kathryn had been up to during her errand. Quite deliberately Kathryn averted her face and walked in the opposite direction. She needn't have worried. With half her hair escaping from her bonnet, a smear of dust on her chin, a soil-stained dress, and the presence of the exceedingly dirty sack on her hip, she appeared more like one of the inhabitants of St Giles's Rookery, and not anyone connected to the respectable household of Mr Henry Marchant.

A close shave. Without further ado she disappeared behind the breadth of a large oak tree. It was only here that she laid down her burden. Hidden quite well as she was from view, she not only sat herself comfortably on the grass and leaned her back against the gnarled bark, but also dispensed with her bonnet and set about repairing the worst of her hair.

Lord Ravensmede reined his horse to a standstill, unable to quite believe his eyes. Surely that could not have been Miss Marchant he had just witnessed vanishing behind that oak? The slight figure certainly bore a striking resemblance to her graceful form, even bowed as it was with some large and weighty object. Perdition, he was becoming obsessed with the chit. First, she had been in his thoughts for the past week. Now, he was imagining that he saw her at every turn. It did not sit well with his lordship. His hand moved to twitch Rollo's rein, then stilled. What if it really was Miss Marchant? He had a thing or two to say to that young lady. No matter how much Ravensmede might deny it, he felt aggrieved by her snub, especially in view of the effort he had made to silence Amanda White. His leg slid over the saddle and he jumped down to the ground.

Having securely tethered the gelding to a nearby tree, Ravensmede proceeded on foot with some caution. Thus, he walked directly to the opposite side of the massive oak without the slightest noise. He heard the hushed melody from her lips before he saw her: 'Ach! Du lieber Augustine.' It had been playing when he danced with her at Lady Finlay's ball. The memory tugged a smile at his mouth. He moved leisurely around the trunk.

She was sitting on the grass, her legs drawn up beneath her, intent on scraping her mass of red-brown hair up into a chignon. The hairpins were held at the ready between her lips. And all the while her soft humming filled the air. At her side lay a lumpy and rather grubby sack. Ravensmede stared, intrigued with the sight. What an earth was the girl up to?

He stepped forward. 'Miss Marchant, a pleasure to make your acquaintance once again.'

Kathryn jumped, dropped the hank of hair she was attempting to secure, and almost inhaled one of the hairpins. The remainder of the pins scattered on the ground as she exclaimed with undisguised horror, 'Lord Ravensmede!'

Ravensmede watched while she scrambled unceremoniously to her feet, brushing any remnants of grass from her skirt. In one glance he took in the worn shoes caked in dust, the soiled dress, and the fatigue in her eyes. The bridge of her nose and cheeks were smattered with freckles that had not been there a week ago, and dirt streaked her chin. He held out his hand to take hers. Kathryn stared at it as if it held a dagger. 'Miss Marchant,' he said with the utmost politeness, and with slow deliberation touched her bare fingers to his lips. Not only was she gloveless, but her hands were reddened and rough, almost as if she had been scrubbing floors or laundering. A frown flitted across his brow at the thought.

Kathryn saw the look and, snatching her fingers away, clasped her hands behind her back. 'What are you doing here?' she blurted, then, remembering her manners, 'I mean…I didn't expect to meet you here.'

'Apparently not.' Ravensmede's gaze dropped to the sack and wandered back to her face. Crimson washed her cheeks and he thought he saw a flash of anger in her eyes before it was masked.

She held his gaze boldly. 'Please don't allow me to interrupt your walk, my lord.' Her cheeks burned hotter.

Ravensmede smiled lazily. He was not to be dismissed so easily. 'I assure you it's no interruption. Perhaps I could join you.'

The girl seemed speechless for a moment at the audacity of his suggestion. He was fully aware that it was rather inappropriate. 'I'm afraid that's not possible, my lord.' As he knew it would not be. Her voice was firm, her body poised for flight.

'Indeed, I must be getting back to Green Street. I've been away too long as it is.' Her eyes scanned for the pins, and, having located them in the soil by an exposed tree root, she bent to retrieve them.

Ravensmede saw her purpose and, with surprising agility for a gentleman wearing such tight-fitting buckskins, stooped to reach them first. Their fingers brushed; an intense awareness tingled in the air between them. He stared into the widening clear grey eyes. Realised that he wanted her, even dressed as she was in the guise of a servant. A determined interest stirred. Jaded boredom faded. His gaze dropped to her lips.

Kathryn withdrew her hand as if she had been burned. 'I do b-beg your pardon,' she stuttered, and rose swiftly to her feet.

Ravensmede followed, his eyes still trained on her face. The pins lay forgotten in the dirt. He closed the distance between them and reached out for her.

A woman's laugh sounded from the other side of the oak. 'Come along, Mary, we mustn't be late.'

It was enough to burst the growing bubble of tension.

Lord Ravensmede recovered first, dropping his hand to his side, and did not move. He was so close he could see the dark sweep of her eyelashes and the glitter of perspiration on her cheekbones.

One step back and then she halted, an expression of confusion on her face. 'I should leave.'

Ravensmede was not fooled by the small gruff voice.

She stepped aside and bent to retrieve the sack.

'Wait.' His hand stilled her outstretched arm. Neither the material of her dress nor his fine leather gloves dampened the arc of excitement that sparked between them.

She looked pointedly at his fingers; only when he removed the offending articles did she raise her gaze to meet his. 'My lord?'

'May I be so bold as to enquire the nature of your burden?' His horsewhip flicked towards the sack.

Her eyes lowered only momentarily before her chin raised a notch, as if in challenge. 'Potatoes.'

'Potatoes!' That would explain the preponderance of sandy soil about her person. 'You've been sent to buy them?' His lordship asked the question with a nonchalant air, as if lugging a huge sack of the damn things was an everyday occurrence for a gently bred companion.

She nodded once, that fierce little gaze never faltering for a minute.

'I see,' murmured Ravensmede with a sudden clarity of perception. The sinister hand of Mrs Marchant loomed large. 'And this is one of your usual chores?'

'No.' Her fingers plucked nervously at the material of her skirt.

Ravensmede waited in silence, a look of expectation upon his face.

'I'm assisting Mrs Moultrie in the kitchen this week.'

'And last week too?' he asked in a gentle tone. He suddenly understood why Kathryn had not accompanied her cousin and aunt on any of their recent outings.

More plucking at the material. 'Yes.'

'Surely Henry Marchant is not so strapped for cash that he cannot employ a kitchen maid?'

She said nothing, just looked at him.

'It seems that you are out of favour with your aunt of late.'

Her eyes held his for a moment longer before glancing away.

'Kathryn?'

She shivered.

The tips of his fingers brushed against hers. 'Why might that be?'

She shook her head in denial.

'Kathryn,' he said again, more gently this time. 'Will you not tell me the reason?'

A soft sigh sounded in the air. 'Please, Lord Ravensmede, I must—'

'You have not told her of our study in astronomy at Lady Finlay's ball?'

Her cheeks reddened. 'Of course not!' Indignation flashed

in her eyes. 'I don't wish to sound rude, my lord, but the reason that I'm assisting in the kitchen is none of your consideration.'

Ravensmede looked at her with growing intensity. 'On the contrary, Miss Marchant,' he said quietly, 'it is everything of my consideration.'

Miss Marchant ignored his remark and continued, 'Now, if you will please excuse me, my lord.'

'No,' he said with a wicked glint in his eye.

The poor girl paled.

'How long is this…punishment to endure?'

A guarded look closed over Miss Marchant's face. 'I didn't say anything about a punishment.'

His eyes held hers. 'How long?'

Her gaze flickered away. She made to step back.

Ravensmede touched his fingers to her chin, guiding her focus to his. 'Let me help you, Kathryn.'

For an instant, just one fleeting moment, he saw the softening of her expression, the hope that shone in her eyes. 'Help me?'

'If you were to be under my protection…'

A pause, followed by a dawning realisation. And then it was gone, replaced instead with hurt disbelief, and finally furious humiliation. 'Certainly not!'

He had never had such an offer so adamantly refused.

She jerked away, leaving his fingers suspended in mid-air. 'I don't need your *help,* Lord Ravensmede.' Her voice was cool, her words clipped. 'I bid you good day, my lord.' She bent to retrieve the sack of potatoes.

But Ravensmede was there first. He watched her cheeks blanch and her eyes widen.

'My offer stands, Miss Marchant. If you should change your mind, you need only send me a message. Perhaps in time you will view matters differently.'

Her nostrils flared with fury. Her small breasts rose and fell with the quickening of her breathing. 'I will never accept such an offer!' Her hand tugged at the sack.

But Lord Ravensmede held firm. In one easy motion he tucked the sack neatly beneath his arm. 'My horse is tethered close by. We'd best fasten this to Rollo's saddle and make our way smartly to Green Street if these potatoes are on this evening's menu.' There was a teasing note in his voice, and the suggestion of a smile. Then off he sauntered towards the gelding, leaving Kathryn staring after him.

The sack was securely attached to the horse when he heard the rustle of her skirt behind him.

'Lord Ravensmede, surely you cannot seriously mean to accompany me home?' The glorious spread of hair had disappeared beneath a bonnet that matched the unfashionable brown coloration of her dress. The glare of sunlight exposed the fragility of her face, highlighting the smudges below her eyes.

A muscle twitched in Ravensmede's jaw. 'But of course, Miss Marchant. It would not be gentlemanly to do otherwise.' He'd be damned if he let her struggle beneath the weight of that load.

Panic rose in her voice. 'No, it won't do. You mustn't! Please pass me the potatoes at once.'

Ravensmede turned to face her, a twinkling in his clear green eyes. 'Have no fear, they're fixed firmly in place and shall not dislodge.'

'My lord,' she said in a stage whisper, 'I must insist that you return my potatoes and cease this…this…' she plucked the word from the air '…madness, at once!'

The corners of Ravensmede's mouth twisted upwards. 'I believe that I've already explained my position, Miss Marchant.' He tried not to laugh. 'The potatoes are quite safe.' One dark eyebrow arched. 'Now, if you wish to avoid a scene I suggest that you take my arm and let us be on our way.'

Several murmurs alerted Miss Marchant to the interest growing around their conversation. At least two ladies were staring. She sighed and tentatively touched her fingers to his sleeve, only to find them firmly tucked within the crook of his arm.

With Miss Marchant secured on one side, and Rollo and

the precious cargo on the other, Lord Ravensmede made his way towards Green Street.

Blast the confounded man! How dare he take such a liberty! She'd have rather balanced the potatoes on her hip to Stepney and back than endure this. What could he be thinking of? His offer of help? Help, indeed! Like a fool she had thought it an honest offer until the truth of his meaning had dawned. What kind of woman did he take her for? Well, he would soon learn that Kathryn Marchant had no need of his sort of help, not now, not ever!

She sneaked a look up at his face. His strong handsome features showed not the slightest hint of discomfort. In fact, if she hadn't known better, she could almost have sworn that he was actually enjoying himself. Such behaviour was only to be expected from a man with Ravensmede's reputation. Not that she knew exactly what it was that he was actually guilty of, only that there were many pursed lips and raised eyebrows at his arrival, and that he had a penchant for women, gaming and drink…in that order.

Her eyes dropped to the burgundy coat, the matching waistcoat and immaculately arranged neckcloth. And lower still to the buff-coloured pantaloons that hugged the muscles of his thighs in a quite indecent fashion. The pristine condition and expensive cut of his clothing only served to emphasise the tawdry state of her own. Realising that she was staring at his lordship's thighs brought her gaze rapidly up, only to meet with an amused pair of green eyes.

'Do I meet with your approval, Miss Marchant?' His voice was a slow delicious drawl.

'Most certainly not,' she snapped, feeling her cheeks begin to burn. Then, realising just how rude she sounded, added, 'I appreciate that your intention to relieve me of my burden is one of kindness. It is, however, quite unnecessary.'

That slightly mocking gaze found hers once more. 'On the contrary, Miss Marchant, I assure you that I'm never kind.'

Emerald lights danced in his eyes, rendering them such an unusual colour that it took the immense application of Kathryn's will-power not to stare.

Not trusting herself not to deliver him a sharp retort, she bit her tongue. They strolled along in silence and all the while she took care to keep her face turned from him.

It was some minutes before he spoke again. 'It appears that I've unwittingly offended you, Miss Marchant. Or have you just a natural aversion to my company?'

Her head swung round with surprise at the directness of his question. It was a big mistake. Those alluring eyes were on her again. A tingling sensation crept across her skin. Her tongue tied itself into knots and she quickly glanced away. 'I…I'm…'

His voice lowered, so that the words would reach her ears alone. 'It did not seem so at Lady Finlay's ball.'

She stared at him aghast. 'You appear to be labouring under some false impression of my character, my lord.' Her hand tried to wriggle free of Ravensmede's arm.

He did not release her. 'Where precisely have I erred?'

As an elderly lady peered down at her from a passing carriage, Kathryn ceased her struggle.

Keeping her expression carefully bland as if they were discussing the weather, or other such matters, she whispered, 'How can you ask such a thing?' She glanced around and recognised that they were close to Green Street. 'Please hurry, my lord. I have kept Mrs Moultrie waiting some considerable time.'

If anything, Ravensmede's feet dragged.

'My lord, I'm very late.' Agitation raised her voice, and she tugged at his arm to propel him faster.

His lordship stopped stock-still. 'What are you so afraid of?'

'Nothing.'

A cynical brow raised. 'I'll speak to your uncle. The situation may change if he realises that your shoddy treatment has not gone unnoticed.'

Kathryn paled at the very thought. Heaven forbid that he

should do such a thing! 'No!' She licked her suddenly dry lips. 'Thank you, but no. It would serve only to make matters worse.'

Ravensmede looked at her, then slowly resumed walking towards Green Street. Once they reached the Marchant residence he loosened Rollo's load and made to mount the steps up to the front door.

'Lord Ravensmede.' Kathryn gently pulled at his arm.

'I won't see you struggle beneath this weight.'

Her fingers tightened around the broad band of muscle. She looked up into his face and bit at her bottom lip. 'Very well. Then please come this way.' She made to walk around the side of the house.

The Viscount of Ravensmede showed no sign of moving. 'I find I have a preference for the front door. I've never used a servants' entrance in my life, and I don't intend to do so now.'

Kathryn's heart missed a beat. The blood drained from her face. She composed a breath. 'Please, my lord.'

The green eyes held hers, and in his gaze was understanding and determination. 'It's better this way,' he said softly, and, tucking her hand into his arm, walked up the steps.

The bell rang. And in that moment of waiting, Kathryn was never more aware of the absurdity of her situation. The tall handsome aristocrat by her side, a sack of potatoes under one arm, her own hand tucked in the other, standing at the front door of the house in Green Street for all the world to see. Footsteps sounded from within. The trickle of fear surged and she felt suddenly that she might be sick. She tried to remove her hand from Lord Ravensmede's arm.

His lordship's hold tightened.

The door opened.

Kathryn swallowed hard.

'I'm here to call upon Mr Marchant,' said Lord Ravensmede and thrust the sack into the unsuspecting manservant's hands. The sack was followed by Ravensmede's card.

The manservant stared first at the potatoes, then at Lord

Ravensmede, and finally at Kathryn. He blinked once or twice, seemingly unable to find words.

Ravensmede gestured Kathryn in ahead of him. 'After you, Miss Marchant.' Once within the hallway he raised Kathryn's hand to his lips. 'So fortuitous to have met you again,' he said gallantly, and finally released her.

'Lord Ravensmede,' she said, and gave a small curtsy. Even her breath was shaky.

'Ever your servant,' he said and bowed.

With a very straight back, and very precise steps, Kathryn walked away…while she still could.

Only then did the manservant remember himself enough to stop gaping and fetch the master of the house.

Lord Ravensmede was wiping his hands on a pristine white handkerchief when Henry Marchant entered the drawing room.

'Lord Ravensmede! What an unexpected pleasure.' Mr Marchant bustled forward, unable to believe just who had called upon him. His lordship might be considered one of the worst rake-hells in London, but, as the current Viscount of Ravensmede, heir to an exceptionally wealthy earldom, and in receipt of a considerable allowance, he was not a man that Henry Marchant felt any inclination to snub. Ravensmede made the Marchant monies look like a pile of pennies, and he was what Henry for all his hard work could never hope to become—an aristocrat. As the initial surprise waned Henry began to calculate just how advantageous Lord Ravensmede's visit might prove. Mr Marchant was, after all, in possession of a young and attractive daughter, and his lordship had ever been known to have an eye for a beautiful woman. The possibilities danced before him. 'Please take a seat. Would you care for a drink?'

'Brandy, if you have any.'

'Most certainly,' said Mr Marchant. He poured the brandy into two crystal glasses and passed one to Lord Ravensmede.

Ravensmede made himself comfortable in the chair and leisurely perused the surrounding room before turning his attention to Henry Marchant. 'Perhaps you may be able to assist me, Mr Marchant.'

Mr Marchant's chins wobbled in delight. 'Of course, my lord, in any way that I can.'

'It is the most peculiar of situations.'

'Indeed?' The older man leaned forward.

'I chanced upon your niece while I was out. She was carrying a sack of potatoes.'

There was the smallest silence before Mr Marchant spoke. '*Potatoes*, you say?'

'Most definitely potatoes,' said Ravensmede, and waited.

A subtle pink coloration crept into Henry Marchant's complexion. 'I don't understand. What on earth would Kathryn be doing with potatoes?'

'My question precisely, sir. Naturally no gentleman would allow a lady to carry such a burden.'

'No, no, of course not,' Mr Marchant added in bluff agreement.

'I therefore carried the potatoes in her stead.'

'You?' said Mr Marchant weakly.

'Me,' said the Viscount of Ravensmede, and smiled grimly.

'Good God!' came the whispered reply.

'Financial straits are always embarrassing, sir, but it is a gentleman's duty to spare his womenfolk.'

The colour of Mr Marchant's cheeks deepened to puce. He stuttered so much as to almost choke on the words. 'M-m-my finances are all in order. You are mistaken, sir, in your thoughts. I employ a house full of servants.'

'Indeed?' Ravensmede paused. 'Then why was Miss Marchant sent to do a servant's job?'

'I've no idea, but rest assured, my lord, I shall discover what this business is about.'

'I'm glad to hear it.'

'Kathryn is very grateful for my family's charity and tries to make herself useful in return. Perhaps that was her intention in this instance—well meant, but poorly judged. There is, after all, no fathoming the workings of the female mind!' Mr Marchant laughed. It sounded false and uneasy in the room.

Ravensmede raised a single eyebrow.

Mr Marchant hurriedly cleared his throat. 'As I was saying, I mean to get to the bottom of the matter. Kathryn came to us when my brother tragically died some number of years ago. She has been welcomed into the bosom of my family. I've never been one to flout my duty, my lord, and I trust that no one would suggest otherwise.'

'Heaven forbid, sir.' Ravensmede took a swig of brandy and stood to leave. 'You stock a fine brandy, Mr Marchant.'

Soothed by Lord Ravensmede's response, Mr Marchant sought to redeem something of the situation. The thought of a match between the Viscount and Lottie was still rather tantalising. 'If you would like to call again, my lord, under more auspicious circumstances, I have some rather splendid cigars.'

'How very kind,' said Ravensmede with an irony that was lost on Henry Marchant, and departed.

Lord Cadmount attacked the game pie with obvious exuberance. 'Nothing like an afternoon practising the pugilistic arts to fire up a man's appetite. Didn't mean to land you such a planter.'

'You got lucky. It was a very respectable left hook, and my mind was elsewhere.' Three hours' boxing had not taken the edge off Ravensmede's disgruntlement. It was a sentiment that had failed to shift since his earlier encounter with Miss Kathryn Marchant.

'So I noticed.' Cadmount forked a great mound of meat into his mouth. There was nothing but the sound of cutlery scraping against plates and noisy mastication coming from Cadmount. He licked a smear of gravy from his lip. 'Ain't been happy for a while. Can see it in your face. Been winning at the card tables; cellar is stocked with the best of bottles; plenty of luck with the ladies too. But something ain't right.

Known you too long for you to pull the wool over my eyes.'
Cadmount resumed his attack on the enormous piece of pie
before him. 'Pressure from the old man getting too much?
Is he still trying to force that heiress upon you—what's her
name—Pitten?'

'Francesca Paton.' Had it been anyone else sitting across the
table, Ravensmede would have quelled them with an arrogant
stare. Archie Cadmount was different. He was one of the few
people that Ravensmede trusted. The two men were as dissimilar in temperament as they were in looks. But since their
youthful days at Eton they had remained true friends. And
because it was Cadmount, Ravensmede spoke the truth. 'And,
no, things are no worse than usual. My father can say what he
will, but I'll be damned if I'll let him dictate my life.'

'Still sore about him forbidding your commission?'

'While you were risking your life in the Peninsula to put a
halt to Boney's forces, I was here doing what I've been doing
for the last twelve years, what I'm still doing. Men are dying
for England and I'm here drinking, gambling, whoring…
What's the bloody point?'

'Ain't your fault that you're heir to the earldom. Ain't your
father's fault either. Maybury just wants to ensure things are safe
for the future. Only son and all that. Can't have you going off
and getting yourself killed. Can't blame the old man for that.'

'Maybe not,' said Ravensmede. 'But tell me this, Caddie—
if you hadn't been obliged to come home because of your
brother, would you choose to still be out there fighting, or
sitting here in London leading a comfortable existence?'

'Point taken. But if you ain't happy with things as they are,
perhaps it's time for a change. Perhaps Maybury is right,
perhaps it *is* time for a wife and a nursery.'

'Hell's teeth, Caddie, not you too! I'll marry when I'm good
and ready and not before.'

'Stubborn to the bone,' murmured his friend. 'Always were,
always will be. Stubborn and wilful.'

Ravensmede gave him a crooked smile. 'You know me so well.'

A little pie remained on Cadmount's plate. He set about remedying that with one final flourish of his fork and pondered on his friend's unhappiness. Clearly a change of subject was required. Something to cheer Ravensmede. Something with which the Viscount was enamoured. He paused to savour the richly flavoured gravy. 'By God, but that was good. If you ever tire of Lamont's cooking, send him to me.' The claret was drained in one gulp and he eyed Ravensmede. Inspiration came to him. 'Made any progress with the Marchant chit?'

Ravensmede sipped his wine with a nonchalance that he did not feel. 'I happened to chance upon Miss Marchant while I was out this afternoon. She's not treated well within the Marchant household, but refuses to consider possible ways out.' He looked away to conceal the depth of his emotion. 'Blasted girl's pride will be her downfall.'

A snort of laughter sounded in the dining room. 'Turned you down again, did she?'

The blue-shadowed jaw-line tightened. 'Something like that.'

Cadmount snorted again. 'Good for her.'

Ravensmede did not want to reveal the full extent of his encounter with Kathryn Marchant. He knew full well what he had offered the girl. Could still taste the sourness that the ignoble offer left upon his tongue. And yet he wanted her, even here, even now, knowing all that he did. Any mention of what she had been doing or her tired appearance would be an act of betrayal. Instinctively he knew that Kathryn would not want others to know of her circumstance. Living as she did could not be pleasant. He thought of her lugging the sack of potatoes across St James's Park, of her seeking refuge behind the old oak tree, ashamed to be seen. Despite her dusty worn clothes and her red chapped hands she had been happy, humming that tune, with a faraway look in her eyes. Happy, at least until he had arrived. He set his fork down upon his plate.

Cadmount eyed him with interest.

Ravensmede's finger tapped thoughtfully against the stem of the glass. 'There must be something I can do, Archie. I'll be damned if I'll just leave her to that family's devices.'

Lord Cadmount knew things must be serious. Ravensmede never, but never, used his given name. It looked as if Kathryn Marchant might be just the tonic that Ravensmede needed. 'She turned you down, old man, and if she ain't under your protection then there's nothing you can do. Unmarried lady and all that. And she *is* a lady,' he said. 'Wouldn't look too good for li'l Miss Marchant if you start charging in there, pistols blazing. Not to put too fine a point on it, Ravensmede, any association with you is likely to leave a lady's reputation a little the worse for wear. No offence intended.'

Ravensmede thought grimly of his meeting with Mr Marchant. Hardly charging in with pistols blazing, rather a case of letting the man know that his treatment of the girl hadn't gone unnoticed.

'Best thing you could do is to stay away.' A large dollop of puréed potato was scooped into Cadmount's mouth. It did not prevent his continued conversation. 'Unless, of course, you're prepared to contemplate a more respectable alternative.' The adroit blue gaze slid to Ravensmede.

Lord Ravensmede picked at the fillet of sole, before pushing his plate away.

'Stands to reason,' Cadmount released a loud and resonant burp, 'why did you turn down the splendid Mrs White if your interest in Miss Marchant isn't in earnest? I mean, the Winsome Widow's practically offering herself on a platter. Don't think that I'd send *her* packing. And from where I was standing, it looked like you were about to devour the Marchant chit on the dance floor. If it ain't serious, why else did you waltz with her?'

Ravensmede's eyes glowered in the candlelight. 'Why indeed?'

Cadmount affected not to notice. 'I know you'll go your own way, you always do. But for what my humble opinion is worth, if you've any regard for the girl you'll stop sniffing round her skirts and leave well alone. There's no family to hush a scandal, and no man waiting in the wings to salvage her reputation. Don't ruin her life, Nick…unless you mean to offer her marriage.'

One haughty eyebrow cocked. 'Still on that old theme? I'm beginning to think that you're in league with m'father.' He savoured the taste of the claret against his palate. 'I've no intention of marrying Miss Kathryn Marchant or anyone else.'

'Good thing you'll be leaving her alone then. Besides…' he looked pointedly at Ravensmede '…I don't suppose the chit is quite what Maybury has in mind for your bride.'

'Don't push it, Caddie,' Ravensmede said quietly.

Cadmount laughed, and shrugged off his serious garb. 'Then it's to Brooks's this evening and the faro tables.' He slapped the table and belched again, grinning all the while. 'It's not as though Henry Marchant will starve or beat the girl.' And with that parting comment Lord Cadmount went to relieve himself.

Ravensmede remained alone at the dining table. Starvation. Beatings. For some reason the thoughts weighed uneasy on his mind. He rubbed at his chin and tried to banish the image of a small heart-shaped face. His dark brows puckered. Damn Kathryn Marchant's pride, and damn Archibald Cadmount's warnings. He could no sooner leave the girl to her fate than he could pluck out his own eyes. Whether she wanted it or not, Miss Marchant was about to become the recipient of his help…whatever guise that it might come in.

Chapter Four

It was ten o'clock and Kathryn was busy helping Nancy wash the linen. The coarse soap stung at their hands as they scrubbed within the cold water, but neither woman complained. They chatted about Nancy's young man and her sister's new baby boy.

''E's as bright as a button, miss, truly 'e is. All downy black 'air and big blue eyes, and such a big smile for a little fella.' The front door bell sounded. 'Wonder who that could be?'

Kathryn tucked a stray curl back up into her cap with a soapy finger. 'It's rather early for visitors. Unless, of course, there was some scandalous affair last night at Lady Campbell's after Aunt Anna and Lottie left. Just think what they might have missed!'

The scullery filled with their chuckles.

'You ain't 'alf a laugh, miss.'

A delicious aroma of eggs and chops and toast wafted through from the kitchen. Kathryn's stomach growled so loudly that Nancy pulled a face.

'Lawk! Sounds like someone ain't had no breakfast!'

Kathryn just shrugged and carried on with the scrubbing. Her stomach protested at being ignored.

Nancy peered suspiciously at the other girl's pale face. ''Ave you ate somethin' this mornin', miss?'

'There was a to-do over the potatoes yesterday that displeased my aunt. Breakfast is forbidden for the next week.'

Nancy knew exactly what the 'to-do' was about. Indeed, the servants had talked of little else since that fancy lord had brought Kathryn and the potatoes home. But Nancy was wise enough to make no mention of it.

'Don't worry. I'm not really hungry. It's just that smell causing all the rumbling down there.' Kathryn's eyes dropped down to indicate her stomach.

'But you didn't 'ave no dinner last night neither. Let me get you somethin'.'

Kathryn's soapy hand reached out towards the maidservant's, and squeezed it affectionately. 'Thank you, but no. I don't want you getting into trouble on my behalf, and it would be just like Mrs Moultrie to spot what you were about. She seems to inform my aunt of every detail. No, Nancy, kind as your offer is, I shall last very well until lunch.'

'She's a bloody bitch, that one,' came the sharp reply. 'Sorry, miss. I know I shouldn't be swearin' in front of you, but I couldn't help myself. She's a mean-hearted woman.'

Kathryn smiled at what a shock it would cause if she were to ask Nancy to which woman precisely the maid was referring. Swallowing down her bad grace, which she feared was getting out of hand, she changed the subject. 'When will you visit your sister again?'

The maid was just about to reply when the clatter of footsteps sounded from the kitchen. Mrs Moultrie's scowling jowls appeared in the doorway.

'The master and mistress are up early this morning so you best get upstairs and strip the beds. It's a fine day, so don't be dallying.' A jaundiced eye stared smugly at Kathryn. 'No outdoor chores today, miss. Mrs Marchant says as there's plenty to keep you busy in here.'

'I'm sure that my aunt is quite correct.'

Mrs Moultrie sniffed and waddled back to her kitchen.

* * *

Upstairs the visitor was being shown into the dining room by a somewhat awed footman.

Even the master of the house had lost his normal staid countenance and was eyeing the doorway of the dining room in a rather apprehensive manner. The *Morning Post* lay discarded upon the table.

Anna Marchant recovered from the shock first and greeted their guest with a feigned smile and a nod of her golden head. 'Lord Ravensmede, what a pleasant surprise and so early in the morning. Please do join us for breakfast.'

'Indeed,' agreed her husband a tad too heartily. 'Make yourself comfortable, my lord.'

Ravensmede passed his beaver and gloves to the footman and sat himself down at the table. The dark ruffle of his hair and colour in his cheeks bespoke a man who had been up since the crack of dawn. He wore an aura of strength and vitality, quite unlike his host and hostess, who had not long crawled from their beds and were still feeling not quite up to scratch.

'Sorry to trouble you at such an unearthly hour,' he drawled with absolutely no hint of sincerity. An invisible speck of dust on the sleeve of his impeccable dark green coat required his attention, leaving Mr and Mrs Marchant perched on the edge of their seats.

'Will you take something to eat, my lord?' Mr Marchant's chins stretched into a smile.

Ravensmede's waved his hand in a dismissive gesture. 'No, thank you, sir. I've already broken my fast.' He watched the shadow of anxiety cloud Henry Marchant's face.

Mr Marchant cleared his throat. 'Regarding the matter you brought to my attention yesterday, my lord, it was a silly misunderstanding and shall not happen again.' His gaze flickered to Mrs Marchant, then back to the Viscount.

His wife looked on coldly, dislike bristling beneath her pleasant veneer.

'Good,' said Ravensmede, 'But I'm here for quite a different purpose, sir. I wondered if I might call upon Miss Marchant this afternoon to accompany me for a drive in Hyde Park.'

'Yes, indeed you may, sir.' The words were out before Ravensmede had even finished his sentence. 'Lottie's the apple of my eye. A darling girl. And a diamond of the first water, even if I do say so myself.'

His lordship did not immediately correct the man's mistake. He thought of Lottie Marchant and her bland prettiness, so like a hundred other young women. He checked the twitch at his lips.

'My daughter will be more than happy to accompany you, won't she, my dear?'

Anna Marchant inclined her head in agreement.

Lord Ravensmede's haughty brow raised just a little. 'But, sir, you misunderstand me. I was speaking of Miss Kathryn Marchant.' He paused to watch the shot go home.

Henry Marchant's countenance coloured and his wife was staring as if the very devil had just appeared.

'My niece?' The words ground slowly from Mr Marchant's mouth.

'I take it you have no problem with my request.'

Unless he had gauged the Marchants wrongly, then they would do nothing other than comply.

Mr Marchant nodded once. 'Fine by me, sir.'

Anna Marchant's top lip curled with disdain before she forced it once more to the semblance of a smile. 'Unfortunately, my niece is indisposed with a chill. It will take some days before she's fully recovered, and I doubt that the outdoor air would be advisable for her state of health.'

Ravensmede's expression did not alter from unassailable boredom. It was the one he used when engaged in card play and it had never failed him yet. 'Indeed, madam, I send my condolences. In that case, I won't waste any more of your time.' He executed the tiniest of bows and made to leave.

Mr Marchant made haste to repair any damage. 'I'm sure she will be recovered by next week, if you would care to call then.'

If looks could kill, Henry Marchant would have been a bloodied corpse upon the rug, a victim of his wife's malice.

'Perhaps,' said his lordship ambiguously and strolled out into the hallway just in time to see Kathryn Marchant running down the stairs with a basket full of crumpled sheets between her hands.

'Miss Marchant,' said Lord Ravensmede, in a tone of absolute correctness. 'I trust you're feeling well enough to be out of bed?'

Kathryn stared at the tall athletic figure that had just emerged from the dining room. 'Lord Ravensmede?' Was she dreaming? Her fingers loosed their grip on the wicker strands, leaving Anna Marchant's dirty sheets to tumble out in full display down the staircase before her.

The lady screeched in the background. 'Kathryn, what are you doing up there? No doubt she has developed a fever to make her behave in such an obscure manner. I cannot begin to think what on earth she is doing with that linen. Leave it at once and return to your room.' As Nancy appeared over Kathryn's shoulder she added, 'You, girl, why are you using the main stairs? Get this mess sorted out at once! I'll speak to you later.'

Aunt Anna's harsh words pulled Kathryn's attention from the Viscount. 'Aunt, please do not be cross with Nancy. I insisted that we come this way. These baskets are so wide it makes the servants' stairwell difficult to squeeze down. I did not think…' The words trailed off and she glanced apologetically in the direction of Lord Ravensmede.

'You never do,' came her aunt's withering reply.

Ravensmede looked directly from the sheets to Mr Marchant. A flush appeared on the older man's cheeks.

Ravensmede allowed a small awkward silence before turning his attention back to Kathryn. 'You appear to have recovered from your chill, Miss Marchant,' he said in a voice that was silky smooth.

Kathryn's brow wrinkled in bewilderment. 'I'm quite well, thank you, my lord. Whatever made you think that I was not?'

Ravensmede cocked an eyebrow in Mrs Marchant's direction.

'Kathryn, you silly girl, you don't know what you're saying! It must be the fever.' Anna attempted to shoo her niece back up the stairs. 'And have a care not to waken Lottie.'

'Shall I send my own physician to attend Miss Marchant?' The deep voice arrested the ladies' progress. He stepped forward, extending his hand to touch his fingers against Kathryn's forehead. 'How strange, no heat at all. A miraculous recovery wouldn't you say, Mrs Marchant?'

Anna Marchant's mouth compressed with fury.

Her husband tugged helplessly at his neckcloth. 'Just as you say, sir, a speedy and fortuitous recovery.'

Ravensmede stepped back, fixed his beaver hat on his head and carefully donned his gloves. 'Then I shall call at four.' The piercing gaze rested on Mr Marchant, 'Good morning, sir', flitted to his wife, 'madam', and finally alighted on Kathryn, 'Miss Marchant.'

The three stood slack-jawed and silent as Lord Ravensmede sauntered from the house in Green Street.

Kathryn had changed into her best walking dress: a slightly faded blue muslin purchased five years ago. It was dated in appearance, but clean, and she knew that the colour suited her well. Her hair was caught back in a knot at the nape of her neck and was well hidden beneath the mud-brown bonnet, which had been a gift from Aunt Anna when her own had fallen apart. A fichu, a rather tight spencer, sturdy walking shoes, darned gloves, and a small home-made reticule, all in a matching shade of greyish brown, completed the ensemble. Standing in front of the mirror, Kathryn surveyed her reflection with a critical eye. Her face was so pale that even her lips had lost their rosy hue. She looked exactly like she felt: tired and washed out. And she had yet to face an afternoon in Lord Ravensmede's company. The prospect was really rather daunting. Why would a man like him be interested in a woman like her? The answer was plainly evident. He had made his intent very clear. Raising her chin a notch, she determined to set his lordship firmly in his place with regard to that. A noise sounded behind her.

'Ah, Kathryn, getting ready for Lord Ravensmede?' Lottie swept an appraising gaze over her cousin. 'You look…like someone far past her last prayers.'

Kathryn said nothing, just watched while Lottie flounced into the bedchamber and sat herself down upon the single battered chair.

'There's only one reason that Ravensmede would be taking the likes of you for a drive, and we all know what that is.' One pretty slippered foot swung repetitively. 'Let's just say that it's certainly not marriage he has on his mind.' A snigger escaped her. 'What have you been up to with his lordship, Kathryn?' Lottie leaned forward, a smug gloating look upon her face.

'Stop it, Lottie. I didn't ask Lord Ravensmede to take me driving. Indeed, I would much prefer not to spend any time in his company. I was as surprised as you to hear that he had made such an offer.'

'And is that the only offer he has made you?'

On seeing the barb hit home and two patches of colour flow into her cousin's cheeks, Lottie continued, 'That night at Lady Finlay's, when he waltzed with you, where were you when you stormed off out of the ball room? In the retiring room? I don't think so. More like reaching an agreement with the Viscount of Ravensmede!'

Kathryn turned, eyes flashing, fists clenched to control her fury. 'Lottie, how can you make such wicked allegations? You know very well that it's nonsense.'

Lottie did not reply, just smiled knowingly.

'Please excuse me, Cousin.' Kathryn could not bear to stay in the room a minute longer.

A snide laugh followed her. 'You may run, Kathryn, but you won't get very far. Mama has a little surprise planned for you.'

She sat alone and tense in the drawing room awaiting the sound of the bell. If Lottie thought such a thing, then the rest of the world was likely to view it in much the same vein. She would have to deter Lord Ravensmede in no uncertain terms. Her gaze fixed on the blackened fireplace. She forced herself to relax, to breathe deeply. In, and out. Tension ebbed. *The fireplace disappeared. Her mother's face smiled kindly. A soft hand reached out to softly stroke her hair. The wind whipped at her face, sea air inhaled deep into her lungs. Mama was laughing and pointing to the shimmering water and the rolling white waves. Lottie's cruel words receded into oblivion. Meaningless. Gentle fingers stroked her cheek. 'Kathryn,' Mama whispered. Kathryn smiled beneath the caress. 'Kathryn.' The voice was deeper, slightly more insistent, not like Mama's at all. She touched her hand to Mama's.* Her eyelids fluttered open, and she looked up into the clear green eyes of Lord Ravensmede. A gasp sounded, her own, and she was up and out of the chair, breathless with confusion. 'Lord Ravensmede, you startled me!'

'My apologies, Miss Marchant. I did not mean to.' He was regarding her with such scrutiny as to set Kathryn's cheeks aflame.

'Good afternoon, Lord Ravensmede.' Mrs Marchant breezed into the room. 'We seem to have found Kathryn at last. I shall tell Lottie she can call off the search.' The bright blue eyes narrowed as they flicked over Kathryn's reddened face.

Ravensmede extended his arm in Kathryn's direction. 'I shall return your niece safely before six. Try not to concern yourself, ma'am. I shall see to it personally that there's no deterioration in her health.'

'Indeed, Lord Ravensmede, I don't doubt it. But I will, of course, be present myself to witness your attentions. Lottie and I will accompany Kathryn this afternoon.' Mrs Marchant almost cackled at the deliverance of her cunning plan. 'It would be unseemly to allow my niece out without a chaperon.' She did not add the words 'and in your company'. She did not need to.

Lord Ravensmede delivered the woman a glare of such glacial proportions that she actually stumbled back. 'Such a thought is anathema to my sensibilities. Which is why I've brought my grandmother in just such a capacity. She preferred to wait in the barouche while I came in to collect Miss Marchant.' The inferred insult was obvious. 'Perhaps you would care to step outside to meet her?'

Anna Marchant moved swiftly to the window and looked out at Lord Ravensmede's barouche complete with an elderly lady dressed entirely in gaudy purple.

Kathryn looked from her aunt to Ravensmede and back again.

'But of course, Lord Ravensmede,' Mrs Marchant uttered between gritted teeth. 'How very thoughtful of you.' Every step those daintily clad feet took on their way out to the barouche warned of a mounting violence. 'I shall await Kathryn's return with impatience.' She slid a meaningful look at her niece.

Kathryn did not miss the promise held so clearly in those cold blue eyes.

The day was warm, but that had not prevented the frail little lady being almost hidden beneath the thickest pile of blankets.

'Grandmama, may I introduce Mrs Marchant, Miss Kathryn Marchant, and…' he indicated the sullen-faced young woman who refused to leave the doorway '…Miss Charlotte Marchant.'

Anna Marchant dropped a graceful curtsy, hid the malice from her face and smiled charmingly. 'Such a pleasure to meet you, Lady Maybury.'

The old lady subjected each of the offered females to a piercing stare from eyes that were a faded version of Ravensmede's own, and let out a cackle. 'The little chit looks nothing like the other two. I fancy Mr Marchant may have been cuckolded there.' Then, as if she hadn't just dropped a monumental insult, she dabbed a lilac lace handkerchief to her nose and declared in an imperious tone, 'Nicholas, how much longer do you intend to keep me waiting? Even the greys are getting bored.'

For the first time since meeting her Ravensmede bestowed a smile upon Mrs Marchant, then he took his leave of her, lifting Kathryn neatly into the barouche and bowling off down the road at what could only be described as a reckless pace.

The entirety of London's *ton* had decided to partake of the afternoon air within the green surround of Hyde Park, or so it seemed to Kathryn when they entered. So many pairs of curious eyes turned upon her, so many hushed whispers and veiled finger pointings. She hid her discomfort well and smiled at Ravensmede's eagle-eyed grandmother. The old lady fussed around with her blankets, oblivious to the heat of the day, raised a withered hand in the direction of a distant carriage and then turned her attentions to Kathryn.

'Well, let me have a good look at you, gel.' A quizzing glass appeared from beneath the blankets. One greatly enlarged faded eye gave a close scrutiny, missing nothing of the worn attire or the way Miss Kathryn Marchant kept her head averted from her grandson's person. 'Not got the fair locks or the silly prettiness of the other two,' came the succinct observation.

Kathryn heard the sharpness in Lady Maybury's voice. Those unused to her ladyship's company had been known to quail under her blunt comments, but Kathryn sensed no malice beneath the harsh veneer. 'No, my lady. Mrs Marchant is my aunt, and Charlotte, my cousin. I've lived with them since my father died.'

'And your father was…Robert Marchant?'

Kathryn's eyes opened wide. Forgetting her reserve, she twisted round to face Lady Maybury. 'You knew him?'

'No. When you've been alive for as long as I have, there's not much you don't eventually get to hear of. Refresh my memory.'

'Grandmama!' said Ravensmede, remembering Archie Cadmount's brief account of Kathryn's history, 'Miss Marchant may not wish to speak of her family.'

'Tush and nonsense, Nick!' exclaimed the old lady heatedly. She then bestowed a look of obvious affection upon her favourite grandson.

For the first time since leaving Green Street Kathryn looked directly at his lordship. 'Really, I don't mind, my lord.'

Ravensmede kept his eyes upon her. And in his breast rose that same inexplicable feeling that had enveloped him on seeing Kathryn Marchant seated all alone in the drawing room with her mind a thousand miles away. Who was it that she saw behind those closed eyes? Someone who had the power to make her smile, someone she was happy to have caress her cheek. A suitor from the past, or some secret lover? The thought did not please him. That velvet-smooth skin washed with the merest hint of colour as she turned once more to his grandmother.

'As you said, my father was Robert Marchant, the elder brother of Uncle Henry. My mother was Elizabeth Thornley, from Overton. She died of consumption almost eight years ago. Soon after, my sister died too, of the same illness. My father…' Her voice wavered. 'My father suffered an accident.' She couldn't bring herself to tell them the exact nature of the 'accident', or how she had spent the time since his death trying to forget the horrendous image that seemed branded on her memory. 'He's been dead for just over three years. Uncle Henry and Aunt Anna were kind enough to offer me a home.' Her fingers tightened against the seat.

'What of your mother's relatives? Have you no contact with them?' the Dowager Countess demanded, but there was a distinct mellowing in the sharpness of her tone.

Kathryn's fingers plucked at the muslin of her skirt, and her lashes swept low before she answered, 'They didn't approve of my parents' marriage. I've never met them.'

'I see.' Lady Maybury raised her quizzing glass once more. 'And why are you not yet married?'

Kathryn blushed. 'There was never time for that.' She did not speak of the pain of nursing her mother and sister, nor of the years of caring for her grief-stricken father. Neither did she mention the torment of her father's death. 'And now I'm my cousin's companion.'

A tutting sound escaped the crinkled lips. 'Stuff and nonsense! No time indeed!'

On seeing the deepening hue of Kathryn's cheeks, Ravensmede came to her rescue. 'You mustn't tease Miss Marchant so, Grandmama. It really is quite cruel of you.' Besides he didn't want his relative getting ideas about arranging a marriage for the girl with the first convenient man; not when he had other plans for Kathryn Marchant.

Of all his family Ravensmede was closest to his paternal grandmother. Even so, that did not mean he was blind to her tendency for bossy dominance and interfering in matters that did not concern her. Not that it was a family trait by any means, or so he told himself. He made a mental note to have a word with her at a more opportune moment.

The dowager snorted, but changed the subject all the same.

They stopped on several occasions to allow Lady Maybury to converse with other ladies, to all of whom she insisted on introducing Miss Marchant. The afternoon was progressing splendidly and even Kathryn had begun to relax and enjoy the bright sunshine and wonderful cooling breeze when the unfortunate incident occurred.

The tiny ragged figure appeared as if from thin air to materialise directly in front of Lord Ravensmede's barouche. Even with the wealth of his driving experience and his renowned skill with the ribbons, there was little that Ravensmede could do to stop the team in time. As it was, his expertise allowed him to pull the team hard to the right-hand side of the path and, in all probability, it was this reflex that prevented the collision and saved the child's life. As the horses ground to a halt, he glanced round to check that his passengers had not been dislodged by the abruptness of his stopping. Kathryn was tucking the blanket around his grandmother, who was complaining in a most querulous tone of voice. Her gaze met his as he heard the soft murmur of her voice reassure the old lady.

He moved quickly, reaching the child in a matter of seconds. With firm but gentle hands he examined the body lying so still upon the ground before him. She was a small girl, three or four years of age at the most. Her hair was dark and matted; her clothes dirty and ragged. There was no blood, and no lacerations of the skin. Neither were her limbs twisted. She looked unhurt, as if she were just sleeping. He heard the commotion as his grandmother struggled to climb down from the carriage. 'Stay where you are, Grandmama. The child does not appear badly injured, but I don't yet know the extent of the damage caused. You may find it distressing.'

Lady Maybury spluttered her indignation. 'Fiddlesticks! If you're bent on shaking me around this carriage as if I'm a bowl of dried peas, then at least have the decency to allow my curiosity!'

Ravensmede recognised the stubborn tone of her voice. Resistance would be futile, and more to the point, a waste of time. With a barely stifled sigh of frustration he ignored her comments and turned his attention once more to the child, only to find Miss Marchant crouched on the opposite side of the poor motionless body. And the concern clear in the gaze that met his caused a peculiar sensation within his chest.

Her darned gloves were unceremoniously cast aside and two little work-worn hands were engaged in feeling the length of the child's body to measure the extent of the hurts, just as he had done. Upon her face was a look of such focused intensity of which Ravensmede had never seen the like. He heard the movement of his grandmother behind him; felt her hand touch briefly to his arm.

'Is the child…?'

Kathryn glanced up for the briefest of moments. 'Thank the Lord, she's not dead. But I fear that she may have broken her leg.' She raised the little girl's skirts to expose her ankles and shins. 'See how swollen and red it is below her knee. Mercifully she's fainted and so cannot feel the pain.'

'It's fortunate indeed that she was thrown clear. She ran straight in front of me. There wasn't much I could do.' A frown wrinkled Ravensmede's brow. 'She should be seen by a doctor. Let's hope that the leg is not broken.'

A moan escaped the little girl's lips.

'Hush, child. You're safe now.' Kathryn rubbed the child's dirty, scrawny arms. 'You've had an accident and hurt your leg, but everything is going to be fine. Can you tell me your name?'

'Maggie,' the child whispered, scarcely loud enough to be heard.

'Well, Maggie, just you lie still until we can get your leg mended. Be a brave girl.'

Ravensmede watched in amazement while Kathryn gently stroked the child's filthy hair, her voice crooning softly to calm the little girl's panic. That a grubby, unknown street child could engender such a tender, caring response! Most young ladies of the *ton* would have run a mile rather than touch such an offensive specimen of the lower classes. But then, again, why should he expect Miss Kathryn Marchant to be like most young ladies, when she had so far proven herself quite dissimilar in every aspect? It seemed she was determined to provide him with further evidence of her rather unique qualities as she began to strip off first her spencer, then her fichu.

He felt the flicker of the familiar hunger that he'd come to associate with her. Without thinking, he licked his lips. Anticipation hardened the angles of his face. And then he remembered where he was, and that his grandmother was at his shoulder. 'Miss Marchant, what do you think you're…?' The question trailed off unfinished as he watched her wrap the garments around the child's body.

'No doubt it's the shock that has chased the warmth from

her. We mustn't allow her to become chilled.' Kathryn appeared
to be so completely focused upon the little girl that she betrayed
not the slightest inhibition at her partially disrobed state and
spoke as if tending an injured child was an everyday occurrence
in her life.

Lord Ravensmede stared at what had been exposed by the
missing fichu. He stared at the tender skin above the shabby
dress's neckline. He stared as he had never stared at any woman
before. And the expression on his face was not one of lust or
desire; rather, shock more aptly described the sensation. Shock
that was rapidly progressing to anger. For Kathryn Marchant's
skin bore marks that should adorn no woman.

'Nicholas.' A firm hand touched to his shoulder. Elderly
green eyes gazed down into his, and he saw in them the reflection of what he felt. Lady Maybury gave a barely perceptible
nod of her head before subtly drawing her grandson's attention
to the rapidly massing crowd.

An indefinable curse growled from the Viscount of Ravensmede before he hastily shrugged off his coat and swept it around
Kathryn's shoulders.

Wide grey eyes met his with blatant surprise. 'My lord?
There is no—'

Ravensmede smoothly cut her off. 'It would not do for *you*
to catch a chill, Miss Marchant.'

'But it's a warm day and…'

The full force of his powerful gaze turned upon her. Anger
spurred his actions and hardened his voice. Those marks, in
faded hues of blue and purple, green and yellow, were still
vivid enough against the white of her skin. Bruising. Made
perhaps a week or so ago. Made by cruel fingers, if the pattern-
ing was anything to go by. What the hell had happened to her?
Who was the scoundrel that had hit her? He slammed the brakes
on the route his thoughts were taking. Hyde Park was neither
the time nor the place.

He was brought back to reality by his grandmother's voice.

'Wrap the child in one of my travelling blankets. There's plenty warmth in those.'

His eyes fleetingly met Kathryn Marchant's once more, before he gathered up the urchin in his arms, complete with Miss Marchant's draping clothing, and walked to the carriage. 'I'll have Dr Porter treat the child at the house.' And, so saying, he deposited the small bundle into one of his grandmother's travelling blankets, ensured that both ladies were safely aboard, and set off for Berkeley Square.

Kathryn's eyes opened wide at the magnificent mansion before her. Ravensmede House was quite the grandest abode she had ever seen. And this was only one of his lordship's properties. She did not dare to think of all of his other houses. The image of one of London's most infamous rake-hells carrying the swaddled bundle with such care up the grand stone stairs would stay with her for ever. In that moment it seemed that the summer breeze had stilled, and her breathing too. The liquid warmth of tenderness erupted in her heart. It was obvious that there was very much more to Lord Ravensmede than his reputation suggested.

Ravensmede withdrew the toe of his boot from the fender and his elbow from the mantelpiece, and turned to face the drawing room chairs in which both Kathryn Marchant and his grandmother were seated. 'Dr Porter has been up there for some considerable time. I hope that the child's injuries are not worse than we thought.'

The dowager arched a quizzical eyebrow at her grandson.

Ravensmede seemed not to notice. 'Little Maggie seemed most reassured by Miss Marchant. Perhaps if Miss Marchant were to go to her… But no, I'm being too presumptuous…'

Kathryn carefully replaced the fine china cup upon the ornate saucer. 'No, not at all, Lord Ravensmede. I should have thought of such a thing myself. It was very kind of your housekeeper to sit with Maggie, but the poor child will be feeling frightened and alone.' She brushed down her skirts and rose, all the while remembering similar feelings from the years following her mother and sister's deaths. It was not something that she was content to let any child suffer. She pushed the memories away and concentrated on the child lying up in one of Lord Ravensmede's guest bedchambers. 'If you do not mind, I will stay with her until the doctor is finished.'

'Of course, Miss Marchant,' Ravensmede said politely. 'It's for the best.'

He reached over and rang the bell.

He did not speak again until the maid had arrived and escorted Kathryn from the drawing room.

'Well?' the dowager enquired of her grandson.

Ravensmede moved to sit on the sofa close by his grandmother's chair. 'Well,' he threw back at her. 'Judging from the bruises covering her neck and chest, I think that someone has tried to throttle Miss Marchant.'

'I'm not blind, boy!' she snorted. 'I saw them all right. I'm quite sure half of London did too when she whipped off her spencer and fichu in the middle of Hyde Park!'

'She was trying to help the child.'

'And exposing herself in the process.'

'She was unaware of what she was doing.' Ravensmede's eyes darkened. 'It would seem that I'm required once more to call upon Henry Marchant. The man is in need of guidance when it comes to his treatment of Miss Marchant.' He cracked his knuckles and balled one hand to a fist.'

'And have the whole of London gossip as to why the bachelor Viscount of Ravensmede is intervening in that man's treatment of his niece. Damn it, Nick, you don't even know if Henry Marchant's your man. She might have got the bruises elsewhere.' Lady Maybury drained the tea from her cup and swiftly refilled it.

'Indeed she might have. But as her uncle, it's his responsibility to ensure her safety. Whether he lifted his hands to her or not, the blame still lies with him.'

The dowager watched her grandson closely.

'I'll be damned if I just deliver her back into his hands. I suspect that his wife lies behind the problem. Mrs Marchant had her niece in the kitchen and laundering the bed-linen, as if she were a blasted maid of all.' Belatedly he remembered to whom he was talking. 'Please excuse my language,' he muttered.

Nothing had stirred Nicholas to such a passion in a very long time. Lady Maybury's focus sharpened. 'You seem to have developed rather a concern with Miss Marchant.'

Ravensmede lay back languidly and stretched his legs out before him. 'What I'm concerned with is righting an injustice,' he said in a lazy tone. 'Hitting a woman goes far beyond the pale for any man, least of all the most charitable Mr Henry Marchant.'

'I agree entirely, but you had no notion of Kathryn's bruises when you asked me to act as chaperon.'

'I enjoy her company. She's an interesting woman.'

'And an attractive one.'

'A very attractive one.' Ravensmede met his grandmother's gaze.

'Her mother was a Thornley of Overton,' she said. 'Kathryn Marchant is a lady. And a young, unmarried lady at that.'

Ravensmede knew the turn the dowager's thoughts were taking. 'She is indeed. I do not mean to ruin her, if that's what you're thinking.'

'Then what exactly is your interest in the gel? Marriage?'

A dark eyebrow quirked in disbelief. 'Certainly not. I like Miss Marchant, and suspected her situation was unhappy, although I had no notion of the extent of her mistreatment. My interest in the girl, as you so aptly put it, is purely philanthropic. Would you have me turn a blind eye to her suffering?'

They looked at one another for a moment longer, before

Lady Maybury finally said, 'So what exactly is it that you are proposing?'

Ravensmede's mouth formed a charming smile, and then he proceeded to explain his plan in full.

Chapter Five

A soft knock at the door heralded Kathryn's return.

Lord Ravensmede slipped from the room to speak with the physician.

Lady Maybury patted the empty chair by her side. 'Come and sit here, Miss Marchant. Tell me how the child fares.'

'Thank you,' said Kathryn, and sat down where the dowager indicated. 'The doctor says that Maggie's leg is not broken, only bruised. As Lord Ravensmede said, she's had a very lucky escape.'

'Lucky, indeed,' said her ladyship.

'She doesn't seem too distressed, but the poor little thing is exhausted. The doctor says that she needs rest. She was dozing off as I came away.'

'Excellent.' The dowager beamed. 'The child could not be in better hands. Dr Porter attends all our family and is one of the best physicians in London. Treated Nicholas when he was a boy. I remember twenty years ago when…' She went on to reminisce over her grandchildren's childhood ailments and the antics that caused them, much to Kathryn's amusement. In light of Lady Maybury's stories her aristocratic family did not seem quite so daunting. They were still laughing when Lord Ravensmede returned.

The clock on the mantel chimed six. 'I hadn't thought it so

late,' said Kathryn. 'I must return home. My aunt was expecting me before now.'

'Oh, but we have not even begun to discuss the other matter.' The Dowager Countess's small eyes brightened.

Kathryn did not miss the conspiratorial look exchanged between Lady Maybury and her grandson. She felt herself stiffen involuntarily and eyed the elderly lady with suspicion. 'What other matter?'

Lady Maybury crowed a small sharp chuckle. 'Well, my dear, you're nothing if not blunt!'

'Please do forgive me, my lady.' Kathryn looked away awkwardly at her sudden lapse in manners.

'It's a trait I admire,' declared Ravensmede's grandmother. 'Can't stand these milk-and-water misses who are scared to say what they think. Would agree with anything I say. Faugh!' The sunburst of wrinkles deepened as the top lip curled with contempt. 'Much prefer a gel who'll tell me the truth!' A smile replaced the frown. 'So, Miss Marchant, how do you find me?'

The grey eyes widened and she stared at the dowager. 'How do I find you?' she repeated with rising incredulity.

'That, indeed, is the question,' affirmed Lady Maybury with a twinkle in her eye, and the same mischievous look that Kathryn had seen cross her grandson's face on occasion.

A short pause sufficed to frame Kathryn's reply. 'Why, I find you to be very nice, and I've enjoyed your company greatly this afternoon.' It was the truth no less.

'Splendid!' her ladyship returned in increasingly exuberant tones. 'Then you'll have no objection to accepting my offer.'

'Your offer?' Kathryn said slowly, aware that she sounded rather like a simpleton who could do nothing other than repeat the questions asked of her.

The faded green gaze locked on to hers. 'To become my companion for the next two months of my visit.'

'Oh, no, my lady. I'm afraid that would be quite impossible. My aunt and uncle—'

'Nonsense!' chirped the grandam. 'I've already made my mind up and I don't mean to take no for an answer.'

'But—' She tried again, to no avail.

'I've a need for a companion. Can't stay in London with only Nick for company. He'll drive me mad before the week is out.' She snorted in the direction of her grandson.

Kathryn glanced over to see a smile curve Lord Ravensmede's lips.

'I'm afraid that my grandmother is quite right. All those wild card parties, the brandy, the gambling... She needs someone to keep her on the straight and narrow. I confess it's a job beyond my capabilities. Why, just look at the shocking influence she's already had on me.' The straight white teeth flashed and one dark eyebrow raised in a crooked gesture.

For all that she tried to resist, Kathryn felt the smile tug at her lips and looked abruptly away from temptation. Was it possible? Could she really just leave the torment of her life within the Marchant household? A brief flame of hope flickered...and then expired. Uncle Henry and Aunt Anna were her relatives, had offered her a home, albeit a miserable one, for the last three years. Wasn't it her duty to act as Lottie's companion until her cousin was successfully married? And if Aunt Anna had her way, a husband for Lottie would be netted before the Season was over. Perhaps then she could... Such thoughts were futile. Lady Maybury desired her as a temporary companion only during her visit to London. And afterwards? It was quite beyond question. She raised her eyes once more to Lady Maybury. 'I thank you for your generous offer, my lady. Indeed, it's most kind of you to even consider asking me, but I'm afraid that I'm forced to decline. It's my duty to act as Lottie's companion until she's—'

'Surely Mrs Marchant attends all of the society events along with her daughter?' The elderly voice was severe in the extreme.

'Yes, but—'

'Then, what does the chit need a companion for? As an unmarried and young lady you can hardly be expected to act as her chaperon can you?'

Kathryn felt the net closing around her. 'No, but—'

'I suppose I should not be surprised that you prefer to accompany a pretty, young chit to dances than spend your time assisting an old woman who is not much longer for this earth.'

The dowager seemed to shrink before Kathryn's very eyes, her narrow shoulders closing in, her velvet cheeks growing gaunt. A hollow cough rent the air.

Guilt stabbed at Kathryn's breast. 'No, it isn't—'

'Do not worry yourself, Miss Marchant.' A blue-veined hand dabbed a delicate lace handkerchief to each faded eye. A sad little sniff…and then the dowager played her trump card. 'I shall contrive my best to attend the injured child upstairs, but at my age…' The words trailed off. 'Such a strain on my health, the worry of it all…' Lady Maybury sniffed again and a tremor quivered upon her lips.

Dear Lord, but the old woman was clearly distraught and in danger of working herself into a fit of the vapours! Kathryn leapt forward and took one frail old hand within her own.

'That poor urchin…' There was what sounded to be a definite sob in her ladyship's voice.

Kathryn gently rubbed the paper-thin skin covering the back of Lady Maybury's hand. How could she make her understand that it really was not her choice at all? That she would much rather leave behind the house in Green Street and live her life as the dowager's companion? But it was not a matter of want. 'Dear Lady Maybury, please do not think that I don't want to accept your kind offer, or help little Maggie. There's nothing I would rather do, but—'

The old lady clung to her, her eyes brightening of a sudden. 'Oh my dearest gel! I knew that you would see sense; that you wouldn't be so heartless as to sentence an old lady to a season of loneliness and ill health. I cannot tell you the relief!' Ravensmede's grandmother's smile was wonderful to see.

'But—' started Kathryn uselessly, and stopped. The old lady was looking at her with such expectation that she could not correct the mistake. It would be a cruel and heartless woman that could shatter such joy. Who knew the effect such a shock would have on the lady's health? Kathryn swallowed down that sinking feeling and forced a smile to her face. And not once did she allow herself to look in the direction of the lady's grandson standing so tall and silent by the fireplace.

The small girl lay still within the great bed, her brown pansy eyes trained upon Kathryn's face.

'How old are you, Maggie?'

'Four,' the little voice whispered back.

'And do you remember where it is that you live?'

'Whitecross Road, the top room in Number Sixteen.'

'Good girl! You're really very clever. I'll send a message to your mama and papa so that they know where you are and aren't worried about you.'

Two fat tears rolled down the cheeks that Kathryn had just cleaned. 'Want to go home. Want me ma.' A hiccup sounded.

Kathryn wiped the tears away. 'Of course you do, moppet. And when you're better, so you shall. The doctor's looked at your leg and do you know what he said?'

The question distracted Maggie away from the sobbing she was poised to commence. 'What?'

'He said that it isn't broken at all, only bruised, and that it will get better very soon. But until then you're to rest in bed and eat lots of food.'

Maggie's eyes opened wide at the prospect. 'Lots an' lots of food?'

'Lots and lots and *lots*!' confirmed Kathryn with a grin. 'And I'll be here to tell you stories and talk to you, so you won't be lonely at all.'

Maggie smiled up into the kind face that hovered above hers.

A creaking of the door and Lord Ravensmede materialised

by the bed. Kathryn struggled to get to her feet, but was stayed by a warm hand touched to her elbow.

'No need to get up on my account.' His voice was both deep and melodic, without a hint of the practised drawl he used when he was out.

She raised her eyes to his and felt a shimmer of excitement ripple down her spine. Just his proximity caused her heart to race. Her fingers fluttered to rearrange the fichu that she had recently replaced. Averting her face, she sought to turn her mind from inappropriate thoughts of the Viscount of Ravensmede. 'Maggie is a very clever girl and has told me where she lives.' With great gentleness she stroked the child's forehead.

Ravensmede smiled. 'Very good.'

Whether this remark was addressed to herself or Maggie, Kathryn remained unsure.

Maggie was regarding the tall dark-haired man solemnly. 'Are you the pa?' she asked quite suddenly.

'The pa?' Ravensmede looked rather bemused.

'Are you?' The round dark eyes had not wavered from his face.

Ravensmede glanced with amusement at Miss Marchant.

'You *must* be.' The strands of black hair so carefully combed out by Kathryn bobbed up and down as the child nodded. 'And you must be the ma,' added Maggie with certainty to Kathryn. 'Where are your little girls an' boys?'

Crimson flooded Kathryn's cheeks. 'Hush now, Maggie, you're tired and need to sleep. I'll come back and see you later.' A small kiss was dropped to the little girl's forehead.

'Promise?' the baby voice queried.

'I promise,' vowed Kathryn and rose to her feet, casting the child's previous innocently uttered questions from her mind.

Ravensmede opened the door and waited for her to pass through, before following her out into the passageway.

A throaty laugh sounded. 'Ma and pa!' And the look that

smouldered from those green eyes caused a dancing sensation deep in Kathryn's belly.

She kept her gaze straight ahead, concentrating on each step, the pink-and-gold patterned carpet, the pale gold-coloured walls with their wall sconces and elaborate gilt-framed paintings, anything other than the man walking by her side. He was so close she could almost feel his heat scorching the full length of her left-hand side. Living in the same house as Lord Ravensmede was going to prove difficult in more ways than one.

Firstly, there was the simple fact that he was a bachelor, coupled with the not-so-small problem of his reputation. Secondly, Aunt Anna and Uncle Henry were not likely to receive the news of her move well. Finally, and perhaps most importantly, was the strength of her own inappropriate reaction to the Viscount. From their first encounter over Miss Dawson's shoe, to that unwitting kiss and the subsequent calamity with the potatoes in St James's Park, Kathryn was well aware of the trouble resulting from that very reaction. The more she thought on it, the more she came to realise that, even as Lady Maybury's companion, living under the same roof as Lord Ravensmede was likely to prove a dangerous pastime—and one that she could not afford to risk, even if it did mean an escape from Aunt Anna's cruel treatment. All she had left was her reputation, and that wasn't something that she was prepared to jeopardise. She did not want to hurt Lady Maybury, or leave Maggie for that matter, but the alternative was far too threatening to contemplate. The decision made, she pressed her lips firmly together and stopped abruptly.

Ravensmede had stepped past her before reacting to her halt. 'Miss Marchant?' He sauntered back to stand beside her.

'My lord, I…' The words were rushed before her fragile resolve could fail. 'I know that I agreed to your grandmother's most kind offer, but upon further reflection I'm afraid that it is—'

Ravensmede took her hand within his and raised it lightly to his lips. 'For your kindness to my grandmother you have my gratitude. She's very dear to me and I would not like to see her ill or distressed. Her heart is weak and the family have been advised that she must be spared all that we can. Any shocking news, any great disappointment is to be avoided. That's why I'm so relieved that you have the generosity of spirit, Miss Marchant, to indulge an old lady's whim.' Warm lips pressed against the roughened red skin of her hand.

Kathryn felt the breath catch in her throat. She blinked several times to clear her head. And stifled the groan.

'Grandmama is rather set in her ways. As you may already have noticed, she's very much determined to do things in her own style, even if it does rather fly in the face of what is deemed convention.' He smiled. 'She often takes irrational sets against people, but rarely have I seen her warm to someone as she has to you. My grandmother likes you, Miss Marchant, and that really is quite an achievement.'

It seemed that there was no way to extricate herself from the agreement. *But surely the Viscount himself can see the position in which I would be placed?* Kathryn's thoughts flitted back and forth. 'My lord—'

'Please, call me Nicholas.'

Kathryn recoiled as if he'd slapped her. Call him by his given name? Indeed she would not!

The smile deepened. 'Or Ravensmede, if that is your preference.'

She gritted her teeth and started again. 'Lord Ravensmede…' Confound the man, but he was laughing at her. Anger flushed her cheeks and she raised steely eyes to his. 'This is a serious matter, not some tomfoolery for your amusement.'

His mouth straightened but those mesmerising green eyes were still brimful of laughter. 'Indeed, Miss Marchant, I assure you that I had no such thought.'

With a tug she rescued her hand from within his. 'You cannot be unaware that living here as your grandmother's companion would place me in a somewhat awkward position.'

The green eyes opened wide and innocent. 'Whatever can you mean, Miss Marchant?'

Her anger deserted her of a sudden and she sighed. 'Just that you are a bachelor and that, as an unmarried lady, perhaps I'm not best placed to accept the position offered.' There, she had said it. She found sudden fascination in the patterned carpet.

'How old are you, Miss Marchant?'

She looked up in surprise. Of all the answers she had expected this had not been one. 'Four and twenty, my lord.'

'Ravensmede,' he corrected.

Two spots of colour burned high in her cheeks. 'Ravensmede,' she repeated softly.

The corner of his mouth squinted up in a boyish gesture. 'Then you're hardly a schoolroom miss, and quite old enough to be considered suitable as a lady's companion. That, coupled with my grandmother's lineage, will ensure that no disadvantage attaches itself to your reputation.'

Her cheeks were glowing with all the subtlety of two blazing beacons. 'I'm well aware that I'm considered to be left on the shelf, but that has no bearing on the concern that I've raised.' The thump of her heart echoed throughout her body and she wished that she were anywhere but here, standing beside Lord Ravensmede, listening to him confirm his notion of her as an old maid.

He watched her closely. 'That was not my meaning, Miss Marchant. I'm sure that there's many a gentleman who would be only too happy to make you his wife.'

Kathryn swallowed her embarrassment well and attempted to force the conversation towards safer ground. 'You mentioned your grandmother's lineage?' she said demurely, as if her face were not aflame.

That not-quite-serious expression was back on his face. 'She's the daughter of a duke, and the widow of one of the wealthiest earls in the country. If Grandmama is for you, Miss Marchant, no one will dare be against you.'

She digested this information in silence for some minutes.

It seemed that Lord Ravensmede had just removed the last of her reasons to refuse Lady Maybury's request. 'Then I hope I may prove useful in my new position.' Quite deliberately she turned and walked slowly towards the staircase, throwing the words over her shoulder as she went. 'When does Lady Maybury wish me to start?'

'Immediately.'

She nodded once. 'Then, I shall return first thing tomorrow morning.'

'I fear you misunderstand me, Miss Marchant. My grandmother needs your assistance *now.*' His gaze held hers.

'Very well. I'll return to my uncle's house to inform him of what has happened and pack up my clothes.'

'There's no need. I will dispatch a letter to Mr Marchant. Your clothes may be sent over later.' There was a determination in his voice that she did not understand.

'I cannot just leave for a drive in the park one afternoon and not return! It's a preposterous suggestion!'

A hand on her shoulder spun her round, and she found herself imprisoned by his grip on her upper arms. 'And what of your aunt and uncle, what of your cousin—is their treatment of you not equally preposterous?' His eyes stared down into hers.

Her skin scorched beneath the touch of his hands. 'I…I've never said so.'

'You don't need to.'

Surely he could not know? She had spoken to no one. Her heart was beating wildly within her chest. 'I won't renege on my agreement with Lady Maybury, if that's what you're afraid of.'

'I know you would not hurt an old lady's feelings, Kathryn.'

Her eyes widened at his use of her name.

'Nevertheless, I cannot permit you to return alone to Green Street. As I said, I will write to Mr Marchant with a full explanation.'

His confident assertion pricked at her pride. *'Cannot*

permit?' Her tone was incredulous. 'I don't think that it's your place to say such a thing, Lord Ravensmede.'

The green eyes did not betray their surprise by as much as a flicker. 'If you're bent on such a journey, then I must insist on accompanying you. My grandmother is quite fatigued by the drive and subsequent incident with the child. Trailing her back across town is quite out of the question. Therefore, we should ready ourselves immediately, Miss Marchant, unless you would prefer to wait until it is dark…'

Kathryn knew very well what his lordship was saying. Arriving alone with Lord Ravensmede to take her leave of them, no matter Ravensmede's assertions as to Lady Maybury's influence, there could be no doubt what it would look like. Aunt Anna and Uncle Henry would have an apoplectic fit. She ground her teeth. 'I have no need of your escort. I'm perfectly happy to go alone.'

'No.' The single word was decidedly emphatic.

'Lord Ravensmede, you're behaving most unreasonably.'

A dark eyebrow raised. 'Are you so very eager to return there? Do they treat you so well that you're loath to leave them?' There was an undercurrent to his words that made her shiver.

'It's not so strange a request.'

'You haven't answered the question, Miss Marchant.'

There was silence.

'It seems that you leave me little option, my lord. Write the letter if you must.'

And this time he did not chide her for the use of his title.

It had been several hours since a letter had been dispatched from the Viscount of Ravensmede to Mr Henry Marchant and still there had been no reply. Kathryn eyed the soft white cotton of the borrowed nightdress with some reticence. She was still uneasy about her sudden new-found position and the means by which it had been effected. Ravensmede's refusal to allow her to return alone to Green Street worried her. Undoubtedly he was stubborn and arrogant and used to getting his own way, but she had never thought him to be so downright unreasonable. It flew in the face of all she knew of him. But then she had to concede that her knowledge of Lord Ravensmede was remarkably scant. And he *had* made her a most indecent proposal in St James's Park.

Her fingers reached out and lifted the garment to her lap. Lady Maybury had seemed to think nothing remarkable in her grandson's overbearing attitude; indeed, the old lady appeared to positively encourage Ravensmede. She was still half-expecting Uncle Henry to come charging over, demanding to know what precisely was going on. But hadn't her uncle always been too keen to court the favour of the aristocracy? If she knew Uncle Henry, he'd be carefully weighing up the best response to further advance his own schemes. She sighed just as a light knock sounded at the door and a young maid entered.

'I'm Jean, miss. Come to help you undress for bed.' She bobbed a little curtsy.

'Thank you, Jean, but I'm used to dressing and undressing myself.' Kathryn watched the crestfallen face and suddenly realised why. 'Are you an abigail?'

The thin face flushed. 'No, miss, I'm a chambermaid, but I'm a quick learner and…' The maid waited to be dismissed.

'Perhaps it would be nice not to have to struggle round to reach the buttons on this dress,' Kathryn said with a smile. 'Do you mind if I change my answer?'

'Oh, no, miss, not at all.' And Jean bounded across the bedchamber to begin work in the lofty realms of a lady's maid. She started with the careful removal of Miss Marchant's fichu, folding the worn length of material into a neat pile before turning to tackle the buttons of the faded blue afternoon dress. It was only then that the smile dropped from her face, replaced instead with a look of shock. The narrow brow wrinkled in consternation and the brown eyes rounded as two new pennies.

'Is something wrong?' Kathryn eyed the maid with some concern.

The gaze dropped to the floor and two small spots of colour mounted in the thin cheeks. 'No, miss.' She skirted round to release the back buttons that secured Miss Marchant's dress, taking care not to meet the lady's eyes. The dress, petticoats and stays were removed in a matter of minutes. 'Shall I help you into your nightdress, miss, before brushing your hair?' The slender hands strayed towards the folded nightdress.

'No thank you, I can manage from here myself. Thank you, Jean, I shall see you in the morning.'

The maid bobbed a curtsy and almost ran from the room, leaving a rather puzzled Miss Marchant looking after her.

Still clad in her threadbare shift, Kathryn unpinned the heavy coil of her curls, sat down at the dressing table, and began to brush her hair using the silver-backed hairbrush from the set laid out on the mahogany surface. The golden glow from the fireplace illuminated the room, and the candle still sat where she had left it on the small table beside the bed. Her eyes glanced up to the oval looking-glass and froze. The brush ceased its action, hovered in mid-air and quickly resumed its position upon the dressing table. And all the while Kathryn's gaze did not waver.

From the mirrored glass a pale thin figure stared back, a ghost of the woman she had once been. Her stomach tightened and sank at the sight. For there, in front of her very eyes, was the obvious reason for the maid's strange behaviour. How could she have so easily forgotten? Reddened fingers reached up and cautiously traced the large purple black smudges adorning the skin around her collarbone, then shifted down to touch each and every one of the bruises peppering her thin arms. Beneath each eye was the faintest trace of shadow and her cheeks had about them a slight gauntness, lending her whole face a look of worn fatigue. Indeed, she looked little better than the poor child recovering in the bedchamber further along the passageway. Little Maggie, who had lain so still and cold on the ground in Hyde Park as to chase every thought from Kathryn's head save for those concerned with the child's welfare. Little Maggie, over whom Kathryn had so readily draped her fichu and spencer. And, by removing her fichu, she had unwittingly exposed her shame for all to see. Dear Lord! The bruises could not be missed. Not by Lady Maybury. And certainly not by Lord Ravensmede. So absorbed had she been in the accident and all that ensued that not once had she remembered the presence of those ugly telling bruises. A groan escaped her at her own ineptitude. She knew now why the Viscount had been so downright stubborn in his refusal to allow her to return to Green Street. He had seen the bruises and drawn his own conclusions.

Humiliation scalded her cheeks and caused an aching in her heart. Her fingers kneaded at the worn linen of her shift. But Kathryn did not cry, even though Ravensmede had viewed the shameful marks upon her body, even though she now knew herself to be an object of pity and curiosity. Jean's eyes had been telling enough and she did not doubt that by tomorrow morning the story of her darned underclothing and smattering of bruises would be the main topic of conversation below stairs. Her chin jutted out as she held her head high. Let them talk. She had survived worse than a little tittle-tattle, much worse. Gossip would not touch her, as nothing had ever touched her since her father had placed the muzzle of a Manton in his mouth and pulled the trigger.

She had cried then, for days—or was it weeks? When the tears had finally stopped she had vowed they would never come again. That was when she had discovered the power of daydreams. Dreams that took her away from the pain of reality. Dreams that made life bearable. And the worse things got, the more Kathryn dreamed. Resolutely she raised the brush to the thick hank of chestnut hair curling over her shoulder and began slowly, steadily, to brush.

'I like this toast. Is there more?' Maggie demanded as she sat plumped up in the big bed. Sunshine shimmered on her black locks, coating them with a blue sheen and bleaching her small elfin face white.

Kathryn laughed. 'Of course, moppet, but first you have your ham and eggs to eat. Let's see what room you have left when they're gone.'

The brown pansy eyes widened in awe. 'Ham *and* eggs *and* toast?'

'Most definitely.' Kathryn positioned the full plate on the child's tray.

A large grin spread across Maggie's face and soon she was too busy eating to manage more than the odd unintelligible word uttered through a mouthful of half-chewed food.

Kathryn sat in the chair beside the bed. Sipping the hot coffee chased away the thick-headed feeling that had troubled her since waking. The bed had been both warm and comfortable, a far cry from the hard, lumpy truckle bed in her room at Green Street. But she had slept poorly, tormented by worries, and nightmares from the past. Her escape from the bosom of Henry Marchant's family was not likely to be that simple. She nibbled at the toast, finding that the previous week's starvation rations had rendered her unable to eat much before her stomach protested its fullness. A crumb was displaced from the bodice of her blue muslin dress with the flick of a finger before she caught sight of Maggie's little face looking at her with a rather guilty expression. 'Is something wrong? You seem to have stopped eating?'

The black head shook in denial. The dark eyes peeped up through long lashes. 'You ain't got no eggs or ham. You can have some of mine if you want.'

Kathryn knew what it had cost the child to make such a generous offer. A child who was no doubt used to going hungry. 'It's very kind of you to offer, Maggie, but I've already eaten some eggs before I came to see you,' she lied. 'I'm afraid you'll have to eat them all yourself!'

Maggie wasted no time in complying. 'Where's the pa?' she questioned between mouthfuls of egg.

The thought of Ravensmede in the role of a father brought a wry smile to Kathryn's face. 'Lord Ravensmede is probably still sleeping.' She had no idea when he had returned, or, indeed, if he had returned at all. 'He was out late last night and is bound to be very tired this morning.'

The gentleman in question chose this precise minute to make his entry. 'Good morning, Miss Marchant, Miss Maggie.'

Maggie giggled, spluttering a piece of half-chewed ham down her chin.

Kathryn remedied the accident with a starched white napkin while returning the greeting. For someone who'd been up half the night, he was looking bright-eyed and refreshed.

'The ma said you was in bed 'cos you was out last night. But she was wrong, 'cos you're here.' Maggie smiled up at the tall dark-haired man, not intimidated by his lordship in the slightest. 'Where was you?' she asked sweetly.

'Maggie!' Kathryn admonished. 'You mustn't ask Lord Ravensmede such questions.' But her cheeks glowed and not just because the child had unwittingly revealed that the 'ma' had noticed his absence the previous evening.

Ravensmede sat himself down on the bed and tousled Maggie's hair. 'I was very busy, but now I'm back to check whether you're eating up all of your breakfast.'

If the Viscount's reputation was true, Kathryn had a very good idea exactly what Lord Ravensmede had been 'very busy' doing throughout the night. She sought to change the subject. 'Maggie's leg is much better this morning. Dr Porter will be pleased when he calls again this afternoon to decide whether she may go home.'

'Home to *my* ma and pa,' declared Maggie in a cheerful tone.

'Indeed so. They were very worried when I told them about your sore leg. If you're to stay here much longer, they'll come and visit you.' The Viscount's eyes twinkled.

Kathryn could not prevent herself exclaiming, 'You've spoken to them yourself?'

His gaze met with her incredulous stare. 'But of course. What else did you expect?'

She smiled. 'From what I've heard, certainly not that.'

'Then you should not believe everything that you hear, Kathryn.' He said her name like a caress.

'And you should not seek to encourage an unwarranted reputation, sir!' The smile deepened to a most unladylike grin.

His lordship arched a dark eyebrow and said, 'I assure you that my reputation is most deserved, Miss Marchant.'

If it had not been for the glimmer of the smile that lurked too readily behind his lips, she would have withdrawn. As it was, Miss Kathryn Marchant, who had for the past three years striven to be as quiet and unnoticeable as could be, was engaging in what could only be described as a rather flirtatious conversation with a notorious rake. But he was so damnably arrogant that he deserved to be taken down a peg or two. 'Indeed, sir? Perhaps it is rather overrated.' Had she just said such a comment? It barely seemed possible. Surely she must be in the grip of some madness. She most certainly knew she was when she saw his lips slide into a sensual curve.

'Would you care to put it to the test?' The suggestion in his gaze caused the heat to rise in her cheeks.

Standing up abruptly, she smoothed her skirts down with the palms of her hands. 'Certainly not. Now, if you'll excuse me, I had better get on.' And, so saying, she gathered up Maggie's tray containing the emptied plates and cups.

A pair of strong arms reached across the bed and deftly lifted the tray away. The teasing sensuality had vanished. Instead, the stark contours of his face contained what looked to be anger. 'You are a guest in this house, Miss Marchant, along with my grandmother. I pay my servants well to do such things.' The tray was deposited unceremoniously on an occasional table and the bell pulled. 'If you would be kind enough to attend the library in ten minutes, there is something which we must discuss.'

A shiver stole down Kathryn's spine. Clear grey eyes raised to meet green. 'My lord?'

'My name is Nicholas, Kathryn, I would that you used it,' he said soberly and softly closed the door.

Chapter Six

Ravensmede was about to ignore his grandmother's advice. The source of the foul markings on Kathryn Marchant's skin was like a needle that pricked at him constantly. Even during last night's journey to Whitecross Road to call upon little Maggie's parents he could scarcely concentrate on what he had to say because of the blasted matter. Hitting a woman, any woman, was something that sickened Ravensmede to the pit of his stomach. The fact that it had been Kathryn on the receiving end of someone's vicious temper exacerbated that response a hundredfold. He controlled his mounting fury admirably.

Someone had been liberal with their fists, that much was evident, and there was no point in meeting Henry Marchant until he knew the truth of it. No matter what Lady Maybury said, Ravensmede had every intention of getting to the bottom of the sickening assault...and today. Waiting for Kathryn to tell them in her own time was simply not soon enough. The brandy hit the back of his throat like a brand. He swallowed it down. Too damn early in the day, but he needed something to dampen his temper.

A quiet tap at the door sounded and the subject of his concern presented herself. She was still dressed in the shabby muslin gown that she had worn yesterday. He noticed that the periwinkle blue coloration brought out the creamy white hue of her skin, and the red lights in her hair. The fichu had been arranged to cover every trace of the bruising. She was so slender as to appear fragile, something he had no memory of either on that first night at Lady Finlay's ball, or later in St James's Park. No doubt the bastard had been starving her as well. The thought of Henry Marchant curled his fingers into fists. With calm deliberation he forced his hands to relax. A deep breath, and he was ready to face her.

'Kathryn.' He smiled and gestured towards one of the two large wing chairs around the fireplace. 'Sit down.' As the day was fine and warm, and showed every promise to continue as such, the hearth was empty. Sunshine flooded in through the large bow window, highlighting a halo of red around the rich brown of her hair. He positioned himself in the opposite chair, stretching out his long, pantaloon-clad legs before him.

She sat demurely, hands folded motionless in her lap, as if she were a model of relaxed serenity…as if she had not been beaten and starved by her so-called family. Her eyes glanced up, but the question in them remained unasked. He would have to tread very carefully. 'Would you like some tea?'

'No, thank you, my lor…Ravensmede.' Her fingers gripped tighter and then relaxed.

'Then I will come straight to the point. Mr Marchant has arranged to call here at three o'clock to discuss your new position. My grandmother will explain the urgency of her need for a companion. In view of her age and the injured child upstairs, I'm sure that your uncle will understand why it was imperative that you commence as Lady Maybury's companion with immediate effect.' And if Henry Marchant dared to raise the slightest objection he'd see to it that the man was put firmly in his place.

Her gaze was trained on the blackened grate. The rigid tension across her narrow shoulders tightened at his words. 'Will he be accompanied by my aunt?'

Now why should that matter so much to her? For suddenly he knew that to be very much the case. 'In truth, I do not know. Do you wish to take your leave of her?'

There was a pause, just long enough to be obvious. 'Naturally. They are my family. It's only polite, after all that they've done, that I take my leave of them all.' And still her focus did not waver from the grate.

'And what have they done, Kathryn?' The question slipped softly from his lips.

Startled eyes raised to his and quickly looked away again. A whisper of pink touched to her cheeks, before the small chin was thrust defiantly up. 'Why, they took me in and offered me a home when my father died. I…I'm very grateful for their charity.'

The time had come to say what must be said, to discover the truth. He leaned forward by the smallest fraction. 'But it wasn't charity they had in mind when they dealt you your bruises, was it? And I would hazard a guess that it wasn't gratitude you felt in receipt of those markings.' His voice rumbled low and quiet, each word enunciated clearly, no hint of the practised rakish drawl.

The chestnut-coloured head whipped round to face him, her breast rising and falling dramatically beneath the outmoded gown. Within her eyes flashed anger and something else that had gone in an instant. She faced him with her fear concealed. It seemed for a moment that his words had rendered her speechless, but she recovered herself well, forcing her emotions back under control. When her voice finally sounded it was quiet and careful, as if she were attending to his grandmother or the child that lay upstairs. 'Lord Ravensmede,' she began, 'you are mistaken. The…bruises…that you happened to see upon my person are the result of a small accident, nothing more. Through my own clumsiness I tripped and fell. The blame rests entirely on my own head and no one else.' The slender fingers began to twist themselves together.

His eyes flitted to her hands, saw more than he was meant to see, and returned once more to her face and the darkened gaze that had been rapidly averted while she told her story. 'You make a very poor liar, Kathryn.'

The colour heightened in her cheeks and she shot him one brief infuriated glance. 'I'm telling you the truth, sir. You've drawn the wrong conclusion.'

'I don't think so.' He watched the small white teeth nibble delicately on the fullness of her lower lip and did not speak again until those stormy grey eyes slowly dragged round, as if not quite of their own accord, to meet his.

'We have nothing further to discuss, sir. I shall be ready to meet my uncle at three o'clock.' With that she rose and made to step away.

But Ravensmede had no intention of letting Miss Marchant evade him quite so easily. Within an instant he was towering over her. 'On the contrary, we've only just begun. Is that your best effort? I would not have thought your imagination to be so lacking.'

A slight gasp escaped her lips before they pressed firmly together with annoyance.

Before she could retaliate he pressed a hand to hers. 'Do you always cross your fingers when you lie? Who told you that it saved you from the sin? Your nurse?'

Rosy stain flooded her face and the fingers encased beneath his straightened themselves. She shifted her feet uneasily. 'How did you know?'

'Mine said the same, much to my father's disgust!'

She smiled a small smile at that.

It seemed a shame to destroy the sudden rapport that had developed between them, but he could do nothing else if he meant to know just who was responsible for her hurts. A suspect loomed large in his mind, but he would not confront the man without first hearing Kathryn's side of the story. He lowered his head to hers. She was so close that his breath fanned a ripple across the curls framing her face, so close that the sweet scent of her filled his nostrils. One finger moved to tilt her chin, until her eyes were looking up into his. Ravensmede swallowed hard and resisted the urge to place his lips upon hers, to kiss her as thoroughly as he'd kissed her that night in the moonlit room. Temptation pulled him closer, beckoned him down a path he knew he had no right to tread. So close, so sweet. It seemed that her lips parted in invitation. He felt the stirrings of other interests and reined himself back with a self-denying hand. She was here for his protection, not the practised art of his seduction. But when he looked into Kathryn Marchant's face there was nothing practised about the erratic thud of his heart or the overwhelming urge to take her in his arms and never let her go.

He wondered as to his assertion to his grandmother. *I do not mean to ruin her*, he had said. But the woman standing so close that he could have plucked a sweet kiss from her lips stirred his blood like no one else. He wanted her. Had wanted her since that night at Lady Finlay's ball. A woman he could not allow himself to have; a woman who deserved better than the hand life had dealt her; a woman he had just made his grandmother's companion. Mentally he dowsed himself with cold water and focused on the matter in hand. And that was confirming Henry Marchant's guilt in the abuse of his niece. She was still looking up at him with such trust that it quite smote his jaded heart. With the gentlest of movements he touched his lips to the coolness of her forehead, before scanning her eyes once more.

'Will you not trust me with the truth?' he said softly.

For the beat of a heart he thought she would do just that. Her mouth opened to speak and then closed again. Her gaze dropped and the moment was gone. 'I cannot,' she whispered.

At least there were no more lies.

'What happened is in the past and will not happen again. I know that you only mean to help me…Nicholas…but…please, just let the matter go.'

His stomach somersaulted at the sound of his name upon her lips. What a glorious sound it was. 'I cannot do that, Kathryn.

You've been treated most cruelly and I cannot let any man get away with such injustice.' Beneath his fingers her hand trembled and she sighed a sigh of such fatigue and sadness and disappointment. 'Kathryn?' The word held an intimacy that he had no right to.

Slowly she shook her head and stepped back. 'No.' Her shoulders straightened and her face was filled with firm resolve.

He made no move to reclaim her. Just watched, and waited.

'No,' she said again with increasing determination.

There was nothing else for it. 'Then you leave me with no other option.' He waited for her response. Knew that it would come.

Her voice was small and tight. 'What do you mean to do?'

The slightest pause. 'I will speak with Henry Marchant until I know the whole of it. And then I'll decide what to do with him. Perhaps I should call him out.'

'No!' Her eyes widened in horror. 'You must not!'

'He does not deserve your sympathy, Kathryn.'

'No, please!' Her hands grasped at his arms, tightening, enforcing her will. 'You're wrong. It wasn't him…he's done nothing!'

Not Henry Marchant? His focus narrowed. 'Then who?'

Nothing, just the pressure of those slight fingers.

'Hell's teeth, Kathryn, tell me!' he growled with more force than he intended.

'Aunt Anna.' A faint whisper, barely more than the expiration of a breath. Cheeks so pale he thought she would swoon.

He moved to take her arms, unmindful that she still held his. A mirror of her stance, unnoticed in the incredulity that enveloped him. 'Are you telling me that Anna Marchant inflicted those bruises upon you?' His voice sounded cold and hard and distant even to his own ears.

'Yes.' Her body recoiled from his, and she stepped back until the chair was between them. 'You have what you wanted. Are you happy now?' The slight figure turned and fled, leaving Ravensmede staring at the library door that had just been slammed so adamantly in his face.

* * *

Kathryn stood still as a statue and stared down from the window of her bedchamber, although quite what made it hers she could not be sure since there was nothing of her own in it. A calm, light-filled room that was furnished with the finest furniture, or so it seemed to the woman who had made do for as many years as she could remember. It was as close to a sanctuary as she had come, even if it was owned by the man who had just caused her to reveal that which she had promised never to. But she could not have allowed him to meet Uncle Henry thinking what he did. The thought of exactly what Ravensmede had threatened to do twisted in her gut. Call him out. There was no doubt in her mind that he would have done just that…and more.

Her fingers kneaded at the tight spot developing behind her forehead, trying to forestall the headache she knew it would become. What would the Viscount do with the knowledge? *Oh, Lord, please do not let him speak of it, not to Uncle Henry, and certainly not to Aunt Anna herself. It would only make matters worse. Aunt Anna will deny all, cast me as a liar. I have no proof and they have provided me with a home all this time. And the scandal! Perhaps I should speak with Nicholas… Dear Lord, have I so quickly come to think upon him in such familiar terms?* The thought was really rather shocking. She pressed the cooling palms of her hands to her eyes. *Think, Kathryn, think!* She willed herself. *I have created this problem and therefore I can solve it.* So engrossed in her task was she that she did not hear the chamber door brush against the rug as it was pushed hesitantly open. Indeed, it was not until something tugged at her skirts that she jumped and gave a small exclamation of surprise.

'Why are you crying?' The pansy brown eyes were regarding her with concern.

One slender hand pressed to her breast before Kathryn bent and clutched the child to her. 'Maggie! You startled me. I didn't hear you come in.' She rearranged the locks of hair around the girl's forehead and kissed her. 'You were as quiet as a little mouse.'

Maggie smiled and touched small fingers softly to the shadowed areas beneath Kathryn's eyes. 'Why was you crying?' she repeated.

'I wasn't crying, moppet, just thinking.'

But the child persisted. 'But you was sad, wasn't you?'

'Just a little, but I'm not any more. Now, Miss Maggie, what are you doing out of bed?' Kathryn chided in a voice of mock severity.

Maggie was not fooled for one minute. 'Looking for you to tell me another story.'

Kathryn placed her hands on her hips and looked stern.

Maggie laughed.

'Oh, very well then, but only if you get back into bed. You must not get up until Dr Porter has checked your leg this afternoon.' Secretly Kathryn was pleased that the child felt well enough to wander. And, from the way she was jumping rather excitedly up and down, it appeared that the injury to her leg was perhaps not as bad as they had first thought. With one arm cupped protectively round Maggie's shoulders, Kathryn guided the small girl back along to the room from whence she had come.

The day passed quickly for Kathryn in her new role as Lady Maybury's companion, and she did have to admit that her first impression of that employment found it to be infinitely preferable to anything she had experienced in the house at Green Street. Ravensmede's grandmother was loud, opinionated and had evidently taken rather a shine to Kathryn. Beneath the old lady's harsh exterior was a heart of gold. She brooked no nonsense and did not suffer fools gladly, but when it came to her grandson it was quite clear to Kathryn that he held a special place in the lady's heart. It was just before three o'clock when the doorbell sounded. Miss Marchant was still seated at the lady's writing desk situated within Lady Maybury's rooms. With pen poised in hand and rather ink-stained fingers, she was waiting patiently for the dowager to dictate the next line of the letter. Her ladyship showed no sign of having heard the bell.

'Lady Harriet sounds to me to be indolent in the extreme. You must not hesitate to chastise her as such, my dear Frances, else you will never get her married off.' Lady Maybury was seated comfortably upon a pink chair. She paused to allow Kathryn to copy down her words, her head cocked to one side like a small lively robin.

Kathryn finished the sentence and glanced up. The clock on the mantel chimed three.

Lady Maybury ignored it. 'Lady Gardiner's daughter was quite the same, and look what became of her.'

The grey eyes drifted to the clock face.

'No, Frances, you must stand firm. It's the best advice I can offer.' Lady Maybury nodded her white curls forcefully. 'Do not pen the next words,' she instructed. 'They are for your ears alone. Harriet Kiddleby was an indolent child and she's now an indolent young woman. I blame Frances, of course. She always was too soft with the gel. If she doesn't act quickly, she'll be saddled with the wretched gel for the rest of her days. Frances never did have much sense.' A tap at the door interrupted Lady Maybury's tirade.

A footman entered and addressed himself to the dowager. 'Mr Marchant has arrived, my lady. He's in the drawing room with Lord Ravensmede.'

The snowy head graciously inclined. Only when the door had closed did she resume her conversation. 'Now, what was I saying? Ah, that's right, I remember now.'

'Should we not…?' Kathryn looked tentatively at the old lady.

'Make them wait!' came the abrupt reply. And so she did. It was some considerable time later and with a degree of mounting agitation that Kathryn came finally to pen the words, *remember me to Lady Augusta. Adieu—Yours ever, Eleanor Maybury*.

Ravensmede's grandmother offered no apologies for her tardiness. Rather, she cast a piercing eye in Henry Marchant's direction as if it were he who was making unfair demands upon her time. Kathryn sat at the old lady's side on the sofa and prayed fervently that the Viscount had not made any mention of her bruising. Her uncle looked distinctly uncomfortable, a sign that did not bode well. The tension in the room was thick and suffocating. No one spoke. She forced a smile to her face. 'Uncle Henry, how good of you to come. My aunt is not with you?'

'No.' He did not return the smile. 'Unfortunately she is otherwise engaged.'

Another awkward silence.

Her eyes sought Ravensmede's. His face was stern, forbidding even, but she thought she saw a softening in that shared moment. It was gone before she could be sure. His attention returned to the man sitting uneasily in the chair with his back to the door.

'Mr Marchant. As I explained in my letter, Miss Marchant has been kind enough to agree to become my grandmother's companion. You understand, of course, the honour that Lady Maybury is conferring upon your family with such an appointment?' Ravensmede had resumed the habitual arrogant drawl that had been missing for the past two days. A dark eyebrow winged as if daring Henry Marchant to disagree.

Henry cleared his throat and looked away. 'Quite. I have no objection to my niece accepting such a position *per se*.' The gruff throat cleared again and the large hands gripped the chair arms. 'However…' Henry looked at the marbled fireplace. 'My wife and I are concerned with the manner and speed with which the offer and acceptance have been made. Kathryn is like a daughter to us and naturally we can only be greatly concerned when she leaves our home for a drive around Hyde Park, and fails to return.'

'I understand your…*concern*.' The stress was on Ravensmede's last word. There was an iciness to his tone that Kathryn had never heard before. 'Indeed, it really is most commendable.'

Mr Marchant's gaze shifted uncomfortably.

Ravensmede's drawl intensified. 'The accident involving

the child that occurred during the drive has left my grand-mother quite exhausted. At her age, I hardly expect her to oversee the child's care amidst all of her other activities. Thus, the immediate requirement for a companion to assist her arose. Miss Marchant was the ideal candidate.'

Henry Marchant gave a little cough. 'And Lady Maybury will be staying here with you?' The question dropped danger-ously into the air.

Kathryn's stomach tensed. The unspoken inference was obvious. And, if her uncle thought it, then so would everyone else, despite all of Lord Ravensmede's persuasion. The Viscount turned a glacial focus upon Mr Marchant.

Mr Marchant drew back against his chair.

'My grandmother has taken a house in Upper Grosvenor Street for the Season,' said Lord Ravensmede.

Kathryn could not suppress a surprised glance in his lord-ship's direction. Hadn't Lord Ravensmede led her to believe that they would be living here in Ravensmede House? His face betrayed nothing.

'In that case, I can raise no objection. My niece is four and twenty, and many years beyond the age at which she would require my permission.' For the first time since entering the room Henry Marchant looked at Kathryn. 'I hope that you'll be happy in your new position.' His gaze skittered away. 'I'll have your trunk sent round.'

'Thank you.' Kathryn had never been one to shirk her duty and she did not do so now. 'I will call upon my aunt and Lottie tomorrow to take my leave of them.' Belatedly she consulted her new employer, 'If that is acceptable to you, my lady.'

A scowl flitted over Lord Ravensmede's face, and disappeared.

Before Lady Maybury could reply, Henry Marchant cleared his throat and repeated the words that his wife had instructed, 'Regrettably, both your aunt and cousin will be out tomorrow.'

A small silence followed.

'Then the day after, perhaps?' Kathryn suggested.

'I believe them to be engaged on that day also,' he said awkwardly, and shifted in his chair.

Kathryn made to reply but Ravensmede was there first. 'How good of your family to be so understanding of the situation.'

Confusion clouded Mr Marchant's face.

The Viscount leaned forward towards the older man in a confiding manner. 'Some people are embarrassed by class differences, but clearly your lady wife is not one of them. Now that Miss Marchant is companion to my grandmother, she must exercise more discernment in her choice of those with whom she associates. It is well that Mrs Marchant understands that.'

Henry Marchant's cheeks stained a ruddy red at the insult, but he said nothing.

Seeking to alleviate the growing tension, Kathryn spoke to her uncle. 'Please send Aunt Anna and Cousin Lottie my regards and my thanks for all their kindness over the years.' From the corner of her eye she saw Lord Ravensmede's jaw twitch, and she almost smiled. Then Kathryn remembered Aunt Anna. If she had thought her aunt to be an enemy before, she had best have a care and watch her back from now on. Anna Marchant was not a woman to forgive or forget.

Henry Marchant nodded once. 'Of course.' He cleared his throat again and looked uneasy.

It was Ravensmede who finally brought an end to the charade. 'Then we bid you good day, Mr Marchant.' He stood over a head taller than Henry Marchant and looked down into the man's small eyes. 'Your niece will be safe with my grandmother, Mr Marchant. Have no doubt of that.' And beneath the polite reassurance was the veiled threat of something dark and dangerous. Henry Marchant felt it too and scuttled from the room with a speed surprising for a man of his girth.

Sunshine flooded the breakfast room the next morning as Ravensmede sipped his coffee. A plate containing the remains of kedgeree lay abandoned before him.

'It's quite impossible, Nicholas. I barely slept a wink last night, most probably as a result of that infernal Marchant rat. What kind of man stands by and allows his wife to beat his niece? He's despicable! Little wonder I was tossing and turning throughout the night!'

'Grandmama,' the Viscount admonished gently, 'you promised that you wouldn't speak of it. Kathryn did not want us to know of her aunt's guilt.'

'Fustian!' exclaimed his grandmother. 'The gel's still up with Maggie. She'll not hear me from there!' She winced. 'It's no good. I'm really not myself this morning. You and Kathryn will have to take the child home.'

Ravensmede's eyes narrowed. 'I'll send for Dr Porter.'

'No! There's nothing wrong with me that a few hours' sleep won't cure. Stop fussing, Nick. I'm not dead yet!' The old lady drew him a fierce stare. 'Just make sure you look after my companion.'

Ravensmede's mood lightened at the thought of Kathryn and a closed carriage. He quirked a smile. 'As you wish, Grandmama.' A small bow and he turned to leave.

'And Nick—' Her voice stopped him at the door. The faded green eyes glared a warning. 'Remember that Miss Marchant is under *my* protection.'

He raised an ironic brow and was gone.

Kathryn's arm tightened around the child sitting by her side. 'I promise I shall come and see you again very soon.' The carriage rumbled through the streets leading them to the rookeries in Whitecross Street and the little girl's home.

Maggie eyed her hopefully before looking over at Lord Ravensmede on the opposite seat. 'And will the pa come too?'

'I don't know about that.' She laughed. Somehow she could not imagine the Viscount of Ravensmede visiting a four-year-old girl in a street of overcrowded slums. But, come to that, she had not thought he would have paid for Maggie to have the best of medical treatments, cared for her within his own house and then personally delivered her to her parents.

Ravensmede leaned forward. 'Of course I will.'

'Good.' Maggie snuggled closer into Kathryn's side, feeling in the pockets of her new apron. The pretty white frills around its edge contrasted nicely with the matching pink-and-white high-waisted frock worn beneath it. An apple was produced and the carriage soon reverberated with the sound of Maggie's crunches.

'That's what I like to see, a good healthy appetite.' Kathryn stroked the little girl's clean, shiny hair, fixing the pink satin ribbons as she did.

She felt Ravensmede's gaze upon her and looked up to meet it. His mouth was not quite in a smile, and there was a solemnity about his eyes that made her feel peculiar.

The rest of the journey continued with Kathryn pointing out landmarks and shops to Maggie. Ravensmede made no effort to join in, just sat back and watched the woman and the child. Once they had arrived, Kathryn did not miss the purse that he pressed into Maggie's father's hand, or the kind words that he uttered to the child's poor work-worn mother. A kiss on Maggie's cheek and they were gone. Kathryn waved until the little girl and her family were just a speck in the distance, and wondered at what she could never hope to have. A child of her own. A family. She thrust the thought aside and looked at Lord Ravensmede. He had not spoken since their return to the carriage, just sat looking from the window as if his thoughts were elsewhere.

'You should not have said that you would visit her. She'll look for you and be disappointed when you don't come.' Kathryn spoke the words gently, not to chastise but merely to show him the error of his ways. What did a man like Ravensmede know of a child's fragile trust?

Then his eyes were on her, casting a spiral of excitement into her breast and down deeper into her stomach as they ever did. She ignored her body's response as best she could. 'What makes you think that I would lie to the child? Do you think so little of me?'

She felt the colour rise to her face at his continued scrutiny and the accusation in his voice. 'No, I just thought…'

'I know what you thought, Kathryn,' he said.

Anger flared. 'On the contrary, Lord Ravensmede, you know nothing of what I think! Don't presume to do so!'

He smiled at that. 'Ouch,' he said. 'The kitten has claws.'

He really was the most infuriating man alive. Deliberately she turned her face to watch the passing houses. And ignored him.

'You think me infuriating,' he said with unnerving accuracy.

'I didn't say so.'

'You didn't have to. And you think that I make promises I won't keep.'

'No.'

A cynical eyebrow raised.

'Very well, yes.'

His eyes did not leave her face and a sensual tone crept into his voice. 'I always keep my promises, Kathryn.'

Her blood tingled.

Anticipation grew in the punctuating silence.

'It seems that you have much to learn of me.'

Kathryn's heart thudded in her chest. Blood surged through her veins, visibly throbbing at the pulse-point in her neck. 'Lest you had forgotten, Lord Ravensmede, I'm companion to your grandmother. There is no need for us to know anything of each other.'

He did not appear in the least discomposed, just stayed leaning back against the seat with his legs stretched out before him. 'On the contrary, I care for my grandmother, and, as such, it's only natural that I take an interest in her health, in her life and…in any companion that she may have. Indeed, I would be failing in my duty if I did not undertake a thorough appraisal of your character, Miss Marchant.'

Her cheeks scorched scarlet. 'I do not think that is necessary, my lord.'

'Oh, but I assure you that it is. I am most determined to know you.' The words were low and mellow, scarcely audible over the rumble of the wheels and the passing shouts from the street.

She faced him defiantly. 'I do not care for the turn this conversation is taking, sir.'

He shrugged his shoulders as if to say that her consideration did not matter.

The balance of Kathryn's temper tipped. With one hand gripping the travelling strap, she reached up and banged twice upon the carriage roof. 'Stop!' she shouted loud enough for the coachman to hear. Her fingers tugged at the window. Her head whipped round in Ravensmede's direction. 'I'll walk the rest of the way.'

The carriage showed no sign of slowing.

'Perdition, Kathryn! Are you trying to kill yourself?' He grabbed at her hands, pulling them away from the glass. The carriage bounced over some bumps. She staggered, striving to keep her balance, and toppled over straight on to Ravensmede's knee.

'Dear Lord!' she gasped and tried to escape. But Ravensmede's arms had already closed around her. 'Unhand me at once!'

'And let you fall out of a moving carriage? I do not think so, Kathryn.'

'I was going to wait for it to stop,' she said with indignation.

'Really?' he said drolly.

'I refuse to stay in here a moment longer with you!'

No reply, just that nearly smile upon his face.

'Lord Ravensmede!' she gasped.

'Miss Marchant,' he replied.

He held her gently but firmly throughout her struggles until at last she realised their futility and relaxed against the hard muscle of his body. Still his arms wound around her, barring any route of possible escape. His clean scent of bergamot surrounded her and she was growing increasingly aware of the muscular thighs on which she was sitting and the tautness of his stomach and chest hugging the contours of her back. The pulse still leapt in her throat, throbbing with a speed that made her ragged breathing seem slow in comparison. It was no longer anger that drove her reactions, but something quite different, something that she most definitely should not feel.

He was a rake! He would take what he could, and cast her aside. To a man like Ravensmede she was easy prey, a nothing, a nobody. If his grandmother found out, then Kathryn knew that she would lose her new home and position…not to mention her reputation. And then where would she be? The thought gave her the strength she needed. Quite suddenly she pulled away from him and attempted to break free. At first she thought she would succeed. It seemed her stillness had lulled him into a false sense of security. But even as her body made to rise the large arms clamped her back down. The breath shuddered in her throat.

'Keep still, Kathryn. I would not have you hurt yourself.'

The words were so close as to tickle her ear. The sensation shuddered down through her core. Whatever she knew of Nicholas Maybury, it was not enough to still her traitorous body's response. She could have cried aloud. Instead, she forced herself to calmness, letting the seconds become minutes. When at last she had some semblance of control she spoke. 'Lord Ravensmede, you may release me now. I give you my word that I won't try to leave the carriage.'

Only the sound of his breath whispered past her ear.

'My lord?'

He did not speak. Slowly his arms relaxed and opened in a gesture of release.

Kathryn knew she should leap across to the opposite seat, but she stayed quite still, only swung her legs round to the side and moved her head so that she might look into his face. His gaze was trained on her, glittering with a force that made the breath catch in her throat. For in those eyes, those alluring green eyes, was a look of such tenderness as to shatter every belief Kathryn had of the man. A large hand moved to cup the back of her head, his fingers untied the ribbons of her bonnet and, casting it aside, threaded into the silkiness of her hair. She knew what he was going to do and still she did nothing to stop him.

With calm deliberation he manoeuvred her until their lips met. And in their caress was the escalation of passionate need. His mouth moved with slow sensuality, sliding and sucking, coaxing and nipping, until she found her lips lapping against his, giving as much as receiving. Just when she thought she was melting in the heat of his embrace she felt the tantalising tease of his tongue, sliding against her lips, invading her mouth, seeking her own. Tongue touched tongue in warm and moist intimacy.

A long low groan issued deep in his throat and his hands moved to stroke her back, sweeping down to cover the swell of her hip, pulling her closer against him. Breast against breast. Even through the layers of clothing that separated their two bodies Kathryn felt the strong steady beat of his heart. Her skin warmed and blossomed against his until there was an aching tightness in her breasts. Not knowing what she did, she rose against him, arching instinctively until their hardened peaks thrust against the firm muscle of his chest. His roughened jaw-line rasped at the scorch marks left by his lips.

'Kathryn!' The whisper was a shuddering caress, full of desire. His fingers wove their magic through the muslin of her dress, sliding round to move against the flatness of her stomach, and up, further, until they reached their goal. He groaned again, a low guttural sound. 'God, but you're beautiful.'

She touched her lips to his.

The coach ground to a halt. The thump of footsteps sounded and, not a moment after Kathryn found herself dumped unceremoniously on to the opposite seat, the door swung open. Ravensmede House loomed large in the background. A footman positioned the steps and stood back to await his lordship's descent.

The green eyes raised to hers. 'Kathryn…'

She didn't wait to hear the words. She didn't need to. Before Ravensmede could stop her she had clambered out of the carriage and was fleeing up the stone stairs to the front door.

Chapter Seven

If Lady Maybury noticed that her new companion's colour was rather high, or that the girl's lips were swollen from being thoroughly kissed, she kept such observations to herself. There was much work to be done with organising the packing and arrangement of her ladyship's luggage for the move to Upper Grosvenor Street. And the dowager seemed to be in a rather cantankerous mood with everyone except Kathryn. It was somewhat surprising that the lady's favourite grandson was also being included under this edict. The dowager's disposition had not improved by the time both she and Miss Marchant came to take their leave of the Viscount.

'Nicholas.' Lady Maybury presented a small withered hand to be kissed. 'You may call upon me next week and not before. I will be busy ensuring that all is in order and have no desire for a distraction. Do I make myself clear?' A rather chilly focus fixed itself upon her grandson.

Ravensmede was not indifferent to his grandmother's mood, but, not trusting exactly what that perceptive gaze of hers had fathomed, he did not enquire as to its cause. 'Perfectly clear, Grandmama. Never fear, I shall not disturb you before the appointed time.' He pressed a kiss to the papery hand and moved to face Miss Marchant, who to all intent and purpose was attempting to hide herself behind the tiny frame of his grand-mother. 'Miss Marchant,' he said politely, 'I trust that you have found your stay to be comfortable?'

'Yes, thank you, my lord.' There was nothing in her manner to suggest that all was not as it should be, apart from the slight tremor in her fingers when he pressed them briefly to his lips. Ravensmede felt it keenly, but could do nothing as she withdrew her hand and stepped away.

He suffered the baleful stare of a faded green eye and then the two women were walking down the steps to the heavily laden carriage and the journey that would remove them from the house in Berkeley Square. The door closed with a thump, leaving Ravensmede alone, save for the creeping sense of loss.

'Heard Lady Maybury has taken li'l Miss Marchant on as her companion. Rather convenient for you, I'd say.' If Lord Cadmount lounged any lower in the chair he would be in danger of slipping out of it. The brandy glass balanced delicately on one thigh as he gave his friend a knowing wink.

Ravensmede grunted and loosened the neckcloth that his valet had spent twenty minutes in tying. 'Then you'd be wrong.'

The pale eyebrows raised as high as they could. 'How so? Could it be that you've already bedded her and found her not to your taste?'

A dry laugh. 'Hell, Caddie! You know that I haven't.' The memory of her slender body pressed against his, the softness of those pink lips, the sweetness of her tentative response, intruded all too readily. He felt a stirring in his lower regions and clamped it down with frustrated determination. A gulp of brandy warmed his throat before he continued. 'As my grand-mother's companion, she should be safe from any such specu-lation.' He made no mention of the vile family from whom Kathryn was also now safe.

'Not quite,' argued his friend. 'There's always room for that wherever the woman is placed.'

'Not when my grandmother is involved,' replied Ravensmede.

'I agree that Lady Maybury would make a most formidable foe.' Cadmount sipped his drink and mulled his thoughts. 'Strange that Henry Marchant never looked to make a marriage for the girl. I know she's no schoolroom miss, but neither has she reached her dotage. Must have been keen to keep her in the bosom of his family. A charitable chap, wouldn't you say?'

Ravensmede's eyes darkened. 'Hardly that. Marchant lacks a backbone; he does little more than dance to his wife's tune. A less charitable couple I've yet to meet.' Something of the darkness lifted from his mood. 'Neither was their home a suitable place for a woman like Miss Marchant.'

Cadmount smiled. 'Ah,' he said softly. 'I think I begin to understand.'

The green eyes raised to his. One corner of his mouth flickered up. 'I doubt very much that you do, my dear Caddie.'

'And therein lies the rub.' A finger stroked thoughtfully at his chin. 'You still want her.' It was a statement rather than a question.

Ravensmede did not deny it. 'She's my grandmother's companion now, and even if she wasn't…'

'It would take a rake of the lowest order to seduce a woman who lost her mother and sister and found her father with half his head blown off.'

'Hell, I didn't realise that Kathryn saw her father after he shot himself.' Ravensmede's brows drew together.

'The chit found him all right. Couldn't have been a pretty sight. Had an interesting chat with Bertie Devon. He remembers the whole thing.'

'No woman should have to suffer that.'

Cadmount paused, then asked in a stolid tone, 'Do you mean to seduce her?'

Ravensmede blew a languid sigh. Seduce her? He had come damn near to doing so a week ago in his carriage. He gave Cadmount a cynical look. 'Do you think that I will?'

'I honestly don't know.'

A wry smile. 'My grandmother will take good care of her. She'll be safe there.' Safe from Anna Marchant, but was she truly safe from him?

Cadmount leaned over the chair and, catching his somewhat wrinkled coat up from the floor, set about rummaging in the pockets. 'Strikes me that the girl brings out the protective streak in you.'

Ravensmede crooked an eyebrow. 'Too much brandy, Caddie. Your imaginings run wild. Next you'll have me attending lectures by the Humane Society.'

'Now that would be something worth seeing.' Cadmount laughed. 'Are you telling me that you have no care for Miss Marchant?'

'I'm saying that the woman's suffered enough. She deserves to have some little happiness.'

The two men looked at one another.

'Undoubtedly we need another drink.' The Viscount walked without a hint of unsteadiness to retrieve the decanter.

'Won't help, old man.' Lord Cadmount shook his head sagely. 'Happens to us all sooner or later.'

Ravensmede rubbed at the darkening shadow of stubble on his chin as he refilled their glasses. 'Enlighten me.'

The finely painted miniature box nestled on Cadmount's palm as he regarded it with a knowing expression. 'Love.'

'You're most definitely foxed, Caddie.'

'Indeed I am,' said his friend, helping himself to a generous helping of snuff. 'But it doesn't mean I'm not right. Fancy a pinch?' The box was dangled enticingly towards Ravensmede.

'Why not?' He helped himself to some snuff and snapped the lid shut again.

Golden flames leapt high in the hearth, causing the logs to crackle and spit. The two men sat in comfortable silence, Cadmount knowing when he had pushed far enough, Ravensmede brooding on the growing fascination that he felt for Kathryn Marchant.

* * *

'Read me the last verse again,' Lady Maybury instructed.

Kathryn glanced up at the dowager's smiling countenance and then, lowering her eyes once more to the book, began to read.

> Whate'er the theme, the Maiden sang
> As if her song could have no ending;
> I saw her singing at her work,
> And o'er the sickle bending—
> I listened, motionless and still;
> And, as I mounted up the hill,
> The music in my heart I bore,
> Long after it was heard no more.

'No poet is quite as lyrical as Mr Wordsworth, and no lady reads poetry quite so well as you, my dear gel. You have a wonderful voice.'

Kathryn blushed at Lady Maybury's generous praise and lowered the book to her lap. 'Thank you, my lady. My father always liked to hear my sister and me reading, and we did so most nights in the parlour. Poems, essays, novels, anything would do, even the newspaper. Papa would listen as if he had never heard anything so interesting in all the day.' She paused and smiled, before adding quietly, 'They're happy memories.' She did not think of the bad ones.

'And did you read to your aunt and uncle when you came to London?' the old lady asked.

The rich brown curls swayed as she slowly shook her head. 'Oh, no, Uncle Henry reads the *Morning Post* and Aunt Anna does not much care for reading at all.'

'And the cousin? What did you say her name was—Lettie?' The ancient tone had sharpened imperceptibly.

'Lottie. I'm afraid my cousin finds reading rather irksome. She's of a more musical disposition, being very fond of singing and with a voice that's lovely to hear.' Kathryn carefully turned the page in the book nestled upon her lap. 'Indeed, my aunt is holding a musical evening very soon at which Lottie will be singing to Mr Dalton's piano accompaniment. Lottie has been practising for weeks.'

Lady Maybury showed not the slightest interest. 'I've just remembered our appointment with Madame Dupont. Come, we had best ready ourselves. She's rather high in the instep for a dressmaker, but I've never patronised anyone else in the last thirty years. Her designs are very much to my liking.'

Thus it was that, precisely two hours later, Kathryn and Lady Maybury came to be sitting within the tiny backroom of Madame Dupont's elegant establishment in highly fashionable Bond Street.

'But, my lady, it is such a colour as to bring out the fire in your eyes. A dark green silk will make the gown, damask is not at all right for this style.' The tall thin woman with the severe white chignon spoke passionately in an accent that still held the lilt of her Gallic origins. 'Most definitely *non*!' She shook her head defiantly.

For the first time since their meeting Kathryn saw Lady Maybury capitulate. 'Very well, Marie. I'll allow you to have your way in this one respect. A small turban in green and black should go very well, don't you think?'

'Indeed, my lady, very well indeed. And I shall add a few small ebony plumes as the finishing touch, yes?'

'Yes. Now that's enough for me at present, Marie. My companion Miss Marchant requires an evening dress for the same event. And we had better have a couple of afternoon dresses and another evening dress while we're at it.' Lady Maybury's small veined hand was pushing Kathryn forward in no uncertain terms.

Her companion, on the other hand, had very different ideas. 'My lady, it's really not necessary, I have a very serviceable evening gown and several other dresses too. I must insist that there is no need for anything more.' Kathryn thought of the few outmoded shabby dresses that had arrived in her old trunk from Green Street. She thought too of the six shillings hidden at the bottom of the trunk, next to the small battered bible that had belonged to her mother. The sum of her worldly savings would not suffice to pay for one of Madame Dupont's gowns, let alone four. 'Thank you for thinking of me,' she added hastily lest Lady Maybury think her rude.

The dressmaker's dark eyes swung back to the dowager.

'Kathryn,' Lady Maybury began, and Kathryn recognised it as her most autocratic tone. 'It is in the role of my companion that you require several new items of clothing. The choice is mine as is the reckoning of the account.' There was definitely more than a hint of the same imperious tone Kathryn had witnessed in the old lady's grandson.

Kathryn's cheeks flushed at the barely veiled implication. Lady Maybury did not care to be seen in the company of someone dressed so poorly. It was also evident that the dowager knew something of her companion's meagre means and thus felt compelled to pay for the clothing. Kathryn could not dispute that her dresses were probably of a state to cause her employer some degree of embarrassment, but she was also very aware of the pride that was lodged stubbornly in her throat. 'Thank you, my lady, but, kind as your offer is, you must know that I cannot possibly accept it. I will pay for the dresses myself.' The defiant little chin thrust up as she waited for Lady Maybury's reaction.

'Very well, my dear. It seems that you have your mind set over the matter.'

With a calm demeanour Kathryn nodded her gratitude and turned to face the dressmaker. She would worry over how to obtain the money later, when she knew the full sum owing.

If Lady Maybury felt any irritation towards her companion's insistence she hid it well and thus, at the end of the afternoon, they finally departed Madame Dupont's on very good terms with the promise of two completed evening gowns for the following week, and the rest to follow later.

* * *

The days passed with an easiness and speed that Kathryn had not experienced for many a year. Life with Lady Maybury was pleasant indeed. The old lady could be demanding in the extreme, but she was also kind, interesting and in possession of a rather wicked sense of humour, as her companion quickly discovered. Even Lord Ravensmede's visits to his grandparent failed to blight Kathryn's growing happiness. From the time of his arrival until his eventual departure she kept herself busily employed in tasks well away from the drawing room where Lady Maybury entertained. There was, after all, no point is jeopardising the harmonious existence into which she had fallen within the dowager's rented townhouse.

As Kathryn found contentment in her new life, her day-dreaming diminished. There were still times when, in her mind, she was the sole recipient of a certain nobleman's heart—a nobleman who did not want her as his mistress, but as his wife and the mother of his children. But this time, she kept the tall, handsome Viscount strictly confined to her dreams. Kathryn had learned her lesson well. Neither Lord Ravensmede, nor anyone else for that matter, would be allowed to ruin the chance she now had for happiness.

Warm golden sunlight spilled across the deep rosewood table in the parlour of the house in Green Street, highlighting a patch of dust that had escaped the maid's cloth and beeswax. Under ordinary circumstances such an omission would have been enough to earn the poor girl a clout round the ear and a thorough tongue lashing from the lady of the house. But, fortunately for the maid, matters within the Marchant household that afternoon were anything but ordinary. For Anna Marchant, sitting alone and bolt upright in the comfortable armchair beside the unlit fireplace, was reading the contents of a letter that had just been delivered by the letter carrier. A small gasp erupted into the emptiness of the room. The colour drained from her complexion. Her mouth gaped liked a landed fish. 'No!' she whispered aloud. 'It cannot be…' She smoothed the paper out upon her lap and then, grasping the sheet so tightly that her nails dug into her palms, made to read the small, neatly formed script once more.

26 May 1815
Amersham
Buckinghamshire

Dear Mrs Marchant

I beg that you will forgive the nature of the tidings that I write to impart, but I have just heard such news that renders me, in good conscience, unable to remain silent.

I was very pleased to make your acquaintance at Lady Finlay's recent ball, and I do not think that I was mistaken in finding that you are a lady of impeccable taste and judgement. However, word has just reached me here at my sister's residence that your niece, Miss Kathryn Marchant, has accepted the offer of a position as the dowager Lady Maybury's companion. As you will be well aware, Lady Maybury is the grandmother of the Viscount of Ravensmede, a nobleman of renowned repute. For reasons that I dare not put into writing, my dear Mrs Marchant, I am compelled to warn you against allowing your niece to take up Lady Maybury's offer. Suffice to say, I have evidence that, were it to become public knowledge, would most certainly jeopardise her reputation. I fear that Kathryn is not of the same genteel mould as you and your sweet daughter Lottie, but of that I will say no more lest this letter falls into the wrong hands and risks your family's embarrassment. It is unfortunate that I am forced to remain here in the country for a few days longer on account of my sister's confinement, but I assure you that I will return to London with haste and call upon you as soon as is possible.

With all good intentions
Your friend
Amanda White

By the time Mrs Marchant finished reading her mouth was quite dry and her heart rate had kicked to a canter. What on earth had that little bitch Kathryn been up to? Making a fool of the family that had saved her from destitution on the streets, if Amanda White's insinuations were to be believed. Mrs Marchant folded the letter up and went to hide it in a safe place, all the while musing on why she disliked Kathryn so very much. The deed was done: Kathryn was already installed in the dowager's house in Upper Grosvenor Street. Nothing in Mrs White's letter could undo that, not without serving the entire Marchant family up to the gossipmongers. And that was something that could not be risked. A sneer contorted her mouth, and her eyes were filled with spite. Anna Marchant had no intention of meekly awaiting the return of the widow to discover just what was going on with Kathryn, no intention at all.

Kathryn stared at her reflection in disbelief. She tried to speak, her mouth even shaped to say the words, but none were forthcoming. Her delicately shaped eyebrows rose and fell expressively and when still she could not speak she whirled around and in three steps had gathered Lady Maybury into a spontaneous embrace.

'I take it you're pleased with Madame Dupont's creation!' chuckled the old lady.

Kathryn finally found her tongue. 'Indeed, my lady, it's quite the most beautiful dress I've ever seen. When I look in the mirror I see a stranger looking back at me. I'm nothing like myself!' A slender hand patted the dowager's arm once more. 'Thank you for allowing me to repay your loan with such reasonable terms.' As Lady Maybury's companion she was not entitled to a wage as such, but her ladyship had insisted on giving her a generous sum, all of which would now be consumed in paying for the outfit in which she was now attired.

'You are very welcome, child.' Lady Maybury smiled. 'I do believe Marie was right when she insisted upon this colour. It complements your eyes.' Her head perched to one side in contemplation. "Yes, Kathryn, you shall do very well.' One snowy eyebrow arched, mimicking the gesture so often used by her grandson. 'Very well indeed.'

For once in her life, Kathryn Marchant thought that perhaps that might just be true. The dress was of a sheer violet silk, high-waisted and cut so that the skirt draped enticingly to the floor with the merest suggestion of the curves hidden beneath. With a low décolletage it revealed rather more of Kathryn's other assets than she was used to, but her bruises were gone; when she suggested the addition of her fichu, Lady Maybury snorted and turned a more-than-querulous eye in her direction.

'There's no need for any such thing.'

Sprinkled liberally over the bodice were the tiniest cream pearls, which led the eye down to the broad cream satin ribbon that adorned Kathryn's waist as well as the edge of her short puffed sleeves. On her hands she wore an elegant new pair of cream gloves that reached up and over her arms to past her elbows. Her neck was bare save for the few chestnut tendrils that nestled about it. The mass of her curls had been gathered up high on the back of her head and fixed in place with pins and cream-and-violet coloured ribbons. A matching cream shawl and reticule completed the elegant ensemble. Little wonder that she scarcely recognised the woman looking back at her from the dressing mirror. Suddenly aware that she had been entirely absorbed in her own appearance, Kathryn turned to the dowager, who was resplendent in the forest green silk. 'You look lovely, my lady. Madame Dupont has truly worked her magic here tonight. We shall be quite the finest dressed ladies at Lady Cooper's ball.'

'I never doubted it for a moment,' said her ladyship in reply.

* * *

The ballroom was glowing with the light of a multitude of candles balanced in four enormous crystal chandeliers. Lady Cooper's affair was proving to be quite a success judging from the mass of people squashed within the confines of her ballroom. Kathryn and Lady Maybury had been fortuitous in finding seats close by the floor-length windows, which were opened in an attempt to remedy the stifling heat. Mrs Lee and Lady Hadstone soon arrived to monopolise the dowager's attention, leaving Kathryn to watch the proceedings upon the dance floor and around its periphery. She sipped her lemonade and enjoyed her contemplation. *The oppressive heat of the ballroom vanished, the air grew cool and sweet, scented with the freshness of grass and earth and blue sky. Instead of the press of sweat-drenched bodies were spacious marble chequered floor tiles and a flood of sunlight. Across the floor stood one large figure, immaculate in full evening dress, his green eyes light like tender young leaves, smiling his heart-rending smile...for her alone.*

'Kathryn!' The dowager's hand touched to her arm, and the spell was broken.

She looked at Lady Maybury, an expression of guilt blazoned across her face. 'I do beg your pardon, my lady. I'm afraid my thoughts had wandered a little.'

But the dowager's focus had shifted and was fixed quite firmly on someone else, someone that stood directly before Kathryn, someone of whom Kathryn was becoming rapidly aware.

'Miss Marchant,' he said. The deep melodic tone teased a shiver down her spine. 'A pleasure to see you again.' His bow was superbly executed.

'Lord Ravensmede.' She made her devoirs and tried to ignore the warmth that had suddenly pervaded her cheeks. *Distant and polite, stay distant and polite at all times*, she reminded herself. But it did not slow the thrumming of her heart or the acrobatic antics of the butterflies massing in her stomach.

He was dressed as if he had stepped straight out of her daydream: a finely tailored black coat worn with pale pantaloons that clung rather revealingly to his long muscular thighs. Well-shaped calves and ankles were encased in white stockings, leading down to a pair of highly polished black buckle slippers. A white satin waistcoat overlaid a snow-white shirt and neckcloth, beneath which it was clear that there had been no need for padding of any description. Nicholas Maybury was indeed a man of impressive physique. He turned to his grandmother and smiled. 'I trust this evening finds you in good health?'

'Never better, my boy. I have the constitution of an ox, as well you know.' Aside to her cronies she added, 'He's ever hopeful that I will shuffle off this mortal coil, but I do not intend to accommodate him for quite some time.'

Kathryn listened to the conversation continue for some little time, with Ravensmede politely exchanging small talk with all three elderly ladies. Notably he did not attempt the same with her. Indeed, his neglect was rather marked. Two strangers in a ballroom. Their kisses had never been. Respectable. The Viscount and his grandmother's companion—a class apart. It was what she wanted, after all, so why did it bring a heaviness to her heart? And then, at last, Lord Ravensmede's attention was upon her, and it was as if they were the only two people there.

His eyes met hers.

Her heart skipped a beat. It was her dream becoming a reality. She wetted her suddenly dry lips. Tried to shake off the enchantment in danger of overcoming her. Knew that she was staring at him in a highly inappropriate fashion. None of it made any difference. Kathryn glanced around, looking for a way to extricate herself from such temptation.

'Miss Marchant,' he said, and her name sounded like a caress upon his lips.

His lips… Her eyes were on them, tracing their outline. Firm, chiselled, with a hint of sensual fullness. Lips that had kissed her with such expertise. Her own mouth parted at the memory. Anticipation fluttered in her stomach. The breath trembled within her throat. She swallowed hard. Fought to regain some semblance of self-control. 'Lord Ravensmede.' How could she sound so calm, so unaffected, when she wanted so desperately to feel the press of his mouth against hers, the strength of his arms around her?

'The next dance is the waltz. I understand it to be a favourite of yours.' He did not appear to be in the grip of any such torrent of emotion. But there was something in his gaze that made the hairs on the back of her neck stand upright.

Kathryn's cheeks warmed. 'I…um…that is…' Her fingers slid to twist at the violet silk of her skirt. 'I do not think that…'

A corner of his mouth twitched. 'Grandmama, may I borrow Miss Marchant for the next dance? I promise to return her safely and I'm sure that these two beautiful ladies…' he turned the full force of his rakish good looks upon Lady Hadstone and Mrs Lee '…will engage you in such interesting and witty conversation that you shall not note her absence.'

Lady Hadstone and Mrs Lee giggled girlishly and fanned themselves with fervour.

Lady Maybury knew better. The tone of her voice was harsh, but the look in her eye was one of endearment. 'Why the blazes should I object?' And she turned her attention back to her friends.

Ravensmede smiled at that, then faced Kathryn again. 'Miss Marchant, would you do me the honour of partnering me for the waltz?' His eyes lingered at her lips before rising to meet her gaze.

Her throat was in danger of sticking together. The pulse at the side of her neck throbbed wildly. She prayed fervently that it would not show. 'Thank you, Lord Ravensmede,' she uttered weakly. From the corner of her eye she could see Mrs Lee and Lady Hadstone positively agog. For the sake of good manners she could not refuse him, and neither did she want to. 'I would be delighted.' And in her heart she knew it was the truth.

A large hand extended, closed around hers and tucked it securely into his arm. He did not speak until the music started and they were gliding effortlessly around the room. 'Are you happy with my grandmother?'

Her lashes swept up and she regarded him with surprise that he could ask such a question. 'Of course, my lord. Lady Maybury is very kind to me.' He smelled of soap and bergamot and something else that was uniquely him.

'It seems you have a short memory, Kathryn.'

She swallowed hard, aware that she remembered all too well a moonlit room and the dimmed interior of a coach. 'I don't know to what you are referring, sir.'

His eyes glinted with emerald lights. 'My lord? Sir? I think we know each other rather better than that would suggest.'

Her cheeks grew hotter. Did he know what he was doing to her? From the look on his face, most probably so. 'On the contrary, Lord Ravensmede, I'm companion to your grandmother. Any other mode of address would be quite inappropriate.' Despite the traitorous reaction of her body to his proximity, she was determined not to let her mask of polite indifference slip. Such a path was the rocky descent to ruin, nothing more.

'Do you deny then, *Miss Marchant*—' he stressed the use of her formal address '—that which has passed between us on two separate occasions?' His eyes held hers with an intimacy to which he had no right.

She bit uneasily at her lower lip, unsure of where his words were leading.

'Surely you do not forget that as well? Shall I remind you of the kisses that we've shared?' he teased.

She gasped and glanced self-consciously around. 'Ssh! Someone might hear you!'

'Then you do remember, after all.'

'Of course I remember,' she snapped. 'I'm unlikely ever to forget!'

'Why? Do my kisses affect you like no other's?' Ravensmede laughed.

She could do nothing to prevent the intensifying rosy stain that scalded the fairness of her skin.

'Your face betrays you, Kathryn.' And for some reason he looked extraordinarily pleased about it.

'You are no gentleman to say such things!' she said, afraid of what she had revealed.

'I assure you, Kathryn, I'm no gentleman at all.' A wicked twinkle set in the green eyes. 'But that is something of which you are, no doubt, already aware.'

'Lord Ravens—'

A dark eyebrow arched. 'Tut tut, Kathryn, what must I do to make you use my given name?' His gaze dropped pointedly to her lips.

'Nicholas!' the whisper ejected with alacrity.

He smiled. 'Much better. So now that we've sorted one small problem, let us deal with another. Why have you been avoiding me?'

Her denial was too quick. 'You're mistaken.' The chestnut tendrils cascading around her neck shook. She was not wanton. No matter the strength of his left hand surrounding hers, or the undeniable heat that emanated from the touch of his right against her waist. No matter that she quivered with the hope that he would kiss her, as he had before. She must strive to show him that he erred in his opinion.

'I've visited my grandmother on five occasions and not once have you been present. Do you mean to tell me that she sent you away when she knew I had arrived?'

'No. I was simply engaged with other chores.'

'I've told you before, Kathryn Marchant, you make a poor liar.'

Her eyes met his at the shared memory of the last time he had uttered those words.

His hand tightened upon her waist.

She trembled beneath it.

'I owe you an apology, Kathryn. That day in the carriage, I should not have taken advantage of you. Forgive me.' The edge of his thumb delicately caressed her fingers.

Right at this moment in time she would have forgiven him anything. 'I was not entirely blameless in the situation,' she admitted. 'I should not have…' She glanced away. 'I ought not to have…' Was there any polite way of saying what had to be said? Silver eyes met smouldering green once more. 'You know very well what I'm trying to say, Nicholas.'

A knowing smile was her only answer.

She cleared her throat nervously. 'No such thing must happen again. I'm Lady Maybury's companion, and even if that were not the case…' Anxiety widened her eyes. 'I would not have you think me anything other than respectable.' There, she had said it.

The music filled the silence between them.

'I do not think anything else,' he said, and a strange expression came over his face. 'And as you rightly said, you're my grandmother's companion. Do you think that I would do anything to dishonour her?'

'No.' It was the truth. There seemed to be a genuine bond of affection between the Viscount and his grandparent.

He was still looking at her in that peculiar way. 'Are you truly so averse to my company, Kathryn?'

She sighed. The lie refused to form upon her lips. 'I'm averse to any impropriety that might blight my reputation. My good name is all that I have left.'

'I do not seek to damage it,' he said softly.

She should treat him with the cool distance that propriety demanded, but she could not. 'If we are agreed that no such thing should happen again between us, then there is no reason that we cannot be friends.'

'Friends?' He rolled the word around his tongue in careful consideration. It would certainly be a novelty. 'Friends do not avoid one another, Kathryn.'

'No, they do not,' she said quietly.

'Well, in that case…' the side of his mouth quirked '…we shall be friends.'

The last bars of 'Ach! Du lieber Augustine' sounded in the ballroom.

Kathryn had no opportunity to speak further with Lord Ravensmede that evening. It seemed that his taking her on to the floor had acted as a signal as to her availability as a dancing partner, for no sooner had she taken her seat once more than she was approached by first one young man and then another. She tried to decline as politely as possible, knowing that she was present only in the capacity of a companion, but Lady Maybury was having none of it and, at her insistence, Kathryn was forced to accept each and every one of the flood of dance invitations. While partnering Captain Brent for the quadrille she became aware of Lord Ravensmede's scrutiny and during the Scottish reel with Mr Parket she saw that he had stood up with an elegant young blonde lady. After that he disappeared and Kathryn focused her attentions on remembering her dance steps.

Chapter Eight

Ravensmede carelessly dropped the neckcloth on to the chair and massaged the knot of tension at the back of his neck that had been growing all night since witnessing Kathryn in the arms of another man, or several other men to be precise. He sighed and loosened his shirt, glad that he had instructed his valet not to wait up. The night was still young, certainly for someone of the Viscount's lifestyle, but he had no inclination to attend his club, and still less to visit Millicent Miller. He wondered whether he had been a trifle hasty in paying his latest mistress off. He paced around the bedchamber, restless, discontented. Each time he closed his eyes an image appeared—Kathryn smiling at someone, and that someone wasn't him. Little wonder he'd been forced to leave early. He poured himself another large and aromatic brandy and lay back still clothed upon the bed.

Perhaps Millicent was exactly what he needed. A pretty face and willing body to ease his frustration. But the thought went no further. The need that gnawed at him was specific, and he was quite sure that only one woman could remedy it. He had no notion for any of the women that had served as his mistresses. Indeed, he had no notion for anyone or anything other than his grandmother's companion; a woman whom life had treated harshly, who, until he had quite literally stumbled upon her at Lady Finlay's ball with that dreadful blonde cousin, had battled alone through life's trials. The thought of what she had witnessed after her father's suicide, and, worse still, at the hands of the woman who called herself her aunt, nipped at Ravensmede. Yet Kathryn had endured and refused to be either cowed or embittered by her experiences.

Perdition, but she was beautiful. He had known it from the first, when she was hidden behind that monstrosity of a grey garment that passed for a dress. His grandmother's influence had unmasked Kathryn's real beauty for all to see. She was not pretty in the mundane sense of the *ton*. Rather her eyes had a silver sparkle, and that smile… He had scarcely been able to draw his eyes away from the sight of Kathryn, encased in the violet evening dress that emphasised the gentle curves of her figure.

And when he'd first approached her, only to find her with that faraway look in her eyes, he wanted nothing other than to pull her into his arms and kiss that delectable mouth that moved so readily to laughter. It had nigh on been his undoing, causing as it did certain physical reactions that were hardly appropriate at a society ball, least of all in front of his own grandmother. He'd been forced to concentrate his attentions on his grandam's cronies in the hope of preventing what could have been an embarrassing situation for them all.

His fingers raked the dark ruffle of his hair. What was this obsession he felt for Kathryn? A desire to bed her, and yet he recoiled from treating her in such a despicable way. He was growing soft. Never once in all the years of playing the rake had he suffered such a revelation of conscience. And all because he'd developed a fancy for his grandmother's companion. Truth to be told, much more than a fancy.

It was time he took himself in hand. She was just a woman, like any other. The brandy trickled down his throat, soothing the edge from his emptiness. A smile crooked across his face. Yes, Kathryn Marchant was definitely all woman, but she was nothing like any of the others. Maybe, just maybe, Kathryn had already offered him the solution to his problem. It was almost as if he heard again the soft whisper of her words within his bedchamber, *there is no reason that we cannot be friends.*

Slowly and carefully he placed the empty glass upon the bedside table, stripped off the remainder of his clothes and crawled beneath the covers. For the first time in ten years Ravensmede was sound asleep before the clock struck midnight.

The sunshine flooded the breakfast room, basking both Kathryn and Lady Maybury in its golden light. Her ladyship was devouring a plate of chops, her appetite being disproportionately large for so small and frail a person. Her companion was satisfied with a mere egg on toast. Behind Kathryn's plate was propped *The Times*, from which she was reading aloud the announcements, between mouthfuls of breakfast.

'Lord Barclay has the common sense of a flea. Engaged to Wilhelmina Turbet? Mark my words, the girl will bore him rigid in less than a month. Just like her mother—nothing between the ears, I'm afraid.' Lady Maybury helped herself to yet another slice of toast.

Kathryn poked an errant curl behind her ear and smiled mischievously. 'But I thought that's precisely what a gentleman demanded of his wife. Did not Lady Hadstone say there's nothing less attractive than a clever woman?'

'Ho!' screeched her ladyship at the top of her voice. 'Amelia's three daughters couldn't hold a single thought in their heads between them. She's not likely to say anything else! Fortunately for her, their dowries were large. Had them off her hands in no time, even though they each had the brain of a small carp, and the face to match.'

The two ladies were laughing at Lady Maybury's scathing observation when the footman entered to announce the Viscount of Ravensmede, followed closely by the man himself.

'Grandmama, Miss Marchant.' He gave a nonchalant bow.

'Forgive the early hour of my call. I wished to catch you before you made arrangements for the day.'

'Nick,' murmured the dowager with pleasure. 'Come and join us for a spot of breakfast.' She indicated the empty seat to her right-hand side and rammed another mouthful of pork into her mouth. 'I'm sure Miss Marchant will not object.'

Kathryn smiled at both grandmother and grandson. 'Of course not.'

Lord Ravensmede helped himself to a little toast and some coffee.

'What's wrong with you, boy?' The dowager's brow wrinkled. 'Picking at your food like a sparrow. Are you sickening for something?'

Ravensmede took his grandparent's jibes with good nature. 'I've already broken my fast. I'm merely accommodating your hospitality, ma'am.'

Lady Maybury grunted, but the faded green eyes remained unconvinced.

'Have you made plans for today?' Ravensmede sipped his coffee, but abandoned the half-eaten toast.

'Apart from attending the Opera House tonight, we are as yet undecided.'

'Then perhaps you'll allow me to accompany you on a visit to the exhibition of the Society of Painters in Oil and Watercolours. From there we could travel to the British Museum.' His gaze flitted from his grandmother to her companion.

The old lady smiled, a fiery light appearing in her eyes. 'What do you say, Kathryn? Shall we attend?'

Kathryn could barely conceal her surprise in being asked. 'My lady, I'm happy to abide by whatever you should decide,' she said with the utmost diplomacy.

'Don't flannel me, gel! Do you want to go or don't you? It's a simple enough question.'

The heat rose in Kathryn's face, creating two small spots of colour. 'I would very much like to see the paintings.' With calm deliberation she folded the newspaper over and laid it on the table.

'Good,' announced the dowager, and then said to her grandson, 'Come back in an hour, we shall be ready then. Haven't had time to finish m'breakfast,' she grumbled. 'Blasted interruptions aren't good for the digestion. Off with you, then!' And the formidable little lady held her cheek up for Lord Ravensmede's kiss before shooing him from the room.

It was very different from the last journey she had made in this same carriage. Kathryn drew her mind carefully away from that avenue of thought. Seated beside Lady Maybury with a well-behaved Lord Ravensmede opposite, things could not have been more dissimilar. Despite the warmth of the fine summer day and the firmly closed windows, Lady Maybury insisted on being covered with the vast expanse of her favourite travelling rug. Its woollen folds overlapped on to Kathryn's legs, making her feel hot and sticky before they'd even arrived at Spring Gardens. She still wore the shabby blue muslin gown as her new afternoon dresses were yet to be delivered; a fact for which she was grateful, given the coolness of the simple material. Fortunately Lady Maybury had not demanded that her companion wear a spencer, although the mud-brown bonnet was an absolute necessity. They arrived at the exhibition while it was still relatively quiet and so were able to enjoy an unimpeded appreciation of the fine collection of water-colour and oil paintings.

'I simply must sit and have a closer look at these paintings,' said her ladyship, seating herself on one of the green-and-pink painted benches within the gallery.

Kathryn touched a hand to the dowager's arm. 'Are you quite well?'

A snort of disgust greeted her concern. 'You're getting as bad as m'grandson, miss. Can't I enjoy the merits of Mr Fielding's work without those around me becoming fixated on m'health?'

'I beg your pardon, my lady, I didn't mean to—'

'No one ever does, it is—' said the dowager with mounting exasperation.

Ravensmede's voice interrupted smoothly. 'Grandmama, allow me to suggest that I accompany Miss Marchant around the room, while you view Mr Fielding's paintings in more detail.'

Kathryn looked rather uneasily towards Lord Ravensmede. 'I—'

The old lady did not shift her gaze from the paintings on the wall before her. 'Very well, Nick.' And then, as if remembering Kathryn, she turned her head and mumbled, 'Go ahead, gel.'

Without further ado Kathryn felt her hand being tucked into the Viscount's arm, and then she was quite literally whisked to the other side of the expansive airy room.

His voice was deep and mellow, laced with a hint of amusement. 'Please do forgive my grandmother, Miss Marchant. I'm sure she didn't mean to be so…forthright in her opinion.' Given that they were in such a very public place, he released her arm and stood back to consider the painting before them.

'Your grandmother is honest and always speaks her mind. It's a trait that I much admire,' she said in stout defence of her employer, and stepped likewise to view the same work. With her head perched to one side she studied Mr Robson's watercolour showing a rather sombre scene of a castle on a rock. 'Mmm, it's a very atmospheric scene,' she said. 'Do you like it, my lord?'

'It's well executed and undoubtedly of excellent technical expertise, but as to actually liking it…'

'Can you not feel the sheer rugged rock on which Stirling Castle is built, the bleakness of the vast view, and the humidity of the grey cloud-layered sky?'

A nearly smile hovered at his mouth. 'Enough to make me feel an inkling of gratitude that I'm here instead of there,' he said drolly.

Kathryn's eyes lit with passionate enthusiasm. 'But *there* is freedom unbounded, wildness untamed—see the mountains in the background. And *here* is something altogether different.' Her eyes met his and she smiled. 'Mr Robson has succeeded very well in showing us that. He truly is a great artist.'

'You sound as if you have a real interest in art.'

Her lips curved up in readiness. 'I know very little of the subject, but when I was younger I enjoyed painting very much.'

'And now?'

A shrug of the shoulders. 'And now I have other things to occupy my time. What of you, my lord? Do you paint or sketch?'

Ravensmede laughed. 'Not at all. Let's just say my talents lie elsewhere. But I appreciate good art, especially that depicting the sea.'

'Really?' The genuine surprise was evident in her voice. 'Seascapes are my favourite too. I remember once, many years ago, my father took us to Cornwall to visit his old friend. All those rugged sea views, it was bliss!'

They looked at Mr Robson's painting in companionable silence, each caught in their own thoughts, unaware of the other bodies that drifted by. And by the time Kathryn had been returned to Lady Maybury's side she felt quite sure that beneath the rakish exterior of Nicholas Maybury lurked another man altogether: a man who was infinitely likeable.

'I'm sorry that you didn't get to see more of the museum, Miss Marchant.' Lord Ravensmede's voice dropped in volume. 'My grandmother's constitution is not what it was.' He glanced ahead to where Lady Maybury was tottering down the pathway of Montagu House. 'Perhaps we could return another day.'

'That would be most agreeable, my lord.' Kathryn caught up with the dowager just in time to hear her cursing.

'Where the hell is the blasted carriage?'

'Edwards will be walking the horses. He shall arrive presently,' Lord Ravensmede reassured his grandmother.

'Lady Maybury, Lord Ravensmede,' said a coldly polite

voice. And then added, 'And, of course, Kathryn.' Anna Marchant and her daughter stopped before the Viscount and his grandmother.

'Aunt Anna, Lottie.' Kathryn inclined her head in greeting. It had been some weeks since she'd left Green Street and in all that time she had never once set eyes again on any one of her relatives. She was surprised at just how easily their memory had been erased from her life. Now it was as if that miserable time had never been. Both Marchant women were immaculately dressed, their golden-blonde curls peeping from beneath their splendid bonnets. But the perfection of their appearance did little to hide the coolness of their eyes. 'How nice to see you both again.' It was gratifying to find that her time with Lady Maybury had not blunted Kathryn's ability to play a part well.

Unfortunately Anna Marchant was not gifted with such thespian skills. Her narrow lips pursed to a fine line across her face, and the fair eyebrows could not quite prevent their involuntary scowl. 'Indeed, dear Kathryn.'

Young Lottie's gaze was having trouble detaching from Lord Ravensmede's visage. When eventually she managed to prise it away, it flitted back and forth between the Viscount and her pauper cousin. 'We're on our way to the dressmaker. Mama has promised me a new gown for my musical evening and Mrs Thomas wants one final fitting before it will be complete.'

Mrs Marchant looked pointedly at the familiar old gown in which her niece was garbed.

A movement from the Viscount drew her attention, as he stepped forward, partially obscuring her view of Kathryn. 'How very interesting,' he uttered in a voice that would have curdled the freshest of milk.

'Dear Kathryn.' Mrs Marchant ignored him and managed to force a smile to her mouth; it did not extend anywhere near as far as her eyes. 'What good fortune that we've chanced to meet like this.'

Lottie's jaw dropped and she stared with puzzlement at her mama.

'We've missed you so, haven't we, Lottie?'

Lottie looked at her mother as if she had run mad.

'Haven't we, Lottie?' said her mother again and pressed a forceful hand to Lottie's arm.

'Yes, of course,' said Lottie.

Kathryn looked from the false geniality on her aunt's face to the perplexity on that of her cousin.

'We wanted to be sure of your attendance at Lottie's musical evening,' said Mrs Marchant.

Lottie positively scowled at her mama.

'Things just wouldn't be the same without you, dear Kathryn. And your uncle would so like to see you again.'

Her uncle had revealed no such inclination at their last meeting, thought Kathryn grimly. Nor did she relish the thought of spending an evening in the house in Green Street. But there seemed to be no way to decline the invitation graciously. 'Thank you, Aunt, I shall enquire of Lady Maybury if it is permissible.' She prayed that her ladyship would judge otherwise.

Mrs Marchant glanced at the dowager. 'I promise we shall take very good care of your companion,' she said with forced jollity.

Lady Maybury's eyes brightened. 'A musical evening, did you say? They are quite my favourite form of entertainment. We shall be happy to come.'

Kathryn's heart sank.

'How delightful,' said Mrs Marchant weakly, and the smile on her face appeared to be suffering under the strain. 'It shall, of course, be the smallest and most modest of affairs.'

Lady Maybury appeared undeterred.

'Then I shall send you a card with all of the details,' Mrs Marchant said. 'And now we really must rush. We cannot keep Mrs Thomas waiting. Please do excuse us.' With one rapid inclination of the head she placed a hand behind Lottie's back and pushed. 'Goodbye, Lady Maybury, Lord

Ravensmede, Kathryn.' And without another word she steered her daughter towards their carriage as fast as she could manage.

Lord Ravensmede raised a cynical eyebrow at his grandparent. 'An interest in musical evenings? I seem to recall that you were afflicted by no such tendency last Season.'

'Fiddlesticks!' declared the old lady. 'Your memory's going, boy. Never missed an invitation to a musical event in m'life.'

'I had not thought you would have included Mrs Marchant in your circle.' His lordship's voice never normally betrayed emotion. But on this occasion Kathryn thought she could detect the subtle undertone of disapproval.

One faded eye glittered rather threateningly in Ravensmede's direction. 'Would you have Kathryn go without me? I have a notion to hear the chit sing, nothing more.' Then fatigue showed in her face. 'Take us home, Nick. I must have my nap in preparation for tonight's outing and time is getting on.'

Anna Marchant was up to something, Ravensmede was certain. Why should the woman suddenly be so eager for Kathryn's attendance…and seemingly on her own? The invitation had been issued to Kathryn alone. His grandmother had taken the liberty of inviting herself. Mrs Marchant's lack of enthusiasm for Lady Maybury's presence had not escaped his attention. For the rest of the day Ravensmede found himself to be pondering the question. It was the foremost matter in his mind as he dispatched the note to Cadmount. He had still not resolved the issue when a footman announced Lord Cadmount's carriage. Five minutes later the two men were *en route* to Haymarket.

It did not take long for Cadmount to become aware that his friend's attention was otherwise engaged. Conversation was scant for the duration of the journey. Cadmount had his suspicions as to the cause of Ravensmede's somewhat brooding mood, but knew better than to test them at that precise moment.

It was only when they had seated themselves within the auditorium that Lord Cadmount understood Ravensmede's sudden urge to attend the opera this evening.

'Isn't that your grandmother with li'l Miss Marchant over there?' The fair brows indicated the direction of the sky-blue box not so very far from Cadmount's own.

'It appears you may be right,' drawled Ravensmede. 'Shall we…?' He did not wait for the answer, but was up and threading his way through the crowds with leisurely determination.

'Lord Ravensmede.' Kathryn could not prevent the sudden gallop of her heart.

'So you decided to join us,' said Lady Maybury quite matter of factly. 'Lord Cadmount.' The snowy white head dipped, sending the deep red plumes balanced thereon into a frenzy.

'Your servant, ma'am,' said Lord Cadmount and bowed. 'You look as exquisite as ever, dear lady.'

'Flatterer!' shrieked her ladyship, but she smiled and fanned herself all the same.

Kathryn tried hard to keep a straight face. It appeared that Lady Maybury had rather a soft spot for her grandson's friend. Her eyes flitted once more to Lord Ravensmede, who was looking devilishly handsome. 'You made no mention, sir, that you planned to attend tonight.'

'No, I did not.' His gaze held hers for a moment longer, raising in Kathryn the peculiar tension she had felt before when he had held her in his arms or pressed his lips to hers. She looked away, unwilling to allow such feelings to resurface.

For the rest of the evening nothing in Lord Ravensmede's manner or speech was anything but formally polite, but she could not dispel the odd sensation that he was, by his very presence, lending her his protection, and not at all in the scandalous way he had once suggested. And when, at the end of the evening, Ravensmede and Cadmount assisted Lady Maybury and herself to her ladyship's carriage, Kathryn was surprised to find that she did not wish to say goodbye.

* * *

The next day Kathryn entered the breakfast room to find a parcel and a small box sitting on the breakfast table.

Her ladyship barely raised her eyes from *The Times*. 'Could they print this confounded news any smaller? I can't see a damn thing!' she complained.

'Would you like me to read to you?' Kathryn knew how her ladyship hated to admit just how much her eyesight had deteriorated. It was their usual routine, Kathryn reading aloud, the dowager interrupting with comments, both learning the news of the day, both discussing their subsequent views and opinions. 'I'm sorry I'm late, my lady. I overslept a little. I hope I haven't kept you waiting long.'

For morning time Lady Maybury appeared to be in an unusually good mood. 'It's of little consequence. My stomach can't be kept waiting for breakfast and I knew you would arrive shortly.' She helped herself to another chop and a couple of devilled kidneys. 'Couldn't sleep then, gel?'

Kathryn lifted the coffee pot. 'No. I slept like a top,' she lied. 'I can't think why I didn't waken. It must have been all the excitement of yesterday.' She most certainly was not about to admit that she had lain awake half the night thinking about the lady's grandson.

'What excitement?' asked Lady Maybury between mouthfuls of kidney.

'Why, our visits to the painting exhibition and the museum, and, of course, the opera.'

Lady Maybury smiled. After a few minutes in which Kathryn sipped her coffee and ate some eggs, the elderly voice asked, 'Aren't you going to open them?'

'Open them?' Kathryn asked, rather unsure of herself, and her eyes drifted to the packages sitting across the table.

'It is your birthday, is it not?'

Kathryn let out an exclamation of surprise. 'Yes, but how did you know?'

'We Mayburys have our ways.' The old lady smiled, and pushed the small dark box towards Kathryn. 'A small token of my affection, gel.'

Kathryn stared at the box, her hand touched to her lips.

'Open it.'

The box was shallow and rectangular in shape, with an external covering of blue chinoiserie painted silk. Inside, on a lining of plain white silk, lay a strand of ivory pearls and two matching single-pearl drop earrings. Kathryn gasped. 'They're beautiful!'

Lady Maybury's smile broadened. 'Happy birthday, Kathryn.'

'I…' The words faltered and then she was up out of her seat and throwing her arms around the dowager. 'Thank you,' she whispered in a voice thick with emotion, 'it is a long time since anyone remembered my birthday, and never with such a truly lovely gift.'

Lady Maybury patted Kathryn's hand. 'I'm glad that you like them. Now, open your other present.'

Still standing, Kathryn looked at the large parcel on the table.

'Hurry up, then. My curiosity's getting the better of me.' Lady Maybury resumed her attack on her breakfast. 'When one gets to my age one's family take steps to curtail all excitement. It has the effect of making some ladies, not to put too fine a point on it, overly inquisitive.' One ancient hand removed itself from the cutlery for long enough to push the parcel further in Kathryn's direction.

The brown paper crinkled beneath her fingers as she picked at the knots in the string.

'For heaven's sake, gel,' huffed her ladyship, and, extracting a small, finely crafted pair of scissors from a pocket in her dress, she reached across and snipped the string. 'You'll be there all day with those knots. No point in wasting time.' Lady Maybury attacked her chop once more, but her eyes were trained firmly on the parcel.

Kathryn peeled back the wrapping to reveal a wooden box

filled with the brightest range of water-colour pans. Inserted in cunningly designed compartments within the set were small pots for holding water and a narrow drawer containing the finest sable brushes. 'It's wonderful!' Her fingers traced the contours of each and every part, touching with a care that suggested reverence.

'What's that beneath it?' A silver fork stabbed towards the paintbox.

With the box positioned carefully on the tablecloth, Kathryn saw that the parcel also contained a pad of cut paper sheets and a box of sketching pencils. 'Who on earth could have sent me…?' The letter was folded in half and lay at the bottom of the pile. Even before she read the words her heart leapt, for there at the top of the paper was the Viscount of Ravensmede's crest. Fingers fluttered to her cheek as her eyes skimmed the boldly penned script.

Her ladyship laid down her cutlery upon the emptied plate, dabbed a napkin to her lips, and emitted a small burp. 'Do you like m'grandson's gift?'

Kathryn's emotions were in quite a flurry. Abruptly she found her chair, and stared at the pile of art materials before her. 'It's…exquisite! But…' She plucked distractedly at the apron of her dress before running her fingers across the beech paintbox. The clear grey eyes raised to the dowager's. 'I can't accept it.'

'Why ever not?'

'It's not that I'm not grateful, because, of course, I am. It's just…well… not quite appropriate that I receive a gift from a…' She couldn't very well describe Ravensmede as a rake to his own grandmother, so she searched frantically for a suitable word, and found one: '…man.'

'Man!' Lady Maybury's tone cast the word in derision. A cackle rent the air as she seemed to find Kathryn's statement of extreme comic value. When she had stopped laughing long enough to speak, her ladyship helped herself to more coffee and said, 'I thought the fact he's reputed to be one of London's most notorious rake-hells might have influenced you more.'

Kathryn balked at the lady's words and flushed with embarrassment. It seemed that nothing similar affected Lady Maybury's sensibilities.

'It's all a load of stuff and nonsense, of course. Rebelling against his father's hand and the like. Wanted to fight for his country. Tried to buy himself a commission. Charles, m'son, soon put paid to that. The two of them have been at loggerheads ever since. Nick's not cut out to be a rake and a wastrel. He's just bored; there's nothing and no one to tax his mind. Never had a real challenge in his life, errant puppy that he is. Things have fallen too easily into his lap all along.' The distant look in her eyes faded. 'For all of his reputation, Kathryn, I'm certain that, in this at least, Nick is well intentioned. It is a birthday gift, nothing more. I see no impropriety. My advice to you, gel, is to accept the art materials with grace. Besides, I enjoy watching others paint. It soothes m'nerves.'

In all the time Kathryn had known the dowager she had seen no evidence to suggest that the old lady was afflicted with anything that could be remotely described as a nervous condition. The paintbox was very beautiful. She cast a longing look at it.

'So you'll paint for me this afternoon,' coaxed Lady Maybury.

Using the water-colours and brushes and paper that Lord Ravensmede had bought for her? His letter wishing her birthday greetings was still clutched between her fingers. She folded it and placed it on the table. 'Yes, my lady, of course I will.'

A week later Lord Ravensmede was standing in the library of his grandmother's rented townhouse, browsing through the water-colour studies that lay upon the table. The assortment mainly consisted of still-life studies, carefully contrived arrangements of flowers and fruits. All were of a good artistic standard, but what really caught his eye was the single sheet at the very bottom of the pile. Kathryn Marchant had captured every aspect of his grandmother's personality in those few brush strokes. The intelligence and perception within that gaze, the kindness and loyalty beneath that harsh façade, and, most tenderly of all, the hint of vulnerability in the grand demeanour. It was something that Ravensmede guessed few others besides himself had ever glimpsed. It was not a posed portrait of rigid formality, but a natural moment frozen in time. His grandmother looked as if she were watching Kathryn, but without the consciousness so usual in those sitting for a portrait. Ravensmede found it hard to draw his eyes away. A noise at his back signalled Lady Maybury's entry.

'Quite the little artist, isn't she, Nick?' Then, without waiting for an answer, she continued, 'I didn't know my face was so revealing. Seems that our Kathryn has a very real talent when it comes to portraits. Unlike most, she can look beneath the veneer we present to the world.'

Our Kathryn... The expression hit Ravensmede like a bolt from the blue. *Our Kathryn*... It seemed so right that she was one of them, a part of their family. Aware of his grandmother's scrutiny, he shook the thought from his head and looked directly at her. 'Grandmama...you do know what you're about with Anna Marchant tonight, don't you?'

'Of course,' she said. 'Thought I would send her into that viper's nest on her own, did you?'

'No, I thought that you might find an excuse that Kathryn need not endure such a farce,' he said wryly.

The old lady chuckled. 'Doubting your old grandam's wisdom, Nick?' She caught his large hand and held it sandwiched between her own. 'Kathryn's attendance this evening will put paid to any suggestion that all is not well between her and her relatives. We do not want any gossip arising over either that or the haste of her move to Upper Grosvenor Street.'

'Indeed not,' said Ravensmede. 'But Anna Marchant seemed too eager that Kathryn attend Lottie's musical. Given the fact that the woman can barely conceal her dislike for her niece, I wonder why that might be.'

'As I said, it would be commented upon if Kathryn were not present. And the Marchant woman is determined to curry favour with the *ton*.'

'Maybe,' said her grandson, 'but I have the feeling there is more to Mrs Marchant's invitation than meets the eye.' His lips curved in a mocking smile. 'I fancy that I too have a notion to hear the chit sing.'

A voice floated in from the hall.

'That will be Kathryn.' The dowager drew him a strange little look. 'The aim is to stamp out gossip, not start it. Is your presence really necessary?'

'Absolutely,' answered her grandson.

The two moved towards the door.

Kathryn's sense of dread that had fast been escalating over the past week had reached a pinnacle. No matter how many times she told herself that she was being foolish, no matter how much she insisted that Aunt Anna would never behave with anything other than congeniality before the dowager, Kathryn could not rid herself of the fear. She did not want to set one foot back in the house in Green Street. Even just thinking about the place brought a cold nausea to her stomach. The memory of the three long years that she had lived there would not be easily erased. It was one thing meeting Aunt Anna out in the street, quite another venturing back into her aunt's own domain—where all the power was, and always had been, in Mrs Marchant's hands. Nothing bad could happen, not in Lady Maybury's presence, or so Kathryn reassured herself. But despite all of her efforts, she could not quell her mounting apprehension. It was therefore with a considerable amount of relief that Kathryn descended the staircase of the dowager's house to discover that Lord Ravensmede had every intention of accompanying his grandmother and her companion to Miss Lottie Marchant's musical evening.

* * *

'Kathryn…and Lady Maybury,' gushed Anna Marchant with a sickly smile plastered across her face. 'So pleased that you could both make it to our little gathering.' The ladies were in the middle of their devoirs when Mrs Marchant spotted the tall dark presence by the doorway. 'Lord Ravensmede!' It was all she could do to prevent the smile slipping from her face. 'What a pleasant surprise.'

'Mrs Marchant,' he said lazily, and watched her through narrowed eyes while she led them across the room to where Lady Finlay was chatting with Lottie.

'Lottie dearest, look, some more guests have arrived to hear you sing. Cousin Kathryn, Lady Maybury, and…and Lord Ravensmede.' Anna Marchant looked up to see his lordship smile. It was something that bore a startling resemblance to one of the great black wild cats in the royal menagerie, being unaccountably menacing. The Viscount's eyes held the suggestion of a threat.

Lady Finlay stared short-sightedly at Kathryn. 'I can't say that I remember meeting you before, Miss Marchant.' She peered long and hard. 'Have we been introduced?'

Kathryn raised her chin a notch and endured the scrutiny. 'No, indeed, my lady, I don't believe I've had the pleasure.'

'My cousin was present at your recent ball as my companion, but that was before she was persuaded into Lady Maybury's establishment.' The words were innocent enough, but no one present was in any doubt as to the intention behind them. Charlotte Marchant intended to set her cousin firmly back in her place.

'Indeed,' drawled Lord Ravensmede from Kathryn's side. He looked at Lottie with an air of utter boredom. 'My grandmother insisted that Miss Marchant is such delightful company that she simply would not hear of anyone else as her companion.'

Kathryn felt her hand being tucked into Lady Maybury's arm. 'Such a lovely gel,' said the dowager.

With such overt championing, who would dare to stand against it? Certainly not Lady Finlay. Especially when Lady

Maybury leaned forward and hissed in her loudest stage whisper, 'Her mother was one of the Overton Thornleys.' The snowy white curls nodded knowingly.

Anna Marchant looked as if she would have liked to throttle the dear old dowager there and then. 'Ah, here is Mr Dalton. Now we can all take our seats for tonight's entertainment. I'm sure that no one will be disappointed with my darling girl's performance.'

'I'm sure that young Lettie will not let you down,' said Lady Maybury.

Lottie's baby-blue eyes squinted in displeasure and she looked demandingly at her mama.

'Lottie,' said Mrs Marchant with emphasis.

The dowager's smile contained all the warmth of a hooded cobra. 'Yes, indeed, dear little Lettie. Let us hope she's as talented as her cousin.'

'Her name is Charlotte, which the family shorten to *Lottie.*' Anna Marchant positively snapped the sharp retort.

Aristocratic cheeks were sucked in all round and a knowing look passed between the ladies of the group as they ambled to take their seats in Mrs Marchant's drawing room.

Kathryn found herself seated between Lord Ravensmede and Lady Maybury in the row of chairs furthest back in the room. His lordship sat closest to the door, as if he hoped to make a quick escape should Lottie's musical ability prove not to his taste. Kathryn hoped fervently that he would not leave. Just his presence made her feel safer, allaying the worst of her fears regarding her aunt and the house in Green Street.

She sneaked a look up at him through downcast lashes. He was relaxed in the chair, as if he had not a care in the world, long legs stretched out before him, dark hair worn fashionably short, and an expression of bored indifference upon his face. His attire was immaculate as usual. A deep blue tail-coat, above which showed a white high-pointed collar and a snow-white neckcloth tied in a simple but stylish knot. Her eyes slid lower to where one hand rested on his thigh. A light sprinkling of dark hair showed on the back of the hand. His nails were short and clean, his skin a light honey coloration. It looked to be a strong squarish hand; a hand used to taking what it wanted, and one that Kathryn knew was capable of the most tender caress. Her abdomen gave a little flutter and she swiftly moved her eyes on from his hand to the thigh beneath it. That did not help matters. Not when the thigh, encased in tight buff-coloured buckskin, was so long and muscular, and the front of his coat was so very short. Her cheeks grew warm and she quickly raised her gaze to find herself staring directly into his eyes. Something warm quivered deep inside her. He smiled, and the quiver became a somersault.

'Are you comfortable enough, Miss Marchant?' There was something in his look that made her think that he had more than an inkling of her thoughts.

'Yes, thank you, my lord, quite comfortable.' She nodded and glanced away, unwilling to let him see just how much he affected her.

Fortuitously Mr Dalton sounded the first notes upon the piano and then Lottie began to sing, and Kathryn was saved from any further embarrassment.

Chapter Nine

Lottie had just finished her third rendition to rapturous applause when Anna Marchant threaded her way quietly to the back of the drawing room, to stand beside the Viscount of Ravensmede's chair. She ignored Ravensmede, smiled sweetly at his grandmother and leaned towards Kathryn. 'Dearest niece,' she whispered, 'may I have a minute of your time?'

Kathryn's heart began to thud within her chest and a certain uneasiness started to squirm within. A sense of foreboding rippled down her spine. For one awful moment she was seized by the sudden overwhelming desire to just run through the door and keep on running—far away from Aunt Anna and this house. Her eyes flickered towards the door longingly. And then common sense prevailed. Kathryn knew very well that there was no way out. She could not refuse to speak to her aunt. So she took a deep breath, looked at the dowager, and said quietly, 'Please excuse me, my lady.' Then she nodded and rose to follow Mrs Marchant.

Ravensmede stood to let her leave. As she squeezed past she heard the silk of her skirt slide against his legs, and smelled the clean citrus scent of him. She looked up to read the unspoken question of concern in his eyes, and tried to hide the fear in her own. Then she had passed him and was following Aunt Anna across the floor and out of the drawing room.

Anna Marchant waited until Kathryn was seated in the small room before closing the door behind her. The click of the latch echoed in the silence.

Kathryn recognised it as her aunt and uncle's own personal parlour. It was much smaller than the drawing room and nowhere near as ornate. The décor was a cool combination of duck-egg blue and pale grey, with no hint of warmth or welcome. A small pile of tinder, sticks and coal dross had been set up within the hearth in readiness for a fire. The temperature of the evening outside meant it had not been lit; the chill in the parlour suggested that it should have. Kathryn suppressed a shiver. Nothing of the summer warmth pervaded the little room. The light of the candles in the wall sconces flickered within the gloom. She noticed that the heavy blue curtains had been pulled to shut out the daylight. Everything about the place felt dim and dank and claustrophobic. Her fingers smoothed nervously over the silk of her skirt. 'You wished to speak to me, Aunt?'

'Yes.' Mrs Marchant took the chair between Kathryn and the door. Now that they were alone all pretence of amiability had disappeared. Her eyes were a cold hard blue; her lips pursed to a thin, narrow line. 'I wish to know exactly how matters are between you and Lady Maybury.'

Distrust tutored Kathryn's words. 'Why, they are very well indeed. Lady Maybury is both kind and thoughtful. I could not ask for more.' She waited to see what this game was about.

'And how fares the child?'

'The child?' Kathryn stared at her aunt.

'The child that necessitated such a sudden and immediate move to Ravensmede House.'

Kathryn's fingers pleated the violet silk of her skirt between them. 'Lady Maybury's house is in Upper Grosvenor Street,' she said carefully. 'Maggie, the little girl who was involved in the carriage accident, is recovered and back living with her family.'

'How fortuitous.'

Kathryn said nothing. A horrible suspicion was forming.

'Does Lord Ravensmede spend much time visiting Upper Grosvenor Street?'

'No.' The violet silk twisted tighter in her hands.

'But I've heard he's inordinately fond of his grandmother.'

Kathryn could guess where this was leading. Perspiration beaded cold upon her skin. 'We're missing Lottie's singing.'

'So we are.' Anna Marchant smiled a vicious little smile. 'Then I had best come straight to the point, hadn't I?' The faint strains of music and a high pitched melodic voice drifted through the barrier of the door. 'Certain rumours have come to my ears, Kathryn, rumours involving you and some very improper behaviour.'

The blood rushed in Kathryn's ears. She felt the tripping of her heart. Her eyes widened in shock.

'If you are intent on destroying your reputation then I have a right to know exactly what you are up to.'

Kathryn rose from her chair, her cheeks scalded with embarrassment and anger. 'How could you say such a thing? Any rumours to which you may have listened are false.'

'Don't give me that, you little bitch,' snapped her aunt. 'I know that you're lying; it's written all over your face.'

'I think I should return to Lady Maybury now,' said Kathryn with a great deal more control than she felt.

'Oh, no, I haven't finished with you yet, miss.'

Kathryn hid her growing fear and made to move towards the door, only to find her way blocked by her aunt.

'You're going nowhere until you tell me exactly what's been going on.'

'Aunt Anna—'

'Don't "Aunt Anna" me! You leave here with Ravensmede and his grandmother on the premise of going for a drive in Hyde Park, and the next minute you're installed in the old woman's house as her companion, without so much as a by your leave. The first that your uncle knows of it is a letter from Ravensmede!' Mrs Marchant advanced towards her niece.

Kathryn instinctively backed away.

'Do you think I know nothing of his reputation?' The older woman's mouth twisted to a snarl.

'The child's leg was injured in her fall, and Lady Maybury was in need of immediate assistance,' said Kathryn with force.

'And what of Ravensmede?'

'He could not be expected to look after a four-year-old girl.'

'But he could look after you, miss, very well indeed.'

Kathryn stiffened at the insult. 'You malign both his lordship and me!' She thrust aside the memory of just exactly what she and the Viscount had shared.

Mrs Marchant stepped closer. 'He's the only man to have shown an interest in you, though God knows why he should have taken notice of so plain a creature. And why else would her ladyship have taken you up? It stands to reason, if you're indulging Ravensmede's interest.'

'Lady Maybury would never stoop to such a scandal. Her reputation is beyond reproach.' The eyes that were normally a clear pale grey became dark and stormy.

'Lucky for us all,' said Anna Marchant, 'else your reputation would be in tatters, miss.' She took another step towards her niece.

Kathryn felt the press of the wall against her back. 'My reputation is unblemished.' A sliver of guilt stuck in her throat.

Mrs Marchant stepped closer still. 'That's not what I've heard, and I mean to have the truth from you, you selfish little trollop. You have no thought in your head for anyone other than yourself.'

Kathryn scanned the room for an escape route, but the only way out was the same way through which she had entered.

'If you cast your reputation to the gutter then what of Lottie? Innocent of all blame, yet she'll suffer just the same.'

'Aunt, you're mistaken—'

Anna Marchant's hands closed hard around the tops of Kathryn's arms. 'Tell me what you've been up to, girl, or, so help me, I'll have the truth from you one way or another!'

'Leave me be!' Kathryn struggled to free herself, but her aunt was much larger and stronger.

'Tell me!' Anna Marchant said again and tightened her grip.

Kathryn's ordeal went no further: the door of the parlour swung open.

Anna Marchant spun to face the intruder, her hands dropping to her sides.

'Mrs Marchant,' said the man's voice, but for all its drawl there was in it an unmistakable flint-like quality.

Anna Marchant flushed to the roots of her golden hair. 'Lord Ravensmede,' she said, unsure of quite how much the Viscount had seen or indeed heard.

His expression was one of cold contempt and every line of his face held the promise of retribution. Mrs Marchant surreptitiously backed away towards the corner of the room.

His gaze slid to Kathryn who still stood, as if pinioned, against the wall. Her face had drained to a powder white. 'Miss Marchant, my grandmother has need of you.' The words were innocent enough, but the tone was loaded with danger. 'You appear to be somewhat distressed. Has someone upset you?' His focus drifted questioningly towards Anna Marchant, and the colour of the woman's cheeks darkened to a deep puce.

Kathryn's hands kneaded at the violet silk. 'No!' she almost shouted, then more calmly, as if regaining control of her emotions, 'No, I am quite well, thank you, my lord. I was just about to return to the drawing room.'

'As I'm sure is Mrs Marchant,' he said smoothly, and waited for the golden-haired woman to cross the floor before them. Anna Marchant did not look back. Only then did he place a supportive hand on the small of Kathryn's back and guide her in her aunt's wake. Lottie was still singing as they quietly settled back into their seats. No one commented on the ladies' short absence.

Kathryn never knew how she made it through the rest of that evening. Certainly the knowledge that Lord Ravensmede was never far from her side gave her strength. She could hazard a very good guess at what would have happened within that horrible little room had he not interrupted. A nausea was rising in her stomach and she longed for nothing more than to flee from the house in Green Street. One look at Lady Maybury's face told her that was not possible. The dowager seemed to be in her element, relaying stories of Kathryn's artistic abilities, introducing her new companion to all and sundry, ensuring that everyone knew just who Kathryn Marchant's mother had been. Through it all Kathryn endured with a smile, a murmur of the right response, and an interested expression as the most trivial of stories were told; and all the while she was conscious of the Viscount standing so very close by, guarding her with his presence.

Strangely enough, at the end of the evening it was not Lottie's musical achievements that were talked of by all the best people. Rather, the sudden emergence of the quietly refined Miss Kathryn Marchant, with her water-colour talents, held that coveted spot, thanks to Lady Maybury.

Anna Marchant had some inkling of the matter and it did not please her. 'It was a mistake to invite your cousin,' she conceded to her daughter in the few quiet minutes they had alone. 'I learned nothing, and, because of that battleaxe dowager, Kathryn has managed to steal your thunder.' She flicked a gaze at her daughter. 'For heaven's sake, don't you dare start crying. Do you want them talking of your hideous red blotchy face instead of tonight's performance?'

Lottie's pouted lips trembled, but she swallowed back the tears that threatened to fall. 'I saw you take her out of the drawing room. And then Lord Ravensmede went and fetched you both back.'

'Interfering villain! I fancy that I must be right in my sup-position.'

'Mama?' Lottie's still-watery eyes opened wide and round in bewilderment. 'I don't understand.'

'No, you never do.'

Lottie's lips began to quiver again. 'But that mean cat has ruined my evening.'

'She could ruin a whole lot more than that,' said her mother ominously.

Fortunately the comment was lost upon Lottie, who continued unabated with her complaining. 'Only see how Mr Dalton is looking at her, I'm sure he means to offer for her instead of me. Oh, I shall never forgive her if he does. How I wish she was living back here, then you could box her ears and none of this would ever have happened.' Lottie's voice whined close to hysteria.

'Calm yourself.' Her mother moved a blonde ringlet from across Lottie's cheek. 'Unlike you, my darling, your cousin is a nobody.'

'But Lady Maybury said Kathryn's mother was one of the Overton Thornleys, and everyone was much impressed,' she snuffled.

'Elizabeth Thornley was a strumpet and her family disowned her. The Overton Thornleys wanted nothing more to do with her or her children. Why else do you think we were forced to take Kathryn into our home? Just because Lady Maybury has her in favour does not alter that fact. It was not so long ago that Kathryn was scrubbing floors and washing your linen. Hold that memory close. She may have tried to steal this evening from you, but I don't mean to just stand by and watch that little bitch get away with it, or anything else for that matter, my dear. No. Cousin Kathryn may find she has a little surprise coming to her.' Mrs Marchant's hand turned to stroke her daughter's bright golden locks. 'Just you trust your mama, Lottie. I shall see that Kathryn gets her due, be very assured of that.'

'Such a delightful evening, thank you, Nick. You may call on us tomorrow,' said the dowager when Ravensmede's town-coach halted outside her house in Upper Grosvenor Street.

'I'd rather call on you now.' Lord Ravensmede's eyes flickered towards Kathryn before returning his grandmother's gaze.

'As you will,' she said.

Only once they were all seated within the dowager's drawing room did she speak again. 'Kathryn, my dear, could you go and fetch me a suitably interesting book from the library? I've a mind to hear you read a little before I go to bed—that is, if you're not too tired.'

'Certainly, my lady.'

Lady Maybury waited until the door closed behind Kathryn before turning to her grandson. 'Well, out with it. I take it you want to tell me what went on between Kathryn and her aunt.'

Ravensmede didn't even comment upon his grandparent's bluntness. 'Anna Marchant had her pinned against a wall and was threatening her when I found them.'

'Good gad! Little wonder the gel looked powder white when you brought her back through.'

Ravensmede looked directly at his grandmother. 'I need to talk to her…alone.'

A white eyebrow arched high.

'I would know exactly what Mrs Marchant was up to this evening.'

The faded green eyes held his. 'You know that I should not allow it,' she said quietly.

'And you know I would not ask were it not so important.'

They looked at each other for a moment longer.

'Very well,' Lady Maybury uttered at last. 'I need not say the rest.'

Ravensmede nodded, and dropped a kiss to the lined velvet cheek. 'Thank you.'

When Kathryn returned to the drawing room, complete with book in hand, it was to find Lord Ravensmede standing by the unlit fireplace. Of Lady Maybury there was no sign.

She hesitated halfway across the rug, as if a little unsure of herself. 'My lord…where is Lady Maybury?'

Ravensmede saw the pallor of her cheeks and the signs of fatigue around her eyes. 'Sit down, Kathryn.'

'I think she'll like this one.' She gestured to the small leather-bound book gripped within her hand. 'It's a collection of works by Lord Byron.'

He said nothing, just waited for her to sit down upon the sofa.

'Perhaps I should check if she needs my assistance.'

'Kathryn…' and the word sounded like a sigh on his lips '…my grandmother has retired for the night. I want to speak with you before I leave.'

Her eyes widened. 'I do not think that's a good idea, my lord.'

He shrugged. 'I disagree.'

She was still wearing the violet-and-cream evening dress. He noted how well the colour became her, how enticingly it fitted around her small bosom. The neckline was plain, the violet silk a fine contrast to the exposed smooth white curves of the tops of her breasts that rose and fell at such regular intervals. Suddenly conscious that he was staring, he dropped his gaze lower to where her fingers plucked at her skirt. He knew then the level of her unease. 'You need not be afraid, Kathryn. I only wish to speak to you.'

'What do you wish to discuss?' A note of caution sounded in her voice.

'That which happened this evening at your aunt's.'

Her fingers tightened around the violet material. She swallowed. 'There is nothing to say about that, sir.'

'Oh, but I think there is, Kathryn.' He watched a hint of panic flit across her face.

Silence stretched between them.

'Kathryn.' The word acted as a prompt, as he knew it would.

'We…we had a disagreement, that's all.' Her focus shifted away to study the pattern on the rug.'

'Then it must have been a very heated disagreement; she had you against the wall when I walked in.'

'She was merely making her point, rather forcibly.'

'She was threatening you,' he said succinctly.

'No…she was just—'

'Damnation, Kathryn, why are you trying to protect her?'

She glanced up at him then and he caught a glimpse of guilt and embarrassment in her eyes, before her gaze skittered away again. 'I-I'm not.'

'Then you're hiding something from me.'

'No!' The denial did not ring true, and he knew it.

The violet silk was suffering a thorough pulverisation beneath her fingers.

He leaned back against the mantel, rested his booted foot upon the fender, and watched her. 'Your lying does not improve with practice.'

She rose swiftly from the sofa. 'It's late, Lord Ravensmede, and I have much to do tomorrow. Please excuse me, sir.'

He pushed off from the fender and moved swiftly to stand before her. 'No.'

Indignation stared from the silver eyes. 'I beg your pardon,' she said stiffly. 'It's not seemly that we're here, alone, at this time of night.'

Exasperation rose in Ravensmede's throat. 'It's not seemly that you're lying to me,' he growled.

'Lord Ravensmede,' she said primly.

'Miss Marchant,' he countered.

She made to turn towards the door.

'I did not excuse you.' He saw the slight body stiffen. Felt a scoundrel for what he was doing. Knew he must do it for Kathryn's own sake.

'I can stand here all night, my lord, and there will still be nothing more to say.'

One step, and the distance between them disappeared. 'Tell me,' he said roughly. His hand closed around her arm. He felt her start beneath him, try to pull away. She looked up at him, fear blazoning in her eyes. Shock kicked in his gut at the realisation of just what she thought. 'I'm not going to hurt you!' One by one he uncurled his fingers so that she was free. 'God help me, I could *never* hurt you.' They were standing so close that the hem of her skirt brushed the gleaming toes of his long black riding boots; so close that he could hear the whisper of her breath and smell her sweet scent. 'Don't you know that by now?'

Her eyelids fluttered shut.

Next to him she was so small, so slender. It pained him that she believed he could have struck her. 'Forgive me if I frightened you, Kathryn.'

There was a catch of breath in her throat and then those beautiful eyes raised to his once more. 'I'm sorry,' she said, and her, words were so quiet as to scarcely catch his ears. 'I didn't mean to…'

'Hush.' With great tenderness he cupped one hand against her cheek and stroked a delicate caress across the silken skin. It seemed that there was a great stillness within him and a peculiar ache across his chest. It was a novel sensation for Ravensmede. Beneath his fingers her skin was warm and smooth. And her eyes clung to his like a woman drowning. She made him feel both powerless and omnipotent at the same time. 'You need not tell me if you really do not wish to. I sought only to save you from the worst of your aunt.' For all that he wanted to help her, he could not bear her pain.

Her eyes shuttered. 'Oh, Nicholas,' she sighed. 'You, of all people, cannot.'

He touched his lips against her forehead, not kissing, just resting them there, trying desperately to give her some small comfort.

'Aunt Anna said…'

He pulled back, rested his hands loosely, lightly, against her shoulders, and watched the hint of a blush stain those pale cheeks. Kathryn would not meet his gaze. 'What did she say?' he asked as gently as he could.

A deep breath. A tremor of tension beneath his palms. 'She said that there were rumours.'

There was a sudden coldness in the pit of his stomach.

'She implied that I…that we…' Her hand moved to worry at her skirt. But his moved faster, catching her fingers back up and threading them through his own. 'That we?'

'That we have behaved improperly.'

Only the ticking of the clock on the mantel punctuated the silence in the room.

'She wanted to question me on the matter.'

'I see,' said Ravensmede. His fingers pressed a gentle reassurance against hers. He controlled the anger rising within him, didn't want to distress Kathryn any more than she was already.

'And she's right, isn't she?' said Kathryn quietly. 'We haven't behaved as we should.'

'Perhaps I haven't behaved entirely as I should, but you've done nothing wrong.'

Her chin came up and she squared her shoulders. 'I'm every bit as guilty as you, Nicholas. I wasn't unwilling.' Colour flared in her cheeks.

His blood quickened at her bold admission, and his heart gladdened that she was not indifferent to him. 'Your aunt can know nothing for certain; she's fishing for trouble.' But even as he said the words, Ravensmede thought of someone who most definitely knew enough to destroy Kathryn's reputation. The fact that he had parted with a hefty sum to buy the woman's silence did not make him feel any easier. Amanda White's discretion could not to be entirely trusted. He could only be thankful that she had been persuaded to leave London for a while.

Kathryn sighed. 'I only hope that you're right.'

How could he reassure her? He traced his thumb against the inside of her wrist, slowly, intimately. 'We shared a few kisses, Kathryn, nothing more. There's nothing so very wrong in that.' A few kisses…it sounded so innocent, but Ravensmede knew better. Kathryn Marchant's kisses were fit to overwhelm a man's mind. One taste of her lips was enough to snare a fellow for life. And even had that not been the case, even if her mouth had been hard and dry and unyielding so that he never touched her again, he had already done enough to sully her name if the truth were to come out. He thrust the thought aside. 'You said yourself it will not happen again…and now we are just friends.' It was what she wanted, what she *needed,* to hear; or so he told himself.

Hurt flashed in her eyes, and then was gone so quickly that he thought he must have been mistaken. She stared down at her feet.

He squeezed her hands in what he hoped was an encouraging manner; struggled to ignore the smell of her perfume drifting up from her hair, and the tantalising touch of her fingers still entwined within his own. Ruthlessly he quelled the desire to wrap his arms around her and crush her to him. Loosening his hand, he took her chin between his fingers and gently raised her face so that he could look into her eyes. 'I look after my friends, Kathryn,' he said slowly. 'I won't allow Mrs Marchant to hurt you again.'

She nodded. 'Thank you,' she said softly.

He could resist no more. Sliding his arms round her back, he pulled her into his embrace, and then just held her, with the softness of her curves pressed against him, and the smell of her filling his nose. She made no protest, just clung to him as he clung to her, her breath warm and moist against his chest. He dropped his lips to rest against the top of her head. And they stood there, as if they would merge together as one for all eternity.

In the days that followed Miss Lottie Marchant's musical evening Kathryn heard nothing more from her aunt. It seemed that Ravensmede had been right in his assertion that Mrs Marchant had been untruthful about the existence of injurious rumours, for, from the very next day following the event, it became clear that Kathryn had been taken into the bosom of the *ton.* Invitations to balls and routs and parties arrived at the house in Upper Grosvenor Street by the score, and all were extended to both Lady Maybury and her companion.

For the first time in her life people looked *at* Kathryn instead of *through* her. There was definitely no danger of her being ignored. People who had previously not deigned to notice her were suddenly keen to be seen chatting with Lady Maybury's protégé. She lost count of the number of requests she received from people asking her to paint their portraits. And a number of gentlemen took to calling in the hope of fixing Miss Marchant's attention. It was akin to the past fantasies played out in her head, unreal in every aspect except that when she opened her eyes it did not vanish. Kathryn should have been happy, and, indeed, she was content of sorts. But something was missing, and that something left an emptiness within.

Since that night when he had held her so tenderly in Lady Maybury's drawing room, Lord Ravensmede had been careful to avoid being alone in her company. He was a model of polite consideration. Indeed, Kathryn would have gone as far as to describe him as the very epitome of gentlemanly behaviour. But there was a new distance between them, as if he had withdrawn from her. It was the right thing to do, the proper thing to do. Especially for a viscount to his grandmother's companion. So why did she feel a constant ache in her heart?

We shared a few kisses, he had said, *nothing more*. Was that all it had been to him? Didn't he too feel that the world had turned upside down? Clearly not. But then he was a rake. Everyone said it. A man who was used to taking what he wanted from women and moving on. Just the thought of that was enough to turn her blood cold. She should be glad that he was behaving with the utmost respectability. And then she remembered the dark smoulder in his eyes when he kissed her, the gentle insistence of his lips upon her, and the tenderness of his touch…and she knew that against all rhyme and reason, what she really wanted from Nicholas Maybury was not in the least respectable.

'Oh, it has been an age since I was in Brighthelmstone. Such a good idea of m'grandson. To escape from the infernal smells of the town will be a blessed relief. I only hope the sea air is not too cold. At my time of life one cannot be too careful about catching a chill.' Lady Maybury drew her shawl around her as if she already felt the gusting of the bracing sea air, instead of the stifling heat of London. 'Are you finished, my dear?'

Kathryn was engaged in yet another portrait of the dowager, this time a sketch in charcoal and chalk. She bobbed her head to the side, considered the work carefully, and, after a stroke here and a smudge there pronounced that she was.

The briefest of knocks sounded upon the library door behind Kathryn and then footsteps sounded upon the wooden floor.

'Nick!' Lady Maybury's face illuminated as her grandson came forward to sweep a kiss to her hand.

'Grandmama,' and, turning to the slight figure half-hidden behind the large wooden drawing board, 'Kathryn.' He made to politely lift her hand, but she pulled it back before he could reach it.

A smile lit her face as she set the board down on the floor and wiped her palms on the dark stained apron covering her dress. 'I'm afraid that I'm quite covered in charcoal.' As if to prove her point, she extended one hand and several slender fingers dangled temptingly in front of his face. It was clear to see that Kathryn was telling the truth, for her hands were indeed ingrained with a thick black dust.

'I've seen cleaner hands on a climbing boy,' he laughed and, before she could protest, plucked the dirty little hand into his and kissed it. 'Let it not be said that Lord Ravensmede could be deterred from his manners by a few grains of charcoal.'

'Your manners are quite impeccable, sir. I don't think you need worry that such an accusation could be levelled at you.'

Her grin was less than ladylike, but it smote Ravensmede's heart just the same. Several wild curls had escaped her chignon and were draping artlessly around her throat, the grey eyes were clear and bright, and her skin, beneath the daubs and smudges of black dust, was of a creamy luminescence. There had been too many days of polite formality, too much self-restraint. Before her appeal the Viscount's will-power began to crumble. In a moment of weakness he touched one thumb tenderly to her cheek, and then, suddenly conscious of exactly what he was doing and his grandmother's perceptive gaze, said lazily, 'More charcoal.' A large snow-white handkerchief was produced and he quickly wiped at the offending mark. 'That's better.'

Lady Maybury's mouth shaped as if to catch flies, before she snapped it shut. Kathryn said nothing, but could not prevent the flood of colour that warmed her face. The skin that he had touched with such betraying intimacy burned as if branded.

Ravensmede replaced his handkerchief, unwittingly transferring a small quantity of charcoal dust on to the pocket of his coat in the process, which he then proceeded to inadvertently share between his chin, and his cheek. He wandered away from the faded green scrutiny and feigned an interest in a shelf of books. At the other side of the room he could hear the scrape of Kathryn's chair and the movement of the drawing board upon a table.

'If you would be so kind as to excuse me, my lady, I'll attempt to remove the worst of this mess. A good shake of my apron outside and a hand scrub should suffice. And then I'll wipe the floor in here just in case—'

Lord Ravensmede glanced up from the book he had just extracted from the shelf. 'My grandmother employs servants to do that, Kathryn; you are not one of them. Is that not so, Grandmama?'

Lady Maybury looked from her grandson to her companion. 'Yes, of course.' Then, waving her hand in a dismissive gesture, 'Mary won't mind a little extra dust to sweep in the morning. Don't bother the gel just now.'

'Very well. I'll go and clean myself up. I'll come back later when you have need of me.' Kathryn started towards the door.

'Kathryn.' The single word stopped her progress immediately. 'We plan to discuss our forthcoming trip to Brighthelmstone. I would have you here.'

Kathryn had frozen halfway across the library floor. When she turned around, Ravensmede could see the deepening colour of her cheeks.

'Fustian, Nick! Must you always be so high-handed? I don't know where you get it from. Let the gel tidy herself. We can wait for her return before we start upon the plans for Bright-helmstone.' Lady Maybury peered down the length of her short little nose at her grandson. 'Besides, I can't think of a thing until I've had some Madeira and cake. Be so kind as to ring the bell.' She turned to Kathryn, who was still standing rather awkwardly in the middle of the room, unsure of what to do. 'Well, what are you waiting for, gel? Off you go.'

The door closed quietly behind the slight figure and the dowager and her grandson were left alone. Neither spoke. The slow steady tick of the grandfather clock marked the passing of the seconds.

And then the faded green gaze fixed its focus upon Ravensmede. 'Are you going to tell me what's going on?'

'Nothing's going on.'

'You seem uncommonly concerned with m'companion.'

A dark eyebrow arched. 'I'm merely being polite.'

'Polite, my foot!' sniffed the old lady. 'You fancy the gel!'

Ravensmede laughed. 'You've been reading too many romantic novels, Grandmama.'

'Don't try to flannel me, boy, I'm not so old that I can't see when a young man's ardour is up, even if he is m'own grandson.'

'Whatever I feel about her is irrelevant—she's your companion, nothing more.' The broad shoulders shrugged.

'I'm trusting you to remember that, Nick,' she said and fixed a belligerent eye on her grandson. 'I've put in a lot of effort to establish Kathryn in the eyes of the *ton*. Got plenty of respectable young gentlemen interested in her. Won't be long before one of them makes her an offer.' She sniffed. 'But one whiff of scandal and that will soon change. I don't want you ruining things for Kathryn, or for myself.'

'I've no intention of ruining anything,' Ravensmede drawled. 'As I said before, my interest in Kathryn is purely philanthropic.'

'Then you should take care to remember that until I can find her a husband,' said the dowager.

The thought of Kathryn marrying one of Lady Maybury's young gentlemen did not please the Viscount. His grandmother clearly had the bit between her teeth and was progressing her plan at an all-out gallop. It was time that Ravensmede slowed things down a little. 'Have a care you don't tire both Kathryn and yourself out, Grandmama. I've never seen you attend so many balls and routs as in these last weeks. When was the last time you spent the evening in?'

'Stuff and nonsense!' declared the old lady with a considerable degree of venom. 'I'm not in m'coffin yet. Why should I want to be sitting in here all evening when I can be out enjoying m'self. And as for Kathryn, the gel's as strong as a horse. We'll go out every night if we damn well choose!'

'You already do. But just think, if you make yourself ill what will happen to your plans for Kathryn then? She cannot go out alone.' That made Lady Maybury think; he could tell by the closed look that settled upon her face.

'It won't be for much longer,' she said. 'I'm very close to success. Indeed, if it were not for our holiday to Brighthelmstone I would be expectant of her receiving a proposal in the next few weeks.'

Ravensmede secretly blessed the forthcoming trip.

'Mr Roodley and Mr Williams have both been attentive and I have been warned that Lord Stanfield and Lord Raith have expressed more than a passing interest in my gel. She'll make a good marriage before this Season is out, or I'll eat my hat.'

'Roodley and Williams would bore Kathryn silly within a week of their company. As for Stanfield…the man's one of the biggest lechers in the country. And Raith's old enough to be her father. Are any of them really a suitable match?' Ravensmede flashed a lazy smile. 'I don't think so, and when you think about it, neither will you.'

Her ladyship cast him a determined look. 'I fully intend to catch her a husband, Nick.'

Ravensmede examined his nails, as if the matter was of such little importance to him. 'I fail to see the rush. Couldn't you just take her home to the dower house at Landon Park with you, and bring her back again next year?'

'The gel's four and twenty! Another year shan't be in her favour. I have Kathryn's best interest at heart when I say that I mean to secure her an offer as soon as possible.'

A wave of disgruntlement swept over the Viscount. The thought of Kathryn Marchant married to another man goaded him to irritation. For all that he'd sworn he would not touch her, for all his good intention for friendship and nothing more, he knew them both for the lies they were. Nothing and everything had changed from that moment at Lady Finlay's ball. He wanted her as much as ever—no, if he was honest, even more so. Then, her standing had been little better than a servant, and now, thanks to his grandmother, she was an eligible young lady on the marriage mart. Eligible to everyone other than himself. He gave a dry little smile and continued to sip his Madeira.

Chapter Ten

With a tap at the door, Kathryn walked into the room. She had changed into one of her new afternoon dresses and tidied the wayward curls of her hair. Her hands were still pink from being scrubbed with soap, but all signs of the black dust had disappeared. As soon as she entered she had the feeling that she had just interrupted an awkward silence. 'I hope the Madeira has refreshed you, my lady.'

'Never more so,' replied her ladyship. 'I was tempted by a second slice, but managed to resist.' She passed Kathryn a slice of sponge cake on a delicate painted plate. 'Help yourself to Madeira, my dear.'

Kathryn did as she was bid and then settled herself down in the empty chair next to the table. It was positioned beside the dowager and directly opposite the Viscount, so that she could not help but obtain an excellent view of his face. He certainly looked to be pondering something. She wondered what his grandmother had said to make him so. Perhaps more strikingly, though, he had a faint thumbprint of charcoal dust upon his chin and a smaller but similar mark upon his cheek. Her eyes flitted towards Lady Maybury who seemed to have observed nothing out of the ordinary with her grandson's appearance. Kathryn's fingers twisted at the skirt of her dress. What to do?

She couldn't let Nicholas leave the house like that—he'd be a laughing stock within five minutes. But to point it out when his grandmother had failed to do so was to risk embarrassing both the dowager and her grandson. Perhaps Lady Maybury would notice before that time came. True to form, the old lady was suffering none of her grandson's silence.

'Well?' A haughty brow rose. 'We are waiting for your discussions on Brighthelmstone.'

Ravensmede seemed to shake the contemplative mood from him, and started to recount the arrangements he had made. 'My servants shall travel down tomorrow to ensure that all is ready for us upon our arrival. We will leave on Thursday, take a leisurely journey with one overnight stop on the way down, thus arriving on Friday. No point in making the journey uncomfortable for you.'

His grandmother made what sounded to be a snort of disgust at this point, but he ignored it and continued undeterred.

'Once in Brighthelmstone I've rented us a house for the month. I'm told it has a good position with unimpeded views of the sea. It's on The Steyne and not far from the Prince's Pavilion.'

'Sea views?' Kathryn could not keep the excitement from her voice.

Ravensmede's mouth curved into a smile, the first since she had returned to the room. 'They're reported to be most scenic.'

Her face lit with delight. 'I can scarcely wait.'

'You will be taking your sketching and painting materials?' He was looking at her with an unfathomable expression.

She smiled. 'Of course! Nothing could stop me. You know how I treasure them.'

His voice was a low husky murmur. 'Yes.'

Their eyes met across the table and held.

'Kathryn, my dear,' Lady Maybury interrupted. 'Do you think I have enough shawls? I should so hate to catch a chill. They do say that the sea air is rather invigorating.'

'Perhaps we could check this afternoon, and if you're not

happy we could go shopping for some more.' Kathryn ignored the flush that had leapt to her cheeks and turned her attentions to the dowager. 'Are you warm enough just now? If not, I could fetch you a thicker shawl.'

'I'm pleasantly warm and cosy,' said the old lady.

A subtle knock at the door and a footman appeared. 'Lady Kiddleby to see you, my lady. I've taken the liberty of showing her to the drawing room.'

The dowager's brow wrinkled. 'Frances here? I wasn't expecting her.' She turned to Kathryn. 'This is not like her at all. I had best go to her at once. Come along, gel.'

The footman gave one delicate cough. 'Lady Kiddleby asked that she see you alone, my lady.' He coughed again. 'Her ladyship appears somewhat distressed.'

'Dear, oh, dear,' muttered Lady Maybury. 'No doubt Harriet has been upsetting her mama again. This shouldn't take long.' She drew her grandson a warning stare. 'I trust Nick shall not make a cake of himself in my absence.' She stared at him a moment longer before rising from her chair and leaving.

A silence.

The moss green eyes were on Kathryn.

'Would you like another glass of Madeira? Some more cake, perhaps?' She lifted the bottle.

'No, thank you.'

Another silence.

'I wondered if I might speak bluntly to you, Kathryn.'

The butterflies flocked within her stomach. She netted them down. 'Certainly, Nicholas.' She saw the tug of his mouth at her use of his name.

He touched a finger to his lips in a gesture that she had not seen him use before. 'I'm concerned about my grandmother's health. You see how much she hates to admit the slightest weakness and would never tell either of us if she were unwell. All these late nights are taking their toll on her. For all her protestations, she's in her eighty-first year with a weak heart, and I fear her hectic lifestyle of late is in danger of making her ill.'

The hand of guilt laid heavy on Kathryn's heart. 'I'm afraid you may be right. I know Lady Maybury enjoys going out but…I cannot help but wonder that she has my interest too much at heart.' She nibbled again at her lip and wondered if she should be confessing such things to her employer's grandson. 'At many events she's insistent that I accept every invitation to dance. Indeed, it's now quite common that I spend the evening upon the dance floor and not in Lady Maybury's company at all.' The grey eyes raised to Lord Ravensmede's with mounting anxiety. 'I have tried to refuse, but she won't have it. I feel that her fatigue is, in part, my fault.'

'My grandmother is forthright in her opinions, and once set upon a course is not easy to dissuade. You must not blame yourself, Kathryn, and, indeed, I did not mean that you should do so.' He reached across the table and gently took one of her hands.

'Is there anything I can do to remedy the situation?' She thought she saw something akin to guilt flicker within his gaze and then it was gone.

'The only way my grandmother would be persuaded to stay in on an evening is if you, yourself, Kathryn, were to feel unwell.' It was there again, an uneasiness in his eyes.

She understood very well what he was asking her to do. 'Yes. The odd headache…' Her words trailed off and she stared at the charcoal dust smears upon his face. She touched a finger to those imprinted places, but upon her own face instead of his. She couldn't let him leave like that, and the dowager's poor eyesight was unlikely to notice. Her finger tapped very deliberately against her chin. 'You have a little…' The finger tapped harder.

Ravensmede's focus sharpened like that of a starving man shown food.

'And here.' The finger had moved to poke a spot on her own cheek.

'Kathryn?'

'A little charcoal, just here.'

The dark head shook its denial. 'No, your face is quite clean,' he said slowly, and licked his lips. The green eyes had darkened considerably and were watching the movement of her fingers intently.

'But yours is not,' she replied with a wry smile. 'Somehow you must have touched the charcoal dust. And it's now on your face.'

A large hand rubbed ineffectually at a clean patch of skin on his cheek.

'No, it's over some more.'

'Here?' The fingers slid too far to the left.

'No, back a bit.'

Again he missed the mark.

'Move forward a little.' Before she could contemplate and dismiss the impulse she half-rose from her seat, reached across the table and moved her hand to touch his face. Then slowly and with what amounted to a caress she rubbed her thumb against the square edge of his chin until no trace of the charcoal remained. From there her fingers slid to his cheek. She could feel the roughness of the first hint of stubble on his skin, was so close she could smell the bergamot of his scent. With calm deliberation she kept her gaze fixed on the charcoal-shadowed skin. A sharp intake of breath that was not her own made her forget her purpose. His eyes were a deep, dark green, and in them was a hunger that made her forget where she was and just what she was doing.

'Kathryn,' he whispered. And contained in that single word was both pain and longing.

She could not speak, could not move, just stared into those dark mesmerising eyes.

His face crept towards hers until she could feel the warm stir of his breath tickle her cheek.

Chest compressed. Heart expanded. A sudden rush of blood to her head.

The smouldering gaze dropped to her lips.

Yes, she wanted to shout, but no words came. His skin brushed hers. Cheek touched cheek.

'Kathryn,' he said, and it was almost a growl. The need in his voice mirrored that in her soul.

Yes! Please. Did she have to plead? Their noses nestled. Lips so close to imagine their feeling. Touching…almost. Nothing existed outside that single moment. Locked in time, alone. 'Nick!' her voice was hoarse, barely recognisable as her own. She wanted *him,* nothing more.

His mouth claimed hers in sweeping possession.

A sigh and her lips opened in sweet surrender. Wanting all he would give, giving all he would take. Urgent. Demanding. The table jabbed at the front of her thighs as he pulled her into his arms. She felt the press of his hands upon her back, warm, caressing.

Footsteps sounded outside the door. A knock.

Before she could even register what was happening, Kathryn found herself quite suddenly pushed back into her chair.

By the time the footman entered the library it was to find a rather startled-looking Miss Marchant sitting bolt upright in her chair, and Lord Ravensmede lounging rather too comfortably back in his. 'Beggin' your pardon, my lord, but her ladyship has asked if Miss Marchant would be so kind as to come through to the drawing room.'

Kathryn's legs were shaking so badly that, had she not already been seated, she was positive she would have fallen. Her heart pounded in her chest. 'Yes, certainly. I'll come right away.'

Lord Ravensmede gave a nod of his head, and the footman retreated. 'Kathryn.'

A blush coloured her cheeks and her fingers plucked at the material of her skirt. She did not raise her eyes. 'I…I must go.'

Ravensmede stood. 'Until Thursday then,' he said politely and bowed.

Only when she reached the door did Kathryn look back to meet his eyes and see that they held a most determined promise.

* * *

Mrs Marchant was busy at her needlework within the drawing room of the house in Green Street when the visitor arrived. No sooner had the maid whispered the lady's name in Mrs Marchant's ear than the lady herself appeared in the doorway.

'My dear Mrs Marchant!' gushed the female voice. 'Anna. I came as quickly as I could. I'm only just returned to town as of last night.'

Anna Marchant's eyes widened momentarily and then she regained her composure. 'Amanda.' She smiled. 'Please do come in and take a seat.'

'Thank you. You're too kind,' said the widow and arranged herself on a stylish gold-covered armchair.

'How was your visit to the country?' enquired Mrs Marchant with politeness. 'I trust your sister is well again.'

'I cannot stand the country,' confided Mrs White. 'The roads are in a terrible state—it takes an age to travel anywhere; there is a dearth of anything remotely interesting; and the assemblies are positively backward in terms of their fashion and the clodhoppers who patronise them. All in all a thoroughly boring experience.' She did not mention that her ennui more specifically arose from the absence of rich young men to fawn over her beauty. The country squires and parsons in the vicinity were all elderly or grossly overweight or both. Amanda White had found much time to brood upon matters in Amersham…and subsequently the insult Ravensmede had dealt her in that little room at Lady Finlay's ball had become honed and magnified in her memory.

'And your sister?' prompted Mrs Marchant again.

'Delivered of a bawling son,' came the curt reply. 'But that is not of what I came to speak. My letter—'

'Came as a great shock to me. I must confess I'd no notion of that which you suggested. My niece has always behaved with the utmost decorum,' Anna lied.

'My dear Mrs Marchant, it pained me to have to be the bearer of such bad tidings; I felt I had little choice but to warn you of the danger.' The afternoon dress was cut to display Amanda White's curvaceous figure to perfection, its deep ruby-red coloration complementing the lush darkness of the widow's elegantly coiffured hair, and the smooth sheen of her pale skin. 'Not long after I'd sent the letter I learned that Lady Maybury has indeed taken the girl up as her companion.'

The accusation hung in the air between them.

'Your letter arrived too late,' said Mrs Marchant crisply. 'Kathryn had already accepted the position, and, whatever you might suggest, Lady Maybury has a lineage without blemish. The Mayburys are not without influence.'

The widow pouted her pretty lips while a sly expression slid across her eyes. 'Indeed, but it makes no difference to what Miss Marchant is about.'

Much as Anna Marchant disliked her niece, she realised full well the consequences of any slur on Kathryn's name. The Marchant family would not escape unscathed. And so it was with this in mind that Mrs Marchant prepared to defend her niece's reputation. 'Kathryn is a young lady of impeccable values. I must insist that your fears as to any improper behaviour are quite mistaken, Mrs White.'

'I saw her with my own eyes, Mrs Marchant, behaving little better than a common whore.'

A sharp inhalation of breath. 'Mrs White! I must protest!'

Both women rose to their feet.

'I thought to tell you only because I know you hold a fine and respectable standing within society; I did not think that you would want your own reputation jeopardised by your niece's scandalous behaviour.' She shrugged her beautiful shoulders. 'But if you are not interested in your niece's dealings…' Mrs White made to leave.

'There is no need for such haste,' said Anna Marchant with feigned sweetness, as she moved swiftly to block her visitor's exit path. 'Your concern for my family is admirable.' It was a lie, of course. The pretty young widow had no concern for anyone other than herself. Anna knew quite clearly that Amanda White's world revolved singularly around herself and her pretty looks. Not that it made one blind bit of difference to Mrs Marchant. But it did make her wonder as to exactly what game Amanda White was playing with her letter and her visit. A smile moved across Mrs Marchant's lips. 'Sit down again, Amanda,' she said. 'I would hear what you have to say.' Before the afternoon was out Anna Marchant intended to have the answer to all of her questions in full.

Mrs White swished her skirts and sat back down before the words were even out of her hostess's mouth. It was clear that she had had no intention of going anywhere. Mrs Marchant's smile stretched wider. 'If you can bring yourself to tell me all, my dear,' she added.

'Dearest Anna,' simpered Amanda White. 'I shall strive to do what is right.' And proceeded to describe the scene she had interrupted between Lord Ravensmede and Kathryn Marchant at Lady Finlay's ball. Every possible embellishment was added, so that not only was Ravensmede kissing Miss Marchant with a passion (which of course was true) but he was kneading upon her breast and clutching her against him in the most carnal of manners. Mrs White gave no mention as to her own assignation with the Viscount and said she had wandered into the room quite mistakenly.

'Why did you not tell me at the ball?' asked Mrs Marchant, barely able to hide the rise in her temper.

'Lord Cadmount whisked me away just as I was about to. And then Ravensmede practically bullied me into going to the country. I was fearful to do anything other than he bid.'

Anna Marchant had trouble in believing that. The young widow was a woman more used to controlling men than being controlled by them.

'You must have enough influence over the girl to bring her to her senses before it is too late. Surely you can make her give up this ridiculous affair and move back here with you? You're her aunt; she'll listen to you. Forbid the girl any further contact with Ravensmede. It's not too late to salvage some semblance of her reputation. The fact that she's his mistress has not yet become common knowledge. There's still time, if you act now.'

So that was what Amanda White wanted: Ravensmede...for herself. Mrs Marchant said somewhat coldly, 'Kathryn has always been disobedient and stubborn. There is, and always has been, little love lost between us.'

'Oh, dear,' said Amanda without the slightest emotion. 'It would be such a shame if anyone else was to learn of your niece's indiscretion. Especially now that she's Lady Maybury's companion, it wouldn't take much for the whole town to deduce that she's Ravensmede's mistress. Poor Lottie, I suppose she shall not remain unaffected by Kathryn's shame.' Mrs White looked slyly at the older woman. 'And you had such hopes of a good match for your daughter.'

Anna Marchant's teeth clamped tightly shut. Her top lip curled with unconcealed contempt. She knew very well exactly what Mrs White was about: blackmail. Get Kathryn back to Green Street, or the widow would spread her gossip. And the thought that Kathryn had allowed her to be put into such a position fuelled the hatred already burning in Mrs Marchant's breast. 'Very well, Amanda. Since you place me in an untenable position, I will do as you ask, but I must warn you it may take some little time.'

'The longer you take, dear Anna, the more chance there is that I may inadvertently let something slip. I can be such a forgetful puss at times.'

'Then the sooner I start, the better,' said Mrs Marchant.

Mrs White took the hint and soon only Anna Marchant sat alone in the drawing room, cursing the widow, trying to think how she could lure Kathryn back from Lady Maybury, planning just what she would do to her when she did.

The journey to Brighthelmstone was pleasantly uneventful. Although the road appeared to be dreadfully busy with carriages and carts, Ravensmede assured both Kathryn and his grandmother that the level of traffic was quite normal. The journey, having been designed not to tire Lady Maybury, was conducted at a leisurely pace. Ravensmede's large closed carriage was well sprung and he had ensured not only a mountain of travelling rugs for his grandmother's warmth but also a basket of provisions including the most refreshing lemonade Kathryn had ever tasted. Lady Maybury alternated between watching the passing countryside, chatting and napping, the latter activity occupying the greater part of her time, thus leaving her companion to fill her own time as best she could. As far as Kathryn was concerned, it was fortuitous indeed that Lord Ravensmede had chosen to ride alongside the carriage rather than travel within its small interior.

Following what had flared between them in the library, being alone in the Viscount's presence was not something with which Kathryn trusted herself. And she had only herself to blame. It was true that he had kissed her, but she was well aware that her own actions had precipitated such a response. Touching her fingers to his face…whatever would he think of her? Kathryn gritted her teeth at the all-too-obvious answer to that question. How could she repay the dowager's kindness by encouraging her grandson, for there was no doubt that that was what her behaviour amounted to? It was behaviour in keeping with Aunt Anna and Cousin Lottie's taunts. Tired fingers kneaded against her forehead, and she sighed. The passing hedges and fields became nothing more than a distant green blur.

'Kathryn? What's wrong? Are you sickening for something?' Lady Maybury's voice interrupted her reverie.

She glanced up in surprise, thinking the dowager to have still been sleeping. 'No, my lady. I have the slightest of headaches, nothing more.'

'Then we must make a stop at the next inn and allow you to wander and stretch your legs. Perhaps it's being cooped up in here that has brought it on.'

'Oh, no, please do not.' The thought of having to face Lord Ravensmede again so soon was not something with which she felt comfortable.

The faded green eyes narrowed in their focus and lingered upon Kathryn's anxiety-ridden countenance.

Blood scalded her cheeks under the scrutiny. 'I mean… please don't stop for me. I would rather press on with our journey.' She plucked at the material of her skirts. 'I'm so looking forward to arriving in Brighthelmstone,' she said with false brightness.

Lady Maybury remained singularly unconvinced. 'Indeed,' she said drily. 'We've first to spend the night at Horley Common.' Not once had that relentless green gaze faltered.

'Yes.' Kathryn did not know what else to say. The old lady was looking at her as if she could see her innermost thoughts. If that were indeed true, Miss Kathryn Marchant would find herself turned off without so much as a reference, and then what would she do? Half of London's bachelors would not be dangling after her then!

Neither woman spoke and the dowager had not shifted her attention.

'Has Nick done something to upset you?' The question fired out of the silence.

Kathryn's heart missed a beat. She forced herself to stay calm. 'No. Lord Ravensmede has been nothing but polite at all times.' She chewed at her lip. 'What makes you think so?'

'An idle thought, nothing more.' The dowager tucked the blanket higher, so that it almost reached her chin. 'Still, if you say there's nothing in it…' One white brow raised in enquiry.

'Nothing at all, my lady,' Kathryn speedily replied. 'I…I'm very happy as your companion, Lady Maybury. Indeed, I've never been happier, and hope that nothing will jeopardise my position.'

The snow white curls nodded once. 'And I'm very happy to have you as my friend.' Lady Maybury relaxed back against the seat and snuggled beneath her blankets. Within a matter of minutes her eyelids had shuttered and the gentle wheeze of her snoring filled the carriage.

That night in the King's Arms coaching inn and for the entirety of the journey Ravensmede behaved with the utmost propriety. Nothing in his speech or manner betrayed in the slightest that he felt anything other than the appropriate civil concern for his grandmother's companion. Neither did he suggest at any time that he should share the carriage, even when he was subjected to a rather heavy rain shower. So by the time the small party arrived in Brighthelmstone to take up residence within their rented accommodation, Kathryn had managed to rein her wayward emotions under sensible control once more.

The episode in Lady Maybury's library was banished far from her thoughts, and she was able to relax, firm in the belief that she would not tempt fate by allowing herself to spend any time alone in the company of Lord Ravensmede. The trip to the seaside resort was the chance of a lifetime and she did not mean to spoil the opportunity with silly worrying. She would not shatter Lady Maybury's trust in her. And as for her own trust in herself, she knew that now, where Nicholas was concerned, that was something on which she could not completely depend. If she did not want to ruin her new life as the dowager's companion, then Kathryn had better have a care...especially here in Brighthelmstone.

'I trust you find the house to your liking?' Ravensmede sipped at his coffee the next morning and watched the ladies across the breakfast table.

Lady Maybury's ferocity of attack on a pile of carved ham mellowed slightly. 'I'm never anything but completely uncomfortable when anywhere but Landon Park, but...' she sniffed '...I suppose I will suffer to endure it.'

'Kathryn?' the Viscount asked politely.

'It's beautiful both inside and out, and our every comfort has been thought of. You spoke truthfully when you promised splendid views of the sea. I haven't seen the like for many a year.' She paused and looked at Lady Maybury. 'It was very kind of you to arrange that my bedchamber was seaward facing. It's a dream come true to wake up each morning and look out at the shoreline.'

'If you would be so good as to pass me that dish of eggs, Nick.' The dowager pointed to the silver heated dish on the serving table and waited expectantly. 'Had nothing to do with me, dear gel. It was Nicholas that took care of all the arrangements. Gave us the scenic chambers, took the one at the back for himself.' She helped herself to four large poached eggs and several slices of toast.

'Grandmama…' Ravensmede laughed '…I swear your appetite is expanding for a lady of such sylph-like proportions.' He did not want to discuss the sleeping arrangements, or the fact that there was a scant four feet of landing separating his chamber from Kathryn Marchant's. Such thoughts were dangerous and that was a direction in which he could not afford to wander if he did not want to disgrace them all. And anyway, hadn't his grandmother determined that Kathryn would be spoken for before the Season was out?

The old lady laughed. 'You'll not get round me with such flattery. Quite how these young females survive on fresh air and lemonade I shall never know. It's not natural. In my day we ate all we could and our stays did the rest. Wretchedly uncomfortable to wear, but a dashed necessity. Didn't pick at our food like sparrows then, I can tell you.'

'I fear you're embarrassing Kathryn.'

'Stuff and nonsense,' replied his grandparent. 'Kathryn's not some milk-and-water miss just out of the school room. Likes a good serving of food herself. No silly nonsense with this gel, is there, Kathryn?'

'I hope not, my lady.' Kathryn smiled at the dowager.

Ravensmede remembered Kathryn Marchant's collarbone outlined starkly against her bruised skin, and her gaunt cheeks when they had first brought her back to Ravensmede House. She had no need to starve herself; Anna Marchant had only been too willing to undertake that task, and her cruel treatment had had nothing to do with slender figures, of that he was quite sure. He brushed such disconcerting thoughts aside and forced his mind to more pleasant avenues. 'I've already paid my respects to the Master of Ceremonies and we are therefore welcome to attend all balls at both sets of assembly rooms. Those in the Castle Inn are on Mondays, and on Wednesdays the balls are in the Old Ship. Card parties are on Wednesdays and Fridays, and on Sundays there is a promenade and a public tea. There's also the theatre in North Street, and of course Brighthelmstone races. If you let me know which you prefer, I will make the necessary arrangements.'

His grandmother nodded. 'Yes, indeed. I think a shopping trip is first in order so that we may familiarise ourselves with the town. A walk along the pier, and a closer inspection of that monstrosity that the Prince Regent calls his Marine Pavilion would also be of benefit. I've a notion to view the new stables and riding house built in the Indian style. Thereafter, we'll see which cards arrive.'

'And the theatre?' her grandson prompted.

'I shall think about it,' the old lady pronounced.

And so their holiday by the sea began very well.

The Castle Inn suite of rooms were superbly adorned in the classical decorative style of Robert Adam. It seemed that the fine weather had brought out all of the town's polite society, for the rooms were filled despite the departure of many local families to London for the Season. It was a cosier affair than the grand London balls with less of those who called the tune that the rest of the *ton* were happy to dance to, nevertheless

Kathryn hovered close to Lady Maybury. Despite arriving as a stranger, Lady Maybury soon discovered some old friends, through which numerous introductions were made. Thus, as had become usual, Kathryn's dance card was soon filled.

Nicholas chatted politely to the rather awestruck young men who flocked to meet the notorious Viscount of Ravensmede. He danced with the flustered giggling débutantes and made great efforts to ensure that his grandmother's friends' grand-daughters were not ignored. And through it all he watched every move that Kathryn made, knew every man with whom she danced. It was a self-inflicted torture to which he readily ascribed. Indeed, he had taken great pains to ensure that they were not too much in each other's company that evening. He had brought her here to enjoy herself, to let her paint the sea scenes so dear to her heart. Damn it, but the girl deserved some little joy in her life. The last thing he intended doing was allowing some uncontrollable instinct spoil the whole set-up they had worked so hard to achieve. He'd damn well not risk both her and his grandmother's happiness, not to satisfy some selfish whim of his own. But he had to admit that his growing obsession with his grandparent's companion had never felt less like a whim.

'Your servant, Miss Linton.' Ravensmede delivered the sim-pering girl back to her mother, bowed and beat a hasty retreat. The chit's mama's eyes were positively ogling with speculation. 'Grandmama, you seem to be in high spirits.' Lady Maybury was fanning herself with an exuberance he'd rarely seen.

'Of course I am,' she crowed loudly. 'I haven't seen Jane Ballantyne for an age. All her granddaughters are married and she has twelve great-grandchildren to boot. I have only a paltry four to compete. What is that compared to twelve? And you show no signs of obliging me.'

'You begin to sound like my father, ma'am,' the Viscount replied. 'It is a favourite topic of his and has been for the last few years.'

The volume of her voice dropped somewhat. 'You cannot blame him, Nick, he does not wish all that he has worked for over the years to pass to the dreadful Herbert.'

Ravensmede thought of the selfish connivance of his cousin Herbert and was forced to agree. 'Neither do I. But I'll marry when I'm good and ready, and not because m'father wills it.'

The dowager raised one cynical white eyebrow. Any reply she might have made was forgotten when Lady Farrow, who was seated some six feet away, gestured at Lady Maybury and shouted, 'Is not the next dance the waltz?'

'I do believe you're correct, Hetty,' came the reply.

Just the mention of the dance was enough to have Ravensmede glancing around for Kathryn. He soon spotted her across the room partnering some fair-faced youth for a country dance. The final bars sounded and soon the couple were making their way back towards Lady Maybury. No sooner had Kathryn been deposited beside the dowager than a most insistent Mr Silverton appeared to spirit her away.

Her eyes turned to Ravensmede in question. The action was not lost on Lady Maybury, who seemed to positively encourage the young gentleman's interest in her companion. 'Off you go, Kathryn,' she said before turning to her grandson. 'He seems a delightful young man.'

Ravensmede could do nothing while the woman who had come to haunt his dreams was led out on to the floor and allowed herself to be held quite properly and at the allotted distance by Mr Silverton. She had never danced the waltz with anyone other than himself. And now she was in Silverton's arms. It was for the best, her best, or so he told himself.

'Nicholas,' Lady Maybury said, 'I have a need to seek the retiring room. Be so kind as to watch over Kathryn until I return. Do *not* let the gel come after me, and make sure that she dances with the next gentleman whose name is upon her card.' Lady Maybury drew him a fierce look and then disappeared across the room, leaving only the lingering scent of her lavender perfume.

Ravensmede was forced to watch Kathryn and Mr Silverton dance the whole of the waltz, before that young man returned her to him.

She smiled and a spasm of desire shot through him. 'Is all well with Lady Maybury? She is not here.'

'A visit to the retiring room. She'll rejoin us shortly.'

'Then I should assist her.' Without waiting for an answer she made to move towards the door.

His hand caught her arm. 'No, Kathryn. She has asked that you stay here. You know how she hates a fuss.' With a gentle tug he pulled her back towards him.

'Yes, you're right. I should wait for her to return.'

Sliding his fingers down to meet her hand, Ravensmede delivered a gentle squeeze. 'Did you enjoy your waltz?' The cream silk of her glove was smooth beneath his fingers. His hand encompassed hers possessively.

She glanced up at him, the hint of a blush just beginning on her cheeks, then peered around to check that no one was close enough to see what was happening between them.

'Nicholas,' she whispered, 'I—'

Whatever she intended to say was cut short by the return of Mr Silverton, followed closely by the dowager.

'Sir…' Lady Maybury tapped her fan in fake reproof against the young man's sleeve. 'I do believe you've already stood up with my companion not so very long ago.'

Mr Silverton smiled a charming smile. 'That is indeed the case, but with a lady as beautiful as Miss Marchant all others pale to insignificance. I would be honoured if she would stand up with me again.'

Lady Maybury smiled in her most agreeable manner. 'Well, as it's you,' she said indulgently.

'You have my undying gratitude, my lady,' replied Mr Silverton and moved to face Kathryn. 'I do believe you've granted me the honour of agreeing to partner me for the quadrille.'

'I…I…' Mr Silverton's name was indeed written upon her

card against the quadrille. Kathryn shot a glance at Ravensmede. The expression on his face was unreadable.

'Don't dally, Kathryn,' urged the dowager.

She had little option but to place her hand in Mr Silverton's and allow him to lead her out on to the dance floor…again. 'Thank you, sir.' Kathryn's impression of Harry Silverton from their waltz was confirmed during the quadrille. He seemed a pleasant enough young man, even if he was prone to a rather overly dramatic turn of speech. It was all Kathryn could do to keep a straight face when he waxed lyrical on the extent of her beauty. She was sure that he lavished the gush of compliments upon every woman with whom he danced. She endured a eulogy on her fine eyes, but when he started to compare her hair to a cascade of rich autumn leaves she laughed and begged him to tell her something of the town of Brighthelmstone instead. When at last the dance was over Mr Silverton returned her, breathless and smiling, to Lady Maybury.

Mr Silverton bowed low to both the dowager and Kathryn. 'May I have your permission to call upon your companion, my lady?'

'*I* have no objection to your calling, sir,' said Lady Maybury, 'but you have yet to ask Miss Marchant her opinion on the matter.'

Three faces turned to Kathryn, who was looking both surprised and a little awkward.

'I…I think perhaps…'

'Thank you, my dear Miss Marchant, I shall count the minutes until we meet again,' said Mr Silverton.

It was then that Kathryn noticed the dangerous darkening of Lord Ravensmede's eyes and the glacial stare that he drew Mr Silverton. Harry Silverton saw it too. With a speedily executed bow the young gentleman was gone, leaving Kathryn to face Lord Ravensmede.

Chapter Eleven

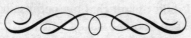

The journey home was rather stilted. Lady Maybury seemed drained of energy, and lay back against the seat with her eyes closed. Lord Ravensmede's ill humour did not recede. His manner was distant and he seemed loath to converse. Only Kathryn, balanced precariously next to the dowager, was desperate for a chance to clear the air. She looked hopefully at Lady Maybury, but the old lady's eyes remained shut. And the Viscount had not yet glanced in her direction. Silence reined supreme. She cleared her throat in an attempt to draw his attention.

The dark profile did not turn from the window.

'Nicholas,' she said softly.

He looked at her then, but she could scarcely see his face through the darkness.

Where to begin? 'I…' It was clear that Mr Silverton's presumption had annoyed him. She was being paid as Lady Maybury's companion, not to court a suitor while the dowager sat alone and fatigued. She tried again. 'I did not encourage Mr Silverton's attentions.'

'Didn't you?' He sounded quite unlike his usual self. There was a distance in his voice, so different from anything that she had heard previously. And exactly what did he seem to be implying?

A gentle snoring sounded from the dowager.

'Of course not! We came to Brighthelmstone for the sake of Lady Maybury's health.'

Ravensmede did not correct her misconception.

'I'm her companion. It isn't right that gentlemen should call upon me here.'

'Then why did you not refuse your permission?'

She faltered. Why indeed? Shock, disbelief. She had fully intended to do so, but Mr Silverton had been too quick in his assumption. 'I didn't grant him my permission,' she insisted with a degree of stubbornness.

'I don't think that Mr Silverton understood that to be the case.'

He was taunting her! How could he change from the caring, passionate man she knew to the arrogant goading creature that sat before her now? Kathryn felt her temper rising. Not only had she to somehow contrive to get rid of Mr Silverton, but she now also had to explain herself to the Viscount. 'Then he's a fool,' she snapped.

'Kathryn, you must have given him some sign to encourage his attentions. Believe me, I know when a gentleman is intent upon securing a lady's interest. And you appeared to be enjoying his company immensely,' he said meaningfully.

'Indeed I did, sir, but with the exception of being civil, I assure you that I have given that gentleman no indication that his attentions would be welcomed.'

Silence.

She could just imagine the arrogant arch of his eyebrow at her reply, and it irked her, as did his ridiculous assumptions. 'How could you even think that I would encourage him?'

'How indeed?' Irony laid heavy on his words.

An exasperated sigh escaped her. 'You're being unfair, my lord.'

'And you're being completely fair, are you, Kathryn?'

A blush rose in her cheeks. 'I know my place,' she said quietly. 'Be assured that I have no intention of receiving Mr Silverton as a visitor.'

'Really? I think that my grandmother may have other ideas on that matter.'

'Then think what you will, Lord Ravensmede,' she said, 'your mind is clearly made up, far be it for me to try to change it.'

'Kathryn Marchant, you are the most infuriating of women.'

'Of that I'm most heartily glad!' she retorted.

The volume of Ravensmede's voice increased. 'God help me, you drive me to—'

'Nicholas?' Lady Maybury's croaked through the darkness.

'Grandmama,' the Viscount replied with forced serenity. It sounded as if his teeth had ground together.

'Why are you shouting at my companion?'

'I beg your pardon, ma'am.'

Kathryn felt the old lady raise herself up on the seat. 'It isn't my pardon you should be begging,' she said quietly. 'I haven't a mind to find myself a new companion quite yet.'

A slowing of the carriage. The crunch of footsteps outside the door.

'Forgive me, Miss Marchant.' Following his stiff words, the Viscount opened the door and jumped down from the carriage before the steps were in place. He waited until they were fitted before helping first Lady Maybury, and then her companion, out into the gloomily lit darkness. The glow of the street lanterns was not sufficient to safely light their path up the stone stairs to the front door of the house so Ravensmede took both ladies' arms in his to act as guide.

Kathryn felt the tension in the muscles beneath her fingers, though her touch was light as a dragonfly and knew the man beside her was angry beyond belief. What she did not yet fully understand was why. Assuredly she should not have answered him back, but his accusations were silly in the extreme. As if she would encourage any man's attentions! Her mind flitted back to the passions she had shared with Nicholas. Oh, heavens! She began to have an appreciation of his point. If she could respond so readily to him, then he had every reason to believe her a woman of loose moral fibre. Oh Lord, what a web she had spun herself into!

Mr Silverton waited only as long as the following afternoon to call upon Miss Marchant, and had the audacity to bring with him quite the most ridiculously outsized arrangement of flowers that had been seen for a long time.

'Ah, Mr Silverton.' Lady Maybury sounded encouraging.

'Lady Maybury, a pleasure to see you again, ma'am. Is Miss Marchant—'

The dowager smiled a smile of sweetness and light. 'She is almost ready. A young lady's *toilette* must never be rushed, sir. The result would be too disastrous to imagine.'

'Indeed, my lady. I didn't mean to hurry Miss Marchant. I'm happy to wait upon her leisure.'

'I'm sure you are.' The smile deepened.

Mr Silverton smoothed his neckcloth. 'Is Lord Ravensmede at home?'

'Why, did you wish for a word?' her ladyship asked.

'No, no,' Mr Silverton said with undue haste. 'I was merely being polite. No need to disturb his lordship.'

'Quite,' agreed Lady Maybury, and then confided, 'It is for the best. He can be prone to a cantankerous disposition when disturbed by unannounced visitors, although I'm sure that would not be the case with you.'

Mr Silverton appeared to have developed an irritation in his throat. He coughed loudly and shifted from one foot to the other.

The awkwardness of the moment was alleviated by the appearance of a maid who quietly informed her ladyship that Miss Marchant was feeling unwell and would not be able to receive Mr Silverton.

The dowager's brows knitted. 'What nonsense is this?' She peered at the unfortunate maid. 'She was as fit as a fiddle not half an hour ago. Tell Kathryn to come down this instant or I shall be forced to fetch her myself.'

Five minutes later Kathryn entered the drawing room to have the huge mass of flowers suddenly thrust upon her.

'How kind, Mr Silverton. Perhaps if I were to just put them down here until—'

The dowager interrupted. 'Of course, my dear. The maid shall see to them. What's all this about feeling unwell? Perhaps it would be better to postpone the drive until another day.'

A look of hope entered Kathryn's eyes.

'I shall ring for tea and cakes and leave you young things together.' She smiled again at Harry Silverton. 'And ensure that Lord Ravensmede knows not to disturb you.'

The young man coughed and glanced around nervously as if he thought Lord Ravensmede was about to appear..

With Nicholas's accusations still clear in Kathryn's mind, Lady Maybury's suggestion seemed unbearable. 'Thank you, my lady, but there's no need. I feel quite recovered.'

'Well, if you're sure,' said the dowager somewhat doubtfully.

'Absolutely positive,' said Kathryn.

'In that case, be sure to have a lovely time on your drive.'

Kathryn eyed Lady Maybury anxiously. 'I shall not be long, my lady.'

'Take as long as you like, dear gel.' The old lady's hand waved imperiously. 'No need to hurry back.'

Mr Silverton's nerves vanished in an instant. He beamed his gratitude at the dowager.

'Off you go, then,' said Lady Maybury from the other side of the drawing room.

The couple walked across the brightly decorated rug.

Just as Mr Silverton's hand touched to the door handle the elderly voice boomed, 'You will bring m'gel back safely, won't you, sir? I fear that I have a tendency to overprotectiveness when it comes to m'companion.'

The young man flushed an unbecoming shade of puce, and announced dramatically, 'Indeed, my lady. I shall guard Miss Marchant with my very life.'

Lord Ravensmede did not enter the drawing room until he had heard the bang of the front door. He strolled nonchalantly to the window and watched while Harry Silverton drove Kathryn away in a hideously over-decorated green-and-black painted phaeton.

'I fancy Mr Silverton is quite taken with her. If I'm not mistaken, an offer will be forthcoming before we leave for London,' said his grandmother from behind his shoulder.

'Unfortunately it appears that you may be right,' he said.

One white brow lifted. 'He's heir to a small fortune, I'll have you know.'

'True, though it's earned through trade.' Ravensmede's eyes were still trained upon the diminishing dot in the distance.

'What's wrong with that? He may not be an aristocrat, but he's wealthy enough to provide her with a life of comfort.'

'Harry Silverton's father owns a string of coffee houses across the country, as well as a sugar plantation in the West Indies. The family are from Bristol and are here only for a short break.' Despite the bright sunshine in the room a sombre aura clung to Lord Ravensmede. 'I've a notion that Kathryn wouldn't approve of the Silverton family's interest in slavery.'

His grandmother frowned. 'Good gad!'

'It's also rumoured that they have significant investments in the overseas slave trade, although if Lansdowne's bill goes through that won't last for much longer.'

'Blast! That means Silverton won't do at all. Can't have her marrying into a family like that.' She eyed him sharply. 'I suppose I should be thankful that you've been thorough in your enquiries, m'boy.' The old lady wandered across the room and sat herself neatly upon the sofa. 'Is there any gentleman either here or in London that you would recommend as a husband for Kathryn?'

'No.' The Viscount's reply was definite.

Lady Maybury's eyes were focused upon her grandson's face. 'But if you were to give the matter some thought, perhaps you would be able to come up with a suitable candidate.'

'I do not think so, ma'am.' Ravensmede's lips compressed into a hard line.

'It's unlike you to admit defeat with such ease,' his grand-mother goaded.

An ache was growing in the Viscount's chest. 'I'm not normally asked to play matchmaker.'

She sighed. 'Does not Kathryn deserve this little happiness? A husband, children of her own?'

'She's happy as she is. There's no need for her to marry.'

'You wish her to stay a companion to me for ever? And what when I'm dead, what will happen to her then? Servant to another old woman? Or, worse still, mistress to some man? Believe me, Nick, when I tell you that it's no life for a girl like Kathryn. I know this is not easy for you, boy, but it's for the best. So, please, just give the matter a little thought.'

He sighed, running his fingers through his hair. 'Very well. I promise I'll give serious consideration to what you've asked.'

The faded green eyes held his with a sudden intensity. 'I sincerely hope so, Nick. I've come to care very much for Kathryn, and as an unmarried lady she's vulnerable...in all sorts of ways. I cannot rest easy until I know the gel is settled in marriage.'

'Grandmama, you've saved Kathryn from a life of misery, and offered her a home with you. What harm can come to her? She's safer now than she's ever been.'

'Is she?' she asked in a strange tone of voice. The old hand moved to clasp his, and she sighed. 'Life is never that simple.'

At last Kathryn saw the blessed emergence of the familiar front door. If the phaeton had not stood so high upon the ground, she would have leapt down herself without having to suffer the indignity of Harry Silverton's hands around her waist.

'Mr Silverton!' she chided when he seemed reluctant to relinquish his hold upon her person.

The gentleman's corn-gold hair glistened in the sunlight. His deep blue eyes held admiration. 'You're such a vision of loveliness as to make a gentleman forget himself.' But he released her nevertheless. 'Will you be attending Lady Richardson's ball tonight?'

'I don't know what Lady Maybury has planned. As her companion it's my duty to accompany her in whatever her wishes might be.' She struggled to remove her fingers from Mr Silverton's clasp and attempted to hurry up the stone stairs to the front door.

Mr Silverton matched her every step. 'May I be so bold as to suggest that I call again tomorrow? We could perhaps drive further out into the country.'

'No. I don't think so, sir.' Kathryn wished to spare Mr Silverton's pride; had seen the effects of her cousin's cruel words too many times not to feel some sympathy for the young man standing so hopefully beside her. 'I believe Lady Maybury has already made arrangements for tomorrow.'

'Then I shall call the following day.' They were standing beside the heavy wooden door.

Kathryn made to press the bell, but not before his fingers plucked her hand to his lips. 'No.' She surreptitiously tried to pull away, while taking care not to create a scene. 'I thank you for your kind invitation, and indeed I've enjoyed our pleasant drive today, but I cannot accompany you again any day this week.' Mr Silverton's grip was surprisingly strong.

'Why ever not, Miss Marchant?' The blue eyes held hers with rather too much intimacy than that with which she was comfortable. 'Without you I shall fade as a flower deprived of sunlight.' He pulled her closer.

'Because she'll be accompanying me,' a deep voice drawled as the door swung open.

Kathryn had never been so relieved to see Nicholas. 'Lord

Ravensmede,' she uttered faintly, unsure of how much of the conversation he had overheard.

In one swift movement he had plucked Kathryn to stand behind him in the hall, leaving the golden-haired young man upon the step. 'I bid you good day, Mr Silverton.'

Harry Silverton lingered only a moment longer, then, with a low and elaborate flourish of a bow, he was gone.

The door slammed in his wake.

'Oh, Nicholas, thank you!' Relief swamped Kathryn. She wrapped her arms around the Viscount's body in a bear hug and pressed her cheek to the broad expanse of his chest. 'I thought he would never go. He was so very insistent and I didn't wish to be unkind.' Freshly laundered linen, and soap, and bergamot tickled her nose. She relaxed against him. 'I can only pray that he doesn't mean to make me an offer!'

His hands touched to her back in a gentle gesture.

Her eyes were still closed, her body nestled into his.

Ravensmede stood very still. It seemed that even his breath had halted.

There was the sudden rattle of china and a footman carrying a heavily loaded tea tray appeared at the top of the staircase leading up from the kitchen.

Kathryn's eyes sprung open, her body tensed for flight.

The footman did not look in the entwined couple's direction once. He merely trotted across the hallway, tapped politely on the library door, and waited until a loud female voice bid him enter.

'Thank you, Toby,' said Lady Maybury. 'I thought I heard a carriage outside. If Miss Marchant has returned, have her come through for tea.'

By the time the footman had reappeared to impart this message Kathryn was standing innocently by Lord Ravensmede's side. Meekly she turned towards the library door.

'Ah, Nick as well,' said the dowager and raised an eyebrow. 'You had best come in before the tea grows cold.' Only once three cups of steaming tea had been delivered in the finest of saucers did Lady Maybury continue between sips, 'Why, my dear gel, has Mr Silverton overtaxed you?' The faded green eyes peered sharply at her companion's face. 'I do declare that your colour appears unnaturally high and you seem to be a little out of breath.' The dowager appealed to her grandson. 'Am I not right, Nick? Pray do examine Kathryn's visage.'

It was true that Kathryn had indeed appeared a trifle flushed upon entering the library, her embarrassment due to the realisation that she had just thrown her arms around Lord Ravensmede and her wholly inappropriate action had been witnessed by a footman, who was now guaranteed to delight in informing the whole of Ravensmede's staff of what he had seen. Beneath the dowager's blatant scrutiny the faint rose bloom intensified to a scarlet flame of colour. Had the dowager heard her words to Nicholas? Did she have any inclination of exactly what her companion had just done? Kathryn forced herself to meet the faded green gaze. There was nothing of shock or anger there, only a little sadness.

'Grandmama, I'm sure Kathryn's cheeks are flushed only from the fresh air.'

'Perhaps,' said Lady Maybury. 'I'm all-agog to hear the news regarding her drive with Mr Silverton. Pray tell all, my dear.'

Kathryn took a fortifying gulp of tea. 'We travelled along the coastal road in order to enjoy the views. They are indeed quite spectacular.'

'How far along the coastal road?' said the Viscount.

'To a place named Rottingdean, whereupon we turned around and came back by the same route.'

Lady Maybury frowned. 'I had thought Mr Silverton's drive to be limited to the park.'

Kathryn did not want to cause trouble for the young man, but neither was she prepared to risk giving the impression that she liked him. 'He thought that I would prefer the scenery along the coast.'

'And did you agree to this change of plan?' asked the dowager.

A pause. 'No.'

'Shall Mr Silverton be calling again?' A white eyebrow raised in enquiry.

Ravensmede's gaze slid to Kathryn's.

'No,' she said, 'I hope that he will not.'

The old lady sighed. 'It is just as well.'

Kathryn's eyes widened. 'I thought—'

Lady Maybury leaned towards Kathryn. 'I had high hopes for you and him. He seemed such a personable young man too. But that was before I learned where his family's money comes from.' She sniffed disapprovingly. 'Slavery,' she said succinctly.

Kathryn's cup clanked back down against her saucer, and said quietly, 'Then it is for the best that he will not be coming back.'

A silence followed.

'You said the views along the coastal road are impressive,' said Ravensmede.

'Yes, they're wonderfully scenic.'

'In that case, why don't we travel the route ourselves? We could spend the day on the beach, Cook can pack us a basket of food…and you can take your paintbox. Would tomorrow suit?'

Kathryn's eyes lit up, and she smiled before waiting politely for Lady Maybury to deliver her verdict.

'It's certainly a splendid suggestion, but Kathryn and I will go alone. We've been monopolising you, Nicholas, and we should allow you to pursue your own interests for the day. You will grow bored with constantly escorting an old lady and her companion.' She faced her grandson. 'Is that not a better idea?'

Ravensmede returned his grandmother's look in full. Something unspoken flashed between them, something slightly dangerous that conflicted with the smiles upon their faces.

Sensing the underlying current, Kathryn felt unease prickle between her shoulder blades.

'A veritable genius.' replied Lord Ravensmede. 'Your concern for my welfare is admirable, Grandmama, but I am of a mind to enjoy the beach tomorrow too. You would not forbid my interest?'

Faded green eyes locked with bright green, in a battle of wills, and then the dowager inclined her head. 'Not this time,' she said.

Anna Marchant left the maid to close the gaping front door and hurried towards the parlour at the back of the house, pulling off her gloves and straw bonnet as she went. Just as she expected, she found her husband sitting comfortably spread out upon the sofa reading a newspaper. He glanced up briefly as she shut the door firmly behind her, then resumed his examination of the article in which he appeared engrossed.

'You're back sooner than I expected,' said Mr Marchant without taking his eyes from the paper. 'Did the visit not go well?'

'The place is empty. A serving girl told me that Lady Maybury and her companion have gone to Brighthelmstone.'

'So?' Mr Marchant could barely keep the boredom from his voice.

'With Lord Ravensmede.'

'So?' he said again.

'Oh, for heaven's sake!' snapped Mrs Marchant. 'Must I spell it out for you?'

Henry Marchant slowly lowered the newspaper from before his face and looked at his wife with an irritated expression. 'Madam, I'm sure that is what you intend, so hurry up and be done with it.'

'Lord Ravensmede has hired a house for them all in Brighthelmstone. He is living in the same premises as Kathryn!'

'And his grandmother,' pointed out Mr Marchant.

'It's all of a sham, I tell you. He's taken Kathryn as his mistress under the guise of her being Lady Maybury's companion.'

'Nonsense! Eleanor Maybury wouldn't risk her reputation with such a thing. And I doubt that even Ravensmede would drag his own grandmother into such a scheme. Besides, if Ravensmede wanted Kathryn as his mistress, he would have taken her by now, and as blatantly as he did all of the others.'

'Whatever you say, the rumours are already starting, Henry!'

she snapped. 'Think what they'll do to Lottie. Where will her chances of a good match be then, when her cousin is publicly denounced as a slut?'

'I'm sure you're mistaken, Anna.'

'There's very much more danger than you realise.' She thought fleetingly of Amanda White's threat. 'I'm sure that a trip to Brighthelmstone is in order.'

Mr Marchant's eyes rolled up into his head. 'I think you're overreacting, my dear.'

'You'll see who is overreacting when your niece is the talk of the town and your own daughter's chance of marriage is ruined because of it. Hasn't Kathryn lived as part of this family for the past three years? Do you think I've learned nothing of the girl's nature? I've said all along that she is a sly and wanton miss, and now I'm proved right. Will you let her destroy Lottie's chance? Are you content to let your brother's daughter ruin everything for your own flesh and blood? Mark my words, if one hint of this comes out before Lottie has made a match, then she'll be on the shelf for ever!' Mrs Marchant pressed a small lace handkerchief to her eye and gave a sniff.

With the weary resignation of a man who knew full well that his wife would give him no peace, Henry Marchant closed the newspaper, folded it in two and sat it upon his lap. 'What do you wish to do?'

'Fetch Kathryn back from Brighthelmstone. Have her live here with us.'

'You dislike the girl immensely, Anna. Why do you want her back here?'

'If she's under our control, then we can limit any danger she might do. She's safer where we can keep an eye on her.' She made no mention of Mrs White and what the widow had insinuated. 'For the sake of my daughter's future I'm prepared to suffer Kathryn's presence.'

Mr Marchant digested his wife's words. 'Kathryn is now

four and twenty. We cannot force her to come back with us. The last time I saw her she seemed determined in her role as Lady Maybury's companion. And I don't suppose she can have too fond a remembrance of this house.'

'Why should she should think of us with anything less than gratitude? Had it not been for this family Kathryn would have ended up in the gutter. However, I concede that she always was a selfish, addle-brained miss, and perhaps that has biased her memory,' said Mrs Marchant. 'That's why I have a plan.' For the first time since entering the parlour she smiled. 'You need not worry, Henry. A little family trip to partake of the sea air and Kathryn will return with us to Green Street.' Her smile broadened. 'And then she'll be sorry, very sorry indeed, for all the trouble that she's caused.'

The day was fine and warm with a pleasant sea breeze. They had encamped on the beach at a secluded spot not far removed from the town of Worthing, and enjoyed a tasty lunch from the depths of the hamper. Lady Maybury, having battled valiantly against the combined effects of fatigue, heat and a full stomach, lost the struggle and finally succumbed to sleep beneath the shade of her parasol.

Kathryn sat on a small stool placed upon the sand. The wooden drawing board was balanced on her thighs, and she stared completely entranced by the vast expanse of sea that stretched before her.

'Do you mind if I watch while you paint?' Ravensmede sat down beside the slight figure that seemed dwarfed beneath the drawing board. He could not see her face beneath that hideous monstrosity of a bonnet. Momentarily he wondered why she was still insistently wearing the mud-brown hat; he knew full well that his grandmother had been doggedly trying to add to her companion's wardrobe piece by piece.

She turned then and looked up. 'I don't mind, but I warn you that it shall not take long before you grow deeply and thoroughly bored.' The small pink mouth curved in a tantalising smile. An errant curl fluttered across her cheek.

She was teasing him! One dark eyebrow arched wryly. 'Perhaps. I've never watched an artist at work. This will be a new experience for me.'

'Then I hope it will be an enjoyable one.' She fixed her paper into place and, after checking the sharpness of her pencil, began to sketch.

'I thought you meant to paint the scene.'

'Yes. But I'll draw it out first in pencil so that I may rectify any mistakes I make. Only when I'm happy that I have the proportions correct will I begin to paint.' All the while her hand moved swiftly, lightly against the paper, her gaze flickering constantly between the sea and the white patch of paper.

Ravensmede's gaze flitted from the view to the paper to the fine bones of the woman's face. She was clearly intent on her task, her gaze never wandering once. There was an openness about her expression, as if she had let fall the careful guard of politeness. This was the Kathryn that he'd witnessed humming behind the tree in St James's Park, who had gazed unseeing at a blackened fireplace in her aunt's house, and smiled when he touched his fingers to her cheek. It was the first time she'd knowingly let him witness her escape, to wherever it was she went when she looked so faraway. He could see the same look in her eye, as if she were present in body only and her mind somewhere else altogether. 'You must have had a very good drawing master!' The faint marks on the paper were beginning to take shape.

A laugh that caught on the wind was carried out to sea. 'I taught myself! Anyone can sketch if they practise enough, and believe me I practised!' Still her gaze moved methodically between the lapping water and the white page. Her eyes were narrowed and her face crinkled against the sun. 'Have you tried your hand at it?'

'As a child, never since. My mother said it was quite the most ugly picture she had ever seen. My talents lie elsewhere, or so I am told.'

Only then did she pause, and look up into his face. 'I'm sure your mother was wrong.' Her voice was quietly serious and her eyes filled with compassion. Then she smiled and the moment was gone, as quickly as it had arrived. She resumed her scrutiny of the view. 'I can teach you if you like.' It was uttered lightly, as if it were of no importance. The pencil scraped against the page, making a vertical line here, a horizontal line there.

A blossoming of warmth erupted in Ravensmede's chest. He longed to lay his arm across her shoulders, to hold her to him. 'I would like that very much, Kathryn.' Since his dismissal of Harry Silverton he had felt extraordinarily happy. Knowing that she held the golden-haired youth in no regard and had sought his own protection gladdened his heart. It was better than winning a fortune night after night at the gaming tables. Better than an evening spent drinking with Caddie and the boys. And infinitely better than any time he had spent in any other woman's company. He watched while she covered the entirety of the page, excepting the odd patch here and there, in pale blue paint.

As if in answer to his unasked question she offered an explanation. 'It's a wash to unify the background. It should also stop the glare from the sun bouncing up from the page and dazzling my eyes. Conditions today are perfect and it should dry in no time. Would you like some paper and a pencil?'

'For now I'm content to watch you. But I'll hold you to your promise of sketching lessons.' The sun beat down with a relentless strength. 'Kathryn, would you mind if I removed my coat?'

She did not look up from mixing her paints. 'Of course not. You must be melting beneath all that wool.'

He peeled off the offending item and laid it down by his side. The cooling breeze fluttered through the fine lawn sleeves of his shirt, and he toyed with the idea of removing his waistcoat and neckcloth, but thought better of it. Daubs of paint were stroked on to the paper by her delicate hand. Just watching fascinated Ravensmede. The slow repetitive action, sometimes tentative, sometimes bold, held his attention so that he could not look away. A sheet of calm sparkling water, clear and deep, of quite the brightest turquoise coloration he had seen. Small waves lapping against the shoreline in the distance. Cloudless blue sky stretching out far to the horizon. She captured it all. And the air of peace that surrounded them. Nothing sounded except the soft rush of the sea on the sand and the cry of the gulls circling high overhead. It was enough just to sit by her, to be in her presence. No need for words. Soft sugary sand warm to the touch, all yellow and fawn, golden and white. On and on she painted, as if driven by the magic of the place to set down a record of what had existed for this one afternoon. And all the while Ravensmede sat by her side.

One last brush stroke and she cocked her head to the side. 'Mmm.' It was a gentle sigh of consideration. With deliberate care she set the board aside and clambered to her feet. 'Pins and needles in my legs.' She wiggled and stamped her feet to ease the numbness and, unmindful of her bonnet ribbons that were flapping around her chin, pressed the weighty drawing board into the Viscount's hands. 'Please can you hold this, just so that I may check that I haven't missed anything. I always find looking at it from a distance helps.' Without waiting for an answer she moved several paces away and turned to inspect the painting.

Ravensmede looked down at the drawing board. 'You've captured the view splendidly.'

'And you, sir, are looking at it upside down!' came the cheeky reply.

His mouth curved to a grin. 'I beg your pardon, but I can imagine how it will appear the right way round.'

'Here, let me hold it while you look.' Just as the board was halfway between them, a gust of wind lifted Kathryn's bonnet clear off her head. She loosed her grip on the board in order to catch it back, just as Ravensmede engaged in the same idea. The drawing board dropped to the sand, bouncing on its side before fortuitously landing on its back. The ties that had secured the painting dislodged in the fall, and, before either Kathryn or Nicholas could move, the sheets of paper were sent flapping and tumbling along the sand. 'Oh, no! That's all the paper I have left!' The bonnet forgotten, Kathryn scrabbled along the shore, and successfully captured the newly finished coastal painting along with four blank sheets. Another five blew ever further away.

Nicholas caught her elbow. 'You have the painting. Let the others go. We can buy some more.'

'No, paper is costly and all my money is accounted for. Please!'

With that look in her eyes and the long wind-blown hair tumbling in a cascade of curls reaching far past her shoulders, Ravensmede would have granted her anything. In a gallant gesture he chased the sheets until at last he had caught each and every one. His exertions had taken him quite some distance along the beach, but when he looked round the slight figure was running towards him. Her hair glinted a reddish golden brown in the sunlight and was billowing wantonly in every direction. A pair of finely shaped ankles and calves were visible each time the wind gusted around her skirts; moreover, the material was blown to cling revealingly against the shape of her thighs and hips. As he collected the papers into a tidy pile, one caught his eye. It was not blank, but contained a pencil drawing executed in great detail. The breath caught in Ravensmede's throat. His eyes raked the picture a moment longer before he bent low to the ground as if catching the papers up to him, and slipped the folded sheet into the secret inner pocket of his waistcoat.

'Nicholas!'

He glanced up and, with a smile upon his face, closed the empty distance between them.

She was breathless and pink-cheeked, wild and wind blown, and, judging from the look on her face, enormously glad to see him. Lord, but he could have taken her in his arms and tumbled her upon the sand there and then.

'Did you catch them?'

'Every last one!' He passed the sheets into her hands, and, unable to help himself, caught her to him and pressed a kiss to the top of her head.

She did not chastise him. Rather one small hand reached up and squeezed his arm. 'Thank you,' she said simply.

'Come on, we had best get you back to Grandmama. She won't be pleased when she wakens.'

The silver-grey eyes were lit with pearly hues. 'Perhaps she's still sleeping and has not seen this débâcle.'

The Viscount laughed and gently swept his thumb across the bridge of her nose. 'I was thinking more about your freckles. Although, personally, I find them quite delightful.' He cast her a wicked grin, held her hand in his and walked back towards his grandmother.

It was fortunate that the Viscount spotted Kathryn's hairpins in the sand close by her abandoned drawing board, and more fortunate still that the young lady had managed to secure her hair in some vestige of a respectable style before the dowager awakened. Alas, the mud-brown bonnet had been swept far out to sea, a mishap that caused his lordship much rejoicing. Indeed, Lord Ravensmede could not remember a more enjoyable day.

Chapter Twelve

It was one quiet afternoon close to the end of the second week of their holiday when Lady Maybury announced her intention to host a ball at her grandson's townhouse.

Lady Maybury continued, 'I haven't told him of m'idea yet, and I don't want you letting the cat out of the bag, young lady. It wouldn't do to pester him with all the details when we can sort those out ourselves.'

'But shouldn't we check that he's happy to host such an event first, before making any arrangements?'

'He shall not be hosting the ball. That's my job,' said the dowager. 'I assure you, Kathryn, he'll be most pleased with my efforts.'

'But…'

Lady Maybury raised an eyebrow. 'Are you questioning that I know what's best for m'own grandson?'

Kathryn saw all the warning signs and sought to pacify her employer. 'No, not at all, my lady. If you've made up your mind then—'

'My mind is made up,' came the adamant reply. 'Fetch paper, pen and ink and let us begin the list of guests. There's no time like the present. And remember that it's to remain, for the minute, a secret from Nicholas.'

'Of course.' Kathryn did as she was bid and waited.

Soon the dowager was reeling off names. 'Lord and Lady Radford, Lord and Lady Finlay, Lady Hadstone, Mrs Lee, Lady Farrow, oh, and Mr and Mrs Barchester and the Misses Barchester, but most certainly not Mr and Mrs Palmer—they're too vulgar for words.' She sighed and waited for Kathryn's neat script to stop. And then the pause stretched a little longer. 'Naturally, when Nicholas is married, his wife will take over such duties. This is likely to be the last time I'm able to play hostess for him.'

Something cold wrapped itself around Kathryn's chest and squeezed. She was quite unable to move. 'I didn't realise that the Viscount was betrothed.'

'Oh, he isn't…well, not officially.' Lady Maybury leaned forward and lowered her voice. 'If I'm not mistaken, that is something that will be remedied before the Season is at a close.' She gave a sage nod of the head. 'M'son Charles—that is, Nick's father, Earl Maybury—thinks it's more than time that the boy settled down and all that, what with him having sown more than his fair share of wild oats.' She sniffed.

A tinge of colour touched Kathryn's cheeks.

'Still, the least said about that side of things the better. Afraid us Mayburys are not a patient lot, as you may already have guessed, m'dear. But even Nick can't hold out much longer against his father. Charles's practically got it all arranged. Gel is from a decent family, good breeding and money too. Can't think why Nick's being so confoundedly stubborn. Wretched boy's got to marry at some time or other.'

Kathryn reeled as if she had suffered a hard blow to the stomach. 'May I…' she steeled herself to ask the question, knowing full well that she should not, that it was none of her business '…enquire as to the name of the lady that the Earl has in mind?'

The old lady's eyes washed bright with compassion. 'Her name is Miss Francesca Paton, my dear, and m'son is very determined that Nick weds her.' She stretched out one small hand and touched it consolingly to Kathryn's.

The slow terrible thud of Kathryn's heart intensified, and deep within the pit of her stomach she tasted the sourness of nausea. It seemed that there was a ligature tightening around her throat.

'There may very well be two weddings. Your future should be assured.' The dowager smiled a small smile. 'I'm very determined to catch *you* a good match.'

'No, my lady, that really isn't necessary,' Kathryn gasped. 'I'm here as your companion, not to find myself a husband.' In her distress she gripped the pen as if she would snap it clean in two, her fingers inadvertently touching too close to the nib and bleeding a large stain of ink across her skin.

'Tush! Don't you want a husband and children of your own?'

'I...' She struggled to keep the emotion from her voice. 'I'm happy here with you.'

'As I'm happy to have you here. But you deserve a life of your own, gel, and I mean to see that you get it.'

The flow of black letters upon the page began to swim. A strange dizziness was rolling up towards her head. She forced herself to inhale deeply, slowly, willed herself not to yield to it. Determination clamped her teeth hard together, and made her lips stiff and immobile. Surely she wasn't about to faint? She *never* fainted. Not Kathryn Marchant. But the dizzy sensation was expanding and black spots danced in the periphery of her vision. Sweat prickled down the length of her spine, and her chest felt so tight that she feared she could not draw the air into her lungs. She shut her eyelids tightly, struggling to regain control, doggedly telling herself that she would not faint, not here, not now, not when the dowager might guess the terrible truth.

'Kathryn.' The old lady's voice was soft. 'It is for the best.'

One breath, and then another. In. And out. She forced herself to breathe deeply, fingers clinging for dear life to the arms of the chair. Slowly the darkness receded, but the terrible weight upon her chest lay there still. It took great strength to hide the utter bleakness that swept over her. The constriction in her chest had spread to her throat, wherein the lump was making it difficult to swallow. But for that terrible tightness all else had grown numb, a creeping lack of sensation that rendered her trapped upon the Sheraton-style mahogany armchair. She could no longer see the words that she had penned so carefully on the neatly cut sheet, could scarcely see the paper itself. 'Please excuse me, Lady Maybury. I fear I'm feeling a little unwell,' she managed to say through lips that could barely move.

'Unwell?' A concerned old hand touched to Kathryn's arm. 'You have gone very pale of a sudden. And you feel so hot! Mary shall take you straight to bed. You'll feel better after a little rest.'

'I'll finish the guest list in the morning,' murmured Kathryn and laid the paper and pen down carefully beside the inkstand on the desk.

'Stop worrying over that. There's time enough yet.' The old lady tried to look severe and for the first time failed miserably. 'I'll brook no disobedience, gel, so off to bed with you.'

'Yes, thank you, my lady.' Kathryn kept her eyes averted, frightened of losing her last vestige of control, and quietly hurried from the room.

Not one last drop of blood lingered in Kathryn's face as she climbed the central staircase towards her bedchamber. Slowly, methodically her fingers worked at the material of her skirt, pleating and smoothing and pleating again, in a rhythmic repetitive motion. And all the while, with each and every step that she took, she wondered why it had taken such a revelation for her to realise the truth. Not that Lord Ravensmede was to marry. As Earl Maybury's heir that had always been a foregone conclusion. Perhaps she hadn't expected it to happen quite so soon, but that in itself was not the issue. No, the truth was much worse than that. In her time as Lady Maybury's companion, she, plain, penniless Kathryn Marchant, had fallen head over heels in love with Nicholas Maybury; a man who was not only an aristocrat and enormously wealthy, but also a rake. And the reward for such a foolish action could only be a broken heart.

At the same time as Kathryn was treading silently up the central staircase by the maid's side, Lord Ravensmede was sitting at the small reading table by the window of his bedchamber in the house in Brighthelmstone. Before him, spread out upon the fine polished cherry-wood, was a drawing. The piece had been executed with a fine attention to detail, capturing every nuance of the sitter, conveying, by the skilled use of line and shade, that person's precise character. Ravensmede studied every last pencil mark upon the paper until at last he sat back in the chair and smiled. It was clear that the artist viewed the model in a positive light. Indeed, he would go as far as to say that there was a distinct tenderness in the rendition. And that thought was a most appealing one to the Viscount, given that the artist was none other than Kathryn, and the model—himself.

Quite when she had secretly sketched his likeness he did not know. These last weeks in Brighthelmstone had only confirmed what he knew of her: that she was kind and compassionate and imbued with a freedom of imagination that allowed her to escape the mundane, the tiresome, and the downright painful. Whether it be through the pictures set down on paper or those that she wove in her head, Kathryn was an artist, and a passionate one at that.

Beneath that meek and mild exterior was hidden an ardour. But Ravensmede had seen beneath the mask, had known the essence of her from the very first night of their meeting, when he'd mistaken her for Amanda White—as if there could ever be any comparison. Mrs White was little better than a courtesan who sold herself to the highest bidder. Kathryn was quite simply the most amazing woman he had ever met. Lust or desire did not go near to explaining the compulsion he felt for her. Just to be near her, to make her laugh, to ensure her safety, to hear her voice, and hold her within his arms… It was far and beyond anything he had ever known.

A door opened across the corridor. Female voices. One that sounded to be the maid, the other so quiet as to almost hide its owner. But he didn't need to hear Kathryn's voice to know that she was near. Awareness coursed through him. And he knew that he could no longer ignore his need to see her, to watch her smile, to touch his lips to hers. Sandwiching the portrait between two blank sheets of paper, he hid it carefully under some papers within a drawer. Then, waiting until he heard the maid make her way along to the servants' stairwell, he quietly opened his door and stepped across the corridor to Kathryn's bedchamber.

Kathryn heard the light knock at her door and scrambled up from the top of the bed. 'I'm just coming,' she said in a small controlled voice. Before she had taken one step further Lord Ravensmede entered, closing the door noiselessly behind him. Her hand clasped at the bedside table. She could not speak.

'Kathryn!' Shock widened his eyes. Whatever he had been expecting to see, it wasn't the state of distress that he now witnessed. He reached her in two strides and without the slightest hesitation pulled her into his arms. Scanning her face, he took in the unnaturally white cheeks, and the haunted look in her eyes. 'What in Hades has happened?' His clasp was gentle, his hands firm and reassuring against her back.

'Nothing at all. You need not concern yourself with me, sir.' She struggled to release herself from his embrace, but he was having none of it. 'Lord Ravensmede, I must insist that you unhand me. It isn't fitting that you should be here in my bed-chamber or that you have your arms around me.' The pale lips pressed tight together as she spoke the words quietly and with as much dignity as she could muster.

'What is this nonsense, Kathryn? I had thought us to have reached an understanding. Are we not friends?'

She lowered her face that he might not see her pain. 'Indeed we are, sir.'

'Then I would know what this about.'

'I made a mistake,' she said, choosing her words carefully. 'We cannot go on as before…even if we are friends. I'm your grandmother's companion…and I'm happy with that.'

'Have you had word from your aunt?' he asked suspiciously.

'No, of course not. She doesn't even know that I'm here.'

'Is it my grandmother?'

'No.' The word was determined and defiant.

'Then why are you so upset?'

'I'm not.'

A single dark eyebrow arched. With slow deliberation he traced a thumb down her cheek.

'No!' She twisted her face away. Then with more control, 'Please do not.'

His hand stilled in mid-air, then dropped back down to her arm. 'Tell me what's wrong, Kathryn.'

'I cannot.'

Silence hummed.

'Kathryn,' he said.

Slowly, unable to help herself, she looked round at him.

His eyes were dark as the depths of a forest where the light does not reach.

Beneath his gaze Kathryn felt her resolve waver. For there she could see concern and kindness…and something else, something for which hope flared…then died when rational thought intruded. It seemed that she had to drag the breath into her lungs, force it back out again. Pain burst anew into a thousand piercing shards at just how much she had come to love this man.

She could not tell him. Had to preserve some scrap of pride. He desired her…as she desired him, to touch, to kiss, to hold. He liked her, of that she was sure. But he did not love her; could not love her as she loved him. Before the summer was out he would be betrothed to another woman…married even. And

Kathryn would be alone once more. She chided herself for the fool that she was. Even as he looked at her as if he could see into her very soul, she lowered her eyes.

She wanted to scream and cry and beat her hands upon the breadth of his chest. She wanted to condemn him for each kiss, for every caress of his hand, the very smile on his face, the tender light in his eyes. How dare he tempt her to love him knowing full well nothing decent could ever come of it! The pain seared across her chest, tightening her throat. Through all the storm of emotions she held herself erect, clinging to her dignity, never once yielding to the sensations that battered her. 'Please leave now.' Those three small words so quietly, so politely spoken were more devastating than if she had roared at the top of her voice.

'No, not until you tell me what's going on.' One hand slid up the length of her arm to grip upon her shoulder.

She trembled beneath his touch. 'Please don't touch me.'

The green eyes widened, but her heart was so wounded she did not see his hurt.

His grip loosened until his fingers were nothing more than a featherlight touch. They lingered for a matter of seconds longer and then slowly, as if by an act of immense will-power, they were gone. And now, even though there was nothing holding her to him, she felt the warmth of his proximity, felt the urge to wrap her arms around him, bury her face against his chest. Her breath was uneven and shallow, coming in fits and starts, gasps and shudders. She forced herself to step back, to reject temptation before it caught her completely. One tiny step backwards, and then another.

He made to follow.

'Lord Ravensmede,' she said as coldly as she could.

Frustration boiled. 'Damnation, Kathryn, just tell me!'

For one tiny sliver of a moment she nearly did, and then common sense came to the fore once more and she shook her head.

She composed her face, unwilling to have him witness the

full extent of her humiliation. 'I fear I have the headache, sir. If you would be so kind as to leave me to my rest.'

Nicholas's gaze did not falter. He made no move.

She swallowed hard. Her heart shuddered. 'Please, Nicholas,' she whispered. 'Don't make this any harder than it already is. Just go.'

He looked at her for a moment longer, then turned and walked towards the door.

Ravensmede only suffered Kathryn's new cold formal treatment for two days before a visit from Harry Silverton forced a change in matters. The Viscount was staring moodily out of the library window, sipping his brandy when the footman arrived.

'Beggin' your pardon, m'lord, but her ladyship sent me. Mr Silverton has arrived and is refusing to leave until he's seen Miss Marchant.'

The ejection of Mr Silverton was to prove rather more problematic than Lord Ravensmede anticipated.

'Ravensmede, you dashed scoundrel!' Harry Silverton bellowed upon Ravensmede's entry to the drawing room.

'Mr Silverton, I must urge you to refrain from shouting when my grandmother is present.' Ravensmede looked meaningfully at the dowager perched uneasily on the edge of the sofa.

The younger man swayed a little unsteadily on his feet. 'Where have you hidden her?'

'If by *her* you're referring to Miss Marchant, then I regret to inform you that she is at present not in to any visitors, nor is she likely to be so in the near future.'

'You confounded cur!' The young gentleman's words had a distinctive slur to them. 'You mean to keep her for yourself. To have her as your mistress when a decent man like me would ask for nothing but her hand in marriage!' The stench of alcohol pervading the room intensified as Mr Silverton staggered closer.

Ravensmede's eyes narrowed at the insult, but he had no intention of bandying insults with a young man who was quite clearly well and truly foxed. 'I will ask you to leave, Mr Silverton, before you make even more of a fool of yourself than you have already.'

'Damn you, Ravensmede, but I love her, and I ain't leaving until I've seen her to tell her so.' He scrabbled about in his pocket and produced a sheet of folded paper. 'I've written a poem to her beauty. I mean for her to have it.' He tried to focus on the sheet for several minutes, but to no avail.

'I shall not ask you again, sir.' The Viscount's voice cut sharply through the room.

'I've heard all about you. Who hasn't? The infamous Viscount of Ravensmede and his affairs with the ladies, and the gaming tables.' The youngster sneered. 'A rake, a libertine and more! I've seen the way you look at Miss Marchant and I don't like it.' The dramatic effect of this little speech was somewhat ruined by the enormous belch that succeeded it. 'I do beg your pardon,' said Mr Silverton.

'You've said quite enough for one night, sir. And if you won't leave of your own accord, then I will throw you out, you insolent dog!' Lord Ravensmede moved to effect his threat.

'Stay where you are!' Silverton produced a pistol and waved it in the Viscount's direction. The poem fluttered unnoticed to the floor.

Lady Maybury, who had hitherto been silent throughout the two men's exchange, leapt to her feet. 'How dare you threaten m'grandson, you odious toad! Put that infernal thing away this instant!'

Mr Silverton looked momentarily at the barrel of his pistol as if he were surprised to find the object in his hand. 'I do beg your pardon, my lady. I was just trying to explain to Lord Ravensmede that I…' he hiccuped and waved the pistol as he spoke '… am here to prevent him ruining Miss Marchant. I mean to have her as my wife, you see.'

'Yes, I see only too well, sir, that you are going about courting m'companion in quite the wrong manner. Not only are you rather the worse for drink, but I'm offended by your presence.' Lady Maybury sniffed and cast him the haughtiest of looks.

'I didn't mean to insult *you*, my lady. *You* are not a rake of the worst degree.' He gestured the muzzle in the dowager's direction as he stressed the word *you*. '*You* do not mean to keep her from me.' The pistol pointed directly at Lady Maybury, the young man's finger lingering unwittingly around the trigger.

Ravensmede had seen enough. He knew exactly how dangerous a weapon could be, particularly in the hands of a man who had clearly spent the best part of the day in the consumption of brandy if the reek was anything to go by. His grandmother was at risk and that was not something he was prepared to tolerate. Moving with a speed and agility that surprised them all, Ravensmede launched himself at the golden-haired visitor, placing his own body between the pistol and the old lady at whom it was levelled. The momentum of his flight carried both men to the floor, but not before an almighty roar reverberated around the drawing room. The stench of gunpowder arose, along with a plume of blue smoke.

Lady Maybury screamed.

Ravensmede clambered up from the prostrate body.

Harry Silverton's bright blue eyes stared up, round, unblinking.

The dowager scrabbled towards her grandson. 'Thank God you're safe!'

The door swung open. Pounding steps as the butler and two footmen clattered in.

'Escort this gentleman from the house. A carriage shall be required to send him on his way.' Ravensmede bent to retrieve the pistol from where it lay discarded upon the floor. 'He no longer has need of this.'

A soft gasp came from the doorway.

She was by his side, hands on his sleeve, eyes wide with fear. 'Nicholas?' No polite and distant 'Lord Ravensmede' this time.

He smiled a lazy smile, and pulled her against the right-hand side of his body. 'Mr Silverton was just leaving.'

Kathryn grabbed both of his arms and stared up into his face, all thoughts of propriety forgotten in her concern. 'What happened?'

An unmistakable wince, and an involuntary withdrawal.

'Nicholas?' With an escalating dread Kathryn let her gaze travel slowly to where her right hand clutched.

The material of his coat was warm and wet beneath her fingers. She drew them back, swallowed hard and looked down at the glistening red stain. The grey eyes swivelled to meet his. 'You're bleeding.'

'The smallest scratch, nothing more.'

Lady Maybury stepped closer, her bony fingers clutching to her throat. 'You're shot,' she whispered in disbelief.

Her words seemed to rouse Harry Silverton from his faint. The gentleman raised himself cautiously to his elbows, terror dawning upon his countenance. 'Was an accident.' And with that he groaned and gingerly replaced his head upon the polished wooden floorboards.

Time ceased. The moment stretched unending, until at last the dowager gave a frightened little mew. 'So much blood.'

'Grandmama.' Ravensmede stepped forward to reassure the elderly lady who was tottering rather unsteadily on her feet.

As if awakening from a stupor Kathryn sprang to life. She moved to gently, but firmly, place Lady Maybury in the closest armchair. 'My lady, please do not alarm yourself. It's as Nicholas says, a flesh wound that bleeds prolifically.' Even as she uttered the reassurance her own fears, her own darkest dread, were being thrust deep down, hidden far out of sight. But from across the years came an image of another man she had loved, of the faint lingering smell of gunpowder, and the raw stench of blood…and her father's lifeless fingers resting upon his desk, still wrapped around the handle of the pistol. Her eyes shuttered. Dear God, not Nicholas, never Nicholas. He could not die…she would not let him. Determination rose. She gritted her teeth hard, shock still kicking in her gut. Pushed away all memories, all thoughts of fear and panic. Allowed instinct to take over. Kathryn would do whatever she had to…for Nicholas's sake. So, having dealt with the dowager for the minute, she instructed the butler to send for a physician, the first footman to fetch boiled water and clean linen strips, and the remaining footman to collect four warm blankets from the press upstairs. Only then did she turn her attentions to Nicholas.

For all of the bemused expression that he presented to her, she could see the pallor in his face. It seemed that something grabbed hold of her heart and squeezed until it was tight and painful. She breathed deeply, squared her shoulders, and moved towards him. 'Nicholas, we must remove your coat.' Her voice was surprisingly calm and controlled. 'Here, let me assist you.'

'I assure you, Kathryn, there's no—' The deep voice got no further.

'Assure me only of your compliance, sir,' she said quietly.

A dark eyebrow arched, but before he could utter his protest she was peeling the fitted coat from his body.

She removed first the sleeve from his uninjured arm and then, without pausing, she caught him unawares and pushed him back on to the sofa.

'I think I might manage on my own,' he said wryly.

But her small bloodstained fingers were already on his arm, easing the cloth away from his wound. The coat was delivered close to the dowager's feet in a heap. His neckcloth and waistcoat received similar treatment and soon lay on top of the crumpled coat. Kathryn worked with a calm quiet efficiency that belied the frenzied beat of her heart.

She cleared her throat. 'Now for your shirt.'

'I beg your pardon?'

'Please remove your shirt, Nicholas.' Arms akimbo, smoky grey eyes that glistened with determination…and something else that she could not quite hide, Kathryn was unaware that she presented a most formidable sight, enough to make a man's pulse race, especially a man whom she'd been avoiding for the past two days.

The sensual mouth grinned wickedly. 'You're putting my grandmother to the blush, Kathryn.'

'I'm sure that Lady Maybury will forgive me this once,' she said with a great deal more confidence than she felt. 'Please, sir, for I don't mean to ask you again.'

His smile deepened and he deliberately lay back upon the cushions, and waited.

'Very well, my lord.' She swallowed hard, gathered her courage together in both hands, and, stepping forward, effected her action in one fell move. The tear of linen sounded loudly in the room. Shock showed upon his face. And she knew that, whatever Nicholas had been expecting, it was not to have her quite literally rip the shirt from his body. Having disposed of the front and one arm of the garment, she lingered over the injured limb, gently easing the material away from the wounded area. The sight of the bloody mess of flesh was almost her undoing. *The smallest scratch* he had said, but Kathryn's heart turned over at what she saw once the last vestige of shirt had been removed. A few inches over and the ball would have lodged itself in his chest. A wave of dizziness swept through her at the thought.

'Kathryn!' Lady Maybury gave a weak protest.

Kathryn took a deep breath and pulled herself together. Such weakness would not help him. 'Don't worry, my lady. I know what I'm doing. All shall soon be ready for the physician's arrival.' Kathryn flung the words of reassurance over her shoulder, but there was no such assurance or confidence within. She forced herself not to think, just to act. 'Once we have this cleaned up, he shall be able to see the damage clearly.'

When the first footman eventually returned with two basins of boiled water that were still steaming and a small pile of linen strips, it was to a scene in which his master was lying semi-clothed upon the sofa with his grandmother's companion clasping his arm. It was the same footman that had witnessed Miss Marchant and the Viscount embracing by the front door not so very long ago. The man was wise enough to keep his thoughts to himself and made no sign as to having observed anything remotely untoward.

'Very good, Toby. Place the basins down here by me and the rags close by. Thank you.' She gave the footman a little nod and moved the bowls to exactly where she needed them. 'And Toby, send Mr Silverton home in the carriage as Lord Ravensmede instructed.' A nod of her head indicated the young gentleman's prone body.

'Yes, miss.'

Then the second footman returned with the blankets and, having sat them upon the table, made to help carry the inebriated man from the room.

Kathryn washed her own red stained hands thoroughly in one basin before wetting the linen rag. For the first time since removing his clothes she sought Nicholas's gaze. Kathryn was unable to help herself; her hand fluttered to lightly cup his face. 'Although I'll be as gentle as I can, Nicholas, my cleansing of the wound is bound to cause you pain.' Her thumb stroked a gentle encouragement. 'I'll contrive to act as quickly as is possible.'

His eyes held hers. 'This isn't work for your hands, Kathryn.'

'Perhaps you're right,' she admitted softly. 'But I'll finish what I've started all the same.' She looked at him a moment longer, wanting to kiss the worry from his face. One last stroke of her thumb, a little smile, and then her hand left his face, and her gaze dropped once more to his injured arm.

'Dear Lord, but I'm too late!' a mumbled utterance escaped Mr Silverton's lips as the footmen manoeuvred him through the doorway. One pink-lined eye fixed itself on the woman bending low over the naked torso of Ravensmede. 'Miss Marchant!'

Kathryn did not divert her attention. Nothing else mattered save for Nicholas and his wound.

By the time Nicholas's arm had been cleansed and the deep furrow ploughed by the trajectory of the lead ball exposed, the Viscount lay back upon the sofa white-faced and with a grim line to his mouth. Perspiration beaded his forehead and upper lip, but he made no sound. There was a nausea in Kathryn's stomach at the pain her cleansing and probing had caused him. But the task was done now. The wound was tightly bound. And Kathryn could only be relieved. Taking his hand in hers, she guided it to lie across the top of the sofa back, allowing her fingers to linger when they should not have, desperate to give him some small comfort. There was nothing of embarrassment, no sense of impropriety at what she had done. Her thoughts were with Nicholas, and Nicholas alone.

His hand closed around hers. There was no strength in the light touch of his fingers, only the gentleness of a caress.

Green eyes met grey, and the smile they shared was both intimate and loving. It lasted only a moment, but it was enough. Kathryn tucked two warm blankets snugly around him, placed a cushion placed behind his head, and moved away. She had done what little she could; now there was Lady Maybury to attend to.

As she bent to hand the hot sweet tea to his grandmother, he could see that some of her hair had escaped her chignon, and was curling around her neck and shoulders. The long sleeves of her dress had been rolled back down into place, but the skirt and bodice were still marked with a liberal application of his blood. He knew that she had not been unaffected by what had just happened, had felt the slight tremble in her fingers, and admired her all the more for her courage. Her voice, quiet and clear, soothed, as did the slender scrubbed fingers carefully adjusting the mountain of blankets surrounding the old woman. He wondered that someone who had received so little care throughout her own life had so much to give. His grandmother looked pale and infinitely older than usual. A frown crinkled his brow.

'Kathryn,' he said.

She hurried across.

His gaze twitched to the dowager and back to the woman standing above him.

As if reading his mind, she bent her face lower to his.

'My grandmother should not have witnessed this. Her heart… She needs to rest. Help her up to her bedchamber.'

The grey eyes were filled with compassion. 'Nicholas, Lady Maybury has suffered a great shock. What she needs now is to know that her grandson is safe, that you've taken no great hurt and will recover,' she said quietly.

'I told you, it's nothing more than a scratch.'

'Maybe so. But you bled like a stuck pig. You must reassure her yourself by behaving as normal. It would be better if we did not retire until the physician arrives.' And with that she hurried back to attend to his grandmother.

He gave a slight nod in acquiescence, and smiled. Kathryn Marchant had courage and honour…and his love.

Kathryn stood alone by the window in her bedchamber and stared out at the expansive shimmering sea views. The water had a turquoise-green hue reminiscent of that captured in the many paintings of Mediterranean subjects that she'd seen over the years. The rhythmic sweep of the waves lulled and pacified her. White spray frothed where the waves broke upon the shoreline. Cool sea air flooded in through the open window, filling the room with its own peculiar scent: salt and seaweed and freshness. Curtains billowed in the stiff breeze and several strands of hair fluttered unnoticed across the pale skin of the woman's cheeks. Still, silent, outwardly serene, the image she presented was far removed from the turbulent emotions twisting within.

No matter that the physician had declared the Viscount to have been extremely lucky or that the damage to Lord Ravensmede's arm was minimal. Rest, clean dressings, and it would soon be healed, or so the doctor had said. The memory of Nicholas's blood smeared upon her palms would not leave her. So much blood that she could have cried her fears aloud on the spot. She had wanted to clutch him to her, to take his pain upon herself, anything but face the awful terror of that moment, when her mind was filled with the worst of imaginings.

Death. It had a starkness about it that pared everything else to insignificance. So she had done what she had to, in order to remedy the situation, with no consideration for propriety, without the slightest notion of how her actions might be construed. He was alive and well. Now she could think of nothing else except how close she'd come to losing him. And that cast quite a different light on all of her best-made resolutions. Her façade of coolness and politeness and distance had crumbled to dust. Nicholas might well marry Miss Paton, but that didn't change the fact that Kathryn loved him with a love so strong that it frightened her. She knew now that she couldn't just turn her back on him, and walk away as if their friendship had never been. Not for all of Lady Maybury's warnings, not even for the sake of her own good name. Kathryn Marchant was changed for ever.

Chapter Thirteen

Kathryn's hand trembled before she clenched it into a fist and knocked lightly against the mahogany wooden panels of the door. Her heart was thudding fast and loud, and she swallowed to alleviate the dryness in her throat.

'Come in.' His voice alone caused a fluttering within her stomach.

She smoothed her skirt down with nervous hands and, before her courage could desert her, opened the door and stepped into Lord Ravensmede's bedchamber.

His eyes widened momentarily at the sight of her standing there so awkwardly by the doorframe. 'Kathryn?' And then, as if catching himself, 'Please…come in.'

Her fingers betrayed her, plucking at the pale green of her afternoon dress, in small furtive movements. For a moment it seemed that she had not heard him, for she stood stock-still and cautious as a deer scenting the wind. Then, just when he would have spoken again, she did as he bade, shutting the door silently behind her.

'Nicholas.' There was a silver light in her eyes and the first hint of a rose blush in the apple of her cheeks. The rich russet brown of her curls had been arranged up behind her head tidily as if she had only just combed and pinned them. Already two curls had contrived to free themselves to dance enticingly against the creamy white skin of her neck. She stopped short of the bottom of the bed, her eyes flitting between him and the floor.

He could see her unease and the tension that ran through her slender body by the repetitive touch of her fingers to her skirt. Yet there was something in her gaze when it rose to meet his, something new, something that was both soft and generous yet, paradoxically, with the same determination he had witnessed the previous day in the drawing room when she had tended his wound with such calm competence. His senses tingled. She should not be here, in his bedchamber, while he sat beneath the bedcovers clad only in a nightshirt. He held his breath and waited for what she had come to say.

As if reading his mind she started, 'I know that I shouldn't be here, but I wanted to check that you…that your arm has not worsened.'

'It's the smallest scratch, nothing more. I'm only in bed today to satisfy my grandmother, and of course my own slothful nature.' He stretched out his injured arm, clenching and unclenching his fist as if to demonstrate the proof of his words. 'But thank you for your concern.'

The colour bloomed in her face. 'I should go.'

'No.'

The word hung between them.

'Kathryn,' he said a little more gently, 'come and sit here beside me. I would speak with you before you leave.'

She showed no sign of complying.

'I want to thank you for what you did yesterday. The physician said that your quick action saved me much blood loss from the wound.'

'Anyone would have done the same.'

'Even to the point of forcibly unclothing me? I do not think so,' he said with a roguish smile.

Kathryn's cheeks were now blazing a fiery hot red. 'Yes, well…' she muttered and stared down at her feet. 'That couldn't be helped. The wound needed my attention and you weren't proving to be of much assistance. I'm sorry if I embarrassed you.'

It was the same expression that she had used at Lady Finlay's ball, for the slip in her dance steps…and their shared kisses in the moonlit room. Ravensmede felt a warmth expand within his chest as the memories flowed. 'You could never embarrass me, Kathryn.'

The clear gaze slid up to meet his, and he felt a flood of desire and need and tenderness. A shy smile spread across her mouth.

'The other day when you sent me away, what had happened to upset you so much?' It was a question that had worried at him since walking in to find her in that state within her bedchamber. For all that she had endured he had never seen her so affected, not until that day. The sight of her pain and the sound of the formality in her voice had made him want to snatch her into his arms, to kiss her long and hard and passionately until she told him what was wrong. And that whispered plea, *Please, Nicholas, don't make this any harder than it already is*, had torn at his heart. For Ravensmede, a man used to taking what he wanted, when he wanted it, such impotence was frustrating. His grandmother knew what the matter was about, with her little looks of feigned innocence, and contrivance to keep him away from her companion. But the old lady had stubbornly refused to be forthcoming and doggedly changed the subject each time he had mentioned Kathryn's name.

He watched her fingers catch at the material again, grip it hard. 'It's of no consequence,' she said.

'Kathryn…' He raised one eyebrow and peered at her as if he would fathom the truth in that way.

But her head just shook a quick denial. 'It doesn't matter, not now.'

He heard the slight breathless catch in her voice, watched her take a single step closer. His right hand stretched towards her, reaching out for her, a gesture of conciliation and more.

It seemed that she hesitated, her gaze unmoving upon his

hand, her face impassive. Then her eyes flickered up to his and he could see their colour had darkened to a soft smoky grey. The moment stretched. Time stilled. Awareness narrowed until there was only the two of them in existence. Thud of heart, flutter of pulse. Her small hand slid into his, his fingers closed around hers. From there he did not know quite how she came to be in his arms or his lips pressed against hers, possessing and yielding all at once.

She was warm and soft, an alluring mix of innocence and passion. His hands swept the length of her back, down to the curve of her hips, pulling her closer. Her mouth opened beneath his, inviting further exploration. The tip of his tongue slipped within, teasing, tantalising. Tongue touched tongue, lapped together, twisting, licking, sucking. All rational thought fled. She was his, to pleasure, to worship, to love. Even as he clutched her closer he heard the little mew sound in her throat, felt the nuzzle of her breasts against his chest. All of Lord Ravensmede's good intentions were lost.

His lips traced a pattern along the delicate line of her jaw to find the tender skin beneath her ear. She gave herself up to the sensations rippling through her. From the strange ache down deep and low in her pelvis to the pulsating heat in her thighs, Kathryn embraced what was happening to her. This was far beyond any dream. It was urgent and wicked and wild, but Kathryn wanted it never to stop. She needed to feel Nicholas's arms around her, wanted his mouth on hers. Her fingers caressed against his cheek, stroking down over the rough stubble of his chin. All the love that she felt welled up and flowed out to him, spilling over in every touch, in every kiss. And in her mind the silent words whispered again and again, *I love you, I love you,* until she knew not whether she gasped them aloud.

He plucked the pins from her hair, one by one, until the glorious mass of curls hung free. His fingers tangled within the heavy chestnut tresses, revelling in their glossy softness. Her hair smelled fresh and clean as if she'd rinsed it in a wash of lavender water. His hands followed her hair down to where it brushed against her breasts, cupped the two small mounds, massaging them through the material of her dress with gentle passion.

The soft white skin grew more sensitive with each caress, every stroke, until she thought that his heat would scorch her. And then when his fingers eventually found passage beneath the pale green bodice, to burrow under every layer of separating material to capture the bare skin of her breasts, she could not contain the sudden sharp inhalation of breath. Instinctively her back arched, thrusting her taut nipples hard against him, seeking more of something that she did not understand. Each and every touch sent sparks of pleasure writhing deep into her stomach. Rational thought had long since fled.

The groan growled low in his throat and his arms locked around her as he twisted and pushed her down so that she lay on the bed beside him. 'Kathryn,' he gasped her name as if it was air and he was a man suffocating for want of it. 'Kathryn,' he whispered again as he rolled his length on top of her.

'Oh, Nicholas,' she sighed and wrapped her arms around him.

A voice sounded from the direction of the stairs on the landing beyond the door of Ravensmede's bedchamber. 'What do you mean I can't go in there! I don't need you to announce me to m'own grandson,' bellowed Lady Maybury. 'If I want to see Lord Ravensmede I'll damn well see him!'

Kathryn and Nicholas froze as the full realisation of their situation hit them.

The dowager's small feet thumped noisily down the corridor, growing ever louder as she made her way to her grandson's bedchamber.

Kathryn's eyes widened in horror. She tried to scramble up, to repair the loosened bodice, the long curls that flowed wantonly over her shoulders. But Nicholas's hand stayed her frantic panic. He shook his head, touched a finger to her lips, and imprisoned her wrist with his other hand.

A sharp knock sounded at the door. 'Nicholas, are you decent?' Lady Maybury's words came clear through the mahogany.

''Fraid not, Grandmama,' said Ravensmede with a lazy drawl. 'I wouldn't want to shock your delicate constitution by the sight I present at this minute.' His eyes glowed wickedly as he looked down at Kathryn lying beneath him.

'Don't be absurd,' came the withering reply. 'I've seen it all before. Had you naked on m'knee before you were in breeches.'

Despite the predicament they found themselves in, Ravensmede smiled at his grandmother's words. 'Grant me ten minutes,' he said laughingly.

A surly-sounding grunt. 'I'll be back in five,' the dowager said, and the footsteps receded back along the landing.

Only then did a very white-faced Kathryn release the breath she had been holding. Realisation of her predicament screamed loud. And now that her ardour had disappeared without a trace, she was suddenly shamefully aware that she was on Lord Ravensmede's bed, with the man himself lying atop her. Nicholas had not the least look of embarrassment; indeed, he was smiling down at her in what could only be described as a positively dangerous manner. Her eyes widened with growing horror. 'N-Nicholas…' her tongue stumbled over his name, as she tried to free herself from her position.

The wickedness of Nicholas's smile intensified and slowly his face moved towards hers…to drop the smallest, innocent kiss on to the tip of her nose. 'Kathryn Marchant, you are quite the most beautiful, beguiling woman I've ever met.' Without another word he rolled off her and, leaning down, helped her up to her feet. In one fluid action he had reached around to the back of her dress and fastened the buttons he had undone not so very long ago. Everything about him was smooth, lazily efficient and supremely confident.

The same could not be said for Kathryn. Not only was she in a state of abject shock at the extent to which passion had pushed her, but her hands were shaking so much she could barely fashion her hair into some semblance of order.

'Here, let me,' he instructed, and simply turned her around, coiled her hair into a neat chignon and pinned it into place with much less fuss than any abigail would have caused.

'How do you—'

'Don't ask.' He spun her round, delivered a final kiss to her mouth, took her by the hand and guided her towards the door. 'And now you had better go before my grandmother decides to return.'

'Nicholas…' Kathryn bit at her bottom lip.

'We'll talk about this later, Kathryn.' Opening the door by the smallest crack, he scanned beyond, then, giving Kathryn's fingers one last reassuring squeeze, pushed her towards the door directly across the landing; the door that led into her own bedchamber.

It was exactly five minutes later that Lady Maybury made a reappearance, and an hour after that when she finally left him to his rest. And all the while Lord Ravensmede was forced to pretend that he had not just reached a decision of monumental proportions. Not until his grandmother left the room did he allow himself to think back on the woman who had come to him out of concern and whom he, in return, had practically seduced. Had not his grandmother come knocking at the door of his bedchamber he wondered if he would have had either the strength or the sense to stop what he was about.

Kathryn absorbed him, totally, completely. Just touching her, kissing her, made him forget all else. What chance had he then when she lay beneath him on his bed? It was enough to drive any man mad. For all these years Nicholas Maybury had called the tune when it came to women. And heaven knew he had practised it often enough, on rich women, powerful women; all of them widowed or well experienced at their profession, some of them even other men's wives.

Now one woman had changed all that. One woman alone

could have called any tune she wanted, and he would have danced to it a thousand times over. One woman alone had the power to gladden his heart, to make him feel dizzy with desire, or to cast him into a doldrum of depression. She was neither wealthy nor titled, neither fashionable nor flirtatious. As Cadmount had so accurately observed, she was not even his type. None of it made any difference. Nicholas loved her. And he meant to marry her. The woman's name was Kathryn Marchant.

It was only later that same evening when he made enquiry of his butler as to the whereabouts of his grandmother and her companion that he discovered them to have departed for a dance in the local assembly rooms. First instinct told him to seek them out, check that Kathryn understood that his intentions were honourable—hadn't he given her every reason to think otherwise? Second thoughts suggested he wait where he was. Care must be taken to ensure that no contrary gossip linked Kathryn's name with his. As his wife she would be safe, but until then... Reputations were a fragile thing in the hands of the *ton.* He was sure that his grandmother already had her suspicions about his relationship with her companion, and was warning him off. Why else was she doing her damnedest to keep them apart? It was for the best that Kathryn be seen in Brighthelmstone without him. Soon they would be together. Ravensmede would have to content himself with that. But had he known what was unfolding in the assembly rooms, the Viscount would have decided very differently.

The air was unpleasantly stuffy and hot within the assembly rooms, and the fact that her dance card was full did not help matters. Lady Maybury was chatting with lively animation to a group of elderly ladies, and looking very pleased with the fact that Kathryn had not yet been off the dance floor. Parson John Andrew, who had a keen interest in lepidopterology, was describing to Kathryn in some detail the differences between the

Red Admiral as compared to the Blue Butterfly, a feat to be much congratulated as they were engaged in dancing a robust Scottish reel at the time. The tempo of the music increased, urging the dancers to skip faster, twirl their partners with more force. Reverend Andrew's face grew redder, and his breathing more laboured. Sweat dribbled down his cheeks and chin. By the end of the dance both Kathryn and Reverend Andrew were much relieved. The gentleman mopped at his brow with a large white handkerchief before setting off to fetch two glasses of lemonade for the delightful Miss Marchant and himself.

'Kathryn?' The woman's voice inflected with surprise. 'Is that really you? What a surprise to find you here, my dear.'

The skin on the back of Kathryn's neck prickled. It was a voice she knew well, and one she had not thought to hear in this part of the country. She looked up to meet the cold blue eyes of Anna Marchant. 'Aunt Anna, the surprise is mutual.' Then, as Lottie stepped from behind her mother, 'And Cousin Lottie too. I had not thought to meet you both here in Brighthelmstone.'

The harshness in Mrs Marchant's eyes faded and she looked almost contrite. 'Our visit is not one of pleasure,' she said in a hushed tone. 'It is Mr Marchant…'

It seemed to Kathryn that her aunt was smaller than she remembered. 'What of Uncle Henry?'

Mrs Marchant swallowed, and compressed her lips as if trying to control some strong emotion assailing her. 'He…'

Guilt and concern pricked at Kathryn's conscience. She noticed the pallor of her aunt's face as she waited for what was to come.

'He has taken an inflammation of the lungs.' Mrs Marchant clasped her perfectly manicured hands together and held them to her mouth. There was a suspicious sheen about her eyes. 'The doctor is not optimistic. He said…' Her eyes squeezed momentarily closed, and, when they opened again, there was in them a vulnerability Kathryn had never seen before. 'He said that clean sea air was our best hope. Hence I brought Mr Marchant here with all haste.'

Lottie clasped at her mother's hand and let out a little sob. 'Poor Papa.'

'It came on so suddenly,' said Mrs Marchant. 'One minute he was fine and well, and the next…' She glanced anxiously at Kathryn.

'I'm so sorry. I didn't know.'

'He insisted that I bring Lottie here tonight. Was so adamant that I dared not refuse him for fear of bringing on another coughing fit. We will not stay long and then we will get straight back to him.'

'Please send my uncle my best wishes that he recovers his good health as soon as possible.'

'Of course,' nodded Mrs Marchant, then paused before she added, 'Mr Marchant would benefit from your visit, Kathryn, that is, if you can find the time to see him. I believe it would make a difference to him.'

'I—I'm not sure—'

But before she could say what she would have, Anna Marchant interrupted, 'I haven't always treated you fairly, Kathryn, and for that I beg your forgiveness. Only now do I see things in a different light.'

The two women looked at one another, before Kathryn nodded and gave a small smile. 'If you tell me where you are staying, then I will visit my uncle.' So shocked was she by the news of her uncle's illness and the drastic change in her aunt that Kathryn failed to notice the gentleman until he stood directly by her side…rather closer than was seemly.

'Sorry to interrupt, Miss Marchant…' and he bowed '…but it's imperative that I speak with you on a matter of privacy.'

'Mr Silverton!' She could not keep the shock from her voice. The last time she had seen Harry Silverton he was being carried in a drunken stupor out of the drawing room of the rented house on The Steyne and into Lord Ravensmede's carriage. An image of a blood-soaked Nicholas flashed into her mind, and fear flickered. Both Aunt Anna and Lottie were looking at Mr Silverton with expressions of curiosity. Kathryn deliberately edged herself away from the young man's proximity, while making the necessary introductions. 'Aunt Anna, Lottie, this is Mr Silverton, whose family are enjoying the summer in Brighthelmstone. Mr Silverton, this is my aunt, Mrs Marchant, and my cousin, Miss Lottie Marchant.'

Mrs Marchant's devoirs went unnoticed as Lottie stepped forward into Harry Silverton's line of vision. 'Miss Lottie,' he said with awe, and stared at Lottie as if she was an apparition. 'Is this an angel I see before me?' And before the stunned Lottie could reply, he plucked her hand into his and placed upon it a reverential kiss.

Kathryn looked from Harry Silverton's stunned visage to her cousin's flushed excited one. Lottie was ogling right back at Mr Silverton.

Mrs Marchant cleared her throat. 'We must be going, Lottie, come along.'

'But I've only just arrived,' protested Mr Silverton, 'and not yet had the pleasure of dancing with the beautiful Miss Lottie.'

Lottie's lips moved to a pout. 'Mama, we are scarcely here.'

Kathryn had no wish to speak to Silverton, especially knowing all that he had done to Nicholas, but she was wise enough to realise that the young man could be dangerous. It would be better to hear what he proposed to say over the matter. 'You wished to speak to me, Mr Silverton?'

Harry Silverton blinked like a man struggling to free himself from a drugged daze. 'Did I? It's of no matter, now.' He bestowed his most charming smile upon Lottie, and held out his hand for her dance card. 'May I hope to secure a dance with you, Miss Lottie?'

Kathryn could see quite clearly the way that things were progressing, especially after her aunt learned of the Silverton family's wealth. She was, therefore, considerably relieved when the Reverend Mr Andrews, carrying two glasses of lemonade, finally found his way back to her. And even more relieved when that same gentleman informed her that Lady Maybury had developed a headache and wanted to leave the assembly rooms.

During the journey home in the carriage Kathryn thought about her uncle's ill health, and the change in her aunt's manner. She thought about the sudden and rather overt attraction between Mr Silverton and Cousin Lottie. But most of all she thought about Nicholas Maybury, and of what had happened between them on his bed that very afternoon.

In the days following Nicholas and Kathryn's illicit tryst not one opportunity presented itself for them to speak together privately. Lady Maybury guarded her companion with all the tenacity of a terrier. Naps were forgotten. The independent old lady vanished. Her temper did not. She developed a need to have Kathryn with her at all times, from breakfast time to dinner. The very night of their return from the assembly rooms, she developed a nocturnal fear that necessitated Kathryn moving into Lady Maybury's bedchamber to keep her company. Matters grew even worse the next morning when Kathryn asked for leave to visit her uncle. The dowager embarked on what amounted to an inquisition over Uncle Henry's illness and Aunt Anna's invitation—and then claimed that she could not spare her companion even for half an hour. Every evening there were dances and trips to the theatre—all very public affairs—all with Ravensmede very much consigned to the background if her ladyship consented to his company at all.

In a way Kathryn was thankful to the old woman. She both desired and dreaded the time when she would be alone with Nicholas. She loved him, knew now that she could deny neither him nor herself. It was just a matter of time. Lady Maybury's tactics were only deferring the inevitable. Kathryn had her suspicions as to how much the dowager knew, loved the old lady all the more for trying to protect her poor companion.

Nausea rose at the thought of what becoming Nicholas's mistress would mean: a slap in the face to Lady Maybury for all that she had done to help Kathryn, and the loss of her own good name. No matter how hard they tried to keep the affair hidden, it would come out—such secrets always did. And what about when he tired of her, when he found some other woman to fill her place? The thought churned cold in her stomach. She was a fool a hundred times over, a fool caught between the devil and a high place…with little idea of how to solve her quandary.

Within the drawing room of the rented townhouse in Brighthelmstone Mrs Marchant was pacing with a great deal of excitement. 'You're certain, Henry, that Mr Silverton means to ask her?'

'Yes, he asked my permission to pay suit to Lottie. The boy is clearly besotted with her and wants to marry her.'

'Very good. Lottie will be married before either of us thought,' purred his wife. Her blue eyes narrowed and her slash of a smile broadened. 'I like Mr Silverton immensely. He has such very interesting tales to tell…particularly concerning our niece and Lord Ravensmede.'

Mr Marchant worried at his chins. 'There is an indecent haste about the affair. Mr Silverton is talking as if he means to marry Lottie tomorrow. They have only known each other a matter of days!'

His wife delivered him a withering look. 'What's to know? Harry Silverton is an only son; he has two sisters, and his parents are elderly. He stands to inherit his father's chain of coffee houses and sugar plantation in the West Indies. Not only that, but he's currently worth fifteen thousand a year, and will receive a large and fashionable new townhouse in Bristol as part of his wedding gift from the old man.'

'But he's trade, and I thought you wanted better for Lottie; a baronet at least, you said.'

'Bah, half the aristocracy have pockets to let. Fifteen thousand. And think what he stands to inherit.'

Mr Marchant nodded in agreement. 'I concede it to be a fortune.'

'Although I should prefer Lottie's wedding to be a grand affair, I would not want to stand in the way of true love.'

Her husband rolled his eyes.

'And there would be other advantages to them marrying sooner rather than later.'

'I see none,' said Mr Marchant somewhat sourly, 'other than the cost to my pocket.'

'There is the little matter of Kathryn. Have you forgotten about her?'

'The chance would be a fine thing,' he muttered beneath his breath, then spoke out loud, 'What difference can Lottie's marriage make to Kathryn?'

Mrs Marchant cheeks grew rather red from excitement. 'Why, if Lottie has already caught herself a husband, and we distance ourselves from Kathryn, then any damage that attaches itself to her reputation will not affect us.'

'She is still our niece.'

'We will publicly disown her. And with Lottie safely wed and sent to Bristol, then what harm can Kathryn do us?'

'Then I can cease this pathetic charade of illness in an attempt to lure the girl here?'

'Yes.' Anna Marchant beamed. 'We no longer need coax the little trollop back to London with us.' That had only been to please Amanda White and that woman had just been rendered powerless. She laughed aloud at the good fortune Harry Silverton had brought them.

'Hallelujah,' said Mr Marchant with sarcasm.

'You must concentrate on persuading Mr Silverton to London. He needs to visit Doctors' Commons as soon as possible—and come to Green Street with a special licence in his pocket. If we play our cards right, we should have Lottie married by next week. And then I can turn my attentions to Kathryn. I'll send her a note today telling of your unexpected recovery and that we have to leave Brighthelmstone. Do you know that I actually had to apologise to the little bitch the other day? How I'm longing to make her suffer for that. She's made her bed, and now I mean to make sure that she damn well lies in it. By the time I've finished, Kathryn Marchant will wish that she'd never been born.'

Less than a fortnight later and Lady Maybury was proving to be as demanding as ever. The two women sat at the breakfast table, the dowager consuming a second helping of ham and eggs, Kathryn sipping her coffee and reading aloud from the notices in *The Times*. Of Ravensmede there was no sign. Kathryn was trying hard to keep her thoughts from his possible whereabouts when one particular marriage announcement caught her attention. Her words faltered. The coffee cup stilled its motion halfway to her mouth.

Lady Maybury glanced up from her plate. 'Pray continue with the next one. I want to see if Mrs Pearsall's granddaughter's marriage to young Fox is in there.'

With exaggerated care Kathryn set the coffee cup down upon the table. There was the tiniest of pauses, and then she started to read again. 'On Friday June 25, at her father's house in Green Street, by the Reverend J. Blundell, Charlotte, only daughter of Mr and Mrs Henry Marchant of London, to Mr Harold Silverton, only son of Mr and Mrs James Silverton of Bristol.' Lottie had married Harry Silverton!

'Good gad!' exclaimed Lady Maybury. 'I thought they only met at that wretched dance the other week.'

'They did, but it was immediately apparent that their interests were captured.'

'Well, never you mind, Kathryn. He's a nincompoop. Showed his true colours when he came round here, brandishing that pistol in m'face. You'll catch better than him. Mark my words.'

'I don't understand.' Kathryn's brow rumpled in perplexity. 'Aunt Anna was different the last time we spoke. She seemed changed: softer, kinder somehow. She wanted to put the past behind us, to start anew. And then when she sent that letter telling of my uncle's sudden recovery and their intended return to London, she made no mention of Mr Silverton. I thought...' She shook her head. 'It doesn't make sense.'

'You thought what? That your aunt would at least inform you of your cousin's wedding?'

'I should know her better than that,' said Kathryn.

'So you should. A leopard doesn't change its spots,' replied the dowager, giving Kathryn a strange little look. 'What a surprise that your aunt was up to organising a wedding so soon after Mr Marchant's recent illness. But then the speed of your poor dear uncle's recovery was truly miraculous. Such a shame I couldn't spare you to visit him...' She raised her eyebrows with just the faintest suggestion of cynicism, before turning her attention once more to her breakfast plate. 'Now read the rest of the announcements before m'eggs grow cold.'

The first leg of the journey back to London was, as Kathryn expected, both slow and tedious. There was little conversation between the ladies as Lady Maybury managed to sleep almost continuously with no regard for the jolting of the carriage. Despite his recent injury Lord Ravensmede accompanied the carriage on horseback, the thud of his horse's hooves never far away.

He watched her pale face at the carriage window.

She studied the dark figure that rode so close by.

Green eyes met grey, again and again, binding the man and his woman together, promising what was to come.

She worried as to his arm, and that he should be riding.

He worried as to why she should look so anxious when he meant to claim her for his own.

Mile after mile. So close as to almost touch, so near as to almost whisper. Yet they could do nothing. By the time the coach entered into the yard of the King's Arms at Horley

Common, the tension between them was unbearable. The party was shown to their bedchambers, given some little time to refresh their travel-stained selves, then the landlord showed them to a private parlour and dinner was served.

At the first opportunity Ravensmede addressed himself to Kathryn, 'How did you find the first part of your journey?'

'Comfortable, thank you, my lord.'

'Don't lie,' interrupted the dowager between mouthfuls of salmon and boiled potatoes. 'It was damnably uncomfortable. It was all I could do to manage the briefest of naps. You really must have that carriage seen to, Nick.'

'I will do so upon our arrival in town,' he replied.

A silence descended upon the little group.

Kathryn poked at the small mound of potatoes on her plate, and tried not to look at Nicholas. She could feel the burn of his gaze upon her, could feel her face colour beneath his scrutiny. Surely the dowager would notice if he continued to stare so? She sought to distract her employer. 'My lady, how do you find the fish? Is it to your taste?'

Lady Maybury shovelled a large portion of the salmon steak into her mouth before replying. 'I'm afraid to say that it's barely edible. When one's appetite is as fragile as mine, it's important that only the best quality of food be consumed.' A large swig of wine passed her lips. 'The potatoes are hard, the pie is lacking in flavour and the soup is too poor to comment upon. I'm forced to nibble upon a meagre portion to sustain my strength.' The shrewd pale eyes swept over Kathryn's barely touched food. 'You would be wise to do the same, my dear, for our journey tomorrow will be as long as today and you heard what the landlord said of the weather.'

'It's going to rain,' supplied her companion quietly, and ate a little more of the pie.

Ravensmede drew a mocking smile at his grandmother. 'Perhaps then you will agree to let me travel awhile inside the carriage, instead of banishing me to the road.'

'The fresh air is good for you, boy,' she said. 'Besides, I thought you enjoyed riding.'

He raised an eyebrow and glanced across at Kathryn, before refilling all three glasses with claret.

Kathryn concentrated on watching the pale red liquid slosh against the glass. Within her chest her heart had kicked up to a canter. She ignored it, along with the peculiar battle of wills that seemed to be going on between Ravensmede and his grandmother. 'May I suggest an early night, my lady. You must be very tired and tomorrow will be more fatiguing than today.'

For once the dowager appeared to be in agreement. With a shrewd expression she patted Kathryn's hand. 'Go on ahead, gel. I shall not be long. Just want to finish m'wine, then I'll be up.'

Kathryn nodded and began to rise, but Nicholas was there before her. 'I'll escort Miss Marchant to her room.'

The blush in Kathryn's cheeks intensified. The flurry of her heart hastened. One glance up into those green eyes that glowed so bright beneath the flickering flame of the candles and she froze, for there was everything of intimacy and possession in Nicholas's gaze. It was as if a hand reached in and squeezed Kathryn's heart. 'Really, there is no need, my lord.' She felt his fingers brush her arm, felt too the instinctive sway of her body towards his. 'I—'

The dowager interrupted. 'Kathryn is right, Nick. Besides, I want a word with you.' She fixed a belligerent eye upon her grandson.

Kathryn's eyes shuttered for the briefest moment. Every nerve in her body was vibrating and taut. What she had feared was about to pass. For Kathryn could not shake the unassailable conviction that Lady Maybury knew. As surely as they were sitting here within the little parlour, as surely as the attraction that flowed between Nicholas and herself, the dowager knew. Why else was the tension wound so tight between the three of them? Dread weighed heavy on her chest. She rose swiftly to her feet, unwilling for either Lady Maybury or Lord

Ravensmede to witness her fear. 'Thank you, my lady.' With every last scrap of dignity that Kathryn possessed she turned and, without a backward glance, walked quietly from the room.

'Well?' said the dowager.

'Well?' said her grandson.

'Enough is enough, Nicholas. Don't think to fob me off this time with some tale of "there's nothing going on". I'm not in m'dotage yet, and I'd have to be deaf, blind and stupid not to see what's right in front of m'very nose.'

'I have not compromised her, nor do I intend to,' said Ravensmede.

'You came damn near to doing so. If it ever gets out that she visited you alone in your bedchamber, then I can assure you that she'll be well and truly ruined…and even I won't be able to save her.'

Ravensmede was genuinely shocked. 'You knew?'

'Of course I knew. What do you take me for, some kind of gibbering idiot? You've been looking at her like you're going to eat her. Why else do you think I've had to resort to guarding the gel night and day? Shouldn't have to do it from m'own grandson.'

His fingers raked through his hair. 'It's not what you think.'

'It's everything that I think and more. Hell's teeth, Nick, I thought you had some semblance of care for her. Couldn't you have just kept your breeches on for once?'

'They've never been off,' he protested, and then he remembered that he had been wearing his nightshirt the day that Kathryn had come to his bedchamber.

A snowy white eyebrow raised and a faded green eye stared hard.

'You're much mistaken, Grandmama.'

'Faugh! I know a seduction when I see one.'

'Grandmama,' He pushed the glass away.

'You might not have a care for the gel, Nick, but I'll be

damned if I just sit back and let you ruin her in a public inn of all places, and make a fool of me in the process.' The faded eyes flashed their angry determination.

He lounged back in his chair. 'Contrary to what you think, I care very much for Kathryn,' he said quietly. 'Do you honestly think I would seek to ruin the lady whom I mean to make my wife?'

Lady Maybury's jaw gaped. 'Did you say *wife*?'

'Most certainly so.'

'I had no idea.'

'Evidently not.'

'But…' The dowager shook her head in disbelief, unable to finish what she had started. A silence grew between them, and then, at last, Lady Maybury asked, 'Does Kathryn know of your intentions?'

Ravensmede's mouth crooked. 'For some strange reason I have been unable to find Miss Marchant alone these past weeks to ask her.'

'Well, I wasn't to know. I thought you were planning on bedding her!' said his grandmother indignantly.

'So you won't be insisting on my riding tomorrow?'

'Only if you behave yourself,' said the dowager. 'You aren't home and dry yet. Better have a care until the ring's on her finger.'

'You're taking the news remarkably well.'

'I find myself resolved to the situation. She might be m'companion and without a penny to her name, but she's got breeding; anyone with an eye in their head can see that. Besides, I like the gel. She's good for you.'

Ravensmede set his napkin down on the table. 'I'm glad we agree.'

'However, there is Miss Paton to consider.'

'Any possibility of an alliance between Miss Paton and me existed only in m'father's head.'

'Your father won't agree.'

'So much the better.' He paused. 'My father might protest, but he'll be relieved that I've chosen to marry at all.'

'If you say so, Nick. But the sooner you tell him about Kathryn the better.'

Ravensmede smiled, but gave no reply.

'You know, of course, there's bound to be gossip. It's not every day one's grandson marries one's companion.'

'There's always gossip.'

'Not about my family there isn't!' The dowager peered haughtily at him.

Ravensmede laughed. 'The tabbies wouldn't dare discuss my misdemeanours in your presence, Grandmama. They're really rather afraid of you.'

'I don't know why!' she snorted, but the glimmer of a smile touched to her lips. Then the smile faded. 'If you marry her, you'll find yourself related to Henry and Anna Marchant. You cannot alter the fact that they are her uncle and aunt.'

'The Marchants have no part in Kathryn's life now, nor will they do so in the future. I mean to see to that.'

'Then, your mind's made up.'

'Yes, Grandmama, my mind's made up.'

They looked at one another in silence for a moment.

'To Kathryn, the future Viscountess of Ravensmede.'

Clink of glasses in a toast, and then the wine was drained, and the small private parlour stood empty.

Chapter Fourteen

The next morning, when it came time to depart, Ravensmede was in the process of escorting Kathryn and his grandmother out to the waiting carriage when they came face to face with a lady and gentleman known to them from London.

'Mr and Mrs Parker.' Ravensmede bowed politely.

Ernest Parker's chubby cheeks took on a ruddy hue. 'Lord Ravensmede, Lady Maybury. Arrived last night from town, travelling down for a brief sojourn in Brighthelmstone. Emily has a notion to try one of those bathing contraptions.' His wife's head nodded in the most peculiar manner and she seemed to be having difficulty in meeting the Viscount's gaze.

'We too have been enjoying the delights of Brighthelmstone.' The dowager smiled. 'May I introduce my companion, Miss Marchant.' An elderly hand of surprising strength thrust Kathryn forward.

Emily Parker's expression froze into one of horror. For one awkward minute there was silence. Then, without even so much as a glance in Kathryn's direction, Mrs Parker grabbed her husband's arm in a lock that would have crushed a smaller man, and announced, 'Dear Lady Maybury, I'm afraid we really must leave. Please do excuse us.' And with that she practically ran across the courtyard, dragging her husband in her wake.

Ernest Parker cast a silent appeal at Lord Ravensmede. 'Your servant, sir,' came the gruff utterance as he disappeared into the carriage.

'Well, of all the most ninny-headed females, Emily Parker must take the biscuit!' said Lady Maybury with a scowl. 'Such an appalling lack of manners, I'm not surprised she's not invited anywhere of consequence.'

Ravensmede cast a curious look at the Parkers' carriage, but the door had been shut and the curtain closed across the window.

The dowager's breast puffed dangerously towards high dudgeon. 'How dare she slight m'companion. Kathryn's got more breeding in her little toe than that creature shall ever have!'

'My lady,' cajoled Kathryn from the lady's side, 'I'm not in the least offended. No doubt it is still too early in the morning for Mrs Parker.'

Lady Maybury seemed marginally calmed by Kathryn's words and allowed herself to be steered across the yard to the waiting carriage.

The landlord's predictions concerning the weather proved to be true. The day was quite the foulest that the summer had seen. Blustery cold winds and one heavy rain shower after the other slowed their journey considerably. The roads were muddied and filled with expanding puddles, the sky grey and forbidding with rain.

In contrast to her behaviour of the past fortnight, Lady Maybury showed not the slightest objection to her grandson sitting within the carriage beside her and her companion. Indeed, she positively encouraged Lord Ravensmede's presence, something of which Kathryn could only be glad on seeing the deterioration in the weather conditions. And rather than keeping a close scrutiny upon his person as she had taken to doing of late, the dowager was not five minutes into the journey when she fell asleep beneath her mound of travelling rugs. The snuffle of her snore competed with the rumble of the wheels and the pounding of the horses' hooves.

Kathryn looked at Nicholas.

Nicholas looked at Kathryn sitting at Lady Maybury's side.

He seeming to fill the whole of the carriage with his presence just by sitting on the seat opposite.

'At last,' he said.

Kathryn's gaze flickered towards the dowager.

'My grandmother is an extremely heavy sleeper.'

A tremor of panic fluttered through her.

Something of her feelings must have shown on her face, for Lord Ravensmede moved back to lounge against the squabs. 'I only wish to speak to you.' The smouldering intensity in his green eyes sent a shiver of anticipation from the top of her head down to the very tips of her toes. He did not look like he wanted to talk to her. Everything about his long lean body seemed poised to pull her into his arms and ravage her mouth with his. A lazy lop-sided smile spread across his face and he stretched out his legs so that his booted shins brushed against her skirt.

She waited.

'When you came to my bedchamber in Brighthelmstone—'

'Nicholas…' Her throat was dry and his name little more than a whisper. Her eyes flicked nervously towards the sleeping form of the dowager. 'We do not need to discuss this.'

'I think that we do,' he said.

She gave a little shake of her head, and a curl escaped down to drizzle against her cheek. 'Things need not change.'

'They already have.'

'We could be friends just as we were before,' she said, grasping at straws.

He sat upright and leaned forward, oblivious to the shake and heave of the carriage. 'We both know that there is much more than friendship between us, Kathryn.'

The breaths came small and fast and shallow in her chest. Her gaze dropped to the floor. 'There should not be.'

'*Should* does not enter into it. There is, and it's clear that you cannot remain as my grandmother's companion for much longer.'

She raised startled eyes to his. 'I would not hurt Lady Maybury.'

'Neither would I.'

'Then why…'

'You know why,' he said and, reaching across, laid his hand over hers.

His touch was light yet possessive. He was right. Kathryn knew very well the answer to her question. He could not take his grandmother's companion as his mistress.

The noise of hooves and wheels and rain and snores filled the minutes.

'There is something that I want to ask you.'

Her heart lurched. She withdrew her hand from his, her fingers stumbling to the skirt of her travelling dress and gripping for dear life at the material. She knew what he was going to ask, had known it for quite some time. Now that the moment had come she feared that her courage had deserted her. It was one thing to be drawn into it while in the throes of passion; it was quite another to agree to it in the cold light of day. An arrangement. To suit them both. He desired her. She loved him. And for the sake of that love she would bear the shame that being his mistress would bring. But this wasn't how it was supposed to be. For all that had passed between them, for all that she had tried to convince herself, she knew that if he asked her here, sitting in his travelling coach, with his grandmother asleep by her side, she would refuse him.

'No,' she whispered. 'Do not say it.'

A curious expression flitted across his face. 'But you don't yet know yet what I mean to ask.'

She swallowed hard. 'Even so, I would not have you ask it here, in front of Lady Maybury. That…that would not be right.'

A dark eyebrow arched in the familiar gesture that she had come to know and love, and he subjected her to a long knowing scrutiny. When at last he spoke there was a gentleness to his words. 'I'll warrant my question is not the one you expect it to be, Kathryn. But…' he captured her hand again in his and stroked his thumb against her skin '…if you would prefer I took a more conventional route with my proposal then so be it. I will wait until we reach London.'

She blushed and stared down at where their hands joined. 'Thank you.'

The coach rumbled on. The rain continued to pour. The dowager's snoring grew louder. Nicholas watched Kathryn. Kathryn watched the passing countryside…until they reached London.

The next morning was fine and warm, with no sign of the unseasonable weather of the previous day. Kathryn sat alone in the carriage, content with what she had found during her visit to young Maggie. The visit had distracted her thoughts from Nicholas and had been most enjoyable. The little girl's pleasure at the doll made the selling of the last of Kathryn's papa's books worthwhile, and the tasty biscuits and cakes from the dowager had doubled both the child and her brothers' pleasure. Beneath the warm golden sunlight Kathryn recalled the small hands pressed to hers and the laughter in those large pansy eyes. Maggie was a joyful delight for all her squeals and clambering.

A slender hand pressed to her cheek as she remembered how the child's mother had thanked her for the food parcels that had seemingly arrived with conscientious punctuality every week since Maggie's return home, and for the job in which her husband was now employed. Nicholas. There could be no one else responsible, after all. The knowledge made her smile. Beneath that devil-may-care attitude was a man who cared about a poor child's welfare, a man who doted upon his elderly grandmother…and a man who was going to ask her to become his mistress… just as he had before. Only this time she would give him a very different answer.

A barouche passed close by, travelling only marginally faster than that belonging to Lady Maybury. Miss Dawson's face looked out.

Kathryn raised her hand in salutation through the open window and smiled.

Miss Dawson's cheeks reddened and she turned her head away with a startling abruptness.

She must not have seen me, thought Kathryn, and returned to her musings without the slightest hint of rancour.

It was only later that same day that she had cause to remember the incident and place quite a different interpretation upon it.

It was late that evening when Ravensmede made himself comfortable in the wing chair within the library of his own house in Berkeley Square and accepted the brandy glass from his friend.

Cadmount's white fingers drummed upon the chair arm. 'How is the delightful dowager?'

'In fine mettle.'

'And li'l Miss Marchant?' asked Cadmount a trifle too innocently.

'She's well. I'm meeting them both at the King's later this evening, if you want to come.'

Cadmount coughed discreetly. 'You encountered no problems in Brighthelmstone?'

'No. Should I have?'

The fair-haired man cleared his throat and avoided Ravensmede's eye. 'You did bed her.'

Ravensmede carefully set the brandy glass down upon the table. 'Question or statement? Before you start down that line, Caddie, there's something you should know: I mean to marry Kathryn.'

Cadmount sighed, reached for the decanter and refilled Ravensmede's glass. 'In that case, best drink it down, old man,' he instructed. 'There have been some developments while you were away, and you ain't going to like them, not one little bit.'

The atmosphere within the King's Theatre was stuffy and oppressive, too many bodies crammed into too small a space, and all for Mr Kelly's benefit night. Those in the gallery were in jovial form and were already shouting and laughing even before the play had begun. When the curtain finally rose on the comedy *Road to Ruin* their crude comments grew louder, thus creating a raucous atmosphere in which the actors struggled in vain to portray their parts with some level of decorum. The dowager's face showed all too well exactly what she thought of such a coarse display.

'No sign of Nicholas yet?' Lady Maybury fanned herself with vigour.

'No, my lady.'

'Not like him to be late, but then he does have other things on his mind at the minute,' she said, resting her faded green gaze knowingly upon her companion.

Kathryn glanced uneasily at her employer. Surely the dowager did not know what her grandson was planning? 'Does he?' she asked, trying not to sound guilty.

'Most certainly,' said Lady Maybury with a twinkle in her eye.

A smile, then Kathryn decided to steer the conversation to safer ground. 'Are you enjoying the performance, my lady?'

'Blasted nonsense with those louts crowing in the background. Damnable waste of time,' she pronounced with venom. 'And it's so uncomfortably hot in this wretched place.'

'Would you like me to fetch you a lemonade before the curtain goes up again?'

'Would you, dear gel?'

'Of course.' And so saying Kathryn exited the box, brushing against the scarlet curtains as she did so. She had barely walked more than a few paces when she became aware of the libidinous stares of several gentlemen who were loitering close by the marble pillars. With an averted gaze and a determined thrust of the chin she headed to the stairwell, only to be intercepted by Lord Stanfield.

'Miss Marchant,' he said. 'Enchanted to see you again. I hope that you enjoyed your stay in Brighthelmstone.'

'Indeed, sir. It was most enjoyable.' Something in the man's manner made her uncomfortable, not that his words could be faulted. He was politeness itself, but beneath the polished veneer… It hardly seemed possible that this was the same man she had danced with so many times in the weeks preceding Brighthelmstone. There was a subtle change, something that she could not quite define.

He lingered a trifle too long over her hand, pressed his lips that bit too ardently to her fingers.

She retrieved her hand and saw his focus drop to her bosom where it remained in undisguised and leisurely pleasure. 'Please excuse me, Lord Stanfield,' she said coldly and moved swiftly past. The thump in her chest and heat in her cheeks persuaded her she had not misinterpreted his behaviour. Thrusting the thought from her mind, she made her way down the stairs and started to traverse the crowded hallway to the queue at the refreshments table. A hush descended, marred only by whisperings and snide laughter. On either side men and women slowly, deliberately, turned their backs to her. There could be no mistaking that clear signal, a cut to her face.

With a hammering heart and trembling legs Kathryn held her head up and walked with quiet dignity towards the table. The crowd parted before her, contempt upon the faces of the fine ladies before they turned them away, and something worse upon the gentlemen's. And then straight ahead, barely a few feet away, she saw Mr and Mrs Marchant. Her eyes met those of her aunt, and for a moment she thought that the woman meant to help her, to rescue her from the nightmare in which she suddenly found herself. Anna Marchant smiled, and her eyes were cold, hard chips of ice. There was nothing of kindness and everything of malice contained in her look. Vulnerability had long fled, as had any vestige of all other pretence. With slow deliberation Mrs Marchant turned to present her back. Uncle Henry followed suit. Voices buzzed in the background. Kathryn swallowed down the aridity in her throat and refused to be beaten. She walked on through the cleared route hedged by a line of smartly presented backs. With her eyes fixed ahead she purchased two lemonades and turned to retrace her steps, running the gauntlet once more. Quite how she did so with such cool reserve she would never know, not when the very ground seemed to loom up towards her.

Halfway up the stairwell she encountered Mr Roodley on his way down. Although he did not address her, his knowing brown eyes swept brazenly over her body as he passed.

The safety of the box was in sight when she felt the firm touch of a hand upon her bottom. Lecherous sniggers sounded from a small group of gentlemen lounging against a wall. Kathryn stopped, and drawing herself up to her full height, turned with icy fury. She would never know the image she presented at that moment, with her ashen skin and stormy grey eyes, her small nose flared and full lips parted in readiness for battle, the steady rise and fall of her breasts and the rigid stance of her body. Indignation personified. Deathly silence. The pulse thrummed in her throat, as one by one she fixed her chill gaze upon them, until their leers and smiles vanished and they looked away. Then she turned and walked to the box, white knuckles gripping the glasses for dear life.

'Oh there you are, my dear. Thank you.' Lady Maybury gratefully sipped at the lemonade. 'So refreshing.' The faded green eyes raked her companion's countenance. 'Kathryn?'

She could not speak, sat frozen in a state of shock, the lemonade untouched before her.

The dowager's hand gripped to hers. 'What is it? What has happened? You look as if you've seen a ghost…and you're shaking.'

'I'm feeling a little unwell. I'm sure it will shortly pass,' she whispered. 'Please do not concern yourself, my lady.'

Lady Maybury frowned, 'But I am concerned, gel, and do not give me that old flannel of feeling unwell. You left here fine enough ten minutes ago and return looking like death warmed up. Am I not entitled to some explanation?'

Her hand pressed to her brow. Where to begin? What to say? Blasted, pulverised, unable to think straight. Kathryn squeezed her eyes shut and swallowed hard at the memory of what had just occurred. But what *had* just happened? And why? Her fingers trembled as they pulled at the silk of her skirt. Why? The question sounded again and again in her mind. The reason did not matter, not once Lady Maybury witnessed the sorry state of affairs upon their exit. It was perhaps fortuitous that they had arrived at the theatre early to beat the crowds, thus stalling the inevitability of what was to come.

'Kathryn—' the elderly voice sounded close to her ear '—come, we'd better get you home, my dear.'

'But Lord Ravensmede—'

'Will know where to find us,' finished Lady Maybury. 'There's nothing to worry about.'

At the sound of such genuine concern Kathryn could bear her shame no longer. 'I'm sorry, my lady, so very sorry. You've been so kind, like my own grandmother instead of an employer. I would do anything to save you from… Please forgive me.' Her voice ruptured into hoarseness and she spoke no more, just touched the frail old hand to her cheek in a gesture of affection.

'Come on,' came the imperious command.

'The play is not yet finished.'

'A bigger load of tripe I've yet to see. I'll not waste any more of my time on it. Hurry along now.' Lady Maybury rose from her seat.

'My lady, there's something you should know before you…before you leave this box.' Kathryn's fingers plucked nervously at one another.

A white eyebrow raised in a gesture similar to that so favoured by the lady's grandson.

The smoky grey gaze dropped to the floor. 'It seems that I have…incurred the condemnation of…that is to say, I have invoked the displeasure of…'

'You may explain it to me in detail once we're home. I've no mind to stay here any longer.' Lady Maybury swept from the box with regal elegance, seemingly oblivious to the whisperings and raising of viewing glasses all around.

They passed few people of any significance on their way from the theatre to the carriage, but the manner of those in their path soon enlightened Lady Maybury as to the cause of her companion's distress.

'Of all the most idiotic, petty and malicious behaviours!' The dowager was working herself into a lofty dudgeon. 'How dare they cut m'companion!'

'Their treatment of me is inconsequential, but I'm dismayed to see that Lady Collins was so frosty to you, my lady. I'm sorry that you should be so affected. I will, of course, leave at once to save you further embarrassment.'

'Don't be ridiculous,' the lady snapped fiercely. 'You were quite the toast of the town when we left only a few weeks ago. And while in Brighthelmstone you barely strayed from the view of my beady eye.'

Kathryn thought of the hungry kisses from Nicholas's mouth. She remembered the warmth of his body lying on top of hers and the press of his bed against her back. The memories brought a guilty heat to her cheeks. Mercifully the carriage interior was dim.

'This abominable treatment is without the slightest merit.'

Kathryn said nothing.

The remainder of the journey continued in silence with the dowager brooding and Kathryn in a state of numb disbelief.

The ladies did not have to wait long before Ravensmede arrived at Upper Grosvenor Street.

'Grandmama, Kathryn.' The green gaze saw in an instant the

tension etched upon the girl's face. 'I went to the theatre first. My apologies for being late.'

'Well, you're here now, thank goodness. Kathryn and I have encountered something of a problem.' The dowager threw off her cashmere shawl in a flurry, ordered that the brandy decanter be brought to the library and ushered both her companion and her grandson into that small cosy room.

'If I may be so bold as to comment, ma'am, you appear a trifle put out,' said Ravensmede, trying to gauge just how far the gossip had spread. 'Was the play not to your satisfaction?'

She waved the butler away, shut the door with a decisive thud and poured three glasses of brandy. Kathryn was then pushed unceremoniously down into a chair and a glass pressed firmly in her hand. 'Drink!' commanded the dowager.

It seemed the gossip-mongers had been busy. Ravensmede could see the tremor in the girl's fingers.

A minute's pause and the glass raised to those lips that were so unnaturally pale. She sipped on the spirit, made a face at the strength of its taste, and swallowed it down.

His grandmother wasted no time in emptying the contents of her glass and soon had it refilled.

'Grandmama.' Ravensmede made to take his grandparent's arm. 'Perhaps you should sit down and tell me what has happened.'

'Polite society,' said Lady Maybury acidly, 'has decided that m'companion is no longer acceptable. Kathryn has received the cut direct.'

'I see,' replied Ravensmede without the least surprise.

'And we have no notion as to the cause of this sudden outlandish behaviour,' said the old lady.

His eyes skimmed to Kathryn once more, but she had not moved one inch, just sat with the brandy glass gripped within her fingers, the amber liquid almost untouched. 'Ah,' he said softly, 'I think I may be able to help you with that.'

Two pairs of eyes swivelled to his.

There was no easy way to say what must be said. A dagger twisted in his gut at the very thought, but he rose nevertheless, without a shadow of the anger and pain that troubled him. He leaned back against the small wooden desk and stretched out his legs before him.

Time slowed within the library. No one spoke. No one moved. They sat as statues and waited.

He could defer no longer. 'It seems that there's a malicious rumour circulating regarding Kathryn's relationship with a certain gentleman. The couple are believed to have behaved without propriety.'

The fire crackled in the grate. The soft wheeze of Lady Maybury's breathing.

He looked up at Kathryn's white face, her eyes huge and dark, overwhelmed by the blackness of her pupils.

'With whom am I purported to have established such a…relationship?' The words forced from her bloodless lips.

Ravensmede calmed the leap of his pulse. The merest twitch of the muscle in his jaw.

She was watching him still, a mask of calmness across her face.

'With myself,' came the dry reply.

Silence echoed.

'They think you're keeping m'companion as your mistress?' Lady Maybury questioned with alarming candour.

A sharp intake of air from the slender figure opposite, and the stormy grey eyes with all their hurt, all their fury, all their incredulity, dropped to the floor.

'It would appear so, ma'am,' Ravensmede conceded.

She turned to face her grandson. 'Then you had better speak to Kathryn,' said the dowager, and walked out of the room.

The latch clicked into place. The grandfather clock ticked its slow steady rhythm.

'Tell me the whole of it,' Kathryn said in a small, tightly controlled voice.

'It's better that I don't.'

Her shoulders squared back, her chin thrust out in defiance. 'I need to know.'

He gave a curt nod. 'Harry Silverton has been busy informing anyone who will listen that I was responsible for the ruination of a young lady acting in the capacity of my grandmother's companion. He's adamant that he witnessed you within my arms while I was in state of some undress upon the sofa in the drawing room of our rented accommodation.'

Kathryn's temper flared, 'What nonsense! He's misinterpreting the whole thing. Where is the mention of his drunken state, or the fact that he shot his pistol at you?' Her eyes flashed and colour burned in her previously pale cheeks. 'Can we not discredit his lies?'

'Even if we could, I'm afraid that Silverton's tale is not all.'

'There's more?' An incredulous frown wrinkled her brow.

He reached for her.

Adamant, she shook her head. 'No. Just tell me.' If he touched her, the last of her brittle control would shatter.

In a calm mellow voice the Viscount proceeded to apprise Kathryn of the worst of their problem.

'And you have seen this printed leaflet yourself?'

'Yes,' he said grimly. 'Cadmount kept one copy and destroyed all the others he could find. Unfortunately, it seems that the damage was already done.'

She held out her hand. 'May I see it, please?'

'I'm afraid it is a crude and vulgar piece, not fit for the eyes of any lady.'

'Not even the subject of its story? Have I not a right to know?'

His eyes did not leave her face. 'It is where it belongs, Kathryn, burned to a cinder.'

She swallowed hard, determination and anger and devastation glinting in her eyes. 'What exactly did it say?'

An uncompromising expression slipped across Ravensmede's face.

'Tell me.'

His jaw set firm.

'Would you have me alone ignorant of what all of London is saying?' She saw the flicker in his focus, knew he was weakening. 'Please, Nicholas.'

He sighed. 'It is a tale in which the Viscount of R. and the widowed Mrs W. arrange an illicit liaison in a back room at Lady Finlay's ball. The widow arrives, only to interrupt a scene of impropriety between Lord R. and a certain Miss M., whom he later installed as his mistress under the guise of his grandmother's companion.' He did not tell her that every tawdry detail of the encounter had been obscenely exaggerated.

Kathryn's face paled. 'Only Mrs White knew,' she whispered.

'Mrs White is hardly portrayed in a flattering light within the article. Had Amanda White been responsible, I'd warrant it would have read a tad more in her favour.'

'Who would do such a thing? Pay from their own pocket to print and distribute such a spiteful piece of work? No one else knew.'

The bright green eyes narrowed of a sudden. He indicated Kathryn's barely touched glass of brandy. 'It might be a good idea to take another sip…a big one.'

Kathryn gripped her hands together tightly to stop them from shaking. 'You know, don't you?'

His gaze faltered. 'It is not pleasant,' he said.

'None of it is.' A terrible coldness was spreading through her body, tensing each and every muscle. And the dread of foreboding writhed in her gut. She waited, watching his anger vie with compassion, his rage with tenderness.

There was nothing but the moment and the waiting.

'I've spoken to the printer and the boy who delivered the article and instruction to him.'

'Already?'

His shoulders shrugged. 'I was still late for the theatre, and I would not have had you face that alone for all the world, Kathryn.' Their eyes locked. 'The boy took me to the house from where the letter was sent…'

She wetted the dryness of her lips. Suddenly knew the name that would pass his lips. The blood roared in her ears, so loud she feared she would not hear him.

'It was in Green Street. The woman who paid for the article was your aunt.'

Even as he confirmed what she feared she sat still as a statue in the chair, unmoving, lifeless, her expression frozen, her eyes wide and unblinking. And then her eyelids shuttered.

She did not hear him move, was not aware that anything had changed around her until she felt him kneel before her and pull her into his arms. His warmth thawed her, his strength anchored her. All around her a storm was breaking, and he was her only haven. She felt the wetness upon her cheeks, tasted the salt upon her lips, and did not know that she was weeping. A sobbing escaped her throat before she could catch it back. She laid her face against his chest, felt his hands upon her back, reassuring, protective. They did not speak; they did not have to.

A dam had broken, and all the misery, all the suffering, everything that Kathryn had so carefully stoppered through the past years rushed out. Fear and frustration and fury. Hurt and betrayal and grief. In three long years she had not wept, not once. Now that the tears had started it seemed that they would never cease. She wept until there were no more tears to weep. When finally she stopped there was nothing. Just an emptiness, and the throb of her head and the gritty nip of her eyes.

She noticed then the damp wool of Nicholas's coat lapels against her cheek, the warmth of his arms wrapped around her. Noticed too that she was standing, her body pressed into his, although quite how or when she rose from the chair she could not say. Neither of them moved. Both seemed content just to be, unmoving in the calm hush of peace. Steady thud of heartbeats, gentle rise and fall of breath. It was a place in which she could rest for ever. Seconds stretched to minutes,

minutes dragged to hours, until at last his fingers found her chin, tilted her face up towards his, and Kathryn knew she could hide no longer.

'I never meant for this to happen,' he said.

'I know.'

A little pause.

'You know too that you'll have to marry me.'

A rapid inhalation of air. She should have known it was coming. He was too honourable a man to do anything else, despite all that society thought him. A proposal of marriage from Nicholas Maybury, the man that she loved, the man of whom she had dreamed. She should have been ecstatic with happiness. But she wasn't. He was a viscount, heir to an earldom, wealthier than she could imagine. She was untitled, poor, with neither dowry nor connections. Moreover, he was expected to marry Miss Francesca Paton, if the scandal had not already jeopardised that arrangement. Kathryn could not hope to wed...not as a fallen woman. She was alone, and would stay alone.

There was also the small matter of love. She felt it. He did not. Her eyes closed. She thought of Nicholas's father and the Earl's expectations. She thought of Lady Maybury and of all that the dowager had done for her. She thought of Miss Paton waiting patiently for Nicholas's offer of marriage. But most of all she thought of Nicholas and how much she loved him. Her pulse steadied. When her eyes opened Kathryn knew what she must do. 'No,' she said quietly. 'I know no such thing.'

Nicholas gave a crooked smile. 'You do now.'

'No, Nicholas.' She captured his fingers within her hand. 'I thank you for your kind offer, but I'm afraid I cannot be your wife.'

'Kathryn, you're ruined. You've no other choice but to marry me.'

Slowly she shook her head. 'It's my reputation that's ruined, not myself.'

'You'll exist as a pariah, not received in any decent house.

If you think your treatment harsh so far, it will only get worse.'
His gaze razed her. 'Men will think you an easy target for their
attentions. You'll be subjected to the worst of their lechery.'

Still she did not speak.

'You must know that you cannot possibly continue as my
grandmother's companion.'

Her head bowed. She swallowed hard. 'I understand.'

The green eyes narrowed as if he understood for the first
time the absolute certainty of her resolve. 'Don't be ridiculous,
Kathryn. You've no other option.'

'I can think of one,' she said, and her cheeks burned pink at
the audacity of what she was about to suggest.

A tiny frown creased between his eyebrows. 'Pray enlighten
me,' he said in a quietly dangerous voice.

Her fingers still touched lightly against his. She could not
look him in the eye. Drawing all of her courage together, she
forced the words out quickly before she could catch them back.
'Once before, in St James's Park, you made me…a different
offer. Yesterday, in the coach on the way back from Brighthelmstone, you would have asked me the same thing. If the
offer is still open…I accept.' She felt his fingers stiffen beneath
hers. Saw the incredulity in his eyes.

He gave a spurt of ironic laughter. 'Let me check that I understand you correctly, Kathryn. You'll consent to become my
mistress, but not my wife?'

It sounded so brazen that she felt the heat spread from her
cheeks to burn the very tips of her ears. 'Yes,' a hoarse whisper
of agreement.

'May I ask why?'

She loosed his hand. Stepped back. Met his gaze. 'I would
not force you to a *mésalliance*.'

He said nothing, just waited expectantly.

The explanation came tripping out of her mouth unbidden.
'I am not titled or wealthy. Indeed, I cannot bring you either a
dowry or connections.'

No reply.

'And this is not the first scandal to attach itself to my family name.'

Still he did not speak.

She found herself rambling on. 'It would not be fair to either Lady Maybury or your father.' Her eyes darted away. 'And then there is Miss Paton.'

'What of Miss Paton?' he asked, and his face was leaner and harder than ever she had seen it.

'You have long been promised to marry her.'

'Have I?' His focus pulled her back, never wavering for a moment. 'And what if I say that it is not true? That I have no need of more money. That each and every one of the reasons you list is nothing more than an excuse. And that the proposal I would have made you yesterday was one of marriage.'

She shook her head, knowing that his honour forced him to deny the truth.

'Yet you still offer yourself as my mistress?'

The breath felt trapped within her lungs. Her fingers gripped against her skirt. She could feel his tension as clearly as if it were her own.

'Why would you do that, Kathryn?' he said silkily, and moved closer.

She could not tell him. Would not speak of love. That small last vestige of pride held strong. She stepped back, striving to maintain a distance between them.

'You think that is what you want, do you?' Without any further warning he pulled her to him, crushing her in a brutal embrace. His lips raked hers, punishing, hard, taking what they would. This time there was no tenderness, no teasing affection. It was a kiss to brand her, a kiss of possession.

She was powerless to resist such an assault.

At last he raised his face from hers and the determination in his eyes took her breath away. 'I disagree. Besides, the offer I made you in the park no longer stands, Kathryn.' He released her and stepped away, watching while she stumbled back into the chair. And then he was gone, leaving Kathryn more confused than she had ever thought possible.

Chapter Fifteen

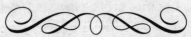

It was early the next morning when a commotion sounded in the hallway of Ravensmede House.

'I don't give a damn what he's doing. I want to see him, and I want to see him now!' A man's face contorted with fury as he strode uninvited into the drawing room. The volume of his voice carried throughout the house.

Within the breakfast room Ravensmede set down his coffee cup. He waved away the footman and without further dalliance moved swiftly and sleekly along the corridor to meet his father.

They faced each other across the drawing room.

The Earl was almost as tall as his son; his silver locks glistened in the sunlight that streamed into the room through the four large-paned windows. 'So it has come to this,' he said, 'as ever I knew it would.' His hand slipped into the pocket of his immaculately tailored coat and withdrew a folded piece of paper. With a deft flick of his wrist he unfolded the paper and, turning it round so that his son might see the printed side, dangled it between the tips of two fingers as if he thought to contaminate himself from its touch.

One glance at the sheet told Ravensmede all he needed to know. It was Anna Marchant's leaflet.

'You've gone too far this time, boy. What the hell do you think you're playing at, dragging your family into your schemes? I didn't think that even you would stoop so low as to attach such scandal to your own grandmother's name.'

Not one glimmer of emotion showed upon Ravensmede's face. Only the slight tension around his jaw betrayed the mask for what it was. 'For that I beg her forgiveness. It was never my intention.'

'God knows I've tried my best to warn you, but you always were intent on going your own way.'

'So it would seem, sir,' said Ravensmede coolly.

'And what of this Miss Marchant?'

'Surely your sources will have told you of her? It seems they have not omitted aught else,' came the gritted reply.

The Earl's eyes narrowed. 'I've heard something of Mr and Mrs Henry Marchant. If that family's character is any estimation of their niece, you are well caught by your own folly.'

'Kathryn has the misfortune to share her name with those people, nothing more.'

A silver brow arched in an arrogant gesture Ravensmede himself so frequently used. 'It matters little,' he said. 'It's one thing to waste your time and your money with widows and harlots, it's quite another to seduce unmarried young *ladies*, especially those that must make their own way in the world.'

Their gazes met and locked. 'For once we are in agreement, sir. Nevertheless, I would have you know that the leaflet is nothing but a piece of malicious spite. Miss Marchant is a lady of unimpeachable virtue.' In his mind he heard again the whisper of her soft voice. *Once before, in St James's Park, you made me a...different offer. If the offer is still open...I accept.* The thought of what it must have cost her to say those words wrenched at his heart. She was an innocent...in every aspect of the word. He would not have his father think otherwise. There could only be one real reason why Kathryn had declined marriage in favour of a more illicit relationship. And Nicholas had a very shrewd idea just what that might be. 'You may say what you will, sir, but I mean to marry Miss Marchant all the same.'

Lord Maybury sauntered to the brandy decanter and poured two large glasses. He lifted one himself and left the other for his son to retrieve. 'I'm relieved to hear that for once you're prepared to do the honourable thing. Whether you laid a finger on the girl or not is irrelevant. To all intents and purposes she's well and truly ruined.'

Ravensmede did not move from his stance next to the blackened grate. 'I assure you that the leaflet does not figure the slightest in my plans, sir. I have intended making Kathryn my wife for some time.' The expression on Nicholas's face was one that the Earl had never before seen.

Maybury grunted. 'And what of Miss Paton?' A swig of brandy disappeared down his throat.

A dry laugh erupted into the silence. 'There was never the remotest possibility that Francesca and I would marry. We would not suit, no matter how much you and her father will it otherwise.'

Silence hissed around them, and from both faces the same green eyes looked out.

The glass banged against the mahogany of the table as Maybury set it down hard. 'I think that I should meet Miss Marchant.'

'We may see her in half an hour's time at Grandmama's house.'

'It's a trifle early to call upon ladies,' the Earl protested.

'The visit has already been arranged: there is someone else whom I want Kathryn to meet.'

Kathryn lay awake all the night through, worrying over what to do. Sunlight was infiltrating the blinds and the birds chirping a lively racket by the time she finally reached a decision. Only then did she succumb to the oblivion of sleep. It seemed only minutes later when there was a knock at the door to her bedchamber, the pad of feet, and the rustle of skirt material. The aroma of freshly brewed coffee and bread still warm from the oven drifted to her nose. Kathryn groaned, pulled the bedcover over her head and rolled on to her stomach.

'Beggin' you pardon, miss, but her ladyship said as how I was to bring you a little breakfast.' The maid set the tray down on the bedside table and moved across to the other side of the room.

'Thank you, Betsy. How very kind.' One bleary eye peeped out from beneath the covers, just as Betsy raised the blind, and bright white sunlight flooded across the room. Another groan escaped Kathryn.

Betsy cast a curious look in the direction of the bed. Lying late in bed was out of character for Miss Marchant, who was normally up and about with the larks. But then again, if the gossip below stairs was anything to go by, the situation that the dowager's companion now found herself in was far removed from normal. The maid wondered if the rumours were true. Lord Ravensmede was a fine-looking gent, and as the old saying went, there was no smoke without fire. Certainly Toby knew more than he was letting on; no doubt his lordship had greased the footman's palm to keep him quiet. 'Are you ill, miss? Shall I fetch Lady Maybury?'

Kathryn pushed herself upright, and sat back against her pillows. 'No, I'm quite well, thank you, just tired. The coffee shall revive me admirably.'

Not by the look of the dark shadows beneath Miss Marchant's eyes it wouldn't, thought Betsy, and then remembered the other message that she had been instructed to impart. 'Oh, I nearly forgot miss, her ladyship would like to see you in the drawing room at ten o'clock.'

Kathryn glanced at the clock on the mantel. 'It's half past nine now!'

'Yes, miss.'

'Heavens! How on earth could I have slept so late?' Kathryn swung her legs out of the bed.

'I'll fetch you some warm water, miss.' And Betsy disappeared.

Kathryn drank the coffee down and ate two bread rolls smeared with honey. There would be no room for weakness in today's dealings. She was under no illusion as to what the dowager wanted to say. The old lady could hardly be expected to keep on a companion whose name had been linked so scandalously with the lady's own grandson. Even Nicholas had said as much.

Nicholas. The mere thought of him made her feel uncomfortably warm. The uncomfortable feeling expanded at the memory of what had passed between them yesterday. Kathryn's cheeks flamed. It was bad enough to offer herself like a common trollop. His rejection was a thousand times worse. She blew out air from between her lips, feeling the sting of shame yet again. He had offered her marriage. Marriage, for goodness' sake! Better than all of her dreams put together. To spend the rest of her life as his wife… How very easy it would have been to say that one tiny word, yes. Yes.

Yes! She should have shouted it from the boughs of the trees. But she had thought better, and now the offer was gone. As was his desire. He had said she was ruined, and so she was. With little money and nowhere to go, Kathryn knew her options were limited. She could only pray that the gossip would not reach Hampshire. Her mother's relatives were her last hope. With a heavy heart she moved to fetch the old trunk she had brought with her from Green Street.

It was only a little after ten when Kathryn was washed, dressed and ready. She had turned a deaf ear to Betsy's protestations and worn her old blue muslin dress. The trunk sitting ominously by the door was as empty as when it had arrived. Madame Dupont's skilfully fashioned dresses, for which Kathryn had not yet fully reimbursed Lady Maybury, were left hanging in the clothes-press. The pearl necklace and earrings gifted by her ladyship sat neatly in the jewellery box on the dressing table. Kathryn was unadorned. Her fingers carefully skimmed her hair just to check that none of her neatly pinned curls had escaped. A deep breath, a squaring of her shoulders, one final smoothing of her skirt, and then she opened the door and walked towards the drawing room…and Lady Maybury's dismissal.

The scene within the drawing room was not what Kathryn expected. She stood for a moment, unnoticed, staring, drinking in the sight before her. The dowager sat in her usual chair by the unlit fireplace, chatting ten to the dozen. Her expression was warm and lively, her manner familiar as if she knew the young woman who was seated demurely upon the nearby sofa very well indeed. In a glance Kathryn could see that the girl was tall and willowy, with silky dark brown hair worn in an elaborate coiffure. Two tiny white pearls dangled from her ears. Her white-and-pastel-blue dress was well cut and fashionably stylish. Everything about her bespoke money and breeding, and she wore it all with an air of effortless relaxation. Kathryn's fingers strayed self-consciously to her own shabby gown. By the window stood two men, both tall, both with the same green eyes, both wearing the same defiant arrogance, one with hair as dark as night, the other whose head had silvered with age. Kathryn's heart skipped a beat as it did whenever she saw Nicholas. It was not hard to guess the identity of the older man standing by his side.

The little group looked comfortable, at ease, like they belonged together. There was only one outsider. For a minute she felt the urge to turn and run, and then the moment was gone. Before she could think any further as to what was going on, she heard Nicholas's voice.

'Miss Marchant,' he said, and made his way to her side. 'Come in.'

She ignored the hammering of her heart and held her head high. 'Lord Ravensmede,' she replied politely, and gave a small curtsy. And then turning to his grandmother, 'Lady Maybury.'

Although she was careful to keep her gaze averted from his, she could feel his scrutiny. Just his voice was enough to set her insides aquiver. She set her face determinedly and prayed that her cheeks did not appear as scalded as the rest of her felt.

He wasted no time in the introductions. 'This is my father, Earl Maybury.'

The man by his side bowed. 'I'm pleased to welcome you to our family, Miss Marchant.' Pleased did not describe the expression on his face. Appraising came closer.

Kathryn froze at the implication of his words. It was clear that Lord Maybury misunderstood the situation. She glanced at Nicholas, waiting for his reaction.

Ravensmede made no notice of having heard anything untoward. He met her gaze with a strange look, as if he was poised, as if he was waiting. There was a pause that was slightly too long for comfort, and then he said, 'Kathryn, this is Miss Francesca Paton.'

Kathryn stifled the gasp, blinked back the black dots swimming before her eyes and breathed deeply. The dizziness diminished. A warm hand pressed against the small of her back. Without looking she knew it to belong to Nicholas. She forced herself to step towards Miss Paton, away from the support that Nicholas offered. 'Miss Paton,' she said, and was relieved to hear that her voice sounded a deal calmer than she felt.

Miss Paton made her reply.

An awkwardness followed.

Then the dowager rose to her feet, and smiled. 'There's something to which I must attend. Please do excuse me.' And she tottered out of the door.

Nicholas stepped closer. 'My father and I must also take our leave of you…for now.' Then they too were gone.

A pair of fine hazel eyes turned upon her. 'Miss Marchant, please do come and sit beside me.' She patted a hand to the cushion to her left. 'Nicholas has told me all about you.'

Not *all,* Kathryn sincerely prayed. 'Thank you, Miss Paton,' she said with as much dignity as she could muster, and seated herself on the sofa.

Miss Paton leaned forward and smiled. 'Please call me Francesca.' Her expression was open and honest and sincere. 'You must be wondering as to the reason for my visit at such an early hour.' Without waiting for an answer she continued. 'Firstly, I came to wish you happy.'

Every muscle in Kathryn's body stiffened. She wetted her lips, unsure of what to say.

'And, secondly, I wished to meet for myself the lady that has finely succeeded in capturing Nicholas's heart.' Her smile broadened and there was a definite twinkle in her eyes.

Kathryn tried to smile, but her mouth seemed unwilling to respond. Something akin to a grimace stretched across her face. 'I fear that you may have misunderstood the—'

Miss Paton let her get no further. Her hand touched to Kathryn's in a gesture of friendship. 'Miss Marchant,' she started, and then said as an aside, 'Or may I call you Kathryn?'

'Of course,' murmured Kathryn.

'Kathryn, let me tell you how heartily relieved I am that Nicholas has at last decided to marry. You know my father and Lord Maybury are great friends, and have for years been trying to force a match between Nicholas and myself.' She laughed. 'Have you ever heard anything more ridiculous?'

It did not sound in the least ridiculous to Kathryn. Miss Paton was heiress to a considerable fortune. Lord Ravensmede was heir to an earldom. There was no disputing that the two were well matched. Kathryn held her tongue.

'Why, my dear Kathryn, Nicholas and I would not suit at all. He's a dear man, and a very great friend of the family, but that is all.'

'I thought…' Kathryn found her voice at last. 'I thought that there was an informal betrothal between you both, an understanding that you would marry.'

'Oh, no, not at all!' Miss Paton exclaimed. 'Besides, my interest lies elsewhere.'

Kathryn watched as two pink patches suddenly appeared on Miss Paton's cheeks. 'You have a *tendre* for someone else?'

Miss Paton's cheeks dimpled, and her face lit up. 'There is a certain curate. He's kind and diligent and of quite the most admirable character. But he's a little shy of approaching my father. Little wonder, for although Papa is the best of fathers, he can appear a tiny bit intimidating in his manner to those with whom he is unfamiliar.' Worry washed across Miss Paton's face. 'I beg you will not speak of it, Kathryn. We have told no one, though now that you've taken care of Nicholas for me, the way is clear for Thomas to speak to my papa.'

A weight lifted from Kathryn's shoulders. 'Your secret is safe with me. And I sincerely hope that you and Thomas find happiness.'

'Thank you,' said Miss Paton.

'No, thank *you*, Francesca,' Kathryn said, and meant it.

They moved to talk of the weather, and then discussed the Duke of Wellington's recent victory against Napoleon. Miss Paton told Kathryn all about the magnificent firework display at Vauxhall Gardens to celebrate the event. From there talk led on to the latest fashions, and then the birth of Lady Harrington's twins. Never once did she make the slightest mention of the most scandalous rumours sweeping every drawing room in London, especially those concerning Lord Ravensmede and his grandmother's companion.

Indeed, when Nicholas returned, alone, it was to find the two women chatting as if they were the best of friends.

Within a few minutes of the Viscount entering the drawing room, Miss Paton took her leave.

Nicholas leaned against the mantel above the fireplace.

Kathryn stayed where she was upon the sofa.

He was careful to keep his face expressionless. 'Did you and Miss Paton find anything interesting to discuss?'

Her face raised to his and he could see that much of the earlier tension had vanished. The silver eyes held a glimmer of mischief. 'Perhaps.'

He moved from the fireplace to take up the seat that Miss Paton had so recently vacated. Kathryn edged closer to the opposite arm of the sofa. He arched an eyebrow. 'Scared?'

'No. Should I be?'

A nearly smile pulled at his mouth. 'Most definitely so. I've just neatly disposed of two of your objections to marrying me. Two more to go and then you're mine, Kathryn Marchant.'

Shock rippled across her face. 'You still wish to wed me?' There was a definite breathy catch to her voice. 'Even after…'

'*Especially* after your proposition.' His eyebrow twitched.

Colour flooded her cheeks. 'It was not a proposition,' she said stubbornly.

He gave her a knowing look. 'If you say so.'

Her gaze fluttered away, and her fingers picked at the skirt of her dress.

He couldn't afford to let himself touch her…not yet. He produced a letter from his pocket and threw it on to the sofa between them. It was addressed to Miss Kathryn Marchant. No other direction had been added.

She peered at it suspiciously.

'Open it.'

A moment's hesitation, and then she did. The wafer broke beneath her fingers and the paper unfolded to reveal the lines of black flowing script. Disbelief creased her forehead. Slowly, concentrating on each word, she read the letter's contents again. 'It's from my uncle. He has enclosed a banker's draft for five hundred pounds…as a dowry.' The paper fluttered to her lap. She stared at him. 'I don't understand.'

'You're his brother's daughter. It is only to be expected that he would supply you with a dowry.'

'But…the scandal…my uncle and aunt have disowned me.'

'It would appear that they have changed their minds.'

Her eyelids shuttered momentarily. She pressed her fingers to her lips, as if to stopper any flow of emotion.

'So it seems, Kathryn, that you now have a dowry…if you should choose to use it as such.'

'I…' He could see her confusion.

His voice gentled. 'Which leaves only your last excuse… your family.'

'You cannot change that, nor would I wish you to,' she said softly.

'Why would I want to, when you have such good connections?' A wry smile curved. 'I have it upon the best of authorities that your mother was a Thornley of Overton.'

She wiped the emotion from her face, fixed her expression to one of blandness. Several heartbeats passed. 'Before you say any more, Nicholas, there is something I should tell you.' Not one movement. Not one betraying flicker of her eyes. 'This is not the first scandal to be attached to my family name. My father…' An image of her papa lying slumped upon his desk, a spent pistol in his hand. She stopped. Cleared her throat. The blink of her eyes lasted just fractionally too long. 'My father…' Again it seemed she could not bring herself to say the words.

'I know, Kathryn,' he said, wishing to spare her the worst of it. Her gaze clung to his. 'How did you find out?'

'Does it matter?'

She shook her head, inadvertently dislodging a few curls. 'No. I suppose not. It's just that I've never spoken of it. Never. But not one day has passed without its memory. So much blood…and the pistol still in his hand…and his face…' She caught at her lower lip with her teeth.

He moved then. Closed the space between them, until their legs touched together on the sofa. Took her hands in his. Gripped them firm. 'I did not mean to remind you.'

'I cannot forget,' she said. 'But with time it grows easier, and there are other things that help me not to think of it.' Such as daydreaming and the man who sat so closely by her side, but she would never say so.

Her fingers were small and cool beneath his. His thumb stroked at the back of her hand. 'Your father's death was a tragedy, but the blame is not yours. It has no bearing on our marriage.' He leaned back against the sofa, keeping her within his gaze, watching the emotion cloud the brilliance of her eyes. 'So,' he said, 'Kathryn Marchant, will you do me the honour of becoming my wife?' Blood pulsed through the pulse point at the side of his neck. Thud. Thud. Thud. His hand still covered hers. Everything was still. Motionless. Breath caught and held, waiting to exhale.

She looked at him, really looked at him, as if seeing him for the first time.

His grip unwittingly tightened.

'Yes,' she said, in a whisper. And a small sigh escaped her.

Whether it was a sigh of sadness or resignation or relief, Nicholas did not know. He pulled her into his arms and dropped a kiss to the top of her hair.

It was Kathryn who pulled back. Kathryn, whose free hand touched to his cheek, her thumb brushing against his lips, tracing down to his chin. He saw her eyes drop to his lips, sensed her need. And then her mouth touched to his, her lips moving in sweet tentative enquiry.

The green eyes sparked. His lips answered her call, sliding and teasing, caressing and tickling.

Her mouth opened in sensual invitation.

The hot moisture of his tongue penetrated. She met his probing with her own. Tongue lapped against tongue.

He groaned and pulled her fully into his arms. 'Kathryn!' The rawness of emotion rendered his voice hoarse. His hands moved upon her back weaving patterns of age-old magic that she could not ignore.

Her fingers threaded through the burnt umber of his hair. Deep within her was an ache of longing. The hardness of his chest grazed her breasts, and she thrust against him and felt the thrum of his heart beneath that warm solid wall of muscle.

His hand moved to claim first one breast and then the other. Much more of this and he would be lost. The last vestige of reason pulled him back from temptation. Gently he eased himself away, looking her full in eyes that smouldered with passion and emotion. 'Sweetheart,' he said, 'it's a good thing I already have the special licence. I don't think my restraint will last much longer.'

With only two days to go before the wedding Lady Maybury decided a mammoth shopping expedition was in order. 'It's such a shame that there's not time to have a new gown made for you. We'll have to make do with a new bonnet and gloves. Oh, and a bandeau perhaps, and stockings…and a matching reticule.' The dowager was warming to her theme. 'And most definitely a new and rather exciting nightdress.' She slid a mischievous look at the young woman by her side.

Kathryn ignored the heat rising in her cheeks. 'It's very kind of you to offer such luxuries, but I already have more than enough.'

'Nonsense,' replied Lady Maybury. 'I can't have my granddaughter dressing in rags. We shall start with Miss Walters, move to Madame Devy, and Mills, then work our way along to Mrs Shabner, not forgetting Millards.'

A sigh was stifled as Kathryn allowed herself to be led into first one shop, then many more.

The day was warm in the extreme. Lady Maybury did not appear to notice. She was busily immersed in yards of ribbons and lace, and had just dispatched their footman to empty his arms of the multitude of parcels into the carriage.

'How dashed inconvenient!' Lady Maybury's nose wrinkled with irritation.

The woman serving behind the counter looked up, shock displayed across her face.

'James has taken the turquoise turban and I need it in order to select the best matching feathers.'

'I'm sure we can make a very good guess at which colours will suit,' Kathryn said.

The dowager raised an imperious white brow. 'Indeed we will not. When he returns, I'll send him back for it.'

Kathryn thought of the rising heat of the day. She thought of the footman's warm woollen coat, and the long walk he would have to reach their carriage. 'He's only just left and cannot have gone far. Perhaps I could stop him in time.'

'My dear gel—'

But the slender figure was already disappearing through the doorway.

The shop assistant sniffed, but said nothing.

Kathryn scanned the street and there in the distance was the retreating footman struggling under his load. Without a further thought she hurried towards him. Her breath became laboured and she felt the sweat bead upon her brow. 'James!' she said in a loud voice.

The footman disappeared around the corner.

Kathryn walked faster still. From out of nowhere an arm snaked around her waist, pulled her into an alleyway and slammed her hard against a wall. Her scream was rendered useless by the hand clamped across her mouth.

'Out walking alone, Kathryn, without even the accompaniment of a maid? What will people say? But then I'm forgetting that your reputation is already in tatters.'

She stared up into the face of Anna Marchant. Kathryn ceased her struggles, the blood draining from her cheeks until, beneath the heat of the day, a cold tremor pricked upon her skin.

The kid-clad hand dropped from her lips, but the grip remained around her wrist.

'Aunt Anna!' she exclaimed, unable to believe who it was that stood before her.

The older woman's lips smirked. 'Why so pale, niece? Did you think to play me for the fool quite so easily?'

'I don't know what you mean,' she whispered, feeling the stirrings of fear.

'Oh, but I think that you do, Kathryn. Sending Ravensmede to blackmail your uncle into paying a dowry.'

'Blackmail? I thought…' The words trailed off.

'You thought what?' sneered her aunt. 'That your uncle paid the money out of some sense of obligation? Affection, even? So sorry to disappoint you, my dear, but only Ravensmede's threats forced Mr Marchant's pen to paper. You could rot in hell for all we care.'

Realisation hit Kathryn between the eyes. 'He used the leaflet.'

'Very good. Did you like it? Really most effective, even if I do say so myself. Because of it, Amanda White dare not show her face. Did you know that she's left the country? Ran away to Italy, so they say. And you and Ravensmede are the scandal of London. All according to plan. Such a shame that he discovered my part in the affair.'

'Nicholas threatened to reveal the truth if Uncle Henry did not supply a dowry?'

'Of course. What choice did we have?'

It made sense. Kathryn looked directly into her aunt's eyes and saw the depths of the other woman's hatred. 'Why did you do it, Aunt Anna? Why should you want to destroy me so much as to publish such a thing?'

A smile stretched across Anna Marchant's face. 'Why do you think? I loathe you. I've always loathed you since the minute you crossed the threshold into my house. Trying to make claims upon your uncle's affection, thinking you were due our hospitality. I saw what you intended from the start. Trying to cast my own daughter into the shade, thinking yourself superior, and always with that look upon your face as if nothing we did could ever touch you.'

Kathryn stared as if she could not believe the words tumbling from her aunt's mouth. 'You are mistaken, Aunt, much more than you could ever know.'

The thing that passed for a smile upon Anna Marchant's face faded. 'No, Kathryn. I know full well what you are.' The ribbons of her bonnet danced in the breeze. 'I never wanted to take you into my home. You may thank Henry and his sense of duty for that. But why should my family and I suffer? It was not our fault that your slut of a mother died, or that your pathetic sot of a father killed himself.'

Instinct took over. Kathryn drew her hand back, and an almighty crack reverberated through the alley.

The imprint of Kathryn's hand, stark and red, appeared upon her aunt's cheek.

For a moment the two women just stared at each other, and then Anna Marchant's voice dropped to a snarl. 'You're going to regret that,' she said, and tightened her grip around her niece's wrist. 'You think to thwart me, but I won't let it happen. Ruined before all of London, and somehow you end up forcing Ravensmede into marriage in an effort to outdo your cousin. Lottie catches herself a decent gentleman for a husband, but you have to go one better with a viscount, and a rich one at that. Do you think after all that has happened that I shall just sit back and let you marry Ravensmede, and worm you way back into society's favour?'

'Take your hand off me.' Inside Kathryn was shaking, but her voice was clear and calm.

'Gladly,' said her aunt, and released her grip on her niece's wrist. She stepped back.

Kathryn made to leave.

'Not so fast.' Anna Marchant drew the small pistol from her reticule and aimed it at Kathryn's forehead. 'I'll see you dead first.'

Kathryn's heart hammered hard enough to escape her chest and her legs wobbled. 'You'll never get away with it. Lady Maybury is in the shop just a few yards along the street. I was merely trying to catch her footman. If I don't return soon, she'll come looking for me.'

'I know exactly where the old woman is. Did you think that I just chanced to be here? I was following you, awaiting my opportunity… which you have very obligingly just handed me.' A low hollow laugh sounded. 'I'll be long gone by the time the footman returns and the dowager realises that you're not with him.'

The pistol poked closer. Kathryn determined not to flinch.

'Just think, dear niece, a lead ball in the head, the same as your papa.' Scrape of metal, and the pistol was cocked.

A thousand thoughts flashed through Kathryn's head in that single moment. Images of her father, her mother, her sister, scenes from throughout the years of her life. But one picture dominated all others: Nicholas Maybury. And her one regret was that she would die without telling him of her love. Her eyes closed of their own volition. Her heart was beating in a frenzy, blood pumping so hard that it sounded like the rush of wind in her ears. Yet somewhere in the middle of the storm of emotion was an unexpected calmness, a silent place, a peaceful place.

'Kathryn!' The deep masculine voice echoed, and all at once she knew she was safe.

Somehow, by some sliver of chance, he was here. 'Nicholas!' she gasped.

'Ravensmede?' Anna Marchant swung to face the tall athletic figure. She paled, gulped and stumbled back in the opposite direction.

Kathryn had never seen such a look upon Nicholas's face. The green eyes glowered dark and menacing, the deep brown of his eyebrows drawn low and angled warned of a mood as black as the devil's. His hair rippled around a face that was the antithesis of colour. Even his lips, pressed firmly together, glowed with an unearthly pallor. Everything about him was still, tense, controlled. Dressed entirely in the deepest darkest black, he loomed a huge stark silhouette against the skyline. A chill stole through the air, the sky dimmed as a cloud obliterated the sun. 'Mrs Marchant,' he said in a voice filled with menace.

Kathryn shivered.

Anna Marchant's eyes widened and with fumbling fingers she swung the pistol towards Ravensmede.

'No!' Kathryn grabbed for her aunt's arm, deflecting the pistol's aim.

A loud bang. Smell of gunpowder. The drift of wispy plumes of blue smoke.

And when the smoke cleared Anna Marchant was lying on her back amidst the filth of the alley, bonnet askew, eyes bulging in terror. The dark figure stood above her, a large pistol trained on her sweating forehead. He crouched lower to look directly into the woman's eyes and when he spoke it was with that same terrible quiet control. 'Death can be mercifully quick, Mrs Marchant.' He touched the pistol muzzle between her eyes. 'And then again, there are ways to make it slow and painful.' The muzzle slid down to rest against her collarbone.

'Please,' came the high pitched whimper. 'Please.'

'Please what?' he asked. 'Do it quickly? I don't believe that the choice is yours to make.'

'No, don't kill me. Please don't kill me.' A sob sounded.

Ravensmede pressed the pistol a little harder. 'Crying for yourself, Mrs Marchant? Do you think that your tears of self-pity will stay my hand? After everything that you have done to make Kathryn's life miserable, to hurt her, even trying to kill her, there is nothing that can do that…'

Anna Marchant began to weep in earnest.

'Save to spare Kathryn the distress of witnessing such an act. She's suffered enough because of you. For her sake, and her sake alone, I'm prepared to offer you an alternative. England would fare better for your absence, madam. Therefore, you should remove yourself, your husband, your daughter, and the slanderous Mr Silverton to a place overseas with immediate effect. I'm sure that Silverton can make arrangements with his contacts in the West Indies. So, what is it to be?'

Mrs Marchant whimpered.

'Speak up, Mrs Marchant. Let us hear your decision.'

'We'll leave the country.'

'Never to return,' pressed Ravensmede.

'Never to return,' repeated a shaken Anna Marchant.

'I'm glad that we both understand the situation. Make no mistake, if you renege on this agreement I'll see you hanged for your attempt on Kathryn's life,' said Ravensmede, and removed the pistol to his pocket. He rose and walked slowly over to Kathryn.

His eyes scanned her face. 'Are you all right?'

Words would not come. Her head nodded, never for a minute breaking their gaze.

And then his arms were around her, strong, and safe. He pulled her to him and held her like he would never let her go.

The sun shone from a glorious cloudless sky as Kathryn made her way down the sweeping staircase of the house in Upper Grosvenor Street on Earl Maybury's arm. She was dressed in a simple gown of cream silk that, with its fashionable high-waist, flattered her petite stature. The décolletage swept low, revealing the gentle swell of her breasts. Tiny shimmering beads adorned the bodice and the edge of the short puff sleeves. Her hair was worn high with the soft curls allowed to drape teasingly down to her neck. Threaded throughout the chestnut locks piled upon her crown were narrow bead-studded ribbons of the palest cream, highlighting the rich red undertone of her hair.

'It's not too late to change your mind. Are you sure you can wed such a scoundrel, even if he is my son?' teased Lord Maybury.

She inclined her head as if deep in thought. 'To wed Nicholas,' she said softly, 'is something of which I thought only to dream.' Then the strange intensity of the moment was lost. She laughed and her curls danced. 'Does he know that you're inciting me to such rebellion?'

His shoulders shrugged. 'Most probably—he would expect nothing less.' The sunlight burnished the silver of his hair. 'I may be Nicholas's father, but for today I also take the role that your own dear papa should have had.' He tucked her hand into the crook of his arm.

'Yes.' A sad little smile stole across her face.

'I'm sure that he would have approved of your marriage.' He patted her small hand. 'That is, once he got to know Nick, of course.'

They laughed and stepped from the staircase on to the cool marble floor of the hallway.

Kathryn stopped and glanced at the door ahead of them, the last barrier that remained between her and Nicholas Maybury. Once she stepped beyond it there would be no going back.

'You plan to keep him on his toes, then?' The green eyes twinkled mischievously. 'Even though you are but fashionably late, he should have started to worry by now. I never thought to see him so tamed.'

Taking a deep breath, she stepped forward and allowed Lord Maybury to open the door.

He was standing facing the priest, with Cadmount by his side. A tall, imposing figure at the best of times, Kathryn thought she had never seen him look so magnificent as he did today. The ebony coat looked to have been sculpted upon his body and highlighted the snow-white sheen of his neckcloth, shirt and waistcoat. Long muscular legs were wrapped in white breeches. Even his deep dark brown locks had been shaped to perfection. Her heart turned over and she felt strangely shy.

Lord Maybury deposited her by Nicholas's side and moved back to sit beside the dowager and Miss Paton.

The palms of Kathryn's hands grew suddenly clammy and her throat dry.

Then the tall figure by her side smiled down at her, and there was such warmth and tenderness in his eyes that she quite forgot her nervousness and relaxed in his protective gaze. And when the priest asked her what she knew he would, she was able to answer in a clear voice without the slightest hint of a tremor. The ring slid smoothly on to her finger as if it had always been destined to fit there.

It seemed that the ceremony had barely started when she heard the priest pronounce them man and wife.

Nicholas's hands moved to take her arms.

She raised her face to receive the chaste kiss that would seal their union.

His lips slid intimately over hers with a prolonged passion that raised the colour to her cheeks.

'Nicholas!' she whispered in scandalised tones and made to pull away.

He held her tight. 'It's quite all right, sweetheart, we're married now.' He smiled a wicked smile and shot her a smouldering glance. And throughout the day when he looked at her she could see the promise in his eyes.

When he entered her bedchamber she was standing by the window as if mesmerised by the luminous glow of the full moon. Curls of chestnut hair cascaded over her shoulders, leading his eye down to the sheer cream gossamer of her nightdress and the barely concealed skin beneath. Small bare feet peeped out from under the hem of the nightdress and the slender hands were held loosely by her side. Although he had not spoken, she must have heard him and glanced round over her shoulder. A shy smile flashed at him, 'Nicholas.' But she did not change her stance, turning her face once more towards the moon.

Ravensmede felt his loins harden at the very sight of her. He had longed for this night for so long and now it was here, finally, at last. Kathryn was his, his wife, to have and to hold, to love and to cherish, for ever. With determined effort he schooled his passion and moved slowly towards her, until he stood so close behind her that the cream gossamer brushed the black satin of his dressing gown.

She shivered.

'Are you cold?' He touched his hands to her shoulders, sliding them down to capture her fingers.

'Just a little. It's this nightdress, it's just so…' She blushed and looked back at the moon.

'So very becoming,' he supplied, and slipped his arms around her so that her back was pressed full against him. The clean scent of her hair drifted up. Unlike most of the women that he had known, she wore no perfume, but her own sweet smell was intoxicating enough. He lowered his face to the red-brown curls and inhaled. By their own accord his hands crept up to cup her breasts. The soft thunder of her heart raced beneath the small firm mounds and he thought he detected a slight tremble in her body. 'Don't be afraid, sweetheart, there's nothing to fear.' A kiss dropped to the top of her head.

'I know,' she said and, twisting round in his arms, buried her head against his chest. 'It's just that there's something I need to tell you, something I should have told you a long time ago, had it not been for fear and for pride.' She laid her palms flat against his chest, and gave her bottom lip a little nibble. 'But when I stood in that alley with Aunt Anna's pistol in my face, I realised that I had been a coward not to tell you the truth: I love you, Nicholas.'

'I know,' he said. 'I've known since you turned down my offer of marriage in favour of a more scandalous proposition.'

'Oh.' Embarrassment warmed her cheeks. Her eyes held level with his chest. 'From all that you've done for me, I know that you must feel some measure of affection, and…and desire…and I want to tell you that it is enough. It doesn't matter that you don't love me in return.'

His thumb and forefinger captured her chin and tilted her face up to his. 'Some measure of affection and desire,' he said and moved his lips to hover above hers, 'goes nowhere near it, Kathryn.'

It seemed that her heart shuddered to a stop.

'I want you…' his head lowered to hers '…I need you…' until their lips almost touched '…I love you…' and they shared the same breath. 'Why else did you think that I went to so much trouble to make you my wife?'

She caught her breath.

'I love you, sweetheart,' he said again in a voice that was low and seductive. 'Completely. Utterly.'

The clear grey eyes darkened to a deep smoky charcoal. A gasp escaped her and his mouth closed over hers.

It was a kiss of longing and of love. A kiss to prove the words he had spoken. A kiss of passion and of need.

The last barrier crumbled. Nicholas loved her. Loved her, just as she loved him. He was her husband, and she was his wife. Kathryn gave herself up to the sweetness of the moment.

Nicholas teased. He tantalised. His hot breath seared the path his mouth had taken, slowly, enticingly, determined to prolong her pleasure.

Beneath the slick caress of his tongue, her lips parted in invitation, offering herself to his touch, his taste. Her palms flattened and crept up and across the broad strength of his back, her fingers sliding on the cool satin of his robe.

His hands skimmed down to her buttocks, the sensual massage a prelude to the grip that pressed her to the hard core of his arousal.

A soft moan escaped her lips.

With shaking fingers he untied the ribbons of her thin filmy gown so that it fell from her shoulders, exposing the pearl lustre of her skin.

Her eyes flickered open and she watched his gaze travel over every inch of her bare body.

'My love,' he said and fluttered soft kisses to her eyelids, her cheeks, across her passion-swollen lips down to the pale column of her neck and further. She arched against him as his mouth moved over the softness of her breast, his tongue washing its rosy peak with erotic precision.

Slender fingers threaded through his dark locks, pulling him to her, guiding him to her other breast. Shallow reedy breaths. Her hardened nipples ached with desire. Something fluttered and contracted deep within her. 'Nicholas.' She whispered his name, not fully understanding the escalating need. A liquid warmth melted between her thighs as he suckled her taut peaks. Then his mouth was gone.

A tiny sound of frustration, and her hands attempted to guide his head back to where it had lain. But Nicholas had other plans. Slowly, deliberately, he traced a line of tiny butterfly kisses beneath each breast then dipped lower, getting down on to his knees to follow the central line of her stomach, down across the soft plain of her abdomen.

'Nicholas!' Her eyes opened wide and round.

The green gaze found hers, and lingered with ardent intensity while his lips slid lower over the smooth silk of her skin towards that most secret of places.

Her legs trembled as his tongue tasted her sweetness and his hands, which had been steering her hips so expertly, gently lifted her and lowered her on to the bed.

He raised his head to hers, their eyes never leaving each other's for a moment, even when their lips met in honeyed reunion. His long, toned body covered hers, the tight muscles rippling beneath the sheen of sweat that drenched his skin.

Naked and hot, their bodies entwined beneath the silver glow of the moonlight. There was no need for covers, the heat of their passion scorched all that it touched. His low murmurs of encouragement caused her breath to come in short pants. She rose against him, unwittingly rubbing the tip of his heated desire. His fingers caressed her hidden moistness, sliding in sensual circles while his kisses played upon the soft whiteness of her inner thighs. Beneath the laboured breaths he felt the urgency of her need.

'Nicholas.' Her arms pulled him closer, until their skin slid together with the moisture of passion. Her lips trembled beneath his, heavy lids shuttered over eyes in which the pupils were huge and dilated.

He moved to take her then, thrusting once into the heat of her molten core.

A sharp intake of air. The grey eyes opened, stared up into his, searching.

He held still. And then his mouth found hers and indulged in slow deep sensual passion. Between those sweet swollen lips his tongue lingered, then lunged in a steady rhythm until he felt her tension loosen. He felt the first tentative wriggle of her hips, and a deep sensuous smile curved to his mouth. When those slender fingers wove a pattern of delight upon the firm muscle of his buttocks he could wait no longer. His muscles tensed to spiral them both into an ecstasy of oblivion for the first of many times that night.

Sunlight flooded the breakfast room. The Viscountess of Ravensmede smiled up at the tall handsome man by her side.

'You should not have risen so early,' he chided. 'I would not have you tired for tonight.' His eyes darkened with simmering desire, as he stared down into the face that he loved so well.

She laughed and, for Nicholas, it lit up the room brighter than any sunshine ever could. 'I promise that I shall not be tired, but what of you, dear heart? I would not want to wear you out,' and her voice held a husky teasing edge. The blush rose in her cheeks at the boldness of her words.

'Minx!' he chuckled. 'At this rate it won't be long before we're able to fulfil young Maggie's expectation of us becoming the *ma* and the *pa*!'

'A child of our own,' she said wondrously.

'Children,' he corrected. 'I don't mean to let you off that easily.' Drawing her to him, he placed a tender kiss upon her lips. His dark glossy hair mixed with the rich red-brown ringlets dancing temptingly at the sides of her beautiful face. He moved back to stare into her eyes, eyes that were of a serene silver coloration. 'I love you, Kathryn Marchant!' he declared with passion and kissed her again, mindful not to spoil the arrangement of her new and highly fashionable lemon silk dress. What was once a dream was now reality.

* * * * *

REGENCY
Collection

*Let these sparklingly seductive delights whirl
you away to the ballrooms—and
bedrooms—of Polite Society!*

Volume 1 – 4th February 2011
Regency Pleasures by Louise Allen

Volume 2 – 4th March 2011
Regency Secrets by Julia Justiss

Volume 3 – 1st April 2011
Regency Rumours by Juliet Landon

Volume 4 – 6th May 2011
Regency Redemption by Christine Merrill

Volume 5 – 3rd June 2011
Regency Debutantes by Margaret McPhee

Volume 6 – 1st July 2011
Regency Improprieties by Diane Gaston

12 volumes in all to collect!

MILLS
BOON

www.millsandboon.co.uk